SONS OF THE PEOPLE

Middle East Literature in Translation
Michael Beard and Adnan Haydar, *Series Editor*

Our Director's Choice program is an opportunity to highlight a book from our list that deserves special attention. *Sons of the People: The Mamluk Trilogy* by celebrated author Reem Bassiouney is a stunning historical epic that was awarded the Naguib Mahfouz Medal for Literature. Roger Allen, who won the 2020 Lifetime Achievement Award from Sheikh Hamad for Translation and International Understanding, brings Bassiouney's rich array of characters to life for English-language readers in this masterful translation.

SONS OF THE
PEOPLE

⊯ THE MAMLUK TRILOGY ⊯

REEM BASSIOUNEY

Translated from the Arabic by
ROGER ALLEN

Syracuse University Press

This book was originally published in Arabic
as *Awlad al-Nas: thulathiyat al-Mamalik*
(Giza, Cairo: Dar Nahdat Misr li-al-Nashr, 2018).

∞ The paper used in this publication meets the minimum requirements
of the American National Standard for Information Sciences—Permanence of Paper
for Printed Library Materials, ANSI Z39.48-1992.

For a listing of books published and distributed by Syracuse University Press,
visit https://press.syr.edu/.

ISBN: 978-0-8156-1141-7 (paperback)
978-0-8156-5548-0 (e-book)

Library of Congress Control Number: 2022932859

Manufactured in the United States of America

Contents

Timeline*

1250	The downfall of the Ayyubid dynasty (founded by Saladin in 1171) leads to the beginnings of the Mamluk Sultanate (1250–1517).
1250–1382	Period of the Bahri (lit. "of the river") Mamluk Sultanate, headquartered on the Nile Island of Al-Roda.
1260	At the Battle of Ain Jalut, the Mamluk commander, Az-Zahir Baibars, later Mamluk sultan of Egypt (1260–77), decisively defeated the Mongol army.
1293–94, 1299–1309, 1310–41	The three reigns of Sultan An-Nasir Muhammad ibn Qala'un (1285–1341).
1294–99	The deposed Sultan An-Nasir Muhammad resides in the Castle of Kerak.
1303	Battle of Marj al-Saffar between the Mamluk army and invading Mongols leads to the defeat of the Mongols and an end to their incursions.
1309–10	The brief sultanate of Baybars Jashankir, deposed and executed by the returning Sultan An-Nasir Muhammad.
1330	Muhammad ibn Baylik al-Muhsini is appointed governor of Cairo.
1347–51, 1354–61	The two reigns of Sultan Hasan, one of An-Nasir Muhammad's sons, who gives his name to the famous mosque in Cairo.
1350s	The plague, often called the "Black Death," reaches Egypt and Europe from the East. The same plague provides the setting for Boccaccio's *Decameron*.
1356	Construction of the Sultan Hasan Mosque begins.
1361	Sultan Hasan is assassinated by Yalbugha al-Umari.

---

* "The Mamluks developed a succession pattern unique in Middle East history. Although a son would often succeed his father as sultan, he usually (especially after 1382) had only a brief reign during which the major factions would fight for power. As soon as one Mamluk party had defeated the others, its leader would seize the sultanate. It should have been the worst governmental system in history; oddly enough, it worked for more than 250 years." Arthur Goldschmidt Jr. and Lawrence Davidson, *A Concise History of the Middle East*, 9th ed. (Boulder, CO: Westview Press, 2009), 124.

1382–1517	Period of the Burji (lit. "of the tower") Mamluk Sultanate, with headquarters in the Citadel.
1382–89, 1390–99	The two reigns of Sultan Barquq.
1384	Sultan Barquq appoints Ibn Khaldun, the renowned historiographer, as chief judge of the Maliki school in Cairo.
1389	Sultan Barquq is deposed by the combined forces of Mintash and Yalbugha an-Nasiri and exiled to Kerak Castle.
1412–21	Reign of Sultan Al-Mu'ayyad Shaykh al-Masmudi.
1516	At the Battle of Marj Dabiq (Syria), Ottoman forces under Selim I defeat the Mamluk army. The Mamluk Sultan Al-Ghuri is killed.
1516	Tuman Bey is appointed Mamluk sultan of Egypt.
1517	After the Battle of Ridaniyya, the Ottoman army under Selim I enters Cairo and executes Tuman Bey.
1517	Khayir Bey, formerly Governor of Syria, is appointed governor of Egypt by Ottoman Sultan Selim I.

SONS OF THE PEOPLE

1. Cairo. Mosque of Sultan Hassan. P. Bergheim. Circa 1860–80. Washington, DC, Library of Congress, Prints and Photographs Division, LC-USZ62-104851.

 THE FIRST STORY
The Mamluks

> I keep asking myself: what happens to "sons of the people"
> in this city? Do they wander around its quarters and blend
> in with everyone else? This city is weird: it can swallow you
> up like the river and rob you of both memory and purpose.
> In the city we're all crazy.
>
> Fatima

AMONG THE NOVEL'S MARGINALIA

The name of the person who designed and built the Sultan Hasan Mosque in Cairo remained unknown until the year 1944. The archeologist Hasan 'Abd al-Wahhab then stumbled across a mural text in plaster inside the mosque's Hanafi school; it mentions Sultan Hasan's name, along with that of the architect who built the mosque. His name was Muhammad ibn Baylik al-Muhsini, a son of the people.

CAIRO: 2005 CE

Ever since she was a teenager, visiting her father in Egypt had been a heavy burden. But now he was dying. This visit was necessary, not simply because of inheritance, but to say farewell and listen to final words of advice. In such circumstances it was possible to tolerate the Cairo dust for a few hours.

Once she had left for Italy with her mother in the '50s, she had only been back to Egypt a few times. Her father had been expunged from her childhood; he had stayed in the Cairene dust, with no farewell and no explanation. That had made her angry, and that anger had still not abated. Now her life and her children were over there. Egypt was just a distant memory; all that remained of its features were a few rocks and pillars. Her father was simply a man about whom she had heard miserable stories from her mother, someone who preferred rocks and pillars to living with her and around her. Many times her mother had told her sadly that her

I

father was a man who had wasted his life in quest of his dream. In the meantime, his mind had become confused, and he had never appreciated the value of things. That is what her mother had kept saying. For herself, she had never forgiven him when he was in good health, and she was not about to do so now he was dying. Death never forgives sins; in fact, it accelerates the final reckoning.

When she entered the hospital, he was sitting up in bed reading some papers. She gave him a token kiss and asked him how he was feeling. She gave him the glass vase that she had bought the previous summer for fifty dollars.

"Where did you get that?" he asked as he looked at it.

She was expecting him to be critical and was ready for it. "In Venice," she replied. "You told me earlier that you like glass."

"I love glass," he said with a degree of enthusiasm. "I love Venetian glass. But, like everything else around you over there, it's cheap."

"Around me here?" she retorted angrily.

"No, over there."

"You're being as critical and demanding as usual, Father. You must be well!"

For a few moments, he was silent, as though he were not listening. Then he asked her the usual question: "When are you coming back to Egypt?"

She gave the usual reply. "There's no way I can come back to a place I don't even know, a place where I've only lived for a few years."

To which he gave the usual response: "You'll regret it. You'll find out."

She had never understood what he meant: why regret could come before knowledge rather than after it.

She stroked his hand. "You're going to be fine, Father!"

For just a moment their eyes met.

"We're always craving satisfaction," he said. "Getting there is impossible. I used to think that, once my task was finished, and I had reached the end of the path to the truth and written the conclusion to the story, I would then feel a sense of ease, if only for a few days. But, along with that sense of arrival and the concomitant end to the process of circling the eventual goal, there comes a feeling of emptiness in the soul and a regret that things are at an end. Aspiration is that much easier than achievement; a desire for the impossible fills the soul with passion and does not rob it of its life. Now I've reached the end, but the void has not been filled, as is the case with you, my daughter."

She did not understand what he was saying.

"I'm happy with my own life," she said quickly.

"No, you're not," he replied. "You've never experienced real joy."

"How can you possibly know," she said bitterly, "when your entire life has only been filled with your scientific books and research?"

"My daughter," he replied, "your bitterness oozes from your words—from your hatred, your anger. You left your husband, isn't that right? In any case, I don't just write research; I write stories as well. I finished them just a few days ago. They were a dream, a quest, life itself, bequeathing me an exultation in my soul unfulfilled by either my human or demonic self—something you'll neither understand nor appreciate."

"You may be talking afresh about yourself, but I suspect that you're actually talking, albeit deceitfully, about my situation and that of your grandchildren."

He was not listening.

"In the year '44," he went on distractedly, "my teacher, Professor Hasan, invited me to see what he had discovered and join him in his research plans. In those days, professors were not like the ones today. He wanted me to do research and understand, and that's what I did. I spent time, a lot of time, doing research."

She looked at him without understanding anything. Was he delirious, was he dying? Or was he revealing some important secret?

"Yasmin, take these documents and get them published. The novel's finished now. Actually, it isn't a novel; it's a true story. I've all the evidence and details needed. First of all, go to the Sultan Hasan Mosque in the city center and search for the name. For years and years gone by, no historian has found out what it was. Then Doctor Hasan discovered it in one of the mosque's colonnades: Muhammad ibn Baylik al-Muhsini. He was the architect who built the mosque. He wasn't a Mamluk; he was a son of the people. Do you realize how important this discovery is? I've spent my life researching it. I've gone to the Mamluk Cemetery, looked at the ruins of the mosque, and examined the names on graves. I've looked at the Qur'an manuscript in Dar al-Kutub (it's still there). I've found everything."

"Father, here you are, talking again about your research. I don't have time now, so I'll come back tomorrow."

"This is my final testament: publish the novel. Go to the mosque and search for the name in its colonnades. It's there, still there, just like the city that swallows, fuses, creates, and is resurrected each and every day."

She stared at him without responding.

"You won't go," he went on sadly. "I realize that. Take your present away with you, Yasmin. You know, don't you, that you've deprived me of the sight of my own granddaughter."

"I asked you to visit us in Italy," she replied coldly, "but you refused."

"I don't like looking at misery and deception."

"What misery? What deception?"

"Your own misery. The deception involved in looking all around you. But never mind . . ."

He finished enthusiastically, although his voice was hoarse. "When you go into the house," he told her, "you'll find a Venetian lamp made of genuine Murano glass. Only scholars and researchers will know how authentic it is and what its historical connection is to us. It's far more valuable than your vase. Give it to my granddaughter Josephine as a present. And get these documents published."

He gave her the documents, but she never had them published. She did not carry out his final wishes, but, before she died twelve years later, she did give the lamp and documents to her daughter. Her daughter published them immediately afterward.

Here they are.

BOOK ONE

RAIDS

With creativity comes transcendence; with the jinn's emergence there follows a slow death for the heart and an opening for the soul; with the fulfilment of a desire, the attainment is bitter and the road is at an end.

The architect

1

1309 CE

This momentous event represented a dangerous and unprecedented occasion:

Merchants and religious authorities came together to discuss the matter and reach a decision. Such were the risks involved, the meeting was closed; everyone who came in was trusted for their loyalty, sincerity, and piety. If news of the meeting was to reach the ears of the Mamluks, the consequences would be dire. Even though the merchant Abu Bakr was renowned for his magnanimity, generosity, and many friends, he was still afraid, as he joined the gathering, of warrior violence. For such people, killing was easy and enjoyable; chopping off heads was easier than greeting people and shaking hands! What really bothered him was not the thought of dying himself, but rather the death of the one thing most precious to his heart.

The senior merchant chided Abu Bakr. "You haven't trained your son and taught him anything," he said. "That's the penalty for your arrogance and pride."

Shaykh 'Abd al-Karim intervened. "The young boy has his own desires," he said kindly. "There's a time and place for training the mind. God is forgiving and merciful. We think of a solution on the path to salvation."

"After the plague," the merchant Abu Bakr said, "my only son is all I have left. Nine of my children died. My son and his sister are the only ones left. People have simply disappeared. If that's not unjust, then what is?"

Shaykh 'Abd al-Karim chimed in quickly. "Don't be so hasty in your negativity toward people. Be careful in this assembly: right now, the word 'injustice' carries consequences. If you disappear along with your son, then who will be around to look after your daughter and wife? Calm down, and read some passages from the Qur'an. God willing, there is a solution. Amir Muhammad is not like the others. At least, he can speak Arabic well."

"He's the worst of them all," the father said hurriedly. "May he roast in hell!"

Everyone stared anxiously at each other. They all stood up to leave.

Abu Bakr now turned to Shaykh 'Abd al-Karim. "Shaykh," he said hopefully, "don't desert me!"

Shaykh 'Abd al-Karim stroked his hand. "People were scared by what you said," he told him gently. "You need to be more cautious. I've never known you to be like this."

"But, Shaykh, he's my son!"

"Don't despair of God's mercy. You haven't heard yet that he's dead."

———

Abu Bakr's tragedy started on the morning of that same ill-starred day.

The plague had left Abu Bakr with two children, a son and daughter—Ahmad and Zaynab. Once he had watched as his children all died, one after the other, he had fled with his two surviving children into the desert. He had stayed there for months, waiting fearfully and abandoning his business, the khan, and Cairo as a whole.

When he came back to Cairo, he resumed his business and reopened the khan; things returned to normal. Once again, the silk trade flourished and his fabrics became well-known. He was paying his taxes, kowtowing to authorities and influential people. His world stabilized, and his two children now became everything he wanted in this world and the source of his happiness.

Ahmad was a good, simple boy, with no real experience of life and no knowledge of his father's trade. The father tried to impart some of that knowledge forcibly, but without success. The daughter Zaynab actually deserved to be the boy. She possessed a superior intellect and eloquence. She learned things and digested books whole—jurisprudence, algebra, everything her eyes fell on. Her curiosity and lively temperament made her her father's darling. Her mother never understood this rebellious streak in her personality nor the behavior of men that she managed to control so well. She used to check her father's accounts; if ever there was a problem, she would offer him advice. Even though she was not yet eighteen, she was his closest companion. In just a week she would be married to her cousin, Yusuf. That was another disaster. Yusuf disappeared along with Ahmad.

When the father asked his son to accompany his daughter to the khan so that she could select some silk and buy some things she needed for her trousseau, he secretly asked his daughter to check on the khan's accounts without Ahmad noticing.

She nodded her head. "As you wish, Father!" she replied forcefully.

The news that she was going to the khan today reached her fiancé and cousin, Yusuf, just as she had wished and planned. Yusuf had been her beloved ever since childhood. When she had stopped playing with him, she knew that he was her lot in life and her wonderful fate. His appearance and manners were both those of an angel; he was the dream of every single girl around her. Their meetings were brief, and, after their childhood, their conversations were terse, but full of passion and love.

She used to wait for him to come; she would watch him from the window and observe him from afar. He would often sense her presence and give her an affectionate smile. On one occasion, he kissed his hand and blew the kiss up to her window. Her heart melted, and she could not fall asleep that night.

Their wedding was postponed for two years because of the plague and death, two things that kept his family and hers besieged.

But now, in just a short while she would be his wife, living in his house, laughing along with him, and playing as they had done in the past. Not only that, but she would be able to touch him, hug him, and even more . . .

All the short distance to the khan her heart was overjoyed. No sooner did she arrive than she fixed the veil over her face and started checking the khan's accounts. All the while, she was waiting for Yusuf to arrive. Meanwhile, her brother was talking to the other merchants, standing proudly outside the khan and fully confident in his own splendid future and settled life.

When Yusuf arrived, he shook Ahmad's hand, then went inside and looked for his future bride, the person who represented everything he dreamed. Their eyes met, and he smiled, while her heart was bursting with sheer joy.

"Just one more week, Zaynab," he said as he looked outside the khan.

"I know," she replied softly.

"I love you, dear cousin," he told her. "Do you know how much I love you?"

She looked at him. "How much do you love me?" she asked.

He looked all around him. Ahmad was talking enthusiastically to another man and not paying them any attention. Yusuf daringly grabbed her hand.

"You're everything I desire in life," he told her.

She withdrew her hand, feeling embarrassed. "We have to be patient," she said.

"My patience ran out from the very first time I set eyes on you, ages ago," he told her. "Your beauty is inscribed in poetry. I've not see anything like it, whether in Syria or Circassia."

"How many girls have you seen?" she asked coquettishly.

"My eyes only ever see you. Take my hand again."

She hesitated for a moment, then stretched out her hand. He understood that he was supposed to take it, but, just then, he heard a loud noise outside the khan. He turned round to find Ahmad talking angrily to a Mamluk soldier.

Yusuf hurried over to Ahmad, while Zaynab refastened the veil over her face. She went back inside the khan, but kept following what was happening outside.

"I'm Abu Bakr's son," Ahmad was saying proudly. "You can't talk to me that way. Either you purchase the silk, or else you leave."

The soldier stared at him in amazement and looked at his colleague. Yusuf's mouth gaped open in sheer fright. The Mamluk soldier grabbed the piece of silk, took out his sword, and cut it into two pieces. Ahmad gave him a challenging look, and their eyes met. With all the rage of youth Ahmad now pushed the soldier who fell to the ground. Ahmad yelled at him to leave.

At that moment all activity in the market came to a halt; the whole world froze in place. The single soldier now became ten, and they surrounded the khan. Zaynab started sobbing in panic.

"What have you done?" she whispered to Ahmad as she left the khan.

Now Ahmad spoke rapidly to the soldier. "Please accept my apologies," he said.

Grabbing a piece of silk, he handed it to the soldier. "Please take this free of charge," he said, "and move on."

The soldier stood up. "Not before you and this mule are dead," he said.

Ahmad opened his mouth to round on the soldier; his youthful fury had managed to overwhelm any common sense or logic. For her part, Zaynab looked all around her in hopeless despair, expecting her life to be over at any moment. Then she noticed the horse outside the quarter's gate, with a man sitting astride it who looked like the amir. There were soldiers all around him. Zaynab ran as fast as she could; all she could feel in her heart was her father's grief over his son who was about to be killed any moment by the Mamluk soldier's sword.

"My Lord Amir," she yelled as she left the quarter, "my Lord Amir!"

The amir looked behind him to see where the shouts were coming from, and looked at Zaynab as she was running toward him.

"Help me!" she panted. "Please, I beg you, help me!"

Her veil had slipped off while she was running; sweat was pouring off her forehead, and her eyes were wide open in panic.

"What do you want?" he asked her, still mounted on his horse.

"It's my brother," she said in a rush. "The Mamluks are going to kill him. He hasn't done anything. They'll kill him. Help me!"

"Mamluks don't kill ordinary people," he replied with a frown.

"I beg you to save him," she said quickly.

He stared at her long and hard, noticing the long hair that almost covered her entire body.

"Where's your veil?" he asked her. "What brings you to this market? It's women coming out to market that has caused the plague and so much death. Go back home before I have you flogged in the center of this quarter to serve as an example to other women."

As she looked around her in search of her veil, she was in total despair. It looked as though her brother was going to die; he was bound to be killed.

She saw her brother, and Yusuf as well, with their hands tied and heads lowered, being taken over to the amir by the Mamluk soldiers. The amir turned to his escorts.

"What did they do?" he asked firmly.

"My Lord," the soldier replied, his head lowered, "this young man assaulted our soldiers right in the middle of this market and in full view."

Zaynab was quick to react. "He did not, my Lord Amir," she said, "I swear to you that he didn't do it. It was this soldier . . ."

"You dare speak to men," he interrupted her, "and walk around the quarter with your face unveiled! Who are you? Some lunatic?"

"Forgive me," she pleaded. "He's my only brother. We're Abu Bakr's children. He has a fine reputation and has never harmed anyone. Please help me, my Lord. Forgive my brother and cousin."

"What's your name," the amir asked bluntly.

"Zaynab."

"Well, Zaynab," he went on, "when members of the public assault soldiers, what's going to happen to the country? Do you realize? There'll be general chaos, and crooked people will be free to cause widespread havoc with no restraints. But you've shown a lot of courage here, so I'll be patient with you."

He now gave orders to the soldiers. "Take them both to prison so I can investigate the entire matter," he said. Addressing Zaynab, he added, "And you should go home now!"

As their eyes met, she opened her mouth to say something, but the expression in his eyes scared her. She felt that he might cut out her tongue if she said a single word.

"Thank you," she said, head lowered. "I shall pray for you, my Lord. You are well known for your sense of justice."

He did not respond.

She ran home, her world at an end and the life she had known now forever gone. But the arrest of Ahmad and Yusuf was the key issue!

The mother screamed and hired a specialist keener to scream all day. This time, the loss of a child was not like all the other times. Neither her husband nor all the other women in the quarter could stop her screaming.

Abu Bakr found it impossible to stay inside the house amid all the wailing, curses at the world, and invocations of the Prophet's family and elders. He closed the khan and stayed all day in the mosque, talking to the shaykhs and religious scholars and asking them to intervene.

One week after the disappearance of Ahmad and Yusuf and their escape from the Mamluk soldiers' clutches, Shaykh 'Abd al-Karim came to see Abu Bakr the merchant.

"I've some news for you," the shaykh told Abu Bakr quietly. "I don't know if it's good or bad."

Abu Bakr was sitting cross-legged, clutching a copy of the Qur'an. "Has he been tortured and died of it?" he asked. "Did they torture Ahmad and his cousin?"

"I don't know," 'Abd al-Karim replied. "In my opinion, my brother, what he did was a crime. He assaulted someone who is protecting our country, showing no respect for people who sacrifice their lives on our behalf. They may have tortured him, but he's still alive. I got the news today."

"Where is he?" Abu Bakr asked anxiously.

"The situation's tricky, my brother," 'Abd al-Karim replied slowly, "in fact unprecedented."

"Give him everything I own."

"Amir Muhammad doesn't need money. He doesn't like imposing taxes either."

"I'll speak to him and plead with him. I'm willing to punish my son myself. I'll flay him in public. He can release him and his cousin."

"The religious scholars have intervened on your behalf," 'Abd al-Karim told him. "They've spoken to the amir. They went to Roda specially to request mediation. My dear brother, the good word is an act of charity. If only people adhered to the dictates of religion, we would be in a different situation."

"Did the amir agree to release him?"

"As I've told you," 'Abd al-Karim continued after a moment's silence, "after the plague everything's become very strange, with all kinds of jolts emerging from the belly of the earth. Now even Mamluks have started behaving in response to their own desires."

"Is he going to release them both?"

"As you know, he waged war on the Mongols and Crusaders on our behalf. There is virtue in admitting the truth."

"Has he promised to release the two of them?"

'Abd al-Karim was silent for a while. "He's going to think about it," he replied.

"Take me to see him. I'll talk to him and ask him to forgive them."

"It's not that simple."

"What do you mean? I'll do whatever it takes to get my son released."

"His request shocked me," 'Abd al-Karim continued. "As I've told you, everything's different after the plague and the departure of Sultan An-Nasir Muhammad ibn Qala'un."

"You mean, his escape."

'Abd al-Karim looked all around him. "Your behavior and your words are going to cost you your own life as well," he said. "Listen, my brother. The amir wants to marry your daughter."

This information hit Abu Bakr's head like a fall of rocks from the Muqattam Hills. The whole thing was not merely shocking; it was completely unprecedented.

"Mamluks don't marry our daughters," Abu Bakr said. "It's a very unusual request."

"I know. It's totally unprecedented."

"They used to leave us to live our lives while they led their own. Neither involved themselves in the life of the other. We paid our taxes and lived in security, while they defended the country and lived in their palaces and fortresses outside Cairo. What's happened and why?"

"I don't know," 'Abd al-Karim replied seriously. "I never expected this kind of request."

"My daughter's betrothed to her cousin. What's this humiliation? He wants to take both my son and daughter. I'll kill this amir with my own hands."

"If you don't stop talking like that, I'm never going to help you. In situations like these, you have to act prudently. Things have to be solved amicably."

"My daughter's betrothed to her cousin; the wedding ceremony was supposed to be today. She'll never agree, nor will I. The idea of tossing her to that Mamluk . . ."

"He's a strong amir with a hundred or more Mamluks at his disposal, commander of a thousand troops in war. Are you out of your mind?"

"But he's a Mamluk. The decision is not his. He was a slave, then he became an amir. He may still be a slave—I don't know. He's a stranger in our land; he's not one of us, and he doesn't know us. We don't know where he's from or what his family background is. However many soldiers he may command, he's still a Mamluk and a foreigner. His loyalty and religious belief are both in doubt. We don't even know what his religious beliefs were in his former country."

"You can't fault his religious beliefs: he's a Muslim and devout. We all belong to God, and none of us can control his own fate."

"My daughter will never marry a Mamluk. They'll kill her. My brother, their cruelty is enough to break your heart in two; we all know that. The Egyptians are free, my dear shaykh. No sultan or caliph has ever enslaved them. How can they possibly marry slaves?"

"The people you're calling slaves, my brother, happen to be your rulers. They're aware of your power, and they'll punish you if you commit wrongs. They don't normally consort with the common people; they prefer women from their own country."

"They can storm around the country as they wish, but they'll not consort with my daughter. We're being ruled by slaves—okay. But they won't be our relatives or become part of us. That's impossible and inconceivable."

"My brother," said 'Abd al-Karim, "the amirs are well aware of the fact that we call them 'Mamluks' because they weren't born free. The label doesn't bother them because they say that authority belongs to God alone, not to anyone else; we all belong to God. I believe they're right. As I've told you, authority belongs to God."

"My, my," Abu Bakr responded sarcastically, "they're so amazingly devout and pious! Here now we see a single Mamluk imposing his tyrannical authority over me for the rest of my life."

The shaykh paused for a moment. "Amir Muhammad is a virtuous man," he said. "I've only ever seen him doing what is good."

"It'll never happen."

"As I've told you, we're thinking of a way out of this problem so we can rescue Ahmad and Yusuf. He can only marry her with the sultan's permission."

"Which sultan is that? The one who fled or the usurper?"

"What's the matter with you? This is a trial. In stressful times you have to be patient. How can the sultan allow him to marry a girl from the Egyptian populace?"

"Does he have a Mamluk wife?"

"He doesn't have a wife."

"How has he seen my daughter? Has he actually seen her? How did he find out that I have a daughter?"

"Mamluks know everything. Perhaps he hasn't seen her; he just heard about her. You should know, my brother, that the amir has said that he's ready to release Ahmad and Yusuf if he's married to your daughter."

"This is the disaster to end all disasters. I'd drown her in the river before making her suffer this fate."

"We need to come up with a plan so that he'll release the two men and not marry your daughter. We don't want the Mamluks to start thinking about our women. Once that idea took root, it would be all over for us, for sure."

⁓

Zaynab sat there, listening in silence to what her father was saying. Her mother could not stop crying. His father looked downcast and hesitant. She had only ever seen him in such a state when he had had to bury one child after another because of the plague.

"I'll never sacrifice your life, my daughter," he said feebly, "in order to save your brother. It'll never happen. You're more precious to me than your brother."

"You're not going to sacrifice her," Zaynab's mother said dryly, "you're going to marry her off. There's a big difference between the two."

Fatima, Zaynab's cousin, stroked her aunt's shoulder. "Calm down, Aunt," she said. "Ahmad's fine, I'm sure."

But the mother did not stop crying, and Zaynab did not utter a single word.

"It's a strange request," said Abu Bakr, rubbing his hands together. "I'm used to Mamluks asking for bribes and gifts, but this request is peculiar. If only he'd asked for my entire fortune rather than this. If they execute anyone who expresses an opinion about them that they don't like, then how on earth do they treat their wives? I can't see you with a Mamluk. Where did he see you? Where did you see him? Do you know him?"

Zaynab said nothing, but withdrew into herself, something she did whenever she felt helpless. Lately she had been dealing with a good deal of weakness, death, and despair. It was only a week ago that she had had a meeting with the love of her life. Everything had been ready: clothes and furniture had been bought, henna had been applied, and she had spoken to her mother about the wedding night and loss of virginity—what would happen, what would be, and what she was supposed to do and say. She belonged to her beloved, in mind and spirit.

What devastation and destruction was hitting this country; and what unhappiness was now hers!

Plague was rocking the very foundations of life; grief was gnawing at everyone's heart. Everything, absolutely everything was in ruins. If only she had never left the house on that fateful day; if only the amir had never set eyes on her; if only her fiancé had not gone to meet her; if only, if only . . . Regret is a useless trait, and trials such as this one demand a calculating mind, one that can understand and adjust quickly.

She stroked her father's hand. "Father," she said, "be strong. There has to be a way out of this."

"I'll not marry you to the amir," he responded stubbornly. "Let him do whatever he wants."

"She's going to be married to him!" the mother yelled nervously. "She has to be married to him. If she doesn't, he's going to kill my son. She's a girl, she can be sacrificed. We only have one son."

"And one daughter."

"She's not going to die."

"He'll be killing her every day a thousand times over. If only she could die . . ."

"How do you know that? The things we hear about the Mamluks are not true. They're human beings just like us. They saved us from the perils of the Mongols and Crusaders. They maintain order and security. Don't talk like Ahmad and Yusuf, the kind of stupid things that young men who aren't strong enough to bear arms keep saying. Who would dream of marrying an amir!"

"She's not going to be married to him," he replied forcefully.

"Zaynab," the mother said to her daughter, "say something."

But Zaynab remained silent.

"Shaykh 'Abd al-Karim will talk to him," the father said. "Religious doctrine will surely reject him."

Even though he was not yet thirty years old, Shaykh 'Abd al-Karim was both clever and erudite. He had come to Cairo from the countryside, studied with senior scholars, and learned through them all the various doctrines. Even so, he was not entirely convinced by the explanations of his teachers or by all their assumptions. His problem was the mild vain streak inside him, something that he never showed in public but could never forgo. It stayed inside him, like a precious trinket hidden from jealous eyes. Whenever he heard an interpretation that he did not like, he would smile sarcastically to himself but not say anything. When he saw his teachers lauding the Mamluks, talking about their accomplishments, and overlooking their transgressions, he would again smile and say nothing. His upbringing in poverty and his remarkable intelligence were the root cause of his every endeavor. For him, knowledge was more important than wealth; he viewed power as lying in understanding, not the sword. Praise deprived the religious scholar of his value and made him the equal of poets and sultans.

Along with his innate perspicacity he was also astute. He was never hasty in his criticism of religious scholars or amirs. He would listen patiently and assess people's inner thoughts. Having examined their inner selves, he would sift and categorize them.

As might be expected, some of his teachers were jealous of him from the outset; they did not like his opinions or his mode of argument. They devoted themselves wholeheartedly to putting an end to him and his future. Shaykh 'Abd al-Karim found himself transferred to another mosque far removed from his teacher. At the time, the city of Cairo was wide enough for the entire world and flourishing for all eternity, with three million inhabitants. The shaykh had to find a mosque where he could preach, one that was far removed from his teacher who kept pursuing him with both heart and arm, the goal being to use his knowledge to put an end to the shaykh's future. However, it seemed that Cairo was too small for 'Abd al-Karim. His teacher's arm extended far enough to encompass all Cairo's gates. Every time 'Abd al-Karim tried to settle in a particular area of Cairo, along with his wife, mother, and children, he would find financial resources blocked and nasty tongues wagging against him like rulers' swords. When he finally settled in this particular quarter, he was greeted by a welcome from Abu Bakr and his family and the people of the quarter. They were all more educated and literate. Eventually, it seemed to 'Abd al-Karim that his teacher, whose primary goal had been to finish him off, had forgotten about him. Now, life was on an even keel and opening its doors to him. It took less than a year for Shaykh 'Abd al-Karim's calm demeanor and eloquence to make him a much-beloved figure, and, at the same time, made senior religious scholars feel somewhat jealous. For his part, 'Abd al-Karim tried to deal with it all patiently. He started adjusting to his new life and decided to avoid the mistakes he had made previously and suppress his former vanity. He deliberately hid both his knowledge and vanity, and made a public display of his desire to learn from his elders, and to form a pact with Mamluks, sultans, and everyone in Cairo.

Shaykh 'Abd al-Karim sat with the religious scholars, among them being Abu Bakr who was feebly asking for their help. They all decided that the religious obstacle might rescue the merchant's son from his fate. Mamluks respected and revered religious scholars. Some of them had been taught by the scholars, while others attended the scholarly seminars and gave them encouragement, building endowments and schools for them to use. It would be the scholars alone who could convince the amir to release the two young men and forget about marrying an Egyptian woman from the populace. The Mamluks had their own womenfolk, hailing from the same origins and country, not to mention slave girls as well. The Egyptian populace paid their taxes and respected all legal regulations. So why was there this interest in their daughters?

The religious scholars agreed to invite Amir Muhammad to their mosque to attend the Friday sermon there. They decided that the sermon's topics should include tyranny, prophetic justice, the triumph of the good, the corrupt on earth, authority figures, and pursuit of desires.

On Monday one of their number composed the sermon and read it to the others. Abu Bakr was delighted.

"This sermon will dissuade him," he commented enthusiastically. "It'll remind him of his own wrongdoing."

However Shaykh 'Abd al-Karim sensed that it was risky; if the Mamluks heard it, it might well lead to the destruction of that quarter and Cairo as a whole. He asked that it be changed and suggested that instead the topics should be self-discipline, avoidance of passionate desires, and mercy for the weak and orphaned. The shaykhs reached agreement on those topics, and on Wednesday Shaykh 'Abd al-Karim read it with enthusiasm.

"That's much better!" was Abu Bakr's happy comment. "It's less pointed. It's bound to convince him."

Some scholars still had objections. "Every authority figure will be annoyed by it," they said. "There are even some pointed comments aimed at the amir. If he gets really angry, he'll completely close down the mosque and put all religious scholars in prison. Forwarding complaints to the sultan is never easy, especially at this point in time when everything is unclear and the populace has no idea exactly who the sultan is!"

So the shaykh wrote a third sermon. In it he offered prayers for the Mamluk amirs and lauded their wars and glorious triumphs outside the country—the sacrifice of body and soul in repelling the Crusaders and Mongols. He mentioned the terrors that the Egyptian people were anticipating from the Crusaders, the way they burned houses down, killed people, and butchered babies. He added a short passage about the plague and cursed all those who sought destruction in Muslim lands.

"Where's my particular problem in this sermon?" Abu Bakr asked in despair.

"Patience, Abu Bakr!" 'Abd al-Karim replied. "First of all, we have to encourage the amir. After the prayer we can talk to him. That's a better idea. Nice words may help us. Above all, we don't want to annoy him."

Once Amir Muhammad had sat down in the mosque, surrounded by his soldiers, Abu Bakr went over to him, his head bowed.

"I crave your forgiveness and magnanimity," he said.

The amir looked at him, then turned away. He asked Shaykh 'Abd al-Karim how he was, and if he needed anything. He told the shaykh that he wanted him to have religion taught throughout the land and to conduct innovative scholarship.

"The Mamluks will expend effort and money to bring that about," he said.

"We crave your justice, my Lord," 'Abd al-Karim replied.

He approached the amir. "I'm giving a sermon today," he told him softly. "I have a simple question for you, but please don't blame me for asking it."

"Ask away, Shaykh."

"When I offer a prayer for the sultan, should I name Baybars Jashankir or An-Nasir Muhammad ibn Qala'un?"

"What do you usually do?"

The question took the shaykh by surprise, and he did not respond.

The amir went on. "Or is it rather that you don't normally pray for the sultan as part of the Friday sermon?" he asked. "Tell me, Shaykh 'Abd al-Karim, do you pray for the sultan or not?"

"Yes, I do pray for him," the shaykh replied, "but these days the situation is confused. Forgive me, but is An-Nasir Muhammad still the sultan, or is it now Baybars Jashankir?"

The amir said nothing for a moment, then continued: "Pray for the sultan of Muslim lands, but don't specify the name. Why are you bothered about the name? Does it make any difference for Egyptians whether the sultan is An-Nasir or Bay-bars? Leave such things to the Mamluks and live your lives in peace. In our times, Shaykh, houses have been lost, libraries burned, and mosques destroyed. The only things left in Muslim lands are whatever the Mamluks have been able to save. They have preserved Egypt, standing tall amid all the destruction and loss. They're protecting the Ka'ba and mosques. But for them, the people of Egypt would disappear and vanish into oblivion. You need always to remember that."

"You're absolutely right," the shaykh replied swiftly. "I've always known you to be a wise man, my Lord Amir."

'Abd al-Karim delivered his sermon eagerly. The amir and his men listened to it in respectful silence, then they prayed behind the imam. After the prayers 'Abd al-Karim asked the amir to pay a visit to Abu Bakr in his house so that the present boon and blessing could be shared widely and they could discuss the matter of his son and daughter.

Zaynab and her cousin Fatima looked out through the meshrabiyeh on the upper floor of the house. Zaynab's heart was thumping loud enough to reach the courtyard below.

"That amir's really handsome," Fatima said, sticking her nose into things. "He has nice black hair and a trim beard which make him look fine. He looks thirty or less. If I weren't already married, I'd fall in love with him."

Zaynab managed to stifle her tears. "What woman could possibly say such things?" she asked. "Your husband's just like us; he's not a Mamluk."

"So what's wrong with the Mamluks?" Fatima replied. "They're running the country and the slaves. A man with no authority can't make a woman happy."

"There's only one man in my life," Zaynab managed to whisper hoarsely. "That's Yusuf. He's my husband and my entire life."

Shaykh 'Abd al-Karim spoke and recited some Qur'anic verses.

"Will you permit me to speak freely, my Lord?" he asked the amir gently.

"Dear teacher," the amir replied, "go ahead."

"The Prophet—may God bless and preserve him—said: 'Let none of you propose contrary to his brother's previous proposal.'"

The amir stared at him furiously.

Shaykh 'Abd al-Karim hurried to elucidate. "It is the Prophet who made that statement, not me," he said. "Forgive me, Lord. In Islam, we are all brothers, and, needless to say, stations are preserved."

"What do you mean?" the amir asked, his patience clearly wearing thin. "I don't like what you're saying."

"My Lord," Abu Bakr intervened. "My daughter is one of your servants, of course. Your heritage is an honor that we do not deserve. She's already engaged to her cousin, and the marriage ceremony was supposed to take place last week before the incident in the market. I want to tell you this to assuage my conscience."

"Who is her cousin?" the amir asked casually.

"He's in prison along with Ahmad. His name is Yusuf."

He gave a nod. "He was her fiancé," he said. "You mean, he was her fiancé, but he doesn't exist anymore."

Abu Bakr clutched his heart, and Zaynab was about to shriek but suppressed it.

"We beg your forgiveness, Lord," 'Abd al-Karim said gently. "The engagement will be annulled and, if possible and permitted by your sense of nobility and justice, Yusuf's life will be spared. There's no need to kill him; he's his mother's only son."

For a moment he said nothing, but then he turned to Abu Bakr. "Tell us again, Abu Bakr, is your daughter engaged?"

"No, she isn't," he replied sternly. "She's at your disposal, and you can marry her whenever you wish."

The amir nodded. "The marriage will take place in a week," he said. "Shaykh 'Abd al-Karim can write the contract today."

Zaynab clutched her neck, throttled by sobs, her life about to end. Closing her eyes, she grabbed her cousin's hand.

"Now I want to die," she said.

"Calm down, Zaynab," Fatima replied. "It's all fated, and you have nothing to do with it."

"That Mamluk will never possess me," she said defiantly. "He's a Mamluk, and I'm free. I swear to you, he'll never possess me. My husband is Yusuf, and no one else. God never condones injustice."

"What are you planning to do?" Fatima asked anxiously. "If you turn him down, he'll kill Ahmad and Yusuf today."

"He's not my husband," Zaynab said decisively. "He'll never be my husband."

"Are you going to say that when the shaykh asks you?"

Zaynab paused for a moment. "Maybe," she replied.

"So are you planning to kill your own brother and cousin?" her mother asked curtly. "You're going to marry the amir, or else I'll kill you myself."

Zaynab kept silent. If they died, it would be over. If she sacrificed her own happiness, then she would be living in misery forever.

The mother started slapping her cheeks and bemoaning her fate. Just then, the father strode in, accompanied by Shaykh 'Abd al-Karim.

Zaynab donned her veil.

"You're a brave girl, Zaynab," the shaykh said kindly. "That's what your father tells me."

"This is more than I can stand, Shaykh," she replied softly.

"No, it's not," the shaykh said, looking at her father. "God never charges anyone with things beyond their abilities. It's a trial, for sure, but it's not beyond you."

"Can't we convince the amir somehow?" she pleaded. "Give him everything we own, anything . . . Maybe he could imprison them for a month then release them."

"I've come to ask you a question," he went on with a smile. "Are you willing to marry him or not? I've not come to persuade you."

"Zaynab," her father told her gently, "you have to be married to him so he'll set Ahmad and Yusuf free. Then we can raise a complaint with the sultan, and he'll divorce you. He'll divorce you, I promise."

She stared at her father, then at the shaykh, but said nothing.

"My dear daughter, I promise you," he pleaded. "When he sets them free, he'll divorce you. I'm not going to let you live with a Mamluk amir. That'll never happen."

"How can God call us to account," she asked, looking at the shaykh, "when we have no choice?"

"Maybe we don't have a choice," he replied deliberately. "The amir didn't choose to be a warrior; maybe he really wanted to be something else. Yusuf didn't choose to be in prison, and you didn't choose to be married to the amir. But afterward, you'll have the opportunity to choose your own way of life."

"There'll be no life afterward," she replied forcefully.

The shaykh stood up. "I can't keep the amir waiting," he said. "Mamluk amirs are not known for their patience. What shall I tell him? You have the right not to agree."

"I don't have any choice," she said by way of retort. "He's left me no choice . . ."

"If our lives worked exactly as we wanted," the shaykh continued, "where would be the trial? Sometimes you take a different turn in the road. You need to be patient and explore your own spirituality. There has to be a way out of this dilemma. My dear sister, search for God's peace within you. Everyone who comes to me for help is looking for that peace, but never finds it with me. That peace will never come as a result of words that I might say to you now or charms given to you by some shaykhs. Your father has told me that you read and have an innovative streak. It is that peace which brings with it success and redemption—a God-given gift and struggle. Don't forget to repeat to yourself: 'Through the mention of God hearts can be serene.'"

"If he treats her badly, dear Shaykh," the father asked immediately, "to whom can we talk? He has no family and no country. Should we talk to the sultan? How can we do that? Can I at least ask him not to treat her badly?"

"Dear brother, why are you assuming that he's going to treat her badly? He may be nice to her."

Zaynab hugged herself and bent over. "Shaykh," she said softly, "Yusuf did nothing; he did not assault the soldiers. I saw it all for myself. The amir falsely arrested him, and now he's about to kill him. I heard the conversation you had with him. He's someone who will kill an innocent man in order to get hold of his fiancée and pretend to be protecting us. How am I supposed to live under his roof when I know all that?"

'Abd al-Karim did not respond, but kept his head lowered for a while.

"My dear sister," he said eventually, "I don't have all the answers and don't always know how to advise people. I try my best and strive to achieve a favorable outcome. People's souls have their weaknesses and desires. Humans will forever be fighting and struggling with their soul's desires."

"Tell me, Shaykh," Abu Bakr asked in despair, "what do you know about Mamluk amirs? Did they inherit their authority from a father who was a sultan or amir? No. They grabbed it through fighting and warfare; they achieved it by murdering and enslaving people. Slaves became amirs, while the people of the country had to swallow humiliation. What kind of logic is that, and what times are we living in? They have been raised to fight and kill, with no family of their own. Legends have been written about their greed and tyranny. Now you want me to give them my daughter without even a promise?"

Zaynab looked at her father. He seemed at a complete loss and in despair, looking all around the room for some kind of solution amid the ancient walls. She stood up.

"I agree with my father," she said with determination. "Don't worry about me. As the shaykh says, it's a trial, but it'll be over."

He gave her an appealing look, since she had just rescued him from a weakness that she had never seen him endure before.

The two men left the room.

Fatima went over to her. "What are you planning?" she asked.

"I've spoken to my father," she replied. "If I'm forced to be married to him, I'll endure it till my brother and cousin are released. Then my father will raise a complaint with the grievance court. He'll ask the sultan himself to decide the issue. I'll get a divorce, then I can be married to Yusuf if he still wants me."

"That's a good idea," Fatima said. "You always have good ideas, Zaynab; it's as though you're from some other world. But you're going to be married to the amir and give him your virginity. You understand that, don't you? Your mother has explained everything to you."

"My virginity lies in my own heart," Zaynab said sadly. "As long as I'm alive, no one can touch it except Yusuf."

"What if you become pregnant by the amir?"

"That won't happen. I want you to help me get a drug so that will never happen."

"But what if the sultan refuses to give you a divorce?"

"In that case, I'll kill myself or leave the country. Rapists can never succeed against what is good. That's what Yusuf is—good, whereas this other man is the evil of all ages. But will Yusuf still want me now?"

"He's crazy about you," Fatima said with all certainty. "He understands the sacrifice you've made. Of course, he'll want you."

"How sinful I feel!" Zaynab said bitterly. "I'm responsible for what's happened to him. I've been his downfall, it seems; the reason for his coming and then for his murder."

Abu Bakr started writing his complaint to the Court of Grievances. It was ready to be submitted at the appropriate time. Every time he composed a line, his heart relaxed; life now had a purpose, and love had a goal. He gave it to Shaykh 'Abd al-Karim to read.

"Dear brother," the shaykh told him after he had perused it carefully, "Sultan Baybars Jashankir doesn't attend the court in person. That practice has disappeared ever since he assumed power this year. Indeed, so have a number of other practices."

"Yes, I hear the rumors too," Abu Bakr responded quickly. "But he's also banned alcohol and opened a huge hostel to feed the poor. He must be a just sultan."

The shaykh paused for a moment. "Have the Mamluk amirs asked you for protection money, or not?" he asked.

"They've asked for my daughter," Abu Bakr replied bitterly, "and they've taken my son and daughter. He's just a single amir, combining the evils of all the other amirs. Throughout my life, I've never been bothered about the Mamluks or their amirs. I've been living in peace. One sultan goes, another kills; one runs away, and the other invades and tyrannizes. But still I don't care. So, where has that lame sultan, An-Nasir Muhammad, run off to, leaving the authority to Baybars, just like a bunch of children?"

Shaykh 'Abd al-Karim had nothing to say.

"I'm going to wait till my son is released," Abu Bakr continued, "then I'll present my complaint. In days he's going to take my daughter to his palace, the apple of my eye, everything that I love and adore. I don't know what's going to happen to her there. I'm not sure that my son and daughter are going to escape from this ordeal unharmed."

At first, the question of Sultan Baybars Jashankir did not concern Egyptians all that much, but they had no idea why Sultan An-Nasir Muhammad ibn Qala'un was still in flight outside Egypt for a second time. They started cracking jokes about An-Nasir Muhammad, the skinny lame sultan who, from time to time, would flee the country whenever the Mamluk amirs put pressure on him. When Sultan Baybars Jashankir banned alcohol and built the hostel, people applauded enthusiastically. Poor people headed for the hostel in thousands, and Mamluk soldiers asked them to pray for the new Sultan Baybars. Such prayers shook the foundations of the various city quarters. However, Baybars was personally dissolute, albeit, so it seems, with a certain degree of piety as well; at least, that is what the shaykhs whispered to each other. He seemed more violent than all the other amirs and more prone to cruelty and avarice. He left the reins of power in the hands of his amirs, allowing them to raid the khans at will and demand gifts from merchants. Egyptians became accustomed to seeing people dangling from stakes, and being flayed and beaten till they were dead. These actions happened every day in the city quarters. Those who were not killed by the plague died at the hands of Baybars and his cronies who matched themselves perfectly to his demeanor. However, Abu Bakr knew nothing about all that, in his hope that his complaint to the sultan would result in his daughter's release from the marriage contract.

When Abu Bakr returned to his house at night, he summoned his daughter and told her to read the complaint. She did so calmly and stroked his hand.

"I believe the sultan will treat us fairly," she said. "Don't worry about me; I'll be fine. You know your own daughter."

"Be careful," he replied fearfully, "and use your brain. We've no idea about the limits of their cruelty and evil."

She nodded and then headed for her own room. She looked at the boxes of clothes and her wedding trousseau, all carefully arranged months earlier for her marriage to Yusuf. Opening the boxes, she took out some clothes and looked at them. Sitting on her bed, she kept wishing that the whole thing were a dream, sorcery, or the work of the devil. It would all come to an end, and she would wake up in the morning to discover that she was not being married to the amir and would not be going to a palace tomorrow. She would not be sacrificing herself or selling her body like a slut.

She inserted her hand into one of the boxes, searching for her cotton dolls; when she was a girl, they used to comfort her, and she would talk to them. She looked at them and counted them: eight in all. When a brother or sister died of the plague, she used to count them, blame them and complain, and ask them what they thought. When her sister, who was one year younger than her, died, she started checking her dolls hysterically, searching for the black spots and sensing the plague's proximity to both her and her dolls. The plague does not distinguish between humans and inanimate things, attacking just like ghouls. The death of her closest sister had another effect on her heart: death touched a part of her own self and infected her body too, but it preferred to leave. If only it had not done so! She thought about taking her dolls with her, but decided to leave them in the safety of her father's house.

Her mother came in and looked at the boxes and dolls.

"Zaynab," she said, "you're not a little girl any more. Forget about the dolls. Do you want to take the boxes with you?"

"No," she replied decisively.

Her mother looked hesitant. "Be careful, Zaynab," she said. "If you annoy the amir, who knows what'll happen?"

Zaynab said nothing.

"Do whatever he says," her mother said by way of conclusion. "Make sure, very sure, you don't turn him down. If you do, he'll cut off your neck and kill your brother and cousin. You realize that, don't you?"

Her body shook and, for a moment, her hand quivered. She nodded in agreement.

"If he treats you roughly," her mother went on emotionally, "don't scream or resist. Do you understand? Woman is born to endure suffering; it's her lot in life, my daughter. You'll suffer agony in childbirth or afterward. That's the fate of all women. Suffer it all patiently until the trial is over. I'd like to feel reassured about you. Try to ask him to let us visit you from time to time. No, not that. Rather don't ask for anything until you're certain that he's not going to hurt you."

2

The amir's palace on Roda Island was beautiful. It consisted of three stories and a wide garden with lots of fountains. But her father's house was also large, with its own fountain and three stories. She was not affected by house size and did not look around her. She had made up her mind and come to a decision. This amir was not going to possess her. When he sensed her revulsion, he would get bored with her and leave her alone. Fatima advised her to act frozen stiff during lovemaking. He would then get bored with her and go back to his other women.

If only she could postpone that black day when she would be giving herself to the amir, then so much the better. She would come up with a stratagem to postpone that day—the day she was sold and became a slut, giving herself to someone she loathed and despised. What a dreadful era this was, when slaves ruled free people, and tyrants were free to assault and forgive!

She looked at her room in sorrow, the one where today she was supposed to be in her house equipped with the finest furnishings, nestling in the arms of her beloved who was currently sleeping in prison between life and death.

Sitting on the floor, she prostrated herself, praying to God to save her and give her the strength needed to extricate herself from this hole, this deep well.

She sensed some footsteps behind her. Turning around quickly, she saw him coming, close up for almost the first time. He was in full dress, but not riding a horse. He took a close look at her, as though she were a fly buzzing around his eyes.

She stood up, head lowered.

"What were you praying?" he asked loudly.

"That is between me and God, sir," she replied, sitting on the bed. "Talk between God and His servants is unknown to anyone, even Mamluks and spies."

"You speak as though you know a good deal," he said, sitting beside her. "Did you study in your father's house?"

"Yes," she replied, moving away. "I studied Qur'anic exegesis and jurisprudence."

"What else?"

"Algebra, medicine, and philosophy."

"That's unusual for a woman. Why did you study?"

She moved even further away till she was right at the edge of the bed.

"I like reading and sewing. I learned it all in my father's house."

"You sew as well? Your father's a wealthy merchant. You don't need to learn how to sew."

"I just love doing it."

He stared hard at her. "If you move any further away," he said, "you're going to fall off the bed."

"I'm sorry, my Lord," she replied immediately. "Everything happened so quickly. I haven't had enough time to think about things."

"Think about what?" he asked in amazement.

"My marriage and moving outside the city. My living with Mamluks and in your palace, everything . . ."

"So you think as well. That's astonishing."

He looked at her as though she were his property.

"Loosen your hair a little," he said. "I want to look at your eyes. Your father wasn't strict with you; he let you go to the market and talk to men. Egyptian people are strange. Are all of them like your father?"

"I never spoke to men," she replied straightaway. "It was just that I was with my brother. I only ever went out with him. The veil came off my face. I hope you don't think badly of me."

"What do you do with algebra and mathematics?"

"I help my father with his accounts."

He move closer to her and took her face in his hands.

"Your beauty is different," he said. "I never realized that such a thing existed among the Egyptian people."

Her heart started pounding. "There are other women much more beautiful than I," she said. "My Lord, you deserve someone prettier than me, a noblewoman like yourself. I'm not one."

She moved away and moved his hand from her face in an involuntary gesture.

"Forgive me," she said, "but I'm feeling nauseous and very ill. I can barely breathe. If you can let me be today, I can hope and promise that I'll feel better tomorrow."

She looked pale as she placed her hand on her heart.

He gave her a lengthy stare. "I don't understand what you mean," he said.

Thinking that perhaps he did not understand Arabic very well, she said the same thing again, this time more slowly.

"I said that I'm very tired and sick today. I'm asking you to let me be today."

"I understand your words, Zaynab, but I still don't understand what you mean."

She stood up from the bed. "If you leave me be today," she said more nervously than usual, "then I'll be forever grateful to you."

He looked at her for a moment. She could not tell whether her words had made him angry or he was not expecting to hear such things. He stood up and headed for the door. She sighed in relief, but he locked it with the key.

"How can I possibly leave my wife on our wedding day?" he asked as he pulled her toward him. "Don't ask me for impossibilities. You and your family always ask for a lot."

She swallowed hard as she felt his body close to hers. She had no idea what to expect or what he was about to do to her.

"Please be gentle with me," she begged, "and patient."

He did not answer.

He pushed her on to the bed. She closed her eyes, and her whole body froze, as though it were completely separated from her soul. She turned into a corpse, neither feeling nor resisting. When she felt the pain as he entered her, she closed her eyes tight. In her mind's eye she could see her childhood, laughter, running around for hours with no restraints or fears. She remembered her cotton dolls—how as a little girl she would talk to them for hours, how occasionally she would be annoyed with them and throw them on the floor, only to make it up to them and explain what had made her so nervous. Had her mother removed them from their boxes, she wondered? They should still be in their wooden boxes in her father's house. Perhaps she needed some of them here with her.

Once he had finished with her and moved away a little bit, he gave her a dubious look that scared and confused her.

"Have I annoyed you, Lord Amir?" she asked as she pulled the covers over her body.

"No," he replied, leaning his back against the edge of the bed away from her. "Why would you annoy me?"

His doubtful look still scared her; she had no idea what would happen if he were to get angry. He had not been rough with her or raped her forcibly as she had expected. It occurred to her that, if she could separate body from soul, as she had done today, she could tolerate things, until her father submitted his complaint to the sultan and she could be divorced.

A degree of patience was required. The plan was proceeding as well as could be expected. Closing her eyes, she tried to fall asleep and get some rest. Losing her virginity had not been as painful as she had expected. She had not screamed or begged to be excused as she had originally thought. So, this was what a slut's life was like, selling love, with nothing in either body or soul. She had come to understand today that separating body and soul was not difficult.

She wandered disconsolately around the palace. She swore to herself that, once she was set free, she would forget about this tribulation and erase it from her memory. Life would return to normal, and Mamluks would go back to their fortresses. The Egyptian people would come back to their own districts and live in peace and quiet. She herself would return to her father's house and her true beloved.

Her mind was preoccupied with the Mamluks. She had never encountered them before; all she had seen on occasion were soldiers in the streets and amirs on horseback in the distance, checking on Cairo's quarters. On the anniversary of the sultan's assumption of power, she used to go out to the celebrations, listen to the songs and music, and have a good time with the Egyptian people. She never once asked herself where the Mamluks hid themselves, how they lived, and what they ate. She did hear some rumors. People said, for example, that it was the Mamluks who had forbidden the sale of geese and chickens in the popular markets and left them with cheap meat and vegetables. Mamluks ate the best types of fruit and wore silk and gold clothing. If only the Mamluks did not consume rights and money as part of their digestion, then the Egyptian populace would be much better off. Whisperings within her own family were rare and cautious. Fear of the Mamluks remained unaffected, even when chickens disappeared from markets and their price was as high as gold itself.

Every time there was a change of sultan, she would hear his name once or twice, then forget it. One sultan would be replaced by another. To Zaynab it seemed that in this country sultans were just like chickens; whether they existed or disappeared had minimal effect on people's lives. You could live without them and accustom yourself to their absence. She would forget the sultan's name and have no idea why he came, why he killed, why he vanished, and why he died. Just like Cairo and its districts, Mamluk amirs were around every night of one's life, never absent, never disappearing as time and harsh realities went by. Their fortresses were packed full of weapons, and their soldiers perfected the act of slaughter. Every year they would bring more of them from Turkish lands, train them, and teach them that killing people was essential, the defense of religion and Muslim lands was an obligation, and the Egyptian people could not eat chicken.

Three days passed, and Zaynab took note of her husband's daily routine. Every day he would practice fighting with swords and spears, running and wrestling; it would last for three hours immediately after dawn. She was amazed by his daily dawn activities, his recitation of parts of the Qur'an before exercising, and then his absence from the palace till evening.

She was not affected by the palace or his slave girls. But her instincts made her realize the importance of making friends and allies. She took out some of the money that her father had given her and gave it to the senior servant woman who was in her seventies. Zaynab had no idea where she had come from and why she was living in the amir's palace.

From the very first day, Zaynab noticed an extremely beautiful blonde girl named Sara. Zaynab realized that this girl had a totally different relationship with the amir; of all the women in the palace she was the closest to him. He only spoke Turkish with her, as though it were a secret language between the two of them, one that neither Egyptians nor Zaynab herself could understand.

Sara represented Zaynab's first ray of hope. If the amir was really attached to her, then he would soon be leaving her, Zaynab, alone. She gave Sara an enthusiastic smile, shook her hand warmly, devoutly wishing to kiss her hand and have her seduce the amir. He would then leave her alone and completely forget about her. From the very first day, she kept wondering how she could let the girl know what she was planning and how she could frame her request. She was scared and fell silent, praying fervently to God and awaiting an imminent release from her fate.

A few days later the amir offered to show her round the palace and gardens. He told her about her duties, what he expected of her inside the palace, and how she should deal with the slave girls and soldiers.

She agreed at once. Putting the veil over her face and donning her flowing robes, she accompanied him with her head lowered, praying to God all the while that He would soon be setting her free. Her patience was running out, and she was finding it difficult to play the role of the frozen prostitute. She neither loved him nor wanted him.

"My Lord Amir," she said modestly, "may I ask you a question?"

"Of course!" he replied, as he walked along looking at the flowers.

"Have you released my brother and cousin?"

He looked straight at her. "Not yet," he replied.

She thought for a moment. "I was hoping that you'd be generous," she said. "I thought that you'd release them on our wedding day."

"I'll release them when I feel like it," he responded bluntly.

"Have you seen them both, Lord Amir?" she asked. "I'm very afraid."

He was silent for a moment. "What are you afraid of?" he asked.

"I'm afraid that they'll die under torture," she said softly. "I've heard the way Mamluks torture people. I know they deserve it, but I'm scared."

He gave her an angry look. "You don't trust Mamluks, is that right?"

"Of course I do. The good ones are all over the country. But, just like gossip, fear can enter the heart without permission."

"There you are, using eloquence again! Why didn't your father stop you reading? Some religious scholars suggest doing that. Sometimes educating girls is a menace!"

"Other scholars advocate knowledge," she replied assertively. "It's a form of religious obligation and a sign of spiritual effort. Reading is the key to religion and knowledge."

He stared at her long and hard. "I've never studied medicine and accounting. We only did religious studies. Do you want me to buy you some books?"

"I would like that," she replied enthusiastically. "I would also beg you to check on my brother and cousin. I'd like . . ."

Suddenly she fell silent and looked where the amir was looking. She saw a man in irons between two soldiers. The amir's assistant was dragging him toward the amir.

Staring at the man's features, she made out that he was not either Ahmad or Yusuf. As she observed this scene, one that was teaching more than all the books she had read, she gave a deep sigh.

"Is this the one we've been looking for, Shams ad-din?" Amir Muhammad asked loudly.

Shams ad-din raised the man's drooping head. "He's the one who's slunk into the palace, my Lord."

The amir took out his sword and in seconds cut off the man's head, which fell to the ground. The body collapsed, and blood started pouring out, no longer knowing where it belonged.

The amir gave his sword to Shams ad-din who wiped it expertly. He gave it back to the amir, who put it in its scabbard.

"Put the head in a box," he said, "and send it to whomever sent him. You know who it is."

"As you command, Sir!" Shams ad-din replied.

While all this was happening, the blood had completely left Zaynab's body. She lost her balance and had to place her hand on a tree to help her stay upright. Her voice was totally incapable of emerging from her throat.

The amir gave Shams ad-din a nod, and he took the body and head away along with the soldiers.

He then turned to Zaynab. "You were asking for something," he said. "Remind me: what were you saying?"

She thought about saying something, but could not do it. She remained silent.

"Zaynab?" he asked loudly.

"Forgive me, Amir," she said, still leaning against the tree. "Blood makes me sick."

"It's blood that gives you life," he replied, offering her his hand. "There can be no sickness with death and blood; they're realities, life itself. Will you take my hand?"

As she stared at his hand, she could only think of the killing scene that she had just witnessed. But then she took his hand.

"What did the man do?" she asked.

"Betrayal," he replied. "The penalty for that is death."

"The penalty is death," she repeated. "But he never spoke. He didn't defend himself, did he?"

"You believe I did him wrong?" he said angrily.

"My Lord," she replied quickly, "you can cut out my tongue before I would say any such thing. You never do wrong by people. Who hired the man? Was he out to kill you? Who wants to kill you? Whom are you sending the head to?"

"As I've told you, educating women brings with it a load of problems. I don't like all those questions. You need to pay a visit to the sultan and meet his wives. Some of them don't speak Arabic. Maybe you could learn Turkish. Could you do that?"

He was speaking as though she would be living there forever. Talking in that way about the future alarmed her.

"Of course I can," she replied without thinking. "Whatever you command will be obeyed."

"I want you to understand that this marriage of ours is peculiar for Mamluks. It required special permission from the sultan. So, don't expect any kind of welcome from his wives. They don't even know any Egyptians."

"Why?" she asked spontaneously.

"Why what?"

"Why did you marry me if it was going to be so difficult? I mean, it's my good fortune that you're marrying me, but I'd much prefer that you didn't have to suffer because of it."

"That's an odd question. I didn't expect such a thing from you. Why shouldn't I have married you?"

"Well, I'm not as beautiful as Sara, for example. You don't need an Egyptian woman. You're an amir; you can get whatever you want."

"Yes, and that's why I married you," he replied confidently.

"Because you want to get everything?"

"Maybe. I don't know. I don't like this conversation. Do you like living here?"

"Very much," she replied immediately, "very much indeed. I admire you and feel that I'm very lucky to be with you."

He gave her another doubtful look. "What do you need besides books?" he asked.

"I'd like some thread so I can sew. Your generosity puts me to shame, my Lord."

Killing in cold blood and beheading were both new to her. That night she could not sleep. She saw the body twitching and blood pouring from the veins. Her entire body trembled, and she was overcome with fear. For Zaynab inside the palace, every passing day brought her hope of release that much closer. She did not know whether or not the amir was already bored with her. She made a habit of turning out the lights, closing her eyes, separating body from soul, and resigning herself to what happened. She had no idea either whether or not he was also visiting Sara's room. Every day she prayed to God that he would get bored with her, hate her, and go back to his concubine. Because she was quick on the uptake and adaptable, she began to reap the benefits of her relationship with the palace women, especially Umm Khalil, who seemed to be their leader. She gave her a gold necklace of special design and spoke to her, Umm Khalil being one of the very few women in the palace who spoke excellent and fluent Arabic.

Sara did not like Zaynab; that was obvious. Zaynab avoided her.

When her father, family, and Shaykh 'Abd al-Karim came to visit, it felt as though she had died in the palace and been born into a new life.

Through her meshrabiyeh she looked down on the assembly of men, with Fatima and her mother beside her. She was anxious to hear any news about Ahmad and Yusuf.

"My Lord," her father asked gently, "when are you going to release Ahmad and Yusuf?"

"Soon," he replied. "Don't be alarmed."

Abu Bakr looked at Shaykh 'Abd al-Karim. "My Lord," he went on gently, "we feel that you're one of us now. We have a filial relationship."

The amir looked at Abu Bakr in amazement.

"The basic foundations are still in place, of course," Abu Bakr added quickly. "But there's another matter that is troubling me. I've come here to talk to you about it, carrying my own soul on my shoulders. Even so, *'whoever among you sees something forbidden, then let him correct it with his hand; if he cannot, then with his tongue; and if he still cannot, then with his heart.'* I don't know if I should be trying to correct things with my tongue or my heart. I'll leave the choice to you. I have no desire to spend the rest of my life in prison like my two teachers."

"Go ahead," the amir said. "I'll guarantee your safety."

"I trust your resolve and sense of justice. You promised us to release the two men, but it hasn't happened yet."

---

* A hadith—an authenticated report of a statement made by the Prophet Muhammad.

"Is that why you've come?"

Abu Bakr's and Shaykh 'Abd al-Karim's eyes met.

"Not just for that," 'Abd al-Karim replied. "There's another really serious matter. I will venture to mention it."

"I've promised you safety. Proceed."

"Ever since Sultan An-Nasir Muhammad ibn Qala'un's departure, the country's been in a dreadful state."

Shaykh 'Abd al-Karim looked all around him, then continued. "I've thought long and hard about whether to speak out or stay silent. But the truth will out. Perhaps you could intercede with Sultan Baybars on our behalf. I certainly hope so. Baybars's men are ravaging the land, crushing all rights, stealing food, imposing taxes, siding with crooks, accepting bribes and favoritism with open arms—and sometimes even imposing such things. Yesterday they burned down ten houses in our quarter because their owners refused to submit to their demands. They have hung the heads of honorable merchants on doorposts to serve as an example for those people who let themselves be kidded into saying no in the face of such corruption and tyranny. Prices have become intolerable even for the wealthy. This country used to thrive on everything that is good, but now it is groaning with poverty and injustice. How can a country that managed to defeat the Mongols and Crusaders now be groaning with injustice? The Egyptian people have no choice but to obey the ruler, but, when the younger generation starts whispering about a desire for perdition and moving to another country, then the time has come to stop and talk."

Muhammad listened patiently and did not interrupt him.

"Who's the legitimate sultan," he asked in conclusion, "and who's the usurper? We people have no idea; it's still a secret known only to the Mamluks. When An-Nasir Muhammad vanishes, abandons his duties as sultan, and moves to Kerak Castle, what are we supposed to do? My Lord, you have here guaranteed my safety. If you were to decide to kill me or torture me, I would not care. I've thought about this a great deal and discovered that telling the truth requires risk-taking. If these injustices were confined to just a few people, then I might perhaps be suggesting some kind of intervention and a lenient response. But Baybars has ravaged and taken over the entire country. How much money is stashed away in the coffers of the Mamluk sultans and their allies? By contrast, how much money is there in the people's coffers, people who work day and night just to earn a living in peace? They never interfere or ask for anything. We pray for the sultan every single day, but I can't pray for him when he's burning down people's houses and killing children. What Muslim would ever do such a thing? What mentality comes up with such a plan? My fellow shaykhs extol him because he's forbidden drinking wine, don't they? If you forbid wine-drinking but then spread corruption and injustice, how can you be defending Muslim territories? Wine is forbidden because it impairs the mind, but the actions of the sultan and his amirs, my Lord Amir, are destroying the Egyptian people's sanity. He requires donations. What has happened to the amir's self-respect if they're extracting money from merchants by force? That takes away their dignity and their time."

"I've heard enough, Shaykh 'Abd al-Karim," Amir Muhammad said gruffly. "Do not criticize the Mamluks in my presence."

"Our army and our rulers. It's corruption that I'm criticizing. I've asked for your protection."

"I understand, and I know what you're talking about."

'Abd al-Karim heaved a sigh of relief. "What are you going to do?" he asked.

"Prayers for the sultan are necessary," he said clearly, "and respect for Mamluks is an obligation. But I'll never abandon you. Isn't it enough for you to know that?"

The eyes of 'Abd al-Karim and the amir met.

"When I leave your palace," 'Abd al-Karim asked him, "will I be arrested and tortured?"

"No, when you leave my palace, you won't be arrested. But shortly afterward, you will be arrested. You realize that, don't you?"

For just a moment, Shaykh 'Abd al-Karim again stared at the amir. "Are you going to tell the spies what has happened between us?" he asked.

"I'm never going to inform the spies," the amir replied, stroking his shoulder. "There are no spies in my palace. But you've been talking to other people, and your words have certainly reached the ears of the sultan and amirs. They're going to arrest you, Shaykh. You're well aware of that, aren't you?"

Once again, the shaykh stared at him long and hard. "I've thought about saying nothing as I've always done in the past, but I can't do it anymore. Is it courage or sheer stupidity, I can't tell. Death brings rescue with it, but shirking responsibility in the face of injustice is an offense against God. God is more merciful than sultans, but one should not exploit His kindness and mercy. Do you understand?"

"Yes, I do understand. If you leave my palace now, you have half a day, no more, to gather up your possessions, take your children and valuables, and leave. After that, you will be arrested and dragged through the quarter for everyone to see. Neither your turban nor your learning will be of any use to you. The sultan has his own particular rules and a different set of reckonings. If you decide to escape, I can help you. You could go to Upper Egypt, for example. That way you would not have to suffer the disgrace, with soldiers dragging you through the streets. I would hate to see such a thing."

"I'm not going to run away," Shaykh 'Abd al-Karim replied forcefully. "If I did, I would forfeit people's respect."

"If you stay, you'll lose it too."

"I won't lose it if I stay. Everyone will understand and be aware of what's happening. As you know, tyranny can have days when it prevails, but then it's defeated. My Lord, you have listened to me patiently. I trust you, I don't know why."

For the first time, Amir Muhammad smiled. "You're naïve, my dear Shaykh," he said. "Forgive me, but you're not involved in politics and don't understand power. We're the same age, and my advice to you is not to trust anyone. If you decide not to leave, I can assure you that they'll treat you well in prison. That I can promise you. Ill-treating religious authorities has its consequences, and the Mamluks are well aware of that. I'll talk to the sultan."

"Which one?"

"The one who'll be putting you in prison after sunset."

"What about my son?" Abu Bakr asked.

"I've given you my promise. Be patient and trust me."

"You've just said that it's naïve to trust people," Abu Bakr said.

"But trust in me is all you have. If you didn't trust me, what would you be doing? Take the chance and trust me; you've no other choice."

⸻

Fatima, Zaynab's cousin, was a particular case; she had caused her family a lot of problems. Her father had even given serious thought to killing and burying her. Ever since she was a little girl, she had never wanted to read and write. She had never learned anything or memorized Qur'anic verses. To the contrary, she had a single passion, and that was music and song. Even as a child, she had asked her mother to buy a tambourine and lute. Ever since, she would wait for festivals so she could listen to the music and songs, imitate the musicians, and sing their songs. At first, her father did not stop her. She was a girl, one of eleven children, and she saw little of her parents. She spent most of her time at her aunt's house with Zaynab who was the same age and had a welcoming heart. Zaynab loved listening to Fatima's songs, her stories, her ambitions, and her frustrations. She was Fatima's only friend. In spite of their different personalities, they remained firm friends, enduring plagues and crises. Zaynab was not only calmer and more contemplative about everything, but also less rebellious and frustrated.

That same rebellious and frustrated spirit would have led to Fatima being shunned by her family, were it not for a scandalous incident when she was fifteen. She might well have put a complete end to her family and her brothers' futures, had it not been for the plague which killed off some of her brothers and stopped her father burying her alive.

One day, Fatima had collected some clothes and gold and slunk out of the house at dawn to be a singer in a shadow-play. She had been persuaded to do it by one of the male singers whom she had met at a festival celebration. They had whispered to each other, and he had given her his address, having looked at her lovely face and heard her beautiful voice.

When her mother woke up and did not find her daughter at home, she started yelling and screaming. Everyone started looking for her. Zaynab knew all about it, but she said nothing; she did not know whether she should tell the truth or not. Her dear friend would die in either case, whether she worked with the singers and lived in Bulaq by the River Nile amid all the debauchery and wanton activity or returned to her father's house. Zaynab spent an entire day thinking about what to do. Her imagination assaulted her with terrible thoughts of Fatima being raped by the singer, of her beginning a life of debauchery, and of a future that would be completely over. After two days, she went shamefaced to see her father. She was just fourteen years old. She told him what had happened and that Fatima had wanted to run away for some time. Zaynab believed that she had gone to Bulaq.

Her father gave a silent nod, then informed Fatima's father. The men of the family grabbed swords and canes and went looking for Fatima. After a whole day's search, they found her singing vigorously before a crowd of men. As soon as she spotted her father, she let out a shriek and tried to run away. But the men surrounded her, tied her roughly to a cart, and took her home.

Her father and brothers locked her in her room and started giving her a severe beating. Zaynab was very upset as she heard it all; she did not know whether she had rescued her friend or killed her.

"Father," she begged, "ask them not to kill her."

"She deserves to die, my daughter," was her father's response.

"Killing her won't help them," she reacted quickly. "They'll be arrested by the police, which will lead to even greater scandal. It might be better if they could find her a husband in another district."

For a few seconds he looked at his daughter. "You're always astute, Zaynab, but she needs to be punished first."

"If they mutilate her body," she replied, "no one will marry her."

"Yes, you're right," he replied.

Once they had finished beating Fatima, they left the room, some of them panting from all the effort. Zaynab's father tried to calm them down, then suggested his daughter's idea.

On that very same day, the plague invaded the house and attacked the brothers. Fatima was married only one year after this event. She was happy to sing on her own wedding day; everyone thought that she must have completely forgotten about her shadow-play dream and singing in Bulaq. Now her major preoccupation was her husband's stupidity and her children's selfishness. Even so, she did not stop singing, and the rebellious spirit inside her never dulled.

Every time she met Zaynab, she would start singing, beating her tambourine, and playing the lute. Zaynab would be happy to listen. But then happiness left Zaynab forever; now Fatima's songs crushed her heart and distracted her mind.

⌒

Zaynab's mother looked at her daughter's expression.

"Is everything all right, Zaynab?" she asked.

Zaynab nodded.

"He doesn't hurt you?"

"Provided you think that destroying my entire life is not a hurt," she replied languidly, "then no, he doesn't hurt me."

"I don't like all those words you've been reading in books. They've corrupted your mind. I mean to say, he hasn't hurt you, beaten you, been rough with you?"

"No, he hasn't treated me roughly."

"Are Mamluks like our men," Fatima asked quickly, "or are they different?"

"How am I supposed to know?"

"Of course. Do you hate him?"

She looked around her. "I utterly loathe him," she said. "I've never hated anyone this much."

For a moment, there was silence.

"I don't know what to say," her mother continued. "Do you think your father's hope of a divorce is going to happen? I'm afraid it's not going to happen. Meanwhile, you're living with someone you're going to hate all your life. I don't know, my daughter, is it possible that you'll get to love him a little bit?"

"There's no such thing as loving someone a little bit," she replied assertively. "My heart is still in love with the man whose rights were stolen by the Mamluks. That'll never change as long as I live."

Rubbing her hands together in despair, her mother left the room.

"My sister," her friend whispered to Zaynab, "I've decided to run away. This time, nobody will find me. I'm going to Syria. No one will know me and no one will be able to ruin my life. If I become a famous singer, I'll send you word to come and leave the Mamluks behind."

Zaynab gasped. "But what about your husband and children?"

"Zaynab, I'll go crazy. I don't love them. I'm thinking about singing all the time. They never listen to me. Can you believe it? They don't even listen to my own singing. What am I supposed to do?"

"Be careful! If you do that, I'm sure the amir will kill my entire family and burn all our houses. Do you hear me? I beg you, don't do it. I listen to you singing. Come on, sing now!"

"Do you think I have a beautiful voice? Tell me the truth."

"I believe it's wonderful—more than wonderful."

"My husband says my voice sounds like a donkey, with no spirit or subtlety."

"He's just jealous. I'm listening to you now. Come on, sing, but don't run away!"

"You don't understand," Fatima said sadly. "The gremlin inside me wants to leave. Sometimes I even think of setting myself on fire, just to get rid of it."

"What gremlin?"

Zaynab's mother, who had come back, chimed in. "Fatima," she said, "you've lost your mind. Either that, or you're crazy. We need to have a *zar* ritual . . ."

"My Aunt," Fatima replied, "the problem's my blacksmith husband. How I hate him! If only he would listen to me singing just once; if only he would show any sign of pleasure, I'd tolerate it all. That's why I'm dying or going mad."

"Be patient, Fatima," Zaynab said sadly. "Your situation's better than mine."

"That's what you think, dear cousin. You don't understand the significance of having something inside you that cannot come out or do anything. It rends the heart and cripples the mind."

"Concentrate on your children," her aunt advised, "and forget about your husband."

"How I wish I could forget him. I can't stand him. I might be able to do that if only he'd listen to my singing."

Zaynab looked at her sadly. "Be patient, Fatima," she said, "just as I have to be."

⌒

The day of Zaynab's visit to the sultan was the worst day in her life—following her wedding day, needless to say.

When Zaynab arrived at the palace of Sultan Baybars Jashankir, her husband, Amir Muhammad, stopped her. He looked at the sweetmeats that slave girls behind her were carrying.

"Are those for the sultan's wives?" he asked.

"Yes, my Lord," she replied somewhat fearfully. "When we pay visits, it's normal to bring sweetmeats and food."

He looked around him, then moved closer.

"You can give them to the women, Zaynab," he told her, "but they won't eat them. When you're with the sultan, you don't eat or drink. In future, I'll teach you how to give the food to the slave girls first so they can taste it. Then you can eat at least one hour later. We'll talk about this some other time. Today I'm ordering you not to eat or drink anything in the sultan's palace or in any other palace you visit."

She did not understand what he meant. She had no idea whether or not she had committed some crime in making the sweetmeats.

"I'm sorry, my Lord," she said softly. "I don't understand."

"Amirs have different regulations from other people," he replied casually. "Mamluk amirs don't trust either food or prayers. Both of them are simple and hidden ways of killing people."

"My Lord," she asked, "won't the sultan be annoyed if you refuse to eat with him?"

"No, he won't," he replied with certainty. "He and all the other amirs know full well. He never eats or drinks in my company. That doesn't mean that he distrusts the amirs, but the warriors' desire for killing has its own rules and methods. We all know it and expect it."

For a moment she did not speak.

"But," she continued, "if he really intended to kill us, isn't our very presence inside the palace enough?"

He gave her a long stare, not expecting her to argue.

"I'm sorry, my Lord," she said. "I just want to understand, so I can follow the rules."

"Sometimes," he said, looking all around him, "visits are random. But, when the sultan goes out surrounded by his escort troops, killing him right then is difficult; it leads to war and destruction for the perpetrator. Poisoning food is something else. Now you should go in."

She nodded and headed toward the harem doorway, with his words still ringing in her ears. She could not believe the level of caution and treachery among the people ruling her country.

As a group, the sultan's wives treated her like any slave girl; there was no welcome or handshaking. They looked away, as though she were a tiny cockroach that they could not even be bothered to kill. She stayed there silent for two whole hours. Even though she had brought presents, food, and sweetmeats, had prepared the doughnuts and *kunafa* herself, and had made the drinks by hand, no one thanked her. Zaynab's pride could no longer tolerate such treatment, it being a trait with which Amir Muhammad had polished the pavement of his palace ever since his eyes fell on her!

She stayed silent, not trying to speak or understand whatever they were saying behind her back. She decided not to learn Turkish, so she could save herself the bother of talking to these spoiled women who had all originally been slave girls and Mamluks themselves. She was amazed by these wives of the sultan who were neither free nor as intelligent and well educated as she was. Why was there so much whispering, gesturing, jealousy, and hateful looks? What a truly miserable era this was, this period of time that assigned to these sluts the rule of the Nile Valley. She whistled angrily to herself and turned away, recalling, as she did so, her father's wealth and his influence with merchants, how she had been so spoiled at home, and the way everyone around her held her in high esteem even though she was a girl, not a boy.

Amir Muhammad's visit to the sultan was important; the latter had invited him to discuss a particular matter. The amir arrived surrounded by his escort. Sultan Baybars Jashankir looked straight at him.

"I trust your loyalty," he said.

Muhammad nodded.

"If Mamluks fight each other in front of the Egyptian people and religious scholars," Baybars continued, "they'll lose all respect. They'll be exposed to all kinds of mockery and sarcasm. That's why I'm inclined to make peace with An-Nasir Muhammad."

"I agree with you," Amir Muhammad replied.

"We can solve our problems among ourselves. The Egyptians don't need to be involved. I'm worried about the fact that An-Nasir Muhammad is in Kerak Castle; Syrian Mamluk loyalty is open to doubt. They believe that he's the legitimate heir to the throne. The throne of Egypt is not inherited. The Mamluks have realized that, although no one before them did and maybe no one after them will either. That's why governing authority has to be held by someone who's a soldier and commanding general. So, Muhammad, this is a problem we face. There's a split here: you know the situation between myself, you, and An-Nasir Muhammad. Isn't that right?"

For a moment Muhammad just looked at him. "You and I are both Mamluks," he said.

"We fought together, soldiers and fighters, at the Battle of Marj al-Saffar and defeated the Mongols, as Mamluks had done before. You and I were both in Sultan Qala'un's contingent. As you well know, Muhammad, even though An-Nasir Muhammad is the sultan's son, he's not a soldier and warrior like the two of us. Even since he was a boy, he's never been trained to fight. He's never sworn allegiance to his teacher, as you and I have both done. He's of Mamluk stock, to be sure, of high birth, but he's not a real Mamluk."

Muhammad thought for a while. "Have you sworn allegiance to An-Nasir Muhammad?" he asked.

"I'll swear allegiance to a Mamluk like me, not to a high-born boy; he's the sultan's son, but he's not a Mamluk. You know what I mean. You know the difference between when a Mamluk breaks his leg and the sultan's son breaks his."

That made the two men recall an event long ago: they had spent hours on training, and Muhammad had fallen to the ground. Baybars Jashankir had whispered in his ear: "If your leg's broken, they'll make you a servant."

"Do you remember?" Baybars asked him.

At the time, he had not understood how a boy could control his leg and not break it. His leg was hurting him a lot; it was unbearable. He was eight years old. He suppressed his screams of pain and carried on exercising. When it was over, he sat down on his bed; his bones were burning, and he was in real agony. He told himself and his bones once again that his leg was not broken and his ligaments were fine. Any deformity in his limbs would mean the end of his life as a man. Killing was a craft and an art; rigor involved commitment and structure.

Next morning he was supposed to go outside the Citadel into the sunshine. This did not happen often, and he was going on a tour of the parts of Cairo that he would only see on rare occasions. While the Mamluk children were delighted to run around after being pent up for months inside the Citadel training and learning things, Muhammad sat down on a street, concealing the pain in his leg and not moving.

"If you tell them your leg's broken," Baybars, who was years older than Muhammad, told him, "you know what'll happen."

"It's not broken," Muhammad replied.

"Does it hurt?"

"No, it doesn't. Who says it does?"

"Then why don't you run?"

"I don't run around like children. The real warrior only runs around during battle in order to attack the enemy."

The leg went on hurting for months, but he had to keep it totally hidden. He is not sure what happened afterward. Was it some kind of miracle, an escape from some unknown place? Did the pain decrease? Or was it that an internal fear cured him and saved him from a dire fate whereby he would become a servant—maybe in a women's baths? He had no idea where the force and truth lay. He convinced himself that it was not fear, but rather certainty. Warriors are never afraid. The Citadel's rooms were bursting with warriors. To become an amir, you had to be strict and cruel with people. What was needed was pain, excessive force, and savagery, delivered without the slightest hesitation. Such hesitation was a characteristic of

Egyptian people; mercy was characteristic of the poor; and fear belonged to those people who really needed Mamluk protection.

He was a Mamluk and a slave; and slaves came in different levels. There were slaves owned by the sultan; they would only leave the confines of the Citadel walls for a few days. When one left, he would know the time when he was due back; he would also know the goal, the general aim, and the purpose of training and suffering. Once he grew up, he would understand even more, adapting himself and observing the sheer allure in the amir's authority—ownership of men and palaces, and all kinds of women from different parts of the world. No matter how different the teacher might be, fighting was an essential part of survival. The best kind of fighting involved conflict on behalf of the individual soul's sultanate, not the country's. The lure of the former would serve to titillate and arouse the soul. He had never chosen to be a Mamluk, but he had indeed chosen to be an amir. In becoming an amir, he had beheaded many people, plunged into wars, and both understood and involved himself in intrigues. Some of his colleagues were still soldiers, obeying his commands; being an amir brought with it a magic and passion of its own. He had craved the status ever since he was eight years old. When needed, he had plotted intrigues, joined other warriors in conflicts, and lopped off heads without the slightest hesitation or thought. All he cared about was the target ahead and the authority for which he was alive. Baybars had long since caught a whiff of Amir Muhammad's ambition and was delighted. In it he found a common bond between the two of them. Once Muhammad had become an amir, he thought he would be going out into the sunshine and touring the country. He had no need of sunshine. What he needed was the kind of authority that can tempt and summon the soul . . . the world, with all its wealth, women, and hidden secrets splayed at his feet; nights to be spent relishing his status; men all around him at his beck and call. There would be women of all sorts, but now not selected for him by any teacher and scholar—no indeed, these women he would be choosing himself and possessing whenever he wished and desired; they would be chosen from all parts of the earth. Freedom brought with it its own allure and special passions, but he had the sense that he was still a Mamluk; he had no idea exactly why. Was it the soul's craving for power and authority, or its quest for achievement?

For years, teachers of An-Nasir Muhammad ibn al-Mansur Qala'un, the sultan's own son, had been trying to train him in warcraft and its various aspects. An-Nasir Muhammad broke his foot; he yelled and screamed, but he did not become a servant. His teachers decided that he did not have the Mamluks' build or the strength of Baybars and Muhammad. Doctors were not able to repair his foot, so, for the rest of his life, he was known as "the cripple." Indeed, as far as the Mamluks were concerned, he was "the lame Sultan" and a "son of the people."

That title, "sons of the people," was restricted to Mamluk children. It did not refer to either Egyptian children or Mamluks themselves. Sons of the people were born in Egypt, but were not Egyptians. The Mamluks always came from distant lands and were trained from a young age. Mamluks were never born in either Egypt or Syria. Soldiers would kidnap them from non-Muslim countries; they would be trained by teachers, and their loyalty was to their teacher and religion alone. There was no country, no family, and no wealth to inherit from parents. They would start earning when they joined the armed forces as members of their teacher's contingent. Sultans would always prefer to be training Mamluks, not sons of the people. Mamluks were fighters, and fighters could not leave any trails—money and other troubling things. The Mamluk would have started young and sworn allegiance. That is how things were. They would be kidnapped young and taught religion, jurisprudence, and every aspect of conflict. Some rose to become amirs; others remained as soldiers; still others grabbed power and became sultans.

"I understand your logic," Muhammad said slowly. "I agree with you that there's a difference between Mamluks and sons of the people. What's your point?"

"I want him to send me all his money and Mamluks," Baybars replied. "I want them all to swear allegiance to me as sultan of the country. He's the one who's decided to stay in Kerak Castle and go into exile. It's my duty to save the Muslim lands."

He looked at Muhammad and spoke clearly. "The Mongols and Crusaders are combining to attack us," he said. "They never stop conspiring against us. They don't want just to liberate their church and holy places, Muhammad. Their real target is Egypt. You know that, and so do I. We must be firm and united."

Baybars moved closer to him and whispered in his ear: "An-Nasir Muhammad the lame will never be able to impress Egyptians with his slender frame and twisted foot. What they really need is a genuine, full-bodied warrior who will appear in full dress and uniform. That's the way they are."

He moved even closer to Muhammad. "The difference between you and An-Nasir Muhammad," Baybars went on, "is that, if you went lame, they would get rid of you like some scabby dog because you're a Mamluk. But, if An-Nasir goes lame, he'll be governing and throttling us because he's a son of the people and a sultan's son as well. Where's the justice and logic in that? Let's forget the past. I promise you that what happened between you and me will never be repeated."

Muhammad did not respond, and there was a period of silence.

"I want you to take a letter to the Mongol commander," Baybars said eventually. "We need to confirm the peace pact between us."

"Of course," Muhammad replied. "When?"

"After I've confirmed that An-Nasir Muhammad has returned all his wealth and Mamluks."

Their eyes met.

"Muhammad," Baybars went on, "the amirs prefer to give their allegiance to me rather than to Qala'un's lame son who has fled to Syria. If we weren't involved in his war, we'd be just like Baghdad now, kowtowing to the Mongols and trying to earn their approval just in order to live. I want you too to swear allegiance to me in front of everybody so that I can rely on your men. We must show unity in the face of the enemy. Egypt's Mamluks are God's blessing on the country. So, will you swear allegiance? We can start afresh. Who will you swear allegiance to, the Mamluks or a son of the people? Remember . . . my rule over Egypt is just like that of Sultan Qala'un before me. He was a Mamluk. He snatched power from the sons of Az-Zahir Baibars. The whole country flourished and thrived thanks to a warrior ruler who protected it—a 'complete man,' as he kept saying about himself. Why did his son, An-Nasir Muhammad, inherit the authority from him? His father was a soldier who wrested power from a son of the people, so why did he bequeath to his son the rule of a country that rebels against luxury classes and needs a sultan who's both powerful and just?"

"It needs a sultan who is powerful and just," Muhammad repeated.

"Will you swear allegiance to me?"

"Yes, I will," Muhammad replied without thinking. "I will indeed swear allegiance."

"Your loyalty is important to me," Baybars went on after a pause. "I need your influence. I'm going to marry you to my daughter here in the palace, so you can understand my intentions and trust me."

Muhammad smiled, as though he had been anticipating Baybars's statement. "We learned and trained together," he said.

"I realize you want power and money, but my daughter will guarantee you more than that."

"Can't you be sure of my loyalty without the marriage?"

"Yes, I can."

"But you need to be reassured?"

"Do you really prefer an Egyptian girl to a princess from a Mamluk family?"

"I'd rather choose my women carefully and not sacrifice my pleasure in the cause of power. I've pledged my life and gambled in order to get power. It's enough for me to die for its cause and not live a life that's bound by it."

"What kind of logic is that?" Baybars asked with a laugh. "You've not seen my daughter. Marriage is always tied to influence. That's the way our life is, and you know that full well."

"I'm sure she's extremely beautiful," Muhammad replied. "But, when it comes to women, let me choose for myself and select the ones I want. It's just like fruit: I only eat the ones I like. But, at all events, you have my loyalty."

As Amir Muhammad left the palace, he was followed by a soldier, who approached him, bowed, and handed him a piece of paper. Muhammad nodded and took it.

All the way back to the palace, Zaynab said nothing. When they arrived, she headed straight for her room without a word. He was right behind her. Sitting on the bed, he looked at her.

"Didn't you have a good time with the sultan's wives?"

"I don't understand them."

"I knew that."

"Forgive me, Lord. I'm not giving you a good impression."

He nodded, but said nothing.

Once he had left the room, she sighed contentedly. She prayed to God that he would go to his concubine and save her having to suffer the humiliation of silent submission and endurance. If he left her alone and did not come close to her, life would be a bit easier to bear. She felt that she was one of the Citadel's prisoners, living in perpetual darkness with no hope of salvation. What made her really loathe him was the careless way he treated her, along with the tragedy for which she was responsible. It was as though he had no heart or conscience; for him, human beings were simply tools that he could use and then abandon. He was not releasing Ahmad or Yusuf. She had sacrificed herself, but he had not kept his promise. What did she expect from slaves? To behave like free people? She swore that a day would come when she would yell in his face and tell him exactly what she thought of him. She would use his own sword to chop his body into pieces. The very idea gave her more hope. She closed her eyes. As she envisaged him, dead and in pieces in front of her, she allowed herself to smile for the first time. She fell into a deep sleep.

Yesterday had been the best day she had spent in his palace. He had been kind enough to let her sleep on her own, without the usual suffering and humiliation and without him seeing her body naked in spite of herself and toying with it in whatever way he wanted. She opened her eyes in delight. Perhaps he was now bored with her and had gone back to his concubine. Maybe release was at hand. Maybe she could go back to Yusuf. In which case, the entire crisis would be uncovered, and she would have triumphed in this trial. She had borne it all patiently, sacrificed herself, and done whatever she could to save the other two.

What a wonderful day it was. She did not see him in the morning, nor all day long. For the first time ever, she could eat in peace, sing the songs that she had learned from Fatima, and walk through the garden looking for lovely flowers. If only all the Mamluks could disappear from Cairo! If only the plague could finish them off! If only they could fight to the death! If only the citizens of Cairo could attack them with swords and hack them to pieces! All these hopes were possible. The things that she had witnessed in days gone by required her to record them in a special book and publish it at a later date. So much sheer evil, indifference, arrogance, and egotism! There was nothing like it among the Egyptian people.

"You look very happy today, my lady!" Umm Khalil said.

"Very happy," she replied eagerly.

Umm Khalil stared at her in amazement, then left.

She sat in her room, sewing, reading, and dreaming of the morrow and the end to her suffering. If he did not come to her that night, he must have become bored with her and gone back to his concubine.

She started praying to God, prostrating herself for a whole hour. He did not come. With a deep sigh, she went over to her bed and lay down on it. She was about to fall asleep, her mind full of expectation and hope, when he came.

He sat down beside her and looked at her. She knew and anticipated what he was about to do. Her body had already frozen before he came over to her. Her soul hid itself in some distant location where her innocent Yusuf was imprisoned along with her brother—and all because he had said no and refused to accept injustice.

She could feel her body putting up its defenses and preparing for the fresh assault. She stayed where she was, with the bedcover up to her neck, and looked at him.

"Your brother's all that's left to your father," he said calmly. "I'd hate to cut him into two."

She swallowed hard, trying to look defiant.

"And Yusuf, your cousin. Do you remember him?"

He gave her a really close look, expecting to see in her expression the grief and longing that he had noticed from the very beginning. But she remained silent.

"I issued an order today pardoning them both," he went on. "That'll make you happy."

As she sat up, his eyes could not detect any delight on her part. But she was relieved.

"My father will be very happy," she said. "I must thank you for your generous kindness toward us."

"Zaynab," he told her frankly, "I'll release them both tomorrow after having their noses and ears cut off. Laws have to be obeyed. Your family must serve as an example to others. I'm concerned about the status of this country and I'm anxious to keep it secure for all time."

"I beg you," she pleaded, "my father only has Ahmad."

"Should I save Ahmad then," he asked, looking at his sword, "and kill Yusuf?"

She closed her eyes. "I trust your sense of justice."

"So what do you expect?"

"My Lord Amir," she said, clasping his hand, "I expect you to behave honorably. You promised my father to release both of them."

"I promised to release them," he said as he looked at her. "I never promised not to punish them."

She gave him a despairing look, not knowing what he intended or why he was harboring such hatred.

The hatred that she felt for him was something she did not believe she could feel toward anyone.

"I'll do anything," she said, "anything to get them both freed. Ask me anything."

With a smile he looked again at his sword, running his finger along the blade to check its sharpness and ability to lop off limbs rapidly without pain or screams.

"Zaynab," he asked, "do you know what first impressed me about you?"

She stared hard at his sword and imagined Yusuf beheaded in front of her. She almost stopped breathing and could not say a single word.

"Aren't you listening to me?" he asked.

She looked away so he would not see the agony and despair she was feeling. What could you expect from rulers except deceit and trickery—pledges broken and promises unmet? A slave with no background and no homeland.

"I hear you, my Lord," she said.

"It was your eyes that impressed me," he continued, "pulsing with life and courage. Never in my entire life had I seen a woman with such eyes. I had to have her for myself."

What she really wanted to say was that she was not some kind of merchandise to be bought and sold. She was not a Mamluk like him. She did not kill for a living, nor did she spread chaos in order to rule with an iron fist.

For a while she stared at the sword, again imagining Yusuf's body in pieces in front of her.

"Do you like the sword?" he asked her deliberately.

She looked at him, then again at the sword. "My Lord," she said finally, "you have to choose the sword that's the finest and sharpest."

"Would you like to hold it?" he asked her, reaching for the handle.

She looked at it and then took it in her hand. She immediately dropped it; it was much heavier than she had imagined. So, there was no release to be had that way.

He moved closer to her, as though he fully understood what she was thinking.

"We were talking about your powerful eyes," he said.

She remained silent.

"But those same eyes lose their light when you're in my arms," he continued. "Why is that? Where do you keep your courage and life hidden when we're making love?"

Suddenly she shivered all over. "Forgive me, my Lord," she replied quickly. "I've had no experience with men and amirs. Maybe your eyes have been deceiving you. Maybe I have no strength. Maybe I was just a poor weak girl like others."

He nodded. "Perhaps," he said, "but my eyes never deceive me. If a warrior's eyes deceive him, Zaynab, then it's all over for him. Maybe it's you who is deceiving me, not my eyes."

"I wouldn't dare, my Lord," she replied immediately.

Their eyes met, and he grabbed her hand.

"Are you worried about your cousin?" he asked.

"I'm only worried about him because he's my cousin," she replied at once. "I trust your sense of justice and the promise you made to my father."

"I'll look into it," he assured her as he opened her hand and looked at it. "It would set a dangerous precedent if I released the two of them without any punishment."

"But they didn't do anything," she begged. "You saw that for yourself."

"Do you really believe that?" he asked blandly. "They did nothing? They didn't assault my soldiers? If Egyptians assaulted Mamluks, everything would be finished, and there would be widespread destruction."

"You're right," she replied quickly.

"Will you obey all my instructions?" he asked her, bringing her hand close to his mouth.

"Yes, I'll obey all your instructions."

"The power in your eyes."

"What do you want from me?"

"Release your feelings and love me with the power of those two eyes. If you do that, then I'll let the two of them go!"

She did not understand what he was asking of her, but, even so, without a moment's thought she told him that she would do so.

"I don't want to feel your frigid body today," he told her as he kissed her hand.

"What am I supposed to do?" she asked in despair. "Perhaps it's the way I am. Forgive me, but I have nothing to offer . . ."

"Leave it to me to explore that," he replied with a sarcastic grin. "Don't resist your feelings and keep your body in check as you've been doing every single day. If I feel that your body is frigid today, then tomorrow there'll be no argument; they'll both be dead."

"I'll do whatever you want," she said with an enthusiastic nod.

What happened to Zaynab was something momentous, a tragedy by any yardstick. Clutching her body, she moved as far away from him as she could. Tears were falling silently, and her body still teemed with life and energy. This Mamluk raped her body and soul, then extinguished all good inside her. Her body was overcome by an evil spirit, making it twitch and scream, clinging to an ecstasy to come and repose of a different sort. She dug her nails into his back, not to repulse him but to suppress groans of a particular kind and a new sort of pain—quivers reaching all the way to the soul, sensations that could neither be ignored nor separated from vestigial memories. This kind of killing clove the soul in two or even more.

Once Zaynab had been scattered to the winds like grains of sand and the storm had passed, he gave a smile that boasted his victory and achievement. For a moment their eyes met, then he moved away, turned his back, and closed his eyes.

Zaynab was still shaking as she got out of bed. Tears still falling, she put on a gallabiya, opened the door, and went outside. Yusuf . . . that proud, pure man who did not deserve someone like her. She had not kept him in mind; instead today she had totally betrayed him in an unforgivable way. That evil spirit had totally dominated her. Cairo now seemed dark and distant. Nighttime would bring sedition and encourage prostitution.

She burst into tears and covered her face with her hands. If only she could die now! If only that Mamluk would burn her alive and kill her! Then she could find peace forever. She had heard about Mamluk cruelty before. Their skill as warriors served to excuse any and every aggressor, criminal, entrepreneur, and exploiter. The defeat that she had suffered today was indescribable.

The way in which her body had abandoned all logical principles left her perplexed, as did the lively conduct of every limb without any kind of permission. It all presaged a new kind of curse, a force of a different kind.

She tried not to remember. Memory brought with it a sense of shame, sin, and defeat that were unknown to her. Why had the plague left her and her brother alive? Why had it not carried her off before this sin had been committed?

She was still sobbing as she went back to bed and lay on her back. She did not notice that he was lying on his side and resting his arm on the bed. But then she heard his voice.

"Zaynab," he asked, "you've spent all night on the balcony crying. Why?"

She did not reply.

"Why are you crying?" he asked curtly.

She swallowed hard. "I've been missing my family," she replied nervously. "I haven't seen them for ages."

He nodded his head, pulled her toward him, and hugged her tight.

"Yes, I know," he said.

When he started kissing her again, she knew for sure that he was trying to dominate her completely and would seize every house in the country that showed any sign of recalcitrance or rebellion.

"I beseech you," she begged, the taste of defeat still soiling her vanquished body, "don't do that to me!"

"What am I doing to make you so unhappy?"

"What you're doing scares me."

"That's part of your nature, reflected in you, your soul, and your power. I haven't done anything."

She could feel herself twitching once again with a terrible, deadly desire.

"Let's postpone this discussion till this evening," she said. "It's daylight now and . . ."

"I prefer to see you and feel you," he interrupted.

"I think I'm ill."

"I don't believe that."

Biting her lips, she grabbed his shoulder with her fingers, her body writhing in his arms. The entire country was now facing destruction and imminent defeat. She closed her eyes so as to limit its impact.

"Careful!" he warned. "Open your eyes."

Reluctantly she did so. There is no betrayal worse than that of the body.

He made a point of looking into her eyes at this moment of total defeat. He wanted her to realize that, in this particular battle, the army had been totally annihilated. The entire territory was now his, as was the bounty and all the spoils.

"That's much better," he said, hugging her to his chest. "That's the Zaynab that I know."

"You don't know me," she replied in a crushed tone.

"Oh yes, I do know you," he replied forcefully, "perhaps even better than you yourself!"

"Are you going to release them?" she asked, reminding herself of the root cause of this war.

"As long as you are still as strong and lively as you are today," he replied assertively, "I'll give serious thought to releasing them both."

"How long will it take?" she asked angrily. "When are you going to release them? You promised my father."

"I'll be honoring my promise soon, once I'm sure that you've recovered your will to live."

"And when will you be sure?"

"I don't like being nagged," he said gruffly. "Don't talk to me about that subject again, or else I'll behead them immediately."

"Forgive me, Lord," she said immediately. "I wish you a nice day!"

3

The Citadel dungeon had been built and equipped with extreme care, just like an artist's painting or calligrapher's designs. The eminence of the creative artist was visible in every sector of the building, along with man's capacity for sheer evil. It was as though the building's designer had built it out of a breathless desire for eternity or a love of power, craving an enhanced capacity for brutality that could not be halted by pleas for help or countered by ideas.

This particular architect had won a competition, a huge success. History would be writing about him and extolling his work. But for him, time would never have been spent devising methods of torture and dismemberment. Words need to have a punishment attached in order to serve as a deterrent. Anyone capable of blending the breaths coming out of his mouth with criticism of authority and the sultan needed to know the real meaning of air by being deprived of it. Dealing with words, the tongue would be cut out, and, with shooting targets, eyes would be ripped out. The Egyptian people needed to realize that, if they uttered unacceptable words and continued to poke fun at them and ignore them, then it was both necessary and desirable to teach them a lesson.

The existence of such a prison on the earth implied that the prisoner had committed some ordinary crime, one that did not deserve a severe deterrent sentence. Such a prisoner had not been trying to change the governmental system, to damage the general interests of God's servants, or inject fear and panic into the general public. For that reason this prison had to be inside the Citadel. Access was difficult, and the steps down could not be seen in the dark. If some of them were visible, then they were broken and in pieces. They numbered exactly as many as the people who went down them. Those people who descended them might never get out and climb them again. They might never be able to speak, relating the things they had witnessed and heard and perhaps might never see or hear. The dungeon gloom was inhabited by bats, creatures that love darkness and hate light. Surrounded by bats, prisoners inured themselves to the flapping of countless wings, which would come as suddenly as cuffs from the prison guards, and the sound of stakes, knives, and swords, along with all kinds of slow-working weaponry that crush the soul and never allow it eternal rest—prisoners' screams vanishing into thin air, their smell wafting outside the Citadel gates.

Each prisoner had his own personal cell in accordance with the nature of his crime. A particular concern with individuals was a primary goal here; creativity was needed in order to discover points of weakness and places to inflict pain without actually killing anyone but nevertheless inflicting a form of torture that went beyond the normal bounds—that being a special talent only possessed by the prison guards themselves.

Today marked an especially sad day in the Citadel prison. This was a major event. The person being thrown into prison was not a member of the populace; he was a religious scholar, namely Shaykh 'Abd al-Karim.

The shaykh placed his hand over his nose as a hand pushed him down the steps. He almost fell flat on his face, but put it on the rough wall to stop himself falling down in front of the prison guards. He went inside, and they locked him in. He spent several days outside the bounds of history, unable to tell night from day or the difference between bats flapping and prison guards coming in.

All the time he was reciting litanies and prayers, trying to remember day, month, and year. In the first week things seemed fairly simple, but, by the second week, it was much harder.

He heard the sound of the door opening.

"Torture's not necessary," he said, putting up a calm front. "Sins only lead to frustration, and injustice results in pestilence."

However there was no torture, nor was it the prison-guard who had come in. He noticed a lamp being carried by someone whom he knew.

"Amir Muhammad?" he asked in amazement.

The amir put the lamp down on the floor.

"Didn't I tell you, Shaykh 'Abd al-Karim," he said, "that you should escape to Upper Egypt? Do you remember?"

"I certainly do," he replied.

"So, how do you like escape now?" the amir scoffed. "Sometimes it's necessary."

"You preferred that I run away?"

"Did you prefer to stay underground for the rest of your life?"

"My Lord Amir, what is happening to religious scholars will only lead to perdition. Mamluks need religious scholars, as you well know."

"The Citadel hasn't broken your spirit! What kind of man are you? I've often visited religious scholars after they've spent a few weeks in the Citadel. They were all begging, wishing, and panting as they extolled every Mamluk ever born and even those still in their mother's womb. I wonder, haven't you reached that stage yet, or is it that you never will?"

"Darkness and imprisonment may silence my words, but they can never turn falsehood into truth nor can they dress up injustice in fruity colors and sweet scents."

Amir Muhammad sat down on the ground in front of him.

"What do you intend, using such words?" he asked.

Their eyes met in the lamp's feeble light. Their faces looked red, remote, and fuzzy, with no lines or features.

"Might I ask you the same question?" 'Abd al-Karim said.

"Your words amaze me, Shaykh. You talk like a legalist and preach like a religious scholar. Just like a Sufi mystic, you can roam at will throughout our own reality. I admire your words and ideas; I admire your powerful spirit. While I have seen many people and particularly religious scholars, only a few of them have impressed me. The powerful spirit possesses its own luster; it respects its enemies before its friends. In your eyes there is a mockery of life, a desire to move beyond the void. The vast majority of religious scholars don't have such views, nor do Mamluks and Egyptians."

"When I die in prison," Shaykh 'Abd al-Karim said sadly, "I ask that you remember me for the good I have done and that God forgive me my sins."

"What sins have you committed, Shaykh? If you ask for forgiveness, then what resort can I and all the other amirs invoke to pray?"

"Do you know how long I'll be staying here?"

"How can I possibly know? The order to imprison you came from Sultan Baybars himself, not from an amir or minister."

"So, I'll be staying here forever."

"Or until the sultan forgives you or disappears."

By now, they were used to the meager light from the lamp. Their features were easier to see in the dark room. The shaykh could see the amir's rigid features and piercing eyes.

"Sometimes," he said, "I can see into people's souls. In yours I see a hatred of injustice. Will you give me a guarantee of safety, Amir?"

"You always have that. No one can know how long you're going to live."

"You could kill me right now if you gave the word," the shaykh said. "That would be better. I don't know whether or not I can stand torture."

"You'll never be tortured," the amir replied firmly. "I can promise you that."

The shaykh moved closer to him. "How weak mankind is!" he said sadly. "They can't tolerate much."

"Are you talking about me or yourself?"

"Both of us. The end may be near. My Lord Amir, I want to tell you the truth. Even though you seek and extol justice, you've actually been pursuing your own desires."

The amir drew even closer to him, and their eyes met again.

"Who among us doesn't pursue his own desires?" he asked. "Look inside yourself, Shaykh, and search for the self-delusion and weakness. The difference between us is that I know about my own self-delusion and weakness; I live with them. On the other hand, you bury them in the recesses of your heart. Do you really know and understand everything?"

"Have my words annoyed you?"

"I've been expecting them. I've noticed them in your eyes ever since we met at Friday prayers. A warrior's eyes must never deceive him, or else he's finished. I thank you for your courage, but I don't know if it results from your self-delusion or sincerity or a combination of the two. As a young boy, Shaykh, I learned that, if you didn't grab what you want without hesitation, reflection, self-justification, and conscience, then you'd lose it. That's the difference between Mamluks and religious scholars. Power has its own glitter; grabbing what you want brings you a respect and sanctity that is the fulfilment of desire. At least, that's what you call it. In our language however, it's called risk and achievement."

"I'm not judging you, my Lord. I'm just salving my own conscience."

"What kind of conscience is it that can tolerate the darkness of the Citadel dungeon? Anyone who emerges from down here needs incredible strength. You don't have that. However, do you remember, Shaykh, that I've told you that I'm concerned about your situation?"

"Why?"

"I don't know. Maybe because Mamluks with no religious scholars will have no legality or way forward. I can't make any judgment about the place and length of your imprisonment. But I can make a decision about the light entering your cell, cleanliness, and food, and perhaps even a bit of fresh air. Having some light in the cell will help you counter any kind of dementia."

"I thank you and pray for you."

"Will God hear your prayers, Shaykh," the amir asked with a smile, "when you've so much delusion in your heart? Maybe more light will show you what's hidden there. You deserve better."

"Once again my thanks to you, my Lord."

"I have the feeling that you won't be here long," the amir said as he stood up to leave. "Remain strong till the ordeal is at an end. Isn't that what you preached in your sermons?"

"Yes, I say that, and I'll try to comprehend everything I've said and will say. Fresh thoughts are always fruitful; increased understanding has a light of its own."

———

Zaynab made up her mind not to surrender again. She would resist with all her might, even if he beat her. That would be better. Never again would she writhe in his arms. Why should she desire a man whom she hated? What kind of body was this? It deserved to be burned and stoned! From now on, she decided that he would never be allowed to touch her.

Ahmad and Yusuf could go to hell; he could easily kill or burn them without bothering a bit. She was fighting on her own behalf, the soul that she was bound to save. And yet, she could not do it; her fear of his reaction turned her into a coward; so much so, in fact, that it made her despise herself. There were some people in the Citadel dungeon who were dying for saying things against the Mamluks. Was that what was worrying her or the thought of the Citadel dungeon itself? She didn't know.

Zaynab's crushing defeat made it difficult to concentrate; reading was boring, and sewing was a chore. She started sitting on her own in her room for hours, distracted, blaming herself, chiding her body, and doing her best to understand what exactly had happened during those moments when she had lost control of her body. Why was it that her body was no longer able to freeze up and emerge victorious? She kept trying to shove her soul out of the way and recall her childhood, but she could not manage it. By now, she had almost completely forgotten her dolls. When they were making love, her entire mind was infected by a rogue element that simply scoffed. All that mattered were the amir's touches and kisses. Careful analysis and profound thinking were both instinctive aspects of her temperament. The entire issue and its possible solutions scared her. The final verdict would obviously be against her. What had happened could mean only one of two possibilities: either that Zaynab was a slut and devil, and now her body could writhe with any and all men; or that the amir was the devil, the one who had aroused the body and dug out perdition from the bowels of the earth. Using a kind of magic, he had extracted all the devils of land and sea. She herself was convinced that it was the second of the two possibilities. After all, she was naturally devout, had memorized the Qur'an, and despised debauchery. Her entire spirit was shaken by a sense of self-reproach over the defeat that she had suffered. But then, he had threatened her; indeed threatened that he would kill her brother Ahmad and her cousin Yusuf. Yusuf . . . from today onward, she would no longer be able to say his name. It was on their behalf that she had sacrificed herself. Why was it that her body could not stop twisting and turning in his arms? Every time and after his every touch, her body would be twisting and wanting more. It was all bewildering. It needed more thought—either that or death; she did not know which.

She was sitting beside him at breakfast.

"What's troubling you?" he asks as he looked at her scowling face.

She paused for a moment and avoided looking at him. "I was thinking about wars and invasions," she said. "I wonder, could you use magic in war?"

"Magic?" he replied pensively. "Warriors don't need magic."

She pretended to eat something. "Maybe if they embarked on an impossible conflict . . ."

Taking a strand of her hair, he followed it down to her waist. His touch always gave her a jolt. Feeling bashful, she looked round at all the servants. His brash behavior and the freedom with which he treated her annoyed her somewhat. It was as though she were one of his swords or a stallion that he owned. She could also feel the effects of the sense of magic that never left her. She looked at the servants, but their eyes were glued to the floor.

"There's no such thing as an impossible conflict, Zaynab," he said. "Yes, there can be dangerous campaigns and others that require careful planning and risk. Some require boldness and initiative; others practice and experience in combat. Time and place are both crucial factors. Haven't you read about wars in those books of yours?"

His hand was still around her waist. She felt embarrassed.

"I've never read about wars, my Lord," she said, moving away from him. "The subject doesn't interest me."

He put his hand around her waist again. She moved away again, removing his hand firmly.

For a few seconds, their eyes met. He put his hand around her waist again and squeezed so hard that it hurt her.

"Make sure you don't move away from me like that!" he said.

"I'm ashamed in front of the servants, my Lord, that's all," she said, suppressing her anger. "Let's postpone this to another time."

He pulled her roughly toward him. "I do what I like when I like," he said. "This palace belongs to me, not the servants."

She could envision herself outside of her own body. She imagined her severed head laid out on his table so he could boast about it. This is his palace; that is what he had just said. She was his property just as much as the servants and armor. It seemed that she had sold herself.

She pressed her lips together so as to control the pent-up anger she was feeling. Outright revolt was relentlessly brewing inside her; it tasted as sweet as honey in her mouth. Death was now a sacrifice to honor in the light of the full moon. She would thrust this taste to the fore and yell straight in his face, then stand up proudly and leave his palace. Before she left, she would yell that she was a free woman; he would never tread on her turf. He would never be teaching his swords on it, nor would he ever touch her again. He would never command her nor scare her. Mamluks would come to a known end, one that she herself would designate.

When he looked at her, he could see the revolt in her eyes; it was obvious even from a distance. It was the kind of light that would usually fade when confronted with shouts and sharp swords.

"You're not replying, Zaynab," he said, still squeezing her waist.

"You haven't asked anything, my Lord," she replied defiantly.

"I'm not asking. I'm simply making things clear. I expect you to say just two words: 'Yes, Lord!'"

For a few moments she remained silent.

"Yes, Lord!" she said dryly.

"As you command, my Lord!" he repeated, moving his hand from her waist and rubbing it down her back.

For a few seconds she felt she was going to choke. "That's five words, my Lord," she said. "You only asked me for two."

"You're arguing like a child," he replied, raising his eyebrows, "someone who has no sense of danger and doesn't know the difference between fire and water. Where does this insolence of yours come from? Never mind . . . I just want to hear you say those five words in a single sentence."

He still had his hand around her waist, exerting his authority and erecting his bars around the areas where he had managed to win her in his raids.

"As you command, my Lord!" she repeated slowly.

"Okay," he said as he took his hand off her waist and sat up. "We were talking about wars. You must be attracted to them now. Otherwise, why would you be thinking about them all the time and contemplating their consequences, methods, and goals with a frowning face?"

"I was thinking about magic," she said.

"Magic?" he said after a pause. "Yes indeed, what does magic do? Do you practice it yourself?"

"Never," she replied firmly. "Shaykh 'Abd al-Karim told my father that it is forbidden. But I'm trying to work out how it can destroy the will and lead the intellect astray."

As usual, he stared at her long and hard. She lowered her head.

"That's the real victory," he said. "Things like wine may affect your mind, but they can never break the will. There can be no victory without will. It's in that moment of mastery over the enemy that lies all magic and elation, without any criminal act, intermediary, or magic. So, why are you so interested in magic?"

"There's no specific reason, my Lord. Maybe because I'm missing my family and quarters. Maybe I'm afraid that I might be touched by magic."

"What would you do if that happened?"

"I don't know."

"Think about reading about wars and studying invasions," he said forcefully. "That's more useful than types and purposes of magic. Are you missing your family?"

"It's my friend and cousin that I really want to talk to. If you'd allow me to invite her . . . ?"

He nodded in agreement and stood up to leave.

Fatima came and walked through the palace. When she noticed the listless look in Zaynab's eyes, she was curious.

"What's happened, Zaynab?" she asked.

"That Turkish slave," she replied, her voice full of hate, "how I loathe him!"

Fatima looked at her. "He released Ahmad and Yusuf a while ago," she said.

She opened her eyes wide in amazement. "The mean dog!" she said.

"What did you say?"

"When did he do that?"

"A week ago, I think."

"He lied to me, Fatima. He made me shame myself. I've done disgusting things, Fatima. How I loathe him! I'm not right for Yusuf any more. I've been polluted by Satan. That Mamluk slave has bewitched me!"

"What happened?" Fatima asked again. "Was he rough with you? Some men prefer that. You must be patient and put up with things until the crisis is over. Your father's planning to go to the Court of Grievances. The sultan himself will preside. He will have you divorced and put an end to our family's suffering."

"You don't understand anything," Zaynab said, losing patience. "Divorcing him now won't be enough. I want to tear him limb from limb before my very eyes. You've no idea how much I detest him!"

"Has he mistreated you that badly? You're the daughter of a major merchant. Religious scholars have an opinion on such matters. Do you want me to talk to my aunt? We need the religious scholars to intervene on the divorce."

"I've rejected your advice, closed my heart, and separated it from my body. My pure love for Yusuf is now stored within me. He's the one my heart desired. Why does the heart have to be defeated in these contentious times? We're being ruled by slaves who carry swords around with them. We'll be forever abject servants to them. If I had just one chance, I'd kill him in his bed and relieve myself of his evil, him and all the other amirs. He hasn't left me and gone to his blonde concubine."

"What's he done? Has he punished you?"

"You don't understand. I'm no longer the pure maiden that I was. He's destroyed my spirit and roused all the evil inside me. One day I'll get my revenge on him. But I can't face Yusuf. That Mamluk has finished me. Now I just want to die for my sin."

"I don't understand, Zaynab."

"It's as though my body isn't part of me anymore. He bewitched me, so it seems, and then totally crushed me."

"You didn't freeze up on him? Did you respond?"

She nodded in shame.

"What did you do?" Fatima asked. "Did you seem to be responding to him?"

"It's not in my hands," Zaynab replied nervously. "I don't know what happened to me. At first, he threatened me, then his hand and mouth were all over my body, feeling me. He's evil, and so is his soul. I'm not fit for Yusuf, not any longer. I did my best, but I couldn't. He was the winner every time. Do you understand? Every time, I swear to myself that I'll not yearn for him, shiver, scream, and clutch his body, but I can't do it. For me, this is a new kind of weakness. Do you think he's bewitched me? They're famous for it."

"What's the problem?" Fatima asked, shrugging her shoulders. "He's your husband now."

"He's not my husband," Zaynab responded firmly. "That Mamluk will never be my husband, and you know it full well. He separated me from the man whom I really love, then grabbed me illegally. Never for a single day will he be my husband."

"Zaynab, I don't know what your problem is. Do you love him?"

"No, I detest him!" she replied immediately. "As you know, I've only ever loved Yusuf."

"You'll soon be divorced. Then Yusuf can marry you."

"You don't understand. It's as though I'm a different woman now. After all this, I can't face Yusuf."

"I do understand you. That happens sometimes. Mamluks bewitch people all the time; they're good at it. They have very effective charms. It's not your fault. When you're far removed from him, the magic will wear off. Don't worry about it. When Yusuf is married to you, he won't know anything about your feelings or what's happened between you and the Mamluk. Keep behaving the same way. Don't resist him. He'll get bored with you and move on to someone else."

"It's as though, in their minds, everything can be bought and sold," Zaynab said, as if she was not listening to Fatima. "All humans are either murderers or victims. I don't understand these rulers. Tyranny is part of their makeup, and cruelty is their motto."

"The crucial thing is to take medicine so that you don't become pregnant by him. Are you taking any?"

Zaynab nodded.

"He'll soon be bored with you," Fatima went on, "and move on to someone else or a beautiful concubine. Be patient!"

"I'm not going to wait until he's bored with me," Zaynab said angrily. "What do you mean 'bored with me'? How can you compare me with this concubine?"

"She's been raised alongside amirs like him. She's beautiful, Zaynab. I saw her today."

Zaynab stood up nervously. "What are you saying, Fatima?" she asked. "That concubine has to leave this residence."

"What's happened to you, Zaynab?"

"She hates me and wants to kill me. I don't trust her."

"You're tired. Listen, my sister. Look after yourself. As we've agreed, don't bother about what's happened to you. You're the only one who knows about it. Once you're far removed from him, the magic will disappear. You'll be able to forget everything and soon start all over again. It's a major crisis, for sure, but it'll be over. Look on the bright side!

"Thank your God," she went on, holding Zaynab's hand, "that your husband has no family to ruin the rest of your life. If I married a Mamluk soldier, I'd be the happiest woman in the world—sister of a husband and mother-in-law who would poke their noses into everything you ate and drank and go everywhere with you, as though you're some kind of scorpion that might sting them. But your husband's an amir with no family. Do you know where his family is?"

Zaynab shook her head. "You don't understand," she said. "The Mamluks, all Mamluks, are his only family. All soldiers are his family; he spends all his time with them, talking to them for hours on end. Then give thanks to your God because you have a husband with no concubines. You can't deal with his kind of family, but just imagine a host of other girls with whom he spends time. That's the real disaster, isn't it?"

"What is the matter with you, Zaynab? I thought that concubines spared you having to put up with the amir."

For a moment she said nothing. "I don't want to talk about that now," she said. "Talk to me about your singing. And don't dare to run away!"

<hr>

After her heart-to-heart with Fatima, Zaynab's feeling of guilt began to lessen somewhat. She made a pact with herself that Yusuf need never know what had occurred between her and the amir, what she felt about him, or about the magic and devil that inhabited her body. All that evil would be concealed from Yusuf. Once she left that devil, she too would forget what had happened. The evil inside her would end.

This pact with herself provided some relief and let her accept the defeat with a joyful spirit. She anticipated his touch without restraint or feelings of guilt or danger. After all, her feelings stemmed from magic delivered by a powerful and evil criminal. Once she was free of him, such feelings would stop. It was like a period of her life that was about to come to an end, a previous era.

From time to time, she would give him a smile, and on rare occasions she would even talk to him. One day, he asked her if she would like to ride a horse. She replied that she did not know how, so he put her in front of him on his own horse. Once they were moving, she cried out in panic, her heart beating as fast as possible. Such moments defied memory; she had no idea how to erase them. On another occasion, she was helping him bathe. He pulled her toward the big pool fully dressed. She screamed and laughed, kissing him without restraint. But every night she kept asking herself when this trial would end. When would she return to the life she knew best?

The feeling of sorrow at her defeat never left her; it did not allow her much time to stop and understand. In these times, it was difficult to keep the soul in seclusion. It was under constant surveillance, like a prisoner in a dark dungeon with only one prison guard who would come occasionally.

The amir's relationship with his men was open and well organized. He only addressed them in Turkish; they would stare worshipfully at him, humbly waiting for his commands. She had the impression that, all his life, he had been used to giving orders, educating souls, and inculcating a spirit of defiance in men and women. His long, silent stares at both her and others frightened her, as did the trembling hands that she observed among those people who worked with him and for him. His words were few, and his connection with the Mamluk regiment was such as to deserve close study in schools. The soldiers could understand what he wanted from a mere glance and would set about their task without question or explanation. She frequently asked herself what he expected and wanted from her. Would he soon be bored with her?

She started trying to understand his words which she could hear through the window and to discern what made the soldiers so scared. After a while, she deduced that the amir had a passion for horses; he owned several different ones and sharp swords as well. She was not certain yet, but she had the idea that he used to spy on other amirs. He used to count the number of horses and estates they owned, just to make sure that he owned more than they did and was more powerful. The amirs all used to count up their peers' wealth and were regularly on guard for any warning of treason or revolt. Power was the amir's mode, and weapons were his clothing. You would never see him eating with the other amirs or inviting them to eat at his house.

A man who was this cruel and rigid was never going to appreciate her sufferings. He would never realize how he had destroyed her life; he had no feelings and did not even understand what the word "feelings" meant. When he asked her what she had done that day, she would hesitate and tense up. She had no idea exactly what to say or what her duties were in this miserable prison.

She was afraid of him and did not understand him. And yet, Zaynab's nervousness came with a wayward quality that no one recognized. Her apparent calm had its limits, and anyone who went beyond them would discover the inability to control herself that would sometimes affect her.

She had no idea why the existence of Sara and the way he looked at her and spoke to her in Turkish upset her so much. Maybe because she thought that Sara was the real mistress of the house, while she, Zaynab, was the slave girl; or else she did not understand what went on between the two of them and what they spoke about.

She started yelling at Sara whenever she could, whenever the opportunity presented itself.

One day, she saw him talking to Sara right in front of her own room. The slave girl put her arms around his neck and buried her head passionately in his arms. This was more than she could tolerate. She waited for a few moments and watched as he spoke to her and put his hand around her waist.

At that point, Zaynab confirmed that, from her perspective, the way Mamluks treated women was completely different from the way Egyptians did. Her husband seemed to be treating her as a piece of property, a piece of fabric that he could try on, sometimes decorated with silk and at others with linen and cotton.

Zaynab's eyes remained focused on the two of them. Eventually the amir left her and went to his own room. He had not noticed that Zaynab was there. Her temper and nervousness had been constant features of her disposition ever since she was a young girl, so now she strode over to Sara and spoke to her in Arabic.

"Sara," she said, "you have work to do in this palace. Do you understand? It involves cleaning, cooking, and many other things."

Sara gave her an angry look. "I do all my chores, my Lady," she replied.

"Not all of them, just some of them, the ones you're supposed to do. Who is in charge in this house? I am. I am your mistress. Now what I'm saying is that you need some training, a lot of training. From tomorrow, you'll be going to the kitchen with me so I can train you."

"I'm sorry, my Lady," Sara replied listlessly. "I don't work in the kitchen. In this palace everyone has their specialties."

"Everyone? You and me, for example? We're equals? You're under my command, my servant."

"My Lord's servant, my Lady."

"Are you challenging me?" Zaynab said, her mouth gaping in amazement. "Do you dare to defy me? In this palace you're nothing."

"Not all the female servants are equal, my Lady."

"Yes, they are," Zaynab replied.

"If the amir asks me to do something," Sara said with a grin, "I do it at once."

Zaynab thought seriously about slapping her right on the spot. She made an effort not to do it, and instead, with her throat afire, headed for the room she shared with the amir.

The amir was lying on the bed with his arms behind his head as usual.

"How can you embrace the slave girl," she asked angrily, "and then come to our room, all at the same time?"

He opened his eyes, unable to believe what she was saying or the way she was talking to him.

She tried to control herself. "My Lord Amir," she said, "forgive me, but I saw you hugging that girl. I don't understand why."

"You don't understand?" he replied listlessly. "You've never understood. Who are you to understand? This is my palace. I can embrace whomever I wish and do whatever I like. Have you gone mad or what?"

"My Lord Amir," she said nervously, sitting down on the bed, "I will not stay in the same house as that girl."

He stared at her in amazement, stunned by the bold way she had stated her conditions.

"Sara will stay," he said. "This is her home."

His words only made her more angry. "Then I'll leave," she said.

"Are you threatening me?"

Her anger now blinded her. "She's going to kill me," she said. "I know she's going to do that. Do you want her to do that?"

"No one in this house would dare to kill my wife. Rest assured."

"If you really want her," she said defiantly, "then divorce me."

That made him even more amazed.

"Have you lost your mind?" he demanded.

"I will not stay with her in the same house," she replied firmly.

"You don't get to decide anything here, Zaynab. This isn't your merchant father's house; it belongs to an amir."

"If you loved her, why did you marry me? Why are you so determined to humiliate me? Why are you doing all that?"

"I don't want to hear your voice any longer," he replied firmly. "Not another word on this subject."

"I'm not going to stay in the same house with her," she said again, not listening to him.

"Your father didn't bring you up properly," he said as he headed for the door. "He didn't teach you how to talk to your husband and amir."

As she stood up, all the humiliation of days gone by floated to the surface.

"You're not my amir," she said. "My father is a free man who knows how to bring up his daughter. He doesn't go around trampling on rights, killing people, and splitting heads open."

He gave her a lengthy stare. "Sara will stay here forever," he said. "This is her home. She's the most important woman in this house."

"Of course," she retorted, looking straight at him. "I fully understand."

"What do you understand?"

"I understand about these miserable times when slaves rule over free people, and all so they can determine people's fates and replace them with other slaves."

He grabbed her by the arm and looked at her for a moment, as though he were trying to work out what she was saying. The impact of what she had just said hovered over her, and she had no idea how she had come to say such things and whether he would kill her immediately or wait for a while.

It took only a few seconds for her to regret what she had just said. She blushed in sheer embarrassment at her nervous impetuosity. He raised his hand and slapped her hard on the cheek. It jolted her entire body, and she collapsed to the floor moaning.

"Those slaves," he said decisively, "are protecting you and your people both from Crusaders who are out to rape and burn you and from Mongols who are hell-bent on leveling your country to the ground and burning every single tree and house. Without those slaves, daughter of the free, all trace of you would vanish from the earth's surface and the face of history."

She clasped her cheek, the force of his slap still burning inside her heart. She was expecting him to kill her at any moment. That was what she wanted.

Bending over, he grabbed her arm and stared at it.

"Your skin's soft; it'll wound easily," he said. "They'll have to be very careful using the whip, but Mamluks are expert at using it without breaking the skin. They're obliged to maintain order and educate the general public. Stand here, Zaynab!"

She stood up slowly, pushing her hair back as she did so. She did not look at him now that he had managed to break her once more.

"You need some time to consider the enormity of your crime and then pay the price. I have my own private prison on Roda Island. There are some filthy rooms with no light and others with light for important noble prisoners such as yourself and your family. I'm going to put you in one while I decide what to do with you and how many strokes you deserve for what you just said."

"You're going to put your own wife in prison," she choked.

"What do you expect from a Mamluk like me?" he asked carelessly.

"I beg you not to do it," she begged in a whisper.

"Don't make me hate you even more," she whispered to herself.

He did not hear her.

"Get your things ready," he said as he left the room, locking the door. "Take some books and sewing with you to occupy your time. Time tends to expand within the prison's thick walls. You'll need some kind of distraction."

As Umm Khalil took her to the prison, Zaynab remained silent. Such humiliation had its own particular flavor, but it had always been there, ever since she had set eyes on him. Her life before was one thing, and after, something totally different.

"What on earth did you do," Umm Khalil whispered after a while, "to make him so angry? No man ever throws his wife into prison unless she's committed some outrage."

"He's not like other men," she said quietly to herself. "He's a devil, not even a human being."

"Be careful what you say," Umm Khalil whispered as she opened a small door at the back of the palace. "He'd chop off your head if he heard you. He's been patient with you."

"He hit me," she said, feeling her cheek.

"With a whip?"

"No, he slapped me on the face. I want my father to know and to go to see the sultan."

"Who'll tell your father?"

"You, Umm Khalil. I'll give you everything you ask."

"He'd cut off my head if he found out. I can't do that."

"I can't stay here," Zaynab said as she looked at the tiny room with the sheet on the floor.

Umm Khalil was frightened by her conversation with Zaynab. "I'll bring you food every day," she said as she withdrew.

Umm Khalil closed the door, and Zaynab heard the sound of the big key turning in the lock.

Burying her head in her hands, she cursed the day she was born, the day when she had sacrificed herself in order to save the lives of the men in her family, and the day when she had put herself at the mercy of this Mamluk. Yusuf had been right when he said that they were all killers and fornicators. Getting rid of them was a solemn obligation whether the revolution came from the people, religious scholars, or herself first of all.

She banged on the door and screamed all the curses she knew. She cursed him, Mamluks, the entire country. Once she had calmed down and thrown herself on the floor, she started blaming herself—not because she had lost her nerve and cursed him, but rather because from the very beginning she had not lost her nerve. She would curse him in front of his own men in the quarter. He would kill her immediately. Her story would end with his humiliation. She had to humiliate him.

Her cheek was still burning from the force of his hand. She pounded on the door again, begging her father to come, for time to change, for fate to kill her as it had her brothers.

As her energy flagged once again, she started blaming herself for another reason. Why did she hate Sara so much? She might be just a servant, but, if he wanted her, so much the better for her. Would it not be better for her? Zaynab detested him from the very bottom of her heart and wanted him to stay away from her. So why was she so angry with Sara? Maybe she was not used to having another woman in the conjugal household. Her own father never tolerated beautiful servant girls in the house; he only allowed male servants.

She could not imagine how a wife could tolerate having another woman in her husband's house, consorting with him and loving him . . . and right in front of his own wife! But she was not a wife. She had been forced to accept this marriage. It would soon be over—if she lived, that is.

What had happened to her? Ever since her body had rebelled, everything was different. Was she jealous of another woman? No, inconceivable, impossible.

As she had anticipated, her time in prison passed slowly, filled with loneliness and regret. She had no idea when she would get out or what the punishment to come would be. It seemed that he had finally crushed her. Initially she used to wait for Umm Khalil to arrive so she could learn the latest news and ask her to inform her father. Umm Khalil did not say a lot, as though she were scared or did not trust her. After a week, she was beginning to beg Umm Khalil to intervene with the amir to forgive her. This prison affected the mind. She had finished reading all the books and done a lot of sewing. She could no longer stand being alone.

"If the opportunity arises," she said in sympathy, "I'll talk to him."

But the opportunity did not arise, and she did not talk to him.

"Is he going to come to see me?" she asked once again. "Isn't he coming to see me? I'm dying here. Has he no mercy in his heart?"

"He's only keeping you in prison," Umm Khalil said sympathetically. "He hasn't cut out your tongue or chopped off your hand. You ought to thank your Lord for that, at least."

"Has he done that before?" she asked with a shiver.

"Of course. He does that with every traitor and rebel. All the amirs do the same thing. To my mind, he's the best of them. But he's an amir, and they have their own prestige."

Zaynab opened a book and cut out a page. She wrote the following on it: "My Lord Amir, forgive me. I seek your pardon. I've been stupid. I've now learned, really learned. I cannot remain here. I'll die."

"Please give him this piece of paper," she begged Umm Khalil. "Promise me that you'll just give it to him."

Zaynab took off her golden pendant and handed it to her. "This is for you," she said.

Umm Khalil looked at her, then took the pendant. "I'll try," she said.

"Leave it on his bed."

"If I do that, he'll think that you're in touch with someone. He'll kill you immediately."

"He's spending his nights with Sara, of course," she said hatefully.

Umm Khalil lowered her head. "I don't know," she replied.

"Even if you did know, you wouldn't tell me. Everyone around him has fear in their hearts. What's the point of life amid such an atmosphere of fear? If he really wants the slave girl and prefers her, then he can let me go back to my family.

"You're like a mother to me," Zaynab said, stroking Umm Khalil's shoulder. "I'm going to die here. The words I spoke do not deserve all of this. I didn't commit any crime, stealing or murdering."

"My daughter," Umm Khalil said, clasping Zaynab's shoulder, "it's words that scare amirs. Everything else has solutions and outlets. But words have an entirely different effect. In future, you need to be careful what you say."

"If only I had a future."

It was at night that all the wrath and anger pent up inside surfaced. She cursed the Mamluk slaves and those who had brought them to Egypt. She could imagine a pleasant, carefree life for herself under combined Crusader and Mongol rule; they would certainly be more merciful and human in their conduct.

"I don't believe it," she said in an audible tone. "He gets rid of his wife in an instant, as though she were one of his traitorous soldiers. What man would do such a thing? My father was right when he said that they had no origins and no country. Soldiers hired to kill. How could I give myself to him?"

She blamed her body for responding to him and her mind for sacrificing herself. He had bewitched her; that was for sure. Now he was perpetrating every kind of evil known in existence. Had she not seen him casually lopping off a head, then carrying on his conversation? Yes, she had seen him! Someone unmoved by death will not be moved by anything. She had thrown herself into the ghoul's cave, thinking that she would be safe. But for her there was no safety. The ghoul had taken the fire out of its mouth and set her ablaze. It was over.

Next day Umm Khalil arrived. "I gave him the piece of paper," she said.

"What did he do? Zaynab asked.

"He read it, tossed it aside, and said nothing."

"You're lying. Why are you lying to me?"

"I swear to you, I gave him the piece of paper."

Umm Khalil brought over some books and sewing thread.

"He asked me to bring you some more books and fresh thread."

She grabbed her own hand so as not to damage her wrist as she banged against the wall.

"He's going to make me lose my mind!" she said.

"Be patient, my daughter," Umm Khalil said kindly. "This is a decent, private prison. You don't even know what other prisons are like, the ones where soldiers are put as punishment."

"He punishes soldiers?"

"Of course, rigorously! Sometimes he'll even behead a soldier if he's gone too far."

"I used to think he had a heart. Does he have any feelings, any feelings at all toward me, even a little pity?"

"My daughter," Umm Khalil explained to her, "pleading with the amir is nothing new for him. How many prisoners do you imagine try to plead? It doesn't work with them. I think he knows full well when you'll be pleading with him and when you're prepared to accept the number of whiplashes so that you can rescue yourself from this prison-time. For them prisons are a game, good fun. Do you understand?"

"He knows that I'm going to plead? I'll ask for forgiveness?"

"He's expecting it."

"Then there's no hope for me."

Loneliness is the companion and lover of despair. She started waiting for Umm Khalil's arrival every day so she could talk to her, even if the conversation was brief. She could ask her about the world outside. Sometimes she asked in despair whether the amir intended for her to spend the rest of her life without ever seeing the sun again; did he intend to bring her life to a close amid the insanity of prison life just because of some words she had uttered in a moment of anger? Umm Khalil stroked her hand affectionately and assured her that he was bound to set her free; he probably had a date in mind to release her; she should be happy because he had decided not to have her whipped and to save her from the agony involved.

"Do you believe," Zaynab asked her, "that one day he'll really set me free?"

"Of course," Umm Khalil replied emphatically. "He's stubborn. I'm sure that he's decided that you'll remain here for a specific period of time; that's not going to change. But he'll be releasing you. Be patient!"

"When?" she asked impatiently. "When do you think?"

Umm Khalil thought for a moment. "In two or three months," she replied. "A year at the most."

Zaynab shrieked.

"If he was going to have you whipped," Umm Khalil added quickly, "he would have let you go earlier, but he's not done that. Be patient till he forgets what it was you said."

"If he doesn't forget, I'm going to die here."

Umm Khalil opened her hands in resignation. "I just don't know, my daughter," she said. "You keep asking me things, as though I have knowledge of the unseen. Be patient, that's all you can do."

"I'll just ask you to do one thing," she said hopefully. "I'd like you to ask him when he's going to set me free. Just ask him when he'll release me. Don't intercede on my behalf; just ask him."

"My daughter," Umm Khalil whispered, drawing close to her, "you don't understand Mamluks and amirs. Use your brain!"

"What do you mean?"

"Imprisonment for a limited time is a form of punishment, but prison with no hope of release is in a different category, one that Mamluks like to use. By now, they've grown accustomed to using it; sometimes they'll even use it on themselves. That's all part of their customs and methods. After a while, you'll understand."

"Dear God," Zaynab commented, "so what cruel act, what crime have I committed?"

Umm Khalil smiled sadly. "As I've told you before, it's what your words have done. Be patient!"

Once again, Zaynab collapsed to the floor in despair.

About a month later, Umm Khalil came to see her at a different time, followed by some soldiers.

"I'm not sure," Umm Khalil said, "whether you're lucky or unlucky."

"What's happened?"

"Your father's sick and wants to see you. The amir is allowing you to go and visit him, then return to the prison. Cover your face. The soldiers will accompany you. Don't try to escape. That's what he said. Otherwise, you know what'll happen."

"Is my father alive?"

"Yes, he's alive, but he's very sick."

She could not believe her eyes when she saw sunlight again. She smelled the air, and her heart fluttered as she made her way into Cairo, leaving Roda Island behind with all its palaces and Mamluk fortresses.

No sooner did she reach her father's house than she made straight for his room, doing her best to hold back her tears.

He was lying on the bed. She grabbed his hand and kissed it.

"Father!" she said sadly.

"I'm the one who condemned you to this marriage," he said, looking around him. "I realize that."

She did not respond.

He looked over at his wife. "I've spoken to the judge of the Court of Grievances," he said in a hoarse tone, "and to the religious scholars as well. I'm not going to leave you with him, my daughter."

"I'm fine," she replied wanly. "Believe me!"

"What kind of era is this! How I wish I'd died in the plague before seeing the rulers in our country choosing names for themselves like foundlings—people with no origins and no country of their own. What do you expect from them? Amir Muhammad ibn 'Abdallah! 'Abdallah because he has no father; Muhammad because he has no name of his own and is eager to befriend Muslims and pretend to be protecting the faith. What's his real name and his lineage? Who's his father? They all realize that we despise them and know full well what their origins are."

She looked fearfully all around her. "Father, we're all God's servants," she said softly.

"He puts you in prison, he dares to put you in prison! As though they've bought us all—slaves buying free people!"

She had no idea how her father had found out, but she felt embarrassed by her humiliation in front of her own father.

"Don't criticize the way I've been treated," she said firmly. "We've argued, that's all. Don't start quarreling with the Mamluks. What's already happened is enough. I can take care of myself."

"If your own brother couldn't defend himself," he asked mockingly, "how on earth can you do it when you're still a young girl?"

He looked at her brother, but he simply gave her a silent nod.

"Father," she said quickly, "I don't want to leave the amir. Withdraw your complaint."

"What's the matter with you, Zaynab? Are you scared of him?"

"Believe me. He's my husband, and I don't want to leave him. Don't worry about me; worry about yourself instead. Keep Ahmad away from this amir. In fact, it's better to steer clear of all Mamluks and live the way we used to do before."

Her father looked at her. "Your heart is large indeed," he said lovingly, "and you can tolerate a great deal."

"The sultan won't deal fairly with us," she said despairingly. "He's from the same origins. We'll only make the amir angry, and he'll take revenge on all of us. I'm afraid for my brother."

She looked over at the soldiers who were standing at the other end of the room.

"I don't want the complaint to go forward," she said loudly. "I am happy living with him."

She stood up from her father's bedside, left the room, and went into the women's quarters. She embraced her mother and Fatima, put her head between her mother's hands, and, full of regret and shame, told her everything that had happened.

Her mother put her hand on her heart, and Fatima opened her mouth in shock.

"I know," Zaynab said, "what I've been through is unbelievable. He's put me in prison and beaten me. I'm in prison now, on my own in a tiny room."

Her mother shook her head in denial.

"You've lost your mind, Zaynab," she said. "How could you say such things to him?"

"It's the truth," she replied defiantly.

"What truth? Wake up, my daughter! That amir loves you; he must adore you. Otherwise, he would have lopped your head off at once. What wife ever says such things to her husband?"

"You don't even know, Mother," she said impatiently. "He prefers a slave girl to me; she's the one he loves. What I said was the truth. He's the one who has destroyed my life with this marriage."

Fatima interrupted gently. "Be very careful, Zaynab. That way, he'll cut your head off and give you an unbearable whipping. Forget about the slave girl. Ask him to forgive you today. Try it."

"I'd rather die than do that after he's beaten me," she replied vigorously. "Even my father never beat me."

"He'll keep you in prison for the rest of your life," Fatima again said gently. "Why are you so proud and stubborn? He's your amir and husband, whether you like it or not. You've asked your father to withdraw the complaint, and yet you still want to defy him? Where's the logic in that?"

"He prefers the slave girl to me," she replied immediately. "Don't you understand?"

"He can do whatever he likes," her mother said firmly. "What's this strange talk you're using? He's an amir. He can buy one slave girl, two, three, and he can marry two, three, or four wives."

"I wanted to marry just one man who really loved and desired me alone," she replied, tears streaming down her face. "Not a Mamluk, and not an amir. He's deprived me of that and destroyed my life."

"Do you love Yusuf?" Fatima whispered in her ear. "Do you still love him?"

"I don't know," she replied, wiping away her tears.

"He's here," Fatima whispered again. "He wants to see you."

"No, no," she cried, "that's impossible!"

"I understand. The amir's soldiers are scaring you. But, if you met him in your father's room and he was supposed to be reassuring himself about your father's health, then no one will have any suspicions. He wants to see you. He's asked to see you."

"I'm crushed and humiliated," she replied, as she kept wiping away her tears.

"Come out and see him," Fatima said. "It's not too long before sunset. The soldiers will want to take you back."

Nodding her head, she stood up and walked with a heavy pace to her father's room. He was asleep.

Looking around her, she saw Yusuf with his angelic face and innocent gaze, enveloped in sheer goodness. As soon as he saw her, he smiled silently.

He looked at Fatima. "My uncle's fine," he said. "He has to forgive me. I've been the cause of all this agony."

"He forgives you," Zaynab said, avoiding looking into his eyes. "Of course, he forgives you."

"I wonder," he went on, "can he get his rights restored by the amirs?"

When she did not reply, he repeated the question, looking around him as he did so.

"If he petitions the court and the judge rules in his favor," he said, "then he'll have his rights restored. He deserves better than that from the amirs."

She stroked her sleeping father's hand. "He can't ignore the amirs," she said.

"In this life of ours," Yusuf went on, "fear is useless. It's the root cause of our sorrows and ruin. That's why we're still subservient to the amirs."

"The time for courage is long past and gone. I'm very concerned about you, my dear cousin. God will provide you with what you deserve. Don't think lightly of the agonies of prison, body torture, and the stake. Forget about courage; grievances and the like are useless. Don't die; try not to die! And don't play around with amirs. Their principles are different from ours, and so are their rules."

"If my uncle were genuinely scared, he would certainly be asking whether fear is the reason why he's still alive. Is it prison, or rather that he wants to be still alive?"

She looked around, a tear falling from her right eye. "Fear's blended with a whole load of emotions. My father realizes that there's no going back; the story's over. Forgive my uncle; he's only human."

"Should I forgive him and wait?" he asked gently.

"No, don't wait," she replied firmly. "He's not coming back."

Fatima stared at her in amazement.

Zaynab left the room and went back to her mother's room to say goodbye.

"Zaynab," Fatima whispered, "I can help you escape."

Zaynab was shocked and let out a scream.

"He's going to put you in prison again," Fatima continued, looking all around her. "Run away. As I've said before, he's not your husband. Run away to Syria or some other country. Maybe you can be married to Yusuf and get a divorce. I know a secret vault which soldiers will never find. Let's go there now . . ."

"What are you thinking?" Zaynab interrupted her angrily. "I'm not some slut. Why should I run away? How can you talk to me like that?"

"It's just that I'm afraid for you. I don't know what he's going to do to you. He may give you a hundred lashes for what you said, or leave you in prison for the rest of your life. No one will be able to help you. Do you realize that? Now your father's sick."

Zaynab said nothing. Looking toward the door, she placed the veil over her face and left.

"We can go back now," she told the soldiers.

Yusuf sat in his aunt's room, his head in his hands. He had seen Zaynab for a few seconds, then she had left. How could his life be over without permission, merely on the basis of a gesture from a Mamluk amir? How could it be that the life he had planned and the day he had been looking forward to ever since he was a young boy was now beyond the realms of possibility because the amir had made his decision in a single moment? How could Zaynab have been crushed, overwhelmed, and imprisoned while he had stood by helplessly, unable to do anything? What kind of man was he, and what kind of husband would he have become if he had been married to her? He had often laughed at the Mamluks, poked fun at their language, clothing, decisions, and unknown origins. He could remember the hours that he had spent with Ahmad, counting up instances of their mistakes, slip-ups, and outright tyranny. Now here was Ahmad, preferring peace and feeling grateful because he would not be spending the rest of his life in prison. What kind of gratitude was this when the wrongdoer had not beheaded anyone, but had only broken and smashed things? What sort of gratitude when the amir had decided to release them both and put an end to his life and all his hopes? Zaynab was everything he dreamed of—what hypocrisy, what humiliation, what total surrender! If people kept on giving way to the Mamluks, what would be left? The amir had even taken away his bride. What was left? They would be forever at the mercy of a Mamluk amir who would determine their fate as though they were the slaves. What kind of protection and security was that supposed to be? The profound hatred inside him only made him feel more feeble.

How was the amir torturing her, he wondered. He had her in prison and was beating her. What else was he doing? Raping her? His entire body shivered as he thought about Zaynab at the mercy of Mamluks in the prison where he had been.

He recalled the last night that Ahmad and he had spent in Amir Muhammad's prison. His soldiers had brought in some new types of torture instrument and laid them down in front of both of them.

"Did you see your cousin assault the soldiers?" one of the soldiers yelled at Yusuf.

When Yusuf stared at the sharp knife, rack, and thick sword right in front of him, his entire body shook in sheer terror. But he remained silent.

The soldier now looked at Ahmad and asked him if he had assaulted the soldiers. Ahmad too did not say a word.

The soldier grabbed the knife. "You're not talking," he said decisively. "That's better. Before you get out today, the amir has asked me to confirm one thing. I've two ways of doing that: one's easy for you, and the other's easy for me."

The two of them collapsed to the floor, sweat pouring down their foreheads. For sure, beheading them would be easier for the soldier.

The soldier gestured with the knife, as though he was about to do a swift cut.

"If I cut out your tongue, Yusuf," he said, "then I could be sure that you won't talk and babble away about Mamluks. But, if I cut out your tongue, Ahmad, then I'll know for certain that you've forgotten all about a moment when you imagined you'd assaulted a Mamluk soldier."

They both responded in unison: "We'll do whatever the amir commands."

"The amir wants to be sure," the soldier went on, "that the assault on the soldiers was a bit of devil-inspired craziness. It never happened. Neither of you will ever mention it. If that happens, and one of you talks and says what he did and what he saw, he'll have his tongue cut out. Even if he talks to his mother or wife, the amir will find out."

"Nothing happened," Yusuf immediately replied enthusiastically. "We didn't see a thing."

"You should pray for the amir," the soldier went on, "and extol his generous spirit and mercy. He's decided to release you both today."

With their eyes still on the knife and sword, they both prayed for the amir. Every single cell inside their minds and being was focused on the hope of rescue. But now . . . what kind of punishment would Zaynab have to endure, delicate and affectionate as she was? What had she said to the amir to make him put her in prison? The amir had to know that she loathed him. He had to feel the utter disgust she had shown when he raped her. She must have resisted him, so he had decided to punish her. Weakness had to be expunged, just like poverty and plague . . . and his weakness was that much worse than plague.

What could Yusuf do? He could kill the amir, in which case he would be put on the stake at the quarter's entrance; he would not die for days. Not only that, but blood would stream from his ears and eyes, and his tongue would not be able to speak and confess. Should he resort to the sultan? Why trust a foreign Mamluk sultan? When have the Mamluks treated him fairly? How could he resort to a tyrant in order to be rid of injustice? Zaynab had said that this was the end; their story was over. Had she sacrificed herself for his sake, he wondered, or had she simply submitted to her fate? Bitterness has its own fire that burns everything in existence; weakness has a whistle that induces madness.

Zaynab! If only she had not made that sacrifice for him and her brother. He had not been able to stand spending a life in prison. If she had sacrificed herself, he could not spend a life without her. She had asked him to go on living and forget her. He grabbed his forehead with both his hands.

4

During the lengthy trek amid the gloom, thought was easy enough and solutions were clear. Her chances of being divorced were slim. Her defeat at the hands of the amir was crushing. He had not merely shattered her pride and soul. He had broken her body as well and extracted both madness and lust. Her only hope for release lay in his forgiving her, so that their life together could go back to the way it was. She was not as defiant as Yusuf and Ahmad; she neither hated nor liked Mamluks. She wanted to have a peaceful life. As long as the amir was alive and the Mamluks ruled the country, any idea of returning to Yusuf was impossible. Divorce would be his decision to make, when he was bored with her. The very idea that he might discard her in the garbage after sucking the life out of her did not appeal to her, not in the least. She had no idea why. Did her sense of pride as a woman want him not to ever get bored with her? Did she want to be the only one to control his heart, or was it something else she did not even realize? She detested him; she still detested him. She could never forgive him; that she knew. But she could not endure the idea of going back to prison, nor the loneliness involved. She could not countenance the idea of a slave girl winning, nor the thought of that girl's body satisfying his desires while she meant nothing to him.

That notion prevailed over all Cairo's quarters and every quarter of her mind. Sara could not be the victor; she could not stay in the palace as long as Zaynab was going to stay there and adjust to the situation. There was something . . . she felt it from the very outset . . . the amir did have certain feelings toward her. Her mother had told her that today. Maybe he did not love her, or even know what love was, but he did have certain feelings. If she could exploit that effectively, she would be able to carry on. She would need to do that outside the prison, not inside. In her father's house she had grown up like a princess. Servants obeyed her every word, and her pride remained unchallenged. Her father spoiled her; he respected her and valued her judgment. He admired her intelligence. But now, the amir had shattered her nobility and utterly humiliated her. It was equally obvious that, if she wanted to carry on as before, she would have to leave her own sense of honor on the sidelines. Honor cannot live within the walls of a narrow prison cell, nor can pride show itself amid palace slave girls. This was her life now. She had chosen to take a risky turn, and it looked fatal. She needed to save what could be saved. If she was going to finish this race and come out on top, she needed to have children; otherwise he would keep on going to the slave girls. She would stop taking the contraception medicine and pray to God every day that she give birth to many children. If not, as she realized full well, things would be over for her.

Properly planned ideas always produce positive results.

That said, getting rid of Sara and resuming her own life with the amir were hopes that seemed naïve and remote. Zaynab, with her naiveté and confidence in her own exceptional abilities, was the only one to pursue such ideas. In some wars, defeat meant death; that was a possibility that could not be contemplated. Zaynab shook her head, as though ridding her mind of such doubts.

Yusuf, oh Yusuf! Dream, goodness, childhood, hope. There was no going back to the past. He was fine now; he would forget, marry, and live his life. She would carry on too, albeit with weakened heart and broken spirit. She would adapt herself to her fate and live with it. In her battle today, she had to win by any means possible. The amir had defeated her many times. Now a time had come to return the blows and strike the boats. In this particular raid, either she would defeat the enemy, or be finally eliminated.

No sooner was she approaching the palace than she started running away from the soldiers as fast as possible.

"I want to meet the amir," she was yelling, "my Lord Amir Muhammad, the amir . . . !"

She knew he was there and that the soldiers would not dare touch her. She banged on the palace door. It was opened by a slave girl. She ran toward his room as fast as she could.

He met her halfway and looked at the soldiers panting fearfully behind her. One of them whispered in his ear. He signaled to them to leave.

"I ran hard," she panted, "because I wanted to see you and talk to you.

"Please let me speak to you," she begged. "Just a few minutes."

"Just a few minutes then," he declared firmly, opening the door to his room, "and then it's back to prison."

She ran into the room, closed the door, and looked straight at him. There he was, standing right in front of her, in charge of everything. How could she beat him today?

"What do you want?" he asked, stretching his arm out to the bed. "To intercede again about Yusuf? If that's it, I'll kill you today."

She was still panting a little. She was trying to remember the words that she had thought of and had ready for some time.

"I want to explain things to you," she stammered, "to ask you to forgive me. I want your heart to be open to . . ."

"My heart's not going to open," he interrupted. "Is that all?"

She collapsed on the bed shivering. "Don't put me in prison again," she said. "I'll die."

"Why?" he asked, staring at the window. "You've a heater and food. I've even let you have thread and books."

"If I'm far away from you," she whispered, holding his hand, "I'm going to die. I can't do it."

"Zaynab," he said dryly, "leave now. I don't like women's wiles."

She stood up. "So, is my pledge to you false?" she asked forcefully, still holding his hand. "I've never lied to you before. Forgive me. I didn't mean what I said. I was scared, scared of being destroyed, that you'd torture me. I kept seeing you with another woman. I can't bear it, I can't . . ."

"I didn't ask you for your opinion," he replied. "You don't have an opinion."

It was obvious to her that he did not like talking about feelings, torture, and details. It was equally clear that she was losing this battle.

She threw herself on his chest and clutched his shoulders. "I love you," she said. "Keep me here with you just for today, then you can imprison me for the rest of my life. Let me stay in your arms just for today."

He grabbed her arms to push her away, but she put her hands on his face and gave him a powerful kiss that carried with it all the fear and despair inside her. It was the first time since their marriage that she had initiated a kiss. At first, she had tolerated his kisses and kept them apart from her spirit, but then she had responded and writhed in his hands. But, ever since they had been married, she had never taken the lead in kissing or touching him. If this kiss was to be her every hope of escape, she had to pour all her fears and despair into it.

He did not push her away or hug her. She did not know whether she had surprised him, or he did not want her any more. But then, she began to feel that he was slowly responding to her kiss and putting his hands around her face. A moment later, she lifted her mouth from his.

"I love you," she said, still panting. "Keep me with you today. I won't annoy you again, I promise. Forgive me; that's all I ask."

She felt his arm slip around her waist and smiled happily.

"Hold me," she said, "and, whatever happens, don't let me go again."

"Are you this scared of prison?" he asked, as he squeezed her waist.

The fear of staying in prison was rocking her entire spirit. "I'm scared of being far away from you," she replied, running her hands over his body.

He pushed her away a little bit and looked into her eyes. He could feel her heart pounding, as though it had either just been born or was about to die. She looked just like a rabbit that its purchaser was about to grab by the ears and slaughter. She was giving him cautious looks, fearing the inevitable conclusion. As she stared at him, her eyes widened, imploring and asking for help. But, at the same time, he detected the power still lurking in the depths of her heart; even a prolonged stay in the prison had not dimmed it.

She was still looking straight at him.

"Zaynab," he asked, placing his fingers around her eyes, "what is it you want?"

She pressed her head into his chest and clutched his shoulders.

"My Lord," she said, her eyes closed, "I'll do anything for you."

"That's what you always say when you're scared and in despair."

She did not respond; she did not know what to say. She muttered some prayers to herself, devoutly hoping for rescue.

His mouth was close to hers as he ran his fingers over her lips. "I can kiss you and make love today," he whispered calmly, "and then send you back to prison tomorrow. You know that, don't you?"

For a moment, she said nothing.

"If you sent me back to prison," she replied, "I wouldn't mind as long as you visited me every day and gave me a hug. But your sense of justice and mercy won't allow you to leave me on my own far away from you."

"My mercy? Oh yes, my mercy. You've relied on that a lot ever since I first knew you."

Had she lied to him or not? She did not know. She had won her battle; that was for certain. However, she had exhausted the troops and run out of ammunition.

This was the moment when he would be exerting his total control over her; today she was his. Their eyes met. Weakness and passion both gripped her simultaneously. The force of her ambiguous feelings, her despair, and fear of prison showed in her body's desire and control. She could not tell whether the magic factor had intensified or it was the fear of being alone in the prison. But she was making love with him, as though her life were at an end, and an evil force inside her had made her his slave and closed down her mind. In his glances she could see both surprise and caution. She did not care; she was at war, in conflict. She had to fight.

Once it was over, he moved away as he usually did. She clung to his arm.

"Let me sleep in your arms just for today," she said, putting her head on his chest. "Please let me."

Maybe for the very first time with her, he looked bewildered.

"I'm not used to this," he replied.

He tried to move, but she held on to his arm.

"I've longed for you and missed you," she said. "Just for today, let me sleep in your arms. That's my only request."

His bewilderment was having its effect on his normal competence.

"I told you," he said gently, "I'm not used to this. I won't be sending you back to prison. You can sleep, Zaynab. You don't need my arm."

She was still clinging to him as she closed her eyes. She gave a happy smile, then pretended to fall deep asleep. He stayed quiet, awake but quiet. She did not dare say anything, not yet sure whether she had actually won the conflict. She was still afraid that he might shove her aside, in which case she would still be outside his personal space. In conflicts like these, victory involved plans and cunning. That was what the amir had said and taught her; and she was a swift learner. In raids like these, you needed to cover districts and quarters, not just palaces.

She put her leg over his, as though to pin it down amid the years of her life.

"You decided to marry me," she whispered, "torture me with this love, then to put me in prison. Don't you feel guilty for all this injustice?"

"I thought you were asleep," he replied after a pause.

"I want to enjoy being in your arms. You've not been fair with me, my Lord."

"What is it you want?" he asked with a frown. "To save Yusuf?"

She put her hand on his arm. "I want to stay with you. I'm not worried about Yusuf or anyone else. Don't leave me."

He stayed silent, still frowning. It was as though he realized that he had lost and realized her intentions.

Now she wanted to assess the control inside him over city quarters and narrow alleyways.

"You wanted to see me be bold in lovemaking," she said. "Now you know, and you're aware of the way I've suffered for this love."

"Why have you suffered?" he asked, looking out to the horizon.

She did not respond. She was unsure whether to strike the blow with the sword now, or rather wait for a while to savor the victory and adapt to it.

However, when the enemy's in retreat, you have to strike.

"I know no one other than you," she said, kissing his arm, "and I love no one but you. I'll tolerate anything to make you happy, anything. Even if my very soul dissolves and is crushed for your sake, I'll do it. No warrior other than you will defeat me."

"I don't understand."

"If I sensed you were with someone else, I'd die. You've no idea how often I've felt that way. My soul makes its way along insane paths and devilish touches. But, for your sake, I'll bear it all. I have no one else but you. Do with me as you wish. Kill me if you like, but don't leave me."

"What kind of game are you playing, Zaynab?" he asked seriously.

He tried to stand up, but she hurriedly thrust her head into the bend in his arm. "Let me stay in your arms. Trust me."

"What's happened between you and Yusuf?"

"You already know; your men were in the room. He came to see my father. He can't stand me now."

"But I'm going to kill him," he replied with determination. "You realize that, don't you?"

She kissed his neck and ran her hand over his shoulder.

"Do whatever you think is just, my Lord," she said. "For me, you're the only one who matters. Forgive me for what I may have said without meaning it. I've had no experience of marriage or of amirs. I learn quickly and promise that I'll work on improving my manners."

She looked despondent. "What can I possibly do in comparison to your slave girls? I'm not as beautiful or as clever as they are. I'm just an Egyptian girl. You'll get bored with me, and then I'll die. I know, but I don't care. I'll stay with you till you get bored. Without you, I have no life; when you're with someone else, I have no life. What can I say? When you're in some other woman's arms, you don't realize how much I suffer. There are all those women around you, but I only have you. How is that fair?

"My Lord," she whispered, pretending she was about to cry, "do you know how I felt in prison, every single night?"

"How was that?" he asked glumly.

"Thinking of you in someone else's arms, I just wanted to die."

She did not want to name Sara; the very mention disgusted her. No one had ever brought Zaynab's hatred of her to his attention before, but now she hated her more than ever.

"When you're in another woman's arms," she told him, her voice full of emotion, "I want to die. Every night I die, longing for you, knowing all the while that you don't want me. I'm sorry; I keep repeating the same boring words. I just want to talk to you."

With a sigh, she held his arm tighter, as though she were about to burst into tears. She closed her eyes, pretending once again to fall asleep. She could feel him next to her, wide awake and still frowning. That night, she did not get any sleep, nor did he. She pretended to be asleep, having said everything that she had planned to say. He had let her talk, and that in itself had relieved her. He had remained silent, staring all the while out the window.

When he got up in the morning, she still pretended to be asleep. He put on his clothes and left the room.

She stayed where she was, unsure as to whether her victory yesterday was complete or not. She did not say a word. Would he now order Yusuf to be killed? Placing her hand over her mouth, she hoped that this military adventure had been successful. She could neither analyze nor understand her emotions. Wars had their own set of priorities and materials.

After getting dressed, she ventured out slowly into the courtyard. She heard him talking to Sara. She put her hand over her heart, not sure whether it was out of fear for her heart itself or over what she might see and hear. But she could not hear anything. She saw Sara kiss his hand gratefully, then leave. She did not know whether she should go over to him or go back to the room.

Now her gaze encountered Umm Khalil's.

"How did you get out of prison, my Lady?" Umm Khalil asked her. "You've more power than Mamluk soldiers!"

"Please don't give me any credit," Zaynab replied quickly. "I don't know yet when he's going to send me back to prison."

"Are you annoyed at what he's done to you?" Umm Kahlil asked with a smile.

Zaynab whispered to herself, as though she wanted to make sure that the spirit followed the mind.

"I'll never forgive him," she said.

Umm Khalil did not hear her.

"Now tell me," Zaynab insisted. "Has he been spending his nights with Sara?"

For just a moment, Umm Khalil stared at her. "My Lady," she replied, "it's not my place to talk about things that don't concern me. Forgive me. I don't understand. Why are you bothered by that?"

Their eyes met. "Oh yes," Zaynab said angrily, "you understand full well. But you won't talk. You'll let my anger fester inside me as you always do. Never mind! You're still my friend."

Umm Khalil lowered her head, but said nothing.

Zaynab looked over to the door to Sara's room. "What was going on between the amir and Sara?" she asked without thinking. "Why was she kissing his hand?"

"He gave her her freedom, my lady," Umm Khalil replied.

"Are you certain?" Zaynab asked with a kind of joy that she did not know she would feel.

"He gave her some money and a place to live, then set her free. I pray for the Lord Amir every day."

At that moment, she really wanted to give him a big hug. Clutching her heart, she headed for their room and collapsed on the bed. Matters involving the heart were always strange—confusing and strange.

Just as victory brings with it the taste of defeat and surrender, so does victory after the death of another soldier. Once again, she repeated to herself that she would never forgive him, never.

She did not see him for the rest of the day. She had no idea whether or not he would kill Yusuf, as he said he would. She did not dare ask him or risk getting him angry after this truce between them.

When he came back at night, he was quiet and gloomy. She helped him take his cloak off. "I'll cook dinner for you myself," she said. "I like doing that."

"Zaynab," he said as he sat down.

She shuddered, not knowing why. "Yes?" she said, grabbing his hand.

"Yusuf . . ." he said, staring straight into her eyes.

She kissed his hand. "I'm not bothered with him," she said firmly.

"I didn't kill him."

She managed to hide her relief. "You're always just," she responded slowly. "I'll get your dinner ready."

"You haven't asked me why I didn't kill him," he said, looking carefully at her expression.

"I'll never ask," she replied, again firmly.

It felt as if he were playing fast and loose in a difficult contest.

"Zaynab," he said, "killing Yusuf now would turn him into a martyr. I'm not going to be the one to perpetuate his memory."

She wanted to ask him whether he meant that Yusuf would be a martyr for the Egyptian people or just for her. Did the amir want to erase Yusuf from her memory or that of the entire population of Egypt? She did not understand, but she did not dare ask either. However, he had not said a word about justice or about reflection on the killing of someone who has not committed any crime.

"But, if I happen to meet him again," he said starkly, "anywhere—at your father's house or purely by chance in the market, I'll kill him on the spot, and you with him."

She nodded. "That's your right, my Lord," she replied.

"This house has its own rules that you have to follow," he went on. "Do you understand?"

She nodded again.

"I want you to get to know the Mamluk wives," he continued, "and improve your relationship with them, the sultan's wives, and everyone on Roda Island."

"Your order will be obeyed."

"From now on, I want you to behave like a wife."

"I'll do everything that pleases you."

She was still holding his hand and kissing it from time to time.

"Be careful," he said, looking straight at her, "be very careful not to think you can ever beat me. Make sure you don't try to deceive me."

"I swear to you, I'm not capable of that. I'm not used to lying."

"I set Sara free today," he commented dryly.

"Your decision to make, my Lord," she responded, doing her best to suppress a smile as she kissed his hand.

"It's better for her. I don't want her to feel bitter about you."

Zaynab smiled, but said nothing.

He stood up, still looking glum. "Now we can eat," he said.

"Can I ask you for one more thing?" she asked quickly.

He gave her a suspicious glance.

"I'd like to sleep in your arms again tonight," she whispered, "just for tonight. Forgive me, but the loneliness in prison has made me want to have you with me at night."

"As I've told you," he replied as though talking to himself, "I'm not used to that."

"Do it for my sake," she replied, clutching his hands.

He said nothing.

She did sleep in his arms, laughing and talking to him for hours. He was still gloomy, as though he realized that he had lost and was accepting it quietly.

"My Lord," she asked suddenly, staring straight at him, "where are you from?"

He looked back at her, not understanding what she meant.

"Where do you come from?" she asked again. "When did you come to Egypt?"

"I don't remember," he replied without looking at her.

"You don't remember where your country is?"

"Egypt's my country."

"Of course, and Egypt's honored by your presence. But where were you born?"

"Why is it important to know where you were born, when Egypt is the place where you're living, governing, and everything else?"

"Do you visit your family sometimes?"

Her questions were clearly annoying him.

"I'm sorry!" she said quickly.

"I don't know anything about my family," he stated firmly. "How can I visit them? I came to Roda Island when I was eight years old. The Mamluks are my family."

As she nodded her head, she was thinking about the Mamluks and this amir in particular. She thought what it would be like to be snatched from her quarter at the age of eight, never to see it again, or her brother, mother, or father. What kind of life would that be? The Mamluks were certainly a special kind, one that she found it hard to understand. Snatching them from their mothers' embrace was an unforgivable crime, but how could you kidnap a child and turn him into an amir at the same time? Among the people where he came from, kidnapping children was normal; according to rumors, they could be killed or even eaten in times of famine. But for the most part, they were used to beg for lunatics and beggars. But she still could not understand how a child could be kidnapped and turned into an amir in a country like Egypt. The whole thing needed a lot more thought.

"My Lord," she asked, "have you ever thought about going back to your birth-place? To look for your mother? Have you ever thought of that?"

He put his hand over her mouth. "Zaynab," he said, "all this thinking is not doing you any good. Go to sleep, or else I'll leave you and go to another room."

"I'll do that right away," she said, closing her eyes and snuggling up to him.

Zaynab adjusted to her life and started accepting her fate. However, tackling fortresses sometimes involves problems and shocks.

She had wanted to dig a smooth, quick path toward success, followed by a truce. The process demanded power, ammunition, and careful planning. The round that she had just won would not be the final contest. In such contexts, reading is always useful; in this particular situation reading logic and philosophy. It was impossible to imagine the amirs' wives accepting her, especially those of Sultan Baybars. The reason why Amir Muhammad did not fit the usual pattern lay in his basic mentality, something that maybe he himself did not realize. She had no hope of reaching those Mamluk encampments and participating in their lives. Those lives were self-contained: they spoke to each other in their own language and phraseology. They could remember their training, their instructors, their absence from their original lands, their kidnap, and their propulsion into a strange, new world. They were not merely its overlords, but also its soldiers and weaponry. They had their own private life. The amir would spend hours with other amirs, often talking with them in Turkish—planning, enforcing, writing, and creating offices and ranks. Grades and tasks would be perfectly organized, and the subtle system would manifest itself in every move they made, in every glance and look. There were times when you could witness their ability to train the soul and endure shocks, while at others you could see in amirs' houses every kind of debauchery and depravity—wine-drinking, dancing, and shameful behavior. She was not sure: were amirs different, or did each one have two separate sides—one as a soldier, the other as a governor? She started occupying herself with the question of amirs; the things that she already knew, from the way they passed through markets on horseback and in their fancy uniforms, were scant indeed. In her mind, Amir Muhammad himself was a complete jumble; no amount of reading books on logic was of any use.

She was on her own in the palace, on Roda Island, and among the Bahri Mamluks. The strange thing was that she felt considerably less lonely when the amir returned, spoke to her, or hugged her to his chest. That strange reality could not be explained either; or rather it could only be partially. Zaynab herself explained it by saying that he was the only person to speak to her in Arabic, to talk to her about basic principles, and not regard her as being one of the people, Egyptians. They were people who habitually neglected security measures and were careless about their own protection, never sensing any kind of danger lurking in wait to swallow up everything in their country. They neither knew nor understood anything. Instead they spent all their time on shadow-plays and jokes criticizing Mamluks. They had no appreciation of the enormous sacrifices that Mamluks had made and the conflicts in which they had been involved. They had no idea about the miserable lives they led in the midst of so much luxury.

For some unknown reason, Amir Muhammad was the only person around whom she did not feel such oppression and strangeness. However, amirs had their own rituals and regulations that she neither knew nor liked. On this very day, she was no longer sure whether or not she had triumphed and made the necessary adjustments. Sultan Baybars had given Amir Muhammad two slave girls, among the most beautiful ones she had ever seen. She herself was convinced that Sultan Baybars intended to use the gift either as a way of chiding the amir for marrying an Egyptian woman, or else perhaps to ingratiate himself with the amir. She did not understand.

The issue involving these two slave girls was more than she could stand. Getting rid of Sara had been extremely difficult. It had resulted in the utter exhaustion of all the armies involved: her own and the amir's. If this issue with slave girls was still keeping her awake at night, then she had no life with the amir. So, that was her final decision; she no longer cared about what happened to Yusuf, her brother, and the Egyptian people as a whole. Her own fate involved ongoing suffering and fated injustice.

This time, she needed to be very careful before starting the attack.

She was still feeling glum as she awaited his return. When he came back and took a look at her, he could see that she was unhappy. But he chose to ignore it.

"My Lord," she asked dejectedly, "will you allow me to have a word with you today?"

"You can talk to me any day," he replied.

Looking around her, she put her hand on his arm. "Can I take a walk with you in the palace gardens?" she asked.

He looked back at her. "Of course," he replied.

For a while, they walked in silence.

"Have you seen the slave girls," she eventually asked, "the ones the sultan brought you as a gift?"

"What is it you want, Zaynab?" he asked.

As she thought for a few seconds, she realized that she did not want to talk about her feelings and sufferings, nor anything else unfamiliar to her.

"When you married me," she told him assertively, "you bought me a lot of gold. Your generosity embarrasses me."

"What has gold to do with slave girls?"

"I'll buy them from you."

"You'll buy them?" he said with a laugh. "How?"

"I'll buy them and give them to my brother, using the gold that you gave me."

"Why are you sacrificing your own gold to give the slave girls to your brother?"

"You know why," she replied assertively. "I can tolerate anything," she went on, "but I can't stand there being any other woman in your life besides me."

He stopped and gave her an angry look.

"I know," she went on, "I don't have the right. What I'm asking is unusual. But shall I buy them? What's the problem? I'm prepared to pay the price."

"And what happens when the amirs or the sultan give me other slave girls?"

"I'll buy them too. I'll buy all your slave girls."

He stared at her. "Why?" he asked.

She grabbed his hand. "I don't want there to be any barrier between the two of us," she said. "I want to love you as you deserve, and that's more than all the other amirs. Do you understand me, my Lord?"

"I'm trying. Carry on . . ."

"There's no woman in the entire world," she said, "who gives her whole heart to a man who only gives her part of his. If a man wishes to possess a woman without any bounds or restraints, then he must be ready to belong to her alone. I want to love you as a warrior such as you deserves to be loved. I don't want to live with you because I'm afraid or because you're powerful, rich, and an amir. I want to live with you because you're Muhammad, the only man for me."

"You read a lot and talk like poets and Sufis. You're weird, Zaynab."

"I beg you, give me the chance. You won't regret it, I promise you that. I'll do everything I can to make you happy. I only ask for one thing: to be the only woman in your life."

"That's a peculiar and unfamiliar request. I don't think I know a single amir with only one wife and no slave girls. What kind of request is that? Can you be my wife with a status that's different from the normal position of slave girls?"

"My Lord, there's no such thing as 'status' when it comes to love. Either you love wholeheartedly, or you don't."

Staring at the trees, he repeated what she'd just said: "Either you love whole-heartedly, or you don't love at all."

He looked at her. "Where did you get these convictions from?" he asked.

"I've read about love, my Lord. I've never come across a poet who serenades two women. Qays only ever loved Layla. 'Antar only ever loved 'Abla. Jamil only ever loved Buthayna."

"People who believe poets and listen to them are misguided. I don't know any of them, Zaynab. I believe that, most of the time, words only reflect untruths. For poets, words are their source of income; that's why their words are always delusions, confused dreams. It's only in times of need and weakness that their confidences emerge."

"The heart always believes, my Lord."

He did not reply, but carried on walking without looking at her.

"In my imagination," she continued after a pause, "humans follow their heart and carry out its instructions. If they didn't, then they'd have no sense of loyalty. Pursuing desires only leads to hell. No greed can profit its perpetrator, no meddling gives entry to heaven."

He stared at her for a moment. "The heart is all about desire," he declared. "Whoever follows the heart is following desire."

"To the contrary," she replied somewhat despairingly, "the heart always tells the truth. It's the source of faith and conviction. Desire plays with vision like a mirage. The heart only ever loves a single person."

"Maybe you're wrong this time, Zaynab. Lots of amirs love their wife and marry other women. Many wives love their husbands, even though he also owns a slave girl or two, and up to four wives."

"I don't want anything," she replied hopefully, unable to come up with any further arguments. "All the amirs' wives keep asking for jewelry and silks. I just want you, and that's also unusual."

"That's also unusual," he repeated.

"As is marrying an Egyptian."

"Yes, that too."

"Do you need slave girls?"

He gave her a long, hard stare. "Explain to me exactly what you meant," he said.

"You are mine alone, just as I am yours alone, heart and soul."

"So, in your imaginary world," he replied with a smile, "men are just like women."

She said nothing, thinking about the next step to take, the unanticipated risk. But then, wars sometimes involved such risks.

"My Lord," she said, "my father only knew my mother even though he was a rich merchant. We had slave girls, but they were only for my mother. I can't stand the thought of you being with another woman. I can't keep living with you if that were to happen."

He gave her an angry look. She was afraid he might slap her again or throw her back in prison.

"Of course," she went on, "you can dominate me the way you did when we were first married, but you'll never own my heart the way you're doing now. You'll be placing a barrier between us forever. Forgive me. I realize that my frankness makes you angry."

"Do you dare to threaten me?"

"No, I don't. I'll do whatever you want. I'm only expressing my inner feelings to a man who appreciates me amid this entire world that rejects and hates me."

For a moment he said nothing, maybe thinking.

"Who hates you?" he asked.

"You know, all the Mamluks."

"It's not all the Mamluks, Zaynab. Don't generalize."

She put her hand through his arm. "Yes, it is, my Lord."

"Aren't you afraid of what might happen to you after all these threats you've made?"

"Put me in prison or kill me. As I've told you, that's easier to bear than having you touch some other woman. Believe me, I can't stand it. I'm split in two."

"What kind of marriage is this?"

"I said that it's unusual. You had the courage needed to take it on, and I realize that was hard. I wish you had the kindness to bestow just this one blessing on me. I promise that you'll fill the rest of my life. I swear to you that, as long as I live, I'll not ask you for anything else. My Lord, what I'm afraid of is that the soul will be coerced, something that, with time, will lead to alienation and apathy."

"I'll think about it," he replied after a pause.

She opened her mouth to finish her thoughts, but he raised his hand to get her to stop. As their eyes met, she realized that he had run out of patience; he did not want to hear any more about this topic. She found it difficult to suppress all the words she had pent up inside her. Jealousy was still controlling her emotions, and the risk factor still had to be taken into account. For the rest of the walk she said nothing.

She was on edge for the whole day. As she wandered around the palace, everyone kept looking at her as she sighed and whispered curses and other words that no one could understand. She looked out of the window. He was practicing fencing with some of his own soldiers. She analyzed his demeanor, trying to determine from his eyes or gestures what his decision would be. But he was concentrating all his attention on the training, as though he were fighting his last battle.

She started sewing impatiently; she could not read.

"What's brought me to this point?" she asked herself with a frown. "If only I'd never set eyes on him!"

That same day, he was late. She started to have her doubts, wondering if perhaps he was trying out one of his slave girls. She decided that, if that were the case, she would leave immediately. If he decided to kill her or put her in prison, that would be better.

Her emotions swayed between powerful waves of jealousy and unspeakable fury at his actions. He had put her in prison, and now he might be bored with her, leave her in the room of his own palace, and go in quest of some new adventure. Everything was a jumble in her mind. In the past, she had sworn never to forgive him and then convinced herself that she had to adjust. Now, her entire being was under the sway of her imagination, a truly satanic force that was threatening to destroy and obliterate her.

Staring at herself in the mirror, what she saw were the various faces of slave girls, Sara, and, who knows, others in the future. What kind of hell was this, and what crime had she committed? With jealousy tyrannizing every fold in her heart, she clenched her eyes shut. What would she do if he decided to keep the slave girls? She had no choice! She would stay in her room, fully aware that he was in another woman's arms, kissing her the same way he had kissed herself and listening to her fitful breathing. She would surrender, but would she continue to feel the same longing for him? If she did, she would certainly die on the spot! Even magic does not have the evil ability to rend the soul and hurl it into the abysses of madness. This incipient feeling of weakness that was seeping through her pores was by far the worst ever. She would need to curse the Mamluks and invoke every kind of prayer against them. In the country as a whole, they were the epitome of tyranny and injustice.

There remained a tiny ray of hope that pervaded her weakened soul, that he might treat her fairly. He had done it before! He had defeated her as well, forced her and broken her. She had no idea what he would do with her, even if she put on a show of strength. In the amir's house weakness was her hallmark. Like a person drowning, she kept trying and resisting, but a feeling of despair kept infiltrating the risk-taking soul.

It was after midnight when he came into the room. She was sitting on their bed.

"Have you thought about the issue I raised, my Lord?" she asked as he lay down on the bed beside her.

"You don't even greet me?" he asked in amazement.

"I'm sorry, my Lord," she replied impatiently. "How was your day?"

He smiled, something he only did rarely. "How was your day?" he asked.

She frowned, but said nothing.

"Wasn't it a good day?" he asked.

"No, it wasn't," she replied in a low voice. "It was the worst day in my life."

"The worst day in your life?" he repeated with a show of surprise. "Why?"

She lowered her head, but said nothing.

"You know something?" he told her. "You don't hide your feelings very well; they're always clearly visible in your eyes. I've known that ever since I first saw you. That clarity is really bewildering. Am I the only one who notices it, I wonder, or does everyone else?"

She rubbed her hands together, trying as best she could to control the temper that had put her in prison last time.

"Have you thought about the issue, my Lord?" she asked again, anger raging inside her. "Forgive me, but the whole subject alarms me."

"I've given it some thought," he replied casually.

"What have you decided?"

When he looked at her, he could see the anger and tension.

"I always prefer actions that are unusual," he said, "things that lead to better results and assured success. A wife like you needs a lot of time and attention, enough for a man over two lifetimes."

She hugged his chest, not even knowing her own self.

"Muhammad," she whispered, her sheer happiness obliterating all other feelings.

"You've never called me that before."

"You're the best husband in the entire country."

"Even though I'm a Mamluk?"

"Yes, even though you're a Mamluk."

"Do you want the gold now?" she asked a moment later.

"No," he replied tersely, "I don't want your gold."

She wanted to make sure about the fate of the two slave girls. "What are you going to do with the two slave girls?" she asked.

"I've given them to two of my soldiers," he replied calmly. "There's no need for you to purchase them, Zaynab."

She smiled in sheer delight.

He stared at her hard.

"Zaynab," he said, "tell me the truth. What do Egyptians say about the Mamluks? Make sure you don't lie to me."

His question shocked her, and for a moment she did not respond.

"They protect the country," she said in a subdued tone, "and are prepared to sacrifice themselves and their lives."

"Do the people of Egypt really understand that?" he asked derisively. "Do they understand the dangers involved?"

"Perhaps they only understand the dangers of plague and poverty, my Lord," she replied, her head lowered. "But the religious scholars certainly understand."

"The religious scholars certainly understand," he said, repeating her words, "but what about you?"

"Now I know more about them," she replied without looking at him. "Such appreciation has its own appointed time, just like birth and death."

He pushed her hair back from her face. "Zaynab," he said, "sometimes I get to hear things that Egyptians are saying. Spies relay to me things that I don't understand. Can you explain them for me?"

"My Lord," she replied, scared by what he might be asking, "you speak Arabic better than me."

"Understanding, Zaynab, only comes with certainty, not with knowledge. Egyptians say that Mamluks are slaves from Asian territories—no heritage and no tribe. They spend all their time inside their palaces indulging in debauchery. They're warriors for hire, protectors in return for protection money. They're not Arabs or caliphs. What do you say?"

"I've never heard anything like that," she replied quickly.

"I've always known you to be clever, Zaynab," he said. "There's no use in lying. You've heard it and repeated it yourself, just like other people."

"I swear to you now," she answered definitively, "that you're the very best husband in the country."

"Is that because I don't want any slave girls, or because I'm protecting Muslim territories and keeping the country safe amid so much destruction?"

She had no idea how to answer. At this moment she wanted to please him and to win him over as he had her. But she remained silent.

"What happened to your usual eloquence, Zaynab?" he asked.

"In front of you, my Lord," she whispered, "my tongue often fails me and my mind goes blank. Ignorance blinds one's vision and promotes resentment. If Egyptians were more familiar with the Mamluks, then perhaps their fears might diminish."

He moved closer to her. "Would you know me better too?" he asked.

"My Lord," she replied immediately and spontaneously, "my fears of you and for you will never diminish."

"There's your eloquence saving you once again," he said softly, looking straight into her eyes.

"Were you planning to punish me, my Lord?" she asked.

"I wanted to understand you."

"I thought you were reading my eyes, is that it?"

"In dangerous situations initiative has its value. Confidence leads to defeat. You've never asked me what the Mamluks think of the Egyptian people!"

She smiled. "I don't want to ask about things that might offend or disappoint me," she said.

5

Zaynab made her adjustments. She no longer hated her life; in fact, she no longer understood her own self at all. Occasionally she despised her weak position with regard to the amir and Mamluks, but, at other times, she convinced herself that he was her husband and she was bound to obey him and keep him happy. Amid all these worries and uncertainties, she realized that she was pregnant; that made her indescribably happy. She sent word to her mother and father, and congratulations came pouring in. Her father was dying. When he saw his daughter for the last time, she stroked his hand and told him that she was happy with the amir.

"I swear to you," she told him, "that the amir treats me well and loves me. I know that he loves me. You'll be seeing your grandson soon."

Her father was not convinced. All he could envision was the tragedy of his daughter's forced marriage to a Mamluk amir. He had already left her a large inheritance so as to avoid sacrificing her in order to secure her brother's rescue. Ahmad's ambitions were limited: all he wanted was to stay in their quarter, sell things in his father's khan, and to get himself a wife and maybe some slave girls, if possible.

When her father died, she wept silently.

"I've always known you to be strong and faithful," the amir told her as he stroked her shoulder.

"I'm sorry, my Lord," she replied, drying her tears. "These days, I must be very boring and miserable. Please don't hate me."

"How can I possibly hate you?" he replied. "What kind of nonsense is that? I want you not to neglect your own health. You need to eat and get some fresh air."

She nodded and did her best to overcome her grief. Her father had been her only support in life, the only one who really knew and understood her.

The strange ritual that Zaynab had initiated, with the goal of weakening the amir, was now something she anticipated every single day.

Whenever the amir tried to leave her at night, she would wrap her arms around him.

"I want to sleep in your arms," she would say.

The strange part of it was that, from the outset, she had never hated sleeping in his arms, nor had she felt disgusted by the way he used his powerful arms right from the start. In spite of all the anger and hatred she had felt toward him after her time in prison, she had never hated sleeping in his arms. For the most part, she needed someone to compensate for her loneliness, at least as far as she knew. But now, she needed his arms at night. It had to be the combination of pregnancy and loss of her father that led to such ambiguous feelings.

She kept up her brief visits to the palaces of Mamluk amirs and the sultan. When the amirs' wives learned that she was pregnant, they offered their congratulations in a few short Arabic phrases, all the while giving her supercilious stares. The day when she visited the sultan's women was different. There was a great deal of whispering among the slave girls and wives; it was as though they knew something important about her. A few moments later, the Circassian wife asked her to come over because she wanted to talk to her. She was one of the few women who spoke Arabic well.

"I want to warn you," she told Zaynab, looking around her. "He's going to kill your husband on the journey."

"What journey?"

"You don't know?"

With that, she left her and moved away.

Those words from the Circassian wife penetrated to the very depths of her soul. They kept repeating themselves all the way back to the amir's palace.

When she reached the palace, it was to find Umm Khalil getting cases ready, filled with food and clothing for the amir's journey.

Anger overwhelmed her. Strange words, strange women. He had not told her that he was traveling anywhere. But why should he tell her? It seemed that she was just a piece of chattel inside this palace. What if he were killed? Wasn't that what she really wanted? If that happened, she could go back to her own life, to Yusuf, and her father's house. After so much error and futility, life could once again be put on an even keel. Had she not once said that his death would solve every problem? So, why this anger? Why this feeling of suffocation, as though she were the one about to be killed?

She collapsed on her bed, almost out of her mind in sheer confusion. She waited impatiently for him to come back to the palace.

As soon as he came into the room, he looked into her eyes for a moment, then went out again. He asked Umm Khalil to slaughter some chickens and geese, prepare fruit, put them into large cases, and seal them firmly.

When he came back into the room, he found her sitting on the bed, looking completely baffled and distraught.

"What's happened to you, Zaynab?" he asked, sitting close to her.

For a moment she just looked at him, as though seeing him for the first, or perhaps the last, time.

"Don't go away!" she said loudly, putting her hand on his.

He opened his eyes wide in amazement.

"They're going to kill you," she went on, "I know they are."

"Who's going to kill me? What's all this nonsense? Your pregnancy is having a bad effect on you. Are you feeling well?"

"Listen to me," she said firmly, still clasping his hand. "I know. Sultan Baybars's wife told me today that they're going to kill you. I went to visit them."

"Which wife?"

"The Circassian."

Their eyes met.

"Don't believe her," he said calmly.

"Why would she lie?"

"Why wouldn't she? If they really intended to kill me, would they be letting you know? It's just that they don't want me to go. They don't want peace with the Mongols. There's always somebody who doesn't want peace."

"It would be better if you sent one of your men," she entreated him all of a sudden. "What would I do if they killed you?"

"What would you do?" he asked sarcastically. "You're asking me? You'd go back to your former life and your father's house. Maybe you'd get married to . . ."

She interrupted him. "Why are you saying that when you know full well that it's never going to happen? Why do you want to torment me? Isn't everything you've done to me in the past enough? Throw me back in prison, my Lord, for the offensive things I'm saying this time as well. Come on, don't wait. But don't go away, as though you have no family or child on the way. Don't fool around with my fate any more than you already have. I can't take any more."

He stared at her as though he did not understand. "Zaynab," he said, "I'm not running away. What are you saying? I'll be killed one day; I know that. It's my fate and that of every Mamluk. But I've a duty, a task that has to be done. I was born for that reason; I know no other cause. You must realize and accept that for the rest of our life together."

"That life together is going to be brief, it seems."

She snatched her hand from his and turned away in anger.

He looked at her silently. "Were you really expecting me not to go?" he asked. "What were you expecting? I think you're intelligent. I'm a soldier. Soldiers fight to the very end. I've been trained that way since I was a child. I know nothing else."

She nodded. "Excuse me, my Lord," she said, opening the door. "I need to get your other things ready for the journey."

She avoided looking at him.

"Go!" he told her coldly.

Clasping her body, she sat cross-legged on the floor.

"If that Circassian wife said they're going to kill him," she whispered to Fatima, "then they're really going to kill him. Why would she say that? Why would she be lying? Who wants to kill him, I wonder? Are you listening, Fatima?"

"I'm listening, Zaynab," Fatima suddenly replied enthusiastically. "You're in luck, my girl. So, God has rescued you from him. That's what you've said: only death can save you from him. If he dies, you'll inherit his wealth and can be married to Yusuf. Do you understand? What's bothering you?"

She clutched her heart and opened her eyes wide in shock. "Don't say that," she said, "don't dare say that! He's not going to die. Who said he's going to die?"

Fatima stared at her, totally nonplussed. "You want him to die, don't you?" she asked. "Don't you remember? He's the one who put an end to your future and deprived you of your true beloved. You were forced to marry him, and he put your brother in prison. Not just that, but he imprisoned you as well, humiliated you, and . . . Zaynab, are you listening to me?"

Zaynab hugged herself even harder. "What did you say?" she asked.

"You haven't asked about Yusuf for ages, not even once," Fatima continued, still perplexed. "You've changed, Zaynab. What's happened?"

"Yusuf?" she asked, as though she had not been listening.

"Do you want to know where he is?"

"Who wants to kill him?" Zaynab asked distractedly.

"Who? Yusuf?"

"No, the amir."

"That amir's managed to dominate you completely. Has he bewitched you again? How has he managed to do it?"

"If he dies while I'm pregnant, what am I going to do?" Zaynab asked in despair. "I'm afraid he's going to die and leave me as a widow, with a fatherless baby."

"Zaynab," Fatima said, "you're my friend and my sister. You're not thinking or talking about anyone apart from him. Ever since you came here, you've been anxious and distracted. If he were to die, how would that harm you? Yusuf would marry you and bring up your child."

"Don't say that!" she yelled. "Don't you dare say that. I must do something. What can I do? Can I beg the sultan to send some soldiers to back him up? How can I get to the sultan? Should I ask his wives to help? What should I do? He can't die."

"Why are you lying to me, Zaynab? If you used to love him, why the lies? I no longer trust you, Zaynab. Did you love him from the outset? Did you really love Yusuf? What kind of woman are you? Do you love him or not?"

"No, I don't love him," she replied quickly as she stood up.

"Do you love Yusuf?"

"No, I don't love Yusuf. I hate all men. I hate times past, this country, and everyone in it."

⟜

As she went to sleep on her bed, in an involuntary gesture she felt for his spot. Then she clutched her stomach, pushed her body into the bed, and closed her eyes. She had not thought about Yusuf for ages; memories of him were remote and intractable. She started viewing him from a different perspective, as a little boy who played with her for hours, laughing, chiding, and running with her. He was her friend. What a handsome and wonderful man he was! But now, it seemed, her evil heart had preferred the rapist and warrior. She had betrayed her family, people, and every single corner of her own self. She had lost, retreated, and revealed every location and secret to the enemy. There was a time when she had hated the amir with a passion. He had shaken the pillars of her heart and, so it seemed, beaten her into the ground. If only he had killed Yusuf and put an end to all the youthful longing and bewilderment. However, he had inserted his hand into the recesses of her heart and changed all the plans and contents.

She placed her hand over his sleeping spot. Injustice and trickery both had their own specialists, people who had perfected the game and its cruelties. She knew them, and he was prime among them. Lopping off heads with no restraint, killing without hesitation! What a betrayal, what humiliation, in that she had swallowed her imprisonment and felt a desire for the jailer who had dragged her down into such darkness and degradation! How had he managed to do such things? How had she allowed him to run his hand over the outlines of her spirit and brand her with the very depths of the Citadel dungeon full of bats?

Even if the amir died, it would still be impossible to be separated from him. She despised herself and loathed her fate and all Mamluks. And yet, she loved him, loved him like a teenager. In mere moments, he had turned her into a woman, toyed with her heart, and then broken it into pieces. Afterward, he had settled there, more firmly than anyone else before—whether Yusuf, any other man, or even her dolls, which had come to her aid when she had bidden a final farewell to her brothers. The feeling of shame at being weak had a fresh flavor to it, but, every time he went away or she felt doubtful about his future, passionate love would surge through her veins.

⟜

Next morning, she put on her clothes.

"Umm Khalil," she asked hopefully, "will you come with me to visit the sultan?"

Umm Khalil looked at her in alarm. "My Lord won't allow you to go out while he's away, my Lady," she replied. "You can't visit the sultan at any time; not for our own wishes, needless to say."

"We can try," Zaynab said disconsolately. "Help me save the amir. I'm scared for him. You can help me. You know the sultan's wives really well, don't you?"

"My Lady," Umm Khalil replied warily, "be patient till we hear from the amir. Behaving like that will make him annoyed and expose you to danger—you and your unborn child."

She collapsed on the bed in despair. "He's going to die," she said. "I'm afraid he's going to die. What can I do? We have to try something."

"I'm sorry, my Lady," Umm Khalil responded firmly. "I know for sure that the soldiers will never let you leave without permission from the amir. I also know that the sultan will never receive us. For the sake of your child, please calm down!"

She shook her head and covered her face, but said nothing.

Several hours later, she heard some whisperings next door, so she went over. When she went into the room, it was to find her mother looking at Fatima and a soldier standing with his head lowered. She realized that something had happened.

"Is the amir all right?" she asked in alarm, clutching her stomach.

"We don't know, my Lady," the soldier replied. "Robbers attacked his caravan. They killed some personnel, but others managed to escape. We don't know, but . . ."

He stopped for a moment.

"Carry on," she said.

"The person who brought the news said that the robbers intended to kill him in person and did so. We don't know for sure."

She fell to the floor with a shriek. Her mother grabbed her and felt her frigid body.

"He's not dead, Zaynab," she said gently. "Be patient, my daughter."

At this point, vision failed her; everything looked obscure and different. She closed her eyes and remained silent.

"Don't be afraid, Zaynab," Fatima told her, "don't be afraid."

She did not respond. Her mother took her back to her room, and she lay down on the bed without saying a word. She lay on her side, her eyes wide open. She started questioning herself in an audible voice: "Not sure . . . why did he enter my life, why did he put me in prison, why leave without permission? He had done it all without permission. I was used to life providing no choices, to power always winning. I'll never forgive him, never! He's destroyed me. If he's dead, I'm finished. If he dies, what will I do? I don't want to live anymore."

Fatima shook her. "That way, you're going to lose the baby," she said. "Even if he's dead, Zaynab, everyone dies. What's the matter with you? It's sorcery, believe me."

She moved her body around. "If he's died," she muttered, "I can't go on living."

Fatima rubbed her hands together. "He's bewitched her," she whispered to her mother. "I warned you, Aunt. Just take a look at her glazed eyes."

Zaynab's mother started stroking her daughter's shoulders. "Calm down," she said. "Your pregnancy is having a bad effect on you. Calm down, my daughter. Why? Do you really love him that much? Why?"

"Remember," Fatima pointed out, "he's the one who put you in prison, humiliated you, and . . ."

"I don't want to talk," Zaynab interrupted. "Please, I don't want to talk."

Umm Khalil came into the room. "My Lady," she said kindly, "you should eat something. Are you feeling all right? That soldier didn't say anything for certain. Maybe nothing's happened."

Zaynab said nothing. Still resting on the bed, she closed her eyes and covered her face. Everyone kept trying to talk to her, but without success.

Now, a whole day went by during which Zaynab neither ate anything nor spoke to anyone. Eventually Umm Khalil came in.

"Leave me with her," she told the other two women. "I've brought some medicine that will make her feel better. Give us a few minutes alone."

Fatima and Zaynab's mother both left the room. Once Umm Khalil was sure that they had both left, she closed the door and locked it. Sitting on the bed beside Zaynab, she felt her head and read certain symptoms.

"My daughter," she said, "the lover's heart is always filled with pains. I'm sorry for you. Do you hear me?"

Zaynab nodded, but said nothing.

"Amir Muhammad's fine," she whispered in her ear. "Nothing bad has happened to him."

"Perhaps," Zaynab replied sadly, "perhaps not."

"Listen to me," Umm Khalil said firmly. "Make sure you don't say a single word. If you say anything to your family, he'll die at once."

Zaynab sat up and looked at Umm Khalil.

"He wasn't part of the caravan in the first place," she continued.

"He wasn't part of the caravan?" Zaynab repeated fearfully.

"He's still alive. He's fine. He'll be coming back on time."

The news hit her on the head like a series of successive blows. Grabbing the pillow, she hit it as hard as she could.

"He didn't tell me!" she said furiously. "He told his soldiers, but he didn't tell me. Why? Who am I? A slave girl he bought from the Egyptian people! Who am I? What a liar! What did he expect? That I'd die today, giving birth to his child?"

"He told me to tell you at the right time," Umm Khalil reacted gently. "Once he'd achieved his goal. Don't blame him. He may have been afraid for you."

"Maybe he didn't trust me, or didn't care about me. How I hate him! He's the worst man I've ever set eyes on. Tell him that I hate him; send him word. Tell him too that I'm going to leave him, even if he kills me. I'm not some chattel to be bought and sold."

She leaped up from her place in bed and started looking for things. She threw them to the floor as hard as she could. Her face turned bright red, and her eyes were flooded with tears.

Umm Khalil looked on in silence. "Do you really love him that much?" she asked. "Love of a woman as forceful as you are is dangerous for men. Have some pity on him and yourself."

She collapsed on the bed again. "No, I loathe him with my whole heart," she sobbed. "Do you understand what's happened to me? Yesterday I wanted to die; I craved death. He was not worried about me or the child I'm carrying."

"But he asked me to tell you when the time was right."

"When the time was right?" she replied. "Who's supposed to decide when that is? You? What time? The rogue!"

"Calm down, my Lady!"

"I'll calm down," she said with a nod, "but I'll never forgive him. Everything's spilled over, and I've had enough."

———

The beginning of Amir Muhammad's own story is like that of many Mamluk amirs. He grew up in Turkish territory along with five brothers—to the best of his memory. They lived with his parents in a small village. Both parents worked in agriculture. His early days were spent waiting and understanding. Once or twice, his mother took him to their worship place. He can remember lights, wooden seats, and some obscure rituals of his religious community at the time. At the end of his eighth year, he saw some boys running away as fast as they could. He looked all around him, but could not understand why they were all running away. "Run," his eldest brother yelled at him, "run as fast as you can, or else they'll kidnap you."

He ran as fast as he possibly could, faster than he thought he had it in him. What he did not realize at the time was that it was the boys running hardest whom the soldiers really wanted and would kidnap. His brother vanished in front of him, and the earth shook. He could feel his heart pounding. He was like a wild beast that had fallen prey to a poisonous snake, knowing that his life was coming to an end. He was seized by a powerful hand that grabbed him around the middle. He tried to remove it, but failed. He screamed and cried, but to no avail. The light in front of him disappeared; his running had deprived him of not only his equilibrium, but also his ability to understand and reflect. Or perhaps it was that this particular moment was not completely preserved in his memory, severed as it was from his childhood, village, memory, and mother.

All he remembers is the long journey to a strange land: different faces, a formidable fortress, children the same age as him speaking his language and stroking his shoulder. Older children assuring him that life would begin anew and there was still hope.

"My mother," he asked in tears, "is she going to come?"

"Forget her," said one of the older boys in Turkish. "You'll never see her again. With most human beings, life is measured from birth. But, for Mamluks, life begins from the moment they reach their teacher. You're in luck. Your teacher is Sultan Qala'un in person. Your location is here on Roda Island."

The boy remained silent, neither accepting nor understanding. He was planning to run away and go back to the country he knew and wanted. He looked all around him, trying to spot an escape route out of this gigantic prison. In his memory, his mother was waving at him in her old clothes with their warm smell, with her old hand, veiny from all the hard work. He kept looking for the escape route out of the prison, but did not find one. However, he made a desperate effort, running toward the gate as fast as he could. He was grabbed round the neck by a strong hand.

"Do that again," its owner said, "and I'll cut your head off in front of everybody here."

He cried for help in pain, as all the other boys watched him in despair.

"If you obey my instructions," the man went on, "you'll become an amir. But, if you disobey me, I'll cut your head off in front of everybody. Here obedience turns you into a tough amir. If you want, you can have a hundred men or more under your command. The entire population of Egypt can be at your beck and call."

"My mother," the little boy muttered.

"Stop talking like a woman," the man said, hitting him in the back. "We've chosen you because you're strong. Don't make us regret our choice and make you a servant instead of an amir. Do you understand the difference? Do you want to be a man or not? We castrate servants, whereas a Mamluk becomes an amir, surrounded by beautiful women. Which one do you choose: to be a man or not?"

"To be a man," he replied fearfully.

"And an amir?"

"Yes, and an amir."

"You have to obey all instructions and understand all your lessons."

He swore never to try to run away again. "I will understand all the lessons," he said fearfully.

"Where's your family?"

He thought for a while, imagining that a knife was severing his manhood.

"My family's here," he replied firmly. "I have no other family."

"The sultan's your family and your role model."

"The sultan," he repeated confidently.

"Your patron and your teacher."

The way the teachers dealt with the boys was very strict, but, at the same time, it was full of appreciation and respect. The strict regime meant no talking while at work, no expression of feelings, no crying, and no arguing. The presence of other boys who spoke the same language made everything easier for Muhammad to tolerate. He started learning about religion, Islamic law, principles of prayer, and ablutions. The teacher made sure that the boys all prayed every day, memorized the Qur'an, and learned Arabic.

After a while, he started training in the arts of combat, horseback riding, and fencing. It was tough, and Muhammad almost lost a leg in one of the drills. The ability to endure and persist was one of the most important features of Mamluks as they climbed the ranks and served in the guard of the sultan himself. Each one of them was "fortunate": that was the word frequently repeated by both teachers and other boys.

"What do you want to become?" the teacher would yell. "A servant, just like your father in a tiny village no one's ever heard of? Now, you're a warrior who can govern, and both command and refuse; a commander dressed in silk and wearing splendid swords; eating meat and chicken! Which of the two would you prefer?"

The boys would always shout loud and clear in response: "We want to be soldiers, then amirs!"

Moments of weakness would be rare; he had long since wiped them from his memory. All he could remember were his battles, his strength, his successes, and his promotion; also the quest for influence and authority, and the increasing status of Mamluks. The things that drove the Mamluk to sacrifice his own childhood, family, and country in the cause of defending Muslim territories were far more precious than anything else—of inestimable value and far more than all the taxes paid by the Egyptian people. Amir Muhammad was renowned for his shrewdness in combat, his sharpness in interactions, and the speed of his promotion, something that earned him the envy and fear of other Mamluks.

Some of his soldiers had been kidnapped when they were older and could still remember their villages and family names. They went straight back to look for their family and mother, found them, and either brought them back to Egypt or went to visit them frequently. Muhammad occasionally thought of doing the same thing, but he was afraid of his own feelings and the folly of searching for something so old and obscure, relying on such a faint hope in a wide world. There was a psychological barrier that his teachers had ingrained in his mind for years, namely that any reliance on feeble, degrading hopes, any search into the past, would deprive him of his masculinity and the remainder of his life. With that in mind, he buried the notion deep inside him and accepted reality.

It was customary for Mamluks to stick to the relationships that they had with each other. They were foreigners, and Egyptians did not understand their language. Along with the decision to discard their previous lives there came an attachment to language and race. Their connections to each other as amirs and soldiers and their mutual defense were laudable qualities, but, when the disagreement involved interests and authority, Muhammad's decision to be married to an Egyptian woman was baffling; nobody could understand it, whether friend or foe. The amirs had no idea what he had found in a merchant's daughter that led him to overlook all other women and go against the normal practice of amirs. Muhammad himself did not understand either.

Amir Muhammad left his soldiers on the Kerak Castle border. Spurring his horse into the territory, he entered the fortress of the deposed sultan, An-Nasir Muhammad. He rapped on the gate, and it was opened by some men. When Amir Muhammad went in to see An-Nasir Muhammad, the latter's face gleamed. He quickly hobbled over to Muhammad, gave him a big hug, and patted him on the shoulder. He had been expecting him for months.

"I'd hoped you wouldn't have to see me in this condition," An-Nasir told him. "But never mind; you're my friend."

An-Nasir's body was emaciated. His foot injury was obvious to everyone present at his assembly, but he still had a firm facial expression and penetrating gaze. Lengthy stares would emerge from profound depths and abundant learning.

They sat down together.

"Baybars is corrupting the entire country, isn't he?" An-Nasir asked after a pause.

Amir Muhammad nodded in agreement without saying anything.

"Can you believe it?" An-Nasir exclaimed. "He's asked for my men and my possessions."

"He's spreading it around that you abandoned your authority and ran away."

"As you know, I'd no choice. He was going to kill me at once, get rid of my corpse, and then rule forevermore. At least now, there's some hope."

"My Lord, that was the second time you relinquished your authority."

"'My Lord,' you say! I haven't heard that from Egyptians for a while. Listen, Muhammad. There's no guarantee to be had with Baybars and maybe the majority of Mamluks as well. Power is their goal; for that cause, they're ready to break any pact. They've all grown up with a different set of rules. Conflict is the goal and the method. Loyalty is something to be bought and sold."

For a while, Muhammad said nothing.

"If that's the way you think," he eventually said, "you'll never recover your power."

"What do you mean?"

"Mamluks are the only ones who'll help you," Muhammad declared firmly. "They own the weapons and money, and they're trained to fight."

"It was one of them that got rid of me."

"The Mamluk amirs will bring you back," Muhammad said. "Don't lose them, my friend. They're all you have. They support you and hate Baybars for his greed."

"Will you help me?" An-Nasir asked, stroking Muhammad's hand.

"You've known I would ever since you left."

"He's blocking my food supply," he said sadly after a pause. "Can you believe it? No fowl, only vegetables. Do you realize he's not allowing me any rice or chicken? 'It's too expensive,' he says. The country's at war and needs every penny it can get. When you humiliate the sultan, what do you expect? He's out to break me; I understand that and suffer in patience. It's happened before. As you well know, Muhammad, and as all Egypt knows, the young sultan was hidden from the amirs. It was his mother who emerged to negotiate with them. She begged them to let him live and promised them that he would leave the country. That's what she did. If she hadn't intervened in that way, I'd be dead now. I've never forgotten that, nor will I ever. How can the Egyptians forget? How can the Mamluk amirs forget? What kind of sultan has to hide behind his mother?"

"That happened in the past, but you're no longer a child and you no longer have any choice."

"I've started getting the taste of humiliation in my mouth."

"Be patient with them," Muhammad said. "Careful planning is what's most needed. If you receive the fealty of the Mamluks in Egypt and Syria, Baybars won't be able to remain in power. I've brought you some rice and chicken, so don't worry."

An-Nasir gave a sad smile. "So, how are the Egyptians doing?" he asked.

"Don't ask about them till you can eat."

"They're suffering both ways, I suppose?" he asked.

"If he stays in power for more than a few months, he'll finish off the entire country. They think you ran away and left all the power to him. He's arrested religious scholars, merchants, and tradesmen. He's not left a single man in the city unbroken."

"If I come back, I'll change all that. The Egyptian people deserve better."

An-Nasir looked at Muhammad long and hard. "You've married an Egyptian woman? Have you really done that? Did Baybars give you permission?"

Muhammad smiled. "How can he stop me?" he asked. "He's been very cautious with me. He's trying to keep me happy and get rid of me at the same time."

"Why did you marry an Egyptian? I've never known you just to follow your desires. Did that annoy the Mamluks?"

"What do they have to do with my getting married?"

"How are you going to help me, Muhammad?"

"You talk to the Syrian amirs and get their promise of loyalty," he said decisively. "Leave the Egyptian amirs to me. I'll talk to them, and we'll wait for the right opportunity to bring you back."

"He's already taken half of my men, but, even then, he wasn't satisfied. He wanted all of them. He realizes and senses our plan."

"Swift action guarantees secrecy and success."

"Why will the Egyptian amirs help me?"

"Because the total destruction of the country means the end for them. They know and understand. When the level of injustice surpasses the bounds of logic, then the truth becomes obvious to everyone and consequences become clear even to those driven by greed and corruption. Leave the choice of opportunity in my hands."

"I don't know how to thank you," An-Nasir replied, patting him on the shoulder.

"My Lord Sultan, we grew up together. I was your Mamluk father and brother. If the Mamluks are to survive, then that loyalty must remain their primary quality."

6

Muhammad was eagerly looking for her, and, for her part, Zaynab was keeping away to the extent possible. She had forgiven him for all his previous wrongdoings, but not for this one. She had made up her mind never to forgive him for this.

She closed her eyes and pretended to be asleep. She even covered her head so he would not see her and feel the anguish, mental distress, and murderous feelings that were affecting her entire being.

From deep inside her, she could feel his hand removing the head-cover, his mouth moving closer to her cheek, and his breathing. When he kissed her cheek, the tear that she had been holding inside her for two months seeped out. She kept her eyes closed as he kissed her on the neck. Her whole body recoiled and did its best to escape.

"I missed you," he said with a gentleness she had never encountered with him.

She clenched her eyes shut even tighter and said nothing.

"What's the matter with you?" he asked gently. "What's happened? Are you annoyed with me?"

She still said nothing. If she even opened her mouth, she would burst into tears. Fear and love were rocking her whole being.

"What's the matter with you?" he asked, putting his hand under her head. "Talk to me."

She took her own hand and moved his away. "I'd like you to leave me alone, Amir," she said. "That's forever, not just today. I'm not afraid of prison anymore."

He sat up straight. "What's this nonsense?" he asked. "What's happened while I've been away? Is this the way a wife greets her husband when he been away for two months?"

"Give me an assurance that you won't slap me or whip me," she said, opening her eyes, "and I'll talk."

"Talk," he said dryly.

Her heart was pounding as she looked at him. She really wanted to hug him, to love him, and to kiss him; also to kill him and make him suffer.

"You lied to me," she told him in a choking voice, her heart brimming with anger. "You lied to me, as though I were nothing, a mere chattel inside your palace with no heart or soul. You lied to me. I thought I'd lost you forever, that you were bound to die. I thought the Mongol attack on the travelers' caravan was an attack on you. Can you feel that? Do you have a heart to feel? Are you even aware of what you did to me? Why did you go to the Mongols in the first place, without even letting me know? But then, why let me know? I'm nothing. You've done me in once, twice, three times. Why bother about me and my feelings? It doesn't concern you. You can buy a slave girl who's better and more beautiful than me; you could even kidnap her from her family, then threaten and scare her. Do what you like with me, but from now on, you're not my husband."

He listened to her in silence without interrupting.

"I understand some of what you're saying," he replied slowly, "but most of it is sheer nonsense. You're my wife, as you well know."

She leaped from the bed. "Put me back in prison or kill me," she yelled hatefully, "but I'll never forgive you. In the past, I've forgiven you for everything, all that's happened. But now, I'll never forgive you. I thought you'd been killed and my son would be born with no father. I'll never forgive you for that. You knew and could have reassured me with a single word, but you didn't."

He put his hands around her face. "I can't," he replied forcefully. "You know that."

She could feel his breath close to her and the sense of both degradation and longing inside her. She closed her eyes as his mouth drew close to hers, then turned quickly away. She removed his hand, headed for the door, and left the room.

Zaynab was in her fifth month of pregnancy. Whenever he looked at her, he felt the tender affection that he was now accustomed to whenever he was with her. Her cheeks would turn red, and life would radiate from every part of her body. He was now incapable of humiliating her, something he wanted to do whenever she had one of her stubborn fits of anger. If only he could batter her door down and force her to communicate and ask for forgiveness. Why not? After all, she was his property and under his complete control. So why this soft touch toward her that was now directing his mind and making any kind of severity impossible?

He had consorted with any number of women before her. Like other members of the sultan's guard corps, he had looked for women from his country and village to remind him of the scent of its trees and the atmosphere of his own past life. He had found one after another, but he had never had any sense of fulfilment; neither his past life nor his mind felt settled. Bodily satisfaction never feeds the soul or helps it reach a goal and need no more.

When it came to Zaynab, his passionate love for her poured from his very soul; from the very outset, he had never been able to understand his feelings for her. It was as though she were his single misstep, bringing out all the sentiments that he had suppressed during his childhood and all the instincts and spontaneity that he had buried alive when he clutched the sword as a boy and learned how to fight. The soul's needs were a mystery to him, and at first they scared him. But then, with one particular woman he learned how to adapt to it and cherish it. Her origins were different, and she did not speak his language, but her face glowed with a kind of life, power, and spontaneity that he had been deprived of forever. Zaynab!

For an entire week she avoided talking to him. Every time he approached her, she moved away as quickly as possible so as to avoid collapsing in front of him as always happened. But she often hid behind a door or balcony so she could hear his voice and squelch her heart's insistent longing to feel the smell of him around her. Sometimes he would stop talking and look up at the balcony, feeling her there behind the curtain, looking down at him. That would make her move away as quickly as possible. But at night, she would always lock her door and lie silent on her bed, burning with longing. Her heart would be beating for him, and her anger would be overpowering everything else. She had missed him, loved him, and been frightened for him. As days passed, with her on her own in her room, her inner self started to grind, and love overcame both anger and pride. But she was always strong; or rather, that's what she wanted.

He grabbed her chin and turned her face toward him. With her heart collapsing, she opened her eyes.

"I promise you," he said firmly, "this won't happen again. Don't worry about me, I won't keep anything from you. Don't you still love me?"

Her body betrayed her and sought his help. She lowered her hand, and he grabbed her and rubbed his cheek against hers.

"You still love me, don't you?" he asked.

She nodded, acknowledging her defeat. She grabbed his back with her hands and burst into tears.

"Don't do that to me," she whispered. "Don't ever do that to me again."

He started kissing her lips, her eyes, and her neck. His breaths came in rapid pants, and his love, weakness, and power were all for her alone.

"I've promised you," he told her between kisses, "it won't happen again."

They kept kissing each other, the frenzy of it making it difficult to breathe.

"You don't keep your promises," she said.

"Yes, I do, all of them," he replied. "How I've missed you! I could see only you; as though you were some kind of jinn that had taken control of me. How have you managed to do that? It's as though all the other women in the world don't even exist."

"You're lying to me."

"No, I'm not."

"Will you promise me again?"

"I've so missed your nagging!"

"I can't make you any promises about that."

When she felt him inside her that day, she could not stop crying. She put her arms round his neck, and all the pain evaporated.

"What's happened?" he asked softly. "Why are you crying?"

She had no idea why she was crying. For just a moment, she had thought she had lost him . . . she collapsed in front of him, and her entire being felt shattered. Her life with him before had involved uncertainty and fear, followed by passion and extinction in the face of loss and death. It was death that had robbed her of her brothers and her father. She had not been sure she could carry on living after her husband's death; her awareness of him was an intrinsic part of her very soul. Now he had destroyed the time barrier and extracted all the longing stained with bitterness.

"What's the matter with you, Zaynab?" he asked again.

She had no idea that love could shatter the soul this way, or that fear could rob you of your mind and insert curses in your heart.

She kissed him on the chest. "I love you," she said sadly.

"Why are you crying? I'm with you."

She put her hands round his head to make sure that he really was with her; she had not lost him.

"You have to promise me," she said, stroking his beard.

He smiled, but said nothing. This battle was a fight to the death, and both of them had been losers. They had both completely dominated each other. She was not seeing, knowing, loving, or desiring anyone else. All he wanted in the whole world was to have her around him and with him.

After a while, he hugged her. "Stop crying!" he told her.

"Don't run any more risks," she sobbed. "Promise me that first."

"I promise," he replied without thinking.

She stayed in his arms for hours, neither talking, moving, getting up, nor sleeping. She had her arms around him and moistened her heart with his presence beside her, although her worries and fears about him did not diminish.

Each of them was well aware of the other's ability to win and eliminate the soldiers involved, while at the same time being careful to avoid any harm to heart and soul.

He found these crying fits peculiar; she had certainly cried many times before, but never with such sincerity, grief, and shame. It had never happened when he was inside her, between her thighs, as she clung to him and writhed with pleasure. Such a reaction had never happened before, whether with Zaynab or any other woman he had known. Even his warrior eyes could not understand or penetrate the interior of this sadness. Even so, she managed to shake his entire soul. What love, what fear could inflict such torment?

Next morning, she left her place beside him and got up slowly. He stayed in bed, watching her, with his hands behind his head. She went over to a drawer, opened it, took out a large, decorated box, and carried it back to the bed. He watched in amazement as she opened it.

"Muhammad," she told him, "take it all."

"What's this?"

"The endowment my father left me, along with a large property in the quarter that he also left for me to rent out, and all my gold. Take it all."

He stared at her, thunderstruck. "I don't need your money," he said.

"Take it all," she insisted, "it's yours, a present from me. We'll go away, leave Roda Island, and put a distance between ourselves and the Mamluks, conspiracies, the sultan, assassinations, and murder. We can live in peace."

He shook his head. "Are you joking, Zaynab?" he asked.

"Why would I joke? I've just given you all my wealth; it's all yours. Take it, and let's leave here. If you like, we can go to Syria, the Hijaz, or anywhere you like. We'll be far removed from the Mamluks, the sultan, and the government."

"I'm a Mamluk too, Zaynab."

"They're going to kill you. You realize that Sultan Baybars is going to kill you. He's tried before, hasn't he? He's the one who sent a man to kill you. He'll try again."

"If I turn myself into an Egyptian, he won't kill me? If I let him go on spreading corruption, will God ever forgive me? I was born to fight, not to run away. Only cowards run away. Do you want a cowardly husband?"

"I want a husband who's alive."

"It's that same cowardice that brings about the need for Mamluks. They're the ones with the courage needed to defend everyone. As you well know, I have an obligation and a goal."

She opened her mouth and he put his hand over it.

"I want you to love me the way I am," he told her gently. "When fate finally comes and if I am to die in combat, don't be sad. Dying from a swift stroke is much better than disease, humiliation, and shame. Help me, Zaynab. Don't make things difficult for me."

She said nothing and looked away. "Do I have any choice?" she asked. "You've never let me choose."

"Today I want you to stand with me and give me your help. I love you."

She nodded. "You'll never lie to me," she said, "at least, you'll never lie to me. I swear to you that I'll die before I reveal any secret between us. You realize that. Do you understand and trust me?"

"Yes, I trust you," he replied firmly.

⟵⟶

That entire day, Zaynab set about putting all these realities into a logical order, trying to understand the things she had overlooked since she had lived in the palace. It was clear that her husband, Amir Muhammad, did not like Sultan Baybars. How could she not have noticed? Even when he went to visit the sultan, he surrounded himself with his own men the entire time. Even if he had not gone as far as Baghdad, he certainly went to Kerak Castle to meet Sultan An-Nasir. But why? What was going on between the amirs? What was her husband's role in it all?

In the evening she waited for his return and then sat beside him.

"Are you going to tell me everything," she asked assertively, "as you promised?"

He looked surprised. "I promised you?" he asked.

"Everything."

He looked all around her. "Why did you go to see An-Nasir Muhammad?" she asked.

"Zaynab . . ."

"You promised me," she said loudly, "you promised you'd tell me everything."

He hesitated for a moment, then lay down on the bed and held out his hand.

"Come here," he told her.

She made for his chest and rested her head there. "I'm afraid for you," she said, wrapping her arms around his shoulders. "If Baybars found out, he'd kill you. If he did that, what would I do? I can't go on living if you're gone."

He rested his chin on her hair. "Mamluks have their laws and rules," he said as though he was not listening to her, "principles and teacher. You know that."

"Yes, I do."

"Do you understand how powerful they are and what they've done for the Muslim lands?"

"They defeated the Mongols, I realize, and the Crusaders."

"They've done things that no one before them has been able to achieve. Their system is innovative and shrewd. I want you to understand it and not simply follow what Egyptians say about it. If you understood what I mean, then you'd realize how Baybars and An-Nasir Muhammad are thinking."

"I'm listening," she replied enthusiastically.

"If you're going to fight the Crusaders and the European kings, whether together or separately, what do you need?"

"Men? And a plan?"

"A lot more than that. Even though Qutuz defeated the Tatars at the Battle of Ayn Jalut, the Tatars are still invading countries and causing chaos. What do you need?"

"The same thing: men and plans."

"If you were responsible for all the Christian and Muslim holy places, what would you need?"

"I don't understand you."

"Do you realize why every Mamluk and amir brings fresh men and doesn't rely on Mamluk children?"

"I don't understand."

"In the Mamluk system, soldiers have a sanctity and a purpose. Their life has meaning and specificity. For example, Sultan Qala'un brought me to the palace when I was eight years old. He started my tough training so I could take care of the country; my loyalty would be to religion and teacher. Mamluk children are not strong enough to endure this kind of tough training in the Citadel's encampments. They are free, and have a house, a father and mother, and a history in that country. The only things Mamluks have is a weapon and a teacher; no mother to scold them, no family to love and prefer to war. They have no other affiliations to raise doubts as to their loyalty to their teacher."

"So, our son won't be one of them."

His response was totally clear. "Our son is neither Egyptian nor Mamluk," he replied. "He's a son of the people. I can guarantee his success and influence, but he's not a soldier. He'll never be a soldier; he won't be able to devote his entire life to fighting. He'll have brothers, family, and a country he knows, a quarter where he can walk, and rituals and connections as well. The success of the Mamluks is based on the soldier's ability to fight, and that relies on his training, loyalty, separation from his milieu and environment, and study of jurisprudence and arts of combat. Sometimes, he has to go through some really tough times, so that he can know the real meaning of war and imprisonment. You couldn't do that with our son, could you?"

"No," she replied swiftly.

"That's because he'll be a son of the people and not a Mamluk. Success in governance and war happens because of the Mamluks, not the sons of the people. When the Mamluk sultan passes on the governing role to his son, who really holds the reins of power? That son is a son of the people, not a Mamluk. Sultan An-Nasir, for example, was born in Egypt and grew up there with his parents. He was never kidnapped or trained in the Citadel camp. That's why Mamluks assume that his regime will be purely token; he'll hand over the reins of power to the soldier who knows the meaning of victory, martyrdom, and risk. Do you understand? The successes and military triumphs that the Mamluks have scored in this country were not and never will be achieved by anyone who comes after them. Egyptians have no idea of what Mamluks give up in exchange for spirit and armaments."

"Sultan An-Nasir Muhammad doesn't want to hand over the reins of power to the Mamluks. That's why they got rid of him."

"Regarding An-Nasir Muhammad, the situation's more complicated than that," Muhammad went on after a moment's pause. "He was still a child when he came to power, and the Mamluk amirs had complete control over him. Whenever he tried to get rid of them, they'd take away his authority and threaten him, or else he would be frightened of them and go away. As far as they're concerned, An-Nasir Muhammad's a son of the people. But he's also astute, powerful, and just. There are now some Mamluk amirs who've forgotten the purpose, goal, and conflict. All they can think about is collecting wealth and estates, murder, plunder, and theft. An-Nasir is well aware of that; he's tried to put an end to it, but has not managed to do so."

She gave him a lengthy stare. "Muhammad," she said, "I don't understand. Are you supporting the Mamluk soldiers who hold the reins of power, or the sons of the people, the sultans' children?"

"In Mamluk times governing authority could not be inherited. It was only given to the powerful soldier and Mamluk warrior. But from the very outset, the system has been inherited. That's why any sultan can only hold on to power for a short period, because Mamluks don't trust the inheritance process. Instead they believe in the superiority of the soldier who's prepared to sacrifice his soul, the Mamluk who'll leave his family and home and learn about crises and how to deal with them. But authority has its own particular methods, ones that are full of sacrifices that involve a disregard for everything costly and valuable. If Baybars stays on as sultan, Zaynab, he'll ruin the country. An-Nasir is not only the legitimate sultan; he's also the most qualified, even if he's not a Mamluk."

"But you've just said that the Mamluks are the only appropriate rulers. If he wrests government control from the amirs, what are you going to do?"

He sat up. "Once in a while," he said, "a soldier has to think about losses in war and preserving house and home. There's no point in preserving a house that's been destroyed by fire. Baybars's corruption and greed will do away with the Mamluks before the Egyptian people. I prefer a sultan from the sons of the people to a Mamluk sultan who amasses property and gold and distributes it to his entourage. In making decisions, there are times when you have to consult your conscience and religious beliefs."

She gave him a serious look. "What are you planning to do?" she asked.

Their eyes met. He was not worried that she might reveal his secret, but he did not know either why he had revealed to her the contents of his heart. She had managed to infiltrate his innermost thoughts with the utmost skill.

"Baybars has to be deposed," he replied seriously, "and An-Nasir Muhammad restored."

"If he finds out," she said in alarm, "he'll kill you. In fact, he must know already and is trying to kill you. Why are you doing this, Muhammad?"

"I'll not be able to do anything on my own. There has to be an agreement with the Mamluk amirs."

"Why should they agree?" she asked, both anxious and annoyed. "How can you be certain that they'll curtail their authority and restore a sultan who wants to restrain them? They'll never allow it."

"An-Nasir has no plans to do the Mamluks any harm. He wants to protect them from themselves. Otherwise, their end is nigh. When a life of luxury makes its way into a warrior's lifestyle, he forgets all about wars. He doesn't want luxury to affect them. He's willing to leave them in their positions and won't appoint anybody to replace them. All he wants is to have decision-making in his own hands. He doesn't want to have to ask every amir's permission before he undertakes any action. The control that the Mamluks had over him was fatal, but it was also fatal to the Mamluks before him. If things continue the way they are, then the Crusaders are sure to be back."

"He doesn't want to have to deal with the Mamluks," she reacted assertively, "provided they don't interfere in government affairs."

"I don't know what's going on in his mind, but that's what I believe."

"Why are you helping him?"

He looked at her for a moment. "I'm doing what any soldier has to do when his house is burning. That's my duty and responsibility."

"Muhammad," she whispered, clasping his hand, "I've never seen anyone as brave as you."

"But Zaynab," he joked, "aren't you scared of the Mamluks and their tyranny?"

"I'm still afraid of their tyranny," she replied with a smile, "particularly of a particular man who's changed my entire life."

⌒

The story of Zaynab and Muhammad's marriage was still peculiar, one that perturbed Mamluks and Egyptians alike. Egyptians scoffed that the Mamluk amir was impressed by the daughter of an Egyptian merchant who was renowned for her beauty. He had had multiple women and tried all sorts and types. Mamluks were famous for their greed and malice. He would get bored with her. He would soon shove her aside, put her in a dark room inside his palace, head for his slave girls, and marry one of his own kind. If he did not get bored with her, then that was because she had inherited most of her father's wealth. Mamluks' greed was as deep as desert mountains and as broad as the extent of the Tatar armies. However rich the amir might be already, Zaynab's wealth would still be his eventual goal. He would stay with her until he had acquired everything she owned. Otherwise, why would Mamluk amirs be demanding protection money when they were already wealthy enough? Why impose taxes and extort money from merchants? He's a thief, and thieves never have enough treasure. To fill his gullet you would need at least the water of three whole seas.

The Mamluks were of the opinion that Muhammad had done this to show his own power and influence. He was confirming to the sultan that he could do whatever he wanted. Amir Muhammad could not possibly have fallen in love with a merchant's daughter; she was simply a power toy, something that only amirs and warriors could understand. He would soon be bored with her. He would then kill her, lock her up, or bury her in a room inside his palace. He clearly needed her wealth. Muhammad was well known for his love of horses and weapons and for bringing together men and lands. He was out to strengthen his own private army, and she was just one of his soldiers. He would crush her; once he was finished with her, he would toss her into the desert and mountains to die of hunger and thirst. She knew that she was not one of their number and had no idea about their abilities and customs.

Fatima came to visit Zaynab after the amir's return to check on her and her health. First pregnancies are always difficult and exhausting. They had a furious argument, the like of which had never happened before. In fact, Fatima launched unthinkingly into a nonstop attack, as though pelting her with arrows. Zaynab knew that Fatima could be tense, but she had never experienced anything like this, nor did she know what was causing it on this particular day.

When Fatima looked into Zaynab's eyes, she detected something that the demon had released from inside her ribcage, something new that had to be attacked. In Zaynab's eyes she spotted a contentment with life, a confidence in attainment, and a satisfaction with what time had given her. Zaynab's expressions were different, truly alarming and aggravating.

At first, Fatima tried to keep the demon inside the ribcage. "How are you?" she asked.

"I'm fine," Zaynab replied, putting some juice and sweetmeats in front of her.

Zaynab kept moving around with all the enthusiasm of a little boy who has found everything he had ever dreamed of, all the while showing a previously unknown liveliness and self-confidence.

"What news of your husband?" Fatima asked. "You never tell me anything! Do you love him, Zaynab?"

The question shocked her. For just a moment, she felt anxious about replying, perhaps because she realized that Fatima did not like her husband, or else her own happiness at having him around her was a gift that she did not deserve. She had not really understood what it meant until she had encountered it for herself. Fatima had grown up with Zaynab, and she knew Zaynab well. The delight and assurance that she saw in Zaynab's expression gave her a severe shock. Even though she had known and loved Zaynab since they were children, she had never seen her in full splendor like today.

"You love him," Fatima said. "You lied to me. You lie about everything."

"Fatima," she replied anxiously, "you know full well that the marriage was difficult at first. He's my husband and father of my child."

"So why did you pretend not to love him?" she asked angrily. "Are you worried about jealousy, Zaynab? Scared of my evil eye?"

"Of course not," Zaynab replied quickly. "You're my sister and friend. There were problems at first, as you well know . . ."

Fatima gave a mocking smile. "Did you agree to be married to him from the start, I wonder? Have you loved him the whole time? You've been lying about everything, haven't you?"

"What's happened to you, Fatima?" she asked angrily. "Why are you talking to me like this?"

A woman's pleasure, eyes that could never get enough of the world because she was living with a particular man, those were things that Fatima had never recognized or understood. The basic reason why she hated her husband was that he hated her singing. Every day she would take her revenge on him for the words that penetrated her inner self and insulted the demon. Not only that, but there were times when she believed that love was not her goal; pleasure would never come inside the house's walls or in a man's embrace, but instead when the demon left the heart. She did not want any man, any jewelry, any sweets. What she really wanted was deliverance, something out of reach.

"What sort of friend are you?" she yelled suddenly, pushing the sweetmeats away. "What kind of cheater?"

Zaynab opened her mouth in amazement, but said nothing.

"You think I don't know?" Fatima went on. "You're the one who's ruined my life. You told them where I had fled. I'll never forgive you as long as I live. Why did you do that, Zaynab? Why did you betray me? Is there some evil lurking inside you, or were you jealous of my singing voice? Or was it something else?"

Zaynab still said nothing.

Fatima stood up and pushed the tray of juice and sweetmeats so that it fell to the floor.

"I curse you, Zaynab," she yelled. "Evil's all you deserve! Are you betraying your friend and destroying her life?"

Zaynab still did not understand what had caused this explosion, nor why at first the arrows had been aimed at her. After two days of thought on the subject, she reached a clear conclusion. She loved to think about things and come to an understanding. Jealousy has its own particular rules. Pleasure is the almost unattainable goal. Not everyone is fated to be happy. Love is a special gift that time only provides for particular people. She did not hate Fatima, nor was she angry with her.

It was three days later that Fatima came to see her again, tears in her eyes and head lowered, carrying a whole load of food.

"Forgive me, cousin," she said, giving her a big hug. "It's that miserable man I'm living with. He's driven me crazy."

Zaynab stroked her shoulder. Once in a while, she still felt a little guilty because she had indeed told them where Fatima was when she had run away.

"Not to worry, Fatima," she said. "Sing me a song. I love your voice."

Their eyes met.

"Do you think it's a nice voice?" Fatima asked.

"It's lovely."

Zaynab was not entirely sure that what she was doing was right. If Fatima ran away she would be working as a singer. Maybe she would never achieve her desires in life. But, if she did not escape, she would be miserable forevermore.

As she peered through the meshrabiyeh at the gathering of amirs in her husband's palace, she was still feeling anxious. As she looked at their faces without understanding what they were saying in Turkish, she clutched her heart.

"Something dangerous happened yesterday!" Muhammad said earnestly. "Some of you already know, but others don't. If it continues, what happened threatens to put an end to our era. We must intervene fast. Yesterday, an amir went out with his soldiers to do a tour of the various Cairo districts. The populace came out to see them, assuming that he was Baybars Jashankir. They had knives and rocks, and started attacking the soldiers. Do you all realize what that means? Never in my entire life have Egyptians dared launch an attack on Mamluks, nor on the person that they think is sultan."

Silence prevailed.

"Do you realize why they dared do it?" he continued. "Because the Mamluks around Baybars have never let the Egyptians have what they need to live on. Careful tyranny can usually survive and carry on, but, if it's oppressive, then it destroys the person who implements it. You can sometimes disregard the Mamluks' vices, but the Egyptians are no longer prepared to tolerate Baybars's ruthlessness. Their attack on the amir yesterday showed the sheer strength of people who are utterly miserable and in despair, enough to finish off the Mamluks in short order. Baybars kills, plunders, and imposes protection money on merchants in order to protect them. If the populace pays its taxes, then why is there a need for protection money? It's as though the Mamluks were highwaymen, not amirs. Which sensible sultan will resort to excessive violence? He kills and executes people in public. Not a single house is left without someone being murdered. No business remains where the amirs haven't made off with its goods. When the Egyptian populace came out to confront the amir yesterday—thieves, beggars, lunatics—all of them assuming that it was the sultan, death was all around them. Total despair engenders courage, and death arouses a contempt that starts with the Egyptian populace. It's my duty to ensure that the Mamluks maintain their governance of the country, but, for that to happen, Baybars has to be deposed. Now, before you start speaking . . . he was my friend; we grew up together and came from the same contingent. However, in wartime we need to consult our minds and be effective. The Egyptian people have come out against the Mamluks; they're attacking us with knives."

"Anyone who does that should be killed," an amir responded quickly, "and his body should be quartered in public. We'll say that he's crazy."

"Don't belittle them," Muhammad said. "They hate wars and fear the Mamluks, because Mamluks defend them and regulate their lives. If Mamluks now start eliminating them, what'll be left? What's the point of protecting a house if you're burning it down? The amir's men managed to kill their attackers, but the Egyptians will never erase that incident from their memories. Something similar will happen tomorrow or the day after. Young Egyptians will come pouring out on to the streets, raring to kill Mamluks. We need to save ourselves and not bury our heads in the sand. The lame sultan is much more sympathetic to the Egyptians than Baybars. I'll say it again: what's the point of protecting a house if you're burning it down? If the Egyptians come out to attack the Mamluks, you're going to kill the entire population! Think about that."

All the amirs looked glum.

"What you're suggesting is dangerous," Badr ad-din said. "If someone reveals this secret to Baybars, you'll be killed immediately. You realize that, Muhammad, don't you?"

"Yes, I do," Muhammad responded confidently, "and I'm equally sure that no one will do that. It's in the amirs' best interests for An-Nasir to come back."

"An-Nasir has no respect for Mamluks," Badr ad-din commented.

"He'll never touch them. Without them he's nothing. He hasn't done anything to them before. He'll allow them to keep their power and influence. But we have no choice. The country's being destroyed; you all know that. If we all agree and solemnly swear today to depose Baybars and bring back An-Nasir, we'll get our prestige and respect back. There can be no respect without justice, and you can't exert influence over the dead."

"These days, you sound like a religious scholar when you talk. Forgive me, Muhammad, but I have concerns about your loyalty. Loyalty to whom? Mamluks or Egyptians?"

"Without the Egyptians," Muhammad replied forcefully, "there would be no Mamluks. You understand that, Badr ad-din, don't you?"

"I'm not used to hear you talking about them all the time. You're obviously concerned about their situation and sufferings."

"Badr ad-din," Muhammad reacted assertively, "you can leave and forget everything. Baybars can stay on as sultan. But it's the Mamluks who will feel the impact of the destruction first. I've tried to explain that to you."

Muhammad now looked at the amirs. "Are you concerned about this country's affairs?" he asked boldly.

"Yes," they all replied without hesitation.

"Are you concerned about this country's people?"

"Yes, we are," they all acknowledged.

"Are you with me or Baybars?" he asked decisively.

They all looked at each other, then whispered in each other's ears.

"We're with you, Muhammad," they replied.

"We now swear to help An-Nasir return to power," he said powerfully, "and we also swear to fight Baybars, should that be necessary. We will send a message to An-Nasir to return to Egypt in the company of the Syrian amirs' soldiery. After that, we put our trust in God."

⸺⸻

Baybars sent Muhammad a messenger asking to meet him and discuss an important matter. Muhammad put off the meeting and did not go. He realized full well that his murder would save Baybars; going would be his end. He now kept his own men around him at all times and used all necessary caution whatever he did and wherever he moved.

Two days later he learned that the sultan had ordered his arrest. He was astute enough to confirm Baybars's plan to get rid of him. First of all, he would convince his men that Muhammad was disloyal to Sultan Baybars. The sultan's protection demanded that all soldiers should show solidarity. As far as Baybars was concerned, arresting Muhammad was better than killing him. Not only would that make it easier for him to gain control of Muhammad's soldiers, but under torture Muhammad might confess his disloyalty; that would convince his contingent of soldiers that it was useless to take revenge on behalf of their amir. Who knows?

He read the arrest order inside his own prison and filed it away in his private room. He did not tell his wife. He was sure that she would not be able to handle it; not only that, but he was also totally unclear as to what might happen to her if Baybars managed to lay his hands on him. As a rule, Mamluks respected amirs' wives; the soldiers belonged to the same race and country. Maltreating them would annoy the religious scholars and lose them the respect of rulers and defenders of the faith. But Zaynab was not of the same race, nor would she ever be. There was no way of predicting what Baybars might do with her; indeed the warrior's astute eye could easily envisage some of the eventualities. He might put her in prison in the final month of her pregnancy; in which case she and her newborn would die, and Muhammad's line and his path to eternity would come to an end. He might kill her as soon as Muhammad was arrested, as though it was a mistake that might happen with some boorish soldier. He might make her a gift to a soldier as a way of insulting Muhammad, alive and dead. Baybars would never be bothered by the wrath of Egyptians. He would fight to stay in power. His revenge on anyone who wanted to remove him from the face of the earth would inevitably be savage. Muhammad knew for sure that Baybars would only be able to guarantee remaining in power by exterminating both Muhammad and his progeny. Who knows? Maybe he would decide to split her womb open in the ninth month of her pregnancy so her fate could become an object lesson for all amirs and Egyptians. Maltreating an Egyptian woman was certainly possible; Baybars Jashankir was doing that to the Egyptian people every day. Absolute brutality provides a lesson, one learned by populace and Mamluks alike. That fear could confuse the adventurous soul and tear it to pieces.

He fortified his palace. His men brandished their swords, fully prepared to take on the sultan's men at any moment. Caution and widespread spying would never be of much use to Baybars. Attacking the amir's palace by day or night and starting a war with him were risky propositions, things that Baybars could not easily undertake. He would wait till the amir emerged from his palace or tried to capture him.

Muhammad's strategy was precise; he had been thinking it over for the past several months. Now the goal was near, and An-Nasir's return was a possibility. But the time had to be right, and appropriate precautions had to be taken.

At those precise moments, Muhammad would totally close both heart and mind and turn away. He would sleep in a room by himself, thinking all night and planning the first strike and its consequences. A Mamluk conflict between Baybars and An-Nasir was something he did not relish, an event he did not really want. But it was inevitable, and there was no escaping it.

He needed to be alone, thinking about consequences and losses. After two days had passed, Zaynab knocked on the door. He let her in.

"Muhammad," she asked gently, "are you well?"

"Yes, I'm fine," he replied, without looking at her. "Don't worry."

She hesitated, not sure whether or not she should tell him what she was feeling. She was aware that he did not really understand talk about feelings and fears. She also realized that he needed to be alone. He knew her, appreciated her, and needed her. Even after just two days, she was missing him and wanted to share his thoughts and all his conflicting ideas. He had not told her what had happened with the other amirs, nor had he hugged her at night for two whole days.

She sat on the bed. "Forgive me," she said. "I don't want to disturb you."

"You're not," he replied dryly. "Do you need anything?"

"I need you," she whispered.

"You know how busy I am these days," he replied in the same tone.

"Why do the men have their swords out day and night?" she asked gently. "That's something I don't understand."

Now he looked at her. She was craving some word or glance from him that might show her the way to his inner soul.

"Don't worry about that," he replied softly. "Go back to your own room, Zaynab."

She recognized that quiet, imperious tone of voice. It still scared her sometimes.

"Forgive me," she said. "I'll wait until you've finished your work."

"Okay," he replied without looking at her.

She headed for the door, then stopped and put her hand on her back. She wanted him to call her back. The way that she had relied on him in the past had made her feel strangely weak. Opening the door, she went out sadly.

One night, while she was sleeping on her side, her arms around her body as she felt the baby moving around in her womb, she discovered that he had come in. He lay quietly on the bed behind her and wrapped his arms around her back. She placed his hand on her belly and smiled contentedly.

Next morning, she watched him as he got out of bed beside her. She focused her gaze on his arm muscles, his firm chest, fully prepared for combat, and the blood in his veins that almost burst out of his skin, as though ready to fight.

"Muhammad . . . ," she whispered hopefully after pausing for a moment.

He gestured to her to say nothing, and she understood. She made up her mind that he could come into her embrace every night even if he did not tell her what was going on. Today she did not want to risk annoying him.

He made for the palace gates. News came, the kind he had worried about. Baybars had managed to arrest some of the amirs who had attended Muhammad's assembly; he had also gained control of their contingents. Today he also received a letter with news other than what he wanted to hear. He was expecting An-Nasir to arrive, but the letter was from Baybars Jashankir. One of Baybars's soldiers stood in front of him and read out the contents of the letter somewhat hesitantly, obviously assuming that Muhammad would kill him once he had finished reading it. Baybars demanded that Muhammad surrender and swear an oath of loyalty to the sultan on the spot in front of his soldier. Otherwise, Sultan Baybars himself would come to Muhammad's palace, attack him, and place him under siege. He would burn the palace and everyone in it. Muhammad would be incapable of launching an attack on the country's sultan.

Muhammad listened patiently to the letter. "Baybars is not a sultan of this land," he said. "No pact with traitors!"

Muhammad's soldiers nodded in agreement.

"If Baybars attacks me," Muhammad continued, "it'll be the end for him. He knows that. Tell him that, by attacking me, he'll be destroying himself; war among Mamluks will be ruination for Egypt as a whole. Surrender is his only course."

As the soldier left, Muhammad was waging a war with himself inside his own palace. Following habit and training, he was now risking everything. But this time, risk brought with it a different kind of bitterness; failure had the savor of perdition. There was no hope in a victory accompanied by collapse, no life involving defeat or ignominy, whether dead or alive. His death would be oblivion; in defeat his life would lead him to crave death. His only family was living inside the walls of his palace on Roda Island, all that remained of his loneliness and homelessness.

He spent two more sleepless days, his eyes glued to the palace walls in Roda, expecting an attack and making preparations. Then came news that gave some relief to his troubled soul. The amirs of Syria sent Baybars Jashankir a message, announcing their loyalty to Sultan An-Nasir. They threatened him, stating that they were fully prepared to meet and fight him. Next day, Muhammad received the letter that he had been waiting for: An-Nasir had arrived in Egypt and was heading to Cairo with his soldiers.

For the first time in two days, he lay down beside Zaynab and closed his eyes. She let him enjoy a deep sleep, not saying a word as she wrapped her arms around his back.

For two whole days now, she had watched him at night, lying on his back with his eyes wide open, looking silently at the window. She had not dared ask him anything, or even to touch him without his permission. She pretended to be asleep and did her best to move as close to him as possible, although she did not dare to wrap herself around his body. But today, when she hugged his back, he did not resist. When she settled her body beside his, she confirmed what the tortures of love involve whenever the soul is tormented.

When she looked at him the next morning, she could see a tranquility gradually infiltrating his soul.

"In days gone by," she said, "I wanted to learn your language and understand what was going on all around me and inside you."

"If you learned our language," he replied thoughtfully, "you might be able to understand what's going on around you, but not necessarily what's going on inside me."

Their eyes met.

"No warrior can ever breach the fortress of your soul," she said. "Words and tongues cannot pierce it. It feels as if I aspire to penetrate some of its secrets, but I fail."

He stroked her hand. "You're always safe and sound," he replied, as though he had not been listening.

She had no idea what he meant.

"What's bothering you?" she asked, putting her hand on his shoulder.

He did not reply, having made up his mind not to tell her about the imminent danger to himself and her.

"Has Baybars tried to kill you?" she tried again. "Tell me the truth. You promised me to tell the truth. He's trying every single day, isn't he?"

"He'll never succeed," he replied firmly. "Baybars doesn't worry me. No one can get close to the palace. He won't be there for much longer."

"Are you worried about the amirs' loyalty? Do you think they'll betray you?"

"No, I don't," he replied. "What I'm afraid of is a civil war between the Mamluks, and it'll be my fault."

"Are you afraid that Baybars will resist," she asked after a moment's pause for thought, "and fight An-Nasir in Cairo?"

"If the Mamluks fight each other, then it's the end for Muslim territories and Egypt in particular. The Crusaders and Mongols hope to unite and enter Egypt."

"But Baybars isn't going to fight," she replied assertively as she put her hand on his shoulder.

He stared at her in amazement.

"He'll never fight," she went on, "believe me. You tell me that he may stab you from behind, but he'll never fight, especially when he's going to lose. He'll surrender, assuming that An-Nasir will pardon him. He won't kill Baybars, even though he could. He'll be expecting An-Nasir to not hold him to account and to forgive him."

He stared at her long and hard. "Why all this certainty?" he asked.

"The warrior's eyes don't deceive him," she replied.

"Are you a warrior, Zaynab?"

"What do you expect from someone who lives with you?"

7

An-Nasir Muhammad ibn Qala'un reached Cairo accompanied by his soldiers and Mamluk amirs, fully expecting to encounter Baybars in a lethal battle—with Mamluks fighting each other. Amir Muhammad and his soldiers were at the head of the amirs in Egypt who were waiting for Sultan An-Nasir's arrival in Cairo and for the battle with Baybars and the Mamluks supporting him.

In the morning Muhammad woke up peacefully, with his wife still asleep beside him. He stroked her cheek gently, and she opened her eyes. He moved closer to her.

"Listen to me carefully, Zaynab," he told her softly.

She sat up and looked into his eyes to locate something to calm her heart, but without success. He looked first at her belly, then at her face.

"I'm going out with my soldiers to meet An-Nasir Muhammad," he told her, "and maybe to fight Baybars."

She said nothing.

"I've left half my contingent surrounding the palace," he continued.

She opened her mouth to speak, but he stopped her.

"They'll protect you from any danger," he said. "Remember your own strength and courage, Zaynab," he told her assertively. "They're what I've always admired about you."

"Muhammad," she whispered weakly, suppressing a shiver, "don't leave any soldiers here. You need them . . ."

He looked at her and put his hand on her belly. "You want your baby to have a life, and so do I for both you and him, whatever happens. That'll soothe my heart. You understand, don't you?"

She was eighteen years old. She loved him and did not know if this might be the end. She felt as lost as someone roaming the dark recesses of Citadel prisons, not knowing how to escape or how to withstand the tortures of days to come. She was a mother now and needed her dolls. She wanted to burst into tears.

"Pregnancy is hard for you," he said, realizing her thoughts. "If Baybars's army should besiege the palace, then you'll have to flee outside the country. That's an order from your husband. Shams ad-din won't betray you; he can't. He'll take you to a secret door from which you can escape. He and other soldiers will guard you to the Kerak Castle borders. You'll always be well protected, as I've told you. I've an agreement with my soldiers, whether I'm still alive or dead. They know that. They won't betray either you or me."

She opened her mouth again, but he stopped her again.

"On the way to Kerak Castle," he instructed her, "don't talk to the soldiers or to Shams ad-din. Never ask any questions about me or what's happened to me. Even when you get to Kerak Castle and someone tells you I'm alive and well and want to see you, don't come back to Egypt. If they say I'm in prison, don't ask to see me. If they say I'm being tortured, then block your ears and don't believe them. If they say I'm dead, then raise our child far away; don't ask and don't listen. In Kerak Castle Shams ad-din and the soldiers will take you to a house and give you some money—the money that I have there. Don't ask about your inheritance in Egypt. As long as Baybars is still the ruler, never send a message to anyone here in Egypt."

She covered her mouth to stop herself bursting into tears. All words had been erased from her memory.

"Muhammad . . ." she said.

"You tell me you love me," he told her sternly. "You've said that. If that's true, then you'll do everything I've asked you. You'll behave wisely and courageously. If it turns out that I'm still alive, I'll find you. If I die, then I'll die reassured."

"What if you don't go now?" she asked quietly.

"If I don't go," he made clear, "then we'll both die together. I know that nothing's going to happen, but we have to consider all the possibilities . . ."

He seized her hand. "You're always courageous," he told her. "Will you do what I've told you to do?"

She said nothing as her world swirled around her. Darkness was a blessing, but she could not reach it at this moment.

"Zaynab," he said, "I realize that you're young. Conflicts like these are new for you. You're not used to a life like this. I realize all that. Will you carry out all my instructions and act courageously? You asked me to talk to you frankly about everything. You have to be ready for such a burden."

"I can't," she replied painfully. "I can't not ask about you. I can't just abandon you and leave."

He gave her an angry look. For just a few moments, she thought that he might be about to pour out in front of her all his resentment, anger, and alarm from times gone by.

But he just gave a deep sigh. "You'll carry out my instructions," he told her. "Don't say a word, and don't object. There's no point. What I need is your courage and security for both of you. I don't want to leave here today without knowing what your fate is going to be."

"But I'm not going to know what your fate is!" she responded just as bitterly.

"I'll come back after sunset. Didn't you just say that Baybars will never fight? If you're right, I'll be back; if he does fight and we win, I'll be back. If I don't come back, then carry out the orders we've agreed on."

"We didn't agree. You decided, and you're then one taking risks . . ."

"Zaynab," he said, interrupting her, "I don't have time now. You'll carry out my instructions."

Their eyes met. After a brief pause, she nodded her head in agreement.

"Swear in front of me now," he insisted.

Head lowered, she swore in a muted voice.

Before she could stretch her hand out to give him a hug, he stood up from beside her and opened the door without even looking at her.

"I'll see you after sunset," he said.

She leaped up from the bed.

"Don't come over here," he said, "and don't cry. Watch out!"

For just a few seconds he looked at her, with her arms outstretched to beg and plead with him. He closed the door and left.

She left her arms outstretched for a while. She could not get up or even contemplate the possible consequences of this risky venture and possible conflict. Over the course of months, she had been his prisoner, wife, lover, and now maybe widow. He had blown away her life and future, fragmenting her heart, sometimes with threats and fear, and at others with passion and loss. She grasped her head in her hands, uttering prayers and hoping for rescue. That rescue could only come through him; he would come back, he had to come back. If not, then why had the plague left her alive; why had it not ripped her guts apart and covered her body in black spots? She prostrated herself and begged God for forgiveness. She had never kept her oath, nor would she. Whatever the risk, all she could do was to stay around him and with him. She dearly hoped that she would not have to break the oath she had sworn to him and that he would come back without her needing to go to war on his behalf. At this particular moment, she was feeling tired and nauseous. How she would hate the rest of her life if she had to spend it with someone else. He had to come back.

⟞⟝

However, Baybars did not go out to meet An-Nasir. He remained in his palace, preferring peace to war. Zaynab's words echoed in her husband's ears. He could not believe that this young Egyptian girl could understand all those sultans and amirs. Her mind seemed a great deal wiser than that of all the men he knew. It was not just that he loved and desired her; his respect for her grew as day followed day.

An-Nasir entrusted to him the task of going to Baybars's palace and demanding his surrender. When Muhammad entered Baybars's palace with his Mamluk amirs and demanded that he either surrender or fight, Baybars looked straight at him.

"I'm not going to fight Mamluks," he proclaimed vigorously. "I will not witness them fighting in my era. Your sultan ran away and abandoned his position of authority. Don't blame me if I tried to save the country."

"You'll come with me to the sultan?"

"Yes, I will."

The meeting between Baybars and An-Nasir Muhammad was brief and replete with hatred and envy.

"Will you pardon me, my Lord?" Baybars asked hopefully. "I'm one of your father's own Mamluks."

"Pardon you?" An-Nasir replied. "How can I pardon you? If you'd taken all my own Mamluks and my entire wealth, if you'd deprived me of food, I would have pardoned you. Do you remember, Baybars? You used to tell me that the river was running low and the country was suffering from famines. No meat, no birds. Do you remember that, you Mamluk of my father?"

"I'm asking for pardon in front of all the amirs," Baybars said.

"Rice has disappeared from the country, you used to say. Why so much hatred? Did you believe I would wage war against you if I ate goose? It would appear that, where Baybars is concerned, there's magic in geese."

Muhammad smiled but said nothing.

"But it wasn't just geese you wanted to deprive me of," An-Nasir went on, looking straight at Baybars. "It was life as a whole. You believe that I don't deserve anything. How can I possibly let you live when you really think that I don't deserve anything? You treat me like some thief or beggar, someone who asks for a lot, while the money in his hand poses a danger for Muslims. What would you do in my place?"

"Are you going to kill Mamluk amirs?" Baybars asked. "If you do, who will protect you?"

"Baybars," An-Nasir reacted quickly, "I seek refuge in God from such heresy! It's Mamluks who have brought me here and supported me. I value and respect them. They are the pillar of the state. I'm killing a traitor. I will not pardon you."

"You're going to kill a Mamluk amir," Baybars repeated. "What kind of rancor are you creating between them?"

"I am killing a rebel from the country under my control."

He gave orders that Baybars be killed.

An-Nasir Muhammad ibn Qala'un now went over to Amir Muhammad.

"Muhammad," he said, "I want you to be deputy sultan. What do you think?"

"My Lord Sultan," Muhammad replied firmly, "first pardon the prisoners, amirs, Egyptians, and scholars as quickly as possible. Then we can decide. Pardon the religious scholars. Their imprisonment is destroying the entire state."

"Do you agree to be my deputy? My father was your teacher. I trust your loyalty and morals."

"Let me think about it."

For Amir Muhammad, the release of Shaykh 'Abd al-Karim was an event of considerable importance. His attachment to the shaykh stemmed from respect for his composure, his strength, his conscience, and his sympathy for the common people. After his marriage to Zaynab those same qualities found a place within him. He ordered his soldiers to wait for the shaykh and escort him to his house in the quarter. Muhammad promised to visit him soon.

All Cairo celebrated An-Nasir's return. Egyptians felt that tyranny would be finally expunged and that Mamluk amirs still possessed a certain humanity, dignity, and love for the country; they were not all robbers and hypocrites. Some of them had principles, while others were genuinely worried about the country. Streets were decorated with lanterns and colored paper. Women, men, and children all came out, waiting on the banks of the River Nile to see the lame sultan pass by as he returned to the country in his sailboat. All Egypt rejoiced.

Zaynab gave birth to a baby boy whom she named Abu Bakr, that being the name of her father who had bestowed on her all his love and trust, the father whom she could never forget.

Life now seemed to be moving in a perfect direction, with victims released from prisons and their rapacious Mamluk amir oppressors taking their place in those same prisons. The sultan promised to fight corruption, limit taxes, and listen in person to complaints from the populace every Monday. In the space of a single month the land of the Nile became a paradise as far as Egyptians were concerned, a place for every traveler and scholar to visit. Egyptians were optimistic; they had no other option.

Muhammad was still mulling over the sultan's request. He sat there, watching his wife as she nursed their son.

"The sultan's asked me to be his deputy," he told her. "What do you think?"

She was surprised that he was asking her so directly. He had never done that before.

"What do you think?" she asked, looking straight at him.

"I don't know."

"Oh yes, you do!" she replied.

"What do you want, Zaynab?" he asked.

"Refuse," she replied firmly.

"Why?"

"Muhammad, Sultan An-Nasir will never trust the Mamluks. They betrayed him many times before. For the rest of his life he won't trust them. He'll tolerate them because he has to, but he'll slay any man whom he doubts or who has a claim to fame. After everything that's happened to him, he's now thoroughly experienced; he's cunning and does nothing in a hurry. He'll wait for the right opportunity to get rid of one amir after another, if he can manage it, and most especially those who stand against him or gain a good reputation among the populace. Do you understand me?"

He remained silent for a while.

"You know I'm right," she continued. "I'm scared for you. Egyptians love you and say good things about you. You're famous for being fair. If the sultan were to discover that his deputy is widely loved, he'd get rid of him. Friendship and boyhood memories won't help. When it comes to governing, betrayal is required, and deceit is an obligation. Don't do it, Muhammad!"

He remained silent.

She looked at him, unsure of her own logic. She did not know if her assertive statement about refusal was due to her fear of what the sultan might do to her husband or by the idea of authority itself. If her husband were to become deputy sultan, he would be obliged to marry other women, one, two, or even three. She would not be able to stop him or even see him. For her, everything was a jumble. She was no longer certain about the reason for giving him advice like this: did it spring from her own egotism, or her fear for herself, for him, or for both of them?

Once again, he looked at her as she rocked the baby to sleep. He said nothing.

Next morning he turned down the post in a friendly fashion. He told the sultan that he preferred to operate at a distance from official positions.

The same day, he went to visit 'Abd al-Karim at home. 'Abd al-Karim gave him a warm welcome filled with respect. Muhammad sat down in front of him.

"I want to establish an endowment," he said, "and to designate part of it for you and your children after you. You're teaching your son to become a religious scholar, aren't you?"

"Your generosity humbles me, my Lord Amir," Shaykh 'Abd al-Karim replied.

"I'd like you to craft for me a copy of the Qur'an," Muhammad continued, "and to emboss it with gold-leaf, as a gift for my wife. I want it to be different from all the other Qur'an copies in Egypt."

"That'll take time."

"That doesn't bother me. Take your time."

"It could take years for it to be an artistic treasure."

"I trust you and your abilities. I can wait."

Muhammad was silent for a moment. "I'm troubled by the Bedouin Arabs," he continued. "They don't like systems of government and have no respect for the sultan. What's your opinion of them?"

"Have you come to ask the opinion of an unknown person like me?"

"I've come to ask the opinion of someone who has stared injustice in the face and has not been scared by the darkness of Citadel dungeons or the bats of jail."

"My Lord, you're giving me such praise. Perhaps I've been affected by such vanity."

Muhammad moved closer. "Shaykh 'Abd al-Karim," he said, "you've been outspoken all your life: ever since you challenged your own teacher and spoke out at a time when all the other shaykhs were afraid to do so. I still believe that your undoubted courage springs from an arrogant streak and your conviction that you're the best and the one who knows the inner working of things. But that's the way you are. Your confidence has its appropriate place. You believe in yourself, Shaykh, and, unlike many others, you don't keep questioning yourself about the place of justice. You already know, you live with it. Give me advice, so I can advise the sultan."

For a few moments, he said nothing, then he continued.

"The situation with Egyptians is peculiar. They're used to having rulers and obeying them. But the Bedouin Arabs don't believe in government systems and sultans. Theirs is a life of desert and travel. Nothing scares them; soldiers' swords don't bother them. They live with danger all around them. The Mamluks may be able to stop Egyptians riding horses, but they certainly can't do that with the Bedouin. The horses are theirs.

"I don't want the sultan to wage war on the Bedouin," he continued, "not in the South or in the Delta. I want to advise him, but I need your advice first."

"Talk to their shaykhs and try the friendly approach. You buy your horses from them. There has to be some way of reaching an understanding with them," the shaykh said.

"I don't know why they waylay people and burn crops. How does that hurt the Mamluks? It's the Egyptian people whom they're hurting first of all."

"The Mamluks, my Lord. It's the Mamluks who get their legitimacy from protecting the Egyptian people. If they fail to do that, then the Mamluks may well lose the Egyptian people's respect."

Muhammad remained calm. "So we need to negotiate with them."

"Their shaykhs, the solution lies with them."

"I'm still afraid for you, Shaykh 'Abd al-Karim. But luckily for you, Sultan An-Nasir Muhammad is both fair and astute. I dearly hope he stays in power, for Egypt's sake and for yours too."

Shaykh 'Abd al-Karim's reputation spread as a shaykh who was not afraid of the ruler's oppression or ruthlessness; a mediator scholar who could explain things to the people and challenge other religious scholars using both logic and evidence. Senior figures envied him, while younger ones admired him. While walking around modestly, he would bend his head to the poor before the rich. However, he did not regard himself as in any way insignificant. To the contrary, he felt that he was both more learned and wiser than many others. For the most part, he was right.

Yusuf's tragedy after losing Zaynab was the talk of strangers and relatives alike. He had dreamed of the day when she would be sleeping in his arms and belong to him. He would thank his luck and his world for giving him Zaynab; he wanted no one else. He had little ambition, being timid by nature. He would laugh at Egyptian jokes criticizing Mamluks and watch shadow-plays, understanding their allusions and enjoying their performances. But by temperament he was no rebel. All he dreamed of was a small house with Zaynab; he would inherit his father's khan and continue to work in the quarter with his friends whom he knew so well, amid the quarter's nooks and crannies where he had grown up and spent his entire life. He firmly believed that good lay in safety, while all evil came with risk. However, when the Mamluk snatched away his entire life's dream, put him in prison, and unjustly humiliated him, the whole situation changed. At first, he told himself that the adversities would come to an end, Zaynab would come back to him, and the sultan would deal fairly with him. When he saw Zaynab's crushed expression, he was sure that she was suffering with the amir. It pained him to realize that he could not confront the situation or restore his rights. He hoped she would ask him for help and assure him that she would never forget him. But she did not do that. His fertile imagination drew him a picture of her miserable existence in Mamluk prisons, being beaten with whips and raped on a daily basis. He did not dare claim his right openly, realizing that, by doing so, he would disappear into the Citadel dungeon. Patience and frustration dominated the rest of his days as he tried to come up with a way of fighting Mamluks without being assured of a certain death.

After a year, he decided to leave the quarter and its reassuring pillars. But, above all, he was anxious to pass by Shaykh 'Abd al-Karim who had now sold himself to the Mamluks and never uttered a true word.

He could not spew all his pent-up fury on the amir and Mamluks, but he had to do it with the religious scholars. They were the ones who had allowed the Mamluks to tyrannize people and produced legal opinions for them. Traitors, hypocrites! That is what he thought of them.

He went to the mosque to see Shaykh 'Abd al-Karim, who was sitting on the floor cross-legged. The shaykh greeted him, but he did not respond.

"You're not speaking to your Lord," he said angrily. "He'll never listen to you!"

"My Lord?" the shaykh replied in amazement. "Isn't he your Lord too?"

"I don't know, but He'll never listen to you. You don't speak the truth or do anything. You married her off to a Mamluk. Why? What did you get in return? An endowment to live off? You sold your own conscience, dear Shaykh!"

"There are certain things about him," the shaykh replied patiently. "You need to reconcile yourself to your Lord's judgment, Yusuf."

"It's not my Lord's judgment," Yusuf said furiously, "it's the amir's."

"It's God's decree. How can you know that she's not happy with her husband? Maybe God will bring you the person you deserve. Be patient in dealing with something where you know nothing."

"I don't know anything about anything. They know everything! You hypocrites, you've turned them into gods and started worshipping them!"

"I can understand your pain," 'Abd al-Karim said patiently, "but don't let it overpower you. Don't adopt this kind of attitude. We're all human beings. Take what's happened to you in stride."

"So, Egyptians can show patience, while Mamluks live with all the fruits of that patience. What sheer hypocrisy! What kind of poison are you spouting? You knew that she didn't want him, but you still married her to him. Why didn't you refuse and tell him why?"

"If I'd told him, he would have killed you, then married her. You have to choose your battles carefully, know your enemy, and do your best to meet his demands. Amir Muhammad is not such an evil person."

"He's the devil incarnate, like his master. He's a slave, like the rest of them."

"But he's rescued you from humiliation at the hands of the Crusaders and Tatars."

"Yes, he's saved me from Tatar humiliation, but only to humiliate me however he wants. One day I'm going to kill him; I'll promise you that!"

"Don't be a slave to your baser instincts! Killing him will anger God. Are you planning to kill one soul without thinking about another?"

"No, it's for two: Zaynab and me."

"Yusuf, I don't believe she's been killed. She's given birth to a child of his. She'll give birth to another. She's not the miserable wife that you think she is."

"He forced her to live with him and then raped her. She sacrificed herself for me."

"Maybe she's chosen to live with him. Forget her and move on. Wars have their own rules. Don't throw yourself into perdition."

"Shaykh," Yusuf said sarcastically, "I want to ask you a question and seek your legal opinion. When I was in prison, I prayed for the amir. The soldier was holding a sword over my neck and a knife on the edge of my tongue. Do you think your Lord will respond to such a prayer?"

"Prayers have to come straight from the heart," 'Abd al-Karim stated firmly. "If it came from your heart, and you know better than me whether or not it did."

"It came from my heart, Shaykh, because I wanted to stay alive."

"Your Lord is fully knowledgeable about hearts and intentions. You're asking me questions beyond the scope of my abilities. I can't give you an answer."

"But you pray for him every day, don't you? Why? Because he holds a sword over your neck, or drowns you in gifts? Piety and corruption are now blended into one. Men of religion have now turned into hypocrites and liars."

"Man can lie and make mistakes, but that does not harm religion. Do not blame your perfect Lord for deeds that result from humanity's failings. If your Lord detected in mankind an unalloyed, perfect good, then he would either keep them all in heaven or spread his angels across the earth's surface to proceed in peace. But he has not done that."

"Mamluks are evil personified. People who side with them are hypocrites and liars. In the entire population of Egypt, who is there who can fight the Mamluks and defeat them?"

"Why defeat Muslims, when our enemies are toying around with neighboring lands?"

"The Bedouin Arabs are the only ones who can fight the Mamluks."

'Abd al-Karim looked at him. "They're highwaymen and criminals," he said. "They burn crops and steal cattle. What are you thinking? When there's general chaos, they'll be the very first ones to do you harm and finish you off. They have no loyalties and no order. For them, everything's permitted."

"You seem to be talking about the Mamluks!"

"No, about the Bedouin. Read God's book so you won't be so muddled. Destruction builds nothing, and chaos never leads to glory."

"Ask yourself, Shaykh. Why should Mamluks need the prayers of an aged prisoner caught between prison walls and mosque pulpits, if they have all the power in their hands now that they've imposed their tyrannical and unjust rule? Why have they resorted to shaykhs so that they can sleep soundly at night? Have you ever asked yourself that question? Never mind. You can keep on living, surrounded by Mamluk glory. I'm going to join the Bedouin Arabs."

The memory can select particular moments and collect them in its hands just as a child will collect river water to drink. For the rest of her life, Zaynab would never forget the day when she went to visit the wives of Sultan An-Nasir Muhammad for the first time.

Between Zaynab and her husband there were moments of submission and others of disclosure, all gathered together in her memory. She had asked him somewhat uncertainly whether she could make some sweetmeats for the sultan's wives and eat in Sultan An-Nasir's residence. After all, he was not Baybars Jashankir.

"Zaynab," he replied firmly, "you don't eat in the homes of either amirs or sultans. That's a rule that doesn't just apply to enemies, but to friends first of all."

She looked anxious. "Fine," she replied.

When she went to pay a visit to the sultan's wives, she expected to be received without a warm welcome, and indeed to feel strange. She noticed how beautiful the princesses were and how different their languages and origins were. As she sat there silently, she could feel a lack of confidence seeping into her veins. In the past, she had convinced herself that she was the cleverest and most beautiful girl in her family, maybe in the neighborhood as a whole. But now, everything had changed. The sultan had a princess wife from every country, so how could her own husband continue to do without all the available women in the world, simply for her sake? How long would he still behave that way? Who was she that he would sacrifice all these foods on offer and keep indulging in just one kind? As far as amirs were concerned, were not women just like food, opening the appetite for life, no more, no less?

Not only that, but the sultan's wives drew her attention to the amir's stupidity in not looking for a Mamluk amir's daughter to marry so that he could guarantee the loyalty of friends and sleep soundly in the knowledge that there were amirs who would be loyal to him forever.

An overpowering feeling of strangeness hit her inside the sultan's palace, even though, three years after their marriage, she had given birth to two children, one after the other. She felt proud that they were boys; the amir's lineage was now firmly in place, and he had a family all around him, after he himself had been snatched from family and home. But today, her self-confidence had been shaken as never before.

Once the visit was over, she started keeping herself busy with various things until her husband came home. As soon as he arrived, she greeted him with a gloomy expression and downcast eyes.

When they entered their room, he sat down on the bed. She looked at him, distracted, then sat on the floor.

"My Lord Amir," she said, resting her hand on his leg, "you're my amir for the rest of my life."

He stared at her in amazement. She had never looked so dejected, even when she had asked him to forgive her after spending time in prison. At first, he did not understand what was going on in her mind.

"I never dreamed of being married to you," she said, clasping and kissing his hand, "not because you're a Mamluk amir, but because you're my amir."

He felt completely dazzled as he looked at her, as though he were in some alternative universe or were a magician with all the treasure. Her complete submission left him aghast.

"So," he asked calmly, "what happened when you visited the sultan's wives?"

She did not look at him.

"Now I know and appreciate the sacrifices you've made for my sake," she said, kissing his hand, "and all so as not to humiliate me."

He said nothing, as if, only for a moment, he was savoring her desolation, He fully understood what she meant. The attractions of such desolation, involving a pugnacious woman like her, would be enough to seduce even unfeeling rocks!

"My Lord Amir," she said once again, "I confirmed to myself today that I don't deserve you. Who am I compared with you? You're all I ever dreamed of. I want to spend the rest of my life looking at you and filling my heart with your existence."

He looked at her hair, splayed across his leg, and turned her head toward him so she could look at him.

"Do you realize," he said, "that I hear 'my Lord Amir' from soldiers all the time. But, when you say it, it has a different effect. I love hearing you say it. When a practiced warrior like you surrenders, it has a particular luster to it, a kind of unrivaled elation!"

"But you're my amir," she declared, kissing one finger at a time, "the very best man in the whole country. For your sake, my Lord, I'll do anything."

He smiled. "That's the kind of thing I love to hear," he told both himself and her. "Once in a while, I expect it. But, tell me, Zaynab, what scared you today?"

"I swear," she replied firmly, "that I'll do anything for your sake."

"Don't swear anything," he replied. "I believe you. Have no fear; I don't want anyone else besides you. Ever since I set eyes on you, I've never wanted anyone else.

In fact, you're all I ever see. It's magic for sure, but the kind that can't be fixed by spells or time's passing."

She closed her eyes and clasped his foot. Leaning over, she kissed his foot slowly. Then she moved up to his knee and kissed it repeatedly. He could feel her kisses in his very bones.

"If I were a real warrior," she said sadly, "you would have defeated him long since."

Looking into her eyes, he hugged her. "Zaynab," he said seriously, "I've never seen a warrior as powerful as you."

She did not understand what he meant.

"This particular warrior can defeat me every day," he went on. "Zaynab, your effect is unusual. Every time you look crushed and defeated, I can be sure that I'm the loser. I can feel the taste of it in my mouth."

She lowered her head with a frown.

"Do you realize," he asked, holding her hand, "that there was a day when I looked at those two eyes of yours and saw that you loved me. I hadn't seen that before; I'd been aware of it and hoped for it, but I didn't dare acknowledge the fact and confront my mind with a teenager's craving for the loving looks emerging from deep inside you. When I did notice it, I thought I'd won. Finally I'd triumphed and reached my goal; the whole earth was mine to till. What I did not realize was that I was actually in retreat and had surrendered all my weapons. I can always read your eyes."

Their eyes met.

"It was possible that you didn't love me," he went on. "You were living with me, being loyal, and obeying my every command. I don't know why I was so concerned about your feelings. I'd never bothered with women's feelings before or given them any thought."

"How many women have kissed your hands?" she asked sadly. "How many women have wanted to spend a single night with you? I realize that I'm selfish; my heart has its cravings, and I beg your forgiveness. You've come to dominate my entire soul. I now cling to your heart, as though it's my sole reward. Without it, I've no weapons to protect me, no covering to clothe my vagrant limbs. Forgive me, my Lord, and excuse my heart's selfishness."

He said nothing as he absorbed her words with relish.

After a while he grabbed her hand. "Zaynab," he said sternly, "I don't want to see fear in your eyes."

She opened her mouth. "For Egyptians," she said slowly, "days have their time periods and years their recognized seasons. But I'm scared of seasons that arrive all of a sudden, putting an end to all gains and demolishing minds. If only I could guarantee years and seasons and know for sure that your love will never change or be affected by time like plague-seasons—leading to its demise with no preliminaries, if I . . ."

He interrupted her. "I don't want you to be frightened. That's an order. As I've told you, I don't want any other woman, nor will I ever."

Bending over, she kissed his knees again. "My Lord," she said, "my husband . . . and my beloved."

Then she clasped his legs and rested her head on them to sleep. She had no more to say.

"As a boy," he said, as though talking to himself, "I learned that struggles involve the will and a keen eye. However, the will cannot remain steadfast in the face of torture and execution. Faced with torture, no one can hold out forever, even if they're a priest or worshipper. No one can stop himself begging for mercy at the moment of execution. Humans are strange; they're weak, easy to break; they can be compelled to do anything: die, beg, confess, surrender. But the one thing they can't be compelled to do is to love."

She still had her arms around his legs, but she did not understand what he meant.

He ran his fingers through her hair. "Do you know why you can't compel the human soul to love?" he went on. "It's because you need your entire heart and soul to love someone truly. That's what my wife has told me. Do you remember, Zaynab? Talking about love, you used to say that love had no levels to it: you either loved with your whole heart, or you weren't in love."

She kissed his thighs and knees again, and hugged his legs. "You either love with your whole heart," she repeated, "or you're not in love."

Some of her kisses fired passion, while others stoked nostalgia. But those very same kisses were blended into a total surrender and fear of a whole series of spoils that rapidly infiltrated his very being and fractured his will. He devoutly hoped that she would not realize how his heart was spiraling downward and how totally infatuated with her he was, something he could neither explain nor encompass.

He looked at a strand of her hair in his hands. "You can torture and kill the body," he continued, "but it's hard to gain control of the entire soul. You can break the individual will, but it's impossible to impose love on it. What if you didn't love me? Is that even possible?"

"Muhammad," she whispered sadly, "it's impossible for any woman not to love you."

He was still holding her hand, while she rested her head on his legs.

"Zaynab," he told her firmly, "if you really love me with your whole heart, it means defeat for all time, with no way out. Do you understand?"

She nodded sadly. He in turn looked at her hand in his.

"Do you realize my own defeat now?" he asked, "or only your own?"

At that moment, she could not look into his eyes, realizing that these precious moments would stay in her memory forever. Neither of them would ever mention them again, nor would they ever confront the other with such weakness and surrender. From that point on, open discussion and shaming were ruled out.

Without saying a word, she kept her head resting on his lap. She had no idea how she was going to keep those memories real and alive inside her till her dying day.

She was well aware that her husband did not have a lot to say about love and did not choose to analyze his own feelings. Whenever he spoke about his defeat and love, he linked them both to notions of war and torture. He would establish the truth as though he were a soldier in front of his commanders: he would know the true extent of his defeats and victories.

He put his hands around her waist and lifted her up. For her part, she snuggled into his chest, gasping in surprise. Chiding him as she whispered his name, she hugged his neck. She was trying to wrap up these moments and keep them in her memory forever.

"When did you detect love in my eyes?" she asked.

He smiled as he stroked her cheeks. "As you well know," he said, "soldiers on raids have their own secrets."

"So when are you going to tell me?"

"Maybe never."

She hit his shoulder gently. "Muhammad!" she threatened.

"So, where's the downfall and defeat?" he asked. "How come they disappeared so fast? I wanted to enjoy those moments for longer than this."

Zaynab felt Umm Khalil's hand waking her up gently, but ignored it. She buried her head in the pillow, but Umm Khalil kept disturbing her. She turned her head, eyes still closed.

"What is it?" she asked.

"My Lord the Amir wants you now," Umm Khalil insisted.

She rubbed her eyes. "Why?" she grumbled as she got slowly out of bed.

"I don't know. He told me to wake you up and take you to him now, wearing your head-veil and fully dressed."

She handed her some faded clothing. "He wants you to wear these," she said.

Now she stood up, perplexed and scared, and did what he had asked. As she walked beside Umm Khalil to meet him, she had no idea why he had not spoken to her directly, nor why he had sent her a complete outfit of clothing. Even three years later, she was still scared of him and discovering his world.

Umm Khalil stopped by the door to the room.

"Go in, my Lady," she said. "I'm not allowed to enter."

She went in hesitantly. He was seated, surrounded by piles of papers and with two soldiers standing in front of him. He signaled to the soldiers to leave and locked the door. He looked at Zaynab.

"Sit down, Zaynab," he instructed her.

She sat down slowly. "Has something happened?" she asked. "Have I done something to annoy you?"

Now she remembered what they had said to each other yesterday—his candor and his weakness. She was afraid that he was going to take revenge on her for all those the feelings that were so dishonorable in a soldier.

"My Lord," she asked quickly, "have I annoyed you?"

"No, you haven't," he replied without looking at her.

She lowered her veil from her face a little.

"Keep the veil raised . . . always," he told her rapidly. "Always do that when you enter this room, even if there's no one there but us. Do you understand?"

She nodded, and their eyes met. "Zaynab,"" he said, "you used to help your father with his accounts, didn't you?"

"Yes," she replied enthusiastically and with a deep sigh of relief. "Do you need my assistance, my Lord?"

"Perhaps," he replied with a smile. "But now you've two children. Do you have the time to work with me?"

"My time's entirely at your disposal," she replied firmly.

Standing up, he gave her some papers, a pen, and an inkwell.

"Now you have the number of my men, horses, and estates, and all the soldiers' salaries. How long do you need to check on the figures?"

Her heart was pounding as she looked carefully at the sheets of paper. The way he was trusting her and making use of her—as though she were not merely one of the women in his life but one of his closest friends—was everything she wanted in life.

"By prayer time at noon, God willing, or earlier, I'll have finished," she told him.

"Get started then."

She said nothing as she started on the papers and reviewing the accounts. He watched her without saying a word.

"My Lord," she told him after a while, "I can take them with me if you need to be alone."

"I don't need to be alone," he replied. "I want to see what you're doing. These papers will never leave this room."

She nodded in agreement, feeling a certain tension. "Can I lower my veil a little?" she asked.

"As long as you're in this room," he told her firmly, "you can never lower your veil. Do you understand?

"Your word is my command."

She started adding up the numbers without saying a word, burying herself in figures as she had done in the past. But this time, they were more complicated and tricky. When she had finished, she held out the papers for him.

"My Lord," she said, "I want to remain in your favor."

He took the papers, looked at her calculations for a while, then looked at her again. She noticed a slight smile in his expressions, but pretended to be serious.

"How did you do this?" he asked her. "What kind of woman are you?"

"I hope that I merit your approval," she replied, hiding her pride.

He held out his hand toward her. "Come over here," he said, pointing to the bench, "and sit beside me."

Head lowered, she sat beside him. "If you were a man," he told her confidently, "you'd definitely be the sultan's deputy."

"Don't praise me, my Lord," she replied. "I don't deserve it. I was just trained to do accounting."

"Zaynab."

With that he held out the papers.

"In this room are all the accounts of Egypt and Syria," he said. "If anyone else read them, we would both be dead. Do you understand?"

"I understand, my Lord."

"Those papers contain numbers that don't just pertain to my men, but all Mamluks and the entire populace. To guarantee my continued position, I have to know about the accounts of all the amirs and of Egypt as a whole. The Mamluks have practices that I want you to know. I need you to help me."

"I'll help you and obey your every command."

"Obey my every command?" he said with a smile. "That'll be difficult for you. But you'll help me. I know that."

Yet again, their eyes met. She understood what he meant.

"Give me a week," she said, "and I'll give you all the figures you need."

"How can I reward you?"

"Your trust soothes my personal anxieties," she replied with a smile, "all my worries and concerns."

He nodded and stood up. "I trust you more than anyone I've ever trusted," he said. "We're agreed."

He handed her the key to the room. "Here's your key," he told her. "I don't need to tell you what'll happen to both you and me if it's lost or stolen."

She took the key from him and nodded. Bending over, she kissed his hand.

"Do you realize how much I love you?" she whispered.

He looked all around him, then bent over. "Not only that, I know how much I love you," he whispered in her ear.

Now he pulled her toward him. "In this room, Zaynab," he told her firmly, "you don't know me, nor I you. No one will ever know who you are. That's for our own safety, both of us. In fact, some will know who you are, others will have their doubts, and still others will never know. That's how I prefer it: some having doubts and others not knowing."

She nodded enthusiastically.

"It's not just love that's opened up this room for you," he said as he headed for the door. "It's also your mind, your intelligence, and your knowledge. Such a mind has to be exploited, and it doesn't bother me whether it's a man or woman."

"Your praise humbles me, my Lord!"

"I'm just speaking the truth. Flattery is useless in combat and war, but in accounting and ledgers as well!"

From that day on, Zaynab knew more about Egypt and Syria than the sultan himself. She kept the budgets of Muslim lands hidden in her memory and spent three hours a day working with her husband. The secret of their working together was known to the two of them alone; not even her children knew about it.

⟜

What was strange was that An-Nasir Muhammad decided not to appoint a deputy; not only that, but to abolish the position. He also decided that he would hold meetings with the Mamluk troops, but the deputy sultan would not, something that had usually happened in the past. Muhammad heaved a sigh of relief, because he had listened to his wife and not accepted the post. He had had his own doubts, and had the same misgivings as Zaynab. He started being cautious about his dealings with An-Nasir Muhammad. Friendship has its limits, clashing interests have their cost, and jealousy has its victims. In times of danger, the sultan would relish displays of cruelty, annulling all previous agreements. He had promised to fight corruption and appointed as head of the Justice Office Amir Ibn al-Waziri, someone who was renowned for his loathing of corruption. Now, the entire country started groaning under the impact of instant justice, something the populace had never encountered before—prevention of bribery and pay-backs—to such an extent that merchants and Mamluks started cursing the sultan in their prayers, ruing the day when he came back to the country, and spreading rumors and jokes about him. They dearly hoped that he would leave the country again and that his third period in power would lead to his destruction. His process of dealing with crooks and usurers with an iron fist affected the Mamluks, needless to say, but the way things were flourishing in Cairo and the populace's love for An-Nasir Muhammad combined to block any attempt to get rid of him. Some amirs came to regret giving him their support, others plotted to get rid of him, and still others regarded him as the kind of just ruler that soldiers wanted. However, An-Nasir Muhammad himself was paranoid about his own safety, realizing that he would be spending the rest of his days either under siege or else in flight. His goal should only involve ruling the country; not only that, but his own self-protection.

Egypt was stable and became a model for all the countries around it. Some years were hard, others were easier. Zaynab bore her husband seven children, five of whom lived: Abu Bakr, 'Ala ad-din, Nafisa, 'Aliya, and Muhammad. Her youngest was eight years old, and the oldest, Abu Bakr, was twenty-one. Abu Bakr married the daughter of one of the Mamluk amirs allied with his father, and 'Ala ad-din married the Egyptian daughter of a merchant who was a friend of Zaynab's father. Nafisa was married to an Egyptian merchant, and 'Aliya to a Mamluk amir. The love story between Zaynab and Muhammad never flagged or diminished. Actually, Zaynab started telling her children the entire strange tale: about the Mamluk who forced the girl to marry him, but she then fell deeply in love with him; he adored her and sacrificed everything and all other women in the world for her sake. A truly unreal story, or maybe a genuinely real one, with all its unusual novelties.

Zaynab still slept in his arms every day. If he happened to be traveling or away somewhere for even a day, she could not sleep. She anxiously and eagerly awaited his return.

The only thing she ever saw was a spouse whose exterior was all power and fear, but whose interior was gentleness and affection, something that she was the only one to see, and then only when she lay in his arms. She wove her love as a mesh that enveloped him so as to fill his entire soul. Every time she felt him lock himself away from her for a day because he was worried about something or angry, she would stretch that cover to envelop him even more and thus reprimand every part of his internal self that was rebelling against her or trying to push her away. As the years rolled by, her inner fears that he too might change as the Mamluks had or that he might go looking for an amir's daughter from his own race—those fears diminished. She was now certain that he would never do such a thing. It was difficult to understand or explain the ties that bound them to each other. While her internal fears subsided, the agonies of love, a force whose power over him she did not realize, did not die down. She needed to hear his breath every day and feel his heartbeat, to be reassured that his soul was at peace and she herself could feel calm before going to sleep. He needed her so much that he could not conceive of his life before her. Above all, he longed for a plentiful supply of affection. As time went by, she learned his points of strength and weakness and realized what used to alarm him more than anything else, namely any threat to his power and land. She would listen to him for hours and give him her opinion. She knew the names of all the amirs, how many horses they owned, and how many weapons and men they had. She knew it all by heart and repeated it all for him whenever he needed such information. Whenever he needed to make sure that he was more powerful, she would provide the necessary ammunition, confirming that he was, as usual, the most powerful amir of all. No, she was actually interested in power, but knew nothing about the life of amirs. She learned it all for his sake. Instead of doing the accounts for her father's trade, she started computing the number of men each amir had and the value of his possessions. She would argue with her husband about it all. Some days she worried about her husband, fearing that a particular amir might be conspiring against him or that another one might be accruing too much wealth. Sometimes she became paranoid, staying awake for days while she imagined him dead, imprisoned, or tortured. He was well aware of the situation and felt that she was like the mother of a tiny gazelle surrounded by ferocious lions. She never realized that he was one of them himself and knew them well. When this particular affliction hit her, she would shout out his name before he left in the morning and kiss his hands. She would beg him not to leave. If he did leave, she would beg him to take an escort of his men. All night, she would toss and turn, tortured by the nightmarish thought of living without him. Sometimes he would calm her down, while at others he would gruffly tell her to stop worrying so much. She would then suppress her anxieties till, given time, they disappeared.

Muhammad established an endowment specifically for her, another for his sons, and a third for Shaykh 'Abd al-Karim. He started constructing a mosque in the Mamluk cemetery where he would be buried, along with his wife and children. Shaykh 'Abd al-Karim was still engaged in creating for Zaynab the golden calligraphic copy of the Qur'an which her husband had ordered as a gift for his wife.

Corruption now became something unusual in Egypt, and justice prevailed in Muslim lands. Wars and desolation came to an end. For more than twenty years,

An-Nasir Muhammad consolidated his rule until he decided to fight the corruption of certain Mamluk amirs. But that is another story.

An-Nasir's purpose in fighting Mamluk corruption was to limit their extravagant wealth, and especially their estates which had started to exceed bounds appreciable or accountable by the human mind, and their revenues which exceeded the combined totals of all merchants and tradesmen. An-Nasir waited patiently till his control was firmly established. Then he caught the amirs by surprise. Some of them assumed that he had gone mad, others demanded that he be killed, and still others thought either that his decision was good for the country or else did not care. However, Amir Badr ad-din who had helped An-Nasir return to Egypt regarded the sultan's action as a betrayal of the entire Mamluk state, a total lack of appreciation for the burden that they had assumed in serving him. After all, they had restored him to his position on Egypt's throne. Badr ad-din assumed that An-Nasir had lost his mind; he always belittled the Mamluks and was scared of them. Even so, if it had not been for the Mamluks, he would still be in exile in Kerak Castle for the rest of his life. This decision of his implied massive ingratitude, a dereliction of responsibility. Having been raised in the luxurious environment of sultans, he had no appreciation for the hard life of Mamluks, the tough training, and undivided loyalty. Badr ad-din decided to get rid of An-Nasir as quickly as possible and replace him with his brother or any sultan who realized that the only people who deserved to rule Egypt were the Mamluk amirs who were trained to fight, the very sinews of the country. No one should challenge them, try to impose their own will on them, or set their eyes on their wealth. A carefully planned strategy was needed to get rid of An-Nasir quietly, especially as the Egyptian people loved him; corruption was gradually disappearing and its power over people had been broken, and that even after the crooks had cursed the sultan.

Some Egyptians and amirs were of the same mind concerning the significance of corruption and middlemen in the country and their central role in state affairs. They were agreed that the fight against corruption was hurting a lot of people and only benefited the poor and weak. They could never benefit the sultan in ordinary life and would be permanently without a voice or power. Only the rich and powerful could be useful to the sultan, and yet it seemed that he could not be bothered with them. Their assault on the sultan began with an attack on the currency and the distribution of phony money in the market. Commerce ground to a halt, and Egyptians lost confidence in the sultan who had brought justice back to Egypt, but outside time and history. Merchants became more suspicious and lost faith in currencies, weighing them carefully before trading with them. They started cheating on their scales, and crooks found a golden opportunity to take revenge. Words started to be heard, cursing and blaming the sultan. Egypt was now preparing to overthrow the governing system.

Badr ad-din was in charge of the new movement to remove An-Nasir from power for the second and last time.

8

Yusuf's period traveling with the Bedouin Arabs only lasted for a year. To begin with, he felt, for the first time ever, that he possessed a power greater than all the Mamluk amirs combined. He would be astride the kind of stallion that only Mamluks were allowed to ride and carry sharp swords. Between night and day, he had become a cavalier, riding for hours through the Egyptian desert, his spirit free as the power of Mamluks dwindled. Horses were not theirs alone, a monopoly for soldiers. In spite of all that, however, Yusuf spent the whole year in an ongoing disagreement with himself and his beliefs. Even though he had been convinced at first that his goal was to get rid of the Mamluks and crush their control over the country, he began to realize that Bedouin raids on travelers' caravans and burning peasants' fields was having no effect on the sultan's throne. Indeed, it would never help him personally gain his rights from Amir Muhammad. In fact, there was now little difference between him and any rapist. Now he was the ravager, thief, and wrongdoer. The Bedouin had their own logic and way of thinking, which emphasized the importance of bringing the Mamluks down—something that could only happen when it was made clear to the Egyptians that they would always be incapable of defending themselves and their properties. But, in spite of all that, Yusuf felt a major sense of alienation and barbarity in his soul. He was not convinced that bringing down the Mamluks required crushing the Egyptian people and making them miserable. On the other hand, he was utterly convinced that the idea of Mamluk protection was a phony mirage, but that the populace could gain strength through both Mamluks and Bedouin. Deep inside him, he understood Mamluk power and relished it. As far as Yusuf was concerned, Mamluk power was calculated and could be anticipated. Eras of poverty always came, impacting anyone who resisted or spoke out. On the other hand, Bedouin cruelty impacted any man, woman, or child. It followed no pattern, as though injustice were itself a known system, to which one could adjust.

One day during the year, Yusuf was involved in raids on peasants' fields. He managed to strike a Mamluk soldier with his sword and kill him.

"My brother," his companion yelled proudly, "now you've had your revenge! If only all Egyptians were as brave as you!"

But Yusuf did not enjoy killing people; he did not do it systematically. When he threw himself down on his bed, he could not fall asleep. He was overwhelmed by sympathetic feelings for the soldier drowning in his own blood.

"He wasn't Amir Muhammad," he told his companion. "How have I taken revenge?"

"They're all the same," his colleague replied confidently. "You've crushed them and humiliated them. Why are you feeling so distressed about it?"

He felt sorry for himself, just like Cain before he killed his own brother!

"Woe is me!" his soul screamed. "I couldn't stop and think. There's no going back on killing. My soul no longer has any dignity. If my Lord does not forgive me, I'll remain in a state of sin till the Day of Judgment."

He had thought that, at the instant of killing someone, he would have a power exceeding that of every other human being; he would feel like a sultan over the entire world. As it was, he could feel his own weakness and defeat. His body did not feel the satisfaction that his companion had promised him as he spotted the soldier motionless on the ground.

"You're not a real man!" his companion told him angrily. "Maybe you can recall their amirs who never hesitate to kill and butcher people. What kind of fighter are you? Are you worried about killing one Mamluk soldier, when they all deserve to be killed? If that soldier had captured you, he would have handed you over to the Mamluks. They would have brought in their racks and used them to crush your body till your eyes popped with the pain and blood started squirting from your ears."

He now knew for sure that his journey with the Bedouin Arabs was at an end.

"Let God do what He wills," he muttered. "With all your vanity and power, I only wish that I could know who deserves to die and who to live. Forgive me, my brother. Perhaps I've not achieved your level of courage."

"You deserve to have your girl snatched from you by the amir," his companion said derisively. "You're just like other slaves. It's as though a slave is manumitted by his master and is deciding on a future life for himself, so he chooses to live in his master's house and opts to serve his master."

Yusuf did not respond.

But his sufferings were not over, nor did his heart forgive him. When he departed from the camp of the Bedouin Arabs, he left behind the large amount of money he had stolen; all he took with him were his few personal possessions. He left Egypt for Syria and started working in commerce there. He sent word to his family, reassuring them after being away for a year with no word and no message.

Yusuf settled in Syria, but his heart did not. He purchased beautiful slave girls and lived in a three-story house. He produced two children, a son and daughter, but never married. He could never forget the injustice that he had suffered, nor could he return to Egypt to confront the Mamluks.

An-Nasir Muhammad was playing with little Muhammad, the son of Muhammad and Zaynab.

"He looks like you, Muhammad," he said with a smile. "Leave him here in my household so he can grow up with my children."

"I can't do that, my Lord," Muhammad replied. "His mother will never agree."

An-Nasir Muhammad opened his eyes in sheer amazement. "I can see that you take your wife's advice," he said, "and speak about it openly. How come the Egyptians have authority over Mamluks? I've never married one and I don't know them. But, after seeing the way things are with you, Muhammad, I've no regrets. I'd marry you to one of my daughters, as I've done with the other amirs, but I know you and realize that you won't agree. I can understand you, my friend, and realize what your goals are. You don't want anyone to interfere with your life or to threaten your influence. That's your absolute right and that of all amirs. I don't want to interfere in their affairs. All I want is for the wealth to stay in the bounds of reason. Do you understand me?"

"You don't need to convince me, my Lord," Muhammad replied. "You know me well enough."

"Yes, I do. I'm aware that you won't accept one of my daughters as a wife, and all because you've stinted yourself with regard to all women except her. But you haven't done that where power and prestige are involved. Power's still your primary goal."

"I'm like all the others, my Lord. We were trained as fighters."

"Do you trust my decision?"

"Yes, both it and you."

An-Nasir looked at the little boy who was looking around at different parts of the palace.

"Will you eat with me today?" he asked Muhammad, "you and little Muhammad?"

Amir Muhammad looked back at him, but said nothing.

"In all the years gone by," An-Nasir said, "have you ever known me to betray you? I want the sultan's palace to become a place where Mamluk amirs are safe. No treachery, and no betrayal. Do you think that's possible?"

"With you, yes, it's possible. But you're not just any sultan."

"You'll eat with me then?"

"Yes, I will."

"Don't worry about your son. At a time when I've grown weary of the world, Muhammad, you've given me some hope."

"Why has the sultan of Egypt grown weary with the world?"

"Let's talk about Badr ad-din. He's cooking up a plan against me. I've heard that he's working with some Egyptians and amirs."

"I'm not surprised."

"Egyptians baffle me. I want them to enjoy a life with justice, but instead they're allying themselves with the amirs! Or, at least, some of them."

"Interests don't differentiate between Mamluks and Egyptians. Faced with power and money, people are the same and equally weak."

"At all events, I've no idea why it's so hard to satisfy the Mamluks. What have I done to make them so furious? Have I confiscated any of their vast lands? What's it about? Their salaries, food, everything, are the sultan's responsibility. I've not taken away any of their rights: the chief judge is one of them, as are department heads and governors. I don't understand why they feel so much hatred."

"It's not all of them, my Lord, just a few."

"You're defending them, of course."

"I'm not defending them because I'm one of them. I'm doing it because I know them. The majority of them are with you; they respect you and stand alongside you. You could expect a few of them to rebel."

An-Nasir nodded in agreement. "I'm finding it hard to kill or imprison them," he said. "They're my father's men and Mamluks in his regiment. I don't want to demolish their prestige with the Egyptians. What should I do?"

"The populace values your sense of justice above all else. There's no prestige with injustice. Produce your proof and then bring charges against your opponent. Don't put people in prison under false pretenses. That way, you'll lose the trust of all Mamluks. You need that trust in order to guarantee your own safety and continued existence."

An-Nasir gave him a hard look. "Have you changed, Muhammad," he asked, "or were you like this from the beginning? I don't know. When I knew you as a young man, you weren't bothered about injustice. All you talked about was power. Every single day, you kept increasing your wealth and manpower. Whenever you sensed another amir's envy, you would ready your weapons and display your forces until whoever had decided to challenge you gave way. Power was your goal."

"I'm no longer young," Muhammad replied. "Power may still be my goal, but restricting estates is a project and a desirable goal in order to preserve the Mamluks and sultan. I don't want Egypt to collapse, but excessive wealth will lead to that."

"Indeed, you haven't changed in more than twenty years. You're still at the very peak of your power, but your goals have changed. It's as if you sympathize with the Egyptians and value justice. Who deserves the credit for this change, I wonder? Age or woman? No matter! I need your help once more."

Muhammad nodded in agreement.

"I don't want to get the Mamluk amirs angry," An-Nasir Muhammad continued, "nor do I want to seem to be acting unjustly toward the Egyptian people. I know what's being hatched up against me. You have control of your men and the other amirs. Talk to them, explain things, and show them why I've done what I have, and why I've restricted their land ownership. Assure them that I'm not going to touch their concessions and that Mamluk soldiers are protecting all Muslim territories from Yemen to Syria."

"I will."

An-Nasir looked at him for a moment. "You used to have a spy for every amir," he said. "You knew how many weapons, horses, and estates he had. I used to realize that and understand. Your survival, Muhammad, always depended on your cautious nature and astuteness."

"Don't expect me to spy on the amirs for the sultan's benefit," he replied with a smile. "You know I won't do that."

"You've spied on them your whole life, but for your own benefit."

"Amirs have their own priorities and reckonings, as you well know. There's another way of helping the sultan, but it doesn't include spying."

"Badr ad-din is inciting the amirs against me. He wants to depose me."

Muhammad's response was clear and certain: "It won't happen."

<hr/>

Amir Muhammad had been a soldier ever since he had finished his rounds of the Mamluk citadels. All he desired was power, order, stability, and security. From the outset, his goal had involved conquests and military achievements. Zaynab had understood and confirmed those goals from the very beginning. Whenever she could, she helped him achieve them. She organized her own life around him and with him, while she herself was constantly searching for that particular weakness lurking inside him, specifically involving her. Her instincts and reading combined to convince her of an innate gentleness that no one else saw, one associated with a little boy who had lost everything and was not the soldier type. She loved him with all the strength and life that filled her. But, because he actually was a soldier, when they were first married he would regularly count up his war spoils and appreciate the value of what he had won. Because he was a soldier, he appreciated Zaynab's value. She was fertile land, replete with rich soil and goodness. If he sacrificed her for the sake of other lands, he would never know her; if he picked fewer crops in the lands of poor folk, then he would be losing his profits. He knew his own abilities, and was well aware that he could not lose her. Without him even realizing it, his love of her was now firmly implanted in the very depths of his being. It had snatched his entire soul and forced it to submit without any possibility of resistance. The warrior mentality inside him made him certain of her abilities and her love. Not for a single day did he think about any other woman; he had no need of one. A woman's love was something he knew about; before Zaynab he had savored it a lot. But this veritable flood of power to love and give, this ability to reject and rebel, these were things he had never encountered in a woman. In the past, he had not left her any choice; in that same past, she had not left him any either. She insisted on sleeping in his arms. Her arms were a haven of security, stability, and order, things he really needed in wars, and of true affection, the kind that he had never known or cherished as a boy, then a teenager, then a man. He had started anticipating that resort to her arms' embrace and longing for that moment when he could feel her, gentle and submissive, as she slept beside him. Sometimes he would look at her for hours, sleeping quietly in his arms. He could not understand why there was such trust in him and such an abundance of passion. Once in a while, if he moved away from her while asleep or she felt him looking at her, she would move her body closer to him, as though she wanted to gain access to his very depths, wrap her arms around his neck or back, and cling forever to all the rebellious parts buried inside him. She had gained control of the weaknesses of the boy inside him, the vanity of the warrior, and the rigor of the commander. She was a past that he no longer remembered and a present that he did not want to end. She was all the love that he had never been able to share with anyone. When her eyes dimmed on occasion, that was enough to baffle him, as though he had somehow lost his way. He could still see her as the loveliest young girl, with powerful eyes and hair cascading down her back. Her body had filled out somewhat, and tiny wrinkles now showed around her eyes and on her neck. But all he ever saw was that young girl who had run toward him twenty-two years ago, asking for his help without any shame or hesitation. She had wrapped him in her arms so that now he needed them before he could undertake any action. She had stunned him with her spontaneous gifts, the absence of any caution when expressing her feelings, her strength, and her rebellious streak. She had become the rebel confronting the soldier, undaunted by his weapons; the ascetic in front of the amir, unafraid of his prestige. Approval was not always his main goal; power was his teacher and the source of his inspiration. However, with the passage of time, he came to realize and understand the value and magic of achievement and the serenity of love. Her smiling eyes were that achievement and delight. From the start, he was sure that no one deserved such delight and serenity, especially him. She had managed to overwhelm his very soul because he was lucky and different from the rest of humanity.

Once Zaynab's two sons, Abu Bakr and 'Ala ad-din, were married—one of them to an Egyptian woman, the other to the daughter of a Mamluk amir—she brought them together, along with her two daughters, Nafisa and 'Aliya, and established a set of rules to govern their dealings with each other, a system for food, drink, expenses, everything. She made it very clear that she would be making no distinction between her sons' wives and her two daughters, nor would she be favoring a Mamluk daughter over an Egyptian woman. She would not hesitate to penalize anyone who infringed on the system, even if it were one of her own daughters. She would direct her estate from the palace and make charitable gifts to the poor. She had a small mosque built, and her husband had two built for travelers and indigents where they could eat two meals a day. But, as far as Zaynab was concerned, Muhammad was more important than commerce, children, and details of daily life. If she noticed a call to her in his expression, she would leave the world to its chaos and head in his direction.

She would always listen carefully to what he was saying, frowning slightly as she watched him, as though she were trying to find a solution and hated to see him baffled. He would always tell her everything and go into explanations. The confidence he had in her was more than any other man or woman could even dream of. Always cautious, he would be thinking about risks, soldiers, and weapons. When he was with her, however, he would let a feeling of weakness spill over the surface of things; a gentle sensation would sneak into his heart. He would pile all his anxieties on her shoulders, and she would bear it all with loving patience.

Once in a while, a strong force would emerge from her eyes. She would insist, albeit calmly, on doing something or on the children doing something. She was not scared, nor did she show any inclination to back down from her wishes. She spoke with all the determination of a warrior intent on winning.

She learned quickly not to confront him. That inevitably involved a loss for her; she should never challenge him or blame him. She now commenced a journey of self-instruction blended with experiment and careful observation. If he did something that she did not like, she would think about it quietly and plan an unexpected silent raid: sometimes she would frown and stay out of his way, while at others she would try to convince him by quietly invoking logic and calculation; more often than not, she would abide herself in patience until she could get what she wanted.

She would often take him in her arms and toy with him like one of her babies. Placing his head on her chest and hugging him, she would drown him in an affection that she did not realize she had inside her. It was as if she wanted to melt him into her heart, as she whispered how much she loved him and that she could only feel so much love and affection when his head was resting on her breast, as though he were one of her children.

It was this feeling of her ardent love blended with colors of every kind—soft colors, glaring colors, gentle and violent—that turned him into a warrior who was always on the point of being defeated. He would go out to meet her with an open heart; on some of those raids his own defeat involved her private victory and her stunning beauty.

One day a few years before, she had asked him something concerning her two sons. Abu Bakr and 'Ala ad-din had no gift for horseback riding nor any talent when it came to hard combat. They told their mother fearfully that they wanted to stop their training. At the time, Abu Bakr was fourteen years old, and 'Ala ad-din thirteen. She was well aware of the impact that this news would have on their father. For days she thought about how to broach the subject. She sat down by his side and explained to him gently that the two boys were not soldiers; they would never be like him. This would be better for both of them, because his own life was complex and full of risks. She could feel the anger surging through his veins, but said nothing.

"That's not possible," he declared. "They'll continue their training, whether they like it or not!"

She remained silent. A few days later, she raised the subject with him again, and again he refused. She had the impression that he was losing patience with her and them.

"I don't want to talk about this anymore," he declared firmly.

She nodded. She spent the rest of the day frowning and did not even try to broach the topic again. But he could sense a barrier existing between the two of them. He was sensitive to her moods and knew whenever the barrier came down: sometimes it was thin and transparent, while at others it was hard and dry. He could not annoy her too much!

He could not stand this barrier and had no idea why he felt so sensitive about it.

He sat down beside her. "They can stop," he told her through gritted teeth.

She smiled and stroked his hand. "Don't be angry with them," she said. "Your children are not all like you. No one's like you, Muhammad."

When Muhammad left to suppress the Bedouin Arab revolt and punish those who stole and plundered, she would anxiously await his return and fully understand his objectives. Her husband had three primary goals: order, stability, and security. When he had achieved those three goals, he would be happy and successful. He knew that the country would continue, that goodness and justice would become norms for the Egyptian people. Even so, she did not view those three goals as having the same importance as others that had melted their way into his own heart. She would join him in fighting his wars without either thought or hesitation and listen carefully to his fears of chaos and destruction.

After many years of communal marriage, Egypt went through a sectarian crisis that shook Cairo. Mosques and churches were burned. One particular day was the hardest for her husband. He kept frowning in sheer frustration. Everyone was scared and avoided him, realizing that the consequences would be dire; everyone, that is, except his own wife, who neither avoided him nor was scared. While her children were baffled by their mother's bravery, she went in to see her husband, but did not open her mouth to speak. Instead, she sat down in front of him without saying anything and looked at him from time to time.

"What do you want, Zaynab?" he asked after a while.

"You've not eaten or slept," she replied softly.

"I know," he said impatiently. "I don't want to eat. Don't ask me again."

She nodded and said nothing.

"How long are you planning to stay here?" he asked her after a while, staring out the window as usual.

"Do you want me to leave?" she asked quietly.

"No," he replied without looking at her, "no, don't leave."

"It's the kind of crisis that's happened before," she said softly, her head lowered. "Don't worry. This is a large country. Crises are to be expected."

He did not respond.

"I know that you hate chaos," she went on, "but you've done what you can. The sultan's ordered the instigators to be arrested."

"This kind of crisis is more dangerous than all wars," he replied, as though talking to himself. "The implications are far worse than for the Crusader and Mongol invasions. In an era like ours, when the whole country's encircled by risk and the enemy proceeds to annihilate strong and weak alike, the populace is completely befuddled. They can't tell the difference between an Egyptian Copt and a Crusader. When Egyptians are so utterly confused, then our age and all ages come to an end. Dear Zaynab, fear can dissolve the heart much more effectively than opium or wine. In such ruinous times strong and weak are both crushed. Mamluks must be made aware of the danger. An event like this will give the Crusaders a pretext for invading and staying for centuries."

"Don't take on more than you can handle."

He did not respond. She stayed there, sitting and looking at him with loving affection. Even though he was not looking at her, he could still feel her presence, as if she represented all the affection he had never known as a child or understood as a youth.

"How long are you going to stay like that?" he asked her after a while.

"Till you throw me out," she replied jokingly, "if you don't want me here."

"I can't possibly not want you," he said, still staring at the horizon. "As you well know, I always want you."

She put her hand on her cheek and kept looking at him, like a child waiting for her father to finish work.

"I still look on you as the handsomest man my eyes have ever seen," she told him with a smile. "Do you realize that?"

He suppressed a smile. "You're still talking like a poet and Sufi," he told her, pretending to be serious. "Are you still reading these days?"

"I'm trying."

He looked up at the stars in the Cairene sky. "It seems as though you're way ahead of all men in your knowledge and intelligence," he said. "You talk like a judge and haggle like a merchant. What kind of woman are you? I don't understand how you've managed to turn out this way."

"But I'm not the most beautiful woman any longer," she said softly. "I'm not eighteen anymore."

He looked in her direction. "You're more beautiful than ever," he said. "I've never seen beauty like it. I've told you that before. Ever since I first set eyes on you, I haven't be able to look at any other woman."

Their eyes met.

"Muhammad," she said firmly, "if you dealt with the person responsible for this uprising with determination and justice and in front of everyone, there would be no other implications, no matter what his position or wealth."

"Why?" he asked inquisitively.

"Because justice, just like a flood, sweeps away chaos and drowns sedition. You should not hesitate to hold shaykhs or priests accountable. If you stop to take into account the position of the person responsible or the implications of punishing him, then the consequences will be dire."

He came over to her and held her chin. "What have I ever done to deserve you?" he asked. "You're all the spoils of war gathered in one place!"

She clasped his hand. "Muhammad," she said, "I love you. I know that I've been saying that every single day for years. Forgive me! Every time I've said it, I've relaxed and surrendered!"

He gave a big smile and hugged her affectionately. "I don't know why I deserve all that either," he said.

He had never exchanged those words or told her how much he loved her. For all those years, he had only done it three times. She did not need just his words; at specific moments, she would summon up intimate memories, times when the world all around her exuded the scent of sweet harmony.

"You always amaze me," she said after a pause. "I've never known you to be so modest."

"No, I'm not modest. It's just that, when I'm in your arms, I'm somebody else, a poet as well and a scholar on my own self's secrets."

All those twenty years, Fatima did not change. She saw her children married, and her husband died. She could still laugh and sing with gusto. Of the world around her, she could see waves, flowers, and its broad expanse. She was not bothered about Mamluks and sultans. She still hoped that one day she would be able to escape and go back to Bulaq where she could sing in shadow-plays and festivals—something she had dreamed of doing her entire life. She still brought together family members and friends, banging the drum and singing with a childlike energy that had never left her throughout her life.

She sat in a circle, surrounded by Zaynab's two daughters, Nafisa and 'Aliya, her own daughter, Zaynab, and all her friends. She started singing for hours. When she finished, she sighed.

"In this sad country," she said ruefully, "we don't have any choice."

Sitting beside her, Zaynab smiled but said nothing.

"Just as an example," she continued vigorously, "your aunt here was forced to marry an amir."

Zaynab's daughters' eyes opened wide in astonishment. They had never expected to hear such a thing. People in Amir Muhammad's household had a particular stamp. The amir himself was a soldier, first and last; his speech was terse, and expression was always serious and frowning. He rarely smiled. Even when he was sitting with his children, he never had that much to say. Everyone was scared of him, boys more than girls. Even so, the entire family know that his wife Zaynab was the only one who could penetrate his depths. Throughout the years, she had been the one to act as doorkeeper to the sultans, mediating between the external world and the amir. None of his sons dared ask for anything directly; their mother was always the intermediary, nor did they dare oppose any decision. Their mother also served as go-between. How did Zaynab deal with him? He did not understand his own children. Why did she have this special ability to reach into his soul? No one knew the answer, but neither Nafisa nor 'Aliya had the same ability with regard to their husbands. The children could not understand the exact nature of this relationship, but, from the very beginning, they realized that their father had a particular weakness when it came to one person, namely their mother. The same weakness did not apply either to them or to any other person or thing. The two daughters tried to understand that weakness, but they failed. Before they were married, they both asked their mother what the secret was behind her ability to influence her husband.

"Give with no expectation of reward," she declared, "and love with your whole heart."

They did not know what she meant.

"If a woman gives something to a man," Nafisa commented bitterly, "he objects and starts wanting another woman."

"There are as many types of men as there are swords," Zaynab replied with a smile. "One type goes to pieces in your hands, another tricks you, another is stiff, and still another dazzles you, so you envisage in him the rest of your life so you can appreciate his beauty. That last type will value what you give."

"Then why didn't you find me a man like that?" Nafisa asked resentfully.

"They're few and far between, my daughter," she replied. "You can't find that kind of man; he has to find you."

They never saw their parents touching each other in front of them, but they did see them exchanging the kind of profound looks that can reach to the inner soul and summarize words. They had the impression that such a relationship did not happen very often in the world; indeed it was not being repeated in their relationships with their own spouses. The really startling thing was the friendship and intimacy which bound husband and wife together far more than their friendship with the children who were of their own blood. That too was strange. When Nafisa, Zaynab's daughter, gave birth to her own son, she loved the little boy far more than her husband; she regarded him as a part of her own heart. But, with her mother, she always felt that she loved the amir first, and only then any of the children. It was the same with the amir. They would look into each other's eyes to make sure what it was they wanted, not caring what anyone else may have thought. For the boys, it was a complicated and difficult relationship. In spite of the mother's affection and the father's gifts, there was still a thin barrier between children and parents, and an open space between the souls of husband and wife.

When their Aunt Fatima uttered those words, both Nafisa and 'Aliya gaped in sheer amazement. They could not believe that their mother had been forced to marry their father. He was her entire life.

They both looked at their mother, waiting for her to say something. Zaynab gave Fatima a disapproving look.

"Your aunt's joking," she said. "Who would ever dream of being married to Amir Muhammad?"

"I agree," Fatima said spontaneously. "From the start, I told you that the fancy military uniforms worn by the Mamluks were enough to make you fall in love. But I was the one who understood and realized it."

"Finish your song," Zaynab said to change the subject.

Fatima's frustrations and the need to suppress her artistic gift crushed her ability to give and love. Sometimes she would loathe everything around her; at others, she would be furious at the entire world. As in the past, that hatred for the world was directed at her husband, alive or dead.

Today, when she finished her song, she looked at young Muhammad. He was concentrating on drawing.

"Does he like to draw?" she asked Zaynab. "He's not going to be a warrior like his father?"

"Don't say that," Zaynab told her, looking all around her. "That kind of thing annoys Amir Muhammad. None of his children will be like him. They can't stand training for hours and carrying heavy weapons for days."

Fatima gave her a malicious look. "Is that what you prefer?" she asked.

"One fighter in the house is quite enough!" Zaynab replied with a smile.

Fatima looked long and hard at the young Muhammad. "He looks just like his father," she said. "I'm sure he spoils him more than his brothers."

"He's the apple of his eye," Nafisa butted in quickly. "I've never noticed my father looking at me that way or any of my brothers either. He'll spend hours looking at him; he never refuses him anything."

"Of course, my girl," Fatima said. "He looks exactly like him. As the youngest child, he's bound to be specially loved."

Fatima grabbed the piece of paper from Muhammad and looked at the structure he had drawn so perfectly.

"He can draw like a professional," she said. "Just look!"

"Little boy," she said gently to Muhammad, "listen to your Aunt Fatima. Don't let anyone hold you back and kill your imagination."

"I don't understand you, Auntie."

"Do you want to draw all your life?"

"Yes, I do," the boy replied firmly.

"Then go ahead and do it, and everybody else can go to hell!"

Zaynab gaped in amazement, while the little boy laughed and kept repeating "draw all your life, draw all your life."

Fatima pointed at the boy's ribs.

"Muhammad," she told him slowly, "here . . . inside those ribs there lurks the demon; sometimes he's a dwarf, at others he's a gigantic demon. If you ignore him, he's going to burn you. You've turned out just like your aunt. If you carry out his instructions, you'll achieve happiness and pleasure. Do you understand? A demon inside your ribs."

"But you're happy, Auntie," he replied spontaneously.

"The only time I've ever been happy," she declared, "was when I ran away to Bulaq. Apart from that, my life's been one long hell. Understand what your aunt's saying and never forget it."

⌒

Young Muhammad waited patiently all day for the moments he spent with his father. If a day went by without his father leaning over him, he would be distracted and unhappy; neither other children nor games could compensate.

The day after Fatima's visit, he was looking for his father in the palace rooms and garden. Eventually he found him checking on the horses. He ran over to him and stared admiringly at him, but without saying anything. His father carried on checking a new horse's teeth.

He was used to the sound of his young son's footstep as he ran after him.

"Muhammad," he asked, without even looking at his son, "how are you today?"

The little boy stared straight at his father and swallowed his fear of the horse's open mouth and his large teeth. "I'm fine," he replied.

"Do you want to ride a stallion with me?" his father asked.

The young Muhammad did not want to show how scared he was of horses in general and this one in particular, so he did not respond.

His father looked at him. "You didn't respond," he said. "Do you want to ride a stallion with me?"

"I want to stay with you," the boy replied spontaneously, "if that's possible."

His father laughed and leaned down to his knees so he could look at his son's expression.

"Are you scared of horses?" he asked.

"No, I'm not," the boy replied quickly. "I promise you, I'm not."

"Muhammad," his father told him, "fear is a feeling that you can train, just like horses. It's fine to be afraid, particularly of things bigger and more powerful than you. But I don't want you to submit to your fear."

The boy covered his mouth so he would not start crying. "I'm not afraid," he said.

The father patted him on the head. "If we ride together," he said, "the horse won't be able to hurt you."

The boy's hand quivered. The father immediately took his hand, mounted him on the horse, and sat behind him. As he started goading the horse into a run, the boy did his best to stifle his screams while a flood of tears coursed down his cheeks. Closing his eyes, he gave his newly emerging courage free rein, forgetting all about the horse's mouth and settling into his father's arms.

Eventually the father brought the horse to a stop, took the boy off, and looked at him.

"Father," he said, whistling happily, "you're the bravest man in the whole country. I'm not afraid of the horse. Did you see me just now handling the horse on my own?"

His father laughed. "You're the bravest boy in the whole country," he said, repeating his son's words. "Do you want to ride him again tomorrow?"

The boy thought for a moment. "Maybe," he replied, "but I'm not sure. I have lessons tomorrow. But I'm not scared; I promise you that."

"I believe you. How can a son of mine be scared?"

Then the father spurred the horse again and vanished into the distant horizon.

When Muhammad ran back to the palace, he yelled for his sister Nafisa who took care of him just like his mother. He told her proudly that he had ridden a stallion on his own in front of his father. He had not been afraid, nor had he cried. Nafisa let out a sarcastic laugh.

"Don't you believe me?" he asked her angrily. "My father praised my courage."

"Praised your courage?" she repeated with a laugh. "He's never done that with any of us. So why you? I'm jealous of you, Muhammad. And if I'm jealous, I'm going to put you in the stable with the horse for a whole day."

The boy looked at her, scared and angry. "I'm going to tell my mother and father," he replied.

"I'm teasing you, Muhammad!"

"I don't like it. Do you believe me?"

"Yes, I do. I realize how you use your words and innocent eyes to control your father! Where did you get such cunning?"

"Nafisa, stop it!"

She started tickling him, with him shrieking and laughing in turn.

Zaynab was going over the accounts and ledgers when he came in. Only her eyes were visible, they being his permanent neighbors and companions. Their eyes met. He sat down.

"Have you looked into the impact of the sultan's decision?" he asked. "How will it affect us and the amirs?"

She held out the papers for him. "Just as you anticipated, my Lord," she replied, "it's to the country's benefit. Some amirs are corrupt; they hoard the money and stolen lands that they've seized. If that situation continues, it'll be the end of the sultan and some of the amirs who are allied with him. You already know this; it's been troubling you for some time."

She always addressed him as "my Lord Amir" whenever they were in this particular room with those paper records.

"You're always concerned about Egypt," she declared. "It needs the Mamluks to maintain stability. You don't treat the Egyptian people unjustly, and your conscience doesn't allow you to take bribes, hoard stolen property, and grab land. As a result, if the sultan does not curtail the wealth of those other amirs in order to limit their greed and corruption, then they'll always be wealthier than you."

He stood up. "I was thinking the same thing," he said, fully aware of what she was not saying.

"Not all the amirs are like you, my Lord," she went on. "But there are some who will understand. They'll realize what's to the benefit of the country as a whole and welcome the sultan's orders."

Muhammad held a meeting in which he discussed things with the amirs. Some of them understood and accepted, realizing that An-Nasir Muhammad's just decision would bring stability to the country and serve as a deterrent to its enemies. They regarded Egypt's rising reputation, something that had now reached as far as the rulers of Europe and the Pope in the Vatican (who was planning a visit to Egypt) as a major victory for them. The sultan might be a son of the people, and yet he was an authentic Mamluk. On the other hand, there were amirs who felt that this particular step and An-Nasir Muhammad's initiative were dangerous and radical, something that had to be stopped and resisted. Restrictions on Mamluks' own property and lands were just the beginning; he might also be thinking of depriving them of their actual functions as amirs. altering the entire system and not giving them official appointments. No one could know for sure what was going on in An-Nasir Muhammad's mind; everything he did was unexpected. This division of the Mamluks into two separate camps made Muhammad's task easier to some extent, but also more difficult at times. Meetings with amirs were fraught with risks and possible catastrophe. There was no protection from a stray arrow or poison in food or drink.

All through dinner, Muhammad looked glum. He did not say a word to his children or to Zaynab.

Zaynab locked the door and went over to her husband who was lying on the bed.

"What's the matter?" she asked him anxiously.

He gave her a long, hard look, but said nothing.

She slid in beside him and wrapped her arms around his head. She knew him well and understood. Once in a while, he would shut himself off, even from her. He would go back to a distant past, one that he could not remember and whose features he did not recognize—a stranger in a country that spoke a different language and had different customs. He was on his own, a desolate loneliness for a boy snatched from his mother's arms, never to see her again. His mother used to prepare meals enthusiastically and give him a hug whenever he cried or felt weak. Sometimes he even felt her scent, although he could not remember her features anymore—a face, but with no features and no hair. But he did remember the warmth of her scent, a blend of onions, garlic, affection, coal, and wood. He had buried that same scent, trying not to revert to her memory so as not to feel weak and turn into a servant. No, he had to become an amir, someone with no family to annul his soul, like some monk in the service of country and religion who never gives any thought to his mother waiting for him or a homeland that he prefers. Mamluks have their own magic power and the kind of power that no one else can achieve, either in earlier times or later.

Zaynab . . . this girl who had penetrated his loneliness and memory with her purity, liveliness, and copious love. The balance had been upset, and the warrior had been confused. How strange for a heart to search for memory among the common people, abandoning his own people and soldiers. Only in her arms did he find release; he did not deserve her. He had originally taken her by force from the folds of the earth, but now he needed her even if he did not deserve her!

He put his head on her breast. She hugged him with an affection that extended to every Muslim region and toyed with his hair.

"What's the matter, my darling?" she whispered.

She kissed his head, as though he were one of her children. He put his arm around her shoulder, but said nothing. All the years past, they had not needed a lot of words. She could understand him from his looks, knowing him in a way she had never known anyone before.

On this particular day, he badly needed her overwhelming affection and serenity that had long since enveloped him. He dearly wished to remain in her arms, forgetting all about life's span and his mother's face, something that occasionally faded away, but drew near often.

Zaynab was whispering many things in his ear, shaking him and kissing his head time after time. She stroked his shoulder and moved her hand over his back so he could sleep and relax. For his part, he realized that the past was over, finished, and the rest of his life would not be all wars. His own far distant country was now just Zaynab's arms. They would not let him do anything except think about her and along with her. She would not let him wander far off.

"Don't be worried about anything," she told him gently, her eyes closed. "Nothing is worth that. Nothing needs you to be so glum. My darling, you're more important than the whole world."

Closing his eyes, he put his arms around her shoulders. He was quietly savoring the various hues of serenity, drinking in the affection that he had come to know for many years, a feeling without which he could not live.

For a while he stayed lying on her breast, then he sat up.

"Zaynab," he said, "I have to do something that is going to infuriate certain amirs. I want you to know; you have to know."

She swallowed hard and shivered. "Why?" she asked anxiously.

"I'm doing something which is in the country's best interests. Sultan An-Nasir Muhammad is the best ruler of Egypt and Syria; he's become Islam's hero. His name is being repeated in Baghdad which surrendered to the Mongols, and in Yemen, Hijaz, India, and China. Even the monarchs of Africa have good things to say about him. Justice has a scent like jasmine; it can't be concealed. It shines like the sun to illuminate the world. I can't allow a conspiracy against him to succeed."

She stayed silent. She wanted to beg him, to ask him not to interfere, to leave the sultan to defend himself, and not to risk both him and her. Even so, she stayed silent, fully aware that whatever she said would have no effect.

She grabbed his hand and kissed it. "Muhammad," she whispered, "I can't live without you. Don't put your life in danger. You're all I have. I've grown up in your arms and counted the years of my life from the time we were married."

"Nothing is going to happen," he told her firmly. "Don't worry."

She pulled his head hard toward her breast. "They'll kill you," she said. "Don't you realize that?"

"Maybe, maybe not. You know how it is. As a child, I signed a pledge to live like an amir. My life might be short and full of plots and conspiracies. Every Mamluk signs such a pledge. If I am to die by arrow or sword, that's still better than dying in bed of some chronic disease. I told you all that a while ago. Do you remember?"

"What about me?" she asked angrily. "Aren't you thinking of me?"

He kissed her breast, wishing all the while that he could kiss the very depths of her heart. "You're everything," he said firmly, hugging her even harder.

―――――⌒―

When her husband left next morning, they looked at each other as they always did, and she gave him a smile. But, no sooner had he left the room than she felt a sharp pain in her heart. She ran after him as fast as she could and shouted to him. He did not hear her.

"Muhammad," she yelled, clutching her heart.

He stared at her in amazement.

"Do you have your soldiers with you?" she asked in a panic. "Don't go out today. I beg you, don't do it."

He smiled, something he did not do very often. He took her hand, and she kissed his slowly.

"You're going," she said, "and not paying attention to what I'm saying. Take care!"

"I will," he replied, putting his hand over hers.

All day long, she felt as though her heart were outside her body in some distant place. Her daughter kept on talking and asking questions.

"What's the matter, Mother?" she asked. "You're not saying anything. Are you well? Mother . . ."

She shook her head, but said nothing.

"I was telling you about my husband," Nafisa continued, "and the bracelet he bought for me yesterday. I don't like this necklace, but . . ."

She was worried by how distracted her mother looked. "What's the matter?" she asked again.

Zaynab raised her hand, as though to stop her saying any more.

"I want to go to my room," she said. "I've a headache."

She closed her eyes tight shut, as she recited some Qur'anic verses.

Shaykh 'Abd al-Karim knocked on the palace door and asked to see her urgently. She knew it and felt it; she had ever since the morning.

He sat in front of her, downcast. "The amir!" he said.

He looked round at the amir's children. They were all looking intently at him.

He paused for a moment, but then Zaynab asked him in a loud voice: "Has he been killed?"

He nodded his head. "He couldn't be saved. The arrow hit him straight in the heart. He died immediately. A traitor's arrow! If only the cowardly killer had confronted him and engaged him in combat. The amir was a warrior; he would have respected a warrior like him. But the killer used treachery, a coward like all killers. He killed him inside the mosque after he had finished praying and was looking through the copy of the Qur'an that he had had written for you, my Lady. I've had his body moved to his room along with his soldiers. You're a believer, and this is fate. I'm deeply sorry that . . . the amir has died a martyr and as a result of treachery."

Nafisa started screaming. Both daughters shrieked, as did his sons' wives, and his young son. However, Zaynab did not scream.

"He wanted to die as a warrior," she declared, "and he did so."

The children raced to his room. He was lying on the bed, his eyes closed. There was blood all around his heart, but his expression was serene.

His sons started crying, kissing his hand, and yelling how much they loved him and would miss him! She stood there silently, staring at him. The bitter bile in her throat was hard to describe; breathing had no value.

"Leave me with him," she gasped.

No one paid any attention to what she had said.

"Leave me with him!" she said more forcefully.

The sons left, desolate. After locking the door, she went over to him and passed her hand over his face. She could not remember her life before him, nor could she know or wish for such a life after him. His face was still strong and handsome, but now it looked cold. She ran her hand over his beard with its tiny white hairs blending in with the black, making it even more spectacular.

"Muhammad," she whispered, "my life's darling!"

She gave his mouth a powerful kiss and put her head on his chest, as though she wanted his blood to stain her entire life to come. However, this time she could not hear his heartbeat as she had done in the past.

Standing up, she wiped away a couple of tears that had suddenly appeared.

"Say farewell to your father," she said after unlocking the door. "I don't want mourning women or any screaming and wailing. Your father was a fighter, and he died a martyr."

She shed no tears afterward. Her grief was so profound that it made tears impossible. It was difficult to express or describe the profound abyss in her heart. Her eyes lost their gleam, and her soul was buried.

9

The murder of Amir Muhammad had a profound effect on An-Nasir Muhammad. The amir was not just one of his few supporters whom he could trust. They had grown up together in Qala'un's palace; he had played with Muhammad and known him all his life. Once An-Nasir Muhammad had heard this terrible news, his whole situation changed. For a long time, he stayed in his room, distracted. He did not visit his wives or slave girls. He made the immediate decision to arrest the amirs involved and did not give Badr ad-din any opportunity once they had been arrested. There was a quick trial in which they were accused of trying to overthrow the government system. They were all hung. He was not worried about angering the other amirs nor their loss of prestige. Things were out of hand, and the murder of a friend only a few years older than himself had made clear the realities of mortality and the imminent end of life itself.

An-Nasir now decided to spend some time each day in isolation, contemplating this world and the world to come. He stopped wearing silk and jewelry and spent lavishly on the poor throughout the land. Historians started writing about him without his having to give them presents. They wrote about him as being the greatest Muslim sultan and his era as being one of security and stability. Justice was possible, and combating injustice was an obligation. Seizing goodness from the rapacious jaws of evil was always difficult, but not impossible. There were some Mamluks like Amir Muhammad, and others like Badr ad-din. Egypt fully deserved An-Nasir. He had turned it into a flourishing land, teeming with goodness, sun, and humanity. He had built hospitals and schools, and was aware, unlike any of his successors, that mortality was real and kingdoms fade away.

The sultan asked to have a meeting with his friend's widow and sons. They all went to see him, but the general atmosphere was gloomy.

Zaynab was holding her young son's hand. The gleam had gone out of her eyes forever.

"Your husband was a close friend," the sultan said gently. "I truly value his sacrifice."

Zaynab managed to suppress a tear. "It is our honor, my Lord," she replied.

"I want to reward him," the sultan continued kindly. "I want to make it clear to everyone that he was the best amir."

"Pray for him, my Lord," she said. "Only prayer can help him now."

"Do you know who killed your husband? Amir Badr ad-din did. But for Muhammad, I would now be dead. He was different from all the others."

She did not react. The mention of her husband's name broke her heart and stirred up feelings of love and loneliness inside her.

"I killed Badr ad-din," An-Nasir Muhammad said. "I avenged your husband. He who kills will be killed."

"Your justice spans the entire country, my Lord."

"What's Abu Bakr doing now?" he asked pointedly.

"He's a merchant."

"I'll give him a governorship if he's ready for it. What about 'Ala ad-din? He's studying to become a judge. Amir Muhammad's sons deserve everything that's good. But they must prove that they're ready for such positions. I'd like young Muhammad to grow up here in the palace with my own sons."

Zaynab did not respond.

"You're not saying anything," the sultan said. "Do you agree?"

"Can I refuse a sultan's order? But, if you'll forgive me, I really need him to keep me company in my loneliness. He looks so like his father and reminds me of him, if you'll allow me."

For a moment the sultan said nothing.

"Yes indeed," he commented, "you're as strong as Muhammad always said. Never mind!"

"You're the widow of my closest friend and best amir," he said. "I'm obliged to suggest that you stay in this palace and be married to the sultan. Muhammad deserves that from me."

Her two sons gaped, and Zaynab lowered her head. "That's an honor I don't deserve," she replied slowly. "But Muhammad leaves no space in my heart."

"Are you turning down marriage to the sultan?" he asked incredulously.

"If you'll permit me, my Lord," she said firmly, "the sultan of Muslim lands should marry a woman with a pure, virgin heart, not someone like me. I have been exhausted by a lengthy passion, the vestiges of my heart have been crushed by a perfidious murder, and I'm simply a cluster of flesh and bones chewed over by a lion."

Her two sons exchanged glances, but nobody spoke.

"You're as eloquent as a religious scholar," the sultan said, looking down.

Then he looked at her, and their eyes met for a few moments. Lowering her head quickly, she realized that he was looking at her as a woman, not as his friend's widow. She was terrified of the decision he might make in spite of her.

"I admire your husband and his choice of wife even more," he said. "Now I can understand why he flouted norms and chose an Egyptian woman."

She continued to stare at the floor.

"Mother of Abu Bakr," he told her, "I respect your decision. Your determination and ability to fight is like a soldier's. It's been a while since I've made two requests and had them both turned down. Never mind. Should you need anything, you or any of your children, come to see me immediately. Don't wait for an appointment."

"Your generosity humbles me, my Lord," she replied. "The entire country benefits from your justice and mercy."

As Zaynab left the sultan's palace, she stopped suddenly. She gave her two sons a stern look.

"What happened today in the palace never actually happened," she said. "What you heard the sultan offer is not to be heard by any mortal, jinn, your wives, or sisters. Do you solemnly swear to that?"

They both looked around them. "Yes, mother, we swear."

"If the Mamluks or Egyptians get to hear that any Egyptian woman refused to be married to the sultan," she declared, "it'll be the end for both of you before me."

They both swore silently.

Young Muhammad suddenly started to cry, holding his mother's hand and walking beside her.

"Muhammad," she told him, looking away, "men don't cry. That's what your father always said. He was your age when he left to travel to a country he didn't even know. He left his family forever with no farewells, and crafted his prestige with his own hands. He became an amir, not because he was an amir's son, but because he was Muhammad. I want you to be like him. We called you by his name because you look like him. Remember him always and don't cry. There's no way that crying can cope with his loss, nor can tears rival the loneliness of living after he's died."

She fingered the gold-embossed Qur'an manuscript that her husband had ordered for her as a gift. She felt the gleaming upraised letters with a quivering hand.

"He's wanted to give it to you for a while . . . years, in fact," Shaykh 'Abd al-Karim said. "Forgive me, I've been slow about copying it, more than twenty years in fact. But now, I'm giving it to you in accordance with his wishes."

She leaned over and kissed the Qur'an, muttering some words and prayers that the shaykh could not hear. However, he was certain that they were prayers for the amir, that she too could join him.

She looked at the fountain and mosque, then at Shaykh 'Abd al-Karim who looked particularly gloomy today after the amir's death.

"I want this Qur'an to stay in the mosque," she said, "and I want the fountain to provide water for the poor. He really admired you, Shaykh."

"He was the finest amir that Egypt has ever seen," the shaykh responded assertively.

"I intend to bequeath you an endowment," she declared, "and for your sons after you. I want to visit it every Friday and to be buried alongside him in this mosque."

"Zaynab," Fatima said gently, "your husband died a year ago. Aren't you thinking of getting married again? You're still in your forties. Why don't you remarry?"

"There'll be no husband for me after him," she replied decisively.

"Do you know who asked about you yesterday? Yusuf wants to talk to you just once. He thinks he can convince you that there's still something left to life. He still wants you. You're his only love, and he wants to marry you. Do you realize that he still loves you? He's never forgotten you."

Zaynab smiled sadly. "Are you joking, Fatima?" she asked gently. "I've told you. I've just one husband—a soldier and fighter. I can't think about anyone else; there's no comparison."

"But why stay alone?"

"I'm not alone. I have all my children. I have my work and my business. But most important is that he's still with me and will never leave me."

Fatima opened her mouth.

"My dear cousin," Zaynab went on loudly, "there's a kind of man that a woman can't forget or compare with any other man. It's like chronic diseases and plague that kill with no mercy and do unchecked damage to the heart. Muhammad has not left inside my heart any single part that can be available for any other man. After his death, my entire heart is dead. He had total control over me. What can I say? You never met anyone like him, did you?"

"No, I didn't."

"I don't know whether that's good or bad luck on your part. Abu Bakr has his personality, while Muhammad looks like him. They have difficult and powerful personalities. Amir Muhammad, my dear Fatima, was just like a jinn. He took me into his well as a child and then brought me out as the princess of all creation. He gave me everything, and left me utterly crushed without him."

Zaynab's total rejection of Yusuf's proposal shattered all his dreams and ideas. He had not expected it or even thought of it as a possibility. He had assumed that Zaynab was suffering when she was with the amir; she would never forget Yusuf, as he had never forgotten her. Mamluk tyranny had to place a barrier between her and any feeling of love for the husband who tyrannized, oppressed, threatened, and put people in prison. How could she have done this to him now? He could not understand or believe it. Once again, he tried to arrange a meeting with her and sent her messages. But each time, she sent the same unambiguous response.

She had loved him! Had she loved the Mamluk amir too? Could Zaynab really be betraying him like this? Or was it that he had been spending his entire life in a mirage, one he could neither understand nor contemplate. It felt as if he had never seen or understood; his past life had been without purpose, lost between wandering in delusion, utter futility, and annihilation. How could he not have noticed? She had never asked for a divorce. Instead she had lived with the Mamluk amir for twenty-two years, borne him children, and settled down into her life. She had never asked after him or paid any attention to his affairs. She had betrayed him then, and not just because she was forced. He would return now to Syria and try to understand it all. But, by now he had become used to searching and waiting. After this ending, life had neither meaning nor purpose.

He wandered through the Cairo streets amid the mosques and hostels that the Mamluk amirs had built. Every mosque provided refuge for Sufis, the perplexed, and all those in quest of the right path. He went into a mosque where a servant was enthusiastically distributing food. He handed Yusuf a plate.

"Here, take your food," he said.

He stared at the servant. "Which amir built this mosque?" he asked.

"Amir Muhammad ibn 'Abdallah al-Muhsini," the servant replied. "God have mercy on him!"

Yusuf looked down at the piece of meat that he was about to put in his mouth, as though it was a chunk of his own flesh.

"How come the mosque's coming to his aid?" he asked. "By God, even if that monstrous rapist fed the whole of Cairo, he'd still roast in hell!"

The servant stared at him in fury. The people present looked at Yusuf, then started pushing him, still cursing and swearing, out of the mosque. The anger that he felt inside him would not subside or disappear.

Shaykh 'Abd al-Karim was watching from afar. He could see how his fame and reputation were spreading and people kept coming to consult him whenever they were facing a problem or crisis. Now that Yusuf had decided that his life had been wasted in delusion and revolt against fate, he decided to visit the shaykh again, although he was not sure whether it was to blame him again or ask for his help.

When he sat in front of the shaykh, he looked straight at him and told him about his time with Bedouin Arabs and in Syria. Why, he wondered, had evil won in the end?

"Only God knows the contents of people's hearts," the shaykh replied with a smile. "We cannot know precisely where good and evil lurk in the human soul."

"God will never forgive him," Yusuf declared. "Even if he opened a hundred mosques, God will never forgive either him or all the other Mamluks. God does not approve of tyranny. Isn't that right, Shaykh?"

"In His creation are many things," the shaykh replied quietly. "In the Qur'an, God Almighty says: '*Say: O you people who have been immoderate against your-selves, do not despair of God's mercy. God forgives sins all together.*' Maybe you can't forgive, but God is one who forgives sins in return for repentance."

"Don't ask me to forgive," Yusuf replied defiantly. "I won't do it. No one's ever asked me to forgive and move on."

"Are you happy in your life," the shaykh asked, "now that you know the truth? You know for sure that Zaynab was not forced to stay with the amir."

"I feel as though I cannot taste pleasure anymore," Yusuf replied slowly. "Life has lost all flavor."

The shaykh patted his shoulder. "How can I help you?" he asked. "It takes effort and determination to achieve pleasure in life. It needs hardship and work. No one can ever help you with that, neither I nor anyone else."

"I'll try," he replied. "I've a son and some money. But I don't want anything."

"How are you going to try?"

"I'll pray, give alms, and fast. I'll do everything I can and ask for forgiveness for my sins as well. What else can I do?"

"All rituals are easy and soothing, but they're not what's needed. They're merely the path toward it. What you need is a profound personal effort on your part. Search for satisfaction inside yourself. Your son, money, and even beautiful women will not give you that satisfaction. At the moment, you're counting your cheap spoils and forgetting what's most important."

"What is it that's most important?"

"That's what you need to achieve. Delusion involves the quest that ranges between the extinction of pleasure and pleasure derived from the qualities of eternity that are not extinction. Satisfaction is a feature of paradise. Everything that you own belongs to the realms of the ephemeral world. How can you possibly achieve a sense of those heavenly qualities by way of the spoils of this lower world of ours?"

"I don't understand you, Shaykh."

"I can't explain those words any further: seek, understand, read, and achieve."

---

* Qur'an Sura 39:53 [The Companies]

Two years after Amir Muhammad's death, Zaynab died of nephritis in 1324 CE; she was forty-two years old, or less.

She had started suffering from the disease while her husband was still alive, a few years after the birth of young Muhammad. She was not one to gripe and complain. One day, when the pain was severe, she stayed in bed, clutching her back but not moaning. None of her children was aware of her illness until her husband came home. He took one look at her and summoned the sultan's Jewish doctor, Ibn Kawjak. The amir sat beside her for hours, looking directly at her protruding eyes and holding her hand, waiting for the doctor to arrive.

He told the doctor to come in.

"You can have whatever you need," Muhammad told the doctor in a firm voice that she remembered so well. "I don't want her to feel any pain or to die."

"My Lord," Ibn Kawjak told him slowly, "death has no fear of Mamluk power. Forgive me, but don't ask me to do something that's not in my hands."

"But she's going to live!" Muhammad retorted.

"I'll do everything I can, my Lord," the doctor said, "but I'd like you to know the agreement I have with the sultan. In your religion and mine, life is in God's hands. So, please do not strike me if she dies, or if her pain gets worse and she can't tolerate a situation where I can do nothing. Till I can perfect my skills, that's what I've told the sultan and what I'm telling you now."

"Do whatever you can," Muhammad almost pleaded, "and you can have whatever you need."

But, when he continued, it was more imperious. "But she has to live."

At the time, Zaynab smiled as she listened in pain to her husband's imperious tone. She was also shocked by the pleading in his voice which still managed to fill both ear and soul.

When the disease's intolerable pain made her groan, the doctor gave her some opium. She was raving all night long.

"I'll stay with her," Nafisa told her father shyly.

It was not usual for husbands to stay with their sick wives, especially if they were amirs. But Muhammad insisted on staying with her all night, as she raved and screamed to the consternation of her two daughters. After a while, he sent the servants and children away and stayed with her on his own. He held her in his arms and whispered some words in her ear that she could not recall. But what she did remember were his delicate touches that countered all the pain. Next morning, she felt better and kept her slight pain under control. Carrying on, she could see for the first time in her life the level of worry and fear in his eyes as he looked at her.

"I'm fine," she said softly as she got out of bed. "I promise you."

He pushed her back gently on to the pillow. "But you're not going to get up," he made clear. "You're not going to move unless I let you."

"As you wish, my Lord," she told him submissively. "I always follow your instructions."

He grabbed her hand and kissed her forehead. "Don't ever do that," he replied. "You'll be fine. The doctor's coming back today and every day till I'm convinced you're well."

She recalled that moment nostalgically, swallowing tears that she had not shed since he had died. She was sure this time was the end, and her children felt the same way. They had gathered around her in tears. She had entrusted to them Shaykh 'Abd al-Karim's endowment, the school, fountain, mosques, and congregational mosque that their father had established. She asked them to keep the Qur'an copy in the mosque and then declared that she wanted to be buried beside him in the mosque as they had both planned and agreed. She wanted his sword to be buried alongside her body. She then fell asleep in the desire and hope of another meeting, better circumstances, and a life free of treachery and greed.

The sultan himself attended the funeral for his friend's wife. Once again, he asked Abu Bakr that young Muhammad should join his household and grow up with his own children. By now, Muhammad was ten. Abu Bakr immediately agreed to the sultan's offer, and Muhammad did indeed grow up with the sultan's children.

When Yusuf left his meeting with the shaykh, he felt even more baffled and pessimistic. He had no idea which path to follow. He had tried many of them, but had never reached his destination.

He started wandering his way through the Cairo streets, thinking of wine and hashish. Occasionally they could give him some temporary satisfaction, but they were not what he needed now. He wanted to achieve satisfaction that lasts. He learned about Zaynab's death, but was not sad. He had not forgiven her; in fact, he wanted her to suffer for days, to regret, and to beg forgiveness, and all because she preferred the rapist to him. He discovered a group of people listening carefully to a man standing in front of one of the mosques. He started to listen himself. The man was talking about his travels and the things he had seen and heard in foreign lands. He was praising the Egyptian people, the fine buildings, the generosity of the Mamluks, the dignity of shaykhs, and the just sultan whose repute had now spread through Muslim lands and beyond the seas.

Yusuf listened enthusiastically and asked the man his name, one that he had actually heard before. The name was Muhammad ibn 'Abdallah ibn Muhammad al-Lawati at-Tanji, known as Ibn Battuta. Yusuf went with him as he toured Cairo, then went to Upper Egypt and Alexandria. He listened to all his stories.

"Can I go with you on the rest of your travels?" he asked.

The famous traveler smiled. "Is it possible," he asked, "for someone who lives in the mother of all countries, the seat of Pharaoh, to want to go somewhere else? I've never seen such food, so many mosques, the hospital, such thrift and generosity in any other country. The Mamluk amirs are really concerned about the country and lavish funds on the poor, religious scholars, and Sufis."

"Dear brother," Yusuf said bitterly, "that's to compensate for their crimes. He who is generous in giving is equally generous in taking. Believe me. It may be the mother of all countries, but it's that same Pharaoh in whose shadow I can no longer live."

Ibn Battuta stared at him for a while. "But I thought you wanted to attain something," he said. "Do you really want to accompany me for a while?"

"I want to accompany you all the time."

"That I can't do. Travelers have their own rituals and customs. Journeys always end in loneliness. Come with me then, till we've left Mamluk territories."

"That's my goal and my purpose."

So Yusuf traveled far away. From time to time, he would send news to his family, but, after a few years, no more was heard. Some people said that he had settled in India and married there. Others claimed that he had died at sea.

———

Egypt continued to flourish. Even the European monarchs had the greatest respect for An-Nasir. It was as though time was standing still, and all rights had been restored to their rightful owners. Well-being and blessing pervaded this virtuous land, or so it seemed . . . until Sultan An-Nasir Muhammad died.

It was as though this blessed land could not tolerate or adjust to justice for too long; the world could not remain stable forever. Endings are always more difficult than beginnings!

Shaykh 'Abd al-Karim heard a knock on the door; he was expecting the caller. An-Nasir's era was at an end, and now there was a new one. The dungeon in the Citadel that had stayed empty during Sultan An-Nasir's time was still there, waiting for someone to reopen it with a gleaming sword, new steps downward, and more space to accommodate everyone.

His wife screamed at the soldiers. "My husband's an important shaykh," she said. "He's a religious scholar. Insulting men of faith can only lead to plague and aridity."

The soldiers paid no attention. They took him to the Citadel dungeon. There was no Amir Muhammad alive to ask after him, nor any sultan to call for justice and tolerance and to place limits on influence and corruption.

"What am I charged with?" he asked again on his way to the prison. "What have I done?"

"There's more than one charge against you, Shaykh," replied one of the policemen. "In the Friday sermon, you didn't pray for the sultan. You spoke about injustice and corruption, and incited the people to rebel. You spoke admiringly about the Bedouin Arabs and encouraged people to destroy things."

"I didn't talk admiringly about the Bedouin, nor do I approve of destruction. The people aren't rebelling. Why the fear if they aren't rebelling? The way spies are behaving is weird! They're afraid of the people and what they're saying! They're all carrying swords and weapons!"

"You're the one talking, Shaykh. It would be better for you to ask to be forgiven."

"Forgiveness is something we ask of God. I'm not a child to be dragged in front of people."

"You hate Mamluks. Why do you hate them? Why such irreverence?"

"How can I possibly hate Mamluks, when the endowment for me and my children comes from the Mamluk amir, Muhammad? Where's the logic in that?"

"Beg for forgiveness and acknowledge your faults. Stop giving such inflammatory sermons and pray for the sultan."

"I won't do any such thing. I don't even know who is the sultan to pray for."

"In An-Nasir Muhammad's time you were spoiled. He encouraged you to make dangerous statements. Well, he's dead now; the era of such nonsense is over. Enough of your controversies! There's more than enough sin to condemn you."

The shaykh spent less than a year in prison. After spending time buried in the depths of filth, he died. His life however remained as a model of a man who never sold himself; he always adhered to the truth even when faced with sultans and amirs, but he was never to hear or know about that. His final days, spent as they were in darkness and with no hope, were difficult. No one knew about it, and no one sensed it as he forgot about days and hours and surrendered to eternity which never disappears. At the end, he could not be certain as to whether or not his mind was gone. When he was imprisoned in the gloom, he was forced to suck the light out of his mind and resort to those corners from which the night had already been sucked. All that was left of the mind was darkness; truth had been buried inside the recesses of oppressive hours, with no words and no books, desperate for release. He kept on repeating words and narrating history, saying his names, his work, and his children's names over and over again. He may have caught a fever before he died. He could no longer remember his own name. All names were now jumbled, and history faded into a dark shadow of melancholy hours and the sounds of torture and screaming all around him. He may well have realized that his mind had given up, perhaps recovering its sanity in order to realize and acknowledge that the end was near. It was just that he was not sure.

When Shaykh 'Abd al-Karim died, his son, Ahmad, came to claim his body. He was carrying a lamp as he entered the gloomy prison with tears in his eyes. People say that on the wall some verses from the poetry of Imam al-Shafi'i had been carved into the stone. Ahmad read them, with his tears still flowing down his cheeks:

> Let the days do as they will;
> Should fate so decree, then be of good cheer.
> Be not alarmed by the events of time,
> For this world's happenings are not really here.

BOOK TWO

SONS OF THE PEOPLE

How easily humanity comes to an end! After the plague, I could feel the inanity and insignificance of man. You know, you have to know, that, if wars were never recorded and immortalized by buildings, they would all vanish in the dust. Plague cannot kill buildings nor can perfidy destroy them.

The architect

10

1353 CE

As far as Muhammad was concerned, living in An-Nasir Muhammad's palace was better than watching shadow-plays. He had his own personal weekly routine. The fact that he was a son of the people and not a Mamluk meant that the Mamluks completely ignored his presence. After the sultan's death, he had watched and lived with the arrest of sultans of childhood age, one after another, and sometimes their murder as well. Whenever the young sultan opened his mouth to speak, the Mamluks would get rid of him. As far as they were concerned, he was a son of the people, not a fighter, trainee, or Mamluk.

This scenario kept being repeated. At first, it scared Muhammad, and he made up his mind to leave the palace. But then, he became used to it and even expected it. When he saw Al-Hasan, the young son of An-Nasir Muhammad, being dragged away in irons with his head covered in a black shroud, he felt a lump in his throat. He had thought of Al-Hasan as a younger brother, innocent, spontaneous and life-loving. He did not deserve such cruel treatment, and yet, like other sultans, he had tried to be master of his own decisions. That had led him to prison. By nature, Muhammad liked precision; he kept a close watch on palace protocol and schematized it. For that very reason, the arrest of Al-Hasan shocked him. The arrest of sultans had its own rules, but what had happened with Al-Hasan was unacceptable. Soldiers had dragged him away from his wives, as though he were some ordinary citizen who had stolen a lamp from a mosque.

Once Al-Hasan had been arrested, staying in the palace became a boring routine. By temperament Muhammad hated boredom. On Fridays, he would visit his sisters, and they would all pay a visit to their parents' mausoleum. They would pray in their father's mosque and distribute bread and charity to the poor. Then they would each return to their house. He would always take his two wives with him on the Friday visit. He had two wives who were Egyptian, just like his own mother: one whom he loved to distraction, the other who loved him likewise. He had been married to both of them in the same year. He could not find any way for one of them to do the job of both: the one whom he loved to distraction behaved coldly toward him, while he had to tolerate the one who loved him to distraction because of her merchant father's importance and his three children.

From his sisters he often heard about his father and his strange love for Zaynab, his mother. His father had never owned any slave girls, and had lived with her alone for twenty-two years or more till he was killed in his mosque. He often felt baffled by his father's naiveté and lack of appreciation. How could he possibly stay with one woman, when the women of the world were of such infinite variety?

He trained to be an architect and constructed some Mamluk palaces. He did not need to work a lot because he had inherited more than a single quarter in Cairo that he could rent out, along with an endowment from his mother. That wealth was sufficient to feed his children and wives and meet all his needs. He would frequently wander around Cairo's streets, chatting with vendors and skilled workers, and spend his time drawing things.

He still remembered Sultan An-Nasir Muhammad and felt a strong affection for him. The sultan used to visit him every week in his personal wing, sit down beside him, and talk about Egypt, Muhammad's father, and the Mamluks. He would then look at the pictures he had drawn.

"You're an architect," the sultan told him, "not a fighter. You have to thank God that your father died before he saw his son, Muhammad, who looked exactly like him and had the same name, was working as an architect and was no good at fighting. He'd die on the spot. All your father ever knew was war. The only things that dominated his life were fighting, war strategy, and, of course, your mother. I only saw her once, but she wasn't simple. How did she manage to dominate a Mamluk? I've no idea. God have mercy on both of them! But for him, I'd be dead now. Muhammad, you're an architect. When you build, use stone so your name will be preserved and your edifices will stand forever."

Muhammad used to watch the sultan carefully. From the start, he noticed how his leg was damaged and his body was skinny; his gait made people feel that he could keel over at any moment. He refused to use a cane and kept on walking lame. He knew all about the jokes that Egyptians and Mamluks cracked about him; he heard them and often laughed at them. After a while, Muhammad came to the conclusion that An-Nasir was the shrewdest man who had ever ruled the country. He was calm, and treated the Mamluks with a respectful caution, even though he actually loathed them with an unspeakable hatred. Whenever he found the appropriate moment, he would explain to the amirs why it was necessary to get rid of this or that amir. He would seek their advice and resort to their power. He would surround himself with men of religion and introduce a religious opinion or two. He seemed like a just Sufi whose major priority was pleasing God. He would occasionally spend hours sitting with the Mamluk amirs, but, no sooner had they left, than he would spit to the right.

"Slaves are still slaves," he would tell Muhammad softly, "even if they are carrying swords."

Even so, he kept purchasing Mamluks and spoiled them much more than his father had done with his. He brought them up himself, passing by every few days to check on them.

"The sultan can't do without Mamluk amirs," he used to tell Muhammad enthusiastically on other occasions. "They are guards and army. Your father was one of them. They rescued me and brought me back to Egypt. There are some Mamluks whose piety and courage are unrivaled in Islamic history. You need to be selective in choosing amirs, to pay close attention when making the selection, and to understand ambitions and points of weakness. Every sultan has to respect the Mamluks. Muhammad, my son, your father and mine were both Mamluks, but we aren't. It's all baffling. You know what I mean. We're still swinging between different types of people without belonging to any one type ourselves. I'm not strong enough for nonstop fighting, and you don't like it anyway. Even so, something binds us together. I regard you as one of my sons, Muhammad."

Muhammad came to regard him as his father, someone whose acquaintance he had made rapidly, someone whom he loved with an affection that never left his heart. He still longed for his own father's glances, powerful voice, and soothing scent. Not for a single day did he forget those things, still remembering those moments spent together which he drew with all the perfection of a skilled architect. After a while, he drew a portrait of his father on horseback and another of himself riding the stallion by himself, with his father looking proudly at him. His connection with An-Nasir and the pleasure that it gave him increased day by day. An-Nasir treated him exactly like his own sons; not only that, but sometimes Muhammad felt as though he actually preferred him to some of his sons and enjoyed chatting with him. He could remember as a boy staring at An-Nasir's foot and noticing that he did not walk properly. One day, An-Nasir sat down beside him.

"What do you think about my crippled foot?" An-Nasir asked. "Do you know how it happened?"

Muhammad shook his head, feeling embarrassed. "I was training with my teacher," An-Nasir said, "and this happened. But why should a commander need a healthy foot? What he really needs is a keen mind. I don't try to lean on a cane because people then call me 'the lame Sultan.' I know; I like the name. The best thing for you, my son, is to learn to love yourself for what you are and not to change it just to please somebody else."

Muhammad did not fully understand what he was saying, but he could sense affection in his tone of voice and kept inside him the innocent smile that he was getting. The one day that he will never forget was the one when the entire course of Muhammad's life was transformed. He was sitting in the sultan's council with all his children. The sultan's architect was explaining to him the design of the mosque that he was going to build for him. With great enthusiasm, he placed a huge diagram in front of the sultan. An-Nasir Muhammad listened to him and then nodded in approval.

"Turn it over," he instructed.

The architect looked astonished, but then he did as the sultan had asked. The sultan took his pen and inkwell and started drawing slowly and carefully on the back of the diagram. From where Muhammad was sitting, he looked over in curiosity, then started moving toward the diagram. He kept slinking closer and closer to look at the sultan's drawing, but he felt himself grabbed by a strong hand that pulled him back.

The sultan was still drawing.

"Let Muhammad come by my side," Muhammad heard him say. "He likes to draw."

Muhammad sat unblinking on the floor, still staring at the drawing. Eventually the sultan finished drawing.

"What do you think?" he asked the architect. "Can we build this mosque?"

The architect looked at the drawing. "My Lord," he said, "your commands are always to be obeyed. However, I'm worried about this alcove and the materials we're going to use there."

"So, be creative and think it through," An-Nasir said. "Or rather, think it through and be creative."

"My Lord," the architect replied, "there's nothing to be creative about. The ancients worked everything out."

The Sultan smiled and looked at Muhammad. "What do you think, Muhammad?" he asked.

The boy did not respond, so he asked the question again.

"I like your drawing, my Lord," Muhammad replied, "I like it a lot."

"The design is to the liking of both Muhammad and myself," the sultan stated assertively. "Now carry it out with daring and courage. You'll need both when it comes to making decisions and constructing the edifice."

The construction of An-Nasir Muhammad's mosque preoccupied Muhammad day after day. Whenever the opportunity arose, he would ask the sultan what was happening. The sultan would explain what the architect was doing. Once the building was complete, Muhammad went with the sultan to look at it.

"My Lord," Muhammad said enthusiastically, "your design is better than the architect's."

An-Nasir stroked his shoulder. "Remember," he said, "boldness demands innovation. There are thousands of architects, but only one of them will raise his head like a jinn every hundred years or so."

"Boldness," Muhammad repeated. "Can I keep the diagram? The building's complete now."

"Yes, you can," An-Nasir replied.

An-Nasir ruled Egypt for almost thirty years after his return from Kerak Castle, and Muhammad lived with him for seven or eight of them. He can recall their final meeting, after An-Nasir had performed the pilgrimage to Mecca and washed the Ka'ba himself. He showed the same remote signs of death that he could remember from his mother's last glances. However, An-Nasir was alert and following everything. His eyes met those of Muhammad and he stroked his shoulder. He hugged his little son, Qamari, whom he himself named Al-Hasan later on.

"This thing called death always arrives at the wrong time," he said. "It finishes you off violently, always arriving when mankind is immersed in life's profundities and dragging you away from the midst of waves of the future and beloveds.

"We always leave our children both inheritance and curse," he continued in a despairing whisper. "Even at the point of death, the human soul craves eternal life on earth rather than in heaven."

"Father," his children whispered to him, "don't tire yourself."

"Can I guarantee your life for you?" he went on. "If I charged my son with ruling after me, he'd be destroyed for sure. But, if I charged a Mamluk from my own contingent, all my own children would destroy him. Life is forever eradicating eternity, and pride leads only to destruction. I bequeath the rule of this country to my son, Sayf ad-din Abu Bakr."

When Sultan An-Nasir Muhammad died, Muhammad was very sad. Perhaps that was because of the connection between him and his father whose face and voice he could still remember, a hidden link that he did not understand. Perhaps he had heard more about his father from An-Nasir than he had from his own brothers, who rarely talked to him frankly and expansively. Perhaps also his brothers did not know much about their father. They would spend hours praising their mother and father, blowing words into the air like smoke, words that soon flew out of his mind.

Whenever he spoke to his sister Nafisa about his mother, she would always talk about their parents' relationship.

"Our mother, Zaynab, wasn't like other women," she would say. "Her eyes used to sparkle when our father came into the room, and she would pursue him with her gaze. It was as though she had found water after panting for thirst in the desert. When their eyes met, they would converse for hours without saying a single word."

Sometimes he used to feel aggravated. "You keep talking to me about my mother and about me," he said. "Did she love me?"

"She adored you," Nafisa replied quickly. "She used to hold your hand and take you everywhere. She was scared for you. Maybe she thought that she might die while you were still a young boy. She entrusted you to us. But, after our father died, she too died inside. She was no longer the way she was with him. She cut herself off from the world and us. Do you understand? She neither saw us nor knew us. She had journeyed to some other place. Even when she was hugging you, I had the impression that she was staring at the horizon as though she could see nothing else or was still looking for it. She didn't expect to live long. That mother of ours was a tale and a poem. How are you, Muhammad? Are you happy being with the sultan?"

His sister's words did nothing to quench his thirst. The only thing that satisfied him was to hear the words of the sultan, talking about his father, his bravery, his skill, and his tolerance. Now Muhammad devoted himself assiduously to training as an architect.

Along with his brother, Muhammad would sometimes visit the daughter of his mother's cousin, Fatima. Fatima was now the only person left from his mother's family. He loved her and enjoyed sitting with her. She used to spend hours talking about people whom he did not know and about a historical period that did not coincide with his own. She used to laugh and sing, and her children would scold her for embarrassing them even in front of sons of the people. She talked to him about his mother, her common sense and her affection; the way she had refused to let him go to live in the sultan's house and had stayed with him till she died when he was ten years old—in fact she had died with him crying in her arms. What was strange about Fatima was that the same tale was different every day, depending on her psychological state and her satisfaction with her own children. There were times when she used to curse Mamluks, sons of the people, religious scholars, and every level of society, but then there were other times when she would praise the Mamluks, their resolve, and their sense of order.

"If it weren't for the Mamluks," she would say, "the entire population would have been destroyed, and there would be widespread chaos. They stand against our enemies like a solid wall, repulsing every invader and destroyer."

Then she would start talking about Amir Muhammad. "Your father was a generous man," she would tell Muhammad. "I can remember his Ramadan feasts for us and how much he loved the Egyptian people. This was his only homeland."

Fatima's young son had hated the Mamluks ever since he was a child. He was now the same age as Muhammad. Every time Muhammad visited his Aunt Fatima, he gave Muhammad a nasty look. He talked about Mamluk tyranny and the way they always lied to the Egyptian people. On this particular day, he was talking specifically about the tyranny of Mamluk children.

"Forgive me, Muhammad," he said, "but corruption has its limits. The control that sons of the people have over the country will lead to disasters in the future. They monopolize commerce, purchase land cheaply, and hold all the major posts. It's as though we Egyptians are devil-manufactured garbage. This tyranny will not continue!"

Muhammad did not like discussing politics. For him, palace politics and Mamluk conspiracies were enough.

"I agree with you, 'Ali," he replied nonchalantly.

'Ali stared at him in astonishment. "But you're one of them!"

"I don't monopolize commerce, nor do I purchase land. My mother was an Egyptian."

'Ali could barely suppress his fury. "Why should you need any of that? You can live off your parents' inheritance."

"I'm not bothered about such trifles, money and inheritance. There's something more important."

"Why should you be bothered if you've the entire wealth of the Egyptian people?"

"I inherited the money," Muhammad replied angrily. "I didn't steal it, nor did my father. He fought in wars for the sake of your country and mine."

"No warrior has the right to take over all the country's resources."

"The warrior's country doesn't have any."

Fatima turned to Muhammad, unhappy about what her son had been saying.

"The Mamluks are Egyptians, aren't they?" she asked. "I've never been sure. They don't marry Egyptians, but their children do. With the passage of time they become Egyptians, not just sons of the people. The country swallows them, dissolves them, and alters them. They melt, fuse, and emerge from a steaming hot furnace, now transformed into Egyptians. This country can burn you, smelt you like iron, shape you and kill you. Forgive me, my son. You're Muhammad, Zaynab's son, the Mamluk amir, aren't you?"

"Yes, I am," Muhammad replied, responding as he always did.

She moved closer to him. "I'm going to ask you a question," she said shyly, "but don't misunderstand me."

"Ask your question, Auntie."

"Who's the sultan today?"

As he was answering, she shook her head.

"Is he a Mamluk?" she asked.

"Yes, he is."

"But Mamluks are not born in this country. They're warriors, but they're not sultans, are they? One of the sons of the people like you?"

"Maybe so. You're right: from the sons of the people."

"Why are they different every time? Mamluks don't like the idea of inherited authority. Why doesn't the army commander or battalion instructor grab power?"

"My dear Aunt, do you understand so much about politics? My two wives never talk about it."

"You've two wives? Are you happy with both of them?"

"Yes, with both of them. One complements the other."

She stared at him long and hard, so much so that he wondered if she had forgotten who he was.

"You're like me," she said. "You've a demon inside you. I can remember you: always drawing and drawing—drawing buildings with all the subtlety of a magician. What have you done with that demon of yours?"

He looked at her, but did not respond.

"Your two wives will never satisfy you," she went on. "You won't be happy with all the women in the world or the entire wealth of the lower sphere. Nothing will satisfy you. The curse of that same demon has struck you. Make sure you don't follow your aunt, meandering your way among mankind! Make it come out of you. Get rid of them all, and make it come out! Don't let women distract you. Listen to what I'm saying!"

"Do you need anything, Auntie?" he asked with a smile.

She looked at him as usual. "You're Zaynab's son?" she asked.

"Yes, I am."

"Who's the sultan today?"

<hr />

The plague toyed with Cairo the way the Mongols had with Baghdad. No house was left without its grief, no street without biers, and no pit without corpses. Muhammad fled with his two wives to Alexandria.

He was afraid that his children and he might die, and dreaded hearing the screams of grief that could be heard every moment, coming from the mouths of men even before women. His two wives kept grumbling.

"There's no escaping death," they told him, "and we'd rather die with our families, not as strangers in Alexandria."

But Muhammad was convinced that the sea could purify all plagues and that he understood things that doctors did not. The sea could remain as pure as paradise, no matter how many corpses and how much filth was emptied into it. The sea was both powerful and abundant, capable of immunizing against the plague and curing people around it. The River Nile was long and unpolluted, but it could not dispose of waste. Nauseated and weary, it would spit it all out. The moment Muhammad had arrived in Alexandria, he had ordered them to bathe in the sea in order to purify their bodies. They told him he was crazy.

"Just look around you in Alexandria," the wife whom he loved yelled at him. "More people are dying here than in Cairo. Just look at the number of funeral shrouds by the seaside!"

But Muhammad paid no attention and dived into the sea. When he started hearing the same keening sound, he looked more closely at his body and determined that it was not the sea's fault, but rather that of the thin, weak human frame which would expire even before those of ants and stray cats. The sea was free of plague and human waste. It was humanity that ingested diseases, like dry plants sucking up rainwater. That was the human body that he despised and found so repulsive. It faded and died, and then turned putrid and dissolved. Nothing would ever last as long as buildings and stone. Everything else was ephemeral, destined to disappear. Wars were simply a game fought between human bodies, scattered and torn apart. Plague was a joke played on a weak, flabby body, like a chunk of meat carved from the backside of a gray-haired cow. He was still in quest of bodily pleasures. Eternity had been forgotten. He had not forgotten about the body, but still longed for eternity.

He stayed in Alexandria, not so much to escape the plague as to annoy his two wives. They decided to return to Cairo and stay with their mothers and families. He decided to stay in Alexandria and told them both that he certainly did not wish to die close to his in-laws; he preferred to die by the seaside. The two wives left with their children, and he stayed in Alexandria.

He started building Mamluk palaces there. It was there too that he fell in love with a girl from Sicily, Maria, who had come to sell her wares in the port. She was buying glass bottles and lamps to sell in her own country. But she did not speak any Arabic.

She was bursting with life. Her facial features were severe, suggesting an ability to confront death. Her long fingers spoke of an expertise in drawing and daily practice. From the very first moment, he started talking to her in Arabic and drawing her pictures to explain things. From the same moment, she too started drawing things as she used her own language. Drawing now became their joint, secret language. Revealing secrets became a linked chain, like soft colors in the hands of an artist. She drew for him glass bottles and colorful vials that she was looking for and wanted to use as commerce in her own country; she wanted to know how she could make them in Sicily and her own environs.

He forgot all about his two wives and children and spent an entire month without asking after anyone or talking to anyone. They only exchanged gestures, each one using his or her own language—he in Arabic, and she in Sicilian dialect. They smiled at each other and made love.

He asked her about her family, country, and sea. She used to point at him, sometimes impatiently, and at others with a good deal of patience. She would draw for him things she wanted to express, spending long hours talking and listening carefully. He would tell her a lot of things without limits or aspirations, all the while cursing, swearing, laughing, and remembering.

She told him about her father, whose only child she was. He had been a merchant. A rich man had set his eyes on her father's money, so he killed him and took it all. She had fled to Alexandria and continued her father's trade.

He toyed with her arm and lay down beside her.

"You know," he told her, "I can only remember my own father in two situations. In one, I can see him; I love him and feel that he's alive. In the other, I see him drowning in his own blood. I don't remember anything else about him."

She looked at him, as though she understood.

"It was the day we visited Sultan An-Nasir Muhammad," he went on enthusiastically.

He pointed to his hand. "I stretched my hand out," he said. "Summoning the courage I'd been storing up for days, I asked my father if I could go with him.

"My father looked at me for a moment. He frightened me, and I was afraid of his gloomy silence, his piercing looks, and the things that my brothers said about him. I regretted what I'd said and stared at the floor in silence. My father grabbed my hand. 'Yes,' he said, 'you can come with me.'

"I clasped his hand and looked proudly at my brothers. I went with him; he was tall and walked sturdily. He said nothing all the way.

"'Go in beside me like a man,' he told me as soon as we arrived. 'Don't hold my hand in front of the sultan. A real man doesn't need anyone else's help, Muhammad. He can tolerate things and take risks. You've done that today by asking to come here with me. I've liked that. If you go on that way, you'll become a real fighter, like me.'

"I smiled, full of pride. It felt as though, where I was concerned, my father was beyond the scope of all being: a giant with extraordinary powers. I had heard about his exploits and seen the men around him look at him with the same awe that I myself felt."

At this point, Muhammad stopped and drew an image of his father as he imagined him.

"The sultan's palace was amazing," he went on, "but inside I was only interested in the decoration on doors and the ways that lanterns were shaped.

"When our visit to the sultan was over," he continued, "I had to run to keep up with my father. I felt shy about clasping his hand again. Even so, I told my father excitedly that the sultan's palace had been really amazing.

"My father shook his head, but said nothing.

"'Did you like it too, Father?' I asked him with the same level of enthusiasm.

"He stared at me in amazement, and I detected a smile on his face that he did his best to conceal.

"'You really want to talk to me,' he said, 'and you're not scared? You're as brazen as your mother. Yes, I did like the palace. What always thrills me are the king's swords hanging on the wall. What did you like?'

"'I like the palace gate,' I replied spontaneously. 'It's thick and well decorated. Not even a hundred men could bring it down. How beautiful it is! Could we construct one like it for our palace?'

"'You liked the gate?' he asked in amazement. 'That's all you noticed inside the palace?'

"He looked into my eyes.

"'I didn't look at the swords,' I replied bashfully. 'Maybe I should have done. I'll do it next time.'

"'Do you like swords, Muhammad?'

"For a few moments I said nothing. At that particular moment, I loved my father. I loved him because, for just a moment, he had opened his heart and spoken to me, and because he was from some other world, a strong warrior. For just a moment, he had held my hand, looking into my eyes as though he were really interested in me. I could never be like him, but nor could anyone else!

"'Yes,' I replied, 'I like swords a lot!'

"He stroked my shoulder with his powerful hand. 'You're going to be a warrior just like your father,' he said. 'I was pleased with you today. You were bold and courageous.'

"Then my father receded slowly into the distance, his words moving away before he had finished talking to me and I could clasp his hand again. He vanished from my life. I saw him drowning in his own blood, motionless amid my brother's keening and my mother's silence. I kissed him once or twice; I don't remember. I held his hand, wishing that I could be a warrior, but I couldn't. Do you understand?"

He could remember the day his father died, as though it were today. The smell of fresh blood, his mother's expression totally devoid of life, and his father's face, sleeping quietly amid all the hubbub. He could still feel his fingers intertwined with his dead father's, just as they had done on the day when they had visited the sultan, the day when his father had become his life's companion and the friend of all his days. Their fingers had been linked together, as his tears coursed silently down his cheeks. After a while—it might have been an hour, his sister, Nafisa, crying herself, had grabbed him. But he had refused to move.

"Let him sleep in peace, Muhammad," she had told him gently. "We'll all be missing him. Come with me!"

He left with her in gloomy silence, his tears still flowing. Gradually the images of his father faded, then disappeared, as always happens. Things were now confused: sometimes he would see his father racing with his horse; at others, he would be sleeping amid his own blood. However, Amir Muhammad ibn 'Abdallah was always present, day and night, in both his dreams and frequent moments of distraction.

Maria looked into Muhammad's sorrowful eyes and nodded in agreement. Tears swelled in her eyes too as she drew a woman. "Your mother?" she asked him in her own language.

"I can remember her too before my father died. All I can recall is the day she died after my father's death. She was just as determined, and used to talk a lot and hug me sometimes. The day she died, I just sat there crying. With a smiling expression and eyes that burned into mine but did not reach them, she stroked my hand.

"'You're not seeing me, Muhammad,'" she whispered, her eyes still riveted on mine.

"Then she opened her hand and stretched her arm toward me. I didn't understand, did she want to hug me, was she afraid of me becoming an orphan, or she wasn't referring to me in the first place? Do you understand?"

Muhammad pointed to his own eyes and Maria's.

"I've a sister named Nafisa," he went on. "She thinks she's my mother now. But she's always annoying me. Do you know what she said? She said that my mother was not calling out to me, but to my father. His name was Muhammad too. Nafisa says that, whenever my mother's pain was really bad, it was my father she was calling, nobody else. It was as though he had appropriated her heart the way the Mamluks appropriated estates. What do you think, my darling Maria?"

Maria looked at him, apparently not really understanding.

He spoke to her again, slowly and using his hand to gesture. "When my mother was dying, was she calling me or my father? His name and mine is Muhammad. What do you think? Nafisa is sure that she was calling my father."

Maria thought for a few seconds, then raised two fingers. He smiled and gave her a big kiss.

"You're my darling, as I told you," he said. "You think she was calling both of us. How lovely you are!

"My mother left this world of ours a while ago," he continued. "In my imagination, I see her as an angel. And yet it's my father who's with me every day and resides inside my mind all my days. I don't know why. Because he was murdered? Nafisa says that he used to show his love for me in particular and spoil me more than the other children, because I'd been born in his old age. Maybe he sensed that I might have to live as an orphan amid the Mamluks; perhaps he was scared for me because of the Mamluks or even Egyptians. After all, I don't belong fully to either one or the other. I'm from you and belong to you! But never mind, let's talk about something else. I'll draw something for you."

He drew her a building. "What do you think of it?" he asked her in Arabic.

It was a small mosque that he had drawn with particular attention and detail. She gave an enthusiastic nod and grabbed the piece of paper. She started drawing pictures of houses in her own country and waiting to see what he thought of them.

"I like your country," he told her, "but what I want to do is to build a structure that no one else will be able to build after me. You realize, Maria: I grew up an orphan. I can vaguely remember my mother's face, and there are times when my father's face looms in my memory. In An-Nasir Muhammad's palace, I was a child just like many others. All my life, I've been searching for something specially mine, a special love, a special language, a different woman; a unique structure that will make me too unique and different. People say that my father broke with custom when he married an Egyptian woman. I too want to break with custom, but without being killed. In my country, anyone who is creative and infringes norms without being a Mamluk will lose both his mind and his life. I'm a son of the people, not a Mamluk. Do you understand?"

"In my country," she replied in her language, "there are two kings who have been fighting each other since the beginning of time. We oppressed people in the middle suffer continuous blows. I've no idea what's going to happen."

She showed him two fingers again. "Two kings," she repeated.

He fully understood. "You're still lucky, Maria," he told her with a smile. "We have ten, twenty, fifty . . ."

"There can be a single king," he said, opening his hand, "but many amirs. The king is nothing where amirs are concerned. There can be nothing without amirs, and they need the king for their legitimacy. It's a weird country where the people don't get involved. Do you understand?"

She nodded.

"You're very brave," he told her. "A woman trading with Muslims, and you're not afraid of being accused of treason and unbelief in your own country. I've never encountered a bravery to match yours. My two wives are cowards. What has commerce to do with politics? It's like art, straddling crises and lands."

She looked at him with a smile.

"You're amazing," he whispered, giving her a big hug.

He pushed her away a little. "My sister, Nafisa," he said, "the one I told you about, used to say that my mother's love for my father was beyond description. She loved him wholeheartedly. That kind of love is extraordinary. I was living in Sultan An-Nasir Muhammad's palace when he married a Byzantine, a Mongol, and a Circassian woman. I lived with my father for eight years, and I never once saw him look at any woman other than my mother. I thought all men were like my father! I loved An-Nasir Muhammad and my father. There must be a difference in the way that we love wholeheartedly; love's purpose must also be as varied as humanity itself. Some people love the sultan wholeheartedly, others love money, still others love a woman, and . . ."

He started signing to her to explain what he was saying, gesturing with his fingers and drawing pictures so she would understand.

"This kind of love is very rare," he continued, "but it does exist. I can't abandon my family any longer. What kind of man can forget his wives and children during the plague? Actually, I'd really like to forget about them, but death brings its own rules and obligations. Maria, you are life in its totality. In your arms I can feel that the pestilence doesn't even exist because you are so brave. You have no fear of the plague's horrors and the anger of your family and church. My darling, you amaze me. I would love to spend the rest of my life with you. Do you understand?"

She kissed him with a smile.

"I too can love with my whole heart," he continued, "but I can't love an individual person that way. I love something else, something difficult, oppressive, something inside me that keeps on nagging and is eager to emerge. I don't know how to draw it for you. Forgive me, but my prestige does not come with a love for women. For me, pleasure involves building; it's my entire life."

He left at night while Maria was still asleep and did not go back to her house. He took two pictures with him that they had drawn together: one of his two parents, the other of her smiling as she holds a glass bottle and lamp. Back in Cairo, he found his two wives waiting angrily for his return. He went straight to his room, locked the door, and started drawing, as though life was coming to a stop on the morrow and it consisted solely of this mosque; nothing else could please or satisfy him.

An innovator's feelings are disturbing and painful. There's a constant clicking over his head and between his fingers, while an imp is doing its best to escape from deep inside him. If it manages to do so, it is transformed into a gigantic jinn that gobbles him up and damns him to roam for the rest of his days. The clicking inside Muhammad was enough to drive him mad; no woman could squelch it, no action could silence it, and no death could bring any relief. Even when sleeping in the arms of the wife who dearly loved him, he would squirm in a fit of nerves.

"Stop fidgeting," she said after a while. "I can't get to sleep."

He got up and started pacing the room, like some drunkard remembering his sufferings. He started looking in the dark for his designs.

"I can't find my designs," he yelled. "Where did I hide them? I'm divorcing you now."

His wife leaped out of bed. "Have you lost your mind, man?" she asked. "What designs?"

"Drawings on paper," he said. "Where are they?"

"Are you slurping wine, man, or just going crazy? You wake me up in the middle of the night to ask me about some designs?"

"Just behave like this," he threatened her, "and you'll make me marry a third wife. Take care!"

"In that case," she said, sucking her lips, "look for someone who can tolerate your madness."

Ignoring her, he lit a candle and starting looking for the designs. When he could not find them, he put on his clothes, uttered all the uncouth oaths he could think of, grabbed some new sheets, and left the house. He wandered around the Cairo quarters, listening to the call to dawn prayer and observing the design of the minarets. He started drawing again, but only returned to his house two days later. He was only interested in minaret design; beneath his fingers were plans for four minarets, each one of them different from the others and from all other minarets in the Islamic world.

He left his two wives some money and departed in anger. They did not understand, nor did they sympathize with the demon inside him.

When he visited his sister, Nafisa, she asked him how he was. She complained about the impact of the plague that was destroying the bodies of everyone around her. He could not explain to her how severe was the insomnia that was afflicting him. In fact, he started by complaining about his two wives and his own life.

"My dear brother Muhammad," she said, stroking his shoulder, "you're letting them control and dominate you. A man has to be firm with his wife. I'm thinking of our mother: she would only ever look at our father with respect and admiration. She would never scold him or answer back."

"Maybe she did," Muhammad scoffed, "but it's not that way usually. There's not a woman in the world who won't answer her husband back. Nafisa, you just don't know women the way I do."

"Your luck's been bad, my brother," she replied angrily. "You were orphaned at a young age, and did not find a wife for yourself who felt any affection for you. My poor brother! If my mother were still live, she would deal with your wives. Our mother was a powerful woman; she set up a rigid regime for our father's palace and the wives of Abu Bakr and 'Ala ad-din. If mother were still alive, your wives would not dare spoil your life like this. My poor brother!"

He left, but her words did nothing to soothe the sleeplessness and agony that were tearing him apart.

As would happen whenever the situation was bad, his father's image loomed before him. He would always appear as the jinn from the lamp, then gradually disappear in tufts of smoke. He would be riding his stallion and running away, blending with the desert and disappearing from view. Whenever times were hard, his father would always appear, smiling and leaning over him as he used to do, then vanishing, always vanishing.

The agony continued, and the demon inside him emerged. The innovative spirit reduces body and mind to fragments. He did not eat much, wear proper clothes, or talk to anyone. He would wander through the streets like a madman, measuring the size of minarets and mosque design. He was like someone with a chronic disease that causes permanent pain. He realized that only death would put an end to that pain. Very few people are stricken with the creativity curse. Who knows: is it a blessing or retribution?

⌒

He decided to visit Al-Hasan in prison. They had been childhood friends, and he was the legitimate sultan in a country where sultans are neither respected nor celebrated. Egyptians never rise up against their rulers, so why should they do so when sultans spend their lives in prisons and get involved in conspiracies and never-ending punishment? They watch Mamluks fighting each other the same way they watch shadow-plays. They laugh, scoff, and carry on. For them, existence involves perdition for amirs, always and forever.

Amir Yalbugha agreed to allow Muhammad to visit the young sultan in prison. No sooner had he entered than he gave the sultan a big hug.

"How are you, my brother?" he asked.

"I read," the sultan replied sadly. "They don't stop me getting books, but they do keep all my womenfolk, children, and those I love away from me. Can you believe it? The Mamluk amirs are humiliating me, Muhammad, just as they tried to do with my father!"

Muhammad patted his shoulder. "The best thing about this country," he replied, "is that everything can change quickly. I'll intercede with the amirs on your behalf. There has to be a way out. You must be restored to your throne. If you yielded to them a little, they'd let you stay on your throne."

"I'll never yield to them. They're my father's slaves. He was their teacher. How am I supposed to yield to them? Even if they kill me, as they did my brother Al-Muzaffar Hajji."

"They're protecting you and the country. Don't forget that your grandfather was one of them."

"Yes, he was, but I'm not. I'm not a slave; I have no commander or teacher. They're even stopping my wives from coming to see me. Can you believe it, Muhammad? When I was under their tutelage, the amirs used to give me three dirhams. Three dirhams, when their own salaries top three thousand dinars! What kind of justice is that? What sheer madness! What country would be content with that? If Egyptians had a voice, they would be rebelling against the amirs and choosing the sultan."

"Calm down, and tell me what you're reading."

"I'm reading books on religion, commentary, jurisprudence, Sufism, and the four schools of law. I've learned a lot over the course of the years gone by. Maybe I've needed this isolation in order to learn. How are the Egyptians doing?"

"As you know, the plague has killed over a quarter of the entire population. Houses are deserted, and every home has its personal grief to bear."

"Are your wives well?"

"Unfortunately, yes."

"What are you planning now?" the sultan asked with a smile.

"For some time, I've been thinking about a mosque finer than any other building."

"A mosque finer than any other building?" the sultan repeated.

"More magnificent than any other mosque or palace," Muhammad continued, "its size reaching into the thousands—a mosque and school. It's a dream that's been fascinating me for a while."

"Can I look at the plans?" Al-Hasan asked.

"Here in your prison cell?"

"It'll distract me from my own sorrow and the fact that my wives are so far away. You're reminding me of death and the end. If this mosque is for a sultan, then it has to contain his tomb and mausoleum."

"Yes, the sultan will have to be entombed there."

"Such a structure will turn people's attention away from loss and remind them of the Tiller of Souls and Giver of Life. It'll perpetuate the sultan's memory and guarantee him a place in paradise!"

"No, it won't guarantee him that!" Muhammad responded with a smile.

"Yes, it will. All sins are forgiven when a Muslim at prayer prostrates himself in such a mosque, not to mention every lesson learned by a student and every minaret where God's name is recited. Muhammad, it feels as if life has not been in vain. Give me this book and draw me the mosque's design on this sheet of paper."

The way in which this dream preoccupied Muhammad almost drove him mad. On the way home at night, he often lost his way. He decided to stay there in the mosque alcoves, along with Sufis and ascetics. He would always have with him his papers, calculations, and pen, and would be drawing things.

When he was spending the night in the mosque of Al-Hakim bi-Amr Allah, he heard a voice close by and noticed a beggar standing in front of him, exuding a foul stench, but staring closely at his design.

"What's that?" the beggar asked nosily. "Have you any food to give me?"

He stared at the beggar. "What do you think of the mosque of Al-Hakim bi-Amr Allah?" he asked. "Do you like its design?"

The beggar moved away quickly, convinced that Muhammad must be mad. With that, Muhammad decided to return to his home and normal life, and to resist this demon inside him that kept trying to come out. He returned to his two wives and asked about his children. He had forgotten their names. Next, he went to see his brothers and visit his father's grave. He tried to go to sleep, but failed.

"You're going to lose your mind," he whispered to himself. "You son of the people, go back to your normal life. Forget the life of imagination and innovation. You've started losing both your mind and your way. Design palaces and amirs' mosques, but forget about this dream. You'll lose your mind. Innovation involves oblivion; the appearance of this demon of yours is a slow death for the heart and a chasm for the soul. The path toward what you desire implies the bitter pill of achievement and the end of the road. Son of Amir Muhammad, go back to your normal life. Remember who you are, and go back!"

He started dreaming every day of the gate of the palace about which he had spoken to his father; not for a single day did it leave his imagination untroubled. To the contrary, as day followed day, his dreams about gates only increased. Every day, he would dream about a gate, a colossal gate of gold, opening on to a bronze sun, from which his father would emerge riding his horse, towering and enormous, smiling at his son, then fading and disappearing as usual. Sometimes, he would dream about a bronze gate with delicate tracery, closed at first, but then open to reveal sounds of spiritual conversation and ascetic love. At other times, he would dream about a gate whose external appearance was of everything good while its internal aspect was all evil. And still another would be obscure and boring on the outside, while the inside was full of life, creativity, and noise. Lines and triangles dominated his vision. From it there sprang the innocence and tyranny of creativity, opening and closing life and keeping a record of life's sorrows and humanity's ongoing quest for eternity.

However, he did not value his own life; he neither knew, appreciated, nor wanted it. This curse was tearing his body apart and confusing him. He needed to rid himself of the disease, and that required medicine. He asked to have a meeting with the Mamluk amirs. He met Yalbugha and interceded for Al-Hasan, offering pledges of loyalty on Al-Hasan's behalf.

"Al-Hasan's going to be busy building a mosque," Muhammad told the amir. "He won't be directing the country's affairs. He won't be interested in power, and he won't bother the Mamluk amirs.

"Just talk to him," Muhammad entreated Amir Yalbugha. "He's understood the lesson and taken it to heart. Back then, he was young, but now he's more mature."

"He's done it before," Yalbugha replied. "Even before he was twenty, he tried to get rid of the Mamluk amirs. The son of the Byzantine woman wants to be rid of Mamluks, something his own father had never dared try! Before Al-Hasan was twenty, he arrested the amirs and sequestered their property. What'll he do with them this time? After three years in prison? I don't trust him."

"Talk to him and agree on a system of government. I really want my intercession here to be successful. You knew my father."

"Amir Muhammad ibn 'Abdallah al-Muhsini was my teacher," Yalbugha declared forcefully. "Were he alive, he would never agree to diminished prestige for the Mamluks. He appreciated and realized the importance of warriors. He was one of them himself."

"Go and have a meeting with Al-Hasan," Muhammad suggested gently. "He's become a Sufi ascetic. He won't be directing the country. He's going to be preoccupied building the mosque."

Yalbugha went with a few Mamluk amirs to talk to Al-Hasan. Al-Hasan was serene and looked dejected.

"If I killed you now," Yalbugha stated firmly, "no one would blame me. I can do it, but I won't. In your opinion, who deserves more to rule this country: the adolescent sultan or the warrior amir? The person who knows about politics and has spent years practicing it, or the one who's emerged from palaces, learned within their walls, and spent most of his time in the women's quarters rather than palaces?"

For a few seconds, Al-Hasan looked angry. Yalbugha's words stung him to the quick. His own legacy led him to feel that, at that particular moment, he was a member of the Bedouin Arab rebels. But he made an effort to keep his nerves under control.

"Mamluk amirs are known for their common sense," he said. "I cannot do without them."

"So, why then did you change your name from Qamari to Al-Hasan?"

"I wanted an Arab-sounding name that would bring me close to the people."

"Why did you want to be closer to the people?" Yalbugha asked warily.

"It's the name of the grandson of the Prophet Muhammad—prayers and blessings upon him! Surely there can be no objections to that. If you want me to resume my original name, I'll do it!"

Yalbugha thought for a moment. "Never mind," he said. "Some amirs take Arab names too—Hasan, as you call yourself. If I let you out of prison and you think even once of doing some harm to the Mamluks, I won't put you back in prison; I'll cut your head off immediately!"

Al-Hasan looked around him. "Forgive me, Amir," he said. "If you address me like that in front of judges, amirs, and religious scholars, I'll have no value whatsoever. In front of them all, I would like you to honor me as the country's sultan. That's my only request."

Yalbugha moved closer. "Sultan of the country, yes," he said, "but you're not sultan over the Mamluks. Don't interfere in government affairs."

"I'll do what you command," Al-Hasan stated clearly, "but get me out of here."

After his talk with Al-Hasan, the amir consented. For his part, Muhammad carried on with his drawings and hid them in a safe place. All he could remember was the place where he had put them.

⁓

After his release from prison, Al-Hasan was indescribably happy, a feeling of freedom that only those people who have spent their entire lives in prison can understand. He had promised himself that, when he was released from prison, the first thing he would do would be to head for the embrace of his wives and quench the thirst that he had been feeling for three years. He would then go to the markets in disguise and buy some fruit and sweetmeats. He would walk along the Nile banks at night with no guards, and then visit a small mosque to perform the dawn prayer, thanking God for the boon of freedom and asking for knowledge and understanding.

While he was still a prisoner, he had promised the amirs that he would obey all their instructions and consult them about everything. He swore that he respected the sacrifices they had made, the system they had established, and everything that they had done for the country.

Al-Hasan was in his early twenties. By nature he loved life and religion combined, living his life to the full, enjoying it to the maximum, and immersing himself to the limit in the love of God. In prison, he had learned and understood a great deal; he realized that life was short and knowledge was eternal.

No sooner did he emerge from prison than Muhammad came to visit him with his plans. He looked at the papers.

"I like it," he said. "I love the idea, but today I just want to walk through the Cairo streets. I've lived as a prisoner all my life and spent my childhood like the poorest beggar in Cairo. I want to take a walk with you; we can visit your family. I know who the Egyptians are, and I also know the people about whom the Mamluks keep squabbling, fighting and killing each other all the time. They must be a load of tyrants!"

Muhammad smiled. "I'm not sure that Mamluks squabble with each other about Egyptians," he said. "They're fighting each other about Egypt itself, not its people!"

"What's Egypt without its people?"

"I don't know. I haven't thought about it. The Nile perhaps, its buildings, and its total wealth. Egypt is beautiful, assuming that you can gain control over it, like a woman who won't obey you even though she gives you herself to melt in her arms."

"Can I control it, Muhammad?"

Muhammad smiled again. "No one's done it yet. Every day I dream about the mosque that you want to have built; it dominates my days and nights. I've stinted myself on women, money, friends, everything. All I want to do is to start work on it. I don't want anything else. I can finish it and die, I don't care."

"Take me into the heart of Cairo first. If I like the trip, we can start work. I'll be building the loveliest and biggest mosque in the world. Egypt deserves that of me."

Al-Hasan put on some old clothes and covered his face. He asked his guards to wait for him inside the palace. Slinking outside, he walked alongside Muhammad.

"Do you realize," he whispered to Muhammad, "that my truce with the Mamluks will work to our advantage in this situation? But for that, they would kill me on the spot. I know them well. But I've reassured them and promised to obey their orders."

They strolled along the banks of the Nile together and stopped beside a stall selling sausage and liver. Like a little boy seeing the world for the first time, Al-Hasan looked at everything and whistled admiringly.

"Just look at the water glistening in the dark," he said enthusiastically, "and see how calm the river is. You can savor life's taste in this rich food filled with wonders. I'd like to buy some sweetmeats too and talk to some Egyptians."

He wandered through the quarters, staring at the mosques of his ancestors and sultans of the past.

"Everything they've all built," he proclaimed with enthusiasm, "will pale into significance compared with the one that I'm going to build. I promise you, Muhammad. Just look at the mosque of Qala'un, my grandfather, or even my own father's mosque. They're all tiny and unassuming."

Muhammad smiled. "Where are you proposing to build this gigantic structure? In heaven? There's nowhere in Cairo's quarters and districts to put it."

Al-Hasan thought for a moment. "We need to lean on certain Mamluks," he said. "I have my eye on a particular spot where a Mamluk amir has a palace."

"I'm wary of putting any pressure on them, Al-Hasan."

"Don't worry. If we can do away with them before they do us, then there's no problem. Ah me, if only I could kill one of them every day."

"Hasan, don't run unnecessary risks by making them your enemies."

"The palace of Amir Yalbugha al-Yahyawi in the horse market is enough for two mosques. It's the best and widest location in the city."

"You're setting yourself on fire!" Muhammad exclaimed in alarm. "Your own father built that palace especially for the amir."

"My father behaved generously with them, but they don't deserve it. The Egyptian people are the ones who deserve to be well treated. Just look at their faces, smiling in spite of so much misery. Their children have died and their houses have been destroyed; the plague has not left them with a single moment's joy. And yet, their expressions are still content. Take me to one of their homes."

Muhammad thought for a moment, then decided to take him to his Aunt Fatima's house. He did not want to explain to his brothers what was happening; they knew the sultan and what he looked like, and that would be risky both for him and the sultan. But his Aunt Fatima was bold and reckless. She would forget things quickly and never ask too many questions.

He knocked on the door of her house. She was living on her own now, with some servants. Some of her children had died in the plague, and others had left Cairo. They would visit her occasionally, and the grandchildren would sometimes come as well. These visits from her close relatives made her happy. After all, loneliness was tedious and depressing, especially when combined with old age, sickness, and long life!

She opened the door.

"Muhammad, Zaynab's son, precious boy!" she said as she embraced him. "How are you, my dear? Who's that with you?"

"A dear friend," he replied, pointing at Al-Hasan. "Can we sit with you for a while? My friend's a stranger in the city. He wants to make your acquaintance."

She stared at Al-Hasan. "I want to see your face," she said. "Take off that veil."

Al-Hasan hesitated for a moment, but then took it off. She stared at him for a while.

"I get the impression I've seen him before," she told Muhammad. "Was he working on the shadow-plays in Bulaq? I would go there all the time."

"No, dear Aunt!" Muhammad replied, suppressing a laugh. "But I've spoken to him about you and your beautiful voice."

She grasped Al-Hasan's hand and sat him down. When she offered him some sweetmeats, he looked at them in amazement.

"What's your name, stranger?" she asked him.

"Hasan," he replied with a smile.

"Just like the sultan's name," she said quickly. "What a lovely name! People say that the sultan chose that name to bring him closer to the people."

"That's right," Hasan replied. "I believe he did so."

"The sultan's an idiot. It's the Mamluks he should be getting close to. Who are the Egyptians, and what do they own?"

"They're the people of this country."

She slapped her mouth. "You're weird, my boy," she said. "You must be a stranger here. You don't know much about the rulers or Egypt. Do you want to hear me sing?"

"Yes, I would like that," he replied enthusiastically.

As she started singing, she brought her hand up to her cheek and plunged into the song.

"Have you ever heard the story about the amir who loved Zaynab?" she asked once she had finished the song.

"No, I haven't."

"Muhammad's mother was married to a Mamluk amir. That's unusual in our country. She had five children, and Muhammad is the youngest. They loved each other; for her sake, he had nothing to do with other women. She found her life very hard after he died. Their children weren't Mamluks; they were sons of the people. But do you see what their grandchildren are?"

"Egyptians," he replied immediately.

"I keep on asking myself what's happening to sons of the people in this city. They roam around its quarters and blend in with the rest of the populace. This whole city is peculiar: it swallows people like the river and makes you lose both memory and purpose. We're all crazy. That's why it's better for the sultan to ignore the people and think about the Mamluks."

"Aunt," he said suddenly, without knowing why, "I'm Sultan Hasan."

She stared at him. "You have a nice, round face," she said. "You've green eyes. You're really handsome!"

She did not look in the least shocked.

Muhammad smiled. "She's really old," he whispered in Al-Hasan's ear. "Sometimes she loses focus."

Fatima stood up. "I'll cook for you, my son," she said. "Stay with me today. I want to tell my grandchildren that the sultan spent the night in my house and heard me sing. My husband hated listening to me singing. May he rot in hell! Foul men! Never mind, did you like my singing?"

"Really beautiful, Aunt," he said with a smile.

She went over to him and took his hand. "Do you really want to give power and authority to the people?" she asked seriously. "Are you really interested in the people?"

"Yes, I'm interested, and I admire them."

She moved even closer and looked into his eyes.

"Remember," she said. "They may not realize and understand. Delusion may continue in various parts of the country. You may annoy people with whom you have no influence. Be on your guard and take care. Do you remember Zaynab? Her husband was murdered in a plot. Mamluks may have short lives, but they love living on top of slaves. You love the Egyptians. That's a problem!"

They ate and laughed together. She prepared a bed for him, using her husband's sheet which she had preserved but never used. Next morning, he stroked her hand.

"Aunt," he told her, "I thank you for everything. Do you need anything? Anything at all? A new house? Money?"

She smiled. "What I need is a new life," she replied, leaning on his hand. "I want an opportunity to sing in Bulaq."

He laughed, but did not reply.

"I'd like to kiss you on the cheek, Hasan," she said, pulling him toward her. "Then I can say that I've kissed the sultan's cheek."

He offered her his cheek, and she kissed it.

"You love the people!" she said, stroking his shoulder. "How sad! Go in peace!"

———

Today the sultan's council was something different. The topic of discussion was more dangerous than Mongol and Crusader invasions combined.

Muhammad remained silent as the sultan spoke enthusiastically about the mosque and school and the building that would perpetuate the history of the Mamluk era. He then asked Muhammad to describe the structure that he proposed to build.

Muhammad's heart started pounding as he placed the plans on the table. He started an enthusiastic explanation, pointing to the plans.

"In size, this mosque will surpass all other mosques. It will perpetuate the memory of the Mamluks for all time. I want it to be two hundred and seventy-seven cubits high, and more than a hundred and twenty-five cubits wide. I want to build four minarets, and I want the dome to be higher than all palaces and other domes. I've agreed with the sultan to build four schools along with the mosque for the four schools of law."

He then pointed out each school. "The Shafi'i school will be here, and the Hanafi, Maliki, and Hanbali schools here. This building is not only for prayer; it's for knowledge as well. It's for life, not a mausoleum. I want it to be big enough for more than five hundred students, teachers, supervisors, doctors, and religious scholars."

Now, Al-Hasan spoke again with the same enthusiasm. "I want classrooms and teachers so children can be taught to read, write, and memorize the Qur'an. Knowledge is a goal and path to achievement. From my own funds I will pay for every child that learns and memorizes the Qur'an and for the teacher who instructs him."

Yalbugha gave him a mocking look. "So, your funds won't run out? Where will you get the money? Like the Nile, where the annual flood replenishes it? Which kind of flood are you going to get, Sultan?"

"To the contrary," Al-Hasan went on, "I'm going to pay for the cost of clothing and food as well. My mosque will become a center for learning, jurisprudence, and life, just as Muhammad says. Carry on, Muhammad!"

Muhammad's heart was beating hard. "No king or sultan will have ever constructed a building like this one. The portico of the Sultan Hasan Mosque will be larger than the Chosroes portico at Ctesiphon. The dome will be the highest in the world, whether the building is Muslim or Christian. The minaret will overtop every other building."

"No king or sultan will have ever constructed a building like this one!" Al-Hasan repeated.

The amirs listened in silence, without displaying any enthusiasm. Eventually, Amir Yalbugha asked dryly: "And where do you propose to find enough money to construct this gigantic, fabulous mosque?"

Al-Hasan stared at him for a moment. "I can see, Amir," he said, "that you don't appreciate your sultan or realize his capabilities. I've thought about this issue. All the endowments and now deserted houses where the owners have perished in the plague are the property of the state for us to exploit. We can use the money to build the mosque."

"But why the wanton extravagance?" the amir asked angrily. "Build a mosque like your father's. Why are you so keen on such a vain display, alive or dead?"

"Remember that you're addressing the sultan."

"I'm the one who made you sultan," Yalbugha stated unambiguously. "You too need to remember that, my Lord. The money from endowments and houses won't be enough. A building like this will bankrupt the state treasury. There's another significant matter that needs to be discussed now. On behalf of all the amirs, I need to discuss with you about your close advisors and everyone else to whom you have given positions in the country."

"Speak," Al-Hasan said forcefully.

"You have no Mamluks among your close advisors, my Lord Sultan. Every governor, everyone who sits with the sultan, everyone who makes decisions, and all judges and police are sons of the people. Even the architect whom you have selected is one of them."

Muhammad remained silent as Yalbugha pointed at him.

"I realize that," Al-Hasan replied. "I wanted the Mamluks to be available for fighting wars and dealing with dangers and to leave the governmental roles to sons of the people. War is much more dangerous and important than governing. Sons of the people spend more time interacting with the Egyptians. They come partly from the people and partly from the Mamluks—they're the linkage between Mamluks and people. There's no one better than sons of the people to help me. Do you understand me, Yalbugha? No Mamluk privileges will be affected."

"How can you reason that way? How did you manage to come up with that? What experience do they have? Who are they originally? They've had no training in war, nor have they had to deal with the enemy's trickery. No order, no rigor, no understanding; just a cluster of effete plutocrats incapable of governing a country such as this. They'll never have the ability or power to do it. You're going to destroy Egypt, Syria, the Hijaz, and maybe Baghdad and Yemen as well. Who knows? The sons of the people are incapable of governing Egypt."

Al-Hasan gave him a lengthy stare. "They know the country much better than the Mamluks," he said, "and they're aware of the people's problems and demands. Do not insult the Egyptians, Yalbugha. If they made up their minds and united with the Bedouin Arabs, there would be general chaos and corruption."

"Neither Egyptians nor Bedouins have the courage," Yalbugha retorted. "Our soldiers have often ambushed would-be saboteurs. If sons of the people govern this country, then you're going to lose your prestige. The Mamluks will be dissolved and their regime will be broken up. It'll be finished, like other dynasties before it. Luxury comes at a cost, my Lord. Forgive me, but anyone who spends his time reading, visiting women's quarters, and strolling amid the flowers in his spectacular gardens doesn't deserve to rule over anything."

Al-Hasan rose to his feet. "Get out of here, Yalbugha," he yelled, "before I cut off your head in full view of these amirs. Nothing scares me anymore. Kill me if you want. But I'm committed to the Egyptian people and this mosque. Even if you kill me, this mosque is going to be built. Bahri Mamluks don't normally knock down mosques, or so I'm led to believe."

"Your father ruled for years because he respected the Mamluks and did not betray them," Yalbugha stated firmly. "I understand what you're saying. Or perhaps the sheer stupidity of youth is impairing your vision?"

Muhammad now started planning the mosque. He abandoned his wives and separated himself from the outside world. He could no longer remember how old his children were or what they looked like. It was as if he had gone mad. He started being obsessed with the mosque. He could not sleep or drink without thinking about it. During the night, he would be dreaming about it, imagining its alcoves and schools, the sheer size of it that the human eye could not take in. He kept dreaming about the years rolling by, the perpetuation of his name, and the continuing existence of the mosque as a witness to his genius. He spent his entire life on a quest, trying to understand, finding no pleasure in love, money, influence, or even country and home. His only pleasure involved the recesses of his dreams, battling and conquering time. Eternity lay in creativity, power in construction, miracles in drawing, pleasure and stability in completion of the building. He no longer wanted anything and was not asking for a salary. As he started work, he kept wondering who would visit the building site, who would view it with admiration, who might draw it, and who would lavish praise on it. How many leaders and sultans would pass by and stare at its size in sheer amazement, how many architects and worshippers, how many Egyptians and Mamluks, and how many ordinary folk!

How many people would be conducting research and reading the name Muhammad, son of Muhammad, son of Baylik al-Muhsini, as an architect? A dream, after which life itself and all other delights were trivial. How many lovers have wasted their lives on quests and passions; how many searchers have wasted their lives too, wandering crazily through the labyrinths of delusion!

Whenever Muhammad completed a section of the mosque, he would visit it over and over again. He would stare at it for hours, then look around at his assistants, draftsmen, and craftsmen, inhaling the atmosphere of creativity loaded with both satisfaction and anxiety. Then he would carry on.

He started designing the mosque's bronze door and furnace. To the craftsmen involved he became known for his exactitude, his desire for perfection, and his madness. How often did he demand that they redo something, be it once or many times! How often did he not like the decoration, remeasure the distances involved, and make them redo everything! The workers started muttering curses and even thought about quitting, but they carried on because there was little other work to be had in the country. They tolerated the architect who had bested the amirs with his never-ending demands. It felt as though his building was going to last forever, and the mosque door would open the gate to the earth with all its treasures, overcoming and demolishing time in the process. When Muhammad had finished constructing and decorating the door, he asked the sultan to come in person to inspect the building and admire its innovative aspects. He would be a witness to the demon's emergence from inside and could grant the freedom to improvise at will.

As Al-Hasan looked at the door, he was utterly astonished and delighted.

"Muhammad," he said, "I'm beginning to have doubts about my finishing this mosque and being buried in it. It's costing twenty thousand dirhams a day. The Mamluk amirs are keeping tabs on my funds and checking them."

"But you're building a mosque," Muhammad replied assertively. "You're not spending money on pleasures."

"Yes, you're right," Al-Hasan said confidently. "I'm not going to stop building a mosque. Which sultan would do that? I want it to last forever and witness this country's greatness."

He moved closer to Muhammad. "My dear friend," he said, "they're hatching plots against me every day. If I don't get rid of them soon, they'll kill me, just as they did with my brother and always do."

"You need to be cautious," Muhammad replied, still looking at the mosque door. "Don't get them all annoyed and don't arrest them all at once. Learn from your own father. He tolerated them, then picked them off one at a time. But you need to have some loyal supporters among the amirs, as your father did. Remember, your father used to say: 'Sultans without Mamluk soldiers have neither attacking resources nor legitimacy.' Do you have any amirs who are loyal?"

Al-Hasan looked perplexed. If Muhammad were not feeling the effects of his creative addiction, he would have felt sorry for his young friend. The sultan looked more lonely and desolate than he had ever seen him before.

"Muhammad," Al-Hasan replied, "I have my children, my wives, and a few men around me, but I don't trust any Mamluk amir. I have no idea how they think or what they're planning. I've heard that a date has been fixed for my murder. If I don't move before they do, then I'm lost. We must get rid of them. You know that; you're my only friend and brother. You realize why I trust the sons of the people, don't you? They were born free, they're not slaves. But, more important than that, they were born in Egypt; they marry Egyptians and speak their language. After a few years, they become part of the Egyptian population, even though they're the children of Mamluks. I'm concerned about the Egyptians. I know what's best for them: that's that they not be governed by Mamluks."

'Dear brother," Muhammad replied, "everyone talks about what's best for the Egyptians. Think about yourself first of all. No one knows what's best for the Egyptians. It's an amazing country, one that, at first, seems easy to understand and then bowls you over with its surprises."

Muhammad could not tear his eyes away from the mosque door, but he patted Al-Hasan's shoulder.

"You're my young brother," Muhammad said. "You know that already. My father died when you were eight, and Sultan An-Nasir Muhammad when you were about six. In our times, the death of a father means loss of prestige and power. I feel for you, Hasan, I can sympathize. All the time I'm building this mosque, I'm thinking of you."

Al-Hasan looked over the mosque again. "I didn't realize how beautiful it is. It's higher and loftier than any other mosque."

Muhammad continued building the mosque. He made only one request of the sultan: that his name be recorded as the mosque's architect after the sultan's own name. He no longer received any news about the sultan, nor did he see or ask about Al-Hasan. He built the first, second, and third minarets, but did not finish the entire construction. That would take years and years. But then, something important happened that changed all the plans.

⸺⟋

The sultan opened a part of the mosque for people to pray. Worshippers poured in from all over. All of a sudden, during the prayers, the third minaret collapsed on the worshippers. It seemed indeed as though Al-Hasan had been unlucky ever since childhood.

For Egyptians, the minaret's collapse on worshippers was an even worse disaster than the plague itself. Three hundred worshippers died, and Egyptians completely avoided going to the mosque. The sultan suddenly became an ominous figure for Egypt and Syria. The Mamluks started spreading stories about the misfortunes of the sultan who was affecting the body, the country, everyone. Even mosques were not to be spared the ill luck of the ruler who had dispensed with the Mamluks and handed over the reins of authority to sons of the people, who were spoiled and corrupt and had neither experience nor organization. There would be general collapse, followed by desiccation. It would overwhelm the Nile, just as it did the mosque. The country would be finished. What had Sultan Hasan done to endear himself to the Egyptians? Why did he love the people? These ill-starred fortunes, which were now afflicting all those closely linked to the sultan and his mosque, now spread far and wide. People started being scared and avoiding conversation about him. The sultan was satisfied with worshippers being killed by mistake; he had managed to bankrupt the treasury and run out of money.

During his reign, the plague was rampant; there was widespread poverty, and death was everywhere. People with experience and knowledge moved away, and ignorance spread far and wide. What kind of sultan was this, what kind of mosque, what kind of state?

Egyptians and Mamluks alike started to whisper. When the minaret fell down, and children and the elderly all died while praying, even sons of the people felt anxious. If the sultan was not capable of constructing a single minaret, how could he govern Muslim territory? Who was he protecting? Who would he be blocking? The entire story got out of hand. Here was Al-Hasan, the root cause of injustice, of corruption, the one who wants to boast about his mosque while the country and its army go to ruin. He's only twenty years old, and he's finishing off a country that's survived for thousands of years. Who can be satisfied with that? Who is saying nothing? Who is not rebelling?

Who is rebelling?

Not the Egyptians; they cannot do anything. After the plague there are not a lot of people left to lose. However, if the Mamluks rebel, the people will not be bothered. One sultan leaves, another returns. Who cares?

For his part, Muhammad wandered around, unable to believe this catastrophe. He did not know whether he was the one responsible for it or his assistants. He wept like a young child and visited his parents' tomb. He begged for forgiveness because he had not achieved his goal or been fully aware. But the demon inside him still had to emerge and not judge him. He could not stop now or give in. The problem was not the mosque, or Al-Hasan, or the building process. It was his own soul that was stabbing him, goading him, keeping him awake, and inserting a cold blade into his heart. He had either to complete the mosque or commit suicide. There was no other way.

The building stopped, and it was time for Al-Hasan's assassination.

⟜

No one knew about Sultan Al-Hasan's assassination; nobody cared. Every home had its own disaster; every family in Egypt had its particular goal and quest. Some people went looking for bread, others wanted to buy women's fashions, others were trying to outwit the market inspector, others were keen to smuggle in a bottle of wine along with a pretty girl in the quarter, others had simply given up hope, others were heaving sighs of despair, and still others were abiding in patience and carrying on.

The day when Al-Hasan was assassinated turned out murky and dark, but the way it ended was well-known and easily acknowledged. When soldiers dragged him into his palace to kill him, he did not try to run away or resist. When he stood in front of the amirs, one of them said:

"We're going to kill you because you're a total disaster for this country. Egypt needs someone better. You waste money, build monuments, and designate authority to sons of the people. You fool with the country as though it's a garden you've inherited from your grandfather! This marks the end of using inheritance for the rule of Egypt."

"I love Egypt," Al-Hasan replied loudly. "Egyptians know that and believe it. Go ahead and kill me, but I did it all for Egypt."

"Your problem and your tragedy," the amir scoffed, "is that you're a child who neither understands nor shows any awareness. Egyptians don't understand you or love you. They don't understand or appreciate your lofty goals!"

He struck the sultan's head with a sword. "Were you planning to put all the Mamluks in prison?" he asked. "Do you think we didn't know? You were going to finish them all off today. A teenager, a child who doesn't understand the country or know about the Mamluks. You're going to die with no grave and no tomb. You don't deserve either of them, Hasan. Once you're dead, you will remain unknown and worthless. No one knows you or cares about you. History will forget about you, you lunatic. You no longer exist on this earth."

The amirs assassinated him in the garden of his palace. They put a stone around his head first, and then another around his body. They tossed them both into the River Nile. All trace of him disappeared, and his life story was forever gone.

The amirs decided to stop work on the mosque that had bankrupted the state treasury and caused so much loss.

Once the work stopped, Muhammad the architect became even more unhinged. He started doing the rounds, searching out amirs and sultans, going to see the new sultan, and talking to amirs.

"The mosque has to be finished," he said, "even though Al-Hasan is dead. His death is not important. He wanted to be buried there, but he isn't. The mosque must be finished. The building's endowment is concerned with the relief of poverty and illness. It's God's house, and must be finished so the country will not be afflicted with a fresh plague. I'll finish it. I don't need a salary. Just let me finish it."

The amirs could not leave the mosque unfinished. What kind of evil omen would that be? What calamity would strike them? The mosque was actually finished two years after Al-Hasan's assassination. The architect heaved a sigh of relief, and inscribed his name along with that of the sultan.

He had vowed to visit his parents' tomb on his own and bury the plans in their mosque. In the name of their twin spirits he would distribute bread and sugar. He would not take any of his brothers with him. Just for once, he wanted to meet his two parents without any barrier or commentator on the past. Of that past he could remember what he remembered; of his parents he knew what he knew. He needed to be with them on his own.

Children snatched the sweets from his fingers. He took out the plans and headed for his parents' tomb. He sat down in front of it and lifted the pages in the air.

"Father," he said in an emotional voice, "do you remember the door in the sultan's house? You must remember. We talked about it when we were visiting the sultan. You were proud of me because I was brave. I've built a door a thousand times better. Don't be angry with me because I didn't become a warrior like you. What I've built will perpetuate your memory and remain standing long after human beings have disappeared. How simple that disappearance is! After the plague, I've become aware of quite how feeble and trivial mankind really is. I want these plans to rest beside your head forever. I've drawn the mosque and door for you. I don't know when I'll be coming to visit you again, but I want to tell you how much I love you. I see you in my dreams, tall, fearsome, a just warrior. Everything I hear about you is good. You were different: you took chances and were inventive. I want to be like you in some way. You remember: you waited for years to give the embossed copy of the Qur'an to my mother. You realize, you must realize, that wars vanish like dust unless we record them and memorialize them with buildings. Plague cannot destroy buildings, nor can perfidy kill them off. I know that you're listening to me and are proud of what I've built. I can promise you that your name will be repeated for all time. That's what you deserve. You were an unusual man. I love you. Forgive me for expressing my own feelings like this, as though I weren't a warrior. But perhaps they're worth repeating."

For a moment he stood silently in front of the tomb, then he went over to his mother's tomb.

"I can still remember how you clung to me on the day you died," he said quietly. "I wonder, were you afraid for me or calling out to my father? Mother, your eyes were always filled with affection. I wanted to love with my whole heart. I loved this building. When I finished it, my heart was still wanting and waiting. Perhaps the prostrations of worshippers inside the mosque I've built can forgive sins and compensate for loss and grief. It's all inscribed on grief, so it seems. You understand, don't you! You have to know. Your eyes now traverse the depths and reach a place where no one but you can go. My dear mother!"

He gave her tomb a gentle kiss, then left.

He then returned to his two wives, but he could not find for himself a place in their lives or their children's. Life had gone on its way, and the gap that he had left had been filled. He traveled to Alexandria to search for a female Sicilian merchant, but did not find her. Her house was deserted. He bought himself a house on the seashore and spent the rest of his days contentedly thinking and boasting amid the sands of the sea. From time to time, he would visit the mosque. He used to sit in one of the alcoves, listening to the cries of the people there and silently boasting to himself. The achievement of an objective occupies a special kind of space; from time to time, the cavity left inside him by the emergence of the demon would give him a painful prick. He knew for sure that he would never undertake another innovative project. The creator's tragic dimension is that the demon inside comes cascading out, still tortured at times, satisfied part of the time, but mostly waiting.

All that remained of the young sultan was the mosque, the like of which no other sultan had ever built. He had not been buried in it, nor had he seen it completed in all its beauty. And yet, he was still contributing to the city a sparkling, ascetic tinge, and mouthing many words. He gave witness to the fact that, amid all the conspiracies, creativity still flourished; in the womb of sorrow greatness could be born. Civilizations could spread and flourish between the folds of murder. The mosque itself spoke of life. Nobody knew of Sultan Hasan or how he had died. Egyptians only found out the architect's name after a long life.

For years, the mosque of Amir Muhammad, where he himself was buried along with his wife, was still to be found in the Mamluk cemetery. It was only after years and years that its remains started to fall apart. Children and grandchildren were all buried in the same place; they were all children of the people, not Mamluks. People forgot about them almost completely. Of Zaynab's family only Fatima, her aunt's daughter, was still living. She was over eighty, and could not move. She had lived through one plague after another, one sultan after another.

Her memory started letting her down somewhat, as did her limbs. The children of the next generation forgot about her and only inquired after her on festivals and holidays. On this particular day, celebrating the end of Ramadan, two grandsons were asking to be forgiven and absolved of guilt for neglecting her for an entire year.

In a hoarse voice, she told them that she would forgive them, provided that they took her outside the house for a tour. She had not been out for two years. The two grandsons looked at each other.

"We're worried about you, Grandma," they said. "You'll die if you leave the house."

She smiled and exposed her toothless gums. "What'll happen if I die?" she asked. "What kind of generation are you? Putrid! I swear to you both, take me to the new mosque. I've never seen it before."

They looked at each other again, seriously thinking about leaving her and going. However, the festival day is a day of blessing. If the old lady decided to curse them, their lives would come crashing down even more than all the other breakdowns afflicting the country.

"You want to go to the Sultan Hasan Mosque, is that right?" they asked impatiently.

"Yes, I do," she replied. "Who is this sultan? Is he the ruler now?"

They turned to each other. "No, he's not," they both replied.

"What's the name of the current sultan?"

"Al-Ashraf ibn Hasan ibn Nasir."

"I thought his name was Al-Mansur."

"That's the name of the previous sultan, Grandma."

"When did it change?"

"Last year."

"Where's Al-Hasan?"

"He's dead."

"Are we going to his mosque?"

"Yes, Grandma, we are."

"I'll tell you about my aunt's daughter who loved a Mamluk. Do you know of her?"

"You've told us that story before, Grandma."

"Then you can listen to it again, you neglectful brats! Why this rude behavior? I haven't set eyes on you for a year or two, and you come here and treat me like a mean market inspector! You keep trying to run away as though I'm going to filch your money. So, you're going to listen to me again. Where's the new mosque? Is it beautiful?"

They took her to the mosque, and she looked all around.

"Do you know, you riffraff," she said, "that the sultan himself came to my house a few years back?"

The two grandsons burst into laughter. They signaled to each other that their grandmother was raving; she had completely lost her mind.

"Which sultan, Grandma?" one of them asked her.

"Sultan Hasan. His face was as white as the moon, and he had green eyes, a young man in the prime of youth. I asked to kiss his cheek, and he let me do it. I loved him; I don't know how."

The grandsons laughed again. She stared angrily at them.

"You don't believe me, you stupid idiots! Why should I lie? I'll tell you both something. The architect who built this mosque is the son of my aunt's daughter and my friend, Zaynab, who was forced to marry a Mamluk amir. But then, she fell in love with him. She was very beautiful . . . Zaynab . . ."

They interrupted her. "We know that, Grandma. You've told us before."

"When did I tell you that, bitch? These grim days, there's no respect. Where's Muhammad now?"

"We don't know him, or where he is."

"Who's died in the plague?"

"A lot of people."

"Who's the sultan?"

"Al-Ashraf."

"Is he fair and strong?"

"We've no idea, Grandma. They keep changing every year."

"What's most important, is he a Mamluk?"

"Yes, he is, from their authentic stock. Why are you interested in that? Worry more about your own health. Just look at this wonderful mosque."

"Is Al-Hasan still the ruler?"

"No, Grandma, he was killed a while ago."

"Killed?" she asked shocked. "What sad news is that? He was good, wasn't he?"

"Don't worry yourself about it, Grandma. All sultans are the same."

"Yes, you're right. Who's ruling Egypt now? Remind me again, what's the sultan's name?"

ON THE MARGINS OF HISTORY

The mosque of Amir Muhammad ibn 'Abdallah al-Muhsini, where he was buried along with his wife, some of his sons, and grandsons, was destroyed in an earthquake that struck Cairo at the beginning of the twentieth century. But some of its segments survived, as did the wall of the burial site where the names of Amir Muhammad and his wife Zaynab were located. He only had one wife and owned no slave girls. Doctor Salah al-Sanusi discovered the remains of the mosque in the Mamluk cemetery and read the names on the wall of the gravesite.

As part of this breathless research journey, Doctor Salah al-Sanusi also discovered in the Egyptian National Library in the 1950s the copy of the Qur'an in gold-leaf that Amir Muhammad had made for his wife, Zaynab, daughter of Abu Bakr al-Maqsha'i. After the initial prayer, the dedication was clearly stated: "From Amir Muhammad ibn 'Abdallah al-Muhsini to Zaynab, daughter of Abu Bakr al-Maqsha'i." The book can still be found in Cairo.

The Sultan Hasan Mosque that was designed and built by their son Muhammad ibn Baylik al-Muhsini, along with many assistants under his supervision, still stands today as an artistic jewel of architecture, unmatched by any other mosque in Cairo or any Muslim country. The historian Al-Maqrizi states, "There is no other place of worship in any Muslim country that can match this mosque and its dome, the like of which has never been constructed in Egypt, Syria, Iraq, the Maghrib, or Yemen." Stories about the mosque are endless; it has lived through any number of events and times, both during the Mamluk era and thereafter.

In the year 1416 CE, when Sultan Al-Mu'ayyad Shaykh started building his own mosque (he was a Burji Mamluk), he went looking for the best door in every Cairo mosque to add to his own mosque. He discovered that the burnished bronze door of the Sultan Hasan Mosque, with its delicate tracery, was the one. He had it moved to his mosque in the same year; it is still there.

The account was read by Doctor Salah's granddaughter, who still spends Saturdays inside the Sultan Hasan Mosque, listening to the supplications and praying in one of its alcoves, trying thereby to achieve a sense of satisfaction and understanding. She still brings the lamp that she inherited from her grandfather, made in Venice in the '50s. She takes it with her while she does the rounds of mosques and Mamluk shrines, searching for the names of Sicilian merchants and for light that is sometimes faint and often bright.

Josephine, Doctor Salah's granddaughter, confirmed that the story goes on. Doctor Salah's narrative is the beginning, but not the end. She wrote . . .

The sons and grandsons of Amir Muhammad and Zaynab were indeed sons of the people. His grandchildren are still scattered throughout Egypt. Just people. Sons of the people perhaps—nobody knows.

2. Floor plan of Mosque of Sultan Hasan, Cairo. *Encyclopedia Britannica* (9th ed.), v. 16, 1883, p. 865. See also 11th ed., v. 18, 1911, p. 900.

Key:
1, 2, Main entrance.
3, Court open to sky.
4, 5, Fountains.
6, 6, North and south vaulted transepts (the dotted lines show the curve of the vault).
8, 9, Dikka.
10, Sanctuary.
11, Mimbar.
12, Ḳibleh.
13, Door to tomb.
14, Domed tomb chamber.
15, Tomb within screen.
16, Ḳibleh.
17, 17, Minarets.
18, 19, 20, Various entrances to mosque.
21, Small rooms connected with service of the mosque.
22, Sultan's private entrance.

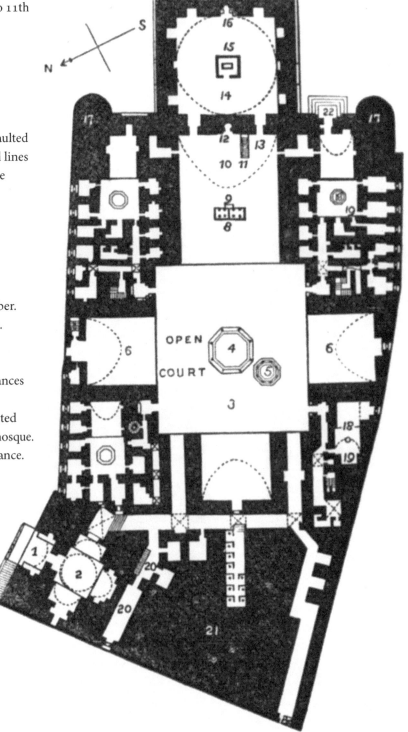

⚜ THE SECOND STORY ⚜
The Judge of Qus: The Mamluks

My son, I know that what you see is always what you want to see. The truth is always hidden, like the new moon before it appears. Delusion! How obvious it is! It glows like the radiant brilliance of morning. All of us follow in its procession. Truth, on the other hand, is all gloomy obscurity.

Woman salt-seller

SULTAN HASAN MOSQUE IN CAIRO, 2017 CE

A carefree heart can invoke both awe and splendor. The concerns of the soul demand courage and independence. Sitting here in this alcove alongside the pulpit long since locked against renovations brings a sense of security, one that I do not feel in any other place. Here is history, and a life lost in the illusions of research and the awareness of failure.

I used to spend hours sitting there. I left the house and my son and chose this corner far away so that I could perhaps achieve my goal and comprehend. Every journey involves arrival and completed story, and every completed story implies success and relief for a vagrant spirit. Love involves complete delusion and salvation; impossible passion brings bitterness and discernment.

Inside this mosque I can recall the enthusiasm of my grandfather, Doctor Salah, and my mother's anger and aggravation, dying alone in a far distant country. I sit here today, searching for two years now for a story like no other, a history like no other, and a past that can help me achieve peace of mind.

Each story contains a part of myself, or perhaps all of it. My misery has many causes, a few of them clear enough, but most of them obscure. It is loneliness, scattered among the recesses of the soul, firmly in place for all time, hating competition and never leaving a space for anything else.

I have done a lot of research for this history, this story: the "Judge of Qus." His name can be found in books and manuscripts: 'Amr ibn Ahmad ibn 'Abd al-Karim al-Manati.

I heard the voice of the shaykh. "Do you need anything?" he asked kindly. "I've seen you here for months. You arrive, you sit down, and you pray."

"I like praying alone," I replied softly. "Being alone involves surrendering to God, something I don't feel in a crowd."

"Are you looking for something?"

"Maybe you know my grandfather. In the past, he used to come here a lot. He died years ago."

I looked at the shaykh who seemed to be in his forties. He could not have known my grandfather.

I still was not sure whether I wanted to talk to him. "My grandfather was with Doctor Hasan," I said, "the one who discovered the name of the architect who built this mosque: Muhammad ibn Baylik al-Muhsini."

He did not seem interested. "Are you an archeologist?" he asked.

"I've been doing research for ages," I confirmed.

"On the architect who built this mosque?"

"No, on the 'Judge of Qus.'"

He stared at me, confused.

"His name came up in a manuscript," I went on, "along with the name of the Sultan Hasan Mosque."

"What does a mosque in Cairo have to do with a judge in Qus?"

"Stories involve beginnings and arrivals. Completing them brings fulfilment to the heart and rest to the soul. Across time and place, minds have become enmeshed, and it's impossible to separate them, however hard we try. But I'm still searching."

BOOK ONE

QUS

Stories involve beginnings and arrivals. Completing them brings fulfilment to the heart and rest to the soul. Across time and place, minds have become enmeshed, and it is impossible to separate them, however hard we try. But I am still searching.

Josephine

1

1388 CE

This sunset is all erasure and oblivion; it brings with it deletion and doubt. People seek help from religious scholars; religious scholars seek help from God. The Mamluks declare that the new moon has appeared and claim to know the absolute truth. Amid the dark shades of diffidence and the certainty of fear, Egyptians decide that the moon has deceived them and is playing tricks—just like the Mamluks and religious scholars. The decision as to when to fast and when to break it has now become a major concern. The people and all other decisions involving their lives are in the hands of the Mamluks and religious scholars. For that reason, the people are divided into two separate groups (or more): one that sees tomorrow as being the first day of the feast; the other that sees tomorrow as the final day of the fasting month.

The truth of things is always patently obvious to Mamluk amirs; aspects of the unseen are regularly disclosed. One or more of them saw the new moon in the Egyptian heavens and notified the religious scholars and Egyptian people. The scholars disagreed with the Mamluks, with all the humility of a dim, unsupported star fading amid the darkness of a starry night. Some scholars maintained that they had not seen the new moon, and thus tomorrow would be a day of fasting. The amirs countered that the new moon had indeed appeared to them; that sighting was sufficient to break the fast. The scholars hesitated. Usually visions only manage to deceive the misguided, and resolute action gives the aura of respect much needed in such turbulent times. For that reason, some scholars came out, albeit somewhat bashfully, and announced that the next day was still a day of fasting, one that would bring Ramadan to a close. The Mamluk amirs had not gone astray or lied; it was just that sometimes visions can mislead those in quest of knowledge, seekers like the majority of amirs. It was the amirs' piety that lay behind their sighting of the new moon, the initiative of the searcher for truth and the preserver of the unseen. However, the religious scholar is always an advocate for the truth, someone who knows the inner workings of things.

Egyptians waited for the sultan's decision and for the celebrations to start. But the sultan had yet to announce his decision; perhaps he was not going to do it. Such confusion was not unknown to the Egyptian people, but what was indeed new was that the decision between continuing the fast or breaking it was in their own hands, not the Mamluks and not the religious scholars. Taking such difficult decisions was frightening and risky. If they decided to go on fasting and the amirs found out, their hands and feet could be cut off; they might well be crucified! But, if they decided to break the fast and that angered God, then they would all roast in hell.

For the first time ever, Jews and Christians felt sympathy and sorrow for Muslims. Their fate was grim for sure!

The people of Qus chased after Judge 'Amr ibn Ahmad ibn 'Abd al-Karim. They were confused and needed to ask him about the new moon, fasting, the festival and pastry. His response was terse.

"Do what the religious scholars say," he told them as he hurried home. "Tomorrow's a fasting day."

That did not calm them down.

"What if the amirs find out?" one of them whispered softly in the judge's ear.

"It's God's wrath that you should be fearing more," he replied firmly as he entered his house. "There's nothing wrong with keeping your fast to yourselves."

He locked the door. He needed to relax after a difficult day, with never-ending disputes. But his day was about to begin, and his life was going to be turned upside down. Time would soon start to rebel, and life was on the point of splitting into two in his own hands—or that, at least, is how it seemed. He had no idea.

On this ill-omened day, there were three women who had managed to make doubt and certainty blend together in a passion in the folds of his mind. The sighting of the new moon was something perfectly normal, nothing to scare or alarm people. Indeed, everything was possible and legitimate. Perhaps it had only appeared to the amirs, but had faded and disappeared for the religious scholars. Maybe the new moon was playing games in order to spread chaos and dig a painful hole in the hearts of Egyptians, populace, scholars and amirs. Three women, who had changed his life, once, twice, maybe more. He could not be certain as yet.

He heard a knock on the door; he was expecting the knock and the question that came with it. A woman in a black dress came in. Her eyes looked dead, those eyes that were so unsettling, as though the soul had departed, but the body was still there; the soul was ephemeral, the body eternal; existence vanished in the face of the scream of murder in her eyes.

She said nothing, but looked straight at the judge, staring at his turban, still silent.

"Have you come to ask about the new moon?" he asked her.

Without asking permission, she sat on the floor. "The amirs lied," she replied softly. "From today on, no new moon will rise in the Egyptian heavens. The religious scholars lied too. No new moon will appear tomorrow or afterward."

He sat down slowly in front of her. His eyes were still staring at hers, which looked like shining glass. He was afraid she was from some other world, a jinn, a demon, or some kind of insanity.

She looked middle-aged. She had uncovered her face without embarrassment and had sat down on the floor with the kind of bold confidence that he had only ever seen in people who had lost everything and were no longer afraid of either death or life.

"My Lord Judge," she whispered, "you're one of the youngest judges in the country. I wonder, is that because you're the smartest and most pious, or the most deceitful and hypocritical?"

"How is it you can speak so brazenly, woman?"

"I can speak . . . I can make a request to God. If you're a servant of God, then you'll listen to me and help me. Not because you're capable of doing so, but rather you're the means to justice and revenge."

"What do you mean?" he asked angrily.

"Hasan was his parents' only child. You need to look into what happened to him."

He now felt a bit more reassured, having discovered the truth of the issue involved. "Are you his mother?"

She ignored his question. "Who killed him?" she continued.

"The father confessed," he replied firmly. "These grim days make me feel sick. He kills his six-year-old son to eat him. What kind of hunger and drought is enough to make fathers in the Egyptian south eat their own children?"

She gave a wan smile. "You're the father of two boys," she said. "Do you really believe that story?"

"The father confessed."

She put her two hands to her head and started rocking it back and forth, but without saying a word.

"If you know something," he told her quietly, "then tell me."

"Why listen to me if you're so sure?" she asked. "Or are you afraid of sighting the new moon and having the truth come out?"

"I'll swear to you," he declared, "that, even if the sultan himself were involved in this crime, I'd still prosecute him."

"Is that youthful enthusiasm, or the piety of a Sufi who has knowledge of the hidden aspects of things? The boldness of renunciation, or the evil of vain boasting and self-deception?"

"Don't keep mouthing off. Who's the killer?"

"I saw him and heard him."

"Who?"

"Jamaq, son of Amir Fakhr ad-din, the governor of Qus."

"Are you accusing him of murder?"

"I heard the screams," she said confidently. "The pleas of that boy, not yet six years old, rang in my ears. He called me mother. When I rushed out to look for him beyond the ancient wall, I found Jamaq finishing up his obscene crime and the boy drowning in his own blood. He ran off down the streets."

For a moment he did not speak.

"That's a serious accusation against the son of a Mamluk amir, governor of Qus. You understand that, don't you. Where's the boy's corpse?"

"Soldiers tore it to pieces and scattered it," she confirmed, breathing hard. "He's my son. I heard his screams, but didn't help him. The man who forced him and killed him is the son of the Mamluk amir. What other punishment for murder is there, my Lord Judge, than killing him? Isn't that so? Or rather, is it the case that unarmed people can be killed, but not those with weapons and governors?"

"I'm not going to repeat what I've said," he declared firmly. "I've assured you that people who kill will be killed. Whatever the case may be, I shall prosecute the culprit. But maybe you're lying, and I need to investigate the matter further."

She stretched out her pale hand and grabbed his arm. He continued to be astonished by her brash behavior.

"He was my only son," she said. "At my age, I can't have another. If he'd died from the plague or hunger, my heart could be calmed and reconciled. But those screams for help have torn my soul. All that's left is my body. They tortured my husband and forced him to confess!"

He removed his arm from her hands. "Which father could ever say that?" he asked.

She grabbed his arm again. "You know I'm telling the truth," she said slowly. "I know you're courageous. No servant of God is ever commissioned except to be victorious. If you apply God's law. I swear before you that I'll be your slave girl and servant till the day I die. I'll clean the front of your house every morning and evening. I'll spend the day looking after your two sons. I'll do everything you ask."

He clasped her hand again to move it away from his arm.

"Justice involves truth," he said, "it's not a mere favor. If Jamaq, the amir's son, committed this deed, then the ultimate penalty will have to be imposed on him. If, on the other hand, he didn't do it, then you've committed a calumny and an enormous sin in accusing him."

She nodded. "If you are convinced," she said, "will you impose the penalty on him, the amir's son?"

"Immediately," he replied without hesitation.

She stood up. "I believe you," she said. "I ask God to assist you in your coming test."

"It's your test too," he added affectionately, "and that's why I'm praying to God on your behalf."

"My test is yours," she replied, opening the door. "My son, my Lord, in this world of ours, fates often intermingle. I have assigned to you a trust, one borne by all God's servants. Whoever bears it pities all humanity."

"I am fully prepared for that," he replied confidently.

Because this night was unwilling to come to an end, or perhaps because of a purpose that always thwarted any attempt to comprehend humans in all their weakness, there came another knock on the judge's door.

"We'll send the beggar on his way, Shaykh," his servant said gently. "It's been a long day."

"As the Qur'an says," the judge responded, "*As for the beggar, do not upbraid him.*" Let in anyone who's asking for help. That's my duty and my goal."

Two women came in, each wearing black clothes that covered her entire body and head. They sat down, waiting for the judge to come in. No sooner did he enter than they both bowed their heads in respect.

"You can both come to my assembly tomorrow," he told them. "That's a better idea for women."

One of the two women seemed older than the other. She was bent over, and her body had filled out.

"Does illness differentiate between men and women?" she asked. "We've come to see you about a disease with no cure."

His mind was distracted, vaguely recalling a promise he had made in a moment of revelation, yet more difficult than the camel passing through the eye of a needle.

"Sister, make your request," he said. "What is it that you need, what is your illness?"

She lifted the veil from her face, and told her daughter to do the same.

"Dayfa," she said, "lift your veil. The judge has to see you."

Her daughter hesitated, but then lifted her veil.

"Why lift your veil, sister?" he asked. "I can hear you and understand you."

"It's the illness I want you to see," she replied. "Raise your head, my Lord."

* Qur'an Sura 93:10 [Al-Duha]

"I cannot look at strange women," he stated. "Tell me what your complaint is, or else leave."

"Dayfa is my daughter," she said. "She's seventeen. She was married four years ago. A man from her father's family contracted to marry her. He's never seen her or touched her. He's left her hanging for four years. Now she's seventeen, and all her friends already have a son and daughter. He won't let her marry anyone else or consummate the marriage. He's never set eyes on her."

"Talk to your husband first," he told her nonchalantly. "Don't come to the judge!"

"That's something else," she replied quickly. "A life wasted, Shaykh. My husband deserted me when I had Dayfa. He's living with his Byzantine slave girl. He never knocks on my door or asks after me. The impetus for our sorrow has come from abroad: white-skinned girls, Circassians, and Byzantines; men much prefer them to their own free women. My coloring is tawny brown like people from the south; my daughter has darker skin. I've been telling myself that her husband doesn't want her for that reason, but he's never even set eyes on her!"

He felt bored. "What do you want from me?" he asked.

"To convince her husband and father to release my daughter. Her husband should divorce her."

"We should start by trying reconciliation. Perhaps that will get her a husband."

He turned to Dayfa, but avoided looking at her. "Have you seen this husband of yours before?" he asked.

She lifted her head and looked at him. "I've never seen him," she replied in a hoarse tone. "I don't know him at all."

"God willing," he told her gently, "he'll come back to you."

"He's never come back," she replied faintly. "Now he's going to return? No, it's black fate, something Egyptians have to suffer, like the color of mud, my color, and that of my mother too!"

"Why are you so pessimistic, sister?" he asked. "We need to change his attitude. We'll give it a try."

"Something else is troubling me, my Lord Judge," her mother added immediately.

"Tell me quickly. It's almost midnight."

She pointed at her daughter. "This daughter of mine is both a blessing and a curse. She's all I have; she keeps me company and gives my life a purpose. But she's not like other girls her age. Her father and mine were Qus merchants, welcoming pilgrims on their journey, buying and selling things. Dayfa is friendly with two women here in Qus, one Abyssinian, the other Yemeni. They both work in commerce and, so I believe, practice magic. My daughter pronounces strange words, as though she can see or know the future. Sometimes she can tell me exactly what's going to happen, as though some jinn has struck her. Maybe that's why her husband has stayed away from her. He may have heard rumors and is scared of her."

For the first time, he turned and looked at Dayfa. She was dark-skinned, with big eyes, thick eyelashes, and features stunning enough to bewitch stones. As he turned away, he was muttering to himself and asking God for protection.

"Ask her to pray and recite God's name a lot," he told the mother. "No jinn can survive amid purity and goodness."

"My husband performed the pilgrimage three times," she reacted loudly. "There's no purity or goodness in his heart."

"Don't curse your husband in front of me," he told her angrily. "You're slandering him and committing a major sin."

When she lifted her arms, signs of whiplashes were clearly visible.

"Yes indeed, you who adjudicate the truth," she responded. "That's the way things are every morning of my life. He married me for my father's money, and then no day went by without him lashing me and his daughter with a whip."

"I never heard from him. I've no idea what you did wrong."

"In that case then, hear it from him. You need to know, Judge of Qus, that love of self brings out its own grudges. A man's hatred of his own wife is enough to bury both her and her offspring. Do you know what love of self is, Shaykh?"

"If I did," he replied forcefully, "I wouldn't be a judge."

"So then, you've managed to overcome it. Counsel the men of Qus about just treatment of their womenfolk. At this moment, injustice is pervasive."

He stood up. "I'll have meetings with both your own husband and your daughter's. May God do as He wills!"

She lowered her head. "You've agreed to take on our burden," she said. "Forgive my boldness and pardon my sin. You cannot know the fire that has never died down for seventeen years. It's stoked by both my love for him and my inability to get near him."

"Leave now with your daughter in God's good care," he said impatiently.

The two women covered their faces again and left.

⁓

The judge of Qus was a shaykh who had won a number of honors from the most renowned and competent religious scholars. He had grown up in a house of learning and piety. He had learned that his grandfather was a man who feared God alone. Several times he had confronted injustice and suffered great hardship as a consequence. On one occasion, he had been imprisoned, then released by a Mamluk amir when Sultan An-Nasir Muhammad ibn Qala'un had returned to power;

and on another occasion, after An-Nasir's Muhammad's death, he was imprisoned again when he was an elderly shaykh and was ill. He had died in the Citadel dungeon. People say that, a few days before his death, he was raving, forgetting his sons and even the verses of the Qur'an that he used to repeat. No one knew for sure whether he had lost his mind in the murky gloom, or whether he had caught a fever and died from it. The prison guards were still talking about the way he had suffered in his final days: some of them were sympathetic, while others accused him of heresy and unbelief. He had opposed sultans and feuded with the religious scholars of his time.

'Amr heard about him from his father, but never saw him. He knew that the endowment that his father had set up for him and his brothers was one that had been specifically established by a Mamluk amir named Muhammad ibn 'Abdallah al-Muhsini for Shaykh 'Abd al-Karim and his sons and grandsons after him. His father had often told him about the firm friendship that had tied the Mamluk amir and the shaykh together all his life. The amir's family and grandchildren still visited the mosque where he, his wife, and some of his children were buried. They were looking after the endowment that he had left for Shaykh 'Abd al-Karim's family.

'Amr grew up in a house of learning and piety. His father kept his distance from government and officialdom, from the issuance of legal opinions, and from currying favor with amirs. Instead, he devoted himself to teaching the Qur'an and jurisprudence. He brought his son up to be like him, a man of religion, not politics; studying laws, but not convinced as to how to apply them; never speaking against rulers and amirs, and never cursing wrongdoers—all so as to avoid his grandfather's fate.

Even so, 'Amr was different; his ambition went beyond that of his father and grandfather. His aspirations were enough to envelop the walls of Cairo and more. He trained, memorized, and studied, and, at the age of twenty, formed close relationships with his shaykhs. He used to sit with the chief judge, treating him with great deference and extolling both him and his learning. At the age of twenty-one, he bashfully asked to marry his daughter. The chief judge agreed. He had never before encountered anyone with 'Amr's piety and intelligence. More important, none of his students and disciples had ever displayed such admiration and praise. The chief judge sipped this laudatory honey and agreed to 'Amr's marrying his daughter without any demands. Not only that, but he started promoting him and preparing him to serve as his deputy when age and prestige permitted.

'Amr was married to the chief judge's daughter. It was an unforgettable day. She was beautiful, pious, and serene. He lived with her for many, many days, content, quiet, tedious, and cool. He could see her father in her eyes; not for a single day did he feel that he was addressing his wife, but rather his teacher and shaykh. Even though she treated him well and obeyed him, her father was still a barrier, whether in serious or playful times. She fell ill ten years later and died in his arms. He mourned her loss and never married again. She had borne him two sons who came to Qus with him when he arrived here three years ago and became the judge of Qus.

His ambitions became a reality and his dreams a certainty. He still raised his head to higher realms. He knew he was not born to be a soldier; he was not of Mamluk stock. No, he was an Egyptian. For that reason, he would never be a sultan. But the chief judge could stand up to sultans. He would know things that they did not, duly protected from mistakes and faults. His word would have authority and efficacy. His suggestions would be a threat and menace to every sultan. Where would the slaves of the earth have acquired the ability to govern Egypt and legal decisions regarding imprisonment and death, if religious scholars and shaykhs had not granted it to them? Without shaykhs, there would be no Mamluks; without religion, Circassians and Turks would have no legitimacy to govern Muslim lands. They knew that, and so did he.

If it was true that the young boy had been murdered by the son of the governor of Qus, then inevitably he would either be done for, or else become a hero and martyr. He did not know yet. In either case, he would be dead. Maybe in time, some people would be accusing him of unbelief, or of insanity. They might claim that he was making a false accusation against the amir's son out of jealousy. Perhaps the amir's son had not done such a thing.

In order to make sure, he had to tread carefully and operate in complete secrecy.

Even before he fell asleep, his strategy was clear and operative. It was possible to achieve the goal.

'Amr made up his mind and made his plans carefully. Memories of his father and grandfather never left him. He craved his grandfather's acuity and courage. He could understand the way his father had given way and worked with the rulers, but he did not sympathize with it. His own ambitions made their way out from his inner self and exerted their influence over Qus as a whole. In fact, they extended as far as Cairo and Alexandria. His knowledge and people's love for him only increased. His quest for knowledge never stopped. Any religious scholar needed ability and power; otherwise, how could he be a fair judge or explain God's book?

Next day, like all other religious scholars, he was fasting. Entering his council, he asked his assistants and scribes to look into the matter of a Qus merchant who had married off his daughter. The husband had been absent for four years and had never consorted with her. He asked them to look for the husband and the merchant. They were to find out about the family; what was the real story behind the magic and jinn who had touched the daughter. He convinced them that this particular problem could explain his own feelings of perplexity and gloom; he could not think about anything else. Godliness was lacking in this particular town. One man treats his wives badly and leaves them *"as though suspended"*; another stays away from his wife and abandons all his responsibilities. Religious scholars and judges are required to "forbid what is wrong" and stop people being mistreated.

They all set off to investigate, while he and a student stayed behind. He trusted this student and was in the process of training him; the student realized full well that he would only obtain the certificate when the judge was satisfied. The judge asked this student to look into the case of the young boy who had died the previous week. He told him to bring the boy's father secretly to the judge, along with all the witnesses, at dead of night and without a single soul knowing about it. Then he would be able to uncover the truth, and perhaps life might for once return to normal.

He was hoping that the mother, poor and ignorant as she was, had been lying. Perhaps she had muddled things up, or she loathed the governor who did nothing to prevent hunger and injustice impacting her life. Hatred and jealousy had obviously led her to accuse an innocent man of a heinous crime. The governor of Qus regularly broke the fast with shaykhs and claimed to respect them. 'Amr himself had never liked him, observing in him a boastful swagger akin to that of pre-Islamic times. Every time he saw him dressed in his gold-embossed clothes, the judge used to mutter to himself *"Walk not on the earth merrily."*†

He was always invoking Qur'anic verses and reciting them as a way of calming his heart and dispensing justice.

He started his investigations seriously and comprehensively. But not a single day had passed before his hopes faded and the new moon appeared. Tomorrow was either a feast day or the end of life. He did not know which. He could not believe what he was hearing and seeing. He asked questions, and asked them again. He gave the people and the father a promise of safety.

"This quest for the truth is not aimed at arresting the governor's son," he said, "but for a particular purpose that the judge himself has in his heart. For that reason, there is no need to fear talking. No scribe is keeping a record, and only the

* Qur'an Sura 4:129 [Women]
† Qur'an Sura 17:37 [Night-Journey]

judge is listening. The judge provides the pledge of safety; he is for them, indeed he's one of them. He wants them to be able to live their lives in peace, hearing nothing and never demanding their testimony."

First of all, he had to swear a solemn oath that their names had been obliterated like light itself; the stories they told would be scattered in the air like dust. Sometimes there could be no harm in telling the truth, provided that it did no damage and did not bite like a rabid dog!

He listened and frowned at what he was hearing. He was scowling too, because he was very frightened. He would essentially be committing suicide.

Jamaq always behaves that way. He goes to the market, looking for a pretty boy. He adores boys; the entire town knows that. Every mother hides her boys before sunrise because they are afraid of Jamaq, the son of Fakhr ad-din, the governor of Qus. It is a story often repeated, and likely leads to the boy's death. At least four people acknowledged seeing Jamaq pouncing on a boy and only leaving him as a corpse. Many people testified that they had seen Jamaq pouncing on a number of children, most of them poor, worthless in themselves and to their families.

It seemed that the entire town was in the know, but the judge had only heard about it today. Realities seemed to appear in a different light to the Egyptian people, to the amirs, and to religious scholars. He begged God to forgive him his negligence and error.

The darkness cleared away, and celebrations of the feast day began modestly. After all, the sultan had not issued a decree, and the amirs had celebrated on their own the day before.

His own feast day never arrived. The sheer weight of what he was carrying on his shoulders was more than any human being could tolerate. His own abilities were feeble. He had no sword and no gold-embossed clothes, only words and verses. In those days, a certain amount of learning was not enough.

But he had made a promise to a woman the previous night; he would never go back on it.

At dawn, he opened his sons' room and woke them up gently. "Get their things ready," he instructed the servant. "They're leaving for Cairo now."

His eldest son rubbed his eyes as he grabbed his shoulder.

"Listen carefully, Ahmad," he said.

"I'm listening, father," his son replied drowsily.

"You're going to your grandfather's house," he told his son. "No matter what happens, you're not going to leave it. You'll take your lessons there and stay inside till I give you permission to return here with your brother. You're a man and the eldest brother. Take care of your brother and keep an eye on him."

"Is something happening?" his son asked anxiously.

"I've a minor problem to solve," he said. "I'll come to bring you back here. Here's a letter to your grandfather, the chief judge. Give it to him and no one else. Make sure you don't show it to anyone. Do you hear me? If anyone else sees it and reads it, your father will be dead on the spot."

The boy shook his head in terror.

His father stood up. "Take your books and inkwell with you," he told his son firmly.

He asked his student to take his two sons and make sure they arrived safely. He gave the student a second letter, not for the chief judge, but for someone else who might well be his last hope.

His assistants arrived full of enthusiasm, with news about the family of Al-Ridawi, his wife, and his daughter, Dayfa.

"The girl is irreproachable," they said. "She never goes out alone, and no one has anything bad to say about her. She is friendly with two old women who work in commerce: one is from Abyssinia, the other from Yemen. They've been settled in Qus for some time. They have no family. She asks after them both, goes to see them, and helps them with everything. The only friends Dayfa has are these two elderly women. People say that she's odd. She's been brought up by three different mothers: Egyptian, Abyssinian, and Yemeni. Her father can't be bothered with her. Al-Ridawi doesn't want either his daughter or her mother. Ever since she was ten years old, she's been learning from strangers; so much so that now she has become strange herself. She talks when she shouldn't and says nothing when she should. Some people whisper about her that she's black, like her mother, even more so than people in Qus. But no one has ever seen anyone so beautiful. Her face has a jinn's power to tempt and command. That's what matchmakers and midwives had to say."

No one knows why the father did not come. After the judge had summoned him, he should have been there.

Her father was actually vicious and rough with everyone around him, apart, that is, from his Byzantine slave girl whom he adored like a teenager. She had borne his children, and totally dominated him. His actual wife, Dayfa's mother, was from a distinguished family in Qus. Her luck was down, and her grief knew no end. Only Dayfa lived for her, and she was her mother's entire existence.

Al-Ridawi, her merchant father, was still bent on acquiring her mother's land and wealth, but she refused to give him anything. Her entire family had died in the plague, and all she had left was what she had inherited. When the family perished, Al-Ridawi's injustice and cruelty went from bad to worse, even though he was already amassing and storing wealth. At the age of nine, his daughter was playing in the markets. She sniffed a hot pepper, sneezed, and fell to the ground. Two women started laughing.

"We see you here every day," they both said. "Who are you?"

People say that the two of them gradually lured her from hot peppers into an unusual kind of friendship. They taught her poetry, reading, and literature. The woman from Abyssinia taught her prophetic hadith and jurisprudence, and the two women worked together on the basis that she was their joint daughter. She has started going everywhere with them and spends a good deal of time with them every day. She takes care of them, their only family. Some people say that they have taught her magic and that she behaves oddly. Her beauty is the work of jinn. Others suggest that she is a feeble girl who can only find affection with strangers, not from her cruel father or her mother who cannot do anything. A strange tale.

No sooner had the man finished speaking than Dayfa herself came in with one of the two elderly women. She kept the veil lowered over her face.

"Help me, my Lord Judge," she said in a muted voice.

'Amr looked around him. "What's happened?" he asked loudly.

"My father's found out that we've asked you to help us," she replied quickly. "He grabbed my mother and beat her. He's broken her arm, and I've left her sprawled out on the bed."

The judge gave one of his assistants an order. "Bring me the father." To Dayfa, he said, "Go back home."

"He'll kill me," she replied immediately.

"No, he won't," he replied firmly. "I've sent someone to look for your husband. He'll be here soon and you'll go to your house. Go back now."

The father was summoned and came reluctantly, his eyes burning with fury. He had sworn to kill his wife and daughter when he went back home, now that they had exposed him to the judge. He was now the butt of jokes from children and teenagers.

He sat down in front of the judge, rubbing his hands together and staring hard at the floor.

"I've heard a lot about you," the judge said calmly. "About your commerce and your generosity to pilgrims on their way to Mecca. God will give you a good reward for that."

He had not expected this kind of praise and said nothing.

"Not only that," the judge went on, "but I can't believe that you performed the pilgrimage to God's house three times. Everyone here envies you."

"It was a tough journey," he said somewhat boastfully. "I was determined to do it, and made a vow every time my wife gave birth to a son who lived even during times of hunger and plague."

"Your children are great sources of comfort and support, I realize that. Did you throw stones at the devil?"

"Of course I did!" he replied in amazement. "Would the pilgrimage be authentic if you didn't?"

"So then, you were victorious over the devil of self and desire. You pelted the devil with stones. Or is it rather that you defeated the devil of the self in Mecca, but, when you came back to Qus, the devil started throwing the stones back at you with a vicious hatred?"

"Who's said that I'm treating anyone badly?" he asked nervously.

"I wasn't talking about bad treatment," the judge made clear. "It's always desire that frightens me. The devil of the self is inaudible and fascinating. It can burrow into the very depths, and there's no escaping it. Adhere to what is and practice charity. That is what God has commanded us to do."

"I'm going to kill that crazy old woman," he said aggressively.

"If you did that," the judge made abundantly clear, "I would immediately cut your head off."

"How is that the judges are now inciting wives against their husbands?"

"Give her the dowry that you've held back, then divorce her."

"I don't have any money to give her."

"Either divorce her or treat her properly. Don't leave her '*like one suspended.*'"

For a few moments, their eyes met, but the merchant had nothing to say.

"If you strike her," the judge told him in no uncertain terms, "or if you break a rib or an arm, you'll be paying a price for it. If you really hate her, then give her what she is due and leave her."

"She's been my wife for twenty years or more," the merchant admitted. "Are you ordering me to divorce her in front of witnesses, my Lord Judge?"

"Treat her properly and be fair, or else leave her. I'll be forcing you to pay the dowry, and you know full well that I can do that."

With that, the judge got to his feet. The merchant left, his feelings a mixture of fury and fear. As it was, he did not beat his wife and daughter as he had expected. Instead, he went, albeit reluctantly, to his wife and asked her to forgive him. He left her room without even laying a hand on her.

The judge was waiting for news of the safe arrival of his two sons and the delivery of the letter to his father-in-law, the chief judge. He had not received any news yet, and his students had not returned with glad tidings. His mind was distracted, wondering what would happen, and what was to be his fate and that of Egypt's religious scholars after him. While he was thinking about all that, a woman came in with an old lady.

"I need to talk to you about a private matter, my Lord Judge," she told him explicitly. "I can't talk in front of witnesses."

He recognized the voice and dismissed the witnesses. Now only she and her friend, the old woman, were left in the meeting-space.

"Has your father been hurting you again?" he asked gently.

She smiled underneath her veil. "You recognized my voice, my Lord Judge," she said. "That's an honor that I don't deserve. First of all, I want to thank you."

He nodded in acknowledgment.

She lifted her veil and stared straight at him. "I've come to make a request," she said. "I'm aware of your sense of justice and your authority."

She looked at her friend, the old woman, who stood up, opened the door, and left.

"Call your friend back," the judge told her loudly. "We cannot be alone."

"The matter concerns me alone," she immediately replied bashfully. "The judge needs to know; he has to know."

"Tell me your problem," he replied disconcerted. "Don't come here again."

"I don't want my husband," she said. "If he's abandoned me for four years and you force him to be married to me, he'd abandon me as my father did to my mother. I beg you to grant me a divorce from him. I don't want to be married, and I can't stand men."

He gave her an angry look. "I assumed that years of your life would give you a bit of maturity, but you're talking like a child!"

She stared straight at him. "I dreamed about you last night, my Lord Judge!" she said suddenly.

He stood up, suppressing the panic that he was feeling.

"Leave now, sister," he told her. "You've said what you wanted."

"Don't think badly of me. It was a lovely dream. You were circumambulating the Ka'ba and hurrying . . ."

He sat down again and stared hard at her. His own pious posture was being affected by what she was saying. He directed his attention to her lips smiling innocently but also seductively, the like of which he had never encountered before.

He looked away.

"But then," she went on, "the Ka'ba faded away, with you still circumambulating something, still hurrying, then waiting. I don't know whether it was good news or not. My Lord Judge, I'm afraid for you. Everyone in Qus is afraid for you.

You've brought down a fire on yourself which will never be cool and safe, like Abraham's fire."[*]

"What do you mean? What are you saying?"

Without even realizing it, he looked at her again, at her eyes and her chin.

"You must be aware that Egyptians are always submissive; they may pretend to forget and claim to be crazy or negligent, but in fact they are always fully aware. There's a difference between knowing something and deciding what to do after you know. Your courageous stance is making the people of Qus feel weak, our men before our women. They're looking into the case of the young boy being killed by the son of the amir and governor. We all knew; we knew who and how."

He said nothing. She looked at him, and, for just a moment, their eyes met.

"It seems," she said, "that the Judge of Qus is being drawn toward a human female, he being the one with insight into the inner workings of things. No doubt, women's eyes are always deceiving them. Love of self always blinds one's vision. There's nothing about me to attract anyone, especially one who knows those inner workings and offers protection from every evil."

He looked down. Her words were still shocking him, as though she were either crazy or heedless—he had no idea.

"Leave now, Dayfa. We have nothing to say to each other."

She stood up, somewhat agitated. "Are you closing the door on a questioner, my Lord?" she asked.

"To the contrary, I'm warding off evil and suspicion."

"I wanted to tell you about my second dream."

"I don't want to know about it."

She shook her head. "I'm sorry," she said sadly. "Words always spill out of my mouth without my thinking about the consequences. I'll try to improve. But I don't want this husband. Divorce me from him."

"I'll talk to him first," he replied without thinking. "Then I'll look into things."

"Nothing's going to change my mind," she said angrily.

"Dayfa," he told her firmly, "our meeting's over."

Opening the door, he shouted for the witnesses, the scribe, and everyone else in the meeting room.

———

Qus is a city with high buildings, constructed by a professional architect and paid for with the wealth of sultans. The city boasted lofty buildings that could rival the

---

[*] Qur'an Sura 21:69 [The Prophets]

ones in Cairo. Human beings could move around in them as easily as bees in a hive. It felt as though life would soon come to an end; the deadline was fated. It was the scheduled time for the annual pilgrimage, a season for commerce and prosperity. Cairo seemed stable: life there was routine and slow. By contrast, Qus was like an anthill. Everyone was working and moving toward a known place and an acknowledged goal. Wealth acquisition was a goal and method at one and the same time. People came in all shapes and sizes, and the smell of incense wafted in the air from one Yemeni merchant to another who was Indian. A few merchants were selling exorbitantly priced carnations and rare spices, while the majority of Egyptians offered different types of bread and sweetmeats to every passerby and traveler.

Qus was life itself and the world. There were different tongues and currencies, varieties of color, some bright, others faded. The world was big and small at the same time. The people of Qus knew the strangers and understood their language. Sometimes they would arrive and settle; at others, they would move on to another deadline.

Like stars, both gleaming bright and dark, love of money mingled with preparations for the journey of the soul. Love of body and sating it with food and women blended with contemplation of the hereafter and the Day of Judgment.

The people of Qus spoke of jinn in the desert and on the seabed. They told each other about their experiences with magic and magicians, envy, and defeat. They talked about heroes, warriors, poets, and Sufis, about people with knowledge of the future, those who had vanished into the earth's fold and had yet to appear, who had been resurrected and been killed, who had loved and who had betrayed. They exchanged stories and parables. The impossible seemed possible, and the possible remote. Journeys only began in order to come to an end. The passage of days usually betrayed and deluded, and yet they too dwindled and surrendered in the face of Qus. Here was the world, colors and voices of all kinds, order, caravans, camels, and food and drink of every kind. Some people were even selling wine in secret, others offering the services of prostitutes. The heart was focused on risk and sin, while the soul was in quest of eternity!

As the days rolled by, the judge of Qus came to know and understand a great deal about evil in people and the heart's egotism. People came to him for help: someone had been swindled and had lost his money; someone's house had been burgled; someone's camel had been killed; and someone else had left without keeping his promise. He was seeing the worst, the most evil aspects of humanity. He became inured to evil and understood the lure of money and the body. He himself had long since stayed aloof from sinful conduct and desire.

The absent husband now came back, and arrived panting and begging for forgiveness. It was the sheer stupidity of youth that had kept him away from his wife all those years past. He had fallen in love with a prostitute in Cairo, but now he had repented and his situation had improved. He could confess his sins because now it was over and done with. He was asking for another chance; he thanked fate and the judge for summoning him back. He had felt ashamed of his sin and of running away for years; he did not dare face the situation. Within a week, no more, he would go in to see his wife and offer her gifts and gold. He would be bringing a house and servants, and would treat her like the queen of all creation. He leaned over and kissed the judge's hand, praying for his help and extolling his justice and wisdom.

He left, happy and enthused about a fresh start on life, a husband telling everyone about his wife's beauty. She was unusual and dark skinned, but she had been well brought up. She would obey his instructions and understand his own temperament.

As the husband left, joy oozing from every pore, the judge was feeling annoyed. He had no idea why he was feeling that way or when it had started. Anger was slinking into his heart, but he shoved it to one side. He had plenty of things to think about. The issue of this young girl's marriage was no concern of his. Perhaps he was feeling aggravated because she had asked him to help her and wanted a divorce. It was a trivial matter of wrongdoing, no more. She did not realize what was in her own interest or appreciate the value of stability.

It was stability that he wanted her to have.

However, anger weighs the heart down and injects doubt. Never mind! The husband will cohabit with his wife, and that will be the end of the matter involving this defiant woman whose spontaneous words emerge without either caution or forethought. She needs a husband to restrain her and fill the rest of her life.

He was frowning all day while he awaited the arrival of the letter from the chief judge. Eventually it arrived with his student.

His two boys were safe and sound with their grandfather. The chief judge was sorry for the situation in which the judge now found himself. It was a terrible calamity, but there would be no point in risking his own demise. The police would side with the governor; they would not obey the judge's instructions. The governor certainly had the authority to dismiss the judge; not only that, but also to punish him and his family severely. There was no hope of arresting the governor's son; that never happened in any town or period, only in stories and legends.

That said, the chief judge was always fair. He therefore proposed that, if the judge was convinced that the young boy had died as a result of this foul and disgusting act committed by the governor's son, even though the boy was only six years old, and the son had shown no remorse or shame, then clearly some form of deterrent was needed. Otherwise, Muslim lands would be turned into havens for obscenity and injustice. Religious scholars and judges had taken off their turbans and headed for Sufi lodges and mosques. They have all become heavily involved in those institutions and have totally neglected the protection of the people and the safeguarding of their interests.

This murder was not deliberate, and so the ultimate penalty could not be imposed. What was needed was a payment of recompense that would have to be paid to the boy's family. The judge could determine the amount for a male child, and the payment would benefit the two poor parents in these hard times. The innocent father would have to be released. The whole thing needed to be handled cautiously and gently. What was even more important was not to anger the governor or any Mamluks. A delay was both desirable and necessary. The judge would need to have an amiable chat with the governor and explain the situation to him. The Egyptians know; they have to know and pretend that they do not. But it involves the governor's repute and prestige. It is the job of both himself and religious scholars to maintain that status. The chief judge instructed him to talk to the governor and persuade him gently to pay the recompense. The judge was then to go out and tell people that the boy had died when the governor's son's horse had trampled on him—no more, no less. Avoidance of intrigue was more sincere than truth itself. The preservation of souls was the judge's obligation.

The chief judge finished his letter with this sentence:

'Amr, you need to realize that your life and reputation, indeed the reputation of all judges, is in the governor's hands. How many judges and religious scholars have been humiliated by governors, insulting them in front of everyone? How many governors have put a religious scholar in prison and then beheaded him? You realize how risky what you are doing is. You must be prudent; your goal should always be safety. Bear in mind that whatever happens to you will have a negative impact on all judges and affect all shaykhs.

He read the letter, folded it, and put it away in a chest. He remained silent. This was a night that would not go away, days imprinted on his heart like graves.

Before he could fall asleep, he heard a knock on the door. He knew who it was.

The mother of the little boy who had been killed arrived with a large broom.

"From now on," she said somewhat hysterically, "I'm going to start cleaning your house. I'll sweep in front of your door and live here as your servant. I'm not going to accept a compensatory payment for my son's death."

He opened his eyes in astonishment. She sat down with dust covering her black garment and her disheveled hair sticking out of her veil, as though she had not combed it for years.

"There's bound to be a payment," she said, "but I won't accept it. Anyone who kills is to be killed, even if it's later."

"Anyone who kills on purpose is to be killed," he told her gently. "How do you know that your son was killed deliberately?"

"If he'd killed him deliberately, I would have accepted the payment. But he humiliated him and us. At any rate, his disgusting crime deserves a stoning. But tell me the truth, my Lord Judge. Forgive me if my words are bitter. If someone were to gouge out your eyes, perforate your ears, and sever all your limbs, then give you five hundred thousand dinars or more and ask you to make good use of them, could you do it? I no longer have any feelings in me; it's just a mouth, one that eats only to stay alive for the day of vengeance, no more. You, who have insight into the interior of things and can achieve justice on earth, are you going to abandon me?"

"It's God who will bring it about, not me. I'll not abandon you, nor will I break my promise."

"I'll seek refuge from the governor's violence inside your house. I'll clean it many times until my heart is soothed and feels more settled."

He did not respond.

This situation continued for two weeks. The woman would sit on the floor holding her head.

"Go home and pray," he told her kindly. "Hand the entire matter over to God. It's a trial certainly, but you have to be patient. Cleanse yourself, then pray."

"He knows what's in my heart," she muttered, "but I don't know what's in His. He knows and forgives; He is merciful and treats me kindly."

He heard a knock on the door. He found her coming in again . . . Dayfa, with her mother, just like a dream being repeated each time, or rather, a never-ending nightmare.

When she lifted her veil, her eyes were glistening with tears.

"You've abandoned me," she said sorrowfully. "I told you I didn't want him as a husband. In seven days' time, he's going to consort with me. Is that justice?"

He looked at her mother, whose arm was tied to a long piece of wood.

"Tell your daughter," he told her, "that the Judge of Qus does not follow passionate instincts. Marriage and divorce both involve principles and rules."

Dayfa fell to the floor. "Is hatred cause enough for divorce?" she asked breathlessly. "Isn't it enough? If I've never loved my husband, why are you forcing me to stay with him?"

"You married him with your own and your parents' approval," he replied casually. "Don't talk about passion like a slut in front of me!"

She grabbed his hand and put her forehead on it. "I beg you to grant me a divorce," she whispered. "I beseech you to intervene. I cannot stay married to one man when my heart belongs to another."

He snatched his hand away and avoided looking at her. "I'll talk to your father," he said.

The tears poured from her eyes. "I beg you to help me," she whispered. "My father will not treat me fairly. I daren't reveal to him the innermost emotions of my heart. If he forces me, I'm going to die. Maybe in the past it would have been possible, but now it's not."

He lowered his gaze and looked at her face, then turned away again and moved away from her.

"Whatever happens," he told her, "don't come to me here ever again. Make sure. Do you hear me?"

She nodded, wiping her tears away. "Will you get me a divorce?" she asked.

"The wiles of women are in a class of their own!" he muttered.

He turned to her mother. "Are you happy with what your daughter is saying?" he asked.

"My Lord," she replied resignedly, "I can't control her. No one can. I've told you before: she's been strange all her life. Her mind wanders and vanishes from our world. She's been touched by the jinn!"

"Can't you convince her," he asked with feigned annoyance, "that marriage provides her with protection?"

"I've tried," her mother replied, "but, ever since the first time we visited you, she's been different. She loses her mind like a maniac and spends hours somewhere beyond our world."

He said nothing, but looked at her. Their eyes met, perhaps for just a moment.

"Fine, you can leave," he told them. "I'll talk to your husband."

The two women left slowly, leaving him distracted. He stared at his hand, her powerful grasp still embracing his heart while her forehead had touched the inner folds of existence itself. He could not sleep. He kept blaming her for an unforgivable sin and for a weakness that he had never encountered and did not know. Next morning he summoned the husband and asked him to divorce her. He assured him that that was what she wanted; she would give him back all the dowry and gold she had received from him.

"I'll not do it," the husband replied with determination. "I've decided to start a new life with her."

She was bound to be angry with him, and she was right. But he was going to show her his generosity and affection. Eventually she would forget her anger and her antipathy toward him.

The judge insisted that he divorce her, and the husband refused. Her father was summoned to the meeting.

"Your daughter doesn't want this man as a husband," he told her father unambiguously.

"The decision is the husband's," her father replied. "He's her guardian. My daughter's always been on the edge, not knowing right from wrong, bright green from sand-color. She has no say in this matter!"

The judge consulted his assistants; that day, he seemed on edge and impatient.

"I'm going to declare her divorced in this very session," he finally declared loudly. "If that is indeed what she wishes, then we can remove any dissension about her. God has given her that right. Is there any objection?"

His assistants looked at him in amazement. None of them spoke. The husband remained silent.

"My Lord Judge," the father said softly, "I want protection for my daughter."

"Look for another husband for her."

"But there's nothing wrong with this man."

"Either he divorces her now, or else I will order it. He can then put his name forward again, if he so wishes. She will have to agree to it, not you alone as her father."

"What kind of logic and judgment is this?"

He did not reply, but issued his verdict, which was duly recorded by the scribe. As the assembly retired, he felt relieved. A sense of ease penetrated his limbs, and those eyes of hers never left his imagination.

2

The judge did not expect the old Abyssinian woman to pay him a visit. He had no idea what she wanted. She knocked on his door, leaning on her stick and bending over unsteadily. Her face was uncovered, and she had a cross tattooed on her hand. She asked the judge to go with her since she needed a legal opinion on a matter that she had concealed from everyone. He told her that he was too busy, but she insisted.

"I've come a long way," she told him. "I've hired a mule just for today. I won't be able to come again on foot to see you and talk to you."

"Why are you asking for a legal opinion from a Muslim judge?" he asked her.

"There's no difference in this case between Muslim and Christian," she replied in a weak voice.

"What kind of case is it?"

"Come with me now, and we'll be back here before the noontime prayer."

He left with her, and the two of them rode for hours on a mule-cart. They went into the Qus desert far from the river and populated area until they arrived at a hut in the desert.

He gave her his hand as she got off the cart. She headed eagerly for the hut. When she opened the door with her upheld hand, she announced that here was her secret: a family that she had brought with her from Abyssinia. She was taking care of them and keeping them fed.

"Are you afraid of what you're going to see?" she asked him.

"Nothing scares me," he replied.

"I realize that. Did you know it, your courage envelops the entire community of Qus? But for the governors it's dangerous. You're emboldening the people and obscuring the difference between Circassians and upper Egyptians. Do you understand what I'm talking about?"

"I'm not sure," he replied immediately.

"People keep saying that the muezzin for your Prophet was black."

"In our faith, there's no difference between white and black."

"Even so, Dayfa's father has preferred his white slave girl to his olive-skinned wife who's the daughter of fine, wealthy people."

"That's just men's desires. It has nothing to do with color."

247

"Men in this country prefer white, although their hearts are black."

"Do you hate men? Why?"

"No, I just hate Dayfa's father. My husband—may God have mercy on him!—was a wonderful man. He died a natural death. But important men don't live long."

"You came to talk about Dayfa?"

"Yes. Her mother doesn't like me. She thinks that I'm a witch who's bewitched her daughter into hating her husband."

"What is it you want?"

She opened the door of the hut and brought out a large basket full of bones. She scattered the bones across the desert space, while he looked on with an unsettled feeling. A colony of hyenas now appeared, backs bent, spots on their skin, and evil-looking ravenous jaws. He stayed put where he was, looking closely at the Abyssinian woman as she fed the hyenas and toyed with them. Then she moved backward and headed for the hut. She indicated that he should come in, and he did so. She sat down and kept swaying from left to right until she found a position that was comfortable for her.

"My Lord Judge," she said, "those hyenas are my family and support."

"What a disgusting family! Those animals are truly evil and despicable!"

"That's what Egyptians think, but in Abyssinia we have a different opinion. I've brought them from my country and settled them here in the desert as protection. They aren't humans, and the only protection again humanity's injustices and the evil spirits that hover all around us lies with God. Only hyenas possess that power. They may be ugly, and yet their hearts are filled with goodness. As you well know, Judge, things that are obvious differ greatly from what remains hidden."

"You seem to have lost your mind. What do you want from me?"

"I've only known you in secret. I've brought you a letter."

"What kind of game is this?" he asked angrily. "It's as though women in this country have nothing to do and no sense of devotion to God."

"Just wait for a few seconds, and I'll get you the letter. You can relax on the wall outside the hut. The hyenas won't hurt decent people."

He went out, rubbing his hands together in despair.

He collided with another Yemeni woman with a thin face.

"My Lord," she said confidently, "I've come to see you. Your activities never leave our alley and quarter."

He stared at her in amazement and not a little anxiety.

"I'm Zubayda," she said, "a friend of Dayfa. She takes care of Maryam and me. She comes to see us every day."

He shook his head and was about to leave. She stood in front of him to block his path.

"In Yemen," she told him, "your children would always be safe."

"My children be safe?" he asked in bewilderment.

"The whispers are getting louder, and people are talking. They're going to punish you for sure. In Abyssinia, there's a king who has his eyes on southern Egypt, and in Yemen another king who's secure in his rule."

"Leave things to me," he said gently.

"Dayfa . . ."

"What do I have to do with her?" he asked in amazement.

"She radiates life from every pore. She's given our life meaning—as both girl and support."

He tried to go around her, but she blocked his path again and pointed to the right.

"Leave here, my Lord," she said, "this way is clearer and closer."

He started walking and could sense her behind him.

He stopped and looked back.

Dayfa sneaked over to the edge of the wall surrounding the Abyssinian woman's hut. Her appearance was like a bolt of lightning to blind the eyes, then illuminate them.

"My Lord Judge," she said softly, "I've come to ask for your opinion."

He looked at her, but was so shocked that he said nothing.

She looked all around her. "You'll never stint in giving advice to someone in question of knowledge," she said.

"There's a time and place for knowledge," he replied with his usual calm. "I don't give lessons in the desert!"

"The scholar has to answer the student at any time," she said, as though the precise topic was important and disclosing it difficult. "If the student is too bashful to pose the question in the judge's council, then it's permissible to ask it at some other time."

He pretended to be angry, but his eyes were bursting with laughter. "Ask the question," he said, "and make it fast!"

Her gaze was focused on him, with her heart in hearing range. "Doesn't God give man freedom of belief?"

"Of course! He's preserved that right for Himself."

"And he's given women the right to make a decision. Isn't that right? The Prophet divorced a woman who was afraid that her faith had been distorted."

"Yes, he did."

"Isn't the heart allowed to love whomever it desires?"

He lowered his head and said nothing for a while. "You're as bold as a sorceress! Why? Where have you acquired such brazen behavior?"

"That brazen behavior shows itself in times of danger. In our country, hearts are being crushed under horses' hooves just like rebels and reprobates. Why? Aren't we supposed to respect and revere love?"

"It depends on the kind of love."

She looked at his hand that he was using to prop himself against the wall. She moved her own fingers a little closer in an entreating gesture. She stopped very close to his fingers and moved no further.

"You need to remember, Dayfa," he told her specifically, "that there are types of love that lead to perdition and heartbreak. Always look after yourself. You only have one heart. Don't do it wrong. Love springs from desire, and the heart always needs to be the victor over desire."

"Love involves stability and certainty," she replied forcefully. "It gives life its purpose and color. Doesn't Imam Shafiʿi tell us that:

Regarding women, most people have stated that love of women is a great trial.
Love of women is no trial. The proximity of those whom you do not love,
That is the real trial.

My father wanted me to live a life of hardship. My Lord Judge has now saved me by granting me a divorce. I want to avoid this type of hardship. I cannot bear it."

"I cannot tell whether you are gifted with wisdom and foresight," he replied as though talking to himself, "or you're simply naïve and foolish. Have you finished your question?"

She moved from where she was standing and sat down in front of him, looking straight at him and holding her chin in her hand.

"Does my Lord Judge never smile?" she asked.

"I'm sorry."

"This was my question. Is it the burden of knowledge and the need to preserve justice that makes your expression so permanently gloomy? Or is it some sorrow that no one else knows about?"

"You're being brazen again!"

He was about to stand up.

"I've not finished asking my questions yet," she said pleadingly. "Forgive me, my Lord. It must be that naiveté and foolishness. It seems there's not much wisdom to be seen."

Their eyes met.

"Do you like Qus," she asked gently, "or do you prefer Cairo?"

"I was expecting a question about knowledge."

"How can a maid in quest of knowledge take time away from a judge, when he's bearing the responsibility of the entire population of Qus? Now that I appreciate your responsibilities and the importance of your time, my tongue fails me. The question fools and deludes me . . . My Lord, your very prestige has made me forget. If you'll give me a moment, I'll remember it."

She started rubbing her hand nervously as she did her best to remember her question. He smiled and suppressed his laughter.

"I'll wait until you remember," he said.

"No one really deserves those rare smiles of yours," she replied eagerly. "And yet, you've bestowed one of them on me. I don't know how to thank you."

"Have you remembered your question, Dayfa?" he asked, trying to make his voice sound assertive, but not knowing why it came out so gentle.

As she looked at him, her heartbeat increased. "I can't remember, my Lord," she replied, short of breath, "but it was something important. Can I talk to you now?"

"You didn't ask before."

"I want to talk to you about my friends and their lives."

In spite of himself, he looked at her, but did not respond. She started talking about Zubayda from Yemen. Her husband had divorced her when she was sixty and married a girl fifteen years old. He had left her with no resources. She had traveled to Egypt to sell incense and spices. Ever since, she's been trading in Qus. The town has become her home, a meeting place between two different worlds. During her lengthy travels, she has been hearing about people in Syria and Cairo. She has never seen Cairo. She has been spreading all kinds of fables about sultans and wars and powerful love stories that traverse time and space. Zubayda loves telling stories; she tells Dayfa one every day, and Dayfa listens with all the attention of a young girl. Maryam, the woman with the hyenas, suffered a great deal in order to smuggle her hyenas out of Abyssinia to Egypt without some passerby killing them or someone else not realizing how important they are, failing to understand that she brought them to repel evil from around her and those she loves. Hyenas may look disgusting, but they actually do no harm. They know Maryam as though she is their mother.

He listened to her without knowing why, and with a childlike eagerness; a kind of joy in seeing bright light for the very first time. He felt a wave of comfort, blended with a craving for something he did not even know. Time passed before it began.

For her part, sometimes she smiled, at others she laughed, and at still others she frowned. Then her eyes laughed.

She leaned down and looked closely at a lizard that was surveying the desert and heading cautiously toward its hole. Her braid fell over her shoulder. Without hesitation he followed her movements. He fixed his gaze on her, on her lush, perfectly proportioned body, and her spontaneous gestures and laughter. He could not control the clutch of clashing emotions that he was feeling. He was the judge and religious scholar. He had read and learned things, but then, in an instant, it had all been erased from his memory. Now, all he could see was her flaming beauty and her laughter, something that could melt the heart and make it throb for the first time ever with desire and passion. How could she possibly be so beautiful and innocent at the same time? What kind of girl was this with a body to kindle flames of desire and a heart as spontaneous as a child's? For a moment, he closed his eyes, then opened them again. She was still talking nonstop as she headed in his direction, while all the while he was praising God that she did not know or feel what was going on inside his heart. The judge could not look away from her face, even for a few seconds. He looked at the sun which was about to set.

Life kept passing. How he wished he could stop it today and tomorrow. He had to rouse himself before sunset.

"My Lord," she told him, innocent and eager, "you've taught us to stifle our admiration for the new moon when it shows itself in all its splendor and purity. So, why is it that I can't stop my tongue speaking the truth when faced with the beauty and stability of the new moon as it hovers in its lofty spot over the whole of humanity?"

"What new moon are you talking about?" he asked her with a tenderness that he could not explain.

"About you," she replied without even thinking.

He stood up slowly. She grabbed a white scarf that she was wearing around her neck.

"Allow me, my Lord," she said.

He stared at her in amazement. She pulled the scarf quickly over his hand, pulled it back into her hand, sniffed it slowly, placed it next to her heart, and hugged it passionately to her body.

He had not anticipated what she had just done and had no idea how to react. For a few seconds, he said nothing while he tried to gather the fragments of his heart scattered across the desert—he did not know when or why. He started walking slowly, speechless. He did not look at her; he could not do it.

He would stop looking at her, even if she tricked him and tried to look at him in spite of himself. He would yell in her face, something he ought to have done from the outset. But what had happened to him? Why was he so relaxed with her around him? Why such feelings of achievement and pleasure when she looked at him? Why was he staring so hard at her gleaming eyes and lips . . . ?

Those lips . . . did he long to kiss them? Had he done it? This entire country was crazy; it could rob you of mind and intelligence. His own wisdom would inevitably triumph. He had to work on his heart.

But why? Tomorrow she could be his. He could be married to her, possess her. She would be his, the way he hoped and desired.

People would be saying: so the judge of Qus divorced the girl from her husband so he could be married to her himself. He had wanted her from the very start, so he had divorced her from her husband for his own benefit.

They would claim that the judge of Qus had lusted after the Ridawi girl like a teenager. He had not been just; he had just followed his passions. They would start whispering that he was a hypocrite and tyrant, just like the governor. But, at least, the governor offered protection with his soldiers and swords. The judge of Qus was supposed to protect people with his knowledge and faith. What total injustice! What utter fraud!

As he lay on his bed, his eyes never left his imagination alone, while his passion kept putting intense pressure on him.

When he whispered her name to himself, his heart started throbbing for the first time and his imagination ran wild without any restraint. He pictured Dayfa in his arms, her eyes full of love, her limbs full of life, and her spirit so innocent and lively. He had to stay. Why had he left? Because he could not guarantee what the consequences would be, because around her he did not know his own self.

No, he would only see her again as his own wife. He was not weak-willed and had now made up his mind. Dayfa was his. People would always be whispering things and making claims. Marrying her would not anger God, and He was the one to worry about. The rest of humanity could go to hell. This kind of happiness and relief merited a certain amount of censure, or rather a lot of it. This heart of his, pulsating for the very first time and shuddering whenever she laughed, spoke, or raged, would definitely nurture his love. He closed his eyes. The sound of her voice filled his entire being and the vision of her body never quit his imagination. He desired her as he had never desired any other woman, dreaming of her at night like a teenager and unable to go to sleep. Sleep would only come in her arms; there would be no peace with her far away. Perhaps she had bewitched him. Or was she the curse of a youth spent with books and learning along with a wife and son?

He remembered the ten years that he had spent peacefully with his wife and achieved everything he had dreamed of doing. She had been a good wife and mother. When he had taken her in his arms in the evening, he had looked at her with respect as the mother of his children and the wife who gave him support. But he had never longed for her lips as he was doing now. His heart had not throbbed at the very sight of her, nor had he ever smiled in pleasure at the entire world. He had always been following his intellect. Bodily needs involved a woman and wife, not a sorceress who could dominate him and make him feel the pulse of passion to his very veins. Such feelings were the devil's work; passion like this was humiliating. Every time he remembered her smile, his heart started beating harder. He buried his head in the pillow. Maybe his mind would arouse itself, and the passion could be throttled. If he were married to her, she would be his, in his arms, and subject to his will. He needed to keep this passion under control and fight it until she was his!

What if her father refused? What if he decided to defy the judge of Qus who had defeated and broken him, threatening him with prison and fines? Would he have to compel the father, like the governor forcing the people to pay taxes? Would he have to dangle the police-sword over him and make threats to get him to agree?

He had made up his mind; he was going to be married to Dayfa. One way or another, her father would agree. Perhaps for once everything would be on an even keel.

He slapped his face with water, maybe hard enough to rouse his wisdom and purge the body which would not leave his imagination alone.

He performed the dawn prayer and read the Qur'an. When he left his room, he collided with the little boy's mother who was sweeping the floor anxiously.

"My Lord Judge," she said as she looked at him, "do you know now?"

"Know what? Go home and sleep. I don't want you to stay here."

"This is the only place for me. The governor will kill me if I don't find refuge in your house. Can you appreciate the true meaning of a craving for the impossible and the passage of time? Time plays with us and arouses a longing for what has passed and been eradicated. Life and soul are both alive. Do you understand me? Today, my son, I can see that your eyes have a different gleam to them. How I pity you!"

"Why do you pity me?" he asked, his heart beating hard.

"As I told you: time stirs up a longing when people leave."

"Who leaves?"

"The ones we love and need."

He looked down for a moment. "Go home and get some sleep," he told her.

"As you know, there's no sleep for me until I've avenged my little boy."

———

Next day, when 'Amr sat in his council chamber, he was feeling relaxed and happy. He had asked one of his close associates in the police to search for the governor's son, find out where he was, locate the places that he frequented, and identify all his friends; and to do it all cautiously and unobtrusively.

His exact intentions were not clear to the little boy's mother or, in fact, to his close associate. When this student came in, he had information about the governor's son: every Thursday he would frequent a tavern in the middle of Qus; he had a young girl whom he would visit every two days. She had short hair and a pale face and used to wear boy's clothing. 'Amr told the policeman that he was to inform the governor's son that he wished to meet him in his council chamber. He wanted it to be a friendly meeting marked by mutual respect and an acknowledgment of his and his father's prestige. It had no connection to the murder of a child or shaykh. The topic would be construction and development.

Imposing the ultimate penalty on the governor's son was going to be a fanciful gesture at best, and not merely because he would never find any policemen ready to implement it, but also because he would not be able to find any policemen willing to arrest the governor's son. If such a self-sacrificing person did exist, the governor's son would still run away or seek protection from his father's Mamluks. How would it be with a minor war in Qus in which Fakhr ad-din's Mamluks killed the police chief, the entire police force, and all Qus men of a certain age? If he could not put Jamaq in prison in a safe location, then there would be no hope of punishment. Even if he did put Jamaq in prison, what then? He had neither weapons nor horses. He had a single horse to ride because he was a shaykh. Religious scholars were a step above ordinary Egyptians. Where could he imprison Jamaq? Where could he carry out the sentence when his father had all the weaponry and soldiers? There was always hope; everything was possible with the right planning.

However, the governor's son got away and vanished. He did not respond to the judge's invitation, obviously sensing a trap in the judge's polite invitation, his flawless career, and his reputation among people for his sense of justice and his opposition to tyrants. In fact, he was very frightened. He got in touch with his father who decided to pay a visit to the judge's council chamber in place of his son. He arrived, decked out in all his finery, and entered the judge's chamber. Everyone stood out of respect, except, that is, for the judge himself, who remained seated.

"What is it with religious scholars," the governor asked, "who are neither knowledgeable nor polite? Don't you stand in the governor's presence?"

The judge smiled. "I think it's the governor who stands in the presence of judges and religious scholars," he replied calmly. "We've heard that about sultans. One sultan stands in awe before the chief judge. Another kisses the shaykh's hand."

"What kind of delusion has struck you? Stand up in front of me, so I don't summon my soldiers to take you in chains to my residence."

'Amr remained seated. "If you were to do that, you'd lose your legitimacy. I'll issue such a judgment, I swear to you."

"Your legal opinion suits your own inclinations. So what's my keeping that legitimacy going to cost? Land or gold?"

"The key to that is justice."

"You have authority over the Egyptian people, Shaykh, but not over the Mamluks. Your authority comes to an end at the boundaries of Mamluk palaces and their sons."

"Mamluks have military judges," he replied calmly, "but not their sons. They're under my authority and protection."

'Amr now stood up firmly and looked at the soldiers surrounding his chamber and the heads lowered in front of the governor.

"You seem to have lost your mind," the governor said slowly. "Your delusion has blinded you. It must be your youth and lack of experience."

The governor now turned to the assembled people. "As you know, people, I'd heard a good deal about the family of Shaykh 'Amr ibn Ahmad ibn 'Abd al-Karim. Even so, I agreed to his appointment as judge of Qus. I agreed to his appointment until the day came when he annoyed my son and alarmed me personally. Egyptians have a strange way of acknowledging a good deed!"

'Amr muttered a verse of the Qur'an that he had memorized, "*When the ignorant address them, they say words of peace.*"*

"What did you say?"

"I was repeating one of God's verses."

"I was talking about your crazy dotard of a grandfather. People say that he lost his mind while in prison. He spent days raving and had no idea who he was or why he was in prison."

He started laughing, and, when he looked at his soldiers, they laughed too out of respect.

"You never met your grandfather," he went on, "but you've inherited his madness."

Their eyes met. "Your verdicts don't follow any law," the governor said slowly. "Yesterday you divorced the daughter of an Egyptian from her husband, in spite of her father's wishes."

"That's the law," he replied. "She does not want him as a husband. How is it that the governor is so concerned about judgments in law? Have you learned to read Arabic?"

The governor purses his lips. "Your turban won't protect you," he said.

He pushed off the judge's turban, and it fell to the floor. The soldiers and entire assembly held their breath, and shocked cries arose. No sooner did the turban hit the floor than the governor trampled on it.

---

* Qur'an Sura 25:63 [The Criterion]

"You are to return to your house," the governor shouted, "and not leave it till I have decided what to do with you: whether it's prison and dismissal, or just dismissal. You're reckless, just like the rest of the people in Qus. Reckless and stupid, demolishing his house with his own hands. No one can blame me for belittling men of learning. They've done it to themselves through their own recklessness and impolite behavior!"

"No one's blaming you, Governor," 'Amr commented dryly. "There's no equivalence between those with knowledge and those without, nor between good deeds and evil."

"Do you want me to drag you behind my horse in chains?"

'Amr did not respond, but lifted his head and looked away. The governor drew his sword, and the whole room went as silent as the grave.

The governor's deputy whispered in the governor's ear.

"I still respect religious scholars," he said after a pause, "but not the lunatics among them. This man, who was judge of Qus, will return to his house on foot today. From now, he will not be allowed to ride a horse, and no one will be allowed to visit him without my authorization."

The governor trampled on the turban again, while 'Amr just stood there in front of him, neither shaking nor showing any signs of emotion.

Their eyes met again. Hatred showed on their faces, and envy was in the air.

"You, 'Amr ibn Ahmad ibn 'Abd al-Karim," the governor shouted, "if you even think of touching my son, I'll go searching for your two sons throughout Egypt and the entire world. I'll get hold of them, even if they're with the Mongols or Crusaders, and flay them alive. I'll chop off their limbs and hang them on the gates of the city till you beg me to spare them the pain and kill them. I shall only listen to your pleas when I've plucked out your defiant pair of eyes and cut out your foul tongue. Do you hear and understand me?"

'Amr did not take his eyes off the governor, but did not respond.

When the governor left with his soldiers, they took the judge's horse with them and left a guard in the chamber to escort him to his house.

No sooner had the governor departed than everyone in the chamber bent over and kissed the judge's hand, apologizing and begging forgiveness for the harsh times in which religious scholars, the ones who gave Mamluks their legitimacy, could be so humiliated.

The judge told them that they were not at fault; they should pay no attention to words declared in sheer stupidity. The governor's son would face the ultimate penalty.

"As long as I have a heart beating inside me, I can assure you of that," he declared. "That's a pledge that I make in front of you. In any case, I was about to carry it out either tomorrow or the day after, before the governor arrived and showed the reality of his ignorance and brutality."

With that, he left and walked alongside the guard. The entire population of Qus left their stores and houses and came out to catch a final glimpse of the judge. Some women started weeping and keening, while others prayed for him. Men stared at him in admiration and envy, fully aware of his courage and steadfastness in the face of the amir's arrant stupidity.

He was walking slowly, his head held high. He had not put his turban back on his head. Men looked at his trim black beard and made up their minds that they would all trim their beards and hair the same way. They would all remember the judge after his departure; his death was a certainty. After today, it would never be easy to see him again.

No one dared talk to him. Just a few inaudible mutterings and some groans from the womenfolk.

Close to his house, the little boy's mother came out carrying a broom. Her head was completely covered. She threw herself at his feet and started kissing them. He stopped and bent down to lift her off the ground. But she stayed glued to his legs without moving. The guard was about to hit her, but the judge grabbed his hand.

"Get up," he told her gently. "Otherwise they'll arrest you and kill you before you can get your revenge."

She stood up slowly and looked around her. She stared at some women who were standing away from the house. One of them was not crying or keening; in fact, she was smiling and her eyes were bursting with life. He turned toward her and recognized who she was. Lowering her eyelids, she smiled again, grabbed the scarf, and pulled it slowly down from the top of her veil. He saw the smile in the lines of her gentle eyes and knew to whom they belonged. He knew them very well. His heart gave a shudder that he could not control.

He turned away, went into his house, and shut the door.

⌒

On the first night of his imprisonment in his own house, he went into his library and sat cross-legged on the floor amid his books. He started reading. He performed the prayers at sunset; his servant came in and asked him if he wanted something to eat. The guard came in and said that Amir Fakhr ad-din was the one to decide what the judge was allowed to eat. All that he had permitted was a loaf of bread each day and water to drink. Fruit, juices, and cloves were all forbidden!

"Thank you!" 'Amr said loudly with a smile. "You're giving me the opportunity to take a plunge into my inner self and leave the world's chattels behind.

Abstinence is an obligation for which I haven't had the necessary time. I'll start fasting from today."

He started fasting, praying, and secluding himself in his room every day. He was not bothered about food. Two days later, the amir got to hear what was happening, and he went crazy. He decided that the judge was defying him once again, donning pious garb while actually being an impious libertine. There had to be some other way of humiliating the judge of Qus to make him beg for forgiveness and approach him with downcast eyes and a submissive heart.

The amir asked the guard how the judge of Qus spent his days. The guard replied that he fasted, prayed, and read all day. He never spoke to anyone or answered any questions. The amir was elated.

"Burn his books in front of him, one by one," he ordered.

"But, my Lord," he pointed out hesitantly, "they are books on religion."

"Don't burn the Qur'an. Only burn the ones written by human beings. Burn his entire library, two books every day, until he begs for forgiveness."

The guard nodded. He started burning books every day. When he grabbed the first books to burn, the judge of Qus looked not a little forlorn.

"You're burning knowledge and scholars," he told the guard. "The very first word in the Qur'an is 'read'."

The guard did not respond.

"Deliberate and think," 'Amr went on somewhat angrily. "Don't obey orders like some donkey carrying documents!"

The guard stared at him, furious. "If it weren't for the fact that the amir has not told me," he said, "I would slap you now for what you've just said."

'Amr shook his head. "Imam Shafi'i says: 'If an idiot speaks, don't respond. Silence is better than a reply.' If a guard can be insolent with a judge, then there's no hope for this country. Do as you wish."

On the first day, he burned two books; the second, four books. In order to hurry things along, since the amir was eager for the judge to give in, the guard decided, on the basis of the amir's instructions, to burn all the books on the third day.

On the fourth day, he decided to limit the judge's movements to his own room; no one else was allowed to enter or leave.

"How stupid your amir is!" he commented with certainty. "Do you think I haven't memorized the Qur'an? Do you suppose that, without any books, I can't understand and know things? As long as there's faith in my heart, no one has any power over me."

"As yet," the guard told him forcefully, "you're not acquainted with the stake and the knife as it cuts into your flesh."

He did not respond. Instead he started chanting the Qur'an, praying and fasting.

A week later, Umm Hasan sneaked into his room, with her disheveled hair and worn-out clothes. She sat down beside him and produced a slice of meat from her clothes.

"You must eat," she said. "Quick, before the guard sees me."

She looked tense as though it were wartime. Her eyes were stony and powerful, as though she were about to win or lose.

"You eat it," he told her blandly. "I don't need meat."

"Yes, you do," she replied firmly. "As yet, we don't know how far the amir's cruel behavior will extend. You must know that . . ."

She looked around her. "I didn't need to come to you for help," she whispered. "I could have killed the wretch with my own hands. Maybe I should have tried, but I was afraid. I was scared in case I didn't succeed, and they'd cut off my head while the man went on living in peace. I would die, knowing that injustice would inevitably continue. Do you understand me, Judge?"

"Yes, I do," he replied firmly.

"Does injustice always win?"

"For a while perhaps."

"It's all tied up with money and power, so it'll last for a while. Now eat the meat for my sake."

He took the piece of meat from her, although he really disliked the idea after she had put it inside her filthy clothes. But he could not say anything. He put it in front of him.

"Maybe a bit later," he said.

"The amir's going to break you and humiliate you. I know that. But, for me, you'll always be the most immaculate human being I've ever seen, the bravest man in all of Egypt."

He gave her a smile. "Before and after, it's all in God's hands," he said.

"He's expecting you to ask him to pardon you," she said, "and forget about his son."

"I know."

"Your determination is suicidal. You're bound to die."

"Maybe."

"What if he kills you?"

"There's a text for every appointed time!"

"You're approaching the idea of death as though you have a plan. Do you have one?"

He did not respond.

"You're going to forget about revenge, aren't you?" she asked quickly. "Are you going to renege on your pledge?"

"After all this," he responded angrily, "is your trust in me really that lacking? What kind of woman are you?"

"No, no," she replied, "I'm not interested in your power and defiance. For me at least, you're God's gift to me. First He tests, then He organizes. You give life a purpose. Which land do you hail from, what are your roots?"

"If you don't leave, the guard is going to kill you and you'll never get to witness Jamaq's death."

"That has to be a touch of madness. How on earth am I going to witness the death of the governor's son? Are you raving after several days with no food?"

He smiled again. "You've lost faith in me pretty fast. Didn't you come to see me because you wanted revenge?"

"It was a moment of sheer madness from a traumatized mother. Forgive me."

"I don't understand you. Do you want me to forget about your son? Will you accept compensation?"

"No. Forgive me, because you're going to be killed, and I'm reminding you of your pledge to me. Farewell, my son!"

After a week, his body looked skinny. At times, he found it difficult to focus, while at others the earth kept spinning. Endurance in such circumstances was a feat of determination. The entire community of Qus kept talking about the brave, crazy judge who was defying the governor, on the point of death, something that was expected and indeed fated. However, the governor ran out of patience. After two weeks, he decided that it was time to bring things to an end.

⟜

As night fell, he was sitting on the floor. The amir had made up his mind that the judge's life would come to an end today. His killing would put an end to corruption and bring about complete stability and the restoration of Qus as the cradle of civilization and citadel for pilgrims, a town known for justice and security, with no crime and no dark secrets. If the judge died in his bed, this story about the governor's ill-fated child would be at an end, and people could go back to their tasks and jobs. Everyone's hearts could calm down, that of the judge being prime among them! Death would be able to calm his ambition and defiance, standing alone in the face of fire and flood, with no support and no salvation. There would be an eternal release from the torture of prisons and episodes of madness that awaited him. The governor would only ever leave him as a lunatic, wandering his way through streets and quarters, shouting out to those who had gone, been killed and tortured, and were now lost. The governor's mind would never rest till the judge had gone mad, and his heart and conceit had been forever crushed.

If the judge had asked for forgiveness, if he had gone to humbly beg pardon in front of his own chamber, if he had renounced his own evil intent and vile plans, he might have thought of some other solution. However, allowing the judge to stay alive would be a disaster for the Mamluks as a group, not just him. If anyone asked him why he had killed the judge, he would explain to them what the judge had done: how he had lost his own legitimacy on the day when he had defied the governor who had appointed him, brazenly opposing the governor of Qus and the governor of Cairo as well. Little by little, he had dared to confront the army's marshal, then the sultan, thus bringing to an end the government of Muslim lands. The danger posed by the judge of Qus needed to be explained. His killing without trial was a mercy and kindly gesture for him, so that the people would not accuse the Mamluks of torturing scholars and men of religion.

The chief judge had to be blamed and reprimanded for choosing such a stupid judge as his deputy from among all the other judges in Egypt and Muslim territories. That was another matter to deal with, with its own day and night, retribution and penalty. Today however, the guard was to stab the judge in the heart three times in his bed, then leave the house, and flee. Who was responsible for his death, they would ask.

Here was the senile old woman, sweeping the house every day and sleeping in front of it. She knew that he had lied to her; he was unable to avenge her son's death who had actually been killed by the father. She would kill the judge because he had released the father and had not brought in the actual culprit. She was going to kill him because, like other poor people in the quarter, she had lost her mind after the plague and drought. She was now confusing good and evil, things lush and withered. The mother had killed him, and she was going to do it as well. She would teach the people of Qus a lesson. After years of famine, abundance would return. The governor would go back to his job, his son would resume his debauched career, and life would resume its proper course.

The guard slunk silently into the judge's bedroom, a poisoned sword in his hand. Perhaps the stabs would not be enough to produce the desired result.

The plan is perfect; the history has actually already been recorded. When 'Amr dies, the people of Qus will be sad for a while. There will be an impressive funeral so that people can calm down and be reassured. He will be buried in an ancient mosque in Qus. Some people will visit his shrine and seek a blessing from him. After a year, the governor will make an agreement with one of the shaykhs, who will claim that 'Amr was a heretic and discuss his strange ideas: how he divorced a woman from her husband in spite of her father's opposition; how he issued legal rulings not based on any Muslim authority, but rather on heterodox ideas. The governor already knows the shaykh who will make these assertions from now on; in fact, he will be talking to the shaykh today even before 'Amr is dead. As soon as the shaykhs decide that 'Amr is indeed a heretic and apostate, they will dig up his bones and remains and throw them for stray dogs to eat. No heretic can be interred in a tomb or mosque. They will be putting the seal on the document recording his disappearance and incineration.

Alive and dead, 'Amr's case is closed. The governor will be guaranteeing the erasure of his career and his punishment in this world and the next. Perhaps he will enter paradise; who knows? But what is important is that the Egyptians are told for sure that he is going to hell. No one can know what will happen to him after death. The historical account has already been written; if he actually died a martyr, that would definitely be dangerous; and, if he died a heretic, then he would be humiliated. How stupid could the judge be, not realizing that his entire fate lay in the governor's hands, and his life as a whole was in his grasp? His career was perfumed with goodness, and now his fate was hell. The amir was dreaming of the day when he could dig up 'Amr's bones with his bare hands, scatter them all around Qus, and proclaim that he was an apostate heretic. The news would soon come that 'Amr was dead; once he was actually dead, information about what had happened would need to be erased from the corporate memory of the people of Qus, not least the way in which the judge had stood up to the governor and the false accusation that he had leveled against the governor's son.

Fakhr ad-din's plan was carefully constructed. The little boy's mother would have to be dragged through the streets and accused of prostitution; she would be cut in two, and the father would die for killing his own son. But it was the mother whose fate had to be exposed to the people of Qus. She would be flayed alive first, then burned to death. Her hair would be cut off and her face burned till she confessed to her prostitution and her foul body and soul. That wretched, malevolent woman who had trumped up evil charges against the son of someone who had bestowed bounty on her through the gift of life and security. What slander, what ingratitude! Once Umm Hasan had been finally dealt with, the amir would devote his attention to the judge's council and his guards. He would station them at the city gates, impose new taxes, and demand that the shaykhs explain the drought as being due to the heresy that had infected the city and witchcraft that pervaded its every quarter. The whole thing was caused by the apostate 'Amr who wanted to alter nature's colors and the course of the Nile. He was turning the sweet water as salty as the putrid fish that Egyptians eat on feast-days. He would impose taxes on the poor first of all, then on merchants. His son, Jamaq, who had been given such a scare by that stupid ape 'Amr, had to be promoted. He would ride his horse through certain quarters, smash some stores, and take the whip to certain salespeople, all so that, whatever happened and whatever he did, no one would ever dare oppose him again. If the scales were out of balance, then ruin was the inevitable conclusion.

'Amr heard the guard come into his room. He caught a glimpse of the sword gleaming brightly in the dark. Death had never frightened him, just loss and deprivation. He was not scared of death today because he was not sure that he was fully conscious. He had lost consciousness for a while, then recovered it. He was dreaming for a while, then awake. He could not stand up. As the guard raised the sword, 'Amr was sitting on his bed thinking about the pledge he had given to a poor mother, one that he would never be able to fulfill because he would be dead. If he kept a knife beside him, he would at least be able to defend himself. But the thought of killing someone had no attraction for him, even if it involved a disloyal guard. Death has its own deadlines and specific days. He wanted to have more time; perhaps there was a way out, but it looked as though this was the end.

He heard the sound of a thick stick striking the guard on the head. It had to be Umm Hasan who had saved him in order to avenge her son. If he died, it would be that much easier for him. Revenge seemed difficult, if not impossible. Even so, he had to swim in the current; self-preservation was an obligation. The killer's death would save him from drowning and madness.

He stayed on his bed, waiting for the fight to be over. All he could see was the sword's shadow; the only sound came from the stick. Then he saw a lamp coming toward him. He heard a loud voice state his name. It had not been Umm Hasan who had hit the guard and dragged him out of the room. It seemed that the second letter that he had sent to someone even more important than the chief judge had reached the person who was to read it.

He heard the command: "To Judge 'Amr ibn Ahmad ibn 'Abd al-Karim from the country's sultan. He demands your presence in Cairo today, indeed now."

For most of the long journey, 'Amr was carried, with guards helping him buy water and food. After several days, he recovered his strength, as he pondered what he would tell the sultan. In fact, he had been thinking about it ever since he had sent the letter to the sultan along with the one to the chief judge. He had taken a chance, lived in hope, and achieved his goal. He was going to meet the sultan. But Jamaq was still free, and the governor was still in charge and exerting his tyrannical hold.

3

"Sultan Az-Zahir Sayf ad-din Barquq," the herald announced loudly.

The sultan entered slowly, his eyes riveted on 'Amr's face. For a moment, their eyes met. Barquq had bulging eyes, and was both tall and bulky. He looked fifty or slightly less. He sat down.

"The judge of Qus," he said as though thinking to himself. "Are you the one who stirs up Egyptians against the Mamluks, and provokes intrigue and rebellion?"

"To the contrary," 'Amr replied immediately, "the one who protects the sultan from damage caused by oppression and rampant injustice."

The sultan gave a sarcastic smile, then spread out his gold-embossed coat.

"Sit here beside me," he said, "while we investigate your activities and explore how the chief judge came to appoint you as a deputy in Qus, even though you're under forty!"

He sat on the sultan's coat. "I'm only a few months younger," 'Amr said. "The amount of time that I've spent acquiring knowledge doubles my age. It's the number of hours spent on learning that we need to count, my Lord. I've never let any time between dawn and evening go by without spending it with legal scholars and books on religion."

"This judge is clearly not to be identified by his modesty," the sultan said, still smiling. "It's his self-delusion that led him to confront the governor and his son."

"As a Mamluk, the governor has another judge, not me," he declared firmly, "but not his son. I am responsible for him."

The sultan nodded in agreement. "The sultan has a project underway," he said, looking at 'Amr. "It's not up to him to solve problems between judges and amirs. But they must cooperate with each other. The information that I have about you leads me to order your dismissal and humiliation before the people. And yet, you have sent me a letter, asking for help and requesting a meeting. What kind of puzzle is this supposed to be?"

*"If a sinful man brings you information, then investigate."**

---

* Qur'an Sura 49:6 [The Chambers]

"Are you accusing the governor whom I appointed of committing sins?"

"How can the sultan expect to probe the governor's inner self and know what he is thinking? People can change, and, as a crime, oppressive conduct can seduce the powerful and mighty."

"Oppression as a crime, those are dangerous words; I certainly don't like them. But you're very brave."

"I've come to ask for your help," 'Amr replied immediately. "You know the governor intends to kill me."

"Are you planning to raise a complaint? I hear you accused him of being ignorant in your council."

"No, I didn't. I simply recited some words from God's book."

"From God's book," the sultan repeated. "Risk and delusion, Judge, risk and delusion, they are the only sources of temptation. They can tempt you just like sin, but not oppression."

"My Lord, you have learned a great deal, studying and becoming familiar with the law. If only your governors would discuss things as you do, duly reflecting and understanding," 'Amr said.

"What do you want from me?"

"Justice."

"Can there be any greater justice than the fact that I'm receiving you in my palace and seating you beside me on the coat that I've spread for you? Religious scholars carry on their shoulders the burdens of this country and its people. I have great respect for them and fully realize how important they are. But they're not immune from making mistakes. Do you agree with me on that point?"

'Amr lowered his head. "No human being is immune from making mistakes," he replied, "but individual interpretation has its own useful role and value. No one does more interpretation than religious scholars."

The sultan looked all around him. "What if a scholar were to issue an opinion that the sultan should be killed? What do you think about that?"

"I've never heard of such a thing before."

"From today onward, you'll be hearing it. You're bound to hear it and understand it. What's your opinion of Sultan Barquq?"

"I've never seen any evil in him."

"Has he done anything to anger God?"

"I don't know the answer to that, my Lord. Not all truths are revealed to me."

"When I responded to the amirs' request and seized power from the boy sultan, As-Salih Hajji, was I a usurper, someone who deserves to be killed? Who's the legitimate sultan? Who inherits the position from his father without any justification apart from his lineage and family? Alternatively, who fights in God's cause, protects the country, and achieves the amir's rank through his deeds and battles? What's your opinion, Judge?"

'Amr remained silent.

"An-Nasir Muhammad's children are not him," the sultan continued. "Even though I can criticize him, he was distinct, an exception to the rule. He was a son of the people, the son of a fighter, but not one himself. In spite of all his achievements, he did not really appreciate the value of Mamluks. Otherwise, he never would have assigned the succession to his own offspring. How has the country come to this pass? Isn't that the case some forty years after An-Nasir's death? How many sultans have lived and survived without there being some intrigue or war? Tell me! What kind of state, what level of weakness and shame have the sons of the people brought to Egypt? Do you know what I want? Egypt deserves better than a mere child as legal heir for the amirs to toy with. Egypt will always need a fighter who is willing to sacrifice himself for the country and Muslim lands and to make it a qibla for religious scholars and a cradle for human existence. Egypt has never had a sultan who ruled through military power, but these sons of the people, children of Mamluks, are incapable of governing. Az-Zahir Qutuz, Baybars, and Qala'un all wrested power over Egypt from the hand of a sultan to whom religious scholars gave legitimacy, solely on the basis of his being a sultan's son. That is even though Islam is not a faith that relies on hereditary succession. In our faith, everyone owns what they have acquired. Isn't that the case?"

'Yes, it is," the judge replied firmly.

"Qala'un is the grandfather figure in all this. He wrested authority from the sons of Baybars. Isn't that so?"

"Yes, it is."

"I'm not looking for such power; I don't want it. No, I responded to the amirs' insistence. The concerns of Muslim lands have been my burden, along with a trust enough to make the very mountains groan. Do you understand what I'm saying?"

"I'm trying, my Lord."

"Religious scholars are not reliable, Judge. They're just like the Mamluks. In this era of ours, their mutual interests are completely intertwined."

"The religious scholar is untouched by any and all evil."

"Can't we agree however that he is not immune?"

"Indeed, he's someone who can get things right and wrong. But the process of interpretation has a distinction and degree that you always understand. Otherwise, you would not have let me sit on your coat."

"Let's return to the matter of the murder of the little boy. I've consulted the chief justice on the verdict of a compensation payment because it was not a pre-planned murder."

'Amr looked all around him. "If the sultan will permit me, I would like to tell him something. But I'm ashamed in front of these other people."

The sultan stood up and signaled to everyone to leave. He then stood in front of the judge, who also stood.

"Give me a guarantee if I speak," the judge said cautiously.

"If you are going to curse amirs and their children, I'll be cutting off your head on the spot, or leaving you to the governor of Qus to do with you whatever he wishes."

'Amr smiled. "Didn't we just agree," he said quietly, "that fighters are different from sons of the people? Mamluks are one thing, and their children are another."

"Now I can understand how you obtained your position: ambition, perspicacity, and cunning—a good deal of cunning. What is it that you want?"

"Give me a guarantee of safety."

"I'll never do that."

'Amr smiled again. "Very well," he said, "I shall speak. But, at least promise me that you'll kill me here in your palace and won't hand over the decision about me to the governor of Qus. Being killed at the sultan's hands is an honor, but, at the hands of the governor of Qus, it's a disgrace that I don't deserve."

"It seems that you're acknowledging me as sultan. Are you?"

"I have always preferred fighters, and still do."

"I promise you that, if I don't like what you have to say, I'll kill you myself and not hand you over to the governor of Qus."

"Egyptians are talking," 'Amr said. "They're cruel about their rulers. Their eyes talk only of defiance; they laugh, they scoff, they pretend to conform. But in their hearts they're always full of disdain, something that only God can see. They separate soul and body. The body may submit to the ruler, but the soul is forever free."

"The Egyptians are in the clear; it's the amirs who have me worried."

"If some amirs conspire against the sultan of Egypt and are joined by a few religious scholars, then it's up to the sultan to clearly establish his justice, absolute and free of all other motivations."

"It's the chief justice who has issued a decree that compensation should be paid in this case."

"The case is much more serious than that. I'm going to speak now with my heart in my hand," 'Amr said.

"What do you mean?"

"My Lord, there's widespread corruption. The governor's son prefers little boys and young men to women. The whole of Egypt is aware of that. What's even more serious is that some Mamluks and their children are doing the same thing. It's reached a point where Egyptians are laughing because, in our era, female prostitutes are losing money; they've started dressing up like boys and shaving their heads to help them find the people they need. I'm speaking freely to you and telling you what I'm hearing and seeing. My heart seeks refuge from Satan. I don't want it to be said that, in the times of Sultan Barquq, a pious Muslim warrior, criminality spread among his own men who preferred boys to women. Were that to happen and Egyptians spread the news far and wide, they would assume that your regime was really weak; your legitimacy would be shaken. Not only that, but Egyptians would start implying that amirs were choosing their Mamluks for their moonlike faces and green eyes, not for their strength. The criterion would be beauty. You surely realize how dangerous this is and what threat it poses to the state and country."

The sultan listened in silence, utter fury surging from his eyes. "How dare you?" he said.

"Kill me, my Lord, if you wish," 'Amr told him. "But it's your own interests that I have at heart, not killing the governor's son. If we execute him, what will the Egyptian people say? That the sultan does not tolerate debauchery and fears God. If Egyptians say that the sultan fears God, then your regime will stay in power until God's determined time for you. You've been talking about warriors who have ruled Egypt, like Baybars. He acquired his legitimacy by fighting vice, confirming his faith, and adhering to God's injunctions."

"How can you think that way? Are you a religious scholar or a politician?"

"A political judge at all times."

"Your malice is alarming; it worries me personally. Your ambition oozes from your eyes. Do you want to be chief judge? Or sultan? Or rather, in your imagination, who do you think has all the power?"

'Amr smiled. "I want to impose the ultimate penalty on the governor's son," he said devoutly. "I want the chief of police to arrest him and bring him here; he's currently a fugitive. I want him to be brought here today. The ultimate penalty will be imposed on him here in Cairo at Bab Zuwayla. Egyptians will come out to celebrate the sultan."

"Aggravating the amirs is no trivial matter. If I behead any Mamluk child, such an action would stir a rebellion against me."

"No, no, it will demonstrate your strength," 'Amr replied gently. "It will deter anyone who's thinking of resisting you or any enemies who are claiming to be friends."

The sultan stared at him. "Who has the real power," he asked, "the sultan or the chief judge?"

"The sultan can dismiss the chief judge," 'Amr replied, "and the chief judge can declare the sultan illegitimate. But, in situations such as those we are now in, the sultan will kill the chief judge in any case, and the Egyptian people will start suggesting that the sultan has no legitimacy. It's a very complicated situation, my Lord, one that relies on both the sultan and the chief judge. Should the sultan issue such a command, he'll seem to be more pious than the chief judge. Not so? Then the chief judge will authorize the payment of compensation. But, if the sultan is to confirm the true nature of his religious belief and the power of his faith, then he will demand that the ultimate penalty be imposed. Egyptians realize that rumors about the Mamluks are false and contrived. They are all sincere and do not prefer young boys; they do not choose on the basis of beauty, but rather of strength."

Barquq looked perplexed. "I'll think about it," he said.

"Too much thinking can befuddle the resolve. The sultan can decide things without needing to hesitate."

"You're kindling an unprecedented fire for both me and you."

"It's a pledge I made to the boy's mother. I have to carry it out," 'Amr said.

"In order to do that, man, are you planning to do away with Egypt's sultan? I've never encountered such vanity!"

"To the contrary, you like it because it reminds you of your power and wars."

"What is it you want?"

"Justice, as I told you before."

The sultan stared at him for a moment. "So, you're fulfilling your pledge and selling yourself to a poor woman who has nothing to give you. Are you a madman or a saint?"

"Maybe both," he replied resolutely. "But first and last, I'm concerned about the sultan. I'm afraid for him."

"What will you give me in exchange for opening the gate that separates us from Yagog and Magog, something that you want to do?"

"My lifelong loyalty," 'Amr replied.

"What if I did something wrong? Would you impose the ultimate penalty?"

"Anyone who has the kind of courage that you do, my Lord, will never do wrong. I'll always support you."

"Because you trust me, or because you want to be chief judge?"

"Everything is preordained," 'Amr said.

"Now you're donning the veil of piety. Never mind! You will have what you want."

The world was turned upside down. The search began for the governor's son, Jamaq, son of Fakhr ad-din. Not only that, but the sultan summoned the governor himself and ordered 'Amr to remain in the palace. 'Amr did not know whether he was a hostage or a prisoner; or perhaps the sultan wanted to protect him. A week later, the sultan summoned him.

"We've found Jamaq," he announced.

"We'll carry out the ultimate penalty on him in full view, in front of the Egyptian people and the religious scholars."

"And the Mamluk amirs?" the sultan inquired.

"Restraint, prevention, and prestige are all properties belonging to the sultan," 'Amr responded persuasively.

"The sultan who doesn't protect his own Mamluks?"

"The sultan who protects all Muslims in the face of injustice."

"You always have the words ready. If I killed you now, wouldn't that be preferable and easier?"

'Amr smiled. "Much easier, of course," he replied. "But it's an opportunity to teach some lessons and establish order. The sultan of Egypt will never miss such an opportunity."

Barquq smiled as he looked at 'Amr. "What do you think?" he asked. "Once the governor's son has been killed, should I get rid of the judge as well?"

"If my Lord has no further need of me, then why not?"

"You know I'll need you."

"And you know that you can always find me."

"Youthful fervor has its own special magic."

The sultan looked around the room. "The Judge 'Amr ibn Ahmad ibn 'Abd al-Karim has the courage of Mamluk soldiers," he said contemplatively, "and the piety of his grandfather, 'Abd al-Karim. I admire you, young man, and the spirit of adventure in your eyes. One day, I'd like to sit down with you and discuss matters of life and death. I've never heard your counsel, nor have I read any of your writings. But now, the penalty of death will be imposed tomorrow after the dawn prayer on Jamaq, son of Fakhr ad-din. You will do it yourself."

"I'm a judge. I don't hold a sword, nor do I cut off people's heads. A policeman needs to do it. I don't hold a personal grudge against the governor that would lead me to kill his son by my own hand."

The sultan nodded and left 'Amr's room. 'Amr was delighted; victory was nigh.

At night, the governor rushed to see the sultan; he prostrated himself at his feet and begged for pardon and forgiveness. If the sultan let his son live, the governor would hand over all his gold, horses, and estates. The sultan lowered his head and seemed to be thinking things over.

"The decision is not mine," he stated. "It's the judge's."

"If anything happens to my son," he responded spontaneously, "I'm going to tear him limb from limb."

"If he suffers any harm," the sultan reacted, "I'll kill you on the spot. From today on, you have no authority over Qus. You've belittled the religious scholars and ruined the sultan's prestige. You'll stay here in Cairo until I decide what to do with you."

The governor looked at him and begged him once again. Guards dragged him out of the palace.

After the dawn prayer and in full public view, the policeman beheaded the governor's son; the head was hung on Bab Zuwayla, with the judge watching. The father's screams emerged from the fiery depths and reached as far as Aleppo and Malatya to the north.

"Go to my house," the judge instructed one of the guards. "You'll find an old woman in shabby clothes sweeping outside the house. Tell her that the Judge of Qus has fulfilled his pledge and imposed the death penalty on the son of the people. 'In retaliation there is life for you, O you people with minds.'"[*]

The governor of Qus took out his sword and swore an oath from his saddle: "By God, if I could do away with the sultan himself, I'd do it. But I'm going to tear you apart, you pride of all judges. I'll watch as your blood flows in front of me. You'll be on the stake, not dying but wishing that you could."

Then he took off on his horse, and some people say that he went to Syria without the sultan's permission, while his scream still shook every quarter of Egypt. Women were whispering, and men shivered. A scene like this was rarely witnessed in Egypt, and so a degree of caution was needed. Perhaps it was just a mirage or confused dream.

Around this encounter the seeds of alarm, tension, confrontation, and anticipation were sown. 'Amr had disagreed with the advice offered by the chief judge; indeed he had opposed it and gone to see the sultan. Such conduct involved obvious insubordination and clear danger to the prestige of the chief judge, his status, and his position. What 'Amr had done was much worse than the crime committed by Jamaq, the governor's son. Through his disgraceful actions, he had challenged his own teachers and defied the community of shaykhs. Going to see the sultan was a sign of something much bigger, a clear desire to curry favor and influence. The chief judge was well aware of 'Amr's ambition, but the fact that 'Amr was married to his daughter, consulted him, and often asked his advice on any number of

* Qur'an Sura 2:179 [The Cow]

issues, reinforced his view that 'Amr was someone who was in quest of knowledge, someone competent who could appreciate the role of shaykhs and religious scholars. He would never be able, nor would he attempt, to distort reality or foment dissent as others had tried. He had always applied himself to serious study, reading closely and asking rigorous questions. In the presence of major religious scholars, he would always look at the floor out of respect, seeking knowledge from whomever he encountered. Now everything was different. The young student had grown up and taken on responsibilities, forcing older scholars to give way. Was this a betrayal? What were his origins? The sultan admired 'Amr because he came from a good family renowned for its piety, faith, and ethics. His father had never stood in front of a religious scholar and had never deceived a sultan. He had worked quietly and cautiously, befriending and reconciling people and never clashing with anyone. His grandfather 'Abd al-Karim had argued with some scholars, but his reputation had done nothing to help him or intercede on his behalf. He had died in the gloomy darkness of prison, a fate that his grandson might share. 'Amr's visit to the sultan was not a fulfilment of any obligation of obedience to the ruler; rather a display of power. Alas for a time when students betray their teacher and mentor! How often 'Amr had claimed to be the chief judge's son. He was still young when his father died, and it was the chief judge who had raised him and taught him things he did not know before. 'Amr was his son by choice and will.

The chief judge pursed his lips, anger eating away at his heart. In fact, he was wishing for a dark fate for his daughter's husband; he would have loved to be able to throw him into the dungeons for a long time.

'Amr did his best to create an atmosphere of peace between them. "I've missed your words and counsel, Shaykh," he said.

"Is that supposed to be sarcastic mockery?" the judge asked coldly.

'Amr was stunned. "What have I done to annoy my father and teacher?" he asked.

The chief judge shook his head and stroked 'Amr's shoulder. "You want to be chief judge, don't you?" he said. "You cozy up to the sultan, spreading your wings, then retracting them. I know."

'Amr was shocked. "I seek refuge in God!" he said. "You're the finest judge and the greatest of scholars. Whatever I do, I can never be half the person that you are."

The chief judge gave him a mocking smile. "You're not concerned about justice and the child's fate. It's a personal need you feel, a conceit in your heart for which there's no cure."

"No, I swear to you: it's a pledge I gave to a woman who has nothing save God."

"You're the executor of God's will on earth?"

"Justice is always His goal. We strive to achieve it, even though '*the soul incites to evil.*'"*

"It's your own soul that incites you to do evil. Your ambition is going to kill you and destroy your future. If you waited a while till the right time comes, then you might attain what you want."

"My shaykh and mentor, my soul is devoted to you."

He was silent for a while as he looked round for his two sons.

"How are Ahmad and Husayn?" he asked.

The chief judge showed a sudden burst of enthusiasm. "They're both fine," he said. "Their aunt's bringing them up as though she were their mother, even more than that perhaps. Her heart's full of goodness. My daughter Ruqayya is a good match for you. She's bringing up her sister's children."

'Amr was stunned by this suggestion. It alarmed him, and he said nothing.

"Are you dreaming of marrying Ruqayya?" the chief judge asked angrily.

"You've honored me once already with a linkage to your family," 'Amr replied. "My grief over the loss of my wife is still with me; no one else can take her place."

"Her sister is just like her."

'Amr put on a display of deep emotion. "Give me time to get over my loss and learn to live with it. There can be no other woman in my life after my wife's death."

The chief judge stared angrily at 'Amr's expression. "You're never going to marry again," he asked, "or buy yourself a slave girl?"

'Amr looked uncomfortable. "I'm not going to get married any time soon. You know what I think about slave girls. I've dedicated my life to knowledge and work. When fate wills it, I'll need someone who can tolerate my burdens. Ruqayya is still young; she wants a simple life with someone who can appreciate her. It's not fair for her to inherit her sister's hardships and take care of two boys and me as well."

"To the contrary, she's the sum of all the linkages between us that you want to destroy. Tell me the truth, 'Amr, has the sultan offered you the post of chief judge?"

"He hasn't," 'Amr replied firmly, "and he won't."

"If he did, what would you say?"

"I'm not qualified as long as you are still here. You're my father and mentor."

"You'd turn it down?"

"Yes, I would," 'Amr responded definitively.

"Will you promise me to turn it down, just as you promised that poor wounded woman to avenge her son's death?"

* Qur'an Sura 12:53 [Joseph]

'Amr was silent for a few moments. "I promise you," he replied, "that I won't accept the position as long as you are in it."

The chief judge nodded. "Now go and see your two boys," he said.

'Amr went to see his two boys, full of longing as he filled his gaze with their young faces and stroked their shoulders. He spoke to them nonstop, his love and worry evident from his words and gestures. He listened to them and quizzed them both, asking about their health, their studies, their aunt, and their grandfather. He wanted to take them back with him to his house in Qus, but he had to be careful; the burden was huge and the trial never ending. They both had tears in their eyes as 'Amr said good-bye. Perhaps for the first time ever, he hugged them as hard as he could. He assured them that, in two months at the most, they would be together. After that, they would never be separated again.

'Amr looked in on the chief judge to say goodbye.

"Youth has its dash and adventure," the judge warned. "You've been betting on the wrong horse, 'Amr!"

"I don't understand what you mean, my revered teacher," 'Amr replied. "I'm not doing anything to anger God."

"Barquq isn't sultan for this country. He stole the throne from the legitimate sultan. He brought his own folk from his homeland. They've made a show of being Muslims, but they're actually adhering to their old faith. He wants to rule the country using his own tribe and coterie, just like the Quraysh infidels."

'Amr look at him in amazement. "Are you comparing the sultan of Egypt with the Quraysh infidels?" he asked.

"Barquq has betrayed his trust. He was the army's marshal, and wrested authority away from the legitimate sultan. He deserves to be killed."

'Amr stayed where he was, incredulous. Was the chief judge jealous, or did he have something else in mind that he did not know about?

"My teacher," 'Amr responded defiantly, "forgive me. I don't understand. Why has he now turned into a traitor after six years of rule, and not from the very beginning?"

"Because he acts without consulting religious scholars, because he's brought in his own tribe and family, because he prefers Circassian Mamluks to Turks, because he behaves like a pharaoh, and because he uses people as factions! I want to warn you, so you won't find yourself opposing religious scholars and shaykhs. Barquq is a traitor and usurper. He bases his choice of people on their lineage and removes scholars from their posts at will, without any kind of religious restraint or respect for their status as guardians of the faith."

'Amr's response was clear and firm. "Forgive me, teacher, but I can only see good in the sultan. Farewell!"

As 'Amr left Cairo on his way back to Qus, he was feeling greatly relieved, but also not a little disgusted at his father-in-law's jealousy and hatred and his preference for personal benefit over that of the Egyptian people in general. It was almost as though he wanted to get rid of the sultan because of his envy for 'Amr. What silliness and arrogance! Truths emerge, and humans reveal feeble heads and weak hearts.

⟶

What had happened was crazy, an event to overturn the scales of history and presage destruction. The people of Qus were not used to seeing justice actually carried out, to such dogged determination and such nonsense. The judge of Qus was an Egyptian: how—not just one, but a thousand hows—had he managed to execute that son of the people, the Mamluk governor's own son? Who could explain it all, and who could compose songs based on such a legendary fable? The execution of a son of the people would inevitably be greeted with skepticism. Jamaq had not actually died; he had disappeared somewhere.

Why did the sultan himself claim he had died?

Why is the sultan scared of the Egyptian people's feelings? Is he even interested in them? Does he want to spread justice among them or to take revenge on the Mamluk amirs? History provides lessons, examples, and stories. Sultans come and sultans go, and the Egyptian people put up with it all. One sultan protects, while another changes things. One of them forbids wine-drinking, builds mosques, and guarantees people heaven, and, all the while, Egyptians are suffering. Another kills people, imposes taxes, and sends out spies to cut out people's tongues, and, once again, Egyptians suffer through it all. One judge pretends to be pious, another claims to have knowledge; they too suffer. A judge tries to spread justice, and along come famines to eliminate the Egyptian people. A sultan lowers taxes, and the plague arrives to finish off anyone trading and conducting reforms. There is no hope of a cure if it is followed by illness, no justice if followed by tyranny, and no piety if followed by debauchery. Then, along comes the judge of Qus, 'Amr ibn Ahmad ibn 'Abd al-Karim. He sifts Egyptians and delivers multiple slaps!

What did he do? What idiocy did he commit? What are the consequences, and who will be paying for them? Inevitably, they will all be paying the price, they and their children. The people of Qus were divided into three groups. One regarded the judge's actions as insanely risky. He did not know what to do with Qus in its entirety. Once or twice in the past, it had happened that one family in a particular town had committed some idiocy, and the powers-that-be had decided to burn the entire town and level it with the ground. That was now bound to happen with the people of Qus. If only the judge had never set foot in Qus, had never known about it or where it was. If only that woman had died along with her son and had not sought the judge's help.

"Let the boy go to hell," they kept saying, "so that the people of Qus can survive."

What oblivion lay in wait for them, and what cost? All the children in the city would now die because of one child. All the women would be widowed because the mother of that boy wanted revenge. The stake would be stuck in every single man, because that rash judge was someone who had killed a son of the people. Their fate had been written long ago.

Another group was worried about what would happen to their trade and the pilgrimage route, to Qus's reputation which had been trampled in the dirt by the judge after being God's blessed land. People in the Maghreb would now be whispering to each other that sons of the people in Qus rape children and the governor of Qus was unable to defend his own son. Not only that, but, if the governor of Qus, with all his power, could not stop his son being killed, then what about merchants from everywhere? If it so happened that one of their children committed such an act, what would be their fate? This was a crime. Qus's reputation had vanished as a result of this shameful action taken by the judge. Justice was for the rich, and the protection of the rich from the greed of poor people. For the judge of Qus to think for a single second that he could wrest from the rich and powerful on behalf of the poor, that would be a reason for condemning and ostracizing him till the day of his death—and, God willing, that would be soon. What trade could make a profit? What money would provide a blessing when rich people could be condemned to death? As though rich and poor were equals, and everyone knows that is not the case.

Still another group—and there were a lot of them—were mostly silent. The amirs thought there were few of them, a paired number no higher than eight. In their opinion, the judge of Qus was the man of justice, and his decisions were a beacon of hope in an era of darkness. As long as goodness was victorious on occasion, then life was worth living. As long as life was stable for a while, the burdens could be tolerated, and the shouts needed to be directed at injustice. Courage was the province of heroes and immortals; cowardice, of everyone else.

When 'Amr entered Qus, people gathered and surrounded his horse and guards. They looked scared and insecure. The mother of the young boy rushed up and called out to him. He stopped and looked at her. She collapsed on the horse's foot and started weeping loudly and keening bitter laments.

"Have faith in God," he told her firmly. "Those who kill will be killed, even if it takes a while. Now pray and thank your God."

She did not react, but kept on crying, maybe for an hour. He could not get the horse to move for fear of hurting her. Eventually she finished.

"People of Qus," she shouted, "this man fulfilled his pledge. In the cause of truth, he has no fear of sword or amir. As long as I'm alive, I'm his servant."

"I seek refuge in God," he responded vigorously. "By God, I only acted the way I did because it's my job and my duty. Come on now, stand up."

She stood up and started running behind the horse. Everyone felt uneasy. Women came out of their houses, and men kept their heads lowered; no one could tell whether it was out of shame, fear, or respect. His eyes were looking for Dayfa's eyes as usual, but did not locate them.

Next morning, he returned to work as though nothing had happened. He listened as his students and assistants praised him, while his enemies feared and dreaded him. He savored some moments of victory and absolute power, but did his best not to swallow too much of it in case it made him drunk.

He did not see her, and she did not pass by or stop in front of his house. She never pretended that she needed to ask him a question, and she did not ask her friends to lure him or see him.

For three days, he hesitated before asking about Dayfa, but he could not keep it up. He had heard nothing about her and was no longer certain about her eyes. The longing that he was feeling inside only increased the longer she stayed away and left him with his doubts. Had her father kept her inside and stopped her going out? Had she been playing a game, and now she was bored with it? If that was the case, then what was he going to do? Would it not be a better idea to forget her and be married to the chief judge's daughter? She could raise his two sons. Why was he feeling so attached to this girl from the far south?

What was it about her that was so different from other women? Never for a single day had he been in love and felt such passion. His primary goal was knowledge and achievement. In his search for a wife, piety and serenity were his principal concerns, not passion and liveliness in the eyes' gaze. He had never simply followed his desires, and, at his age now and with all he had achieved, he was not about to start. Why follow his desires, when he could now make her his own property; why long for her when she could well be in his hands within days? If she could use magic and a different kind of beauty to attract him, no matter. She had done it, and that was the end of it. Perhaps if he saw her today or tomorrow . . . maybe if he could be sure that she wanted what he did. If she wanted to see him, she would be looking for him as she always did. Maybe she was toying with him, as he expected. Such obvious flirting only involves those who like to play, then get bored and disappear. Maybe she was now happy with her husband and had settled down with him.

He did not hesitate for long. He sent one of his assistants to bring the Abyssinian woman to him. When she arrived, he feigned a casual posture in asking how Dayfa was. The woman replied languidly that she was fine, no more, no less.

"Is she married?" he asked nervously.

"My Lord Judge, you'd know if she had been married."

"Does her father stop her going out?"

"I don't know, but I don't think so."

So, she was toying with him. He would close his heart and tear it open if he thought about her again. Today he would forget her, and tomorrow he would be married to Ruqayya. The whole thing with this girl would be forgotten. The power and mind that he possessed were properties of judges. But for that, if he kept panting after her like a teenager, it would be better for him to be a poet wandering around the desert, leaving matters of justice to the intelligentsia.

"Fine," he said sternly. "I just wanted to check on her and make sure her father wasn't harming her. Thank you!"

He went into his room and lay down on the bed. Today he had made up his mind to forget her. Tomorrow he would send a message to the chief judge, agreeing to be married. Why not? He needed someone to look after his two sons, and it did not really matter who it was. Even if Dayfa's laughter and those lips and bright eyes of hers kept looming in his memory, he would still put it all to one side. Not only that, he would scold and punish her and maybe decapitate his own perfidious memory.

That night he almost slept.

Next morning, he started work again. He patiently received congratulations and praise, doing his best to stop the glowing words from reaching his heart. If he allowed that to happen, he would be no different from the amirs. Modesty is a characteristic trait of great people, but a small amount of praise is also desirable. His kind of courage was unprecedented, whether in Qus or Cairo, and during the Ayyubid, Abbasid, and even Fatimid dynasties, a rare courage and a fighter's challenge. He knew and understood; he wanted the praise to be a promotor of justice, and not an impediment to it. He was well aware of the heart's ambitions and its craving for achievement, but he wanted that instinct to work for the defense of the poor and weak, not personal glory. That was a more cognizant and worthy goal.

His meeting came to an end, and he was about to return to his house; his horse, a gift from the sultan, even more beautiful and powerful than the one that the governor had taken from him, was waiting outside. Without asking permission, Dayfa came into the room, as she usually did with her two friends, the women from Yemen and Abyssinia. He only had a student with him.

"An old lady needs your advice, my Lord," she told him quietly.

He smiled. Had he done it? Had his heart started pounding? Had he told the student to leave so he could talk to the old woman alone? Had he really done all that?

No sooner had the student left than the two old women went out and stood by the door, as though to keep watch during the meeting. No sooner had they left than she lifted the veil off her face.

"My Lord has inquired after me, asking how I was," she whispered longingly. "I've come to reassure him that I'm fine as long as he is. While I've not known anything about his fate, I've not been fine. I've been distracted, like cats waiting in the dry Qus desert."

"You have to stop coming here," he told her firmly. "It's dangerous to take risks like this."

She lowered her head and sat in front of him. "I made up my mind not to bother you," she said. "I would stay at home. Pouring out the inner secrets of the heart in front of the judge weakens and humiliates the soul. I don't deserve a mere glance from your eyes, and yet the questions keep nagging me."

He looked closely at her. "Ask your questions," he said.

She looked unsure of herself. "I want to ask about certainty," she said. "How does it enter the heart and soothe the soul?"

He responded without thinking: "Through prayer, application, training the heart, and avoidance of yearnings."

"If the devil were to toy with my heart and give me hopes that I can't handle, what should I do?"

"What certainty are you talking about?"

Their eyes met.

"Achieving certainty demands effort and strength," she said. "Is holding on to an impossible love madness or bewitchment? Or even affliction?"

"We've talked about love before," he replied, trying his best to stay objective. "Think about something else that can restore your well-being."

She moved her hand close to his. "It's as though happiness has never entered my heart before," she said hesitantly, "and suffering has never found my house. I float in the air, like particles of dust; every day between hope and despair, pain and pleasure."

Swallowing hard, he looked at her and kept his gaze on her face. "I used to tell myself," she said gently, "that men in our country preferred white-skinned women from the north rather than dark-skinned ones from the south. What beauty is there in my features, my Lord?"

He stared at her hand, now close to his, nor daring to touch it.

"I wonder, Dayfa," he asked, "what is it you want from me?"

She looked shy and said nothing.

"If I asked to be married to you," he said involuntarily, "would you agree?"

She did not know her own self as she grabbed his hand in hers. She said nothing, totally unable to speak.

Their fingers were intertwined.

"Will you agree?" he asked. "Why? You really want to be married to the judge of Qus? What is it you want? To be rid of your father and his ruthlessness? Why do you hover around me, sometimes blocking out the sun, but also brightening the entire world? Do you admire my sense of justice and my position? Tell me the truth!"

She looked at her fingers entwined in his. "My Lord," she told him, "you don't know a lot about love."

He let go of her hand, feeling as if he had now woken up from his doze.

"You love me?" he asked. "That's not enough. As I've told you before, love weakens the resolve and leads the heart to perdition."

Dayfa stood up. "My Lord," she replied bitterly, lowering her head, "I don't possess your strength of will. I don't know how to control the love that spreads itself through my heart. It's a love that's stripped of all purpose and goal; a love for your heart and soul, not for your position and your learning. From among the whole of humanity, my Lord, I exist from my own heart and for it. Forgive me for speaking firmly and boldly: you're making me like a slave girl, not a free woman. I swear to you that I've only ever behaved this way with you."

He was doing his best to appear resolute. "How do you come to know so much about love," he asked, "when you're only seventeen?"

Dayfa looked away. "I've heard about it from Maryam and Zubayda," she replied gently, "and saw it in the eyes of my tortured mother. I've read some poetry, but have only recently begun to appreciate its true essence. Maryam says that love is like a cruel prison guard. If the beloved disappears, it can block the sunlight; it can lock the heart's recesses to anyone except the beloved. It is always painful, and can raise weakness from the very sea depths. Strength cannot defeat it, and swords are unable to check it. At first, I didn't believe it. I wanted a love that would please me and make me happy; a serene, modest kind of love like domestic cats, not something vicious and scary like hyenas. You've understood and learned, my Lord."

"What have I understood and learned?"

"You've come to understand how the light goes out of my eyes whenever you're far away from me," she said affectionately, as she stared into his eyes, "and how my heart throbs when you're around me. How I'm short of breath whenever I am worried about you, how my breast expands whenever you look at me . . . my Lord . . ."

He interrupted her as her words were breaching every kind of barrier. "You'll be married," he told her.

She headed slowly for the door. He stopped her, his mind in a stupor and his life in her hands for a few seconds.

"Dayfa," he told her softly, "I'll be married to you this month."

She gave him a sad look and was about to open the door.

"That may be impossible," she muttered, "just like achieving perfection. You have ability surpassing that of the Mamluk amirs. Stubbornness and determination make you on a par with jinn and angels. Even so, I don't believe we're in heaven."

"What's that you said?" he asked, part in anger, part in distress. "Why such pessimism?"

She hesitated for a moment and looked first at the door, then at his face. She moved away from the door and buried her head in his chest.

The shock left him frozen in place, not knowing if he should push her away or scold her for this unexpected and unaccountable behavior. Should he be reprimanding her because she had managed to extract so much passion from deep inside him, whereas, for a while, he had been assuming that his mind was what kept things under control? Should he push her away because she was roiling his carefully regimented world? Maybe she was a devil or sorceress come to test his strength, a kind of trial whose dimensions, along with the extent of his own loss, he did not know.

She clung to his chest, her hand resting over his heart. "My father won't agree," she whispered, "he'll never agree."

"He'll agree," he replied firmly. "He has no choice."

As he raised his hand, he did not know whether to push her away or run his hand over her hair and pin it back as he really wanted to do. He left his arm in the air, while his heart was beating hard. With a fresh affection he did run his hand through her hair, while passion scrambled and erased every avenue.

She kept her hand over his heart. "You can extend justice all around you," she said sadly, "but I'm not sure you can give me this dream of eternal happiness in your arms. Perhaps I can feel your heart today, but tomorrow maybe not. Forgive me. How I wish I possessed your power and strength!"

He sighed slowly, stopping himself from hugging her to his chest as she deserved and he wanted. If he put his arm around her waist and felt her breast, he would dissolve and vanish inside his own body. If he ran his hand over every part of her as he was dreaming of doing, if he simply embraced her as he longed to do, if . . . he could not stop this passion.

He lifted his hand, then moved gently away from her. "Tomorrow you'll see," he said. "Tomorrow you'll know that you're mine. That's inevitable."

She lowered her veil to hide her cascading tears. "I love you, my Lord," she said.

He remained silent, trying hard to recover his poise, and, at the same time, regretting that he had not given her a big hug and covered her in kisses as he dreamed. What kind of imagination and heart did someone in quest of justice possess? What was the shame and reproof he was bringing on himself?

She went out, leaving him at sixes and sevens in his own chamber, not knowing how things had reached this point or what would be the end of this curse and passion. If only she had never come, if only his mind had won, if only he had left her and married Ruqayya, if only he had asked the sultan to let him leave Qus altogether, if only he had become chief judge! Many dreams. He stared at his hand and touched his chest where she had been and stayed, where she had traced the outlines of the rest of his life. Such goals involved plans and specific timing. He had to start using his mind again; the heart always blinds the vision. Tomorrow he would summon her father, and he would agree; in spite of himself, he would agree. If people in Qus started whispering about the judge's bullying and oppression, he would pay no attention. Her father's error and hatred were both well known. 'Amr understood both of them and knew how to exploit them. The love element had to remain a secret; the negotiations could go ahead.

———

For just a few seconds, they stared at each other. In her father's eyes he could see the hatred and loathing.

"Merchant Ridawi," he proclaimed loudly, "I've asked to see you today for two personal reasons: firstly, to clarify something for you, and secondly, to offer you my assistance."

The father stared hatefully at him, but said nothing. The judge started explaining to him the legal process regarding a girl's agreement to marriage. That was preferable and more proper even with the existence of a guardian. God's punishment for those who forced girls to marry and treated them like slave girls was severe. Compulsion has no place in religion. If the girl in question is young and does not know her own interests, then attempts should be made to persuade her through fair means. God has demanded that we employ wisdom and good counsel to summon people to His path. When it comes to a lesser goal than that, then it is the father's duty to talk to his daughter and offer her advice.

The people present all nodded in their approval of the judge's wisdom, piety, distinction, and ability to persuade. He continued, noting that the bad customs that people in Qus were following had to stop. Inherited traditions were not religion. As God says in the Qur'an, *"Say, my Lord has ordered justice."** Anything soiled by the suspicion of injustice must be avoided.

The father lost patience. "Is the judge happy for my daughter to stay like this, with no husband and no restraint?" he asked. "She befriends strangers, and people keep saying that she's a sorceress or bewitched."

"She's your daughter," the judge replied firmly. "Talk nicely about her in this company. What's the point of an absent husband who cannot avert temptation or protect her from sin?"

"But he was full of regret when he came back," her father said enthusiastically. "He wanted to cohabit with her, but you made them divorce, my Lord. You made me give him back everything he had paid."

The father was about to go on and say that this was not justice. But he did not dare annoy the judge, so he said nothing.

"We'll search for another husband for your daughter," the judge said in a monotone. "She'll have to consent. Do you hear me? If she doesn't agree, then she won't marry the man."

"My Lord," the father said by way of challenge, "that goes against everything we've been brought up with, and everything that scholars and shaykhs in our country have decreed."

The judge interrupted him: *"When they commit an abomination, they say: We found our fathers doing it, and God has commanded us to do so. Say: God does not ordain abomination. Do you say against God things that you do not know? Say: My Lord has commanded justice. God Almighty has spoken the truth."†*

"What abomination is there in veiling and marrying off my daughter?"

"The abomination comes from the heart's injustice or that of other people. Forcing your daughter to marry is a major injustice."

The father seemed to think that the judge was not from their country or faith. He was talking about love, seeking the impossible, and emboldening women against men. Every Muslim had the right to kill or banish this judge; the sultan's affection for him was only because he was a relatively new convert to Islam and came from a country with no previous knowledge of the Muslim faith.

---

* Qur'an Sura 7:29 [The Heights]
† Qur'an Sura 7:28–29 [The Heights]

"You don't seem convinced by what I've been saying," the judge declared. "No matter. As long as I'm judge of Qus, you'll not marry off your daughter against her will. I hereby make it a condition for every guardian that his daughter has to consent before the marriage."

Everyone present gaped in amazement, but no one dared say a word.

"My Lord," the father said gently, "the people of Qus have their own ancient traditions which cannot be changed. To do so will lead to bloodshed and destruction. From the cradle, my daughter has been promised to her cousin or someone from her household and family."

"I'm not concerned about what the people of Qus do," the judge declared. "Anything contrary to Islamic doctrine is heresy and tradition. It must be stopped."

"What is it you want from me, my Lord?"

"Forget about the husband who's been divorced. I'm going to look personally for a suitable husband for your daughter, someone who will shelter her and give you more gold than that absent husband. There are lots of Muslim men; everyone here would be glad to offer protection to a Muslim girl."

The merchant gave him a hateful look. "Do you really want me to forget about the man whom I chose for my daughter, my Lord, and, while I'm still alive, let the judge of Qus choose a husband for her? What else do you expect, my Lord? For me to expose her face in front of tyrants and every applicant, as though she were a slave girl, and then ask for her opinion, as though she were a man in my own meeting room? Your demands will cause bloodshed."

"Whose blood?"

"My daughter's first, and then her mother who hasn't brought her up properly."

"If you kill her," he said in a vicious tone, "I'll chop your head off and hang your body by the city gates as a warning to all tyrants and slanderers."

"Forgive me, my Lord," the merchant replied fearfully. "I didn't mean that. I was just suggesting . . ."

'Amr interrupted him. "This session's gone on too long," he said. "I've no more time for this. The judge hereby commands you to treat your wife and daughter well and believe in God in the way you behave toward them. He hereby orders you to find her a husband whom she will agree to marry. There's no harm in showing her face to men who seek her hand. But she must agree to it. Do you understand? You must obey my instructions . . ."

The merchant gave him another hateful look. "I will obey your instructions, my Lord."

He gave a nod to indicate that the merchant could leave. Anger was eating his heart, and the battle between the merchant and him seemed to be fully engaged.

He tossed to left and right on his bed, angry at times, and distracted at others, but longing all the time.

He had to be patient. After a while, he would be able to be married to her without arousing too many suspicions. Her divorce was long since passed. It would not be long: a month, twenty days, two weeks. He had to be patient, not too impetuous or hasty. If she behaved like a child, it would be up to him to behave like a sensible adult, or at least to try. She was not seventeen, wandering in the desert with the animals. He had responsibilities, children, and maybe enemies as well. People have to bear their own responsibilities.

After performing the dawn prayer, he headed for his council chamber. He asked Zubayda, the woman from Yemen, to come. When she arrived, he asked her how Dayfa was. She replied that Dayfa was fine. He told Zubayda that he wanted to make sure she was safe and well. He was going to pass by her house every morning on his way to his council chamber so he could see her, until the time came when they would be married. That moment would not be long now. In less than a month, he would be married to her.

In the morning, he passed by her house. She was standing in front of the house with her veil lowered. Her eyes gleamed when she saw him, and their eyes met. A deep affection took root in his heart, and he could see fate smiling in her lovely pupils. Every day eyes only came together and smiled. The promise was renewed, and the heart was soothed till the moment arrived. Now he only wanted to see her as his wife. This time, he would not be able to avoid hugging her to his chest and kissing her as he dreamed and desired. Just days, and he would ask to be married to her. Her father would have no choice.

News reached him that made him very happy. The chief judge of the Maliki legal school had decided to pass by his house on the way to the pilgrimage.

People told him that 'Abd ar-rahman ibn Khaldun, the Maliki judge, had heard about the courage of the judge of Qus, the imposition of the death penalty on the governor's son, and the judge's insistence on the application of justice in spite of threats from the amir and his obvious power. He had also been told about the profuse welcome that the sultan had given to the judge and the way the sultan had spread out his coat for the judge to sit on. The different judges of the four schools of Islamic law kept whispering to each other that 'Amr was about to be promoted to an even higher and more important position; his relationship with the sultan was not as open and pure as some people thought. In return, he was bound to defend the sultan and pray for him in pulpits, even though he was a usurper who wanted to put an end to the lineage of Sultan Qala'un. He had gradually seized control from the young boy, Salah ad-din Hajji. The story told by some amirs close to him was that they had forced him to take over the government of Egypt and Syria because of problems both ancient and modern. Scholars whispered and acknowledged that that was far from the truth.

The amir, the former governor of Qus, had traveled to Syria and attached himself to the deputy in charge of Aleppo, Yalbugha al-'Umari. Religious scholars alluded, with a certain amount of envy and a good deal of certainty, to the fact that 'Amr was ambitious but had little actual knowledge. His decisions were often peculiar; instead of individual interpretation, he was promoting discord and heresy. He despised inherited tradition and customs. 'Amr was not qualified to be judge of Qus or even a mosque teacher. He was a social climber and hypocrite, no more. He did not speak like a religious scholar, nor did he adhere to their opinions. If the sultan were to decide . . . if he were to appoint him chief judge, there would certainly be a revolution, and it might well be the end of the sultan himself.

'Abd ar-rahman ibn Khaldun had heard all this from the judges of the four Islamic schools of law. He listened with circumspection and tremendous interest as he anticipated the opportunity to meet 'Amr and understand his goals. He might be able to make him aware of the enormous danger he was facing, not merely from the amir whose son he had had executed in front of himself, but also from scholars in Egypt and other Muslim lands—something that, if he realized it, was much more dangerous for him.

'Amr welcomed Ibn Khaldun warmly and slaughtered some animals to celebrate. They sat together, eating and chatting. 'Amr seemed excited; he looked happy, as though he were totally unaware of the damage or the likelihood of his downfall; or perhaps instead it was a sign of his youth and passion.

Ibn Khaldun smiled. "Judge of Qus," he said, "your reputation has reached as far as the Maghreb and beyond."

"Ibn Khaldun's reputation is much greater. It's an honor for Egypt that you are the Maliki chief judge."

"I was . . ."

"Excuse me?"

"You're not following the news, my son. Forgive me, but I'll call you 'my son.' . . . I'm no longer chief judge. I was aware and expected it. It's happening in every country. Rivalries are vicious, and human hearts are full of delusion."

"They plotted against you? Which shaykhs? What learning do they possess?"

"There's rivalry everywhere. In Egypt, scholars will accept you for a while and give you the opportunity to work until you say something to annoy them. In that way, they're the actual sultans. 'Amr, beware of trusting any sultan. In scholars' hands, religious learning is like a sword. If it doesn't cement their authority, they dispense with it."

"You mean Sultan Barquq?"

"To tell you the truth, I wasn't referring to him specifically. What's your own opinion of 'Abd ar-rahman ibn Khaldun?"

"He's a scholar who's written books with enough knowledge to fill all the gaps in the libraries of Baghdad."

Ibn Khaldun smiled derisively. "He was imprisoned in Fez because the governor loathed him. This scholar was not allowed to travel or leave the country. He came to Egypt, hoping eagerly to find a new location. He was deprived of his own family because the governor in Tunis kept them as hostages. When the governor of Egypt persuaded him to send them to Alexandria, then . . . everything came to an end."

He was silent for a moment. "This journey is not a normal pilgrimage," he said, tears streaming down his face. "It's to fill up a hole in the depths of my being, one dug with fire and loss."

'Amr lowered his head. "I heard what happened," he said. "It's God's will."

"It's God's will that my wife and son should drown in the sea on their way to Egypt, but it wasn't God's will that I couldn't travel with them from Tunis to Egypt. That was an order from the governor. They have neither decency nor legitimacy. What's the difference between Mamluks, Mongols, and Ottomans?"

'Amr gaped in amazement. "My dear Shaykh, forgive me," he said. "How can you compare Mamluks and Mongols?"

"Timur Lang's a Muslim, right? The Ottomans are Muslims too. Is Sultan Barquq a Muslim? Which of them are Arabs? Neither one, nor the other, nor the other!"

"I've encountered nothing but good from Sultan Barquq," 'Amr insisted. "I'm convinced that the hatred that religious scholars have for him is for their own personal interests. He's protecting the country from ruin and restoring its power. In fact, there's a huge difference between an invader and someone who guards the home. To me, the difference is obvious. The Ottomans have no interest in protecting Egypt or centralizing their authority over it. Timur Lang may have been a Muslim, but he would never have made Egypt a center of Islamic civilization. For him, the country was just spoils, not a particular goal for him. For Mamluks, Egypt is their homeland; they have no other; for them it's mother and heart around which the world revolves. How do you see Egypt at this point, Shaykh?"

"It's the heart of the world," 'Abd ar-rahman replied, "the focus of religious learning and knowledge. There's no doubt about that. In spite of my love for Qus, Cairo is the world's capital and garden of scholarship. Moons and stars get their light from its scholars. To quote the senior scholar in Fez: 'those who have not seen Cairo, do not know the glory of Islam.'"

"That's because the Mamluks spare no effort in promoting learning and building schools. For them, Egypt is the compass of victory. Should it be defeated or weaken, then their wind will be gone forever . . ."

"Perhaps."

"Are you angry at the sultan, Shaykh, because you're no longer chief judge?"

"'Amr, my son," Ibn Khaldun said quietly, "listen to me carefully. Religious scholars and shaykhs should only concern themselves with knowledge. Rulers and sultans can provide no sense of security. What will remain after you die are your books, your knowledge, and your students. Any encouragement that you receive from sultans is for a particular goal and purpose."

'Amr remained silent.

"It could be," 'Abd ar-rahman continued, "that we tend to follow our own inclinations when it comes to the power of the sultan and his enemies. But the need for self-preservation first of all and the continuity of religious knowledge has to be your primary goal; that knowledge always has to come first. If it requires extolling the sultan or criticizing someone else, then no matter. But never forget the main goal."

'Amr did not look convinced. He had pledged his loyalty and believed in it to his very bones. That was to Sultan Barquq.

"Even if the sultan of Egypt is affected by the jealousy of religious scholars," 'Amr insisted, "and has deprived you of your post as chief judge, he's still given you a place in mosques where you can teach your students. He has treated you well, dear Shaykh, and honored you. I'm aware that the Bahri Mamluks hate him, believing that he prefers the Circassian Mamluks to them. But that's no reason to depose him."

'Abd ar-rahman smiled. "When you support him and use him to remove the Bahri Mamluks, what's going to happen to you? Will they kill you? If their hearts are full of mercy, they'll expose you and bring you down as though you're a horse thief, not a religious authority. Al-Muntasir is bound to take revenge on you. That's why you need to look for Al-Muntasir and support him. Barquq's finished, 'Amr. His agreement to execute a son of the people is a final attempt to improve his image, not done out of any love of justice."

"Forgive me, Shaykh, but I don't agree with you. You've met Barquq and know him from up close. We don't need to make decisions based on whims. I support him because I'm convinced of his justice, not out of either fear or risk."

'Abd ar-rahman shook his head. "I know what you mean," he said, "and I respect your opinion, even though it goes against my own. I can support a sultan on the surface, but, deep down, my support is for religious learning and scholars. Sultans and scholars are always engaged in a power struggle. Fair enough. Tell me, 'Amr, how have the Egyptian people reacted to the news of this reappearance of justice?"

"Your sarcasm reminds me of Egyptians. So now, you're one of them!"

"Their sarcasm has a different flavor to it. Their love of order and stability is different from that of all other forward-looking countries. I'm going to write a lot about them, their view of rulers and government, their customs and festivals. If justice has to clash with stability, I wonder what Egyptians will do."

"I don't know. You're the one studying their customs."

'Abd ar-rahman looked sad. "I wonder," he asked slowly, "if I circumambulate the Ka'ba seven times, will that extinguish the love I feel in my heart for my wife and son, or inflame it? Initiative can fill the gap in the heart, and worship of God keeps us calm till an appointed day. That's our world at play, spinning us around as it narrows and expands. All we can do is abide ourselves in patience and keep trying."

'Amr sympathized with him, a feeling mixed with a fear for his two sons and his own fate and hers. He was determined that she would be his, filling his house with her passion and liveliness. His two boys would come back, and he would live with everyone he loved. He would come home at night to take her in his arms and kiss her as he hoped and dreamed.

"I can see love's gleam in your eyes," 'Abd ar-rahman said. "I'm afraid, 'Amr, that you've accelerated your own end and that of the sultan as well. In that case, you have to support him. You've finished him off!"

'Amr smiled. "You're joking again," he said. "Our country's dyed you its color!"

"No, I'm not joking, 'Amr," 'Abd ar-rahman said. "I'm telling the truth. How are your parents?"

"Fine."

"And your wife?"

"I don't have a wife. She died two years ago."

"That glint in your eyes is not for someone who's dead. Loss of a wife is not what's dimming them either. No, they're gleaming with new life."

'Abd al-rahman smiled as 'Amr remained silent.

"Tomorrow I'm going to finish my journey," 'Abd ar-rahman said. "When I come back, I'll pass by again. A longing for what will never return can provide calm."

———

In narration there is originality, and in history a rare resilience. When it comes to sighting the new moon, scholars and amirs differ. It is to be expected that, between quarters and city walls, the versions will differ. In Alexandria, for instance, the sea becomes a hero in the story. In Cairo, the gate that witnesses the execution sees a lot. In Qus, the narrative has several endings, some involving books and rings, others still in the hearts of narrators who are looking for those endings but have yet to find them. There is nothing new about the confusion. It is possible to exclude events or write about them. Difference is a mercy. But the situation in Cairo was not a happy one: Egyptians viewed the conflict among Mamluks with both sarcasm and fear. In Mamluk hands, swords were like balls in a boys' game, kicked all over the place, at any time, and with no thought given to the possible consequences. Observing the conflicts from a distance made people prouder and more scared. Endings involved the death of many people, and the installation of a new sultan who was a more worthy ruler. No one knew for sure why such a decision was made and by whom.

Merchants pursed their lips, and craftsmen complained about a lack of work. Judges and shaykhs made up their minds to overthrow one man. The story of the little boy, Hasan, came up in every version and prevailed in every council. Actually, the story seemed to be different . . . that is what Cairo merchants were saying . . . after reaching an agreement with certain Mamluk amirs.

Rich merchants whispered to each other that Jamaq had been innocent. Why would a son of the people commit such a heinous act when he could have easy access to every young boy in Egypt, Syria, and Iraq? What on earth could have led the son of a Mamluk amir to commit such an act on the son of a poor salt-seller in Qus? It would be sheer madness. The mind told you that Jamaq had to be innocent.

There was something else as well that the merchants could not believe about this narrative. Even supposing that the crime had in fact been committed by the son of the governor, who had already agreed in principle to appoint the judge, then how could the judge dare to contemplate, even in a dream, imposing the ultimate penalty on the son of his benefactor and boss? That was sheer madness. No judge in Egypt had ever done such a thing before. In order for us to tell stories, they have to be realistic so that people will believe and comprehend them. Narrators compete with each to relate tales about jinn, magic, and flying birds. All of it can be believed by the mind because it is permissible and possible. Some people have witnessed flying and bewitched animals, while others collaborate with jinn on a daily basis, eating, drinking, and having sex with them. But the story involving the judge of Qus was unbelievable.

There was laughter, bitter, sarcastic, and hysterical. Even shadow-plays would not be able to act, narrate, or sing this particular narrative. What was it exactly? Some Mamluk amirs started writing alternative versions and asking people questions. The poor salt-selling woman had sought the judge's aid to punish someone for killing her son. How had she reached the judge's house, and who had allowed her to enter? Why did the judge listen to her? If one or two of her sons died, so what? What is the problem? People die every day. During droughts and plagues children die, and their corpses are littered everywhere like wheat at harvest time. What utter madness!

Then what? Had she had refused compensation and insisted that the governor's son had to be killed? Had the judge yielded to her will, challenging the amir and bent on killing his son?

People laughed again. The first part of the story might just be possible, but the second part only provoked sarcasm. What sheer madness!

What next? They say that the governor arrested the judge and imprisoned him. But he did not kill him. They also said that the judge sent a letter to the sultan, telling him what had happened. It seemed that the sultan, who had brought his entire family, surrounded himself with Circassians, and fortified his palace, paid close attention to what the judge of Qus had written about the death of the salt-seller's son, was that right? Still more laughter. What madness!

Who would ever believe this narrative? Even children in mosques would not; itinerant dervishes and lunatics could not repeat it.

The amirs went on to note that what was even more catastrophic and bitter was that the sultan had listened to the Egyptian judge of Qus, then decided to carry out his verdict, and killed the son of the Mamluk amir. Does that make any sense? Who is the sultan pleasing by doing such a thing? The salt-seller, or the judge of Qus? What is abundantly clear is that it is not intended to please God. Sultans are not out to please God. They only build mosques to perpetuate their names, no more; trying to buy paradise, which is not available for purchase. What madness!

The storytellers started doing the rounds of merchants, scholars, and craftsmen, then the poor and Sufis. The narrative had its own special niche, one that could be believed.

The Mamluk amirs stated that the judge of Qus was allied with the usurper sultan, Barquq. He wanted to humiliate the Bahri Mamluks, just as Barquq was doing. He was eager to please the sultan, and perhaps to be appointed chief judge. Who knows? That is why he had decided to fabricate the charge against the son of Fakhr ad-din, the Turkish Mamluk amir; he wanted to destroy the amir's reputation and break his heart. Then the sultan could bring in a Circassian who could govern and tyrannize in his place.

People went on to say that Fakhr ad-din was a wonderful governor; justice was one of his main characteristics. His mercy enveloped everyone. He had annulled taxes, they said, and personally handed out the sweets he had brought to children during festivals.

No other Mamluk amir could rival his piety, not even any Egyptian religious scholar. He had to be dismissed. The judge of Qus had no knowledge of either justice or mercy. A killer for hire. His belly was broad enough to accommodate all the wealth and treasures of Egypt and Syria. They kill the amir's son for personal reasons; today the usurper sultan agrees to execute the son of a Bahri Mamluk amir. Tomorrow he will kill all the Bahri Mamluks. If Fakhr ad-din had been a Circassian, would the sultan execute his son in front of him? How cruel, how iniquitous!

How much money did the judge of Qus make every single day? His house has three stories and a gold fountain. He owns twenty-five slave girls, and his children only wear gold-embossed clothing. His wife is dead; he used to hit her and treat her badly. She was the daughter of that holy man, the chief judge, who today has issued a legal opinion that Sultan Barquq should be killed.

Why had the chief judge issued such an opinion? Because Barquq is a tyrant, someone who loves blood and kills without restraint.

The event involving the little boy, Hasan, the salt-seller's son, was not normal. It was a disaster for Egypt, Syria, and all Muslim territories, not because of the alleged outrage committed by Jamaq, but rather the lies, slander, injustice, and perfidious execution. That was the truth, and it was as evident as the new moon in the month of Shawal. It demanded a contemplation of God's creation.

The execution of Jamaq was definitely enough to warn the heedless and arouse the sleeper. Sons of merchants, craftsmen, and the poor would clearly take notice. If the sultan was bold enough to execute a son of the people, then he would start savoring the experience and kill other people without restraint. Killing had its element of gravity, and especially in the case of killing amirs' children. Where in all this was mind, logic, and sound thinking? When the sultan executes the son of an amir because a salt-seller in Qus has wrongly accused him, what kind of message is the sultan sending? Does he enjoy killing wealthy people? He certainly does not consider the consequences of killing Mamluk children. Will he now start killing anyone who rebels against him and who he personally thinks is jealous of him?

The Mamluks are maintaining that the sultan had hated the governor of Qus his entire life and was jealous of his son's beauty and power. The sultan himself had had weak children who were not fit for combat. It was simple envy between two men, and the judge had given way and sold himself. Does he not fear God? Does he not recall that one day he will be meeting God? Does he not ponder and realize what chaos and evil will be coming to Egypt?

The teller of this story wandered through the streets, his eyes full of tears as he related to them the truth of the story and the background to the execution. The entire world would be turned upside down, with no hope of recovery. The Cairo area would erupt in conflict, and arrows would strike anyone pursuing God's path, male or female. Ruin, poverty, lice, and hyenas would all follow. No produce would grow in the land of tyranny, with this sultan in Cairo.

The execution of Jamaq was a wholesale disaster. Killing a young man of his age in such a barbaric fashion was a totally different kind of happening, a fear of a particular kind. No one knew the salt-seller's son, and nobody saw him. Who killed him? His father. Everybody knows. His father confessed, but the judge forced him under torture to accuse the amir's son. That is the truth.

What is to happen?

The scholars spoke about the incident during Friday prayers. They cursed the tyrant and liar, the one who had falsely and criminally accused an innocent person. None of the shaykhs forgot to boldly curse the sultan at the end of the sermon, after receiving instructions from senior shaykhs and scholars, joined, of course, by certain amirs.

The end of the sultan would be happening sooner or later, but the judge of Qus had accelerated the process. Drumbeats in the markets presaged bad news to come. In the heart of Cairo war was on the brink. The cause was the judge of Qus and the execution of the amir's son. There was no answer to the question. Smiles mocked the judge. People kept asking: if Amir Fakhr ad-din had been a Mamluk in the Circassian palace, would the sultan have killed his son?

The order from the chief judge arrived by mail in every council a day ago, after the Friday sunset prayer. The religious scholars were bound to issue a legal opinion that the usurper sultan needed to be killed. The amirs had composed the narrative. Barquq had been an army marshal, they stated, and he had usurped the throne from Sultan Hajji, scion of the Qala'un family that had brought victory to Egypt and the Muslim lands. The era of their grandfather, An-Nasir Muhammad, a son of the people, who was not a warrior or soldier, gave witness to the superior claims of the Qala'un family and to the killing of his children and grandchildren, whether by fate or judgment; one could not talk about that. But no Mamluk amir had dared appoint himself as sultan.

Maybe the Mamluks would start fighting each other; maybe they were . . . maybe. No one knows exactly. Maybe they had killed a boy sultan once in a while, but they had never dared to grab the rule of Egypt for themselves.

The amirs stated that Sultan Barquq, or rather the one who claims to be sultan, had been unjust and immoral. Had he not executed a son of the people a few days earlier in full view and hung his head at Bab Zuwayla? It was an act of revenge against the boy's father, the courageous Amir Fakhr ad-din. But now, Fakhr ad-din would be coming back victorious and would depose the usurper sultan.

Does the family of Qala'un deserve to rule? Some people whispered bitterly that Qala'un senior had in fact wrested power from the children of Az-Zahir Baybars, had he not? It was a glass that was passed around among governors and sultans. The idea of heritage cut no ice with the army marshal. Was Barquq not army marshal? Had he not made up his own mind about the sultan, keeping him alive and not killing him as others had done previously? They could remember: he had been merciful with Qala'un's grandson. He was the actual ruler. The amirs had persuaded him to take over as ruler in order to save the country. They remembered . . .

Someone else shouted that they should remember who killed Sultan Hasan. Who was it killed the person whose name is attached to the largest and finest mosque in Cairo? Was it not Sultan Barquq and Yalbugha al-'Umari?

No one knows who killed Al-Hasan. He was a martyr. Maybe he drowned on a fishing trip.

Only in this country can fishing trips be a killing field, one where the sultan always dies. Everyone knows that it was Yalbugha al-'Umari who brought Barquq from Syria to Egypt. He had been Yalbugha's teacher, and Yalbugha was the one who had killed Al-Hasan. Barquq had learned about disloyalty and legitimized the shedding of sultans' blood. Either tomorrow or the day after, he would be killing the young sultan, and the judge of Qus would be the usurper sultan's right-hand man. He would attack the Bahri Mamluks and kill their sons. He would let their women live. Poor Amir Fakhr ad-din whose own son had been cruelly and treacherously executed before his very eyes! He would now return victorious and, if he could, kill the judge of Qus, Barquq and all the Circassians.

The judge of Qus did not curse the sultan or issue a legal opinion for his killing. In his Friday sermon he prayed for avoidance of strife, self-control, and self-examination, all so as not to follow in the devil's tracks.

"Killing is easy and even palatable," he told them. "Whenever someone gives life to a soul, it is as though he is doing so for people in general. Wars only lead to pestilence and poverty. The current ruler of Egypt is a just man; we have never seen his like before. Egyptians have no business interfering in the affairs of amirs and copying their inclinations."

"Judge," a member of the congregation yelled, "fear God! Are you thanking a heretical usurper sultan because he allowed you to defeat the amir? Which inclination are you following, and which religion?"

'Amr smiled at him. "I pray that you'll be rightly guided," he said calmly, "and that God will enlighten your vision."

"No," the man yelled back, "it's your vision that needs light. We all know about your conspiracy with the sultan against Amir Fakhr ad-din."

Their eyes met, but the judge did not respond. He understood about this attack on him. Students and other people present held the man back. The judge left the mosque calmly, having made up his mind that he would never insult a sultan who had come to his aid and was not going to carry out the instructions of the chief judge.

In the evening there was a knock on his door. A soldier in Mamluk dress came in and sat down in front of him.

"Shaykh," he said, "I've come to offer you advice. It may be useful in these dust-clogged times."

'Amr looked closely at him. "Who's your teacher?" he asked.

"Do you want to know?"

"Yes, I do, so that I can understand why you've come and why you're giving me advice."

"Amir Mintash."

'Amr shook his head. "Amir Mintash?" he repeated. "He sent you to me? Why? Why is the judge of Qus so important?"

"The judge of Qus is deputy to the chief judge of the Shafi'i law school. His name is being repeated throughout Egypt, alongside that of the usurper Barquq."

"Usurper Barquq?" he repeated in amazement. "Isn't he your sultan anymore?"

"He's only ever been sultan for the Circassian amirs and his family whom he brought from a non-Muslim country."

"If you know all that, what is it you want from me? Do you want to advise me to issue an opinion calling for him to be killed?"

"All the shaykhs and judges have done that," the man replied firmly.

"So, why do you need my opinion?"

"You're his friend, so it means a lot."

"But I'm not his friend. I've only ever seen him once in my life."

"Amir Fakhr ad-din doesn't want to kill you. He plans to kills your sons first. Amir Yalbugha is Fakhr ad-din's friend and ally."

"Amir Mintash is also Amir Yalbugha's ally," 'Amr said. "If I don't do it, is Amir Mintash going to kill them himself?"

"Amir Mintash doesn't kill children, but he can either protect them or leave them for Fakhr ad-din and Yalbugha. Fakhr ad-din knows where they are, and will go to get them."

'Amr was silent for a while. "If Barquq wins this war," he said, "what will happen to you and all those who've announced that he should be killed?"

"Barquq can't win," he replied confidently. "He'll be defeated badly and leave Cairo that way."

"Your confidence scares me. But tell me the truth. A question keeps bothering me."

"Ask it."

"What's the point of scholars issuing legal opinions and Egyptians either accepting or rejecting them, if swords are always in Mamluk hands? This is a battle that will be won with the sword; victory will go to the strongest, not to the most pious or whoever it is the scholars favor."

The soldier moved closer. "Shaykh," he said firmly, "the sword is of no use without shaykhs, nor does it guarantee security for Mamluks. Egyptians are complainers and renegades. For Mamluks to rule Egypt, they have to keep the people happy. That cannot be done using the sword; they need shaykhs and priests. You're being easily deceived by anyone who suggests that ruling Egypt is easy and taming its people is possible without keeping its people happy."

'Amr gave a bitter smile. "But it's a sword edge that is threatening me now," he said, "to make me issue an opinion to suit your wishes."

"It's your choice, Shaykh. I'm giving you the opportunity to save yourself."

"Let me think about it," 'Amr replied firmly.

"There's no time for that."

"I need to think about it," 'Amr repeated.

Once the soldier had departed, 'Amr started making preparations to travel to Cairo that day, in fact, now. He had no plans to issue a legal opinion about killing Barquq. No, he was planning to rescue his two sons.

⁓

People in Cairo locked their doors and windows and brought in supplies of milk and bread. They stayed seated indoors, waiting for the conflict between Mamluks to come to an end so that they could go out into the streets and eat sweets on the banks of the Nile. No one knew when it would all end or indeed begin. People said that the deputy in Aleppo and governor of Malatya had both declared rebellion against the sultan. Syria was the key to Egypt, and rebellion in Syria meant ruin for Egypt and the end for the sultan. People kept whispering that Barquq had to be stupid if he thought that the Bedouin were his enemies, or the Ottomans or even the Mongols. No, the real danger was coming from the north, the far north, in Malatya.

The shaykhs noted that Mintash, the governor of Malatya, was renowned for his courage and bravery. He had joined forces with Yalbugha an-Nasiri in order to depose Barquq and reinstall the legitimate sultan. They were eager to restore justice throughout Egypt and to give government some legitimacy again.

Some sons of the people and Mamluks pointed out that justice was a term that Egyptians hated; all it brought was ruin. It needed to be erased from memory. Had not the judge of Qus invoke it before killing the amir's son? Justice could go to hell, because all it brought were wars and pestilence. Even sweetmeats had disappeared from the markets. Did the salt-seller woman have any feelings? Sentiments among the poor were muted; for them, death was something to be taken in stride, not so? Jamaq's mother would be weeping and would want us to feel how sad she was. But no one knew the slightest thing about the salt-seller woman. What kind of era was this in which everything was being turned upside down? The two amirs would arrive, finish off Barquq in Cairo, and that would be the end of it. That done, they could go out and eat sweets by the Nile banks. End of topic.

Now conflict erupted in the various parts of Cairo. 'Amr had left Qus on horseback, heading for Cairo and only thinking about his two boys.

He set out so fast that he could hear the sound of the horse's heartbeats and feel the vibrations of his own heart. Surely no harm would come to his two sons; they were grandchildren of the chief judge. He would protect them both, sons of his late daughter. He would never allow anyone to seize them or kill them.

In wartime, there is always ruin and chaos. Fakhr ad-din would be bound to seize them in order to get his revenge. Had he not joined Yalbugha's army specifically in order to do that? Why did Cairo now seem so far away, defiant and cruel? Why was it that, every time he was close to the river, distances seemed to lengthen? He could hear his sons' voices. Were they missing him and screaming? Begging for help? At that moment, they were all he wanted. If they were well and life came to an end, so be it.

When he entered the city gates, it seemed empty and deserted. Stores were closed, and the only people wandering around the streets were a lunatic or two, nosily searching the trash, not for food but for the remains of humans killed in the day's fighting. He headed for his father-in-law's house as fast as possible. Night had fallen, and the streets were all dark. The house was dark too, without a single lamp, as though the occupants had left a while ago. Feeling scared, he banged on the door and looked around him for some help. He could not find a single watchman or anyone else to ask, except a lunatic who was hovering around the door, his hair a long tangle, and his beard a large, growing nest for every kind of bug.

He heard his own shout as the sound of his voice bounced off the walls: "Husayn . . . Ahmad!"

Nobody answered. He sat down by the door, not moving. He tried to take it all in and think. Where was the sultan? When had the amirs reached Cairo? If they had already arrived, then there was no hope for the sultan. They would defeat him for sure. In fact, they had already done that, and it was all over. What was happening to his two boys? Had they both fled with the chief judge until things settled down? Maybe they had, and that would certainly be the best plan. Maybe Fakhr ad-din had found them; maybe he was just waiting for the day when he would carry out his threat; maybe they were now prisoners and slaves; maybe they were being tortured and their skins were being cut open.

The muezzin still announced the dawn prayer, but no one came.

He hurried to the mosque to pray behind the shaykh. The prayer came to an end.

"Has the sultan fled?" 'Amr asked the shaykh.

"Nobody knows," he replied, without looking at 'Amr.

"Was he defeated by Yalbugha and Mintash?"

"Yes, he was. That's certain."

"Where can he be? I want to inquire about the chief judge. Do you know where he is?"

"I don't know anything. Some people say that some of them took refuge in the Sultan Hasan Mosque. Others say that the mosque was the site of some fierce fighting. Now the Mamluks are using it as a fortress, hurling spears on to the Citadel from the top. No one dares go there to find out the truth."

"Perhaps the chief judge has sought refuge in the mosque," 'Amr said, sensing a ray of hope.

"There's no refuge in that mosque today, brother," the shaykh replied. "It's a scene for fighting and bloodshed. It's not being used for the recitation of God's name, but dispatching people to meet Him."

As he rushed to the mosque, those words kept on resounding in his heart: "It's not being used for the recitation of God's name, but dispatching people to meet Him."

"My boys are all right," he told himself. "They have to be."

He looked at the mosque. The sun was shining in its alcoves. It always looked lofty and solid, surrounded by hills and surmounting them. Gleaming white stones, thick and triumphant. Brass doors embossed with care, inimitable and unforgettable, opening up to reveal the genius of its designer and the beauty of immortality. From its alcoves there gleamed the delightful colors of life and filigree of perfect love firmly grounded in the depths. How distant now was this architect, how certain of annihilation and death! How he must rue the course of humanity today, with people fighting each other amidst the light, perishing amid such beauty, their blood dripping amid the various hues of love! What sorrow that architect must feel! He had built it so that God might perhaps forgive and be merciful. He had built it for the lover of God's essence, for the abstainer from the world's desires. He never expected that wars fought over those same desires would adopt the mosque as a residence, that the devil would crack the stones and settle among the alcoves of beauty, defiling and humiliating it. Oh, his sorrow, and the judge's as well!

He prostrated himself on the mosque floor, covered his face with his hand, and then prayed to God, asking for forgiveness. Who knows? Perhaps delusion had entered his heart, greed had sunk into his soul, and ambition and conceit had sapped its energy. Perhaps love had shaken the depths of his heart, and it had lost its equilibrium.

Now, here he was again, hoping that his two boys were safe and knowing that the human soul undertakes its journey alone. He would flee from his sons, his beloved, his ambition, and his conceit. Eventually, satisfaction, achievement, fear, defeat, and victory, all involved no question about an element unseen. He could not avoid a confrontation with his errors.

Now he was prostrating himself in prayer before God, only seeking reassurance about his two sons. If only he knew that they were safe and sound, if only God would give him patience as He had with Moses's mother,* then he would know that God was pleased with him. If only he had certainty, just for today; if only he could reside in evanescence, for an hour, a day, or part of a day; if only time were as balanced as scales.

Two tears fell on the floor of the mosque. He wiped them with his finger, then stood up to start his search all over again.

He scurried up the staircase, his ears deafened by the noise of swords, spears, and soldiers cramming the narrow space as they rushed to kill and be killed. He asked himself forcefully what might be the fate of the chief judge and who might be taking refuge in the mosque's schools and fountain area.

"There are only soldiers here, no shaykhs," a soldier told him. "You should look somewhere else."

He reached the top.

"You can see everything clearly from here," another soldier told him. "Every reality is revealed. The enemy can be seen in true colors, and the friend offers you support. Just look over there at the Citadel. The enemy has taken refuge there and is firing arrows. Cairo's citizens are taking refuge in the foothills."

"At the top every reality is revealed," 'Amr repeated.

Just then, the midday call to prayer rang out loudly and on time.

---

* Qur'an Sura 28:7 [The Story]

"It's time for midday prayer," 'Amr said softly. "I'll pray with you before the fighting continues."

They looked at each other, waiting to see what their teacher would say.

The teacher stared at 'Amr. "Where do you come from?" he asked.

"From God's own country," he replied. "I'll pray with you first, and then you can carry on fighting. Remember, this is God's house. Salute His angels here, assuming they're not leaving in order to escape the devil's sojourn."

"Are you a Sufi or a lunatic?"

"Maybe a shaykh."

For a while, there was silence.

"No matter," said the amir, "we'll do a quick prayer. Hurry up with it."

'Amr started praying; he read the Qur'an in a tone full of sorrow and sincerity. For a while, the soldiers forgot about combat; the Qur'anic verses managed to break through the noise of swords. Some of them even had tears in their eyes. No sooner was the prayer finished than some of the soldiers came up to him to shake his hand and seek his blessing.

"Who are you fighting?" he asked, as he shook their hands. "For the sultan or against him?"

"The sultan, of course," they declared. "Al-Hajji, the country's real sultan. Barquq the usurper's been killed today.

'Amr smiled, mocking himself, them, and everything. "I don't even know if I want you to win or not. At any rate, I wish you all to be rightly guided."

He stood up and looked around him, searching for someone to ask or a person who could direct him to the place where his two boys were.

He descended the stairs slowly with a heavy heart and a broken soul, but his faith unshaken. He collided with a man whom he thought he recognized. He had seen him before, but could not remember where.

"Judge of Qus!" the man yelled in surprise.

'Amr stared hard at him and began to remember. A soldier and guard who had stayed with him for two weeks, one of Fakhr ad-din's soldiers and guards.

The guard grabbed his sword. "I've come to finish you off, you unjust hypocrite," he yelled.

He struck 'Amr's head as hard as possible with the edge of his sword. Blood poured out.

BOOK TWO

WORLD EVENTS

Let the days do as they will,
When fate is decreed, be of good cheer!
Be not afraid of the events of night,
The events of this world will not endure.
Be a man, stolid in the face of terrors,
Let your trait be kindness and loyalty.
Deliberation will not diminish your provision,
Nor will drudgery increase it.
At all times let the days deceive,
No remedy can ward off death.

From Imam Al-Shafi'i's poetry

4

Yalbugha al-Nasiri. What an amazingly sincere, pious, and religious man! He came from Aleppo to rescue the Egyptians from tyranny and ignominy. He fulfilled his promise by forsaking power, like some saint or monk. He had no desire to seize the throne and grab the occasion to cement his rule. He restored the governing authority to the illustrious Qala'un family and judicious dominion. He put the young Sultan Hajji back on the throne; thanks to the amirs and their just conduct, he was now victorious.

Cairo came out to celebrate. The sultan had now returned and would be handing out gifts to the people and canceling taxes. The period of Circassian control was now gone forever. Back in power were rulers who were feared by Crusaders and Mongols, and even the kings of Abyssinia and China. At last someone had come to keep the country safe and give Egypt what it deserved.

Religious scholars left their hideouts, joyfully praising God because they had bet on the winning horse; Barquq had definitely been defeated in Cairo.

The sultan returned, and animals were slaughtered. He issued orders for the poor to be fed in local mosques and lamps to be lit in Cairo for several successive nights. If stones had not been forbidden for Muslims, they would have constructed a mausoleum to Yalbugha who had saved Egypt from something that no one could specify exactly. Even so, Egypt had been saved, the sultan had been restored, and Yalbugha had not wanted to assume power.

The very fact that Yalbugha had not assumed power for himself after his victory over Barquq was enough to build him a mausoleum beyond the city gates as a matter of pride and novelty. Barquq had not managed to escape, thank God. He had been captured in order to face his penalty. He was to be executed.

What a wonderful moment, the magic of the Nile waters after dinner, with Egyptians coming out to celebrate.

For the people of Qus, there was a double celebration, at least for some of them. Ridawi the merchant had been spending some of the happiest days of his life, once the judge, who had brought with him ill fortune and shame and had deliberately humiliated him once or twice, had left. Both the judge and the sultan who had supported him were now gone, and life could return to normal.

He slaughtered an animal and handed it out, but only to the merchants, not to the poor. They had stood with the judge at one point, the one who was now dead—God willing! He went to see a shaykh to tell him about the injustice that he, his wife, and daughter had suffered; how the judge had divorced his daughter from her husband in spite of his own opposition, how he had mouthed some peculiar words about a woman's right to either refuse or accept, and how his own wife had defied him after going to see the judge. She had turned totally recalcitrant in every sense of the word, and he was not able to give her instructions; she neither obeyed him nor pleased him. The shaykh listened sympathetically to him, and announced that the judge of Qus had been removed and was no longer alive. His daughter had not been divorced, and her husband had every right to her. He should return the dowry and gifts and cohabit with her, God willing.

Merchant Ridawi had not brought up his own daughter himself; he had abandoned his wife as soon as the daughter was born and had only seen her intermittently. When he did, he had mostly argued with her mother and beaten both of them. His hatred for his wife and his anger was based on her intense love for him, one in which her only fault had been that he had married her; his family made him fully aware of her existence, and he was too scared to divorce her because that would annoy her family and turn them against him. He had no choice but to keep her in his own house. He stayed out of her way as much as possible, while she started spending most of the time in her own family's house. Her daughter grew up with her aunts and uncles. Everything worked according to plan until the judge of Qus arrived, upset the scales, and caused complete chaos. Both wife and daughter asserted themselves.

When he went into his house today, he was delighted. Instead of going to his slave girl's room as he normally did, he went to his wife's. He surprised her, sitting there eating. As soon as she stood up, he gave her a hard slap. He looked at her arm that he had previously broken and punched. All his buried hatred boiled to the surface.

"Today you'll obey all my instructions," he told her, "or else I'll kill you."

She was used to this kind of talk from him, and said nothing. Until the judge of Qus had arrived, she had never expected anything better out of life. He told her to prepare her daughter to cohabit with her husband in a week's time. Grabbing a whip, he made for his daughter's room. She tried to stop him.

"If you whip her now," she told him in a pleading tone, "her husband won't want her with whip marks all over her body."

"She went to the judge to complain," he replied stubbornly. "She kept refusing, talking, and objecting. It was always 'yes or no.' She has to be taught a lesson before she goes to her husband's house."

He whipped his daughter ten times, while she kept back her tears. Now, it was not the pain that was tearing her heart apart. Life was enclosed in circles of fire. If she ran away, her mother would suffer; that might even lead to her being killed. If she stayed, then her fate was surely death. How foul was the death of the human soul!

That done, he went out to the market in all his finery, proud of himself and his strength. He passed by the now deserted house of the judge. The salt-seller, Umm Hasan, was energetically sweeping the front, as though the judge himself was about to arrive and pass by.

"Stupid old woman," he told her dryly, "the person you're working for is dead and gone. We're well rid of him and his injustice. If you only knew it, you're the reason for his ruin."

She stopped sweeping and looked at him. This time, she was wearing a clean, black garment. She collected a load of spittle in her mouth, then spat in his face.

"Shove off, you!" she yelled.

He opened his eyes wide, hardly realizing what she had just done. He kicked her in the stomach as hard as he could, and she fell to the ground groaning. Then she stood up, grabbed her broom, and hit him on the head with it.

"Hit women, would you?" she yelled. "Maybe you'll turn into a man, you piece of shit!"

Before he could recover himself, she had gone inside and locked the door. For the first time since her son had died, she smiled, but then she started crying.

———

Next day, the new judge of Qus arrived, along with his guards, witnesses, and secretaries. He was wearing expensive clothes and enveloped himself in a halo of arrogant superiority. From the very first day, he started oppressing people and issuing swift, cruel judgments. Some people started whispering inside their own homes that a thousand dinars would be enough to save a life, prevent a flogging, or make smoking hashish legal as far as this particular judge was concerned. A few others started whispering that Amir Mintash was imposing harsh taxes and severely punishing poor people and others who refused to pay; they were convinced that darkest night could not be blacker than what he was doing. However, Mintash proved that such was not the case. In fact, if Mintash and Yalbugha were to coincide with the appearance of the new moon in the month of Shawal, that moon would be bound to fear even showing itself; it would stay at home and allow darkness to spread and dominate.

On the first day, the judge welcomed merchants and received plaudits and gifts. Ridawi was the first one to tell the judge about his daughter's marriage and invite the judge to the ceremony. He brought the judge a lavish gift and left, feeling happy that once again normality had finally returned. The salt-seller stopped sweeping the house, and the judge sent her away contemptuously. He told her threateningly that, if she so much as approached the house again, he would imprison her for the rest of her life, till people would take pity on her wretched appearance. With that, the salt-seller disappeared!

The merchant imprisoned his daughter and wife inside the house. He told his wife that the religious scholars had advised him not to let his wife leave the house until she died. Her daughter tried to bind her arm around the wooden splint again, but she realized that her mother could not move her arm, and this time the fracture could not be repaired. She hugged her mother, who did not cry but stayed silent as she stroked her daughter's back.

The wound in his head kept pounding on the door of his mind, like some importunate guest demanding to be let in. For days he neither saw nor heard anything, nor did he know where he was or who was talking.

"I want him alive," a voice that he knew kept yelling. "He has to stay alive so I can take my revenge. The torture hasn't even started yet."

In the recesses of his mind those words kept repeating themselves along with the importunate guest. He kept on hearing nasty voices saying the same thing over and over again:

Barquq gave up . . . Egypt did not treat him right and his soldiers did not protect him . . . he fled to Syria . . . he was taught a lesson there . . . he was betrayed by sons of the people . . . they want a sultan who's one of them and like them . . . not a soldier who began as a slave with no background and no father and mother . . . he was deluded . . . he thought of himself as ruler of Egypt, from the people, scholars, and sons of the people.

The Judge of Qus will be seeing his two sons on the stake first . . . then Fakhr ad-din will rip his skin off and disembowel him so he can shake his hand warmly and then let him die a slow death after spitting in his face . . . The Judge of Qus will say alive for a while, but not long.

Where are his two sons? . . . Fakhr ad-din knows where they are; he knows everything.

The wagon was moving slowly, with him inside. The pains he was feeling were the worst imaginable. His mind was totally confused, voices were a jumble, images were splinters of color, people standing around him. Had he lost his mind forever? His memory too? Had madness infected him? Was he actually dead, buried, and answering to the two angels? What crime had he committed, and what punishment was he expecting? Why was fate not showing any mercy, striking him down with a powerful blow to finish him off and make him disappear? How he longed to be mingled with the dust of the earth and to erase forever what was left of life, one that would be spent in madness, humiliation, shame, and the worst kinds of torture. Where was the salt-seller? Was she still sweeping the house? Maybe she had stopped doing it. He could smell those particles of earth dust everywhere; he needed to brush them off his eyes, head, and body. Dust was all around him, and now the salt-seller had vanished. She could not brush away the dust nor could she predict death. Why had she vanished when he really needed her?

Fakhr ad-din's voice deafened his ears. He disappeared . . . or moved away . . . battles and swords all around him . . . the road was a long one . . . this camel was taking him to some unknown place . . . he was alone, no child, no beloved, and no sword.

In the Kerak Castle Citadel some rooms are bright and clean, while others are filthy and rat infested.

Laughter arose from a voice that he recognized; he could not believe that it was here with him. Night came, the lamps were extinguished, and all that remained was that distinctive voice.

"So, Judge, you've arrived, have you? You're the one whose idea of justice is responsible for this destruction, aren't you?"

These days, everything was confused in his mind. Life seemed like a series of nightmares; years were like days, and places were as different as the flash of an eye.

"Why don't you answer? What do you think of justice now?"

He collapsed on the floor. His health had taken a turn for the worse in recent days, due to the rotten food, dark places, polluted water, and long journey whose purpose and end were unknown to him. What made places and distances feel so distant, within his grasp, and yet impossible? That was the mask over his eyes that stopped him knowing or understanding. The entire universe was a single color, humans had unified features, and shapes were products of the imagination!

Ever since the sword handle had landed on his head and the world had assumed two or more guises, he had closed his eyes, then opened them again. He had heard people whispering: "He's not well. They intend to kill him, of course, but they need to keep him alive so that Fakhr ad-din can take his revenge. Fakhr ad-din . . . he has to stay alive . . . Fakhr ad-din? No, the Judge of Qus."

The water was thrown hard and hit him in the face and arms. It aroused him from a lengthy nightmare. It was dawn, and he was still groggy. Even so, he said forcefully that he had to pray.

"Eat first, then pray."

One of them took off the mask. He looked all around him, and his mind turned toward the qibla. Not being able to pray recently had hurt him more than the mask over his eyes.

The voice moved closer.

"'Amr," it said, "I can't decide whether to kill you with my own hands, or wait till I can see your body torn apart in front of me when Fakhr ad-din decides to kill you."

He could not be sure whether the voice was being serious or was simply joking. Was it friendly or hateful? Whichever it was, he could remember it very well.

"It's not me," Barquq told him, sitting cross-legged. "I'm not your lord, nor am I sultan. I'm a prisoner in a Syrian fortress, that's all. Like you, 'Amr, I'm expecting orders for me to be killed."

Barquq pointed to the other prisoners around him. "These men are Sanqar, Amir Shihab ad-din, and Amir 'Abd al-Hamid. This, friends, is the Judge of Qus!"

They all exchanged whispers.

"Everybody knows you, 'Amr," Barquq said enthusiastically, "even more than the current sultan."

He moved close to 'Amr. "You realize, don't you," he told him quietly, "that they're going to kill you?"

"Yes, I do."

"Do you now regret imposing the ultimate penalty on the amir's son?"

"By God," 'Amr responded forcefully, "if time were reversed, I would do it again."

"For Egyptians, your stubbornness is something strange. No matter."

"How about you, my Lord," 'Amr asked him without thinking. "Would you hesitate before imposing the ultimate penalty on a son of the people?"

"Indeed," Barquq replied, also without thinking, "I'd impose that penalty on all sons of the people. They supported Yalbugha and Mintash, and betrayed their trust. They're hopeless, those Mamluk children!"

"There's no need for 'my Lord' here," Barquq continued. "Time's short, and the end may be already determined. Say: 'Barquq, son of mankind.' Once in a while I like to hear my father's name. Do you realize that most Mamluks don't even know their parents' names? If they do, they never go back to their family locations. For me, no! All the treasure in the world cannot make up for family. Do you have a family, 'Amr?"

For a moment he said nothing.

"I've two sons," he said, "but I don't know where they are or if they're even still alive."

"When I die, "Barquq said, as though he had not heard 'Amr, "I don't want to be buried in my mosque. I don't deserve that. I'd rather be buried with my father, just my father. How about you?"

"My Lord, I don't know if they'll give us a choice. I doubt it. In fact, I don't think we're going to be buried at all."

He looked around him. "Shall we pray first?" he asked.

When the prayer was over, Barquq sat down beside 'Amr.

"Do you know why they didn't kill me after I'd been defeated?" he asked 'Amr.

"No."

"To humiliate me. When Mamluks don't kill you, you need to be scared. Being killed is always a mercy.

"Tell me the truth, 'Amr," Barquq inquired. "When the amirs kill me, will I be a martyr and enter paradise?"

'Amr gave a sad smile. "I sincerely hope so," he replied.

"No, you know, you have to know. Didn't you study the subject?"

"It's your intention that will serve as the basis for your questioning."

"That's always involved the preservation of Egypt—that it should remain the heart of the world and center of the universe."

"Life on earth is brief, and talk is necessary. You preferred Circassians, gave them positions, and brought over your family. Egyptians are not entirely sure that they're actually Muslims."

"Now you're talking like Yalbugha and Fakhr ad-din," Barquq responded with a laugh. "If Fakhr ad-din killed you before my very eyes, I wouldn't care about it. That would be because amirs are totally unreliable and cannot be trusted. My primary goal is the security and stability of the country. I want Egypt and Syria to survive. Fighting the Mamluks destroys countries. 'Amr, only a powerful military marshal in charge of the government can properly protect Egypt, put an end to intrigues and conflicts, and scare the Mamluks. That's because he's one of them and knows them well. Sultans' children are sons of the people. They have no interest in conflict, nor do they possess the power and ability to break the amirs' hold. The warrior, someone who lives for combat and the defense of Islam, is not like a son of the people raised in luxury."

"Supposing you were still sultan," 'Amr asked him, "would you entrust the rule after you to a Mamluk amir whom you trust or to your own son?"

"To a Mamluk amir, of course," he replied without even thinking about it. "My son has no interest in Mamluk conspiracies or confrontations with the enemy whether at home or abroad.

"'Amr," Barquq continued, "it's your job to guarantee Egyptians a place in paradise. It's my job to guarantee them a decent life. Your task is with the world to come, mine is with this lower world. We complement each other. You're protecting them from hellfire, and I'm protecting them from the humiliation of invaders and the cruelty of aggressors. Each of us has his goals, but the achievement of my goals cannot use the same means as the ones you need to achieve yours. If that were not the case, could we swap roles; I'd be the religious scholar and you the warrior? Maybe if we did that one day, would you understand what I'm saying?"

'Amr nodded, but said nothing.

"Do you miss your boys?" Barquq asked him.

"I'm scared about what's happened to them. If only I knew, I could relax."

"Isn't fear of this world of ours and what's in it a sign of weakness, Shaykh?"

"This world is all fear. A child determines the will."

"Before you do anything else, you should think about their fate."

"I've been trying to rid myself of such weakness."

"You never hesitated?"

"No, I didn't."

"What about now?"

"At least, I'm confident that God will take care of them, as He did the salt-seller."

He looked longingly at the huge jug of water. He wanted to wash and have a drink. At this point, water was his primary goal, no other.

As he fell asleep, this conversation with Barquq fascinated him as their friendship grew. Day after day, he was praying the five prayers for the sultan and amirs.

The idea of rescue seemed impossible. Yalbugha and Mintash had cemented their rule and forgotten about them for a while. As month followed month, there was no news and no word to give reassurance about anyone.

Even so, the food was clean and the water plentiful. Lamps lit the place, and there were three windows in the huge prison room.

'Amr wanted to die in prison if his two sons had been killed.

Death soothes the soul and relieves the pain. He recalled the boys' smiles, their words when they were younger, and some situations and events.

When they walked along the Nile bank and laughed as they ate sweet cakes, that was the happiness they had, one that he was now afraid had vanished forever. He was afraid of a dark fate for them and torture that he was incapable of preventing. He remembered their innocence like light itself; it was that quality that he dearly wished could remain for a while.

And Dayfa. He wondered what her father was doing with her. What a despicable man he was, crude enough to make donkeys and other animals run away, his sheer greed enough to overwhelm Qus as a whole! Had he married her off against her will?

He realized that the man would do it. The latent hatred between him and her father was totally unparalleled. He could understand her father's strong desire to break her, rebel against the judge of Qus, and achieve everything that would annoy and hurt him. Was there any doubt in his mind that he wanted her for himself? He wished he had not done it. If he had, he would be even more attached to her. Dayfa had been married, he realized. She was right: happiness never wins in this world; contentment is not humanity's lot in this world. Even though she was young, she knew more than he did. When she put her head on his chest, he had to hug her once, and then again even harder. He told her that she had transformed destiny in his mind and spread light throughout his heart. Her innocent laughter convulsed his being as nothing had ever done before. He had not spoken, nor did he realize that it was the end.

The salt-seller had been right. Impossible love leaves a bloody taste in the mouth, along with fear of what he was going to lose, indeed what he had already lost; the impact of death on the heart, but not the soul.

He would inevitably have been the one to kiss her, hold her in his arms, and stay there for days until his passion calmed down and his heart ceased its craving. It had not happened. He could still remember and taste her tears. She knew and understood, whereas he could do neither. He had assumed that he was capable of anything; his large house could enfold all those whom he loved, his two boys and Dayfa. The salt-seller would stay under his protection, reminding him of his power and abilities. Maybe he had forgotten that, as a human being, he was unable to achieve what he willed; calamity always arrived in the form of loss.

He recalled the eyes of 'Abd ar-rahman ibn Khaldun, that profundity in the wake of utter dejection and the depths of despair, that surrender to fate and continuity, since all roads had gradually narrowed and disappeared. All that remained was a road devoid of all heart and soul, a long road with no crops growing, no animals gamely leaping, no birds bravely soaring, and no life. None of that, just stultifying routine and permanence.

He felt a jealousy invading the folds of his heart at the thought of another man touching her, hugging her to him, and making her his. Given time, she might perhaps respond and come to love him. Who knows? She was young, and her strong emotions might change with the passage of time and the birth of one child after another. She would completely forget about the judge of Qus and erase from her memory those moments of pleasure and repose. In fact, with a husband and son, she might well feel them again.

His end was coming soon. He was ready to die and longed for it more as day followed day.

Every time he remembered his two boys and their voices rang in his ears, he prayed for them and begged for forgiveness. On rare occasions, he would grumble and rebel, but then he would calm down and ask again for forgiveness. His faith remained unshaken, but despair could always find a way into his heart and mingle with the bitterness of defeat.

But he had imposed the ultimate penalty on a son of the people. He had actually done it. That might be his only victory.

As time went by and his friendship with Barquq developed, he started to appreciate and understand his personality. He had not expected him to relish laughter and to poke fun even at himself; or that he was modest and enjoyed life. Indeed, during those tedious hours, Barquq was his only friend.

"Why so sad?" Barquq asked him one day. "For your two boys? What about me? I don't know what's going to happen to my children, my wives, and even me. What do you have to lose, Judge of Qus? Your position as judge? I've lost everything. Aren't I part of your sadness? Or is it that my faith is stronger than yours? Is it a woman whom you love and lost, Shaykh? Or just a son you're worried about? Or maybe both?"

'Amr smiled but said nothing.

"Both of them then," Barquq went on. "You realize, you must realize that there's no escape from this prison. Mintash and Yalbugha possess none of that kind of mercy that we've been applying. In fact, some Kerak Castle amirs, who feel some sympathy for us, are amazed that Fakhr ad-din hasn't come already to pluck out your eyes. When do you think he's going to come?"

'Amr did not reply.

"Doesn't this bitterness of yours anger God?" Barquq asked him. "Aren't you supposed to accept God's will with a pure heart?"

"I do accept His will, but can't a human being be sad? God *'never charges a soul except according to its ability.'"*

"If you could be reassured about your two boys, Shaykh, would your own heart be reassured? Or is it a passionate love for a woman?"

"If I knew the boys were well, I would be reassured," he replied firmly.

"And the woman?"

"Which woman?"

"There has to be someone who deprives you of sleep every day."

He remained silent, feeling ashamed that his passionate feelings were so obvious in his eyes.

"Love and death don't discriminate between shaykh and sultan," Barquq said with a bitter sarcasm, "or rich and poor. The Mamluks have no choice. Women in

* Qur'an Sura 2:286 [The Cow]

our life, 'Amr, are just like battles: we choose what protects us, not what the heart really desires."

"Most people have no choice. As you said, like death itself, it's all predestined fate."

"I've never chosen any of my wives with a lover's heart, but a soldier's. Slave girls are gifts that have to be carefully selected. Some of them are wicked, others are good. Others are poison wrapped in honey, full of intrigue and ambition, with no sense of loyalty to anyone these days. Lucky indeed is the judge who can fall in love and make his own choice. As far as I can tell, you didn't choose your first wife. Was she a slave girl who made you lose your mind or a jinn from the desert who poured you some sweet water without which you are unable to live?"

"Judges can't afford to think like teenagers," 'Amr responded sternly.

Barquq laughed. "In moments of passion," he said, "there's no difference between judges and sultans. They're all teenagers. It's a disease, one that toys with the mind and plays with the will. So give us an opinion, Shaykh. Is there any kind of passion that leads a man to a fate other than hellfire?"

'Amr paused for a moment's thought. "Worldly love has its temptations," he replied. "However, everyone has the right to fall in love and enjoy God's beauty on earth so long as he distances himself from sin."

Barquq gave up trying to find out anything about the woman who had robbed the judge of his mind.

"'Amr," he asked, "do you know that An-Nasir Muhammad is also imprisoned in Kerak Castle? This citadel's only a prison for important Mamluks."

"But An-Nasir Muhammad was a son of the people. He's not a warrior and Mamluk like you."

"As I told you, he's the exception to the rule. There's no disagreement about how important he is. But it's warriors who deserve to rule Egypt. It's the lamp of all lands; no son of the people can possibly control it. It needs someone who can repel all harm and danger, both internal and external. Mamluks, my dear 'Amr, are not free to make decisions: they're first beholden to their teacher, then to authority and country. That said, there's no warrior or believer like a Mamluk. In Cairo, no mosque or school illumines the city as theirs do. Do you realize that? That's because they don't bequeath their wealth to a son or nephew; they come into the world with the sole purpose of defending country and faith. I'll tell you again: only warriors will ever remain on the Egyptian throne. Sons of the people neither know nor understand the country. It's a land that needs strength to plow it. Tell me frankly, 'Amr: is it the fates that give us power, then take it away again, like a ball in a child's hands, or is it rather the things that we do?"

"No, it's the Mamluk amirs."

"If you were giving us a single piece of advice today," Barquq asked eagerly, "what would it be? In just one sentence."

"Stop harming the very self that God has generously provided."

"How can that be? Isn't that what I've tried to do?"

"My Lord, it's a lot easier to stop harming others than yourself."

"You mean myself?"

"Yes, myself and all other selves."

"Explain it for me."

"Explanation robs truths of their beauty and luster. It's like tossing your golden sword into mercury, and the color changes."

"Your eloquence amazes me. Tell me frankly: what are the faults of sultans?"

"Love of money."

"What about religious scholars?"

"Love of money."

"And people in general?"

"Love of money."

"What about arrogance, greed, and injustice?"

"They all involve love of money. As God Almighty says: '*And you love money a great deal.*'*"

"If you were sultan of Egypt, what would you do to get the people to love you?"

"I wouldn't do anything to get them to love me. I'd do whatever would make the Creator of those people love me."

"What would that be?"

"Justice, my Lord, justice. You'll never make the people love you of necessity. But justice serves as a guarantee of strength and courage. No just sultan has anything to fear."

"How many just sultans have been killed and mutilated?"

"Killing doesn't scare Mamluks, my Lord. That's what you told me."

"You're right!" Barquq responded admiringly. "Now it's your turn to ask questions."

'Amr paused for a moment. "My Lord Sultan," he said.

"No, say 'Barquq.' Then I won't feel so sad."

"If Fakhr ad-din were a Circassian and not a Turk, would you approve of the imposition of the ultimate penalty on his son?"

Barquq remained silent, then smiled. "That word 'if,' 'Amr, is the devil's own device. The fates always treat us mercifully."

---

* Qur'an Sura 98:20 [The Dawn]

'Amr smiled as well. "Treat us mercifully?" he repeated.

Now Barquq tried again. "Allow me to ask you a question. Who is it you love so much? Is she your wife?"

"My wife died two years ago," he replied uneasily.

"And you haven't remarried yet?"

"I've been distracted by people's business and my quest for knowledge."

"Lovers always pay a price for perfect work. People who are so good at acquiring knowledge are also good when it comes to love."

"The sultan is showing an unprecedented level of wisdom."

"We learned it at the hands of legal scholars, 'Amr. You're not the only scholar in this room. Now tell me the truth. Isn't the life of knowledge safer than that of Mamluks? Mamluks live short lives. They're fated to be involved in conflict."

"No, the scholar has a short life too. He has no alternative but to fight as well."

"How is that?"

"Doesn't he have to rely on the Mamluks? If Mamluks enjoy fighting and the scholar is living in their midst, then fighting is undoubtedly part of his fate too. So many judges have been killed and imprisoned, and the ones who have compromised have stayed at home."

"If you already knew that, why did you agree to become judge of Qus?"

"God Almighty has said: 'Verily We offered the trust to the heavens, the earth, and the mountains, but they refused to carry it and were afraid of it. So man carried it. Verily he is sinful and ignorant.'"*

"I hope you don't mean trust of authority as well."

"Authority is a trust, and so is judgeship."

"I have to thank the amirs of Kerak Castle because they've thrown you in this prison. Sitting down with Mamluk amirs is very boring; I already know what they have to say. It's like eating the same food every day. Do you know what I want, 'Amr?"

"What do you want, my Lord?"

"I want to have a smell of pomegranate with oil and sugar."

"That's not possible here," 'Amr relied with a smile.

"Nothing's impossible as long as you're imprisoned with Barquq. Can you imagine that, at this point, the sultan of Egypt can't even have a tray of pomegranate? He'll have to come up with a plan of some kind."

He looked up at the lamp, then spoke to the amirs. "Every day let's take a few drops from the lamp," he told them.

---

* Qur'an Sura 33:72 [The Confederates]

So, as the days went by, they collected oil from the lamp. Then Barquq yelled for the guard.

"Tell me," he said gently, "how are things in the Muslim lands?"

The guard stared at him in amazement. "They're fine," the guard replied, "so long as the legitimate sultan is governing."

"But he isn't governing."

The guard looked at him, then turned away. "I'm not allowed to talk to you both," he said.

"How long are we going to stay here?" 'Amr asked impatiently.

"Maybe forever, or till the amirs decide what to do with you."

"If you could bring us a single pomegranate and some sugar," Barquq said gently, "you could be governor of Cairo when I'm sultan of the country again."

The guard laughed. "But you're never going to return," he said.

"If I'm no longer sultan," Barquq said, "then this shaykh will still pray for you. He's a superb scholar. Pray with us today, and you'll hear his lovely voice chanting the Qur'an."

The guard hesitated for a moment. "Maybe," he said.

"Maybe you'll pray with us, or maybe you'll bring us a pomegranate?"

"Maybe I'll pray with you both."

The amirs pounced on the guard with all the enthusiasm of people seeing a demon from another world. They asked him questions, begged him, and offered bribes and properties, leading him to feel angry at times and boastful at others.

"What's your name?" Barquq asked him after a while.

"Tintagha," he replied.

"A nice Circassian name."

Their eyes met.

"The governorship of Cairo might be a bit too large," Barquq said. "How about five thousand dinars if you brought us a pomegranate?"

"How will I get that money?"

"I'll direct you to someone who'll give it to you."

The guard looked down for a moment, then left. A day later, he came back with a pomegranate and some sugar. Barquq took it from him and started peeling it eagerly. He put it into the oil and mixed it up.

"Friends," he said, "in these dark times you need to chew each seed by itself, and slowly. It won't happen very often that I'll buy a pomegranate at that price. Do you realize now, 'Amr, why kings love money? So they can buy a single pomegranate seed to give savor to their life."

They all started eagerly eating the pomegranate. Barquq looked over at 'Amr.

"You are still concerned about your two boys," he said, "so you're not enjoying it, even though the time we're spending on adventures will soon be over. Everyone will go their own way. If they are to die, then you'll soon be meeting them. If they are to live, then too bad for them!"

"I'm afraid about their lives under torture," 'Amr said quickly.

"If they've been tortured, then they're certainly dead by now."

'Amr said nothing and stopped eating.

'Amr," Barquq said kindly, "I thought you were going to place your burden on God."

"It's an unbearable agony."

"You knew, and you chose justice."

"Yes, I knew."

"If they were with the chief judge, then he would have been able to protect them. They're his grandsons. Think about your own time in prison, something that may well last for the rest of your life."

"For the rest of my life," 'Amr repeated.

The joyful celebrations in Cairo eventually calmed down, to be replaced by the burden of taxes and the cruelty of the amirs. This time, the wars in Cairo did not stop. The Sultan Hasan Mosque became the primary focus for fighters and goal for adventurers and mercenaries. In the mosque's different parts, blood poured from countless dead and wounded living. Arrows hit both friend and foe. Egyptians carried on with their daily lives. Some people started muttering that perhaps they had been too hasty in their verdict of the judge of Qus. Maybe Jamaq deserved to die. Who knows? Realities were scrambled and spread to reach the very depths of the earth, where they were hard to understand. What was the problem with Barquq appointing people from his own family and tribe? If he brought in all Circassians, what was the problem with that? It seemed that the now-imprisoned sultan had been doing that to prevent the damage caused by amirs fighting and squabbling with each other. He was appointing people he trusted. Some of them stole things. So what? Some amirs are unjust, others are fair. Aren't they just human? Why should Egyptians fuss about Circassians and Turks? They're all Mamluks. Whether they lived on Roda Island or in Burj, they would still be Mamluks. However, this war in Cairo had to come to an end before life itself did. Even Yalbugha and Mintash seem to be working together just to commit crimes and oppress people, not out of any kind of charity or piety. No sooner had they wrested power from Barquq than their own war started, financed by the wealth of the peoples of Egypt and Syria.

Barquq befriended the guards and promised them equipment, gold, and silver. He asked them about the amirs and wars. He seemed happy, hopeful in the light of the previous few days. In fact, a few days later, one of his supporter amirs arrived. Barquq started making plans to retake Cairo, all in a muted, despairing tone, and in fear of some kind of treachery that would see them all killed.

'Amr did not bother about any of this. He asked the guard for some books, and started reading and explicating verses for the amirs and sultan. Days passed in a desultory fashion, with no hope but no despair either.

Then there came a knock on the door at nighttime. Barquq and the amirs were asked to come outside. Barquq looked at 'Amr. "What about 'Amr?" he asked.

"He's not a Mamluk. I'm not allowed to bring him too. That's the deal I've made with the guards—only Mamluks. Forgive me, my Lord. Perhaps you can rescue him after a while."

Barquq's gaze met 'Amr's.

"I'll come to get you out," Barquq said as he stroked 'Amr's hand. "Don't worry."

'Amr nodded. He was not particularly concerned. He just wanted to be reassured about his two boys. Once he knew that, he could die or be torn limb from limb. He would not care.

Once Barquq and the amirs had slunk out of the prison, the guards came next morning and only found 'Amr. At first they whispered, then said out loud, that the prison was for amirs, and he was their shaykh. Since the amirs were no longer there, he would now have to go to the commoners' prison.

The guard pushed him contemptuously into the depths of the prison darkness, where the foul stench throttled him. He almost fainted. They threw him into a dark room in the depths of the earth. He thought he was dead, or almost so.

⟡

Loneliness was now different. He started repeating the verses of God's word in his head all the time. He recalled his childhood, youth, sons, and beloved. He was afraid that, after a year or two, he would lose his mind. At first, the prison was dark, and there was no clean water or food. The jailer's purpose was perhaps to destroy his pride and crush his vanity. His mind kept hankering after the sound of his two boys and recalling tiny details about each of them. Ahmad had little to say, very like 'Amr in his seriousness and fondness for work. Husayn had an innocent spirit, loved ballgames and sports, and laughed and chatted all the time. On the day their mother died, they did not cry, but stayed silent for fear of being mocked by people present for crying like little boys. No sooner had the mourners left than they both sat on the floor and started crying silently. He did not usually hug them; he wanted them to grow up like himself, strong and willful. But, on that day, he sat down beside them and hugged them both silently. No words could lessen the loss, and no amount of obduracy could relieve the impact of utter sorrow. When he wrapped his arms around them, they started crying even harder and louder, wailing out loud as fear rattled their hearts. He remembers . . . he hugged them even harder and stroked their shoulders.

"Be sad," he told them, "there's nothing wrong with that. But I never want to hear the sound of fear in your voices or to feel it in anything. As long as I'm alive, there's to be no sign of dejection in your eyes."

They both nodded, and, after a long time, they stopped crying. That night, they slept together on the floor in the big hall. They spent the whole week close to their father. He remembers . . . But, yesterday or today, did they cry perhaps? Did they cry after losing their father or because their spirits were crushed?

He had no idea whether or not the memory of the two boys would quickly rob him of his mind, but, at any rate, it certainly melted his heart.

The years would pass in darkness so that he could learn the true extent of his mistake: was it his own arrogance or justice that would humiliate him? Justice works every time. There's no escaping it; it is one of God's attributes and a path toward Him.

He kept reciting the same verses, hoping that they could save him from self-delusion before any other kind. "*O Lord, do not let our hearts veer after you have guided us. Give us mercy from Yourself. You are the Giver.*"*

He repeated it several times every day in a loud voice.

Waiting for the jailer became a goal, like waiting for escape from fire. Once a day, he would listen for the footsteps. The jailer would approach with a feeble lamp. Neither his hunger nor thirst would be satisfied, but his mind would eagerly soak up the weak light and try to remain stable. Once a day, the jailer would come with food and drink, along with a tiny ray of light.

He kept repeating Al-Shafi'i's poetry:

At all times let the days deceive,
No remedy can ward off death.

Words to rouse the mind and prevent delusion. He did his best to use his mind to lap up all shapes in the house and all colors of earth and sky. Occasionally black and white would overwhelm all other colors, something that saddened him like death and destruction. He kept trying to remember: stories, poetry, the

* Qur'an Sura 3:8 [The Family of 'Imran]

Qur'an. Dayfa possessed all colors. She met him in the sandy desert, wearing a dress embroidered in blue and brilliant green. With her body she leaned over like fire and jinn all in one. She scared the hyenas and put an end to the longings of desert snakes. Her colors were brilliant. Every time he remembered her, the black of prison and white of death disappeared. Life shone bright, and its borders blossomed. This was still the lower world, and yet it still only aspired to the world to come. With death, no cure was effective.

At all times let the days deceive.

He was nine years old when he had memorized the Qur'an. He had watched his teacher as he had whispered to his father that his son had memorized God's book. When his teacher left, 'Amr had sat proudly in front of Ahmad.

"You've done well, 'Amr," his father had said clearly.

"How will you reward me, Father?" 'Amr had asked excitedly.

His father stared at him in astonishment. "Why should I reward you?" he asked.

"Because I'm the youngest one in the family who's ever memorized the whole Qur'an," he replied without thinking.

His father was silent for a moment. "Imam Shafi'i memorized the Qur'an when he was seven," his father replied. "He only sought a reward from God. Have you memorized it so you can show off in this world, 'Amr, or in the cause of God? Do you want to become a shaykh like your grandfather and father, or some kind of charlatan and fame seeker?"

"I want to become a shaykh," he replied immediately.

"Today you've disappointed and annoyed me," his father responded in a cruel tone. "You're my eldest son, and I was hoping that you would realize and understand. But you didn't."

The tears welled in 'Amr's eyes. Before he could respond, his father stood up and left the room angrily. He was stubborn and never gave him any encouragement or praise. However, he was fair and consistent. On that day however, his words hurt the young boy for days.

That day, 'Amr started to pray, bowing first, then prostrating himself, then bowing again.

"You know, O God," he entreated. "I didn't do this for reward. You are more merciful than my father. He has wronged me today. You know that I love You. Sometimes he wrongs me. Do You know that? Do You hear me?"

That day, he slept with a wounded heart. Next day, his mother entered his room and gave him some sweetmeats.

"What's the matter, 'Amr?" she asked. "Didn't you eat anything yesterday? Are you well?"

With a shake of his head, he told her he did not want any sweetmeats. For just a moment, he hesitated, then he told her what had happened. She listened sympathetically.

"You spoke to God yesterday?" she asked.

"Yes, I did," 'Amr confirmed. "He knows."

"Shaykhs have their protocols and rigid systems," she told him, stroking his back. "You're the cleverest and best of our children. Your father's afraid that you're going to get too boastful."

He paused, as though day was day and hour was hour. "He knows," he repeated.

Months went by. After a while, he lost count of the number of days. He kept reciting the verses without tears, and now with no bitterness either. Instead, it was all a matter of submission and self-denial, along with a conviction that the end was inevitable. He devoutly wished it would come soon; otherwise he would be losing what was left of his mind in the meanwhile.

He thought about his grandfather whom he had never met, but could picture in his imagination—tall, august, with a thick white beard and white gallabiya. He was broad chested, with a good heart and a cloak replete with both generosity and self-denial. His grandfather, 'Abd al-Karim, had realized that life was inevitably fleeting. Anxiety blinded one's vision, and a craving for extinction was a human trait. Pleasure was a quality of paradise and eternity. He had known. Had he too lost his mind, one wondered, or had he died, happy, calm, and trusting in eternity? He had left this world in preference for the next, searching for what would remain in the midst of what would disappear. He had classified things and sorted them all. In love of this world he had discovered neither good nor achievement. He had preferred eternity and had strived to achieve knowledge. Where was he, 'Amr, in relation to his grandfather? He was still deeply in love with a woman and dreamed about her. He was still scared about his two sons and judgment at the hands of the lone All-powerful. He still wanted to get his position back and return to Egypt; he wanted power and victory. Justice would not be enough, it seemed; that was the beginning of the road, but not the end.

Today he prayed, but forgot the statement of faith. He did his best to retrieve it from his memory, but failed. He was stunned and went into a rage. If his memory failed him, it would be the end. If he went mad, he wondered, would he enter paradise as a martyr? Now that darkness had killed his mind, was a skinny body all that was left? He had to lose his mind in order to find out whether or not he was dead.

At all times let the days deceive,
No remedy can ward off death.

Every day now, he started forgetting the things he had memorized and trying to recover them. He talked to himself so as to hear the sound of his own voice, but, like everything around him, memory forsook him. It happened slowly. Memory is peculiar: it does not follow any rules, and the visual cannot deal with it. Images of things were buried in memory, but words started disappearing. He could remember the designs on pages of the Qur'an and the shapes of letters. He kept trying to remember all the verses; sometimes they would come in a sudden rush, while at others they would move away and disappear. He could remember houses, the Qus market, and his two sons; faces and glances, but not words. He could remember the way defeat looked, but not the echo of its scream. Even images now were vague, distant, and old, and still colorless.

There would be a day when he was aware of existence, and another when he would sleep night and morning; one day eyes closed, another with them open. But he kept on repeating verses from the Qur'an, those he could remember for the day or part of it.

Talking loudly made him feel that he had some companions, but, after a few months, it started to scare him. He started hearing the echo of his own voice when there was silence and during those hours when he could not tell whether it was day or night. He was afraid that he was losing his mind, so he stopped telling stories or speaking in an audible tone. All around him, he started seeing images of people whom he knew and some whom he did not know. He closed his eyes and remembered his convictions. He asked for forgiveness and help as images appeared and disappeared, dithered, then came back. He did his best to control his dreams and the images that he kept invoking: of dead people, worsening his confusion and folly, of the living whose absence was driving him crazy, and of wrongdoers who made life itself a necessity.

If he could divide up the day into segments again, if he could decide when night began and ended, then he could tolerate the situation. Every day starts from scratch. Whenever the guard brings him food, he tries to absorb as much of the weak light as possible. Clinging to the hours, he longs either for them to pass or for him to disappear.

After a year perhaps, the guard came in with a lamp. He closed his eyes, then opened them again slowly so as not to be blinded by the light. After a while, he was able to see the light from the lamp clearly for the first time.

"Come with me," the guard said gently.

He realized that this was the end, the appointed time that he had been expecting.

"When am I to be executed?" he asked clearly.

"Not today. Tomorrow perhaps. Today you're being moved to a brighter room. You'll bathe, eat, and sleep. Tomorrow will definitely be the end."

He nodded and headed for the new room. The sunshine felt just like the woman he longed for but could not reach. His very existence was full of beauty and joy. He bathed, ate, and sat on a clean bed. When night came, he was waiting for the morrow, longing for freedom and termination. With that, he closed his eyes.

———

She was with him in his dream; Dayfa, he did not know why. For some time, he had stopped thinking about her and had concentrated on his two sons. But today, he was recalling her and smelling her scent as though she were with him. Was she with him? He opened his eyes. She was with him.

He closed and opened them again. So he really had lost his mind. He was imagining something and thinking it was real. He was plunging into his dreams, and assuming them to be a certainty. He banged his pillow to make sure he was really awake, but said nothing.

"My darling," she whispered.

"You're just a dream, aren't you?" he demanded.

She grabbed his hand and clasped it tightly. "No, I'm really here!" she replied.

He closed and opened his eyes yet again to confirm what he was seeing.

"How can that be?" he asked.

"You're not going to die," she gasped in a voice full of love. "You can't die."

He sat up and stared at the thick hair encircling her face and her billowing dress.

"How did you get here?" he asked.

She waved a sword and knife in the air. "Kill the guard," she said, "and get out of here!"

"How did you get in?" he demanded.

"I paid one of the guards. I told him I was your wife. I want to see you one last time before you're killed. If you don't escape, they're going to kill you tomorrow. You must escape today."

She put the sword in front of him. "Kill anyone who stands in your way," she told him. "It's your life and mine that you're defending."

"What about my two sons?" he asked.

"They're both fine," she replied quickly.

"How did you find out?"

She looked all around her, then stood up and locked the door firmly with a key she had with her. She sat down again.

"Will you believe me?" she asked.

"I still don't know if you're real, or I've lost my mind."

She grabbed his hand, put it over her heart, and squeezed it hard.

"Do you believe me now?" she asked.

He stayed silent as he listened to her heartbeats.

"Why have you come?" he asked her with a frown.

She kissed his hand. "Do you know why?" she asked. "You can feel me and you know."

He could feel his own body shivering with love for her. He closed his eyes; perhaps it was death's own delirium. Then he opened them again.

Once again, she guided his hand to her breasts, and he slowly withdrew it.

"What kind of insanity is this," he exclaimed, "what sin!"

"If this is to be your final night on earth," she insisted, "then I want you to die in my arms. If I could save you, then nothing could possibly equal your life. Yes indeed, it's crazy . . ."

He looked at her lips. "What do you expect?" he asked. "What do you want?"

"For you to save yourself and promise me that. Maybe to hug you once, then leave, in the hope of meeting you again soon while my love for you still gnaws at my heart."

He was trembling. "You're like temptation and passion personified," he told her. "There's no fear that can influence me, and no money that can buy me. But you . . . are you a demon come to grab my soul, or an angel come to rescue me? I've no idea."

She raised her hand and put it on his shoulder. "I don't know," she said. "Are you going to kill anyone who stands in your way and live for my sake?"

He put his hand over hers. "Go your own way now," he told her with a smile. "Get married, have children, and don't let teenage passions and girlish dreams affect you."

She put her head on his chest. "I love you," she said sadly.

He held her shoulder and ran her hair over his cheek.

"Predestined fates are not in our hands," he said. "Go back and carry on with your life. However long it seems, life is short. Love is fated too, however hard we try to smother it with dust and water."

He clasped her shoulder tighter and felt her lips kissing his cheek.

"Leave now, Dayfa," he whispered. "If you really love me, then leave."

She moved away a little. "You're my only husband," she said.

"Such hints of mirage and erasure really scare me. Don't sell your entire life for such momentary glimpses."

She looked straight at him. "If I give myself to you now," she demanded, "would you still get rid of me? My father will stone me to death for doing it. You have to stay alive and rescue me."

He leaped up from his bed. "What kind of devil is controlling you now?" he asked furiously. "Only a prostitute would be talking like that. Cover your face and get out."

She swallowed hard and grabbed hold of her veil, intending to lower it. But instead, she took it off and then used her shaking hand to undress. Under her dress she was wearing a red, silver-decorated undergarment that showed her arms, most of her breasts, and her thighs. Very little was concealed. It was quite enough to seduce wastelands and cracked rocks. Darkness spread all around him, and the path ahead had no clear lines. Indeed, she seemed to be the entirety of what was left of life.

Once again, he felt as though he must have lost consciousness. He started raving, imagining that some demon was trying to dominate him in his final moments on this earth. After such a life, and now on the very cusp of death, how on earth could he commit fornication? Had he wanted to? Was his body now on fire, rebelling as never before?

He bent down, picked up her dress, and put it over her breasts.

"What you're doing will hurt you first of all," he told her.

"It's not in my hands. When you die, you'll kill me along with you. If I give myself to you, you'll have to come and save me. You won't let my father stone me. You'll defend yourself and come out alive."

"Sheer insanity, crazy logic! It's sheer desire on your part, not a plan to save anyone. Do you really want me to follow my personal desires when I'm about to die?"

"No, I want to make love with you once, and then die."

She grabbed the dress that he had put over her breasts. "This silver dress was made by my mother," she said, "for me to wear on my wedding day. I was dreaming about today, and never imagined anyone else, just your beloved face. If you die today, no one else will ever touch me."

He did his best to sound determined. "What if I die today or tomorrow, and you waste away and the rest of your life vanishes?"

"What we have between us can never be destroyed."

"If today is my last day, should I end it in your arms? How can you even think of such a thing? Put your dress back on and leave."

"Shall I go then?" she asked desperately. She stretched out her arm. "Hold me in your arms just once," she whispered. "Tell me you want me and love me."

His heart started pounding. His whole body shook as she came close to him slowly and put her breasts close to his chest.

She put her arms around his neck. "Do you really love me?" she pleaded. "If you don't, then please tell me now, I beg you."

He put his hand behind her back and kissed her hair. "Yes, I love you," he said. "I long for you and want you. Leave!"

She moved even closer till he could feel her inside his own body. She kissed his cheeks and let her mouth rest there so she could inhale his body scent. He dearly wanted to hold on to them for the rest of her days.

"Maybe you could kiss me once," she said.

He said nothing. He could not push her away, put a stop to his own passion, or stoke it.

She put her lips close to his. "Just one kiss," she said, "then I'll go."

"Dayfa," he muttered to both himself and her, "there's no triumph to be had in my defeat. You know that."

"I don't want to defeat you," she replied. "All I want is some peace for my errant heart."

"This isn't the way to achieve that."

"You're my husband, and I have no other."

He took her face between his hands and gave her a breathless kiss, something he had wanted to do for ages and had resisted over the past months. He could no longer do so. He could not remember when the kiss came to an end or how he came to be entwined with her body, as though she were the life that was coursing through his arms. He had never wanted anything like it, nor had he ever loosened the reins of his passion as he was doing with her. He squeezed her in his arms as though he wanted to absorb her into himself. Then she would melt and stay attached to his chest till death. Her breath came out in spurts. He thought that he had drowned in the deep ocean, disappeared, and dissolved.

When she felt him inside her, she closed her eyes hard to control the pain and bit her lips, fully aware of the enormity of what she had just given. She gasped in shock as she realized what had happened. Their eyes met, and she could see the agony buried deep in his pupils.

"Dayfa," he whispered sadly.

She clung to his back, tears pouring down her face. "My darling," she said, "I have only you."

⌐

She moved away from him a little. Looking away, she clutched her body and hugged herself. It was as if she did not know whether he was going to kill her immediately because she had seduced him and won. Would he pity her and understand her motives and sacrifice?

He stayed frozen in place, trying to cope with what had happened and what he himself had done. Then he held her hand and pulled her to his chest.

She left her head on his chest without saying anything and clutched his bare shoulder. When she looked at him for a moment, she could see that his agony was now firmly in place.

"Forgive me," she told him in a tearful tone. "I was fighting a battle for your life. You're going to kill the guard and escape. Promise me. I swear to you that I would not have done this if I had not been fighting for your life."

He did not respond.

"I can't stand your suffering," she said, kissing his neck. "I don't want it. I need to feel you as part of me, inside me, around me. If you die, I'll never touch you again."

Again he did not reply.

"I love you," she said, kissing him on the lips. "Forgive me, please forgive me!"

He held her face. "It's my own heart I can't forgive, not you," he said. "You're the loveliest thing I've ever seen; you're life itself. If only man could fight for life itself! You need to forgive me! I haven't protected you or shielded you from the evil in my heart."

She looked at the blood on the sheet. "Don't let them kill me," she said. "You have to live so you can save me. They'll know. They'll torture me and kill me. Promise me to come back alive soon."

He gave her a hug. "I promise," he said without even thinking.

They both looked bewildered. She looked all around her, trying to understand what she had just done and appreciate the enormity of her sacrifice and evanescence.

She covered her body with her hands as she stood up. "Don't think badly of me," she said bashfully. "I swear to you, I never imagined I'd be doing this. I was afraid for you. I have no idea how passion managed to paralyze my mind and let my body yield. You know that I'm no prostitute. I beg you to understand."

He nodded in agreement. His mind was drifting far away. It was almost time for dawn prayer, but he had no idea whether to wash and pray or to postpone the encounter so that some time could elapse following his sin or he could commit some other offense. Who knows?

She used her shaking hands to put her dress back on. Her body was still throbbing with his touches, his passion, and his longing for her. He stayed where he was, staring at her for a few seconds in case the dream dissolved and life vanished.

"How did you get here?" he asked her. "How did you manage to get in? How will you return to Egypt?"

"There's no time for that now," she replied confidently. "Don't worry about me.

"Escape today," she told him, holding his hand. "Now, just as soon as I've left. The guard who let me in thinks I'm your wife, and I wanted to spend some hours with you before you die. But he's going to let you get to the walls. I can't do more than that."

She looked at the sword and knife. "In spite of myself," she pleaded, "you're going to be married to me. If you don't come, I'm going to die or run away, or else my father will kill me."

"I'll come," he replied definitely.

She gave him a big hug. "Don't die," she said, "don't forget me! That will anger God more than anything you've done here. How cruel it would be to let me down!!"

He put his hand around her waist. "I won't let you down," he replied.

She took another look at her blood on the white sheet. "Take the sheet with you," she told him fearfully. "Don't leave it here."

She opened the door and vanished.

She disappeared in just a few seconds, leaving him more bewildered than he had ever felt before, a kind of defeat he had never encountered. Maybe it was just an hour she had spent with him . . . maybe. When he looked at the sheet, he could still feel her body wrapped around him and inside him, a lush, soft body to do away with the mind.

Looking all around him, he grabbed the sword and knife and hid them in his clothing. Then he folded the sheet and put that in his clothes as well.

When he opened the door, the guard gave him a signal. "If you leave the Citadel," he said, "you'll find a horse waiting for you in front of the right gate. I can't do more than that."

Whatever happened or did not happen after that was swift. He started running and woke up the guard who started running after him with a sword. 'Amr used the knife to cut him down. He kept running till he reached the Citadel gate. He found the horse, mounted it, and disappeared.

BOOK THREE

THE SEARCH

Striving in the search for truth has a cost that lovers pay.
People who are so good at acquiring knowledge are also
good when it comes to love. Whoever is totally absorbed in
the quest for justice is also in search of a woman who does
not belong to this earth nor does she follow its rules.

Sultan Barquq

5

After spending half the day riding his horse, he stopped to drink some water by a tent, where he was surrounded by men surrounded in turn by sheep.

He was exhausted. "Can I have some water?" he asked.

They gave him some water, and he sat down to sip some milk. He felt that his cloak was somewhat light. The sheet must have fallen out somewhere on the road; had it really fallen out or did it not even exist?

He could still feel her wrapped around him, with all her softness and seductive power. She was different, like a jinn, like fire and warriors' swords.

Was she really with him, or merely seemed so? Had he lost his way or was he safe now? He was not sure.

Was he a lunatic, with jinn toying with his mind, or a fornicator whom angels refused even to look at? He had no idea.

Was this reality or pseudo-reality? No idea.

Which Egyptians would be the most receptive? He had not thought about that yet.

He clutched his head and started checking his gallabiya. He found some money, but had no idea where it had come from. He could not remember. How long had he been in prison? Two years? Perhaps. He had been lucky enough to stay in the amirs' prison for a year, but then another year in the people's prison—that was a hellish grave. It had given him a lot of time to think, waiting for release from an hourly death routine and liberty on rare occasions. He had not lost his faith for a single instant, nor did he regret his sense of justice for a second. However, his fertile imagination kept toying with his fate, giving him some hope that life might return to normal. Why not? He would go back to Egypt, find his two sons, and be married to his beloved. He would have to be married soon so he could forget the sin he had committed or the shadows he had experienced. It felt like a sighting of the new moon that shows itself to some people, but not to others. It was like erasure and licentiousness, pale-colored, life's charm, that ripe red pomegranate, eaten by a prisoner after a year of only having dry bread.

Dayfa, at every single moment she looked out of his heart and overpowered the darkness that surrounded him. He was going to find her.

He asked the man how to get to Egypt and about the sultan. The man told him that the sultan had confronted Yalbugha and Mintash again. The tables had been turned; Egyptians and Syrians had gone through enough hardship at the hands of Yalbugha and Mintash, and now the sultan had won. This time too, people in Cairo had closed their windows and waited inside for the Cairo wars to come to an end. It had been a fierce battle. All Egypt was well aware of how vicious Mintash was and how stubborn was Yalbugha. However, Barquq and his aides had been victorious, and now he was reestablished in Egypt. He had shown mercy to the young Sultan Hajji. He had not killed him, but only limited his residence. Now Barquq was sultan of all Muslims once again.

'Amr had no idea where to go and what direction to take. Should he go straight to the sultan and ask him to help locate his two boys and see him married to his beloved? Would the sultan welcome him? Who was he, 'Amr, now? A refugee? Escaped prisoner? Things that happen inside prisons are bound to be completely forgotten by the sultan. Then, why would the chamberlain even allow him to enter the sultan's residence? When he had been judge of Qus, it would have been difficult but possible to meet the sultan, but now he had no position and no work.

How had Dayfa managed to come and see him? How had she found out where he was? That's impossible. Where is that sheet now so he can assure himself that his mind is still sound? What could assure him about that? She was the one to do it, only she. If he had not made love to her, he would definitely not have killed the guard. How had he managed to get out? Maybe the guard had opened the door on instructions from the sultan. Had the sultan not promised to rescue him? He had not killed anyone or made love to her. There was no trace of the guard's blood, nor of hers, and none on him either.

He did not know whether it was his passionate love for her that was making him search for her now, or whether he wanted to make sure that madness had not burrowed its way into his heart and taken it over.

He spent the night in the Bedouin's tent, then set out on his journey at dawn. As he prayed the dawn prayer, any doubt turned into certainty: prison darkness had toyed with his mind, and Dayfa had never come. He had escaped from prison on his own. Maybe it had indeed toyed with his mind, but every strength has its own weakness. Every certainty starts with doubt. Every intelligent person has a slight touch of madness. From now on, he would put his life in order and forget the two years he had spent as a prisoner.

After arriving at the gates of Cairo, he headed straight for the chief judge's house, searching yet again for his two sons.

He knew that the chief judge had changed. His father-in-law was now living in another house. As he headed there, he was feeling utterly exhausted from the hard journey and worrying about the rest of his life being lost.

His breaths came fast, and his suffering in prison weighed on his exhausted frame; it seemed eager to collapse on top of him. When he finally reached the judge's house, he almost fainted. He banged on the door, and a servant opened it.

When he entered and sat down, his entire head was spinning with the pressure. His father-in-law came in and shook his hand coldly. He seemed tense.

"You were in prison, weren't you?" he asked 'Amr. "We all heard the news. You were imprisoned along with all the people who supported Barquq."

"How are you, my dear Shaykh?" he asked his father-in-law gently. "How are Ahmad and Husayn?"

For a while, he just looked at 'Amr and said nothing.

"They're fine," he eventually said, "but I'm not."

He gave a deep sigh and assembled his next words. "Can I see them?" he asked. "Where are they?"

The chief judge called them.

"As I told you, 'Amr, I'm not doing well."

'Amr's mind was still confused. "I understand, Shaykh," he said.

"The sultan has a black heart. He wants to take his revenge on everyone who stood up to him."

"Of course."

"He's unjustly fired me from my position. That's not right."

"That's not right," 'Amr repeated as he saw his two sons arriving.

"After everything I've done for you, you have to help me."

"Of course I'll help you," he repeated. "First I want to see my two sons. After that, I'll sleep for a while, and then we can look into things."

The chief judge stared at him long and hard. "Did you run away," he asked, "or were you freed? If you escaped, they may rearrest you, and my house . . ."

"They freed me, of course," 'Amr replied immediately.

"You know the sultan, don't you?" his father-in-law asked. "Will you help me?"

"Of course, I will," he replied without thinking. "You're the only one who deserves to hold the post. But first, I need to see my two boys and then get some sleep."

The two boys came in hesitantly and not a little bewildered. No sooner did he set eyes on them than his whole heart relaxed and life returned to normal. He did not say a word and avoided hugging them, something he dearly wanted to do, nor did he tell them how much he had missed them both. There were rules that governed everything, even times of erasure and bewilderment.

"Are you both well?" he asked in a tone that he wanted to sound calm.

"We're okay, Father," they both replied.

"Have you been with your grandfather all these two years?"

The two boys looked at each other. "No," they both replied.

He nodded. Sleep was overcoming all his thinking.

"We'll talk in the morning," he said.

How long did he sleep? When did he sleep? Maybe a day or two? His dreams meandered amid times and people; at times he was flirting with death, at others he was in a tangle with life. His father, mother, and brothers were all with him at a huge celebration, for which they had butchered a sheep belonging to the Bedouin whom he had encountered in the way from Kerak Castle to Cairo. They were all in the man's tent, five brothers, still young, all laughing and eating. Then Dayfa came in with a large tray of pomegranate. Everyone pounced on it, and nothing was left for him. At first, he was angry with them, but then he laughed and gave her a long kiss. With her innocent face and joyful eyes, she was laughing, the way she had been when he saw her for the first time. His two sons were children, crawling around beside him. A shaykh was there, teaching him to memorize the Qur'an, sitting in a corner and reciting this verse: "*I have only created jinn and mankind for them to worship Me.*"*

The shaykh repeated it three times, and then he did the same. Maybe he was six years old, the same age as the salt-seller's son. The salt-seller—how had she managed to break into his lovely dream, with her tattered clothes, her hair pulled up in a messy spiral, and her hard expression? The shaykh stroked the shoulder of the child 'Amr.

"You'll read and learn," he said. "You have to read and learn."

"Who are you?" he asked angrily. "Why have you come here?"

"I belong here. My house is here. I've come specially so you can read and learn."

He opened his eyes and looked around him.

His family had died in the plague years ago. He was the only one left. He can remember the problem of getting them buried. There was nowhere to bury them all; he was seventeen at the time, and looked everywhere. His only goal in life was to have them buried; after that, he could feel an unrivaled sense of peace.

His two boys were sleeping on the floor beside him. He got up, rubbed their shoulders, and woke them up gently.

* Qur'an Sura 51:56 [The Scatterers]

"Were you with your grandfather all those two years?" he asked them again. "What happened to you? I'm sorry for coming after so long. You both understand, don't you?"

They both looked older, more mature, and more settled.

"We understand, Father," the elder one said, now fifteen years old.

"Where were you?" he asked.

"When the war in Cairo started," Ahmad said, "Grandfather decided to move far away. He was afraid that the amirs would assault the chief judge, as sometimes happens. He was planning to travel to the Delta, but, two days before we were going to leave, she came . . ."

"Who came?"

"The woman you sent to us."

He stared at them. "What did she do?" he asked.

"She convinced my grandfather that she should take us away till the fighting was over. At first, he wasn't convinced, but she explained that there was an amir who wanted to kill us. She had come especially because you had asked her to do it. She told stories about you, things that only someone very close to you could know. My grandfather agreed and sent some servants along with us."

'Amr looked at the floor. "Where did she take you?" he asked.

"To Nubia. We were on a boat for two days."

"What did she do with you?"

"She treated us like a mother. She used to spend hours, talking to us in her language. We didn't understand much, and she didn't let us go out a lot.

"'A man is out to kill us,' she told us. 'We must be careful.' We stayed there for a whole year, then came back when Sultan Barquq returned. She gave us back to our grandfather and left. We haven't seen her since."

"What kind of story is that? Don't you know who she is?"

"We were a bit scared," Ahmad replied. "We wanted to see you again."

'Amr nodded. "Of course," he said. "In your place, I would have been scared too. What does this woman look like? Is she thin, with matted hair, and a harsh expression?"

They looked at each other. "No," they both replied.

"How old is she?"

"Middle-aged."

"Was she maybe from Yemen or Abyssinia?"

"No, not from there," they both said. "She spoke a language we didn't know. If she'd taken us there, we would have known."

He nodded again. His brain was now working better after a good sleep.

"No matter," he said. "The past is over, and now we're together again. Do you know why I left you?"

They looked at each other again. "We know all about it," they said.

"God willing," he declared, "we'll go back to Qus. You'll start your studies again, and we'll forget about these two years forever."

The younger one, Ahmad, moved closer to him. "Father," he said, "you were brave. That's what the old lady told us. She said that bravery was a characteristic of religious scholars."

He smiled. "She said that in Arabic?" he asked.

"Those were some of the very few words she spoke in Arabic."

———

He took his two sons to his house in Cairo. As soon as he arrived, he asked to meet his students and assistants. He started asking them questions about conditions in the country and the situation of people in Qus. He learned that there was a new judge who was well known for his arrogance, stubbornness, and crude behavior. People in Qus loathed him, while some of them had found him to be a useful partner in trade and a supporter when it came to collecting money. Such people did not hate him; indeed they offered him powerful support.

'Amr was thinking as he listened patiently to all this. When Hamza the student had finished his account, 'Amr posed him a question. "Was there a gruff merchant named Ridawi? Do you remember him?"

"Yes, of course we know him," Hamza replied. "He used to hate you, Shaykh, and say bad things about you after you'd left. He asked the shaykhs to annul your decision regarding the divorce of his daughter. The stupid idiot did just that and married her to 'Abdin again."

For a few seconds his heart stopped. "How could he marry her off again?"

"As he said, he was returning her to her husband. The divorce had never happened in principle, so he returned her to her husband."

"When?"

"Two years ago. He did it on the day you were arrested."

"She's been married for two years?"

"Yes," the student replied, "I believe so."

He stared at the floor for a while.

"Shaykh," the student asked, "what are you going to do now? Will you stay in Cairo?"

She had been a virgin when she melted into his arms. Maybe it was all a dream, intimation of death for sure. How sorry he felt for his poor, confused, passionate heart! It was all over, or almost.

"Why should I stay in Cairo, when I'm the judge of Qus?" he asked challenging-ly. "I haven't heard from the sultan that he's dismissed me."

The student gaped in confusion. "But Shaykh," he said, "there is already a judge in Qus."

'Amr stood up. "Who is the chief judge now?" he asked.

⌒

He did not allow himself any time for contemplation and understanding, nor for self-pity over his fate and indulgence in sorrow. He had had plenty of time for con-templation over the past year amid the gloomy darkness and deprivation. He could no longer spend a lot of time within the folds of his own mind nor could he place any trust in his deceitful brain. For a time he now wanted to walk amid the trees, sniff the sun's scent, and savor the taste of colors.

Two days later 'Amr had arranged his meeting with the new chief judge. He felt determined as he made for their meeting, fully expecting to return to his position victorious, as he deserved and the situation demanded. The chief judge agreed to the meeting and offered him some food. They ate together. They discussed the general situation in the country, Sultan Barquq, and the new judge in Qus, who had been appointed before Barquq's return and would now be difficult to dislodge. 'Amr listened in silence to the new chief judge, someone about whom he had known a lot ever since 'Amr had been a student.

The chief judge conveyed his respect and appreciation to 'Amr, but he was unable to dismiss the judge of Qus. He had not committed any outrageous acts, he was fair in his judgments, and he spread an atmosphere of peace.

'Amr listened patiently. "My Lord," he said, "you've known me ever since I was a student and earned a certificate to practice from you. I learned a great deal from you."

"I wish that my knowledge had benefitted you," the judge said somewhat superciliously. "However, 'Amr, you're recalcitrant by nature, ambitious, and vain—three traits enough to disgrace any judge and work against him. What you need instead is piety, giving up pleasures, and seclusion ten days a month."

'Amr gave a bitter smile. "I've been secluded for an entire year, my Lord. If only you knew what it was like!"

"I can't help you. I've explained it all."

For a moment there was silence.

"How good is the funding for endowments?" 'Amr asked.

"Fine so far," the judge replied. "However, I'm worried that the sultan wants to control everything."

"I've a house in Cairo," 'Amr said nonchalantly. "I inherited it from my father. I was thinking of placing it at your disposal, my Lord."

Their eyes met.

"I don't understand your intentions, 'Amr," the judge said.

"If religious scholars were to be in need of an endowment," 'Amr said, "I'm proposing to leave it at your disposal. Perhaps things will deteriorate for shaykhs, who knows. These are unprecedented times, and sultans do not realize the power of religious knowledge. We have to feel secure and live cautiously. If the situation becomes more difficult, scholars must present a unified front in the face of tyranny. Transfer the house deed to your name, and it will be at your disposal. You're the chief judge, my teacher, and my shaykh. I trust you as if you were my own father."

"But 'Amr," the judge said, "if it's your house, you don't have another one."

"That's why I've wanted to return to Qus," he replied enthusiastically. "I wanted to donate my house to the cause of religious learning. I'll start working again to earn my daily bread and teach my children. If I did return to Qus, I'd have the judge's house again. I wouldn't need a house in Cairo. It's a beautiful two-story house right in the heart of Cairo."

The judge did not react. "Let me think about it," he said after a pause.

"It's my right and my position," 'Amr said gently. "It was and still is. You're famous for your asceticism and fairness."

"You were never dismissed. Is that right?"

"Yes, I was never dismissed, and the new judge was never appointed during your tenure. That same tenure, my Lord, is the beginning of justice and the end of injustice. Give me back my position. I have suffered dreadfully for two years, without having committed any crime."

"I'll think about it."

'Amr stood up and shook the judge's hand warmly. "I'll start the transfer process for the deed," he said. "I'd like us to have a good relationship, my shaykh and teacher!"

No sooner was he away from the house than he snorted in disgust at time, the present era, and the teacher whom he remembered very well. He realized how he had reached his position and what he wanted. Maybe such achievement had its price, and yet the eventual goal was noble. For justice to spread, injustice had to do so first; asceticism demanded an initial dive into excess.

He returned to his house and, without even hesitating or thinking about it, he started the process of selling it to the chief judge. He told his sons to get everything ready to travel to Qus very soon.

A week later, the chief judge had made the decision that justice demanded that 'Amr had to be restored to his position as judge of Qus; a new position would have to be found for the deposed judge. As chief judge, he was continually in control of both mind and conscience and striving to show devotion to God and put an end to any suspicions. The deed of sale for 'Amr's house in the chief judge's pocket provided a degree of assurance and would always illuminate the truth. The world could never be entirely safe in the Mamluk era. If the sultan decided to punish him tomorrow or the day after, he would certainly go ahead and do it without the slightest hesitation or concern. In this fractious era, there was no fear of religious learning or shaykhs. This lower world had to be dealt with, not just the hereafter. To be sure, the human heart needed to be rid of all worldly desires, and yet life in this world required mankind to protect themselves from poverty, something that could come just as quickly as death and plague. If it did come, then it would finish off everything, whether desiccated or green, and bring people down even more than Mamluk prisons. There was no choice: in this era, precautions had to be taken. Needless to say, 'Amr understood full well why the chief judge had accepted his modest gift, or so it seemed to him.

Today the road back to Qus was long and empty. Once in a while, Dayfa loomed in his imagination, then moved away again. If what had happened had never really happened; if she were now a wife and mother; if she had accepted her fate, loved her husband, and inured herself to life with him, then what could he do? Yes, it might be permissible and even certain. But to allow Ridawi the merchant to annul his legal decree, no . . . that was not going to happen as long as he had a heart beating inside him. To be put in prison for a year or two with no charge, that was certainly possible. To be belittled by the governor of Qus, to have his turban trampled underfoot, and to return to his house on foot, that too was possible. But, for Ridawi the measly merchant to assume for even a second that there was a legal opinion issued by 'Amr that was wrong, and that Egyptians today could issue legal opinions at will, that was something that he would never tolerate.

He paused outside his house and noticed people gathered either to wait for his arrival or eager to watch the confrontation between 'Amr and the judge who might well be leaving today. The judge had already put his property on some wagons. He gave 'Amr a hateful and somewhat derisive look, but did not offer him a greeting. Along with his sons, 'Amr simply waited for the judge to depart, along with his family and many slave girls. No sooner had the judge departed than 'Amr entered the house and ordered the servants to clean it again. During his absence, it had been filled with the dust of injustice and corruption.

He went over to the balcony and looked out on Qus. Women in their black clothes were walking around the markets, and men were haggling, buying and selling—an entire world inside the walls of this town: pilgrims waiting, emigrants listening to the clarion call of staying there for a day perhaps, a year, or an age.

People were arriving from everywhere, lofty houses illuminated by lamps, laughter and screams emerging from them.

His two sons slept soundly, but he did not. Hatred and envy were two emotions he had never encountered before. Resentment and bitterness were new to him, as were arithmetic and algebra, two disciplines that he did not understand very well, but seemed to be important.

Next morning he walked proudly to his council chamber. He listened to the words of congratulations and praise, indeed to the poetry which the people of Qus had composed specially for him. After a while, he cut them off. He gave instructions that Ridawi, the merchant, was to come as quickly as possible and police as well. Not only that, but the police were to arrest the merchant and bring him in irons to the judge today.

The merchant arrived panting, his gaze full of hatred. For a moment, their eyes met.

"I issued a verdict canceling your daughter's marriage," he told the merchant forcefully. "Do you remember?"

"My Lord . . ." the merchant replied.

"When I left," he interrupted, "you married her off. Isn't that right?"

"If you'll give me the opportunity, I'll explain our customs to you."

"Was the contract involving her renewed?"

"No," the merchant replied shamefully.

"It wasn't renewed?"

"The shaykh ruled that the divorce was invalid. I didn't make the decision."

"Which shaykh would ever rule against a judge's decision? Are you out of your mind, man?"

"I swear to you that the shaykh gave the ruling."

"If the contract was never renewed, then this is a marriage that never happened. From this point, you're going to prison and right away."

He now demanded to have a meeting with the husband, 'Abdin. He ordered the police to arrest Ridawi and take him to prison in full view of the people of Qus.

He was still furious, and his heart allowed him no mercy.

The husband could not be found. They would have to wait till tomorrow to search for him.

He tried to make his voice sound calm, but it came out furious: "I want to see Ridawi's daughter and her husband tomorrow."

⌁

These feelings were the devil's doing. He disdained hatred; it meant defeat, no forgiveness, and an admission of weakness. He had no desire to kill even Amir

Fakhr ad-din and did not really hate him. Instead, he sympathized with his stupidity, realizing that he was bound to meet a grisly fate, perhaps in this world and certainly in the next. No, hatred implied a defeat that he neither knew nor relished. He realized that now.

He did not hate anyone as much as Ridawi. It was as if hatred arrives like a flood, tearing up everything around it, even the haughty mountains of the human heart that are there to stop it tumbling into the abyss. There is no escape from hatred.

He kept tossing and turning to left and right as he thought about the dream; was it real or not? Every single day it appeared as sheer fancies, tricks played on the eye that had grown accustomed to permanent darkness and thus managed to weave days that were not days and events that never happened. It was the same eye that had blamed him for neglecting it for an entire year or part of it, and was now bent on revenge. He had not seen Dayfa or killed the guard. Had he killed the guard?

Why was hatred now mixed with killing in his mind? What kind of defeat awaits someone who tries to impose justice on earth?

Ridawi deserves to die, based on principles of both justice and hatred. Did he not force his daughter to do something obscene? That man is not her husband.

He heard a knock on the door; he had been waiting for it and anticipating it. Voices were raised, and Umm Hasan, the salt-seller, was proclaiming that she had to come in to clean the house. The servants thought she was crazy.

He came down the stairs and looked at her. "Welcome!" he said in surrender. "I've been waiting for you ever since I came back."

She pushed the servants away and came inside. "Forgive me, my Lord and master," she said. "There was something I had to do first. Praise God for your safe return! Welcome, now that you're back in our country."

He signaled the servants to leave. "You realize," he told her, "that I didn't expect you to serve me again. I don't need it."

"I know," she replied nonchalantly.

"So, why are you doing it?"

"I made you a promise. You fulfilled yours to me, and I must do my part. Do you remember, my Lord? Mankind was created to be always in a rush. What you don't need today you'll need tomorrow. Maybe you don't understand now, but you will tomorrow."

Their eyes met, but he did not respond.

"Your boys are well, I hope?" she asked.

"Was it you who hid them?" he asked her.

"No, by God, it wasn't me."

"Who did? Do you know?"

"No, I don't, I swear."

"Where's Amir Fakhr ad-din? Did he die in the wars?"

"Those people only ever die in one crisis or another."

He nodded. "I'm going to sleep," he said. "Get a little sleep at least. Choose a room and put your things in it."

"My Lord," she said, "your expression is a tissue of defeat, even after victory and a goal achieved. Why?"

"Go to sleep," he ordered her angrily.

"I told you before the way that passionate love can toy with the heart and bring it down."

"What passionate love?"

"But life never comes to an end when we want it to do so. This life of ours is its own master. There's always justice, but it needs someone who'll look for it and strive on its behalf. Didn't you say that before?"

"Yes, I did," he stated firmly.

"Did you understand it?"

"Yes, I did."

"You go to sleep now, in God's protection. You always have that and tranquility as well.

"Tranquility first of all," she repeated loudly, "then security."

He left her and went into his room. He did not go to sleep, but started walking in circles while the fire in his heart stretched far enough to envelop the whole of Qus. Even if 'Abdin had been married to her, he would give her a divorce from him. He would do that whether she wanted it or not. She could not possibly have loved her husband. She would never have toyed with his heart for years, then toyed with someone else's, as though he had died in that gloomy prison. He would be married to her in spite of her father, and of her as well. He could do anything. He would make do with the application of a law in a country that bolstered the strong and humiliated the weak. It was his law and his heart on whose behalf he was fighting. He would give both father and husband eighty lashes for the crime of making her live with 'Abdin after he had divorced her from him. He would be married to her, without asking her opinion. She had none.

Sometimes he feels like tearing her apart in his hands, slapping her over and over again, then hugging her and never leaving her. Did she come to him or not; was it a dream or reality? She was the dominant factor, the one who had appeared in radiant colors amid the darkness of the grave in which he had been buried.

That darkness had almost driven him mad, but her marriage for two years had now lost him everything. Throughout his life he had recognized the truth and searched for it. She had been sincere in her love for him and her impetuous actions. She loved him; that was certain. But, now that he had been away for two years, did she still love him? Time can always parlay with people, and now, after he had eventually won, that same time was letting him down. But his feelings for her were still the same; his eyes could still picture her laughter, and her scent was still firmly fixed in his imagination, his darkness, his entire life.

He could not lie down on his bed, and stayed awake the whole night. After he had prayed the dawn prayer, he started having doubts about his own logic and decisions. But he did not change his mind; or maybe he did a little bit. His hatred and bitterness did not lessen, but the compulsion that they represented was no part of a judge's task. Even if justice was crashing all around him, he himself was obliged to remain tied to justice in spite of the rest of humanity, or, at least, to try. Compelling her would be both a defeat and disgrace.

When his assistant arrived in the morning, they told him that the husband had not been found yet, and Ridawi's wife and daughter could not come either. It seemed that his wife was sick.

He listened in silence. He then demanded again that there should be a general search for the husband, and he should be brought to him. His assistant asked him if he intended to release Ridawi.

"That's not going to happen," he stated clearly, "not today or tomorrow."

He carried on with his work, doing his best to put right the damage done by the previous judge, listening patiently to complaints and restoring rights to their owners. He sent a message to the sultan, asking to have a meeting with him. Now his request might actually arrive, and he could have a meeting with the sultan.

When he went home at night, he started teaching his boys as usual and helping them memorize what he could. Then he went up to his room to read, without saying much to anyone.

Next day, he heard that the husband would be coming to meet him either that day or tomorrow, along with his grandfather, the policeman. After the noon prayer, he discovered that someone was coming in with hesitant steps. No sooner had he looked at her eyes than he knew who it was.

For two whole years, he had only seen her in a dream that seemed real or a reality with the flavor of madness. Her eyes had lost their sparkle and looked as though the light had gone out of them. She came in with her mother whom she was holding up. Sorrow was all that showed in her eyes; there was no love for him or joy at his return. As he looked at her, he said nothing, afraid that his voice and eyes would betray him. He waited for a moment.

"Dayfa's mother," he announced in a voice that he desperately wanted to sound strong, "welcome to you and your daughter. Please sit down."

His assistant and the witnesses were sitting beside him, waiting for his instructions.

"You know why I've brought you both here, don't you?" he said in the same tone of voice.

"We heard that you had returned, my Lord," the mother said weakly. "Welcome back, and God be praised for your safe return! I'd like you to release my husband. I have no one else."

He opened his eyes wide in amazement. He looked at her arms which she was not moving.

"What happened to your arms?" he asked.

She remained silent.

He looked at Dayfa. "Do you want 'Abdin to be your husband?" he asked her with no preliminaries.

She looked back at him. This time there was something different about her eyes. She did not respond.

"You must say what you want in front of witnesses," he told her angrily.

She still said nothing.

"My Lord," the mother asked again "will you release my husband?"

"No," he replied firmly.

"But . . ."

He interrupted her. "Why didn't your daughter answer?" he asked.

She looked all around her and then at the witnesses.

"Could we talk without witnesses and a scribe being present?" she asked.

"No," he replied. "I can't waste time on this problem. If she wants 'Abdin to be her husband, we can draw up a new contract."

For the first time, she spoke. "I don't want him as a husband," she whispered.

He managed to keep his smile and delight hidden. "Why didn't you say that to begin with?" he asked.

"I thought you would know, my Lord," she replied in a voice that only he could hear. "You don't need to ask. I've told you before."

He gave a deep sigh, the sheer joy he was feeling almost leaping out of his eyes. So, tomorrow would be different, enveloped in a fresh atmosphere.

"That was two years ago," he declared. "I thought you'd changed your mind. Has 'Abdin lived with you as a husband?"

This time, her reply was loud. "No!" she said.

He could no longer keep his smiles and happy expression hidden. He was afraid that the scribe and witnesses might notice it.

"I need to speak to Dayfa's mother alone," he announced, feigning a serious tone. "You can leave, and I'll call you back when I need you."

When they had all left, he looked at her and expected her to lift her veil so he could see her face and be sure of the truth. But she did not do it.

"My Lord," the mother told him sadly, "these two years have been a disaster for us."

"What's happened?"

"A lot."

"Your husband's broken your arm, hasn't he?"

"He's my husband, and I forgive him."

"But why?" he asked bitterly.

"Fate, my Lord. He has the right to be angry with me and Dayfa. But we've done nothing wrong."

"I want to know everything," he insisted, "everything. That's if you want to see your husband and for me to release him."

She looked at her daughter. "What is it you want to know, my Lord?" she asked.

"How is it 'Abdin hasn't cohabited with your daughter?"

She gave Dayfa a scolding look. "She's crazy," her mother said, "and stubborn as well. Maybe she's the one who's spread the rumor about herself, that she's been infected by the jinn. She befriends them and practices magic. 'Abdin is scared of her and has not consummated the marriage. In fact, he hasn't set eyes on her up till now."

'Amr did not take his eyes off Dayfa's. "Infected by the jinn?" he repeated.

"That explains what her father does to her," she went on sadly. "I swear to you, my Lord, she deserves to be whipped."

"What does her father do to her?"

"They've advised him to beat her till the jinn leaves her body. He's convinced that she's only doing it to expose him; there are no jinn in her body."

He looked straight at the mother. "How did her father beat her?" he asked.

She looked down, maybe feeling ashamed at her degradation.

"He really deserves to die. Maybe he'll have to be killed."

She now defended her husband. "My Lord," she said, "Dayfa has ruined his reputation and disgraced him by befriending aliens and practicing magic. Now no one will ever want to be married to her. He could have killed her, but he didn't. He's a merciful father, did you but know it."

"I wish to question your daughter about magic," he said impatiently. "Wait for her outside for a while."

His demand shocked her. Even so, she accepted it and left the room.

Once she was gone, he spoke to her tenderly, keeping his longing for her inside himself. "Dayfa," he said, "I want to look at your face."

She hesitated for a moment, then lifted the veil off her face, her gaze glued to the floor. His heart froze as he looked at her. She was much thinner, and her face had lost its glow. Her bones looked a little prominent. Even so, she was still the most beautiful woman he had ever seen, a sorceress who could toy with the fates and dominate body and soul.

For a while he filled his eyes with her lovely face. "Are you well?" he asked deliberately.

"I'm well," she replied in a choking voice, "as long as you are, my Lord."

Should he ask her now? Should he make sure that she still loved him as she had in Syria? Did she think he was crazy? Had he really been with her as he believed, or not?

"You know, don't you?" he asked. "I was in prison."

"Yes, I do," she replied quietly.

"How did you know? How did you find out where I was?"

Their eyes met, and for a moment she said nothing.

"Which prison?" she asked.

"How did you find out where I was in prison?" he asked again. "How did you know? Did you actually know?"

"I didn't know," she replied decisively.

His sigh reflected anger and relief. So, he had not committed a sin with her. Dreams in darkness. What kind of madness was this? Would it infect him again? If it did, what would he do? When would it pounce again?

"I'm going to be married to you," he declared.

She stayed silent.

"Do you agree?" he asked. "Times have changed, and two years have passed. Do you agree now?"

"Aren't you afraid of magic, my Lord?" she asked somewhat bitterly. "Do you know how to outwit it? You're someone with insight into the inner workings of things."

He looked at her lips, her eyes, and her cheeks. His passionate love was like the dark recesses of prisons.

"Perhaps I know how to outwit it," he said, "the same way it did with me. Do you agree?"

She still stayed silent.

"Don't you want to be married to me?" he asked angrily.

"Your questions always amaze me, my Lord," she replied bitterly. "It's as if you read a lot, but understanding does not make its way into your heart, and you never achieve certainty."

"These days," he said confidently, "I'm not certain about a lot of things, but not everything."

"Have you always consulted your heart?"

"My heart tells me that you've never desired anyone but me, and you still don't."

She stood up slowly and lowered the veil over her face. "Your heart has always been right," she said.

He stayed where he was, but did not ask her to stay or to leave. It felt as though the world was finally on its right course and time wanted him to win. He closed his eyes for a moment, then reopened them to hear the mother's voice asking him if he needed her for anything else.

"No," he replied. "You can leave now with your daughter."

Umm Hasan, the salt-seller, took a close look at him as she always did. She was about to speak, but he cut her off.

"I don't want to hear your opinion every time you see me," he told her. "It feels as though I'm standing before the monarch of death. He keeps asking probing questions and testifying against me!"

She smiled, maybe the first time he had ever seen her do it. "I can see you're happy, my Lord," she said. "You deserve some pleasure."

"Thank you," he said as he looked away. "I'd like you too to feel some pleasure in your heart now that your son's death has been avenged."

"Yes, I feel it now," she replied meekly, "all thanks to God and His servant, namely yourself."

With a nod he went to his room. He savored all of the types of food of which he had been deprived while in prison. He looked forward to the next day with both passion and a certain amount of knowledge, but not a lot. When he slept with her, he would know for sure. He would find out if she were death throes taking him over, or if she were really possessed, doing the impossible and reaching to the very depths of existence.

Tomorrow or the day after, she would be his. This time, he would need to act fast. Wait too long, and time can deceive and play games.

He told the police to accelerate the search for 'Abdin. He was waiting for morning to arrive, full of anticipation and hope. He did not need to force her; she still wanted him. A clarion call from deep down kept bothering him: what if she really did not want him? Would he force her as he had planned? He shook his head so as to rid himself of satanic thoughts and crazy doubts. He deserved to win and be happy.

Next morning, he had a meeting with 'Abdin, at which he informed him that the marriage had never actually happened. He confirmed that Dayfa was not his wife. 'Abdin looked relieved and complained to the judge about the things he had heard about his wife's relationship with the two foreign women, the old woman from Abyssinia and the other one from Yemen. The three of them had bewitched people, turned them into animals such as dogs, and spoken to them. He was scared that she would turn him into a dog or goat and much preferred to put as much distance between him and her as possible. He wanted to get back the dowry that he had given to Ridawi.

The judge listened to him patiently and understood. He then summoned Ridawi and demanded that he give back the dowry again. Now that Ridawi had spent some time in prison without knowing when he was going to get out, he returned the dowry immediately. Once 'Abdin had left, the judge started talking to Ridawi. He explained to him emphatically and resolutely what was going to happen.

"Magic is the devil's doing," the judge told him. "Believers shouldn't be scared of magic." No matter what had happened, spreading such rumors about a Muslim girl was strictly forbidden. The judge hated to see his daughter in such a state. It was part of his duty as judge of this town to offer her his assistance. With that in mind, he had made up his mind to be married to her before the next day. The father said that no one in Qus would agree to be married to her. She was nineteen years old now, and rumor had it that she was consorting with jinn.

The judge said that he did not like such rumors. He was anxious to give the people of Qus an example of sacrifice and nobility. That was why he had decided to be married to her. The contract for her marriage would be executed today, now.

At that point, Ridawi gaped in sheer amazement. He was shocked and realized, perhaps for the first time, why the judge was so interested in his daughter. In any other circumstances, he would have refused the judge's demand. His hatred of the judge was deep-seated, and he would have dearly loved to humiliate this arrogant judge of Qus. But at this point, he was at the judge's mercy, with no way out.

"My Lord," Ridawi said all of a sudden, "this marriage is impossible."

"Don't challenge me again," the judge replied, trying to sound calm. "I've returned to Qus and I'm going to stay . . ."

Ridawi looked all around him. "The judge of Qus cannot possibly marry someone who's bewitched and in touch with jinn. She's my daughter, but I'm more afraid for my country, my religion, and my people."

The judge stared straight at the merchant. "The judge of Qus will marry whomever he wants. It's not up to you to decide who is in touch with jinn and who is not."

Ridawi looked all around him again. "Help me, men," he said. "I'm saying to the judge that my daughter is not right for him, and yet he's determined to be married to her."

'Amr looked at the policemen and ordered them to arrest Ridawi.

"Because I don't trust you and fully realize your evil intentions," he said, "you're going to stay here until we've signed the contract. Then you can return to your house."

Nobody present dared say a word.

"We'll draw up the contract now in the presence of witnesses," the judge said, "then I'll let you go home, even though you haven't acknowledged the true extent of your crime. You didn't realize that, did you?"

"Now I realize it all, my Lord," Ridawi replied.

"Tomorrow I'll be cohabiting with your daughter in marriage," the judge said. "You must consent to the marriage now. I'll be summoning her now to hear her response. I don't trust you, or what you'll say or do to her. After the contract is agreed over the Qur'an, I'll let you return to your house. Meanwhile, if you strike her or hurt her between today and tomorrow, I'm going to put you in prison and you won't be leaving for the rest of your life."

People present all looked at each other. The judge seemed different and was acting more nervously than usual. It was as though he was really concerned about this girl; Ridawi's daughter had somehow managed to bewitch him.

"She's my daughter, my Lord," Ridawi grumbled.

"Within an hour or less, she'll be my wife. She'll be obeying my instructions, not yours. You'll have no authority over her."

"My Lord," Ridawi responded angrily, "judges are supposed to act according to justice, and not follow passion."

The judge looked straight at him. "Believe me," he said, "I'm not following passion. If I were, I'd have killed you by now and on the spot."

6

'Amr sent two guards to accompany Ridawi, station themselves in front of his house, and make sure that he did not beat his daughter that day. Ridawi was well aware that his hatred of the judge was by no means at an end; his contempt was obvious enough. He had to pay the price, but today there was nothing he could do. The wedding contract had been pronounced over the Qur'an, and his daughter had now become the judge's wife. Tomorrow she would be moving to his house. Her departure would give him some peace. Ever since she was born, she had only brought him poverty, sorrow, and scandal. Now she was bringing humiliation to him and his sons. She was leaving the house, and that implied success and peace. And yet, his hatred of the judge had not dimmed and never would.

The judge moved around his house with a lively enthusiasm that many people thought had managed to infiltrate itself into the space somehow. He told the servants to prepare the house to welcome his wife; it was as if the nightmare had now turned into a dream, and the darkness had finally dissolved. Tomorrow she would be his, till the end of his and her life. Tomorrow there would be certainty about his madness and sin.

Sometimes he wished that he actually was crazy and had committed an obscene act. He had never lost his mind. After dinner, he spoke to his two boys and explained things to them. They had no objections and did not seem sad. That relieved him.

Umm Hasan was keeping her eye on him as she cleaned the house even more thoroughly today. He did not give her the opportunity to say anything, nor was he ready to listen to whatever might worry or distress him. Her own despair constantly worried him.

He told the servants to prepare the very best food and fruit. He sat on his bed, in sweet expectation of the day when all doubt would disappear and passion could be satisfied. He was afraid that something might happen to change his plans. After the dawn prayer, he recited some verses from the Qur'an and asked God for forgiveness if he had sinned and for His support in carrying out his intentions in this lower world. Today his prayers only concerned this world. At this moment, the delights of this world were all pervasive.

At sunrise he summoned his guard and asked him to check on Dayfa and her mother. As 'Amr went to work, his mind was completely distracted as he thought about her and the two years he had spent wavering between hope and despair. She and his two sons were everything that he wanted. In the evening, he waited for her to arrive with her mother as agreed. Opening the door, he could see the wagon approaching in the distance. Umm Hasan rushed over to help the bride get off the wagon. Dayfa walked behind her mother, head bowed. Neither she nor her mother said anything. Eventually they reached the house.

"My Lord," her father said, "here is your wife as agreed."

'Amr nodded and signaled to Dayfa to go inside. No sooner had she entered than her mother whispered in his ear.

"Would you allow me to stay at your house for a few days?" she asked. "I'm scared of staying with my husband when he's like this."

'Amr nodded. "You're welcome at any time!" he told her.

When Dayfa went into his room, her mother whispered to him again. "My Lord," she said, "I need to tell you something before you go in to be with my daughter."

He paused and looked at her, beset by doubt once again. "Tell me," he said.

"I want you to forgive me and her," she said. "It's not her fault."

"In what way?"

"The marks on her body. The ones on her back are still fresh and open. He's whipped her a lot, maybe every day. But he didn't do it yesterday. At least ten strokes every day. He didn't care any more about spoiling her body."

'Amr frowned. "If he died," he said, "that would rid the world of his evil."

"Believe me," she whispered sadly, "he's merciful. Any other man would have killed her with no argument."

He opened the door. "Don't worry," he told her. "Now I know."

He locked the door and looked in front of him. There was Dayfa, his dream, his madness, all the stars in the firmament gathered together. She was sitting there in her long gown, her face uncovered and her thick hair covering her arms. The gown was made of silk and covered her entire body.

He sat down beside her and grabbed her hand. She seemed hesitant or scared; he did not know which. She clutched his hand and looked away. This was different from the woman who had so tempted him with her daring and control. Now she was broken and defeated. Deep down he decided that there were three aspects to this sorceress; she had to be one. There was Dayfa the innocent, full of life, speaking fearlessly, running freely in the desert as though she owned the entire universe. That was the Dayfa he loved. Then there was the Dayfa who had tempted him, her body surging with femininity, her eyes inviting him to savor oblivion inside her. That Dayfa was different, practicing seduction and magic. Finally, there was the Dayfa that he was seeing now, broken by her father. That much was certain. Maybe he had defeated her, but maybe not. Even after so much torture, she had not been married to 'Abdin. What will, what love, what madness!

He stretched out his arm and hugged her to his chest. "Do you know how much I've longed for you," he asked, "how much I need you?"

She did not respond, but put her arms around his shoulders. He stayed there for a long time, only wanting her arms, making sure that this time it was not a dream and existence was now back to normal. He put his hands around her face and started kissing her. She moved away gently, as though she knew nothing about love-kisses. So, it really had been madness then; he had never been with her before today. He pulled her toward him again, and kissed her gently this time, keeping his overwhelming passion at bay.

"You still love me, I know," he told her between kisses.

She may have shivered a bit. Her heart was pounding, but she did not speak. Her lips . . . it seemed that he had tasted them before and knew them well. He knew her body and every part of her. He had memorized it by heart.

He took her clothes off.

"Can we put the lamp out?" she asked shyly.

"No more darkness after today," he made clear. "I can't stand the dark. Please forgive me!"

"Maybe you'll hate me," she said in shame.

"How can I possibly hate you?" he asked. "Have you lost your mind?"

"The marks on my body."

"They don't bother me," he told her. "You're all I care about."

He looked at the fresh whip marks. Some of them were red wounds, while others were older with black scabs, and still others red marks that might soon disappear. He was appalled by her father's ignorance and cruelty. In his imagination there had not been any marks on her body; the same body with no marks, and the same woman—or so it seemed.

The same blood on the sheet? So, it had all been a dream, a hallucination from spending month after month in the dark.

Once he had finished, he took her in his arms and rested her head on his chest. He had done it before, or at least so it seemed.

There now prevailed darkness mixed with light. His mind traveled far away; it left, then came back. Sometimes he could not believe that it belonged to him; at others, he recalled something from a particular night and day. Maybe it had only happened in the depths of his soul, in the core of his mind. There were times too when he tried to make certain that she was his and with him.

He closed his eyes, then opened them again.

He heard her voice in a whisper: "Do you still want me?" she asked.

"I always want you," he replied emphatically.

It looked as though she wanted to say something else, but she did not speak.

He smiled and kissed her hair. "I want to know everything about the past two years," he told her.

"I want to erase them from my memory," she responded painfully.

He used his fingers to touch the marks on her shoulders that looked fresh and different; some showed torn flesh, others were turning black. As he looked at her face, he could see that she was pursing her lips to hide the pain.

"Does that hurt you?" he asked.

"No, it doesn't," she replied.

She buried her head in his chest, as though to hide the pain of shame and sin.

"Did your father burn you?" he asked angrily.

She did not reply.

The anger he was feeling overcame any heartfelt pleasure or triumphal joy. "Did he burn you, Dayfa?" he asked again.

She clutched his arm, but still said nothing.

He realized now that she wanted to forget and hide from the desert wastes all around her. Once again, his entire body erupted in his love for her. She had been his for a while now and yet he still felt adrift between a violent desire and years-long deprivation on the one hand, and, on the other, doubts about his mental recalcitrance and the certainty that she was in his arms. If she was now his once again, the fire of longing would die down. In the course of his dreams, he had forgotten how much pain her body had suffered from the whipping and burns, for days, months, and even years on end. How could he not have cared?

He kissed her and ran his hand over her body. "Do you want to go to sleep now?" he asked.

"I want to do anything to make you happy," she replied in a muted voice.

He smiled. This time, he wanted to quench his bodily thirst with her slowly and fully awake.

"No," he said, "it's your happiness I want. After everything you've been through, I don't want to do anything that'll hurt you."

"I belong to you, 'Amr," she said. "I've no one else."

He did not respond. She was now his as he had dreamed. Once again, she belonged to him. This time, he was remembering everything. He could feel her between his ribs, longing, wishing, and shivering in desire for him. To achieve her own rapture, she held her breath, closed her eyes, and buried her head in his arms, as though to conceal the signs of achievement and pleasure.

Now he felt sure of real success. "I told you that you would be mine," he said. "Do you remember?"

She nodded. "I love you," she whispered.

"This time," he said with real conviction, "nothing can ever separate us."

"Nothing can separate us," she repeated, although she sounded both bitter and scared.

He was surprised. "Why are you afraid?" he asked.

"I thought I was going to die," she said with an abrupt sadness. "Sometimes I thought I would die before you arrived."

"Don't say that, take care!" he responded loudly.

He started kissing her. "I'm going to punish you for those words," he told her between kisses, "for your fear, and for years spent far away from you. Today and tomorrow I'm going to put out the fire of my passion for you. You're not going to close your eyes until I've put out the flames of at least two years."

She lowered her eyes, but said nothing.

"Are you listening to me?" he asked between kisses, in a menacing tone that was blended with gentle affection.

"Yes, I am," she replied shyly. "I'm listening, my darling, I hear you."

Smiling, he closed his eyes, content at the world today.

⌇

Next day, he made up his mind not to go to work for a whole week. He would enjoy having her with him and quench the flame that had been burning for ages. He would not meet anyone unless it was absolutely necessary. He told the servants to prepare the very best food and asked her to eat it. Then he asked the servants to lock all the doors. He had promised himself to hold her in his arms every day and all the days to come. She did not object, but her bashfulness surprised him. At first, she was not at all shy; there was daring in those eyes of hers so full of words. But then, she turned all bashful. Why, now that he was her husband? She was never the one to start things by touching, kissing, or hugging him. She would wait until he started sensing her passionate love in heartbeats and body shudders. He spent the night trying to douse the flames of years of passion, but he could not. Every time he made love to her, he wanted her even more. Every time he could sense in her eyes the love she felt and her suffering heart, his thirst only intensified.

She never went to sleep in his arms at night. The week went by, hovering between dream and reality. She was his, silent perhaps and submissive, but passion poured out of his body.

"After years of suffering in your father's house," he whispered to her after a week, "now I've exhausted you. There's no sleep or rest inside my house."

"It's only after I've come to your house," she replied, looking away, "that I've learned to savor real peace."

It was after dawn when he turned away from her and closed his eyes. He realized that he would have to go back to life. Once she was sure that he was asleep, she slipped in beside him and put her arms around his back. She kissed his shoulder lightly and fell asleep herself. He was pretending to be asleep; he felt her beside him and smiled. She was hesitant, quiet, and different, but she was still Dayfa, the woman he had dreamed of, the one who had driven him mad, the most beautiful woman he had ever seen in his life.

Dayfa's mother stayed for a week, closely monitoring her daughter and chatting with the salt-seller. She noticed the passionate glances her daughter was sharing with her husband and his gaze that was doing its best to protect her from every evil. She noticed the way he sat her beside him at meals and how he asked her to eat; how his voice changed when she was with him, becoming gentler and more affectionate; how his gaze kept following her, as though she were a girl he was worried about. She observed all this with amazement, but then she started to feel sad. At first, she did not understand why, but then she remembered bitterly the way her own husband had treated her at first, scolding and beating her only two days after their marriage, how this and that had happened. She had assumed that all husbands were like hers; actually, some of them were a lot worse. She had not realized that someone existed who could show so much affection and have such feelings!

"I understand you," the salt-seller told her. "I know the meaning of deprivation."

"I have a husband," she replied immediately.

"He hasn't touched you in years. If he did, woman, there'd be no affection involved. Don't lie. The salt-seller knows it all. Not all men are like the judge. He's the best at his job and at love as well. He uses his conscience and soul in everything he does. Men are all instinct; that's it, nothing else."

"Where's your husband?" Dayfa's mother asked.

"When it comes to life and men, I've abstained. Now this house is all I have. I've no life, woman."

"I know. It's all fate."

"Your daughter's suffered a lot. I can see it in her eyes. Her heart's been broken, and she can't stand up for herself anymore."

"It's my husband's temperament."

"What kind of woman are you to let her be beaten by your husband that way?"

"What could I do? It's the only house I have. If I left my husband, my family would never have me back. He didn't kill her. After she confronted him and made a scandal, he could have done."

"Maybe he actually did kill her without you realizing it. Do you see me, standing alive in front of you?"

For a moment, her heart stopped. "My daughter's fine," she said, "she's fine. As you can see, she adores her husband."

The woman shook her head. "Yes," she said, "she adores him and more. But she still hates her vanquished soul. In order to reach her goal, she had to pay the price. As far as she was concerned, that involved having her own heart destroyed. I'm sorry for that daughter of yours. She's loved him more than her own self."

"What could she have done?"

"Nothing. If she'd succumbed to her husband's desires, she would have crushed her own soul. If she hadn't, then she would have broken her very self, but kept her heart intact. She chose to keep heart and soul in place. Without the soul, Dayfa's mother, there can be no revival. How about you? Are you going back to your husband?"

"Of course," she replied bitterly. "Do you expect me to stay here, sweeping the house with you?"

"Stay here for a while," the salt-seller told her. "If you can stay, then there's no reason to go back."

He often watched her as she talked quietly and submissively to her mother or his two boys. They both seemed to love her. He had long since tried to understand how it was that a disgusting, hard-hearted man like Ridawi could produce a daughter like Dayfa, with all her intelligence and common sense. From her mother, he had learned that she used to spend a lot of time with the two foreign women, old-timers from Yemen and Abyssinia. Her mother in turn had made sure to teach Dayfa how to read and write, as well as to study the Qur'an and hadith, even though neither her mother nor father could read or write. A month later maybe, the two of them were sitting together in their room, eating some fruit.

"'Amr," Dayfa asked softly, "can I ask you something?"

"Of course," he replied. "You can ask me anything you like."

"I'd like to be able to visit my two friends," she stammered. "I'm all they have. They regard me as their daughter and they need help."

He said nothing for a while. "If you like," he said, "I'll send the servant with some food."

She nodded. "I was hoping," she said, "that maybe . . . maybe you'd let me visit them."

"No, that's not possible," he replied, toying with her face. "Not because I don't like them, but because I must maintain my respect as judge in front of people. Otherwise, all sorts of crimes will start happening in the town. If people start spreading rumors about my wife and her friends, then that will hurt the people of Qus, not just me. Do you understand?"

"Yes, I do," she replied, lowering her gaze.

He opened his mouth, but she went on: "I didn't mean to annoy you," she said. "I won't see them any more if it annoys you."

He was shocked by her total surrender. For a moment, he felt an endless sympathy. Her father seemed to have crushed her will or, at least, part of it. But her frowning expression revealed more than what she had just said.

"'Amr," she stammered two days later, "can I send some bones and meat scraps with a guard to Maryam and Zubayda so that they can feed the hyenas?"

"No, you can't," he insisted. "I told you that we have to be cautious and avoid creating rumors. What will the guard say about the judge's wife who's feeding hyenas in the desert?"

"Yes, you're right," she replied after a pause.

He headed for the door. "Hyenas are predators," he stated. "They can find food for themselves. Don't bother with them or believe fairy-tales about spirits and evil."

Their eyes met for a moment, then she looked away in defeat without saying a word. He was not bothered about hyenas or the two old women in the desert. What he was concerned about was something far more important and risky. He was expecting the letter.

Months later, a messenger arrived with the letter he had been expecting. After two whole years of oppression and humiliation, the world seemed, at long last, to be treating him fairly. He returned to his house and started making preparations for the journey to Cairo.

Meanwhile Dayfa had confirmed that she was pregnant. She let him know with the same unusual shyness. Now he told her that he would be traveling for a few days, not more. He was looking happy and enthusiastic.

All of a sudden she started shivering. "Why?" she asked as he came into the room.

He came in behind her. "Why am I traveling? I have a meeting with the sultan."

"You're going to leave me forever," she said with a determination that stunned him. "You'll get rid of me. I know."

He tried to make his voice sound calm, but he was so shocked that it came out loud and forceful: "Dayfa," he told her, "what are you saying? I'm traveling and I'll be back in a few days."

His harsh tone had scared her, or so it seemed. She sat on the floor.

"Never mind," she said quickly. "I'm fine."

He sat down beside her. For the first time perhaps, the truth came crashing down on his head. Her submissiveness stemmed from some deep-seated fear. Her love for him could no longer provide her with any sense of security or ease. Her father had forever stolen from inside her that sense of security, her ability to run in the desert, and her spontaneous laughter. Meanwhile, life had continued and faded away.

"What's the matter?" he asked her. "What's scaring you?"

She hugged herself, obviously scared of something he could not understand, but said nothing.

He stretched out his hand to her cheek, but she stood up suddenly, obviously alarmed as if he were about to slap her.

He said nothing, but could sense his own weakness; life was not back to normal after all, and the return had not been without its problems.

A bitter feeling made its way into his heart. "Come here, my darling," he said gently, "come here!"

She looked at him, closed her eyes, and then opened them again. She came over to him cautiously.

"If you want to leave me," she said, putting her head on his chest, "I won't be angry. I'll still love you."

"How can I possibly leave you?" he asked.

He put his hand on her hair and then grasped it. "Dayfa," he said after a pause, "do you want to come to Cairo with me?"

She buried her head in his chest and put her arms around his neck. "It's up to you," she replied.

"What do you prefer?"

She hesitated for a moment. "I'd rather be with you," she said, "but if . . ."

He toyed with the curls in her hair. "Are you afraid of your father?" he asked her. "Are you thinking that, if I leave you here, he'll hurt you?"

She clung to his shoulder without meaning to do so. "There's nothing I can do," she replied.

"Oh yes, there is!" he told her. "You have an unparalleled strength, did you but know it. As long as I'm alive, Dayfa, he won't hurt you. Remember: trials always come to an end, and endurance determines how things are resolved. You went through a trial, and now it's over."

She gave an enthusiastic nod. "I wasn't sure you'd manage to escape," she muttered. "I almost lost my mind. What if you hadn't escaped?"

"I wasn't sure either. But now we're together. It's your happiness that concerns me. Are you happy now?"

"Very happy," she replied immediately.

He did not believe her, noticing the bitterness in her expression and voice.

For a while, he was feeling a new sense of frustration. He could not change the past or influence the present. It felt as if existence on this earth was never complete.

In the evening, she was asleep on his chest, but he was still wide awake. What her father had stolen from him was unforgivable. As long as she was enveloped by so much pain and bitterness, he could find no happiness. It was as if she were some other person whom he did not know. She had little to say, and, when she did speak, she looked distracted and fearful at what she was saying. Her head was always lowered, and her smile seemed to have completely disappeared. Was this really Dayfa, or did it seem that way?

He gave a big sigh and snorted angrily. He tried thinking about his meeting with the sultan. He would take her with him. That way, her heart would not be wracked by anxiety and anticipation.

When they both reached Cairo, they stayed with some relatives. He decided to take her on an excursion through Cairo. She had never seen it before. She went with him without saying a word. Every time he spoke eagerly to her, she replied in a muted, monotonous tone, as though she could not envision or feel a sense of delight at anything.

They reached the Sultan Hasan Mosque, then he told her that he was intending to pay a visit to the mosque of Muhammad al-Muhsini, the Mamluk amir who had bequeathed an endowment to 'Amr's grandfather, then his father, and then him. When they arrived at the mosque, he told her eagerly about the amir and his relationship with 'Amr's grandfather; about the gold-embossed Qur'an which he had left for his Egyptian wife, Zaynab al-Maqsha'i; about their love story which people still talked about today. It was her son, Muhammad ibn Muhammad al-Muhsini, who had designed and built the Sultan Hasan Mosque.

He ran his fingers over the letters of the gold-embossed Qur'an.

"It was my grandfather," he told her eagerly, "who did the calligraphy for it over many years. The amir loved his wife dearly. When my grandfather gave it to her, the amir had been killed. His wife died two years after him. Their love was an example of abstinence, nobility, and unusual beauty. What do you think?"

She touched the manuscript with her fingers, tears pouring silently down her face. He did not know how to react and said nothing. Should he be angry with her? Pity her? Was she crying for the happiness that had been forever stolen from her heart, or because the amir had been killed? Or because of her own misery? The last possibility worried him.

"What's the matter?" he asked her angrily. "Why are you crying?"

She wiped her eyes quickly. "It must be the Cairo dust," she replied.

"No," he told her without even thinking, "it's the dust that you leave all around you. It's throttling you."

She gave him a despairing look. He sat down on the mosque floor.

"Are you happy now, Dayfa?" he asked.

"Of course," she replied, "very happy."

"You're lying!" he said furiously. "Why? I've never known you to lie. I've never seen you look happy ever since we've been married. I'd thought that the new moon would appear to the two of us after such a long absence. But it didn't. It never did."

She opened her mouth, but he interrupted her.

"What is it that you want? Tell me. What will make you happy?"

"Don't get angry with me," she begged, tears flowing down her face again. "I swear to you that I love you. Please don't get angry with me."

That made him even more nervous. He stood up. "Stop thinking about my anger," he said. "It's your happiness which seems unattainable. The very sight of you is a defeat that I can't stand."

He looked away. She put her hands over her face as though she was afraid he was going to hit her.

"What's the matter with you?" he demanded. "Do you think I'm going to hit you? How can you even think I would ever hit my wife?"

He sat down in front of her. "Dayfa," he asked seriously, "why are you crying? Is it because we haven't yet found happiness in our marriage? Is there something you want and need that I don't know about? Are you thinking about your two friends? You wanted to pay them a visit, didn't you?"

"No," she replied clearly, "I swear to you."

"Don't tell lies. It won't work. When we get back to Qus, we'll go and visit them together. Does that satisfy you and make you happy?"

She did not respond.

"What's worrying you?" he asked nervously. "Hyenas in the desert? What are you thinking about? Are you thinking?"

She still said nothing, her eyes riveted to the ground.

"I told you that we had to be careful and thoughtful," he continued. "But you don't seem to know what it is that you want. Is it to go into the desert? Is that it? Fine, we'll go into the desert. Does that satisfy you?"

She kept hugging her body and shaking a little. She did not dare say anything.

He lost his temper. "Are you afraid of me?" he asked. "Why did you agree to be married to me if you were that afraid? Did you want to get away from your father? You were keen to be married to the judge, weren't you? Everything you said was a lie. No love can possibly survive amid such fear.

"From the very start, you've wanted to escape from your father's tyranny," he went on, looking straight at her. "I was the means of escape, no more. There's no love in your heart, Dayfa. It's cowardly, and love demands risk and courage."

He wanted her to object, to shout that she loved him, to shudder in shock, but she did not.

He gave a deep sigh, angry and frustrated. "We'll go to the desert," he told her, "then you can relax and your heart can be soothed."

He stood up again and held out his hand. "Come on!" he said.

She moved away unintentionally. He lowered his hand again.

"Come on," he said. "Get up. I won't touch you. I don't have a lot of time."

She stood up cautiously.

She walked beside him without saying a word. The atmosphere between the two of them shrieked of defeat.

$$\sim$$

They did not speak to each other all day. At night he slept in his bed, while she lay alongside him, scarcely breathing for fear of disturbing him. When he closed his eyes, his imagination started rebelling. It had been a dream. What had happened in Kerak Castle had been a dream involving the bitter realization of sin. What was happening now was the bitter realization of the truth. He still wanted her and longed for her. He suffered her pain with her and was amazed that she could have remained so stable in the face of her father's cruelty. But now, his own bitterness was crushing love and passion. His very closeness to her was jangling his nerves and reminding him of a new defeat.

"The matter is for God to determine," he said, "both before and after."

"I don't know what I'm supposed to say," she said bitterly, "so as not to annoy you."

"Just the truth."

"There were days," she said, "when I wanted to die, other days when I expected to be dragged off like some animal to my future husband in spite of my own wishes, others when I thought I'd never see you again, and still others when I expected to be whipped. Sometimes the whippings would be postponed, but then they would come and be even harder and deeper. If my father decided to eat first, and then whip me, he'd take more time over it and eagerly hurt me as much as he could. Sometimes I'd scream in spite of myself. I would plead with him and kiss his foot, but he didn't care. But not for a single instant did I ever think of any man but you."

Her words had seared his heart. "Endeavor always brings success," he said.

Still lying on his back, he stretched out his hand, and she hesitantly put hers in it.

He grabbed it and kissed it. "Endurance determines how things are resolved," he said, "and effort puts an end to difficulties."

He kept her hand over his mouth. "I love you," he said.

She remained silent. Today her tears had been flowing freely. He did not try to hug her or have sex with her. He let go of her hand slowly, rolled over, and closed his eyes. He did not hear her quiet sobbing, but he could sense it and realized that he could not erase the past.

Next morning was his meeting with the sultan.

Barquq still had the same demeanor, enthusiasm, and sarcasm. No sooner did he set eyes on 'Amr than he gave him a big hug.

"The judge of Qus is back again," he said. "Prison companion, I've missed you!"

He dismissed the assembly and sat down in front of 'Amr.

"You went back to your position very soon," he said. "Your experience in Syria did not break you. Does that strength come from your faith, or is it a stubborn streak born of arrogance?"

'Amr smiled. "Perhaps both," he said.

'Amr then moved closer to Barquq. "My Lord," he said, "the chief judge likes money a whole lot, as you well know."

"Yes, I do," Barquq replied slyly. "Didn't I tell you," he went on, "that love of money has its advantages? I sent someone to help you and open the gate."

Now 'Amr knew for certain that the sultan was the one who had sent the guard to open the gate. He was also the one who had sent the horse.

"Now the sultan's view has a different impact," 'Amr said.

He stroked 'Amr's shoulder. "Did you prefer having the sultan in prison with you?"

"No. Egypt, Syria, and the entire Muslim territory needs a powerful warrior like you."

"Egypt has a lot of needs. The most important thing is for it to have permanent security, something that will remain in place and not suffer defeat. Mamluk wars represent a defeat for Egypt."

"The fact that the chief judge has so much money," 'Amr suggested calmly, "involves a corruption that can only be followed by ruin. You're already aware of that, Sultan."

The sultan paused for a moment. "You gave him your house in Cairo, didn't you?" he asked. "Have you come to ask for it back?"

"I handed it over to someone who doesn't deserve it so that I could get what I deserve. He was my teacher, and I know him."

"You're behaving like a politician," Barquq said, "not like a person of faith."

"People of faith have to deal with politicians. War is betrayal."

"You gave him something he doesn't deserve. You know that's wrong."

"I gave him something he doesn't deserve so I could stop people being hurt."

"That's logical too. Sometimes stopping people being hurt costs a lot of money and personal involvement. I'm happy that you're back; I've been looking forward to it. You have all the magic of Sufis and the arrogance of a fighter. What is it you want, 'Amr? To punish the chief judge, or to reclaim your house that he took away from you?"

He looked straight at Barquq. "I want what's best for the country," he said.

Their eyes met, and the sultan gaped in astonishment. "'Amr," he said, "do you want to be chief judge? That's why you've come, isn't it?"

'Amr smiled. "If I say yes, then the sultan will think I'm being arrogant," he answered. "If I say no, will the sultan be wrong to chop my head off?"

"As you well know," Barquq responded, "I'm always concerned about your head. But, every time you come to see me, you ask for a lot and provoke conflicts, as you will recall."

"There may well be something that you dislike, but God turns it into a major benefit. That's the trial associated with your power. You've extended your influence, so now the Mongol kings respect you and the Ottomans are keen to please you. There's power to be had in trials. Getting rid of Yalbugha and Mintash is a complete triumph."

"What man can aspire to that?"

"Didn't the Prophet Joseph ask the pharaoh to put him in charge of the country's granaries? The pharaoh realized that he was qualified to do it."

Barquq was shocked. "Are you comparing yourself with the Prophet Joseph, 'Amr?" he asked. "What kind of arrogance is that?"

"No, it's not that. I'm simply using an example of a person who's asking for something for which he knows that he's qualified."

"Joseph turned his heart away from desires and resisted all temptations. Can you do that too?"

"I'm not a prophet, but I can strive to achieve the goal."

Barquq looked around the palace room. "The chief judge is someone who gives opinions and issues commands," he said. "As you well know, he's issued an opinion to kill the sultan before now."

"What's the point of a judge issuing an opinion, when the swords are in the hands of the amirs? If that were not the case, then the judge would issue a different opinion."

"If I made you chief judge and kept the sword in my own hand, would you accept?"

"If you made me chief judge, then you would be wanting justice and truth. Those two qualities cannot be combined when the judge has a sword over his neck."

"You make demands and impose conditions. You realize that I have strong feelings for you and regard you as a younger brother."

"I would not be asking if I didn't realize the feelings we share."

"You admit that this is what you want?"

"As you well know, my Lord, power has its own magic."

"You've just been saying that love of money is a disaster for rulers. Do you realize that love of power is what destroys them?"

"I have no need of money."

"Do you crave this world, or are you purchasing the next?"

"A mixture of the two is what I want. Even so, I know what I'm capable of doing, and what I'm not."

"You'll get what you want, 'Amr. Your wish is granted."

7

Some news gets spread by Egyptians from ordinary people to scholars and even Mamluks because it is shocking and strange. Other news is spread among those same groups because it seems like a stretch of the imagination, something that befuddles the mind like alcohol. But this particular piece of news was far more significant than either of those. When scholars spoke about it, it was to complain and scoff. They decided to complain to the sultan. When amirs discussed it, there was a sense of bewilderment and alarm. They too decided to complain to the sultan. Ordinary Egyptians were delighted and relieved, and decided to go to celebrations of the Prophet's birthday and watch shadow-plays. The religious scholars all knew 'Amr ibn Ahmad ibn 'Abd al-Karim. Most or of all them had taught him. He was not yet forty years old, and yet his arrogance and ambition were enough to disturb everyone. His dealings with Amir Fakhr ad-din revealed all the recklessness of youth and a lack of concern with regulations. His treatment of the Qus merchant was even worse. He had twice annulled his daughter's marriage, only in order to be married to her himself. He was well known for following his own desires, for his lack of real knowledge, and for his black heart, his harsh treatment of enemies, and his threats against those who opposed him. If only he would show a little gratitude or respect his vows. But no. He had pledged to his father-in-law that he did not want the post of chief judge. He had lied and broken that pledge. He was a hypocrite, for sure, an infidel, and a social climber, and all after his own father-in-law had taken pity on him and restored him to his position as judge of Qus. He had gone to see Sultan Barquq to ask for help, to lie, and to stir conspiracies against the man who had helped him regain his position. What kind of man was this? What kind of nerve could produce such a monstrous person?

His grandfather had been just as deluded, but he surpassed everyone else in his iniquity. He had no interest in religion, nor did he function with the next world in mind. This young tyrant deserved to be stoned and killed, someone who denied all decency, loathed his own teachers, and aspired to positions belonging to other people. They had to get rid of him.

The amirs were genuinely alarmed by what seemed to be a hasty decision on the sultan's part. It seemed that the sultan was rewarding 'Amr for taking a stand with him against Yalbugha and Mintash. He was ignoring the community of religious scholars and turning instead to his friends, giving them the most important positions in the country. Barquq was wrong, and that mistake of his was a crime. From among all the people in Egypt, Syria, and the Maghreb, had he really chosen the judge of Qus, who had been bold enough to condemn the son of an amir to death, all so that he could become chief judge himself? What kind of message was the sultan sending to his amirs? What humiliation! Was a shaykh now going to have legal authority over them and trample all over them, when they were the true guardians of the territory? Barquq had made a bad mistake. He had lost his way and followed his own inclinations.

Reactions among Egyptians varied. Some of them were with the amirs, others with the religious scholars, and a minority said that the appointment of the judge of Qus as chief judge was a clear warning to all tyrants in the country and marked a return to truth and justice. However, even though that might be the case, they were not particularly involved. When had the chief judge ever dealt fairly with them? For that matter, when had the amirs or the sultan? The only person who ever did so was the sweet-seller on the Nile banks, who made life possible and endurance feasible.

When 'Amr returned to Qus, he realized that the fight was only just beginning. He would have to fight to keep the position that he had now gained after a lot of hardship. But then, was not mankind created in suffering? This was the hardship needed for fruition, the process of survival that would humble him.

He had hardly had time to reach his house in Qus before congratulations started pouring in from every household, even from his father-in-law. As soon as he entered the house, he called for his wife.

"I promised you that we'd visit your two friends," he declared. "Do you remember?"

"If that would damage your new position, my Lord," she replied softly, "then we shouldn't go."

"My Lord, you say?" he said with a smile.

"The chief judge is my Lord and everyone else's too," she replied immediately.

She bent down, grabbed his coat by his feet, held his hands, and put them on her forehead.

"Chief judge of all Egypt," she said humbly. "We must all bow down to him, especially me."

He stared at her, not understanding what she meant, but said nothing.

"I wonder what the shaykhs will have to say about his olive-skinned wife from the south," she went on, "the one who befriends sorceresses in the desert."

"You know me," he responded confidently, "and you realize that I fear only God. I'm not bothered by what anyone else has to say."

She kept his hand on her brow and hid her face in his palm. "This marriage is not appropriate for the judge of all Egypt. You didn't marry the daughter of a scholar, an amir, or even a senior merchant in Cairo. I feel that it's wrong, my Lord."

He leaned over and held her face. "You feel that it's wrong?" he asked in amazement.

"Yes, to a certain extent. Your new position is one of awesome respect."

"What kind of darkness is obscuring your vision?" he asked her sternly. "You know . . . you must know."

She hid her face. "The mind is not the heart," she said. "Life is a succession of passing days."

"What are you trying to say?" he asked angrily.

She was both scared and dispirited. "If you get bored living with a girl from Qus," she replied, "I won't get angry. That's your right, my Lord."

He closed his eyes. "If I do get bored living with you, Dayfa," he told her forcefully, "I'll let you know. I don't need your advice."

"As usual, I've annoyed you," she said, standing up. "Every time I tell you what's in my heart, you get annoyed."

"Because you don't understand, you don't realize. Fear has seared your heart, just like the Mongols when they burned Baghdad. You don't have any vision or understanding anymore."

He pulled her toward him. "Do you feel it?" he demanded. "Do you realize how much I want you? How I long for you? What I've suffered for years? Do you know anything?"

She shivered a little, but said nothing. "I don't deserve your distress," she whispered.

"I'm the one who decides whether or not I deserve it," he responded firmly. "Keep your opinions to yourself, Dayfa."

She still said nothing.

"Come on," he told her firmly, "we'll have to leave in just a few days. Let's go and visit your friends at sunset."

She nodded, and her eyes shone, perhaps for the first time.

They made for the hut in the desert where the old Abyssinian woman lived. The old Yemeni woman was waiting for them as well. No sooner did they set eyes on Dayfa than they drowned her in kisses and tears. He stayed back, watching them but not interfering.

He could not hear what they were saying, but he could see his wife crying at times and smiling at others. Then he saw her pick up some bits of meat and bones to give to the hyenas. He rested his chin on his hand and started watching her, as though seeing her for the very first time. At first, she was uncertain, looking all around her and searching for him. When their eyes met, he gave her a smile, as though to say that he was pleased with what she was doing. She waited for the hyenas to appear like a little girl. When they started appearing in front of her, she tossed the meat at them quickly, her heart pounding and her eyes sparkling. The Abyssinian woman stroked her shoulder.

"The hyenas like you, Dayfa," she said. "Your presence drives away the evil spirits. You are everything that's good in this town."

She stared at the hyenas who were devouring the meat, and did not move so as not to scare them. The two old women started talking to her nonstop, while she listened patiently. When the Abyssinian woman almost fell down, Dayfa offered her support and took from her the bags of incense that she had brought specially for her from Yemen. She sniffed the scent and then looked over at her husband again. He looked away, as though he had not been watching her. A short while later, she left the two women and went over to him so they could return to the house.

All the way back, she said nothing, but her eyes were still shining bright. When they reached their room, she handed him the incense.

"Thanks to you," she said. "I realize that you don't like me knowing them."

"No," he replied without thinking, "I do want you to be friends with them. I may have been thinking about what people might say. But it's only God who needs to be feared. Forgive me!"

She lowered her head, but said nothing.

"Dayfa," he said suddenly, "when you called me 'my Lord,' were you joking? I detected some sarcasm in your expression. I'd thought that would not be back."

She seemed to smile. "If you own my heart," she said, "then you're 'my Lord' in any case. Are you happy with that status?"

"As long as you can smile and crack jokes," he told her affectionately, "I'm happy. I'm a bit jealous of your two friends and the way they've managed to put the gleam back in your eyes. I've failed in that regard."

She held his hand. "When you haven't been with me," she said, "my eyes haven't seen anything. You don't realize. You can't even imagine how much I love you."

"Are you scared of moving to Cairo and leaving your mother and friends here?"

She shook her head vigorously. "Something else is bothering me," she said.

"What's that?"

"Cairo has no hyenas to repel evil spirits. Your ascent to the very summit is lighting fires all around you. For your sake I'm afraid of people who are jealous, ambitious, and unjust."

He sat down. "You used to be able to see and know everything," he said.

"Love brings its own special delusions."

Next morning, he summoned Dayfa's mother and told her what was going to happen; they would be moving to Cairo. He offered her the option of going with them, but she refused and decided to stay in Qus. She decided to go back to her husband.

The salt-seller stared at him long and hard. "I'll come with you," she said. "I swore and promised you that I'd serve you till my dying day."

"Stay here with your family," he suggested gently.

"You're my only family," she replied.

From the start, he had known that she would decide to go with him.

He looked at her, anticipating that she would say something alarming. "You've faced a host of problems," she said, "and all because of your pledge to me. You've shouldered the burden patiently. You've also suffered because of your beautiful, angelic wife. Do you realize how beautiful she is?"

"Yes, I do."

She stroked his hand. "Her father broke her heart, but couldn't destroy her spirit. Make sure you look after that spirit in case it slinks out of you and disappears."

"I'm doing that all the time," he replied immediately.

"I realize, my son, that the eye always sees what it wants to see. Meanwhile, the actual truth vanishes like the new moon before its appearance. Delusion, how obvious it is! It can gleam like the brilliant whiteness of morning. All of us walk in its procession. Truth, on the other hand, is all erasure and darkness."

He said nothing as he tried to understand what she was saying.

"All the pain and injustice that have been inflicted on you have not been a real trial. That trial actually begins today, chief judge. Power and ability are the biggest trials and the most vicious as well. But come on, so we're not late for your appointment."

⌁

This year, the new moon was clearly visible, and it was seen by Egyptians, religious scholars, and Mamluks. Everyone celebrated the festival and hoped for a year with no drought, plague, violence, killing, taxes, and oppression. To 'Amr it seemed that things would be improving. His wife would be cured of her depression, and that would remove his sense of defeat. When they reached Cairo, she seemed happy to a certain extent, but she still rarely spoke or smiled. Some of the time or even more often, her eyes looked dim. But there were also a few occasions when Dayfa showed herself as that innocent, alert young woman whom he had loved from the very first moment he set eyes on her. Her eyes would shine like a child's, and enthusiasm would show itself on her lashes and eyebrows. He would wait patiently for those special moments, hoping that they would increase as time went by and the signs of whipping disappeared.

The sultan himself came to the ceremony recognizing his appointment. 'Amr was dressed in the chief judge's headdress. He welcomed the religious scholars, students, heads of Sufi orders, descendants of the Prophet, Mamluk amirs, and city governors. When he returned home that night, he bowed down to his Lord, wishing to be rid of all arrogance, desire, and ambition. His wife was watching him in silence. On his first days as chief judge, she only saw him at midnight, and he did not have much time to chat with her. He was receiving religious scholars and amirs and, after some research and information gathering, beginning the process of selecting deputies. He was spending a lot of time thinking and writing so that he would be able to select the best judges for everywhere in Egypt. Then he gave some thought to the appointment of the supervisor of endowments.

⌒

He looked all around the big hall. He saw drooping heads and pleading eyes. He was not yet sure about the elevated status of his council, but he was viewing the world from its lofty heights and exalted position. Intentions were both uncovered and concealed, but humility showed on everyone's faces and expressions. He was there, sitting at a distance, while his inner self hovered over the assembled company, observing what was hidden, hearing things that souls were keeping suppressed, and searching for truths amid the ventures of sinking hearts. Was he seated there in a place from which to view existence in all its vast expanse, full of pearls and treasures, and yet treasures that did not gleam like lightning and could not be contained in a single place or hall? How many jealous people were there, how many hypocrites, how many wanting a service or advantage? How many of them had actually come in quest of knowledge and justice?

His spirit flew around the space, but did not feel any contact with any kindred spirit in the audience. Instead, it came to recognize and regret the number of petitioners, hypocrites, and people with evil intentions.

They moved toward him, one after another. One bowed out of respect, another wanted to kiss his hands and stay by his feet. Someone else extolled his knowledge and learning. All the while, he said nothing, unaffected by the paeans of praise and poetry. As he sat there, he was well aware that prestige makes its way into the hearts of the weak; confidence and stability were the real sources of power.

He listened to all of it patiently. Eventually, one of the shaykhs of Cairo spoke up.

"Chief judge," he proclaimed loudly, "save me from the Mamluks!"

At that moment, silence fell. Now everyone looked down, and not out of a sense of awe and humility.

"What's this about?" 'Amr asked.

"My Lord," the shaykh said, "the situation's out of hand, and times are very harsh on us."

The shaykh rushed over and kissed his hand. "The Mamluks have left their palaces," he said, "and started spending the night in the Bulaq bars. They sit there with Egyptians, bargaining and intermarrying. The sultan won't hear our complaints."

"The sultan must be mentioned favorably in the judge's council."

"I'm telling the truth," the shaykh insisted. "What are soldiers supposed to be doing, being married to Egyptian girls and living in our quarters and streets? Since when do Circassians and Turks mix with Egyptians?"

The whispers grew louder. Eventually the shaykh went on:

"I'm asking for your protection, so I won't spend the rest of my life in prison."

Hamza approached 'Amr. "He's telling the truth, my Lord," he said. "The sultan has allowed soldiers to form families with Egyptians and be married to their daughters. In fact, he himself has been married to the daughter of the architect who built his mosque. For us, it's all very strange."

"What wrong with that?" 'Amr asked. "For soldiers and Egyptian women, marriage is both shield and boon. Neither lineage, race, nor kinship should matter. What's really important is faith and piety."

"Soldiers have no piety in their hearts," the shaykh retorted loudly. "They have no family and no lineage. They are slaves and warriors. They are not part of us, nor are we of them."

"They are human beings, just like us," 'Amr responded firmly. "What applies to them is equally applicable to us. If one of them does something wrong, then we reform him. There is no harm in creating family relationships with soldiers, as long as their faith and character are unsullied. With regard to their going to bars and drinking wine, that's something else. Penalties will be imposed on them, just like any Egyptian."

All the shaykhs looked at each other. Whispers started doing the rounds, stating that the chief judge was siding with soldiers and was fond of the Mamluks. That was because the sultan had given him a position he did not deserve. On this particular matter, he would never adjudicate fairly.

"I'm afraid of conflict breaking out between the common people and soldiers," the shaykh tried again. "The people will be annihilated."

"It's marriage the soldiers want, not conflict."

"My Lord," the shaykh responded, "more than one father has come to see me, asking for a legal opinion on such marriages. I've always rejected the idea. Marriage has to be based on sharing and family stability. Soldiers can't be trusted."

"Do not forbid what God has permitted," 'Amr replied firmly. "If I had a daughter and someone with no doubts as to his faith came asking to be married to her, I would give her to him. I wouldn't be concerned about where he came from or what his job was. From today on, the chief judge hereby announces that there is nothing to prevent soldiers marrying Egyptians. It is both permissible and sanctioned by religious law."

Once the meeting was over, he stood up and headed for his room.

"My Lord," his student asked him gently, "do you want to see the ledger with the names of Cairo's shaykhs now?"

He nodded and started looking over the names of shaykhs and their various jobs. He stopped at the names of two shaykhs whose behavior seemed particularly bad: Al-Qumati and Al-Tibabi. He asked that the matter of both of them be investigated; if necessary, they were to be arrested.

News of the chief judge's decision spread. It soothed the hearts of mothers who wanted to see their daughters married, but it infuriated shaykhs who could not see anything good in soldiers and regarded their marriage to Egyptian women as being both sinful and ruinous. However, the conflicts died down, and the country enjoyed some stability. It had become impossible for soldiers to stay in the Citadel, so Barquq let them walk through the markets and mix with Egyptians. Amid the various assemblies, they married, traded, argued, and created new families.

⌒

In the first month, he received a visit from Amir Saladun, governor of Cairo, who brought him gifts and slave girls. 'Amr gave him a warm welcome. The governor's servants brought in food, fruit, silk, and cloves.

"I've brought you a Byzantine slave girl," he told 'Amr enthusiastically. "She's the most lovely thing the eye has ever seen."

He asked the girl to remove her veil.

"There's no need," 'Amr replied gently. "Your generosity is clear, and I appreciate and understand it. I don't need a slave girl."

The governor gave him an angry look. "Are you turning down the governor's gifts?" he demanded.

"I've accepted your gifts of food and fruit," 'Amr replied gently, "because I know people who need them. But I have no need of slave girls."

For a moment, the governor said nothing. "I've heard about your house in Cairo that you sold," he said.

The governor looked at the house where 'Amr was currently living. "You need a larger and wider house," he said, "one big enough for you to hold councils and receive Egyptians and amirs."

'Amr smiled. "The governor of Cairo overwhelms me with his generosity," he said. "I realize that he's doing it because he is keen to see justice applied in this city which has always illuminated the world's lamps."

"Of course," the governor responded at once. "I want your legal opinion first on something that concerns me personally."

'Amr looked at him, waiting to see what he was about to say.

"I can't stand fasting in Ramadan. I've tried, but I can't. I get giddy and feel ill. I asked one of the shaykhs, and he asked me in turn whether the doctor had allowed me to break the fast."

"Did the doctor do that?" 'Amr asked.

"No, he didn't," the governor replied despondently. "With that, the shaykhs suggested to me that I leave the country for the whole month of Ramadan. As long as I'm traveling, I have a dispensation for breaking the fast. What is your own opinion, Shaykh? Am I angering God by traveling?"

"You're asking me questions beyond my competence, Amir," 'Amr replied. "God is fully aware of your intentions and capabilities."

"But the shaykh has given me a dispensation," he responded confidently.

"The shaykh can do that, but he can't guarantee either reward or penalty. The entire matter belongs to God, both before and after."

"Your words are not any comfort. They don't make any clear distinction between sin and righteousness."

"My words are clear, Amir. They're not intended to provide comfort or resolution. Instead they require personal involvement and knowledge."

Their eyes met. "Everything I've heard about you is good, Shaykh," the governor said. "I'd like you to think about an important matter, and then show justice in your choice."

'Amr waited without saying anything.

"The judge of Qus," the amir continued.

"The judge of Qus?" 'Amr repeated.

"I don't mean you. I mean the person whom you're now going to appoint as judge of Qus."

"Who deserves the position?" he asked.

"Shaykh Al-Qumati al-Tarzi," the governor replied.

'Amr raised his eyebrows. "I didn't realize," he said, "that governors have enough time to know about the circumstances of shaykhs."

The governor ignored his comment. "Do you know him?" he asked 'Amr. "Have you thought about him as judge of Qus?"

"No, I don't know him. But the shaykh's behavior follows him wherever he happens to be. I shall make inquiries about him."

"There's no need for inquiries if the governor lets you know that he's a suitable choice."

"To the contrary, Amir, it is the judge's job to conduct inquiries and a thorough examination. That's a charge that God entrusts to me."

The governor stood up, not a little angry. "Make your inquiries then," he said, "but he's the most qualified."

'Amr nodded. "Your visit has honored my house," he said.

"I've heard about the way you deal with governors and amirs. I hope you realize that your existence is dependent on them."

"It is God who dispenses bounty," 'Amr said calmly. "I've never depended on them before."

"Arrogance leads to oblivion, 'Amr," the governor replied.

"Oblivion awaits us all, Amir, but it's what happens after that oblivion that is what concerns me in my work. As you well know, God deserves that I fear Him."

The amir looked at him angrily. He told his servants to leave and took the slave girl with him.

For a few seconds, 'Amr stayed where he was in order to quell his annoyance. He looked at one of his assistants.

"Look into the matter of that shaykh. I've discovered a large number of outrages, but I need to be sure."

The assistant nodded and left.

That evening, he called for his wife and two sons and sat them down in front of him.

"This position involves trials and temptations," he told them firmly. "That involves both me and you."

Dayfa lowered her head. She had already heard about his conversation with the governor. As usual, she looked uncertain and fearful. The two boys listened, in respectful silence.

"In a number of years," he told them both, "I'm going to get you both married, God willing. For now, you're going to learn and understand. You'll learn about religion. You need to realize that the devil will always come out looking best and emerge from the heart in order to corrupt it. Many people will have the corruption of the chief judge's two sons as their primary goal. Fakhr ad-din is still alive and is bent on revenge. There are thousands like him both inside and outside Egypt. You need to realize that I'm not afraid of you dying. Life is recorded in a book, and there is no way out of that. What I'm afraid of is that you'll both lose the soul which will deprive you of this world and the next."

He looked at them both. "Ahmad and Husayn," he continued, "you've both now reached the age of choice and knowledge. If it so happens and I find out that either one of you has drunk wine, smoked hashish, or gone to Bulaq in search of a prostitute, I'll carry out the ultimate penalty in this house of mine, and without a moment's thought about it."

The two boys swallowed hard, but said nothing.

"I'm not scared about anything to do with justice," he went on in a harsh tone. "You both have a guard to protect you from the devils of this world, but I can't give you protection from devils in the heart. I have enemies who will think of ways to use both of you to weaken me. How many boys have been enemies of their father, weakening him, sapping his resolve, crushing his heart and lowering it to the very pits! You are both the best of sons! I don't want you bragging about my position or assuming that you're above other people or somehow better than them. It's a position that will eventually disappear; what will remain is just your own actions. I'll repeat what I've just said: I'll impose the ultimate penalty on my own son before any stranger, and without even thinking about it."

"We know, my Lord," they both replied timorously. "We understand."

He stroked their shoulders and smiled. "I'm still your father," he said. "You don't need to call me 'my Lord'."

"We know that, Father," they both replied immediately.

He stood up and signaled to them to leave. Dayfa was still listening, head lowered.

"Dayfa?" he asked inquisitively.

She did not speak. She could see the anger in his expression and realized that the amir's visit had provoked his stubborn streak and arrogance. She understood his moods.

"I want to go to sleep," he told her as he headed for their room. "It's been a long day."

She followed him into the room. "Do you want something to eat?" she asked him sweetly.

"No!" he replied angrily.

She helped him get undressed. "I noticed the slave girl and governor," she said.

"How on earth does the sultan choose such governors?" he asked softly. "I don't know. Did you distribute the food he brought to poor folk around the house as I ordered?"

"Yes," she replied immediately.

Once he had undressed and laid down on the bed, she sat beside him and rubbed his shoulder.

"Shall I massage your shoulders?" she asked. "You seem exhausted."

He did not reply, so she rubbed her own shoulder against his.

"'Amr," she began.

"Yes?" he replied without looking at her.

"Were you telling the truth when you said you'd impose the ultimate penalty on your own sons if they drank wine or consorted with prostitutes?"

"Of course," he replied without any thought.

Her heart started pounding as she continued to stroke and massage his shoulders and neck with her shoulder.

"But they're still young . . . your sons."

"Do you know something about them, or are you scared of the ultimate penalties?"

"No, I don't," she replied, her massaging fingers now quivering. "They're the best of sons. I've never seen any boys like them. I swear to you that I've never seen anything other than good about them. It's just that there are times when I don't understand."

"Don't understand what?"

"How do you manage to keep your heart and work separate? You have an amazing ability to keep your heart at bay. You deserve your position."

He did not respond as her hands on his shoulders were soothing the pains of the day. And yet his anger had not diminished. He could feel her breaths close to his neck. She brushed it with her lips and closed her eyes, full of longing and desire, intending to give him a kiss. But then, she hesitated.

"You can kiss your husband any time," he said. "I don't understand why you're so shy."

She moved away and rubbed his bones with her fingers. "You didn't look at the slave girl he brought for you," she said.

"I'm not interested in slave girls or the governor's gifts."

He was still feeling annoyed. "So, Dayfa," he asked, "why so bashful?"

She moved closer. "Forgive me," she said. "I don't know what you want."

"You do what you want," he replied. "Don't you know that as well?"

"I've annoyed you now," she muttered. "I was just trying to stop you being so angry."

"You didn't annoy me," he said, turning to face her. "What's making me so anxious is the heavy burden I'm shouldering."

He was convinced that he had been created in order to do this work. Justice provided both goal and life. He was the best person for it and the most knowledgeable.

She did not say anything more; with him, she usually had little to say. Their relationship had developed and taken a turn that he had not anticipated. He always wanted her, and she always longed for him, went to pieces around him, and trembled in his arms. She would tell him how much she loved him, and, from the very start, her body had longed for him. But that was the longing of a heart of which she had now managed to deprive him, hours he had spent in the desert with her years ago. Back then, he had thought that the hour was just a moment, sunset was noon, and her every word lit up the universe all around him. She could laugh, play, and happily catch fire. All that was in the past, and now it was over. Her heart had now concealed itself in a place that was difficult to reach. After a while, he gave up trying to reach it and made do with bodily satisfaction. He had been forced to realize that life could not continue without the whipping marks and other signs of pain changing the course of existence and making it slanted and defective. That is our life, one that is only finally stabilized in the oblivion of death. But she was still Dayfa, the one he loved and wanted; Dayfa, for whose sake he had endured more than any human could tolerate.

His love for her was never ending and his desire never dimmed. That was enough. The moon would never be full in the starry sky, and the impossible was beyond reach.

Next morning, he welcomed his assistant in his council room. He brought information about Shaykh Al-Qumati. He told 'Amr that the shaykh was responsible for the orphans' endowment. 'Amr now asked his favorite assistant to bring him all the accounts for the endowment and to prepare for a secret visit to the endowment and the shaykh himself.

After looking over the accounts in detail, he made a visit to the endowment, the orphans, and the shaykh. He confirmed that the shaykh had been stealing funds from the endowment. He ordered that the shaykh be arrested immediately.

"My Lord," his assistant suggested gently, "it would be better to wait. You'll make the governor of Cairo furious."

"No amir has any authority over me," 'Amr interrupted. "Anyone who steals will be punished, whether he be a shaykh or amir."

"He's a shaykh with disciples and students," his assistant said gently. "He's not an amir, someone whom people are scared of and don't really know. He's a shaykh who delivers sermons in mosques and issues legal opinions."

"This matter is something even more serious than an amir who behaves unjustly or violently. Intrigue is much worse than murder. Stealing orphans' money is like a fire in the belly."

"It's your decision, my Lord," the assistant said resignedly.

Dayfa asked him shyly if he would ask her mother, if he could, to come and help her in her childbirth. He agreed at once. A few days later, her mother arrived. She seemed much better. No sooner did the salt-seller set eyes on her than she gave her a warm hug and asked how she was. She then spent hours sitting with her daughter, chatting and giving her affectionate hugs. The time for her to give birth arrived. For Egyptians, that year seemed to be one of poverty and drought. There was no Nile flood, crops withered, and people got used to bread with no butter or meat. The sultan asked for a meeting with all the religious scholars to discuss an important matter. Dayfa gave birth to a daughter, then it seemed that she was not going to live to see her.

The fever grew worse, and doctors were unable to come up with a rapid cure. After two days, she no longer recognized her mother and husband. Her eyes were glazed over and her body was hot enough to be shaking.

Her mother started moaning nonstop, and her screams shook the walls of Cairo. She prayed to God to let her die before her daughter or else to have the earth swallow her alive.

The salt-seller kept on sweeping the house with a frowning visage. She did not try to calm the mother down or talk to her. The two boys tried to keep studying. The very idea that Dayfa might die was enough to upset them and remind them of the death of their own mother before.

The chief judge's trauma began immediately, so it seemed, or came to an end quickly—he did not know which. He spent most of the time praying, not saying a word or eating anything more than absolutely necessary. He sat beside her, reading the Qur'an and reciting prayers for her.

He was fully aware that her death would mean the death of his own spirit and his goals. Her illness had been a blow, like being hit on the face by a rock before death. It had woken him up and left him in despair and anger.

That day, he could not leave her and go to meet the sultan. He could not say much to anyone.

"Her father has to be told," her weeping mother told him sadly.

He looked at Dayfa, at her unfocused eyes and wan complexion, and held her hand. "I'm not concerned about her father," he said.

He put his hand around Dayfa's shoulder, then sat her up in her bed, and hugged her.

"Dayfa," he said, "can you hear me? Your daughter needs you. Can you hear me?"

He brushed her hair off her face and wiped her forehead with cold water. He started talking to her nonstop.

His son knocked on the door. "Father," he said, "there's someone here who wants to talk to you."

"I've left a deputy to take my place," he said firmly.

One doctor after another came in, but she was neither dead nor alive. For days, she did not recognize anyone or give up the ghost.

Her father arrived, frowning, and asked to see her. 'Amr went in with him, his heart still not willing to forgive and his hatred undiminished by the passage of time. Her father looked at her for a moment, then left the room.

He sat there, head lowered and not saying a word.

'Amr invited her two friends to come, hoping that they might be able to help her. Perhaps they had a cure unknown to doctors. They came rushing over with tears in their eyes and stayed in her room and around her all the time.

"She seems close to death," her father said to 'Amr after a while.

'Amr did his best to sound resolute. "It's in God's hands, both before and after."

Her father looked at his wife. "Did you give her the gold you inherited from your mother?" he asked hatefully.

"What gold can possibly replace my only daughter?" she screamed at him.

'Amr remained silent and distracted.

"If you've given her the gold as you've said," he asserted, "then you and I have to take it back. Forgive me, my Lord Judge. If my daughter dies, it has to revert to us."

He almost pummeled the father's head on the spot, but instead he stood up and headed to their room again. 'Amr was furious at her or perhaps at the fact she was so ill—he had no idea.

"Dayfa," he said, "you can't do this. Not now, not after everything that's happened. What kind of woman are you, what kind of wife? Wake up!"

The two old women, one from Abyssinia, the other from Yemen, stared at him in amazement.

He shook her. "Come on, wake up!" he yelled. "Why are you dying now, after everything that's happened? After everything we've been through? This isn't justice, it's not fair."

"It's God's will, Shaykh," the Yemeni woman told him resignedly.

"It's more than we can bear," he replied, just as angry.

She was wiping the sweat from Dayfa's brow. "You're a shaykh," she said. "You know that lives are in God's hands."

Closing his eyes, he muttered some prayers, and maybe some words of blame, plea, hope, doubt, and certainty as well. Then he left the room, followed by her father.

"Have you found the gold, my Lord?" her father asked.

"Get out of my house now," he told him coldly. "You've seen your daughter, and it's all over. I don't want to see your face ever again as long as you live."

Ridawi looked at him, alarmed and full of hatred.

"So, you're taking other people's money?" he said.

"It's your wife's gold," he insisted. "Your daughter is still alive."

Ridawi opened his mouth.

"If you don't leave now," 'Amr told him firmly, "I'll call the police to take you away."

Dayfa's father left, cursing and swearing. But, before he did, he spoke to his wife.

"You're going to find the gold now," he insisted. "If you don't, I'll kill you. I'm not bothered by anything."

The anger that had been building up inside 'Amr now overwhelmed everything else and let all the demons out. He headed for his room, prostrated himself on the floor, covered his face with his hands, and spoke at length to God.

The salt-seller came in slowly. "I know and understand," she said. "Didn't I tell you that love for the unseen tears the heart apart and impairs the intellect? But no matter."

"Leave now!" he told her aggressively.

"Every time you grab the rope," she muttered, "it scores your hands and hurts your heart. Let go of it; be courageous and certain. To be sure, that very certainty can shake up powerful hearts, but then, my son, it comes back sturdy as a tent peg. God is the most merciful of the merciful."

He did not respond. She went out of the room, leaving him still in prostration.

"I must not have reached the goal yet," he whispered to himself. "I didn't understand. Here I am yet again, turning to You on a worldly matter that is completely preoccupying my attention. After that, the world has no point. I have wanted my sons, then my wife, everyone whom I would leave behind on the Day of Reckoning. I haven't been able to rid myself of worldly matters, as I had hoped to do, or to forsake all other love save for You. It's my weak heart. I have begged You before, and You have granted me victory.

"If she dies," he continued in resignation, "then it's Your will, a life that is fated. I realize that and still plead. I'm not good at pleading. My very weakness crushes my heart's arrogance and reforms it. I swear to You, as you already know, that I've tried and taken initiatives. Forgive me my anger and wrath. You have crafted the heart and well know its weakness and aberrations."

He felt a little calmer. It seemed that he had taken control of his heart, submitted, and resolutely accepted fate. When he left the room, he bumped into his son.

"Father," the boy told him gently, feeling scared. "The shaykhs are waiting for you to perform the Friday prayer together as usual. What should I tell them?"

He nodded. "Don't tell them anything," he replied resignedly. "I'll pray with them."

He made for her room and heard her mother's suppressed moans which pierced his ears like arrows.

"Stop moaning!" he told her aggressively.

She continued to wail. "She's my only daughter!" she replied.

He turned away and looked at Dayfa. "She hasn't died," he insisted. "Why are you moaning?"

"She's going to die. I can see death in her blue lips. I can tell."

He looked at Dayfa again without intending to, then bent down and ran his fingers over her lips.

"She's still breathing," he said. "Don't despair of God's mercy."

Repeating to himself some words from the Qur'an, he went to lead the Friday worship, finishing it with a lengthy prayer. He was afraid that his grief might be coloring his tone of voice or that his despair might communicate itself to the congregation.

"My Lord and Shaykh," one of his students whispered in his ear, "we've heard about your wife's illness."

"Endurance determines how things are resolved," he repeated. "It's God's own judgement, one that cannot be reversed."

As he made his way back to his room, he repeated the words of the Prophet: "O God, to You I complain of my weakness and my lack of resource . . . If You are not angry with me, then I care not what happens. Your favor toward me is vast."

He went into his room, locked the door, and continued praying on his own. When it was dark, his heart was calmer, his grief was constant, and the possibility of loss was always there.

He went to her room, expecting the worst. He had steeled himself to accept it, realizing even so that the loss of Dayfa would be like no other; her love was like no other, and his suffering for her was the same. Clinging to his lower world and everyone in it was an act of deceit, the work of dark forces. Everyone was bound to die, and the days rolled on. The achievement of power was the beginning of weakness and the very acme of elation in its termination. Dayfa, to whom he was married, was both victory and defeat. Her father had killed her once and more than once, and perhaps she no longer had the will to live. Ridawi, he had robbed him of everything . . . all his days with her, all his dreams, every gleam in her eye, he had been waiting to see them. Hatred had no place in a believer's heart, so why such hatred in his heart, refusing to forgive? Not merely that, but he was deliberately leaving the wound fresh and blazing, as though he were the salt-seller. Perhaps he was fond of the salt-seller because she was for him and part of him, reminding him of the fire that was eating away at his heart, the sheer insistence that dominated his heart, and the acts of resistance and conflicts that he wanted to engage in. How utterly ignorant he was! How despicable life was! What was the point of hatred and loathing?

"If You are not angry with me, then I care not what happens," he repeated. Words to soothe the restless, anxious soul. His hatred of Ridawi was endless. How would it be if he gave him eighty lashes till he was dead, put him in prison for the rest of his life, or dragged his name in the mud throughout Qus! Why had he not done that? What was the point of revenge? Revenge brought a feeling of requital and even ease, but true success lay in God's mercy.

Dayfa's mother had started moaning again, as the doctor sat down beside Dayfa. She sighed, and he looked at her face.

"Is she alive?" he asked the doctor.

At first, the doctor did not reply. He put his hand on her forehead for a moment and gave her some medicine.

"I think she'll live," he said confidently. "Her temperature's lower, and the fever's gone."

He heaved a sigh of relief and went into his room to pray. He did not emerge till dawn. After that, he went into his wife's room. She was asleep. He put his hand on her forehead; she seemed better. He kissed her forehead slowly, then took a look at the large box that her mother had brought for her. Her mother was still sitting silently beside her daughter, neither sleeping nor eating.

"What's that box?" he asked her.

"The things she loves," her mother replied hoarsely. "She's kept them in that box since she was a child."

He looked at the mother, then opened the box and examined the contents.

"What gold was her father talking about?" he asked.

"Gold that she inherited from my mother," she replied equally hoarsely. "He kept trying to get hold of it, but I left it at my father's house. Then I gave it to her, and she hid it somewhere he could not reach. I only told him I'd given it to her after she was married. If I'd told him, he would have beaten her till she told him where it was."

He was still examining the things inside the box. "Does she have it or do you?" he asked.

She did not reply. He was looking at a cotton doll she had kept, some incense, and a white sash that he remembered very well.

He took out the white sash that she had once passed over his hand and clasped to herself. He put it back in the box carefully and put his hand further inside to see what other things of hers were there. Then his eyes opened wide as life came to a sudden halt.

His fingers clasped the gown, and he tapped his mind to make sure he had not gone really mad. Demons took possession of him. It was that gown, or it looked like it, the red, silver-embossed gown. He rubbed the silver with his fingers.

"What's this gown?" he asked in a quavering voice.

"It's one that I made especially for her wedding night," she said in the same sad tone. "Didn't she take it with her?"

He folded it up. "No, she didn't," he replied.

"Are you feeling okay, my Lord?"

She was kissing him passionately. He could feel in his guts her breasts pressing against his chest and her trembling body. Dayfa, between imagination and reality, erasing the outlines of his life so his sinful act dwindled and was buried—or so it seemed to him.

Had he actually killed the guard or not? Was it deliberate or self-defense? Had he fornicated with her or not? Here was the sorcery that her father had accused her of now toying with his mind, making him see what had not happened and feel what had never been. It had to be magic. How could he not doubt that she was a sorceress? How could he not have thought about her relationship with hyenas and sorceresses? What mind could possibly believe that she befriended hyenas? How had his love blinded him to the truth? If only such a thing existed!

Maybe she is a sorceress.

Why had she bewitched him? She had loved him and bewitched him. Then she had been crushed and broken. Was all that was now left of her just fragments? If she was indeed a sorceress, why had she not put a stop to her father's abuse? Why such fear, hesitation, and shyness . . . so much shyness?

Here was his only chance to understand and know for sure. If that kind of understanding led to oblivion, then the truths would inevitably be erased, things he would be annoyed to find out. For the moment, his mind was in a fog. He stared at Dayfa who was groaning in her sleep. At this point, his affection for her was totally overwhelming all other realities.

"Did Dayfa travel anywhere two or three months before her marriage?" he asked her mother.

"No, she didn't," her mother answered clearly. "Her father wouldn't let her go out."

"Why did he hurt her so much?" he demanded. "What made him whip her like that?"

"It's his nature, my Lord," she muttered, "a stubborn streak that we don't encounter in our country."

He left the room and went to take a look at his little daughter whom he had only seen for a few seconds earlier. She was olive-skinned like her mother, with lovely features and hands clinging to life. He held her tiny hand, looked at her for a moment, then left.

He headed for his council chamber, doing his best to control his feelings, his doubts, and his fear of going mad.

His meeting with the sultan and religious scholars was short and full of tensions. He demanded that the shaykhs give him some funds from the endowments so that he would be able to feed the people after the drought. The shaykhs as a group refused. The sultan observed that the shaykhs were for the most part using money from the endowments to suit their own whims. The shaykhs lost their tempers, and so did the sultan. Eventually a compromise was reached, namely that the sultan could have access to some endowment funds this year only.

'Amr's loyal student came over. "My Lord," he said bashfully, "I've heard about your wife's illness. I hope she's better."

"She's better," he replied tersely.

"I want to tell you something," the student went on reluctantly, "and I hope it won't make you angry."

"Tell me."

"The sultan's let Shaykh Al-Qumati go."

'Amr's eyebrows shot up in sheer amazement. "How, when?"

"The shaykh raised a complaint with the sultan, and he responded. This all happened while your wife was ill. I didn't want to add to your worries. My Lord, you're well aware of how much the shaykhs hate you. I'm afraid for you."

He looked all around him. "Sultans have all the power and force at their disposal," the student said. "Religious scholars don't worry them, nor does any religious knowledge stop them from doing as they want whenever they feel that their authority is under threat."

"What do you mean?"

"I know you, my Lord, and I realize that you won't stay silent. Even so, I beg you not to interfere in this confrontation with the sultan. If you do, there'll be no one on earth to intercede on your behalf."

"God is intercessor for all of us."

"He demands of us that we do not hurl ourselves into perdition. If the sultan removes you from office, then Egyptians will lose more than they do by simply having Al-Qumati exist. You need to choose the lesser of two evils."

For a while he said nothing. "The governor of Cairo seems to have a lot of influence, it would appear," he said.

The student looked carefully all around him again. "He's Circassian," he said, "and from the same clan as the sultan. You can't beat him."

"Is Al-Qumati paying him?"

"He's showering him with gifts and issuing legal opinions as he sees fit."

"Send a message to the sultan, saying that I need to have a meeting."

"My Lord, fighting corruption involves risks and struggle. But self-destruction leads to a totally useless oblivion . . ."

"I understand what you're saying."

He looked at his wife, rocking the baby, hugging and singing to her. He stroked her shoulder.

"Thanks be to God that you're well again," he said.

She gave him a look full of shame, as though she had committed some heinous act.

"I don't know how you can forgive me for what's happened," she said.

"What's happened?" he asked, opening his eyes.

"I've been sick for days, days when you were supposed to be at the sultan's council. If I'd died, you would have been relieved of the burden of being responsible for me!"

Her words, always strange and unexpected, now aggravated him more than ever before, and yet he said nothing. He did not want to yell at her when she was still sick.

"Forgive me for giving you a daughter and not a son," she said as she hugged her baby.

"I thought you were intelligent," he replied angrily. "What's happened to you? Can't you tell men apart? I'm not your father, Dayfa. Daughters are a gift from God."

She gave a bitter smile. "I wonder, if you'd accepted the amir's gift, you'd have had at least one woman if I had died."

He could hardly believe what she was saying. He opened his mouth and did his best to hide his amazement. "Did you want me to take the slave girl?" he asked her. "Would you have tolerated that?"

She remained silent.

"Maybe not," she replied softly. "I might have been distressed. But you deserve not to be distressed."

He said nothing.

"Do you want to be like your mother?" he asked her after a while.

"No," she responded without the slightest hesitation.

He held her hand. "If I'd fallen in love with the slave girl and deserted you," he said, "had you even thought about that? You're talking without thinking about it, aren't you? Why do you regret God's decree?"

Lowering her head, she held his hand, but said nothing.

"Dayfa," he asked, "do you want me to buy a slave girl?"

"I beg you not to," she pleaded.

"You told me that I had to do it so that I would have someone to keep me company if you were sick. Have you forgotten?"

"My illness had a bad effect on me," she replied at once. "If I died, I wanted you to be married to someone else who could make you happy. But I didn't die . . ."

Affection now overruled any feeling of anger. "You didn't die," he said. "Your father came to visit you."

She was glued to the spot, and her hand twitched.

"He won't be coming here again," 'Amr told her casually. "If you want to see him, I'll send a guard with you, but he's not going to enter my house again."

She still said nothing. He ran his fingers over her hand.

"He was asking about your gold," he said. "I didn't know you had some gold, Dayfa. You never wear gold."

She swallowed hard. "It's not my gold," she said. "It's my mother's."

"Your mother's keeping it?"

He stood up. "I want you to keep it somewhere safe. Your father's evil intentions and greed have no limits."

She held his hand tight. "Stay with me for a while if you can," she pleaded.

For the first time, she was asking for something clearly. He sat down beside her.

"How are you feeling now?" he asked.

"I'm fine as long as you are," she replied.

He hesitated. "Do you want me to take you in my arms?" he asked.

She looked down. "If you can," she said, "if it doesn't annoy you."

He smiled and pulled her toward him. "No," he said, "it doesn't annoy me."

She put her arms around his neck and lay her head on his shoulder, not saying a word.

Nagging whispers kept gnawing at his mind. She was a virgin in his dreams, and had been a virgin on their wedding night.

He had never found a blooded bed-sheet, nor was his dream about the red robe real. Perhaps the effect of magic and love had made him see what she was seeing and feeling what she was feeling. Had she not said that he was a part of herself?

"I have to thank you for inviting my two friends," she said after a while.

He stroked her back, but said nothing. Her scent, her touch . . . everything. What magic, what madness!

"If you were feeling better," he said, "I'd go back to our own room."

"I'd really like that," she replied, hiding her eagerness, "if being with me won't annoy you."

"I've already told that it won't."

"I mean, having our little daughter with us, so I can nurse her. She'll wake up at night, and that will disturb you."

"Don't worry. There's nothing to worry about."

He sat there, going over the accounts of schools and endowments with his deputies and assistants. He had appointed someone he trusted to be supervisor of endowments. One particular mosque made him pause.

"Are these the accounts for the Sultan Hasan Mosque?" he asked.

"It's no longer functioning as a mosque, my Lord," the assistant answered. "It's a battlefield for Mamluk amirs and their soldiers. You can see the Citadel clearly from the top, fire arrows easily, and hit the enemy—by which I mean warrior Mamluks. The sultan has issued orders that the stairway leading to the school and mosque should be destroyed so that the Mamluks can't use it in battle."

"What are the Mamluks doing now?"

"They jump, slither, and still use it, my Lord. But all the schools are closed. There's no hope of getting them to stop fighting inside the mosque."

"They're fighting inside a mosque, one of God's own houses, a place with its own sanctity and splendor where angels gather! Perhaps they need someone who will set them on the straight path."

"Sultan Barquq's mosque is fulfilling that function. His schools and fountain are offering education and feeding a lot of people."

"Mamluks possess a kind of piety the like of which I've never seen or read about," 'Amr said. "Their power surpasses that of any other state. We need to think about the mosque. When is our meeting with the sultan?"

"Tomorrow or the day after."

Today's meeting was different. There was a need for caution, and special rules were involved in risk-taking.

Sultan Barquq stood up respectfully to greet the chief judge, then seated him on his own cloak.

"Shaykhs have big stomachs," Barquq said with a frown. "They can eat up people's money without ever getting full."

'Amr looked at him, but said nothing.

"What do you think, 'Amr?" he asked.

"Your words amaze me, my Lord," 'Amr replied softly. "They don't fit with the decision to let Al-Qumati go. Or perhaps you don't know. He's been stealing orphans' money."

Their eyes met.

"Are you accusing the sultan of ignorance or neglect?" Barquq asked.

"Certainly not, my Lord," he replied immediately. "I know the sultan as being fair and intelligent!"

"The news I have about you, 'Amr, is not pleasing. The shaykhs have a lot to say about you. If I listened to them, I'd remove you from your position."

For a moment 'Amr did not respond.

"Your information suggests someone who listens to what's being said, then takes the best of it. Not all statements are alike, and scurrilous rumors are not the truth."

"Religious scholars and shaykhs need to take a stand with the sultan. They make moves, they ask, they refuse, and, all the while, they don't realize the imminent danger posed by the Mongols close by, the burdens of government, and the responsibilities of the Egyptian people in times of drought. What harm is there in having the sultan request some funds from the endowments? Isn't it their money to regulate as they see fit? Not only that, but in dangerous times the entire wealth of Egypt is in the sultan's hands, did they but know it. Who's risking his life? The sultan. He's the one who was put in prison while fighting on their behalf. Which scholar can grab a sword and fight for the sake of religion? Even so, I was patient with them. They've issued opinions authorizing my death before now, and I was still patient with them. I haven't put any of them in prison as Qala'un's sons did. I haven't double-crossed them. They're still making decisions about the poor and schools, as though they themselves inherited them from their fathers!"

'Amr did not respond.

"Why have you come here today?" the sultan asked after a while.

"Forgive me, my Lord, I haven't come to see you. My wife has been ill."

The sultan nodded, although he was still feeling tense. "Is she well now?" he asked.

"She's a lot better."

"Who do you want to discuss, Shaykh Al-Qumati and the governor of Cairo? Do you argue with the governor, 'Amr, every time you go to a city? That's not right."

"The governor tried to bribe me," 'Amr stated firmly. "Al-Qumati is dishonest and has no conscience. He had to be imprisoned. That's a trust that I want to hand to the one who gave it to me."

"And who might that be, 'Amr?" the sultan asked angrily.

"The one who gave it to me," he replied.

"And who gave it to you, 'Amr?"

He thought for a moment. "God, the one who gives and takes away."

"Of course it's God who gives blessings, but, chief judge, I'm the one who entrusted you with the care of the Egyptian people. I'm the one who decides who goes to prison and who doesn't. The shaykhs can have their individual interpretations, but the sultan makes the decisions."

The words were sticking in 'Amr's throat, and he said nothing.

"Tell me your news," the sultan said after a while. "Forget about Shaykh Al-Qumati. The chief judge is too important to be bothered about one shaykh."

'Amr sent guards to accompany the two old women on their journey back to Qus. He asked the guards to find out for sure whether or not the two women had traveled to Syria during the past two years. That would help clarify for him a number of things that were still obscure. However, it was surely impossible for Dayfa to have found out where his prison was located, then to get into the citadel and reach him. No one could have reached a prisoner inside the citadel and spent the night with him. His imagination was playing tricks on him again; the whisperings inside his mind would not give up and were eager to triumph. What if he was left to roam between truth and imagination, what if light disappeared and darkness came to dominate the days to come, what if . . .

If he could not be sure in and of himself, he would be even more under water. But perhaps, if he did confirm things and understood, he might well regret it. What kind of judge was he, what assurer of justice, if he did not even know about the recesses of his own heart and, first of all, investigate his own self?

It was with considerable anxiety that he awaited the return of the guards with news about the two old women. After several days, they came back and gave him some news; they did not know if he wanted to hear it or not. The Yemeni and Abyssinian women were both merchants who traveled to a number of different countries. In the past two years, they had both traveled to Syria once or twice.

The truths now started to shine, like the blinding light of lamps—or so it seemed to him.

When he returned to his house, he did not go to ask about his wife and daughter, as he usually did every day. Instead, he asked to talk to her mother in his council chamber. She came at once, looking alarmed.

"Has Dayfa done something to annoy you, Shaykh?" she asked.

He signaled to her to sit down and locked the door.

"Do you love your daughter, Dayfa's mother?" he asked.

"She's my entire life."

"She traveled to Syria with her two friends, didn't she?" he asked her. "Why are you lying to me?"

"She didn't, I swear to you," she replied with determination. "Her father never allowed her to go out."

He looked down. "Do you want me to send her back to her father now?" he asked her. "Do you want her to die? I'm going to leave her if you don't tell me everything. I'll leave her today . . . now."

"I beg you not to do that," she said in shame. "She's been through enough."

He was on the point of standing up. "No matter," he said, "I'll send some guards with both of you so you'll get back to Qus today."

"Yes, she did go with them," her mother said immediately.

He sank to the floor and sat down. "You lied to me," he said. "Why?"

She ignored him and started swaying back and forth. "Predestined fate," she said. "She was afraid you'd leave her. She loved you more than I've ever seen with anyone else. If you'd wanted, you could have left her with no bother."

"You're going to tell me everything that happened, everything you know."

"Shall I tell you what she did, my Lord," she asked dryly, "or what she didn't do? Shall I tell you what I know or what I don't? When Dayfa met you, I don't know what happened between the two of you. You know that. Or have you forgotten? Or is it that you want to forget?"

It seemed to him that he had lit the lamp and blinded his vision. For seconds he said nothing.

"How did her father let her go? How did she find out where I was?"

"He didn't let her go, Shaykh, he didn't do it," she responded, equally dryly. "She ran away with her two friends."

"How?" he asked.

"Do you realize now how merciful he was with her and why you need to thank him because he didn't kill her? When he told her that she had to be married to 'Abdin, she ran away. 'If that happens,' she told me at the time, 'then I'll die. I can't be married to him.' She told me she was worried about my own lot in life, but she would die if she was married to 'Abdin. I let her have all my gold and let her run away. She lived in the desert with the Abyssinian woman amid the hyenas, and no one could find her for months. Her father went berserk looking for her, then spread the rumor that she was consorting with jinn and was not well. She would leave the house until she was well again or the jinn had left her. He hit me, tortured me, and swore that he would kill her."

He remained silent. He did not know whether to hate himself, despise his own vanity, or prostrate himself in prayer and beg for forgiveness.

She went on: "Merchants have their special ways of doing things; every kind of secret is at their disposal. They trade with Mamluks, amirs, and Egyptians. They know everything. Her Yemeni friend sells cloves to rich people. She realized that Sultan Barquq and all his supporters were imprisoned at Kerak Castle. She discovered that you were imprisoned there too and were not dead."

He stared at the floor. "How did she get there," he asked, "and how did she get in?"

"You know. You must know."

"She sold all her gold?"

Dayfa's mother nodded. "Yes," she said, "she sold all her gold and gave it to the guard as a bribe so that she could see you and make sure you were okay."

"Sultan Barquq sent someone to rescue me."

"Perhaps he did, I don't know. But she paid the guard so that you could have some light and food and she could spend the night with you before you were killed. They were waiting for Fakhr ad-din's instructions to kill you. He delayed things because he was busy fighting and killing—no other reason. It was her two friends who talked to the guards, gave them some really expensive cloves, and confirmed everything."

"Dayfa," he muttered.

"No man deserves that from a woman," her mother said, "not even you. I've no idea why she did what she did and why she made the sacrifice that she did. Delusion and love in her heart . . ."

He still said nothing.

She went on: "When she came back, her father had heard the news. He realized that she'd been hiding with the two women. No sooner did she arrive than he took her with the full intention of butchering and burying her. I was the owner of some land that I'd inherited from my father who had died with no sons. I gave my husband the land so he'd let Dayfa live. For days he tortured and burned her, and her screams were loud enough to be heard in Cairo. Then you came back. When you did, Shaykh, I asked her if she knew where you had been. It seemed that, after all your trials and mishaps, you'd forgotten everything."

"She was a virgin," he mumbled.

The mother did not reply. His mind went back to their marriage night when her mother had insisted on staying with them; Dayfa had gone into the chamber before him. She had deceived him with her mother. It was not her virgin blood. His own previous sin was the reality. Their wedding night had all been illusion and deceit.

"Yes, Shaykh," her mother said vehemently, "she was a virgin. No one had touched her other than you."

"Yes, I know," he replied forcefully.

He stared at the floor in his seclusion room. Qur'anic verses were cascading through his mind as the truth placed restraints on his self-importance and conceit. How many times had he given orders for a fornicator to be whipped? How many times had he condemned to death someone who had killed on purpose? How many legal opinions, how many verdicts? He did his best to be merciful, to understand and pardon. Yes, but now what he needed was a legal opinion from heart and angels. His mind was totally incapable of appreciating or knowing.

There was no purpose in self-flagellation, and running away was generally the shortest path to the truth. He had killed someone in order to save himself. What if the guard had not attacked him? He had certainly done that and was on the point of assaulting him. Perhaps he had not intended to kill him. If he had not killed the guard, he would have tried to arrest him and put him back in the dark dungeons again. The guard must have had a mother, wife, and sons. He was certainly looking down from the heavens now, scolding and blaming him before the whole of humanity. Was it love of a woman that had hurled him into the darkness or attachment to life itself? Had she seduced him, or was she the expression of his own internal desires? Did she truly know him and understand him? What was the purpose of seclusion, of asceticism? This was the lower world, continually toying with him, his control and aspirations. He could seclude himself during Ramadan and for a few days each week, and then spend the rest of his days as a slave to his ambitions and desires. He could not simply dispense with this world and hold himself above it. Asceticism was now something temporary, whereas clinging to life was eternal. What kind of shaykh, what kind of judge was he?

Could he really give up his positions and scrupulously avoid influence? Why do that when he was fully qualified? But then, if he had sinned, he was not qualified.

Mankind was created ignorant. God knows full well that sins always trail human beings and keep them company. God has promised forgiveness in his desire to achieve justice and put an end to suffering. He wants people to "forbid wrong and enjoin good." What had happened was not deliberate. Perhaps it indicated his own humanity. He did not know.

She was under twenty years old. He was a religious scholar, someone mature who knew what he was doing or, at least, seemed to be in control of his own actions. How could she be blamed for being in his arms with no experience or knowledge? All she knew was her passionate love which overpowered every other feeling. So what was the sin?

Dayfa. She had prompted him to kill and to love. She had pushed him toward the abyss, because she wanted him to live. What a woman, what a sin, what an angel and demon! He remembered the scars from her whippings. It was not the whip that had left deep red scars on her arms. No, it was fire and burning. As he closed his eyes, the world seemed far removed, life was short, and permanence impossible.

———————

She was bouncing her baby daughter to get her to sleep, hugging her and looking straight at her, as though she were some miracle on earth. She kissed the baby's cheeks and sang some songs that he did not know.

Standing behind her, he looked down at her for a while. Once the baby was asleep, Dayfa put her in the cradle, then turned round and found him standing there, watching her silently. She gasped in surprise.

"I didn't see you come in," she said after a moment.

Their eyes met. She walked toward him cautiously, her eyes glued to the floor.

"You're still shy with me after we've been married for a year," he asked her forcefully. "Why?"

She bent over, held his hand, kissed it, and put it on her forehead. "My Lord," she said softly, "the chief judge."

"Are you being sarcastic or joking?"

He was sure that her mother had told her about their conversation. Her head was still lowered, and his hand was on her forehead.

"Are you going to impose the ultimate penalty on me, my Lord?" she asked. "You promised to do it to those closest to you if they committed a crime."

"If I did it to you," he replied bitterly, "then I'd have to do it to myself as well. In such a case, killing is the worst possible crime. I did it, not you!"

"Your heart is protected from all evil," she said in a muted tone.

He snatched his hand from hers. "How ignorant mankind is!" he said. "He's so fond of self-deception and makes it a habit. Power and victory come with truth; falsehood means defeat. But self-deception is unparalleled loss. Even so, God's mercy encompasses everything."

"I don't know if I've done something to annoy you. I don't want to do that."

"I want to rip apart the divide that you put between us," he declared impatiently.

"There's no divide between us, 'Amr," she replied firmly. "You're everything."

For several minutes, he just stared at the floor. She had no idea what he was thinking about or what he was going to say next.

She noticed the suffering in his eyes as she had on that day a while ago.

"You betrayed me," he told her forcefully, "and I've blessed that betrayal because the heart prefers love to truth."

Her heart was pounding. "I didn't mean to betray you," she responded firmly.

"Yes, you did," he said. "You intended to do it. You know that."

She rubbed her hands together. "So now, do you hate me?"

"No," he replied, "I blame myself for my errors and inattentiveness. I'm sorry for the heavy burden you've had to bear on your own."

She took his hand again and kissed it. "The judge is scaring me," she said. "Sometimes I can't understand him or reach to his heart. My Lord, might I ask you to look for 'Amr on my behalf?"

He snatched his hand away. "'Amr is the judge," he said.

She looked all around her in despair, like some wild animal that had just been put in a cage.

"Punish me then, my Lord," she said with determination. "The chief judge must strike with an iron fist."

Her sudden defiance astonished him. "How dare you speak to me like that?" he asked in a muted tone.

"Do you really want to scold me, blame me, or flay me?" she asked, getting angry for the first time. "I did what I did, and God alone can hold me to account. He knows and He is merciful. But you . . ."

She looked at him. His expression was dry and stony.

"Give your verdict, my Lord," she told him. "I'll obey your orders. What do you want from me?"

"Tell me everything."

"I didn't expect you to forget. I was furious and seething inside when, after your return, you asked me if I knew where you'd been. It was clear that you didn't want to remember what had happened. Your intellect was rejecting what we had done and shut its doors to the truth. I could neither lose you nor confront you. Confrontation might well be the end. Yes, I was furious, and my anger tore my heart apart. But you were still everything to me."

He shook his head. "Salvation doesn't lie in loss of direction."

"It's your own loss of direction that you've fostered. The truth's always been clear to me."

"No," he retorted firmly, "you're the one who's nourished that loss of direction inside me till it gobbled up truths in their entirety."

Her response was a mixture of fear and anger. "If truth involves the death of my soul and your loss of direction allows me to stay with you, what am I supposed to do?"

"What delusions are controlling you and the way you're thinking?" he asked in frustration. "Did you think I was going to get rid of you? That I'd hate you?"

"If you erase truths in order to live with dreams, then who am I to rouse you? I'm not an angel, and I don't possess supernatural powers."

They both fell silent. There was tension, anger, fear, and love, but it was love buried in the soul that neither shifted nor hesitated.

"You're going to leave me now," she said bitterly. "I know you're going to do that."

He looked at her, as though he had not heard what she had said. It was as though he had disappeared inside his own heart and vanished.

"I wonder how many times you've betrayed me," he said as though talking to himself, "how many times you've lied to me while pretending to be so shy and being shocked by my kisses . . . the light embarrasses you . . . What kind of demon is dominating you?"

"But I've never deceived you," she replied in despair. "You know that. You can understand me. You know I'm a part of you and belong to you. No one else has ever touched me. You know that, don't you?"

"Yes, I do," he replied impatiently. "But I'm not so sure about the sincerity of your desire, your shyness, your love, anything . . ."

"'Amr," she pleaded, "you know that your heart can sense how much I love you and long for you. Don't let that error come between us again."

He did not respond, but stared at a multicolored rug on the floor.

"There was no reason for lying," he said. "It was my sin, not yours. You were young and spontaneous. I was the scholar judge. The sin wasn't yours."

"We can forget the past," she replied immediately.

"From now on, there can be no forgetting. It can't cure the heart."

"Your cruelty has no equal," she sobbed. "If only my father had slaughtered me after all and not left me in your hands, doing my best to reach your heart, but failing."

She stretched out her hand to touch him, but he moved away and kept staring at the colors on the rug. After a while, he made for the door and left her. From the room he went out on to the main balcony in the house's hall, contemplating the night and darkness and muttering prayers.

She threw herself down on the bed, not seeing or touching anything. She could feel her soul leaving her body and the pains of her father's whipping assembled at that very moment. She could see her father whipping her mercilessly, relentlessly burning her while blood flowed fearlessly and her screams never ceased.

She felt her breaths constricted, and there were no tears. There were just sighs and suppressed sobs. She stayed put, not sure whether or not she could get up from now on. But she had to get up and beg him, kiss him, explain to him what had happened and had been. She knew that that was pointless. She herself was his war, his heart, and his struggle.

She held her neck, realizing the enormity of what she would be losing if he left her and how she had wasted her life for his sake. Her father was bound to kill her. Why had he not released her?

After an hour perhaps, he came back to her. No sooner did she set eyes on him than she burst into a flood of unrestrained and fearless tears.

He sat down beside her. "Sometimes," he said gently, "painful truth can bring mercy and forgiveness."

She started sobbing and crying as though she was not looking at him.

"I understand and appreciate the situation," he told her kindly. "It's my own vanity that has stood between the truth and you. Forgive me!"

"But you'll never forgive yourself."

He clasped her hand and opened it. "There's no need for tricks or deceit," he said. "Your courage can mediate for both of us. Your good intentions and innocence are enough to shame the devil."

She looked down at her palm in his hands. "What are we going to do now?" she asked.

He clasped her chin and turned her face up toward him. "Do you still love me the same way you did that day?" he asked.

She nodded enthusiastically.

He kissed her cheeks. "The difference now," he said affectionately, "is that we're together. Today we're only enveloped in certainty."

Spontaneously she wrapped her arms around his neck. Not uttering a word, she gave him a passionate kiss, first on the lips, then cheeks, forehead, eyes, and neck. The tears never stopped flowing.

"That's the first time since we've been married," he whispered, hugging her to his chest, "that you've kissed me with no restraint."

At this point she could not talk. Her eyes could see a lot of colors blended with the austerity of a creative artist who is not afraid to break all the rules!

"Dayfa," he said, stroking her shoulder, "stop crying."

As he kissed her cheeks, her tears were wetting his lips. "If you don't stop," he said, "I'm going to kill every hyena in the desert."

She hugged him hard around the neck and smiled amid her tears.

"Where was all this strength last year?" he asked.

"I was scared," she stuttered, still sobbing, "that you'd think that my love for you was like that of debauched women. After my initial plunge, I needed to be careful."

"It was that same plunge and spontaneity that won me over when I first saw you. It wasn't the kind of love that debauched women offer, Dayfa. What you were feeling was innocent and genuine love."

Next morning, the darkness was gone, and things appeared in their natural colors. Realities drew closer and started to take their place on his difficult journey.

She was sleeping peacefully in his arms. When she woke up, she gave him a happy smile, something he had not seen for some time. When she kissed his chest,

he could see a glint in her eyes and a sense of life in her limbs. The day before, they
had made love as though for the very first time. She had dissolved in his arms, but
had not closed her eyes to hide her shyness nor bitten her lips as a way of blaming
her heart for its delirious passion. To the contrary, she had called him by name,
repeated it, and told him just how much she loved him, adored his touch, and
longed for his kisses. She always wanted him. Once the storm had passed, they
both laughed as they recalled that day in the desert when life had come to a halt,
then reached a conclusion, and started to dissolve.

He sat up and hugged her to him. "You know," he said, "realities are cascading in
front of me, like water that has been kept back for years behind the walls of dams.
Once the dam bursts, realities pour forth. Self-deception has a sweet taste like sugar."

She looked into his eyes. "I'd really like you to stay with me for a while this
morning," she said. "I want to tell you things and talk to you."

"I'll stay with you," he replied with a smile.

She proceeded to talk and tell him things. Her eyes were gleaming, as though
her heart that had been so crushed was now fighting back and had triumphed. Her
soul was joyful, conclusion was feasible, and achievement was assured. She stood
up and brought her baby daughter over.

"Look at her," she told him eagerly. "She looks just like you, my darling!"

As he held her in his arms, she was staring back at him with her round eyes.

"No," he said, "she looks just like you!"

"'Amr," she said with a frown, "forgive me if I lied or was deceitful. Everything
I've ever done stems from the fact that you're my heart and soul, and I was afraid
of losing you. There's something else I want to tell you so that lying will never be a
barrier between us ever again."

"What's that?" he asked seriously.

"I know who took your sons away and kept them safe during the war."

He looked at her, waiting for her to speak.

"But," she went on slowly, "I swore not to reveal that person's name."

"Which woman did that?" he asked impatiently. "One of your two friends?"

She shook her head. "I don't want lying to stand between us," she said gently. "I
swore not to talk. It wasn't either Maryam or Zubayda. Your sons are fine, the war
is over, and not all realities are revealed to us."

"I have to know such realities," he declared firmly, "so that I can make just
decisions."

"You're a judge and know the meaning of an oath. I don't want to break mine."

He nodded after a while.

"You forgive me?" she asked, running her hand over his chin. "Everything I've
done has been for you."

"Of course I forgive you!" he replied calmly. "You've saved my life and brought light back to my days. There are twenty. Do you realize?"

She moved away and stared at him perplexed.

"Twenty burns on your body," he went on, "ten on your right arm, and ten on your right leg. Why did he only choose one side? I wonder if he wanted to control your spontaneity and defiance."

She gave a nervous laugh. "He'd sworn that, if he ever found me, he'd burn me with a spit," she said slowly.

"But he burned you twenty times."

"How did you find out?"

"Do you think I don't know you? I know every part of you, heart and soul. Why did he burn you rather than being satisfied with whipping you?"

"I told you," she replied casually, "that he swore that, if he found me, he'd burn me ten times. I intended to bear it all once I was certain that you'd be coming back. You'd promised me that you'd come back. After he'd burned me the first time, he said that I'd screamed or run into the house to get away, so he was going to do it double. I screamed, of course, cried for help, ran away, and pleaded. Does it upset you to see the burns on my arms and leg?"

He hugged her again. "To the contrary, it brings out feelings that I dearly want to rise above. A gigantic hatred and desire to kill. Are you still afraid?"

She paused for a moment. "Sometimes," she replied.

"You weren't afraid of me yesterday."

"No, I wasn't afraid," she repeated. "I don't know why. Maybe it was my anger, despair, and desire to defend everything you've gone through."

"I still hate darkness and avoid it. Both of us have pasts that are full of defeat and resistance. But now, it's all over."

———

"You're getting your things ready to leave, aren't you?" the salt-seller demanded of Dayfa's mother.

"I can't leave my husband any longer," she replied sorrowfully.

"Wake up, woman! It's almost as though you think that life can only be normal if your husband's beating you! He doesn't want you or need you!"

For a moment, she said nothing. "You're a sharp-tongued old woman," she replied. "I don't know how the judge can put up with you."

Maybe for the first time, she laughed. "Dayfa's mother," she said, "every time you've come to visit your daughter, I've seen the sorrow in your eyes. Don't you realize? Such realization gives you power and pride. It grants you release, woman!"

"Sometimes," Dayfa's mother replied despairingly, "it can also imply the end and oblivion."

"I came to realize that life was over after what happened to my son, Hasan," the salt-seller went on. "My husband would never compensate me. He had neither my strength nor persistence. My fate, I decided, lay with the judge of Qus. I would serve him for the rest of my days. Stay here now to salve my loneliness."

"You don't need me, salt-seller."

"Does being a companion to me make you feel ashamed or sinful, woman? I'm poor! But I'm stronger than you by a number of years."

She nodded. "Why should the judge tolerate me being here?"

"Stay here. He will, and the house is big enough."

"What if my husband asks about me?"

"Which husband, you silly woman? You don't have a husband. He's a stray dog who bites you from time to time. Just take a look first at your paralyzed arm."

She swallowed hard. "Will the judge agree to my staying?" she asked weakly.

"If he's prepared to risk his own life to implement justice, do you think he's going to let you go back to the man who's going to hurt you again?"

⟜

The chief judge held a meeting, as usual each month, with all the shaykhs and deputies and the supervisor of endowments. He wanted to discuss with them endowment funds and how they would be used this year to counter poverty; also the sultan's decisions to lower taxes on Egyptians.

The judges arrived and sat around his council chamber. He himself sat on the chief judge's cushion in his official costume to greet the assembled company. The sultan's decision to lower taxes had delighted the population; it had come at a time when Egyptians were suffering shortages. The religious scholars were not happy that the sultan had interfered in matters relating to endowments, but, to a large extent, 'Amr could understand the motive for such interference. Lowering taxes for Egyptians was his own preference.

He shook hands with one judge after another. Looking around, he did not find the supervisor of endowments.

He questioned his assistants. "He's bound to arrive shortly," they told him.

Soon afterward, a man entered wearing the supervisor of endowment's clothing.

"Forgive me, my Lord, for being late," he said eagerly. "The responsibilities are hard."

Silence prevailed, as though fire had been kindled and could not be extinguished.

'Amr rose slowly from his seat and looked at the man. "Al-Qumati," he demanded, "why have you come to my council chamber?"

"The sultan's appointed me supervisor of endowments," he replied proudly. "I'm expecting to be greeted by the chief judge."

"Have you lost your mind, man? The sultan doesn't appoint the supervisor of endowments. Shaykh Al-Tibini, the supervisor of endowments, will attend now."

"No, he won't," Al-Qumati replied assertively. "I've ordered him not to come. It's the sultan's order, my Lord."

The whispers and complaints started. 'Amr remained silent, doing his best to take in what had happened.

He addressed the assembly. "Shaykhs," he asked, "who has the right to appoint the supervisor of endowments?"

"The chief Shafi'i judge, my Lord," was the unanimous response.

"Leave my council chamber, Shaykh," he told Al-Qumati loudly. "You have no place here, and your appointment has no validity with me!"

"Are you defying the sultan, 'Amr?" Al-Qumati asked softly.

"There are rules and regulations that have been in place before my time and that of the sultan. Leave my council now before I put you back in prison!"

Their eyes met for a moment, then Al-Qumati left. 'Amr said nothing and remained in place, trying to understand why the sultan had appointed a stealer of orphan's funds as supervisor of endowments. To please Amir Saladun perhaps? What ruler would ever do such a thing? Why was he interfering in something that was the chief judge's business?"

Chief judge: younger than anyone before him. The sultan had selected and appointed him. Why?

He closed his eyes for a moment, then opened them again. Why had the sultan appointed him? Did he think he could control him, or that he'd sell himself? How naïve and stupid he was! How heedless and weak his heart was!

He asked the assembled company to leave; the meeting would occur at some other time. He returned to his house, distracted.

⁓

When he sat down with his wife today, he did not eat or say anything. She knew, everybody knew how the chief judge had been humiliated and the sultan had interfered in his actions and business.

"Be careful, 'Amr," she told him as gently as possible.

"When truth is involved," he said firmly, "caution has no place."

"He'll kill you and crush you," she said immediately. "He's the sultan. He can do whatever he likes."

"For thousands of years, this country has had rules. Islam has principles and a system. How can he claim to be protecting the religion, and then interfere in something he doesn't understand? He brings in a thief to supervise money?"

"It's all politics, 'Amr, not religion. Don't turn this into a personal struggle between you and the sultan."

He did not respond.

"All I want," she said softly, "is that you don't kill yourself through this confrontation."

For maybe the first time he started yelling angrily. "What do you expect?" he demanded. "What do you want me to do, dealing with a supervisor appointed by the sultan in spite of my objections? I know he's a thief. Am I supposed to sell myself to the sultan so I can stay with you? Is that what you want?"

"No, I didn't mean that," she replied gently.

She started massaging his shoulder and held his hand. "The position of chief judge is something you've always dreamed of and wanted because you knew you were qualified. The governor of Cairo doesn't want you in the position because you don't steal or accept gifts. However, he has influence with the sultan. By doing this to you, his goal is to get rid of you by provoking a confrontation with the sultan or by moving you out of his way. Perhaps if you ignored this incident, carried on, and tried to implement reforms, that would be better for Egypt. If he removes you from office, then he'll be able to bring in someone who'll work with him."

He looked at her. "So much wisdom!" he said sarcastically. "Maybe I didn't hear your voice for a year or listen to a single opinion. What's happened to you, Dayfa?"

"There are new realities, 'Amr, that are aroused now and instilling the soul with energy again."

He did not respond.

"Your ambition intoxicates your heart just like wine," she whispered, "and you've wanted the position ever since you were a student, haven't you?"

He did not respond.

"It's your decision," she went on.

He looked at her hand that was still clutching his arm. "Do you prefer to be married to the chief judge?" he asked her.

"I prefer to be married to 'Amr," she insisted.

"I don't understand you."

"Do whatever keeps your heart intact," she said. "Don't destroy it, my Lord."

"'My Lord!'" he repeated. "Of course! You've always said that I must tolerate the unbearable."

"I was clarifying my opinions for you, but I know what you're going to do."

"How's that?"

"It's your heart that I've known for some time, the one I dearly want to preserve."

That night, he did not sleep.

Next morning, he asked his assistant for a meeting with the sultan on an important matter. Then the salt-seller arrived and set about cleaning the house assiduously. She was talking to Dayfa's mother and smiling from time to time. Their eyes met, and he expected her to say a word or two, but she did not.

"Go in peace, my Lord," she said with conviction.

———

His anger was clearly visible in his expression. The way the sultan had humiliated him was unexpected and intolerable.

"So the chief judge asks to meet me on an important matter, does he?" Barquq asked with a frown.

"I would like the sultan to dismiss the assembly," he requested firmly.

The sultan gave a signal, and they all left. The sultan took a seat, and 'Amr sat down in front of him.

"Have you come to complain, or just because you're annoyed?"

"I just want to understand. Maybe I didn't realize it. However, I was under the impression that the appointment of the supervisor of endowments was one of the functions of the chief judge. That's the way it's been for hundreds of years. Has it been changed without scholars, shaykhs, and judges knowing about it?"

"As I've told you before, religious scholars are not impeccable. Some of them take bribes and spread corruption. They're just like merchants and Mamluks. No one on earth is completely impeccable."

"But my Lord knows the chief judge," 'Amr said in a voice that he was trying to keep calm. "He knows that the judge is not corrupt."

Their eyes met.

"Every judge has a blind spot," Barquq said directly, "and every human being has a weakness. I can handle corruption and understand it. But vanity and stubbornness are dangerous, 'Amr."

"What vanity, what stubbornness? It's my right, my Lord, in my role as chief judge."

"From today, it's my right," Barquq declared threateningly.

"I don't understand."

"From this very hour, it's the sultan who appoints and dismisses the supervisor of endowments, not the chief judge. Too much power in one man's hands leads to corruption."

'Amr kept his eyes glued to the sultan's. "Too much power in one man's hands leads to corruption," he repeated. "So, does the sultan appoint Al-Qumati who steals from orphans as supervisor of endowments? Why?"

"You don't question the sultan. He doesn't have to explain his decisions."

"The supervisor of endowments is appointed by the chief Shafi'i judge, my Lord. Too much power in one man's hands leads to corruption."

Barquq looked at him for a few seconds. "I should cut your head off right now," he said. "I will not listen to your words."

"No, my Lord, it was your words I was using. I realize that I'm doomed, with no recourse. No matter. I won't work with a supervisor of endowments who's corrupt and a thief. I've a request, or maybe two. If you'll open your heart enough to listen to me."

"I know what the first request is," Barquq said impatiently.

"If it's a case of slander," 'Amr said, "then the sultan is showing a preference for malice over good. However, if it's a preference for someone whose loyalty we can guarantee as a way of avoiding bloodshed, then justice and truth will guarantee paradise before anything else. I hereby relinquish my position and request that you assign to me the supervision of one of your schools."

For a few seconds, the sultan said nothing. "I told you that I intend to kill you," he said.

"If I were still chief judge, that would make sense," 'Amr replied. "But, as a teacher, there's no point."

"You defy me and challenge my decisions," the sultan said. "How brazen can you be?"

"What I'm saying is the truth. I'm guided by God."

"It's as though you're never wrong. How watertight your piety is!"

'Amr did not respond. After a pause, he spoke again.

"If my request is so difficult, then please allow me to leave."

Barquq frowned. "Do you want to teach in the Ibn Tulun Mosque or my school?"

"Supervisor of instruction in the Sultan Hasan Mosque."

"Hasan ibn an-Nasir Muhammad, a son of the people? The one who died at the hand of my own teacher? What's your intention, 'Amr? What is it you want?"

"What I want is salvation for the state, Mamluks, and the Egyptian people."

"The Sultan Hasan Mosque has turned into a citadel for battling Mamluks," the sultan said assertively. "I've had the staircase demolished so they can't fight each other."

"Give me a chance to rebuild the stairs," 'Amr asked, "and we can try to bring reforms to Egyptians, both Mamluks and common people."

"That'll never happen. They'll keep fighting each other. They'll never learn. The Mamluks have their eyes on the Citadel, and the mosque has become a fortress, no more. No one thinks of it as a mosque any longer. That spendthrift young ruler spent the country's entire wealth on building his mosque, but the only beneficiaries of its construction were amirs' soldiers."

"If the sultan would give me the chance, I'd be very grateful."

"It'll be a penalty for you, 'Amr. You might be hit by an arrow while you're teaching your lessons, and then people will be rid of your vanity. By God, if you hadn't supported me at one point and shared some pomegranate seeds with me, I would slay you today and hang your head on Cairo's gates."

"If I'd realized," 'Amr replied with a bitter smile," that the sultan did not plan to kill me today, I would have said a lot more. You have always said, my Lord, that the government of Egypt needs to be in the hands of a Mamluk commander, not sons of the people. You also said that Egypt needs an army marshal, and not an heir to the throne. Do you remember?"

"I'm going to cut your head off, 'Amr!" the sultan said.

'Amr smiled. "You've just promised not to do that," he said. "This is a truth I want to share with you because I realize I'll not be meeting you again. You'll never allow it. Is your son going to take over after you? Barquq's family is going to rule Egypt just like Qala'un's? You're trying to cement his rule in place by placating Circassian amirs. No Mamluks in charge save for the army marshal. That's a statement that's best for you, my Lord."

"If you don't shut up, 'Amr," the sultan said, mixing anger and sarcasm, "I'm going to revoke my promise. Your wish is granted, and don't ask about things that don't concern you."

"I swear to you that I only wanted to offer advice."

"No, it's your anger and malice that are at odds with your status as a shaykh. You always want to take revenge on anyone who challenges or opposes you."

"Allow me to leave, my Lord," 'Amr requested with a sad smile.

Barquq nodded, and the friendship between the two of them faded and crashed to the floor like rocks from the Muqattam Hills.

When he returned to his house with his family, he told them his decision and that they would be leaving that house and moving to a smaller one in Cairo near the Sultan Hasan Mosque. His wife gave a little smile, and his two sons frowned.

"It was a big burden," he said as he entered their room, "but now it's over and I feel more relaxed. I can devote myself to knowledge and teaching."

She smiled again and nodded. He seemed in a bad mood and angry.

"You did the right thing, 'Amr," she said after a while.

He lay on his back. "These days," he said, "shaykhs are not safe, and rulers have no commitment."

His mind distracted, he took her in his arms. She rubbed her hands across his face.

"My darling," she said, "you're right. You've done what you could, but this is a crazy time where good and evil are scrambled. There's no one like you, 'Amr."

He was not sure. Was she inundating him with praise because she loved him or because she was convinced? He had often thought of asking her, but he had not done it. Now her praise was much needed. With the passage of time, he had grown accustomed to it and always felt in need of it.

Next morning he brought Dayfa and her mother together.

"Dayfa's mother," he told her, "there's a trust that I must return to you."

She looked at him but said nothing.

"I want you to stay with us always," he went on, "and I'd like you to accept this gold from me to compensate for what you've lost."

She opened her mouth in utter amazement, and Dayfa looked at him.

"I asked Dayfa about your gold and its weight," he went on. "She didn't know a lot, but she gave me an approximate guess. This isn't the exact amount, but it's a trust I want to return to you."

"I don't own any gold, Shaykh," she replied strongly. "I'm residing in your house and living under your protection. I'll never accept this."

"Dayfa's mother," 'Amr declared firmly, "you have to accept it because it will give me some peace and close the pages of the past. I don't want to start anything new while a debt is hanging over my neck. Life is in God's hands."

"Take it, mother," Dayfa told her sternly.

Her mother hesitated for a moment, then took the gold. She did not manage to hide her utter amazement and surprise.

BOOK FOUR
THE SULTAN HASAN MOSQUE

With creativity comes transcendence; with the demon's emergence there follows a slow death for the heart and an opening for the soul; with the fulfilment of a desire the attainment is bitter and the road is at an end.

The architect

8

News that the chief judge was leaving his position delighted a number of amirs and shaykhs. Indeed, some of them spread rumors that 'Amr ibn Ahmad ibn 'Abd al-Karim had been dismissed for bad conduct; the sultan had reprimanded and threatened him, but, because he always showed mercy to shaykhs, he did not want to expose the judge to any scandal. He had given the judge supervision of a school with no value or purpose. The Sultan Hasan Mosque was a fortress and battleground for Mamluks. There was no way of teaching there or advancing learning. The staircase had been deliberately destroyed to stop the Mamluks fighting one another. What penalty was involved and what crime had the chief judge committed? One of the people who were happiest that 'Amr had left his position was his father-in-law, the previous chief judge, who had always regarded 'Amr as an interloper who knew nothing. He was bent on achieving his goals by any means and prepared to forgo anything in his quest for positions and authority. He regretted the fact that 'Amr had been married to his pious and virtuous daughter. Not only that, but, after being married to the pious daughter of a shaykh, he had then been married to a merchant's daughter who defied her own father and stood in the face of traditions and customs. People said that she was touched and had contacts with jinn. How could any shaykh do that, following his own whims and desires? He had neither trust nor commitment. His arrogance had gone so far that he had even dealt roughly with Shaykh Al-Qumati, who was twenty or more years older than him. He had dismissed him from his position in front of the assembled shaykhs, and then tried to harm him and throw him in prison. One shaykh imprisoning another? Quite how far would 'Amr's overreach and injustice extend? The shaykh's daughter must have died out of grief at her husband's cruelty and corrupt behavior. Barquq had finally woken up and realized the true facts about 'Amr. He had been completely dominated by the judge's honeyed words and his gloss of piety and learning. The truth had shown itself and triumphed. What was strange was that the person who had defeated the chief judge and brought him down was Shaykh Al-Qumati, that noble man and learned shaykh. It had not been Amir Fakhr ad-din from years back. There was a lesson there to be understood. The aged Egyptian shaykh had triumphed over the arrogant young interloper, whereas the Mamluk amir had not managed to do it, but had preferred to escape.

Sweetmeats would need to be distributed to every mosque at this happy turn of events.

'Amr was walking tall and with confident stride. He did not care what shaykhs and amirs were saying, and yet his heart was full of rancor and resentment. He prayed, spent time in seclusion, and did his best to quell the fire of his ambitions and frustrated soul. His was the lower world, days spent dealing with people; at least, that is what he told himself—they change and disappear. So why hang on to corrupting positions and ephemeral gloss, and abandon the virtuous things that endure? He spent a lot of time reading and writing. He had made up his mind that the full extent of his desires involved the acquisition of knowledge and its communication to his students. There was nothing loftier and better in God's eyes than knowledge and learning. At first, he spent two whole months without saying much to anyone; just reading and writing. When his wife asked him how he was, he would tell her that he was preparing his lessons to teach in the Sultan Hasan Mosque. If his sons reminded him that the mosque was now a fortress and battlefield, he would ignore them and carry on with his habitual stubbornness and resolution.

His sons did not understand what had led him to give up his position or why he was so obstinate and persistent. They did not dare talk to him about it, but they did with Dayfa. They complained to her, and she listened patiently. She could understand what his two sons were thinking and how they thought that their father's position had been one of prestige and power. Leaving it was a disgrace and shame. Rumors were making the rounds, and now people were looking at the two of them differently. Even their teachers had started treating them roughly and giving them supercilious and biased looks. They spoke to Dayfa for hours and asked her to intercede with their father so he would talk to their teachers or maybe even try to get his position back.

There were two people in the shaykh's house who understood everything about him and the inner secrets of his heart. One of the two understood because she had been broken into scattered pieces. It had been 'Amr who had collected them, so she had become some kind of human being again, but someone with a good deal of knowledge and understanding, both of which the individual achieves by severing the heart and letting it immerse itself in knowledge. In the case of the second person, it was because she was near to his heart and knew it from close up. Umm Hasan was the first, and Dayfa the second.

Because Dayfa knew and understood him, she did not try to talk to him or divert him from the decisions that he had made. One day, she asked to come into his room while he was reading. She sat behind him and started gently massaging his shoulders, something he loved. She could feel the tension in his tight muscles and gripped them firmly with her fingers.

"You did what was right, 'Amr," she told him. "It's the sultan's loss, not yours."

He did not reply, but pretended to be reading so he would not need to respond.

"Teaching's better than being a judge," she went on, "and safer too. I realize why you've chosen that mosque, and I fully understand."

"How do you understand?" he asked after a pause.

"I know you, and realize that you like to be challenged and to reform what's corrupt. I know that it's your belief that reform brings recompense and reward."

"Do the boys understand that?" he asked blandly.

She stroked his shoulder with her fingers. "You sit here for hours," she said. "Your back and shoulders must hurt."

"You didn't answer my question."

"They understand," she said after a pause. "But they're young, and they need you too. They're a trust, and there is a reward to be had in taking care of them. If only you'd give them a little time . . ."

He looked at her in surprise. "Are you giving me advice and instructions, Dayfa?" he asked.

For a moment, she said nothing. "'Amr," she said, "I'm hoping and begging that you'll sit down with them so they don't hear things about their father that'll upset them. Give them the strength that they need to confront people with an open heart."

"These days," he said impatiently, "I don't have enough time."

She was still clinging to his shoulders and neck. "They're your sons," she told him in no uncertain terms. "They need you. Are you up to the responsibility involved, or is it that you're regretting the decision you've made?"

This was a direct provocation, something he had not expected from her.

"Of course, I don't regret it," he said.

"That's because all you want to do is to please God," she responded slowly and assertively. "Days on earth vanish into oblivion, and the good things that endure are with God. That's what you told me."

"Yes indeed," he confirmed.

"People also have to live their life here on earth," she said. "They have needs and aspirations. But you're more powerful than all of them. You've overcome the weakness in your own heart and chosen the rocky road."

He pulled his hand away. "Why are you saying all this?" he asked.

Their eyes met.

"Are you quizzing me or poking fun?" he asked. "Or did you prefer it when I was chief judge?"

"Yes, I'm quizzing you," she said, "and explaining what I see. Maybe you can't see it. Light reflections can eliminate realities."

"I don't want to hear this," he reacted angrily.

"Okay," she replied immediately.

"You can go to your own room," he told her gruffly.

She stood up slowly and made for the door. He stopped her.

"Dayfa," he said.

"Yes?"

"These days," he said, "you don't seemed scared of me. Aren't you worried I'll beat you or threaten you?"

"No," she replied with a derisive smile. "I know that you'd never do that."

"Maybe I should have done it before!" he said quietly. "Your very confidence leads to my own perdition."

She stopped smiling. "Will you come to our room tonight?" she asked.

He smiled in spite of himself. "I think so," he said, "once I've finished my lessons."

She moved close to him again, sat behind him, and started gently massaging his shoulders. He could feel her breath brushing his neck. She kissed his neck, a long kiss.

"I've missed you," she said.

He could not control his neck or his passionate love for her. She knew it and could feel it. His entire body was convulsed with a desire for her.

He turned to look at her and saw her lovely eyes, the most beautiful he had ever seen in his entire life. He remembered years of suffering, dashed hopes, and feeling that having her to himself was an impossibility.

He recalled endless darkness in prison, going on and on and taking control of the mind. It was as if days were an age, hours were eternity, and death was a mercy. Along with his exuberant triumphs and aspirations, he had forgotten all about both his sufferings and gains.

"I've missed you too," he said as he gave her a big hug.

But this new defeat was crushing and as swift as the arrows fired at the Sultan Hasan Mosque. What did he expect? Had the sultan now turned into a shaykh, and vice versa? What naiveté, what vanity! Now he needed to pray and ask God for forgiveness, because his own delusion had blinded him, not once, but twice. The first time, he had ignored his own sin and hung it in some dark recess of his mind so he would not have to think about its causes and consequences; the second was when he thought he was going to change everything and the power possessed by men of religion could overcome Mamluk power. What utter stupidity, what lies!

So, had he completely lost his sense of purpose, or did it just seem like it?

He moved away from her and looked at her face. She was young, at least eighteen years younger than him. Today, she looked like a young girl, and he looked a lot older. He had turned gray; he knew and understood, and had been unable to reach his goal. With that understanding and failure came a different kind of bitterness. His realization of the truth and knowledge of his potential authority regarding Mamluks and corruption brought with them a double defeat. She had suffered too and been hurt to a degree that men would find unbearable. He knew all that, and yet today her eyes looked lively and innocent. Her expression was that of a young girl triumphant.

Why had she fallen in love with him? How did she manage to know everything about him? Why did she stick with him amid all the insanity while whole mountains caved in and were leveled? What a girl, what a woman! Only a stupid little girl was standing before those toppled mountains, but it was a childish innocence that led her to stick with him, not the knowledge possessed by more mature people. And yet, her love for him was mature enough to rival the knowledge possessed by religious scholars.

He was married, and in his own mind his wife was both intelligent and calm. Her knowledge commanded admiration and respect. But, in that same mind, Dayfa also toyed with hyenas and laughed in the desert whenever she found evidence of life amid death. Dayfa represented the rapacious instincts of wild beasts in her sense of sincerity and loyalty, and the spontaneity of palm trees rising defiant in the desert.

Today he was feeling a lot older than her. Maybe he did not possess her inner strength or her stability in dealing with every defeat.

She was his weakness and strength, the overflow of love inside him. But it was the weakness he knew nothing about that alarmed him. For a while, he assumed that he had won a victory against the devil himself. He knew him and uncovered him while revealing truths of every kind. But he had not realized that the devil himself can lurk in a number of guises, calling to him from time to time from somewhere inside his mind; that the devil plays tricks and cajoles people; that holding high office is intoxicating, and power removes your mental capacities; and that living above God's servants because you are the most knowledgeable, just, intelligent, and sagacious about everything may tickle the human will. He would win in the end. He would strive, endeavor, discover, and eventually win.

He hugged her again and felt her soft, succulent body in his arms. "I'll come back to our room today," he whispered. "Maybe now . . ."

"You'll never leave it again?" she asked threateningly. "You must promise me never to leave it again."

"Never again," he announced, as he pushed her into their room.

That evening, he spoke to his two sons. They listened to him in silence and were not convinced. He explained things to them in Dayfa's presence. Once he had finished, Dayfa asked him to talk to the boys' teachers so that they would change the way they were treating them both. He agreed to do that and ended his month-long seclusion during which he had vowed not to talk to a single person.

⟶

He stood in front of the stunning mosque, along with ten of his students.

"Shaykh," one of them asked, "how are we going to get into the mosque when the sultan has demolished the staircase leading to the school's roof and blocked everything behind the doors with sand and rocks?"

He looked around, searching for a way in. "We'll get in through the school window," he said.

The students suppressed their smiles.

"Shaykh," another of them asked, "why such a difficult choice when there are lots of other places?"

"If you only choose the easy course of action," 'Amr stated firmly, "then it would be better for you to stay at home. The easiest way of all takes you to your own bedroom. You know it well and know what to expect inside."

With that, 'Amr lifted his gallabiya and climbed through the school window. A student stretched out his hand to help him, but he did not take it. Instead, he clambered into the mosque. For a few moments, he paused to feed his eyes on the august nature of the building as he recalled moments of despair and inner turmoil.

The students gathered all around him. "Building a mosque like this," they all said, "requires both hardship and purpose."

He headed for the Hanafi school so he could read the name of the architect carved into the wall. He ran his fingers over the clearly visible words. He read out the architect's name: Muhammad ibn Baylik al-Muhsini.

"He was aspiring to eternity," he said. "Building brings eternity, reform brings permanence, and self- and bodily-preservation brings victory and success."

He left the Hanafi school and went next to the Shafi'i school. The students sat around him in a circle. He started talking about the building and its construction, and how humanity must have as its goal the population of the earth. To kill the human soul, something that God has forbidden except when justified, is to kill a part of your own self. It weakens you, just as it did Cain who, in his weakness, begged for help after he had slain his brother, Abel: *"Woe is me! Have I failed to be like this raven?"*

He told them that Cain's weakness came after he had killed his brother. For the first time, he became aware of his own heart's weakness and mortality. 'Amr had

---

* Qur'an Sura 5:31 [The Table]

not noticed the footsteps following him nor the Mamluk soldier standing behind him in full uniform. He was tall and thin and had green eyes and blond hair. He stood there as stiff as stone, not looking at anyone or paying attention to words.

After a while, 'Amr turned round and noticed him. The students looked at each other, but 'Amr ignored him.

"It seems that the sultan wants to make sure we're talking about religion," he said loudly, "and not politics. No matter! Maybe the sultan's guard can benefit from some lessons and information."

The soldier did not react, but kept looking at the horizon, sword in hand.

The lesson went on for a while, and the soldier did not move. The students asked questions and read. 'Amr asked some of them to read books, among them the one he had written a few months earlier. They agree to meet again the next day.

The lessons continued, and the number of students grew. For the students, entering the mosque through the window turned into an adventure for young religious scholars. 'Amr's always different and challenging words made the certificate that he issued better than ones offered by other scholars. He realized that increasing numbers of students would bring problems and that the jealousy of other religious scholars would trigger poisons. But he did not care. After a few months, his two boys joined the class, and the soldier was always there.

When he was explaining the lesson, he would find the Mamluk soldier standing there, like a bewitched piece of stone.

When he was discussing things with his students, he would find the soldier standing there.

When he was reading his books before and after the lesson, he would find the soldier standing there.

After several months, 'Amr was deeply engaged in a fierce discussion with one of his students. He heard a noise like swords and arrows. Suddenly, while he was sitting there explaining things, he felt something brush past him really close, like a flash of lightning. Before he could move, the soldier leaned over and, swiftly and professionally, parried the arrow with his shield.

For the first time, their eyes met. The students were in a panic and encircled their teacher. 'Amr stood up, his eyes still glued to the soldier.

"Did you just save my life," 'Amr asked, "or is that how it looks to me?"

The soldier's expression was still cold. "I'm sorry, Shaykh," he replied in a monotone, "that arrow must have come from the Citadel and gone astray."

'Amr smiled. "Or maybe the arrow knew its target," he said, "and had been planning my death for some time."

The soldier looked away. "Perhaps," he said.

'Amr looked down. "Have you come here to guard me," he asked, "or to listen to my words?"

"The sultan's orders," he replied directly.

"Yes, I know," 'Amr said, "but what exactly are his instructions? Are you guarding me or listening to what I have to say?"

"You can ask the sultan, Shaykh," he replied mechanically.

He sat down again to continue the lesson. "Yes, of course," he said, "I can ask the sultan. But, as you know, he's annoyed with me at the moment. What's your name?"

The soldier paused for a few seconds. "Shaykh Ibn 'Abdallah al-Mahmudi," he replied.

"Your name's Shaykh? You must have been devout as a child, so they called you Shaykh."

"It's my name, Shaykh."

"So you're not devout then?"

"I don't know, Shaykh."

'Amr turned away and continued with his lesson. Then, right in the middle of the lesson, he turned suddenly and looked straight at the soldier. He had the impression that the soldier might well be listening to the lesson and staring at him hard. All very perplexing!

⌒

When he went home, he did not tell Dayfa what had happened, but his two sons did. The salt-seller and Dayfa's mother listened in. He was expecting a whole load of questions for which he had no answer.

They all asked, and he responded calmly, "Our life is in God's hands. Every timeline has its own record. There's no need to panic."

"Is it Fakhr ad-din who ordered your killing, Father?" the two boys asked.

"Perhaps."

"Maybe one of the shaykhs wants to get rid of you?"

"Perhaps."

"Maybe it was a stray arrow from the Citadel?"

"Perhaps."

Now Dayfa's mother spoke. "Perhaps it's the sultan who wants to be rid of you?"

"Perhaps."

Dayfa was staring at him, looking anxious and tense. But she did not speak.

That evening, they made love with a passion to match jinn and wizards. She realized that her own life was in his hands. He ran her hand over his face and kissed part of it devotedly.

He took her in his arms. "Any day now, I'll be hit by an arrow . . . ," he told her softly.

She put her hand over his mouth so he could not finish. She kissed him, then went to sleep, wrapping herself around him as though he was bound to escape somehow. He smiled as he buried his head in her thick hair. He recalled days of deprivation, fear, and delusion, days that passed and came to an end. But her love still remained, although he did not know why he deserved it or what he had done to gain it.

⌒

He began today's lesson with the term "godliness" and its mention in the text of the Qur'an. He recited God's verses, one after the other:

> Get provisions, but the best provision is godliness.
> And the garment of godliness, that is best.
> A mosque founded on godliness from the first day is worthier for you to stand in.
> And then beware of a day when no soul will compensate for another at all.*

Following discussion of the meaning of "godliness" in the context of those verses and their structure, the students started arguing, and, as usual, it was heated. 'Amr gave them the opportunity to ask questions and talk.

"The Mamluks, for example, obey orders without thinking," one of the students said, "and often kill for the sake of a teacher. Don't they remember God's own words: *'And then beware of a day when no soul will compensate for another at all'*?"

Everyone gaped in astonishment and not a little fear as well.

For a moment 'Amr did not speak, but then he turned and looked at the soldier who was pretending not to be listening to the discussion. Standing as ramrod straight as usual, he turned his head and body.

'Amr was curious. "Shaykh," he said.

The students looked at each other. "Shaykh 'Amr," one of them asked, "how come you're calling the soldier 'shaykh'?"

---

* Qur'an Sura 2:197 [The Cow]; Sura 7:26 [The Heights]; Sura 9:108 [Repentance]; Sura 2:48 [The Cow]

"That's his name," 'Amr replied. "It has to have a purpose behind it. This soldier must be pious and full of knowledge. So what do you think, Shaykh? Do you actually kill without giving it any thought, or do you realize that killing the soul is a major crime?"

All eyes were focused on the soldier who hesitated for a moment.

"No," he replied. "I kill to prevent discord and keep Muslim lands safe. That demands individual commitment."

"You're as eloquent as shaykhs!" 'Amr told him, feigning surprise.

The soldier's response was something of a challenge. "You talk, Shaykh, as though everyone in this country was free in every respect. You realize that fate is what moves us. Choice is only tied to our freedom to do what is right or wrong."

The students looked at each other without saying anything.

"I know, for example," 'Amr replied, "that it's not your choice to stand here for hours on end."

"To the contrary," Shaykh replied, "I've made that choice."

Now the whispers grew louder, and the voices reached 'Amr's ears.

"You've chosen to stand here?" he asked in genuine amazement. "Or did the sultan order you? Don't tell me to ask the sultan. You know I can't do that. Humans can be guided, but not compelled. If I wanted to go to the sultan now, I would not be allowed."

"Shaykh 'Amr, I asked the sultan to be the soldier who would be present during your lessons."

"Why?"

"I know you and have been following you for a while. I want to benefit from your lessons. The whole of Egypt knows you, Shaykh."

'Amr remained silent for a moment. "I'm duly honored that you benefit from my lessons, Shaykh," he said. "Can I call you by your name?"

"The honor's all mine, Shaykh," the soldier replied vigorously. "All the soldiers talk about your courage."

"I didn't realize that Mamluk soldiers have nice things to say about me," 'Amr joked. "I thought they all loathed me because I passed judgment on the amir's son in the past."

"Some of them do loathe you, but others know and understand. It's the same with all of them. Some are shameless, other devout; some braggarts, others modest; some courageous, other cowards—just like all Egyptians."

'Amr nodded. "By God," he said, "you're surely going to do better than my students if you keep on that way. When you get your certificate, will you stop fighting, or become the first-ever shaykh who works as a soldier?"

He smiled gently. "Shaykh," he said, "you know and I know that mankind is guided, but not compelled. I have something to ask you, if you'll permit me."

'Amr looked at him waiting to hear the request.

The soldier continued. "I'd like to speak to you outside the school about an important matter."

"You are welcome at my house any time," 'Amr assured him.

That evening, the soldier knocked on the door of 'Amr's house. No sooner had he entered and shaken 'Amr's hand warmly, than he bent over and kissed his hand timorously. He then sat down in front of 'Amr, awestruck.

"I've wanted to meet you for some time," he began enthusiastically, "for ages in fact."

'Amr smiled. "You look twenty or slightly older," 'he said. "It can't have been all that long."

The salt-seller came in with some juice, meat, bread, and sweets.

"That's Umm Hasan, isn't it?" the soldier asked once she had left.

"You know Umm Hasan too?" 'Amr asked in amazement. "Do you work with spies, or are you interested in my career?"

"All of us know about the salt-seller woman who has vowed to serve you till she dies."

The soldier drank some juice and ate. "It's an event that changed the course of my life," he said sadly.

'Amr listened without saying anything.

"During the war between the sultan and the two rebel amirs, Mintash and Yalbugha," the soldier continued, "I was guarding the sultan, of course. He's my teacher. He bought me a while ago when I was twelve. I love him and respect him."

'Amr nodded and carried on listening. The soldier looked down at the decoration on the carpet. "I know that you spent a year in prison with the sultan," he went on, "and then another year in complete darkness. How was it to be in such darkness, Shaykh?"

"Just like hell," 'Amr responded firmly.

"Did it change you? Did it affect you?"

"For a while I kept confusing reality with imagination. All truths in my mind were obliterated, save for one: my faith in God."

"You were fortunate indeed to have such a powerful faith. We're not all like you. Spending time in the Warehouse of Virtues [Khizanat ash-Shama'il] prison is not like being imprisoned in the Kerak Castle Citadel."

'Amr froze in place. "You were imprisoned there?" he asked loudly.

The soldier looked very nervous. "The foulest prison in Cairo," he said.

"You were severely tortured?" 'Amr asked, as though he now understood everything.

"Before Barquq came back after being rescued," he managed to stutter, "I spent an entire year like a scabby dog tied up in a ditch. Sometimes they burned me, at others the guard would take chunks out of my body. I used to scream like a lunatic. A year or slightly less. But, for me, it was an eternity, the rest of my life."

For a while, there was silence.

"Did you curse everything," 'Amr asked, "and long for the release offered by death?"

"In that prison, there were special rules about torture. The only people who were put there were people who Mintash was scared of personally. I had to be a powerful soldier for Mintash to need to put me in that prison. He was out to break people's spirit, and he succeeded."

"No, he failed. Here you are, standing in front of me, proudly talking about your experience."

"That very experience doesn't let me live or grant me a merciful death. Whenever I picture myself screaming and howling like wolves, pleading with them to get things over quickly and kill me, I hate and despise myself. What soldier can carry on when he's destroyed things as thoroughly as the school staircase in this mosque?"

'Amr stroked his shoulder. "The body can't take a lot of punishment," he said. "It was created weak. However, the soul is inevitably victorious so that it can achieve eternity. Do you read the Qur'an?"

"The problem, Shaykh, is that I hate and despise my self for its weakness and surrender."

"What is your self supposed to do when it is enveloped by the obscenity of other hearts that are themselves both weak and oppressive? So, for a while you surrendered, but not all the time. Those times need to be examined."

There was a lengthy silence.

"Do you know, Shaykh," the soldier asked, "what I'd really like to do?"

"What's that?"

"I'd like the day to come when I could tear down that prison using my own hands. I'd grab an axe and tear it down stone by stone."

"Once you'd done that," 'Amr said, "you'd need to cover over it with another building."

"I've sworn and promised my own heart," he declared vigorously, "to build in its place a mosque unlike any mosque Egypt has ever seen. Instead of screams, there'll be prayers and chants, and the light of the Qur'an in place of darkness. The door will have to be made of brass with inlaid gold, just like the one for the Sultan Hasan Mosque."

'Amr moved closer to him. "You're talking and dreaming as if you're dreaming of being an amir, not a soldier," he said. "In fact, only a sultan could build a mosque such as you're describing."

"Oh no, Shaykh," he responded at once. "I'm only dreaming of destroying the prison. Reform and construction would follow, as you yourself have taught us. You've taught us a lot. But my own heart which I can never forgive cannot succeed. It begged, surrendered, and implored. My body that I now find repulsive was like that of wild beasts, like hyenas eating in a ditch, shitting in the same place, and living in filth!"

'Amr smiled. "There are some people," he said, "who believe that hyenas are the best kind of animals and can get rid of evil spirits."

"What kind of crazy person would believe that?"

"My wife for one."

The soldier was appalled by what he had just said and put his hand over his mouth, but then suppressed a smile. "I'm sorry, Shaykh," he said. "I didn't mean . . ."

'Amr stood up. "Would you like to take a stroll along the Nile bank with me in that uniform?" he asked. "People will think that I've a close connection with Mamluk soldiers and stop trying to kill me again."

"As long as I'm alive," the soldier said firmly, "no one will kill Shaykh 'Amr ibn 'Abd al-Karim."

⌐⌐⌐

They walked together, with the soldier talking enthusiastically about his dream of destroying the prison and putting up a mosque in its place.

"Bab Zuwayla," he continued. "It's going to be near the mosque, and no heads are going to be hung up there. Would you believe me if I told you that I hate killing and prisons? But our fates are always decided. I would have preferred to become a man of religious learning, just like you."

"People are never satisfied with their lot in life," 'Amr replied with a smile. "They're always wanting more, right to the end. To me, you seem good at your job."

"I try."

'Amr was silent for a moment. "A lot's happened in my life," he said. "I've met a number of people. Sometimes I knew and understood, and, at others, I didn't. I'd like to ask your advice about something, Shaykh al-Mahmudi."

"I'm at your command, my shaykh and teacher."

"No, your teacher's the sultan."

"I'm sorry, I'm just used to saying it. Ask your question, Shaykh."

"When the war started and I was put in prison, something strange happened. An old woman arrived and took my two sons to a safe place in the south that they didn't know. I've tried to find out who that old woman was, but I've failed. Can I ask you to help me?"

"I'll bring her to you within seven days," he replied confidently. "That's a promise.

"Will you allow me to listen to your lessons?" the soldier continued.

"You can listen and learn, and then I'll give you a certificate."

"That's not allowed. I'm a soldier."

"I'll give it to you when you've earned it. You don't have to teach or tell anyone about it, except yourself."

The soldier smiled enthusiastically, a reflection of his love of learning.

⁓

Several days later, Umm Hasan heard a knock on the door. When she opened it, a middle-aged woman with olive-skinned face unveiled and pale features came in. Her skin was entirely covered in age-wrinkles, even though she was not yet forty. She asked to speak to Shaykh 'Amr and said that Shaykh al-Mahmudi had sent to her to see him.

'Amr came in and immediately realized from her clothes that she was a Christian. He sat down in front of her and welcomed her to his house.

"What do you need from me?" he asked.

"You're the one who needs me," she replied dryly. "I don't know why."

He looked all around him, trying to understand. Umm Hasan was pretending to be busy sweeping, but she was listening to them both intently.

"Do we know each other?" he eventually asked her.

"You don't know me, but I know you."

"I'm honored," he replied with a smile. "Who sent you? Was it the Mamluk Shaykh al-Mahmudi?"

"Yes, in person."

"You're the one who rescued my sons," he said enthusiastically. "Why?"

She said nothing for a few moments. "That lady, Umm Hasan," she said slowly, "is brave, courageous, and a Muslim."

He did not say anything, expecting her to continue.

"One day ten years ago," she continued, "Jamaq killed my son the same way. He was ten years old. He raped him, then deliberately killed him. But he didn't die in agony as happened with Umm Hasan's son."

Umm Hasan's eyes teared up.

"I didn't dare ask for revenge," the woman went on. "I was poor, and, even more important, I was Christian. Some shaykhs have issued legal opinions to the effect that the ultimate penalty cannot be imposed for killing a Christian. Do you realize that, Shaykh?"

"Yes, I do," he replied clearly, "but I'm not one of them. If I'd been a judge back then, I would have imposed that penalty on him. It's the human heart that God has forbidden anyone to kill, my sister. That transcends religious boundaries and human divisions."

She looked at him for a moment. "I realize, sir, that you possess the courage of the mad and the justice of the saints. That's why I had to rescue your sons. I took them to Nubia in the south till the strife in Cairo would be over."

"How did you know where they were?"

"It's easy for a mother to find out where a father hides his sons, in a safe spot inside their grandfather's or grandmother's house. But Maryam, the Abyssinian woman, helped me. She knows you and your wife. Your wife knew everything."

"My wife always knows everything," he said resignedly and somewhat amazed. "She's like a bottomless well. But why didn't you come and tell me?"

"I didn't do it because I was expecting to be thanked. Thanks belong to God, sir. I did it because I felt obliged after you had avenged my son."

For several seconds, he said nothing. "Bring in lunch," he told Umm Hasan. "Bring the two boys in as well, so they can greet the person who saved them from certain death."

Less than two years later, Dayfa's mother started feeling a new lack of concern on her husband's part. She did not hate him or feel any sympathy for him. She had no desire to see him again; he never asked after her or tried to win her back. It was as if her staying in 'Amr's house was an escape and a good opportunity. She was still feeling a bit anxious about staying in the house of her daughter's husband forever, but, over time, her friendship with the salt-seller blossomed. She had become sister and friend. The two of them started going out together occasionally and visiting the new market that the merchant Al-Khalili had established in Cairo, so it was called "Khan al-Khalili." It had a lot more merchandise than the market in Qus, so much so that Qus merchants started going there and buying things to sell back in Qus. At this market the two women would chat, laugh, eat sweetmeats, and look at the minaret in the rest house and the big square. After a few days, the two old women, the Abyssinian and Yemeni, decided to move to Cairo for a number of reasons, the most significant of which was that they both missed Dayfa and could not live so far away from her. Another sad reason was that the hyenas had been killed by the people of Qus, something that made the aged Maryam very unhappy.

It had made her issue a warning to people around her about disaster to come and a sudden invasion of Egyptian territories. She realized how deluded and stupid the people of Qus really were. How on earth could they kill hyenas and let evil thrive throughout every segment of the country? Both she and the Yemeni woman came to 'Amr, complaining and weeping. Dayfa felt somewhat anxious because she was not sure of her husband's sympathy or even his desire to see the two old women. She apologized to him because they had come. He replied that he was aware of how much she loved them and they her. He understood that she was their daughter and mainstay in Egypt.

One month after the two old women had come to Cairo, Dayfa's mother asked 'Amr to give his agreement to her purchase of a small mosque near Khan al-Khalili, along with a small house. She proposed to use the gold that he had given her. She had decided to make use of the small house for charitable acts which, in her opinion, would be confined to making a refuge available for every woman who wanted to be rid of her husband because he was beating or injuring her. The house would be restricted to women who were either divorced or with divorces pending and no other prospects, but not for widows. She was proposing to live in the house along with the two old women and would charge them both for the rental of one or two rooms. She would charge a minimal rent for those who could afford it; those who could not would stay without charge. The salt-seller started visiting her every day or two.

Some years later, 'Amr asked the salt-seller to come to him. He told her firmly that, from that day on, she would not be cleaning the house; her old age made it impossible, and she needed to relax for the rest of her life. His house was hers, and he would give her food and drink; his wife would take care of her. She objected and insisted on continuing to work, but back pains were making it difficult for her to move about. Dayfa insisted on preparing her food herself. One day, the salt-seller went to see 'Amr.

"You've kept your pledge and promise," she told him, "but it seems that I've not kept mine."

"Yes, you have," 'Amr replied firmly, "and for years. That's enough. I hereby release you from your pledge."

For a moment, she looked at him. "You're a good man," she said, "and God has blessed you with a virtuous wife. God is the protector. I've always wanted to protect you from any evil, but it seems that my old age and sickness will make that impossible."

"You've been protecting me?" 'Amr asked with a smile.

"Of course, I've been protecting you, 'Amr. Protection doesn't mean swords, fortresses, and citadels. It involves the heart, good intentions, and prayer. Don't imagine that I haven't been protecting you."

'Amr hesitated. "You've never said that before," he said.

"You've been a judge and a shaykh. For me, you've been a son and support. My feelings about you are different, the kind of affection and protection that only a mother can feel for her son."

She opened her arms, and he gave her a confused look.

"Come over here!" she said. "I wanted to hug you to my chest just once, and then I'm leaving."

He paused for a moment. "Where are you going?" he asked.

"To Dayfa's mother's house. She's become a sister and friend. She'll take care of me."

He did not move and was not ready for her request. She pulled him toward her and gave him a hug. "Here, my son . . ." she said.

She massaged his shoulder. "May God protect you always!" she said.

She stood up slowly, wiping a tear from one of her eyes. He held her up with his arm.

"These days," she said, "realities are in a muddle and truths are lost. Doubts spread, and poor people lose support and confidence. The very existence of a man such as you is like the appearance of the North Star in the Cairo desert, guiding and directing the lost soul within God's own safety."

Umm Hasan moved to Dayfa's mother's house, lived there for a year, and died quietly. 'Amr and some of his students were the only ones to attend her funeral.

Dayfa's mother lived in the new house, along with Maryam and Zubayda. Others joined them, one after another. They spent their days telling each other stories about cruel men and patient women. They filled the mosque with female Sufis and memorizers of hadith. The two old women's trade flourished in Cairo.

A few years later, the two boys, Ahmad and Husayn, were married by 'Amr. They both lived in his house with their wives until the boys decided to move to a house of their own. It proved impossible for Dayfa and the two boys' wives to live together.

Ahmad's wife had hated Dayfa from the start. She found Dayfa's behavior odd; perhaps she was a witch or possessed. Her dark skin made hating her that much easier and her doubts about Dayfa's tendencies more palatable. Dayfa's lack of concern about other people's opinions, whether women or men, had the same effect as beheading people who carried letters to the Tatars. So, Ahmad's wife defiantly declared war. She would tell her husband that Dayfa was not a spectacular beauty, as some people maintained and she herself purported. She was bewitching their father and giving him a potion blended with evil jinn magic every day. Their father's love for her was merely the result of her dealings with a jinn who would come to the house every day in the guise of a wild dog and stray cat. Her husband Ahmad silenced her forcefully, and yet she continued to talk, her mind being totally preoccupied with Dayfa to the exclusion of the world as a whole. She started complaining to her husband that Dayfa cooked some weird things, she took an interest in stray dogs and fed them bones every day; not only that, but she also took her daughter outside the house to give the animals the bones, without the slightest fear or worry about her daughter. It was as if those dogs had turned into roses and palm trees offering blessing and love. She kept nagging him to complain to his father, but Ahmad replied that he did not dare talk to his father about Dayfa, and he himself had never noticed anything bad about her. But Ahmad's wife continued to hate Dayfa and encouraged Husayn's wife to hate her too. She embellished her tales and stories with lower jinn and sea jinn, the way Dayfa talked to jinn and performed magic on them so their children would die.

The two boys did not dare talk to their father about this particular topic. For her part, Dayfa knew; she was well aware of the way the two wives hated her. She was used to dealing with the hatred of strangers and people whose hearts were locked against the truth. She ignored their hatred and continued to go outside every day with her daughter to feed the stray dogs some bones. She told her daughter about hyenas that could ward off evil and protect Qus. The little girl would listen, eyes wide open in delight.

After a whole month of push and shove, the two boys decided to leave the house for fear that one slip of the tongue on their wives' part might reach their father's ears, and he would be absolutely furious. They realized that their father protected his wife as though she were a child. He would never allow any words to be said that would hurt her. They also understood why he loved her so much.

Their father agreed to their leaving, but, before they did, 'Amr summoned Ahmad, who stood fearfully in front of his father.

"Ahmad," his father told him firmly, "when you get to your new house and start your new job as a shaykh, I want you to start with your own family and change your wife's attitude."

Ahmad opened his eyes wide in alarm.

'Amr continued. "I can see her eyes filled with hatred," he said. "That's a disease that needs to be fought and brought to an end. That's your first task in the new house."

Ahmad felt a bit ashamed. "I'll do it, father," he replied. "Has she done anything to upset you? Tell me, and I'll punish her severely."

'Amr massaged his son's shoulder. "No, she hasn't," he replied. "Change your wife's behavior, my son. Use prudence and wise counsel to put her right."

Dayfa spoke to him when he came into their room. "Don't blame your son's wife," she said kindly. "Everyone realizes that my actions are scary, even though I never hurt anyone."

"They're certainly odd," he said with a grin, "but they're not scary."

"Do you know, 'Amr, why people hate wild animals?" she asked him. "It's because they can't control them and make them obedient. They're free and independent, rejecting submission even if it involves food and safety. Human beings realize that these animals are superior to them, and they hate them for that reason. They know that the animals won't follow their orders, so they envy them."

He could spot the dignity in her expression; she was challenging his will and winning.

He looked into her eyes. "It's as though you're talking about yourself," he said.

"No," she replied at once, "it's about desert animals and . . ."

He interrupted her. "But you're much more beautiful than hyenas," he said. "I suspect that Ahmad's wife was jealous of your beauty."

She lowered her head.

"She's right," he went on. "I haven't been able to take my eyes off you, even though, ever since I first set eyes on you, I've been a scholar with knowledge of the internal workings of things."

"If you'd prefer that I stop giving food to the animals," she said hesitantly, "then I won't do it."

"You've tried before, Dayfa," he replied. "You've known that wild animals never give in and can't be controlled. They die in confinement. I want you alive with me."

⌒〜

Dayfa only gave birth to one daughter, Fatima. The doctor said that her illness after she had given birth may have affected her health. The fact that she has had no more children, he said, may be good in that it lets her live, since he could not guarantee that she could carry a new child to term. At first, that made Dayfa unhappy, but then she poured all her affection into her daughter. She was afraid for her, but from human beings, not animals. Her father taught her everything he was teaching his sons; by the age of nine, she had memorized the Qur'an, which earned her a smile and kiss on the cheek from her father.

"How proud of you I am!" he told her confidently. "You're going to be ahead of all men."

Her mother smiled, although she regretted how young her daughter was: still a child, someone who did not realize her father's real affection or know the love of any other man apart from the one who, years later, would be her husband.

That night, she sat down on their bed and gestured to him to put his head on her thighs. Once he had done that, she twirled her fingers around his chin.

"'Amr," she asked gently, "are you happy now?"

He was silent for a few moments. "What kind of question is that?" he asked.

"Sometimes," she replied, running her fingers over his head, "I get the impression that your ambition is broad enough to encompass the world. You can only feel content with authority, power, and control, as though you were a Mamluk yourself."

He frowned.

"When I look at you at other times," she went on immediately, "I can see a Sufi, ascetic in everything, someone who's dedicated his life to knowledge, books, and worship of God, someone whose only desire is to please God and is unconcerned about prestige, power, money, and children. It's as though the two entities are fighting each other inside you."

"What's this nonsense?" he asked angrily. "It's the world to come that is my goal."

"Doesn't God say: 'Do not forget your share of the lower world'?"*

"I've taken my share and achieved what I want."

"Are you happy and content now?"

"Yes," he replied firmly, "as long as God is content with me."

She took his hand and kissed it. "Forgive me," she said. "Sometimes I read your heart without shame or hesitation. Your very own heart."

"I know. You're always doing that."

"Do you still love me?"

"You're the one reading my heart. What does it tell you?"

"It tell me that Shaykh 'Amr ibn Ahmad ibn 'Abd al-Karim has a stubborn streak and never budges from his opinions. Love involves obstinacy, oppression, and sheer pigheadedness. For some time, it's dominated you, and there's no way out. There's no easy way of changing you, Shaykh."

"Aren't you ever going to say 'my Lord'?"

"I feel that you're a shaykh now. I'll say that again when I feel that you're a judge."

"I've never met anyone like you," he declared. "I still have my doubts as to whether you're bewitched or touched by jinn."

"Each of us has his own special magic," she replied. "Yours managed to capture everyone's heart, and my own heart specially."

Dayfa's words had an unusual effect. She could read the heart like a jinn and tug on the strings of both strength and weakness. She used to spoil him and listen to him as though he were her own child. Perhaps she also managed to tolerate his self-confidence and his avid quest for knowledge. She could acknowledge that he

* Qur'an Sura 28:77 [The Story]

was different: ascetic, genius, writer, shaykh, judge, scholar, and fighter, all in one. Sometimes her expression was full of irony and a sense of maturity as she sensed his weakness and encouraged him to understand and learn; at other times, the expression was one of affection and admiration, as though he were the scholar who could penetrate the inner working of things, able to reach every truth and comprehend things that remained unknown to everyone else. She would always shock and alarm him, leaving him perplexed. He still loved her the way he had on the very first day he had seen her in the desert with the hyenas. Sometimes he was annoyed with her and felt angry if she behaved in an unexpected way; he would lose patience and scold her. On other occasions, she might say something that he did not understand at the time or respond in a challenging kind of way. He would then ignore her and decide to argue with her for a day or two. But most of the time, he could not do even that. Memories of earlier days of despair put an end to any kind of blame. The total failure of torture and darkness to change the heart and force it to submit made such arguments impossible.

Rumors circulated to the effect that, when Ridawi the merchant's wife, Dayfa's mother, left the house, the only person left on whom he could vent his anger and cruelty was his slave girl. He started abusing and cursing her; after a year or two, she too ran away. His male children took over the business and started insulting him. People in Qus became accustomed to hearing shouting matches between father and sons.

When the student Shaykh al-Mahmudi finally earned his certificate, he did not tell anyone, even the sultan. He and 'Amr kept their mutual secret till the end of their lives. Once Al-Mahmudi had been promoted to the rank of amir and been sent out of the country, contacts between him and 'Amr were few and far between. However, both of them, Shaykh 'Amr and Shaykh al-Mahmudi, recalled the friendship they had enjoyed.

For eight or nine years, all contact between 'Amr and Barquq had been severed. Then, a guard from the sultan arrived at 'Amr's house, demanding that 'Amr present himself to discuss an important matter, that very same day and not the next.

His wife and two sons looked alarmed, but he was not worried. He knew why the sultan wanted to talk to him.

He was met at the palace gate by Shaykh al-Mahmudi, dressed in his amir's uniform. He still showed 'Amr the same respect and admiration, lowering his head as he shook 'Amr's hand.

"Meeting you, Shaykh 'Amr," he said, as he put 'Amr's hand on his forehead, "always delights my heart. Forgive me for falling short, but, as you know, I've not been in Egypt."

'Amr smiled. "To the contrary, meeting you gives me some hope in the Mamluks at a time when, as you know, there is no feeling of confidence between amirs and me."

He looked all around him. "Except for you, that is," he went on. "You're a different kind of amir, a scholar.

"The sultan's not well?" he continued.

"No, he's not well," Shaykh al-Mahmudi responded gloomily.

'Amr shook his head sadly, as memories of the year or more in prison with Barquq came back and erased any residual grudge and anger he might have felt.

When he went in to see the sultan, he found him surrounded by his wives and children.

The sultan indicated that everyone should leave. He was lying flat on his back.

"'Amr," he said in a feeble voice, "how I've missed our joint sessions in prison!"

'Amr smiled and stroked his arm. "My Lord will get better, God willing," he said.

"No," the sultan replied, "this is the end; I can smell it. Death has a powerful stench that fills the space, a day when man escapes from his brother, mother, father, friend, and children. Authority also controls the heart, leading it to run away from friends and children. Do you know what I'd really like now?"

"A pomegranate with oil and sugar?" 'Amr responded softly.

"How did you know?"

"Those days we spent together. Each of us knew the other by heart."

"Are you still angry with me?"

"There's no point in being angry."

"You mean, there's no point in being angry when someone's dying?"

"Days we spend being angry and in love soon come to an end."

"I've brought you here today," Barquq said in the same feeble voice, "to ask you whether I'm going to enter heaven or hell. You're one who knows."

"My Lord knows that I don't know."

"You've read and understood. Give me the answer before I hear it very soon. Then I can prepare for the examination."

"It's a questioning process that none of us has witnessed before or knows how to answer. Some of the questions are unexpected. They may occur to us, but in our drowsy lives we don't pay any attention to them. When we do respond, we make our own decisions without knowing the consequences. Instead, we follow the evidence and strive for deliverance. Each of us, my Lord, has something to benefit him."

"But you give opinions and have knowledge. I've built the mosque, school, and fountain. I've done the best I can."

"So why do you have doubts?"

"Mankind sins and covets."

"God's mercy may extend to everyone."

"Your words always bring me relief. Fear is only ever quelled by achieving the goal. Tell the guard to bring some pomegranate so we can eat it together."

⌒

Maryam died, and a year later so did Zubayda. Zubayda did not realize that her forecast of bad times would come to pass; Syria would fall into Mongol hands. Religious scholars in Egypt now realized that their fate inevitably lay in the hands of Timur Lang, the destroyer.

For the first time, it occurred to Dayfa that killing the hyenas was a portent of bad times; things would only get worse in the days to come. She thanked God that her husband did not have a dangerous position. But, where the Mongols were concerned, butchering scholars was both permitted and possible.

The new sultan, Faraj ibn Barquq, was fond of wine; he did not seem to be sober very often. Drought and famine pervaded the country; the Nile had not flooded in years. Fear and doubt were everywhere.

Dayfa was scared for her only daughter. There was no food to eat and awaiting death became a certainty. She shut her daughter in her room and would not let her go outside. Cairo was full of illnesses. Young and old alike were snatched away: selling them became a daily reality. Dayfa's husband scolded her for being too worried, but she paid no attention and refused to listen to him. As year followed year, they had less money and thought hard before eating meat or buying sweetmeats. However, Dayfa and her husband were not unduly bothered about that; their primary concern was the safety of their daughter and the two boys.

They had a visitor, someone they had been expecting for years, but whom the affairs of this world had prevented from paying a visit: 'Abd ar-rahman Ibn Khaldun.

The two men ate together and spent hours sitting with each other.

"The fall of Syria has meant the same for Egypt from time immemorial," Ibn Khaldun said regretfully. "Their fates are intertwined. Timur Lang's a Muslim, but, as you well know, religion will never intercede in wartime. Didn't I tell you?"

"Egypt needs a powerful sultan now," 'Amr replied, "someone like Barquq perhaps. But I'd prefer a sultan who was more devout and less inclined to tolerate corruption."

Ibn Khaldun smiled. "Piety can never stand in the way of kingly might and power's magic," he said. "How about your writing? Are you writing, 'Amr? Your repute has now reached me, and your students know a lot. Egypt injects soul into religious scholars. You need to write."

"I'm trying," 'Amr replied.

"This entire era is one of fear and panic. In such a context we desperately need creative thinking and initiative. Now that my heart is alone and defeated, I have started writing about humanity. At the moment, I'm writing about people's situations. I understand them. They're always what remains as a constant, while monarchs disappear as their regime vanishes and life comes to an end."

"I've read your books," 'Amr confirmed. "It's as if your sorrow and loss only make you that much more creative and knowledgeable."

"That's always the case with loss. In my books, 'Amr, I'm trying to put into words everything I've learned over the past seventy years. History isn't just tales and stories about one tyrannical ruler and another who's more reliable and has dedicated his life to serving his country. History is about people. When a scholar is interested in people and talks about rulers and sultans as human beings, then history becomes a mode of understanding.

"Humanity as a whole has different categories and principles. Every civilization has a different mode of analysis and understanding. If we pursue the scholarly method, we come to understand that history repeats itself and we can learn what will happen in the future. In order to predict the future, we need to understand the present by means of an understanding of different models of humanity and civilization; how rulers make their decisions, what gives them their power, and what elements may either weaken or scare them.

"Scholarly reflection is important, and the link between tradition, land, civilization, and people is essential. The man of religion is bound to be concerned solely with works on religion and jurisprudence, and indeed with evil, so that he can adjudicate between people justly, and appreciate the causes of injustice and corruption and their consequences."

That was the last time he ever saw Ibn Khaldun; he died shortly afterward. The Mongols left Syria, and Sultan Faraj ibn Barquq was killed after a short time in Syria. It was never clear who killed him, but what was clear was that Barquq's family would never rule again. The next son of the people would never be acceptable to the Mamluks. Warrior power was what was needed to retain authority over Egypt, Syria, and the rest of Muslim territories. Egyptians now waited for the next warrior and Mamluk savior. Would he be Circassian or Turkish, from the Bahri Mamluks or the Burji? Would he be imposing taxes, then distributing sweets, or distributing sweets first and then imposing taxes? What madness would they have to endure after Faraj? Rumor had it that raisin liquor had disappeared from Cairo markets because of Faraj, but he had eventually defeated the Mongols and thus saved the scholars and Egyptian people.

The new moon appeared, and so did the new Mamluk savior, a fighter and warrior who knew the meaning of sacrifice and death in God's and the country's cause by defeating the Mongols with his soldiers: Al-Mu'ayyad Abu Nasr Shaykh al-Mahmudi.

People said that Faraj's death was a release; his ruthlessness and ill-luck had almost devastated Muslim territories. If it was Shaykh al-Mahmudi who had killed him, then he had done a good deed. Maybe he had; who knows? Was that normal with Mamluks? A number of sultans are killed, but only Mamluks stay in power. The person who ruled Egypt had to deserve it. The drought disappeared, and people relaxed. Dayfa's daughter was married to one of her father's students.

'Amr noticed the change in his wife. Sometimes she went into a panic about plague and famine, and at others she had a sudden attack of depression. Following the marriage of her daughter and the deaths of her three mother-figures, she locked herself in her room and sat there on her own, clutching her body and muttering that she was alone now and had lost all her loved ones. She asked her daughter's husband to let Fatima stay with her mother, because her daughter was all she had left. However, he refused. Fatima started visiting her regularly, perhaps once a week. Once again Dayfa's eyes dimmed, as she clung to a loneliness that she had known ever since childhood. She surrendered herself to a feeling of desolation and inner sorrow. He would see her day after day, and she did her best to look normal in front of him, smiling and sitting down beside him, but he knew her inside out.

One day, he went in to see her. She was sitting on her bed, staring at nothing.

"You keep worrying about things in this world and what you can lose," he told her, "and forgetting the things you still have. Rouse yourself, Dayfa!"

"Forgive me!" she replied sadly.

"I'm with you."

"I'm afraid you're going to leave me," she said, "just as everyone else has. What would I do if you left me?"

He stroked her hand. "Fear only brings doubt and delusion," he told her firmly. "You're a believer. You have to let a certain knowledge of God trace your days into the future. He never burdens us with more than we can bear. It is devotion that protects me from the fickleness of fate through your own trust in their maker. Do you understand?"

She remained silent.

He continued: "'*No disaster happens on the earth or to yourselves unless it is in a book before We create it. For God, that is easy. So that you may not regret what has escaped you, nor rejoice at what has come to you. God does not love anyone arrogant and proud.*'"*

She looked at him without comment.

"I've an idea," he said eagerly after a pause.

She looked at him.

"What do you think about working with me for a while?" he asked.

She looked at him in amazement. "You mean, as a student—you learning and teaching me?"

She smiled. "What can I possibly teach you," she asked, "when you already know everything?"

"You can teach me about wild animals," he said lovingly, "and I can teach you jurisprudence and hadith."

"You'd be wasting your time with me," she said dispiritedly.

He held out his hand. "There's no time-wasting in learning," he said. "Mankind was created inquisitive. Don't allow anxiety to consume your days like leprosy. That's a disease that buries and disfigures the years of your life."

She clasped his hand. "Sometimes," she told him, "I think you're an angel, not a human being."

He moved closer. "And at other times do you think I'm a Mamluk amir?"

"'Amr," she told him delightedly, "I agree. I'd like to learn from you. I adore you, if you only knew."

'You still love me?" he asked gently.

"It's predestined fate, Shaykh. Teach me. Maybe learning will help soothe a vagrant heart and extinguish the fire of a longing for the impossible."

From that day on, he would spend two hours with her every day, teaching her and holding discussions as though she were one of his students. Sometimes he would get annoyed with her and be unkind if she did not understand something or memorize the material. She met the challenge involved with both strength and commitment. She would argue like a female warrior, affected and calm, filling her days as he wished and required of her. She started reading voraciously, trying to come out on top once in a while. On occasion, he would let her, but at other times he would put her down. She acquired learning with all the vigor of hyenas and made use of an open and creative mind to understand him.

* Qur'an Sura 57:22–23 [Iron]

Gray hairs started to show on 'Amr's head along with the appearance of the new moon. Sometimes his eyes would let him down, and things would look distant or fuzzy. It was more difficult now to read books with small print. He grew old, he wrote, and he studied. He kept trying to keep up his individual investigations of belief. With Dayfa, it was as though time had no effect on her. She had either bewitched time itself, or else had emerged victorious through her pure heart— who knows? But then, perhaps his eyes were deceiving him, and she was no longer as fascinating and beautiful as she had been. One day, he asked her how it was that she had not grown old. No lines had appeared on her face for twenty years or more.

"My dark skin poses a challenge to time," she replied with a smile. "It can overcome wrinkles."

He had no idea whether it was her color or her magic that still made him doubt, but she had never changed. He even started to worry that she would regard him as an old man now while she was still aged seventeen, as she had been when he first set eyes on her. She had to know what was going through his mind.

"Some spirits encounter each other with an appointment for eternity," she told him one day while she was preparing his food, "and they're completely intertwined. My teacher, my housemate, the handsomest man I ever saw!"

"My head's gone all gray, Dayfa!" he replied with a smile.

"No gray hair can ever affect your heart, my shaykh and teacher," she said lovingly. "Colors wash the heart and light up the days."

He gave her a hug, still loving and wanting her as he had for years.

They walked around the Khan al-Khalili bazaar together. Rain was falling and shining light on one mosque after another, as well as a hostelry and small worship space. The mosque of Sultan Barquq was surrounded by Sufis, imbibing sweet water, washing away their sins, and longing to sense a revelation of imminence and a whiff of paradise to come. He ran his hands over the mosque wall and looked at the lamps now lit to blend in with sunset which, each day, would produce its own fresh coloring. He recalled lamp oil, the taste of pomegranate, the ephemerality of rule, the lack of food, and the permanence in Cairo of lofty mosques, themselves witnesses to injustice, victory, struggle, permanence, suffering, longing, cruelty, humiliation, and oblivion; lofty minarets aspiring to distance themselves from every criminal and imprisoner. Where now were those prisons, imprisoners, and prisoners? They will always disappear, whereas the mosques will forever remain.

His eyes now met those of his wife. She could see the memories wafting in front of him like lightning, swift, bright, and invigorating.

"'Amr," she asked him, "what do you want to buy today at the Khan al-Khalili bazaar?"

"You know," he replied confidently.

She smiled under her veil. "A lamp?" she asked.

He stared off to the distant horizon. "Perhaps a number of lamps can help us forget the months of darkness and insanity," he replied.

"I can see that you're always sensible," she said.

"All of us have our moments of significant madness as part of life's journey, moments that batter our mind, then arouse it and crush its vanity. I'd like to pass by the mosque of Al-Hakim bi-Amr Allah to see an old friend. You go and buy the lamp, then we can meet up in a while at the mosque."

She went on her way, and he headed for the Al-Hakim bi-Amr Allah mosque. He went inside and looked for his friend who, he knew, liked to contemplate God in private there: Taqi ad-din Ahmad ibn 'Ali al-Maqrizi.

'Amr tapped him on the shoulder. "Greetings to the shaykh and scholar!" he said.

Al-Maqrizi was busy writing. Looking up at 'Amr, he shook his hand warmly.

"'Amr ibn Ahmad ibn 'Abd al-Karim al-Manati," he said, inviting him to sit down in front of him, "your books enlighten Cairo and its environs."

"'Abd ar-rahman Ibn Khaldun told me about your visit," 'Amr replied softly.

"My teacher and shaykh!" Al-Maqrizi said affectionately. "But for him, I would never have started and continued."

"Have you finished?"

"No, I keep writing and explaining words, all in the hope of conquering time which can erase things like the proverbial flood, leaving nothing to survive unchanged and unerased. You've gone gray, 'Amr. I haven't seen you for years. Didn't I tell you that the passage of days transforms everything?"

"You're recording it all in your notebooks and preserving their history, if only for a while."

"I'm trying. It's as though God's extended my life so I can write and never achieve full understanding. I'm constantly learning, but there's never enough water when the thirst burns my throat."

"That's the way it is with time, my brother. The thirst and longing only intensifies, and yet achievement only comes through extinction."

"Shaykh Al-Manati, your books endeavor to grant imagination a triumph over truth and to distinguish evil from good."

"I also am trying."

"I wish you a life without loss or sorrow. I don't know whether or not I should be asking God to prolong my life. When your son and wife both die, you realize that the days do exactly what they will. As Ash-Shafi'i states, events of this world have no permanence."

'Amr stroked his shoulder. "It seems to me that, when someone like you loses a son and wife, he can give generously, both learning and knowledge, and he can be creative in doing so. It's as if his giving is a reflection of an infinite sorrow. That's the way you are, and the same was true of Ibn Khaldun."

"I learned about humanity from him. I didn't realize that I'd be as sad as him, and even more so. No matter! Rulers have changed, and Mamluks are fighting each other as usual."

"The strong man is now the ruler," 'Amr said confidently. "Only a devout and adventurous person can bear the burden. Al-Mu'ayyad is a shaykh who is able to keep the trust."

"You're putting your trust in him, 'Amr, as though you know him from up close."

"I know him, and I know Barquq," 'Amr replied confidently. "I realize that Egypt is like a fascinating sorceress. All the ruler has to do is to fall in love with her, then spend money and progeny in order to reach her. But she will always refuse to submit. Pray for me, Ahmad. Perhaps we'll meet again soon amid the stones mingled with pulpits, love, passion, and time."

'Amr sat on his bed as usual. Today seemed to be different. She came over and started massaging his shoulders, something he had grown used to over the years and loved without any need for words.

"Al-Mu'ayyad Shaykh seems both pious and fair," he said enthusiastically. "As you know, I taught him myself."

She pressed her fingers against his neck. "Yes, I know," she replied.

"He wants to start a new era of justice and mercy."

"I'd like that," she said. "We'd like it."

"The dangers are growing all around us. It isn't the Mongols that worry me. The war between them and the Mamluks has gone on for a while, and their capabilities are now known. No, what worries me now is the Ottomans. They're a danger for Egypt."

"Why?"

"Did you but know it, there's a huge difference between them and Mamluks. These days, I keep on saying that Egypt is the heart of civilization and the world's minaret. I told Ibn Khaldun that earlier. If Egypt's joined to an empire, then it'll be just a chunk of land, no more. The center of the world will shift to the heart of the empire, as happened with the Abbasids, Umayyads, and other dynasties. The Mamluks have given Egypt a great deal, and still are."

She nodded.

He held her hand and stretched out on the bed, still looking at her. "Al-Mu'ayyad Shaykh offered me the chief judge position today," he said.

She looked at him for a while. "What do you think?" she asked.

"I've devoted my time to learning, knowledge, and teaching," he said resignedly. "The Mamluks can't be trusted."

She shook her head and gave a faint smile.

"I've grown old," he went on, "and I'm tired of fights and conflicts."

He looked at her and noticed the smile on her face. "Why are you smiling?" he asked.

"I'm not," she replied immediately, sitting down beside him.

"Al-Mu'ayyad Shaykh's different," he said. "My problem is that I took the position when I was young, and that made me seem to be challenging the scholars and shaykhs. It'll be hard for them to admit they were wrong. Now my age is more appropriate; I'm a bit over sixty, and I've had a lot of experience. This ruler's been one of my own students. That's significant in itself. But I've told him no."

"You told him no?" she said, eyebrows raised.

"Yes, I did," he replied forcefully. "I've no aspirations to high office any more. I've had my fill of this world's desires."

Their eyes met.

"But it's an important responsibility," he went on. "It demands mercy toward Egyptians and Mamluks. The chief judge can change every kind of injustice and disseminate justice. Al-Mu'ayyad Shaykh was determined and did his best to persuade me. Not only that, but he promised not to interfere is any of my decisions. He said he was prepared to swear to divorce in front of everyone if I would agree. He's different from Barquq. Even so, I stuck to my guns and said no."

She shook her head but kept looking at him.

"My only aspirations now involve learning and teaching," he continued. "Al-Mu'ayyad Shaykh kept on insisting, even after I'd said no. Needless to say, if I become chief judge, I'm going to change a lot of things. The sultan who's willing to put the fear of God before loyalty and amirs is one who needs support. But I'm still not eager to take on the job."

She started to laugh, but put her hand over her mouth.

"You're laughing?" he asked angrily. "What are you laughing about?"

"No, I'm not," she responded immediately.

"Yes, you are. You're laughing. Why?"

ON THE MARGINS OF HISTORY

Shaykh al-Mahmudi assumed the throne of Egypt in 1412 CE and called himself Al-Mu'ayyad Abu an-Nasr Shaykh al-Mahmudi. As he had vowed, he constructed his mosque on the site of the infamous Cairo prison Warehouse of Virtues [Khizanat ash-Shama'il] where he himself had been tortured previously. He stopped having heads hung on the Bab Zuwayla, and decided to take the brass door that he so admired at the Sultan Hasan Mosque and put it on his own mosque. With his assumption of the throne, the lineage of Barquq came to an end. Al-Mu'ayyad Shaykh was a Burji Mamluk and not a son of the people.

Before his death, Al-Mu'ayyad Shaykh had the staircase leading to the school in the Sultan Hasan Mosque repaired and installed a new door to replace the one he had taken for his own mosque. Once again, the call to prayer sounded from the Sultan Hasan Mosque's minaret, but, after his death, the Mamluks started using it again as a fortress and combat zone.

About one hundred years later, in 1517 CE, the Ottomans entered Egypt, and the Burji Mamluk dynasty came to an end.

The new moon appeared in Cairo today, and people started to celebrate.

I sat down in the mosque courtyard to look at the moon.

I still purchase candles and lamps. Sometimes I stroll through the Mamluk cemeteries; at other times, I wander through their mosques. The fates are only ever in balance when I'm among them and with them, around their pulpits and amid their stones. This mosque in particular, built with love, tears, and a craving for closeness to God, the Sultan Hasan Mosque. I am still looking for the person who stole the lamps; I need to know the rest of the story.

I sat down, realizing that the end was nigh and loneliness was depressing. All the stones were warmth.

"Are you still looking?" the shaykh asked me next day.

"I'm feeling better now," I replied, my heart full of sorrow. "For a time at least, bringing this story to a close is both victory and release. But it's still not the final tale. I'm still looking for that. Reaching the goal is never eternal, and truth vanishes as fast as life itself. 'At all times let the days deceive; no remedy can ward off death.'"

"Do you read Al-Shafi'i?"

"It seems that he understands the passage of days better than I do."

3. The Mosque-Madrassa of Sultan Hassan. Photograph © Mohammed Moussa, 2014, CC BY-SA 3.0, https://creativecommons.org/licenses/by-sa/3.0, via Wikimedia Commons.

THE FINAL STORY
Event of Nights: The Mamluks

Writing the truth involves endeavor and success. Recording events brings about an arrival at certainty and stability
for the heart. Fate toys with us and our destinies. And yet,
if we write the truth, then our feet stand firm on antic soil.
We have never concealed either weakness or strength, nor
have we favored brother or kin. Father of blessings, history
stands in the way of oblivion; it warms cold palaces and
provides protection against the wiles of the ambitious—if,
that is, it is written by a reliable hand and recorded by men
of learning and knowledge. I hereby record in your book
that I have witnessed with my own eyes people fighting
courageously, with abstinence and a spark in their eyes,
using all the competence and perfection of hermits and
worshippers and the ardor of lovers and rebels.

> From the testimony of Salar
> the Mamluk

SULTAN HASAN MOSQUE IN CAIRO, 2017 CE

She always reveres lamps, their light gleaming fearlessly and without hesitation,
unbothered by either blame or threat. She had her doubts about the goal and purpose of the search. The intention was always to fill the gaping hole in the depths of
the heart. That urgent quest had run away from the obvious, well-established facts
like light from the lamps. Why had thieves stolen the lamps, she wondered? Why
were invaders even interested in them? And why had the traveler and Sufi written
about them?

Her grandfather, Doctor Salah, had written the first narrative, and now she
had to write the last one.

Josephine, the granddaughter of Doctor Salah 'Abdallah, was searching for
vestiges of light in the various parts of the mosque and recording the source, but

not as history. Her Italian grandmother had died with her sorrow, and her Egyptian grandfather had died too, still yearning for knowledge. During his travels he had forgotten both source and method. She too was inevitably going to die, but she was bound to leave behind her a novel about the three of them, each of whom had their own history and presence, their personal testimony and story. They had told them to the historian Abu al-Barakat Ibn Iyas. He had recorded their words, but they were source, origin, and lamps, always alight but defeated. Hind, the Egyptian woman, Salar the Mamluk amir, and Mustafa Pasha the Ottoman all saw what they saw, and heard what they lived through and suffered. From their inner souls truths emerged amid doubt, defeat, and loneliness. They lived with Cairo before darkness prevailed, lamps were stolen, and souls surrendered. History implies victory amid continuous defeats; recording it brings power amid destruction.

Josephine took her usual seat alongside the pulpit in the Sultan Hasan Mosque. She was reading the book by Ibn Iyas. The shaykh of the mosque knew her very well and felt sorry for her overwhelming loneliness. Such a relentless search on her part implied a large hole in her heart: no children, no husband, no friend, and no family. Maybe they existed, but they had not filled that hole. Perhaps they had disappeared between night and day. Who knows?

"Are you reading Ibn Iyas?" he inquired. "Have you finished looking for the 'Judge of Qus'?"

"Yes," she replied enthusiastically, "I've finished the research, but I've not finished trying to understand. Reaching such a goal requires some interpretation. That's what the 'Judge of Qus' says."

"You seem to have plenty of time. Do you want to know about some of the mosque's programs involving academic circles and lessons?"

"I prefer to learn on my own. For me, knowledge is like the approach to God, a journey undertaken by the individual, without family or clan. If one doesn't do that, then the goal is never reached."

"You seem to like being alone."

"For me, it possesses its own sanctity and purpose."

"Are you writing a new book?"

"No, I'm trying to finish writing my old book first. You have to understand the old in order to do research on the new; to accept the past so as to live in the present. Ibn Iyas (or Abu al-Barakat, as he was known) relied on a number of witnesses. I really admire this scholar-historian. He writes with sincerity. There are three testimonies in particular that interest me."

"Are you trying to confirm their accuracy? Are you a history professor then?"

"No, I want to find out their authors' stories, the final one that will throw light on the way ahead and remove any doubt or anxiety."

"Stories of victory or defeat?"

"That's the way human beings have always categorized their destinies so that the truths may seem clear. But life doesn't have victories or defeats. Instead it's separate days with their mingled colors. There's no such person as a victor alone, eternal, omniscient, protected and fortified against every evil. Needless to say, we have never known a powerful person, for example, who has not been brought low by his own vanity, or someone in defeat who has not been crushed by his dejection. No, Shaykh, I'm not concerned about either victory or defeat, good or evil, rich or poor, powerful or weak. Steady light offers serenity; knowledge leads one to the goal."

"The final story then?"

"The last story of all."

BOOK ONE

THE CONFLICT
Testimonies 1517–22 CE

Mourn for Egypt over what has happened,
An event whose devastation has impacted all humanity.
Its Turkish soldiers have vanished in
The blink of an eye as though falling asleep.
God is great! It is a disaster
That has afflicted Egypt, it's like never before seen.
My grief for those cavaliers, their necks
Severed by the foe when they attacked.
My grief for a life in Egypt, its days
Now past, like the dream that trails from behind.
                                        Ibn Iyas

Hind's Testimony (1)

My Aunt, I am going to tell you about something that happened.

There is defeat in this morning light. Within the specks of this scream lie treason, deceit, and frivolity. It all happened years ago. I shall be telling you the truth and recounting things that embarrass me and maybe even annoy me. The events happened six years ago, to be precise.

I will tell you, Aunt, that what happened was beyond imagination in its profundity and malice. Humiliation may be a feature of existence, but submission has never been part of my own nature. I want you to promise me, my Aunt, that some of the details in this testimony of mine will remain in your heart until God's judgment comes. You will tell my father some of the information, but not all. What happened to me was unexpected. I was spending the day at home, reading hadith and learning principles from it. I was inspiring my heart with knowledge and had no desire to be married. I did not like the idea of house and children, and was afraid that there might be an upheaval and life's blessings might disappear. I had observed grieving mothers and wives weeping over a husband who had died, been killed, or preferred a Byzantine or Turkish slave girl. I decided to devote my life to learning and knowledge. My father knew that, and did not force me to get married. Actually, there were times when I felt that he admired my courage, my steadfast attitude in front of other people, and my desire to memorize and teach hadith.

So, I reached the age of eighteen without being married. I refused to go to the girls' mosque in Cairo, so that I could parade in front of men, praying in hope of finding a husband, something my cousin had done. My mother died a year before her, still alarmed by my gloomy destiny compared with other girls and my remaining as lonely as wild animals in the desert. I devoted myself to teaching my younger brother who was less than five years old when he became an orphan. My days continued without any obvious color or radiant light. That said, they were as secure and stable as I desired.

You can recall the day when I traveled with my elder brother and Shams, my younger brother, to Balbis to visit you. You will remember the ill-starred day when darkness fell, the event happened, and there was no escape other than God.

449

My brother Shams went out, or rather sneaked out, of the house into the street in the middle of the city. Ottoman soldiers were kidnapping boys and stealing grain. Their proximity to Cairo presaged certain death, like ravens when they can smell rotting corpses. What a dreadful day, what a sad year! I went out in a panic to look for him and kept yelling his name in the marketplace. I had a sneaking worry that I might never set eyes on him again and started wondering what I was going to tell my father; what excuse would I have for not keeping an eye on him and protecting him? My sense of wrongdoing overcame my fear of taking risks. I ran toward the soldiers and their encampments, searching for my brother.

What happened next is part humiliation, part shame, part minimal courage, and part maximal bewilderment. Forgive me, my Aunt, for what has happened and is going to happen.

Soldiers can never be trusted. These soldiers are not like the others. I had heard about the Mamluks' cruelty and the way they treated khans and merchants so badly, but I have never encountered or seen this kind of humiliation. Their uniform is imposing, their mustaches are thick like black broomsticks concealing greed and avarice, and their faces are dirty. These soldiers do not have beards to lend them an appearance of piety and devotion.

I ran as fast as I could, holding my brother's hand and dragging him behind me as hard as I could. But one, two, or three hands grabbed my hair; their hands then grabbed hold of me and handled me roughly. I hoped that someone would come—a shaykh, a hero, or even a jinn from another world to rescue me. My mother had told me about amazing sea jinn who would rescue drowning people after they had been asked three questions. If the person drowning failed to answer, he was bound to drown. I tried to remember the questions and answers, but I failed. If only those jinn were questioning Egyptians now. If only the jinn could save them before Ottoman forces entered Cairo. Once they had entered the city, no jinn or shaykh would be of any use. My Aunt, Egyptians must have been too slow in responding to the questions; either that, or else the Mamluks and mercenaries had failed and been defeated. I do not know which.

At this point, I really hoped the sea jinn would come to banish those rough hands, cleanse the city's streets, revitalize the Mamluks, and eradicate greed and treachery. If only they would come to arouse the sleeper, kill, and burn the houses of those mercenaries. If only they could breathe from their wide open mouths, remove the dust of treason and injustice, and restore life to its former state, the one described to us by our forebears. My grandfather used to say that there is no defeat for Mamluks; they do not know what it means. They are the soldiery and pride of the Muslim community. They have done things that no other group has managed to do: liberating the Holy Lands and stopping every invader. There is no other group like the Mamluks, not even jinn. That's what my grandfather used to say.

I wanted the nightmare or life itself to come to an end; whichever came first, I had no idea.

But life must end before everything collapses and is degraded.

Before the stench of corpses and the regular hanging of heads on gates took hold, I took some initiative and tasted the blood that oozed from my lips. I wanted to die before the blood of my own innocence was splattered all over Ottoman soldiers. What those soldiers were going to do to me was hellish, something that would swallow my life forevermore. I kept praying, fasting, and memorizing God's own book. Verses escaped from my head. "I seek Your help, O Lord," I kept saying, "I seek Your help." My hope was that maybe those soldiers would hear me and remember their faith, assuming that they had one.

One of them slipped his hand over my breasts, and another slapped me so hard that for a moment I lost my hearing and could not speak. All around me, existence was making a single noise, the buzz of war silencing all other sounds. My head was spinning, and my eyes could not focus. Even so, I resisted and did my best to stay conscious, fully aware of the crime and assault, with blood gushing in my throat. There were ten or more of them . . .

My scream echoed, but then separated from me. For a few moments, soul left body. I pleaded, I stuttered, but I could not resist. The soldiers did not understand me. All I can remember is the savagery in their eyes, my torn clothes, and hands wanting more.

"My brother," I muttered. "Leave him alone; he's only a little boy."

My Aunt, you warned me about soldiers. They're always after a woman; after months of thirst in the desert, it can be any woman. You once told me, Aunt, that, after a soldier has killed someone, he is afflicted with a strange disease. He needs to take out all his violence, regret, and weakness on a woman and loves to hear the screams. I had to stop screaming, but I could not do it. Maybe if I had stopped . . .

I closed my eyes. "Help me!" I asked in a voice I did not even recognize.

The world started to move away, and feelings retreated. Breathing was now easy.

There were no bodies strangling my own, no hands fondling my breasts, nothing . . .

I have no idea: had I died and been born again?

A strange feeling came over me, and the whole world turned into a jumble, or almost . . .

When I reopened my eyes, everything looked strange . . . the sound of sirens echoed in my ears. The soldiers were still there, but I was moving away from them.

The screams were still all around me, but I was moving away from them as well.

A hand grabbed hold of mine and pulled me away. Unconsciously I put my hand over my breasts to cover what the soldiers had exposed. I swear, Aunt, that I felt the jinn transporting me far away. He took off his cloak and covered my breasts with it. He spoke to the soldiers in a language which he did not speak very well. He was speaking slowly and calmly as he diligently searched for the right words. Then he threw a money purse at them and put me on a cart.

"Don't move," he told me in Arabic.

I obeyed him without saying a word. The cart was filthy, and the donkey was an old one. This particular jinn had come in a strange form, a big surprise, not what I had expected. He was wearing a peasant's turban over a sunny face and a faded gallabiya.

"My brother," I whispered pleadingly, "please rescue him, I beg you. He's still with them."

He produced another money purse and threw it at them too. They pushed my brother toward the cart like a sack of rotten potatoes. He banged his head and screamed, but the peasant put him on the cart and made off as quickly as possible.

I was shaking, Aunt, and it did not stop for an hour. He may have been driving his cart through the fields.

Eventually I spoke. "My brother," I panted, "I don't know how to thank you. Giving you everything we own would not be enough."

He did not respond; it was as though he did not even see me, my Aunt. I started assuming that he actually was a sea jinn who had appeared in this particular guise.

He kept looking all around him, his goal being to avoid soldiers.

After a while, I tried speaking again, with the ringing sound still echoing in my ears. "What kind of era is this," I asked, "one in which a Muslim man can assault a Muslim woman and brother can fight brother? Where are the Mamluks now to protect us? They used to humiliate us as they lied and stole, but we put up with it for the sake of protection. Where's that protection now?"

"Cowards!" I went on hatefully. "They ran away like women and hid like slaves. I'll repay you everything you gave them, my brother. My father's rich."

He did not respond or look at me.

Unconsciously I pulled the cloak up around my neck.

"My brother," I repeated, "I'll repay you everything you gave them. My aunt was on her death bed in Balbis, and I had to see her. She's fine now, but Balbis isn't. Are you from around here?"

The soldiers disappeared from view. The color green now dominated the scene, and palm trees pierced the vague vistas. For sure, life would now return to normal, and the Ottomans would never reach Cairo. Impossible. They would never enter the city today, tomorrow, or till life came to an end.

"My brother," I said after a while, "are you listening to me?"

"I'm not your brother," he responded dryly.

I swallowed hard and started to feel anxious. "Are you from here?" I asked. "Yes."

"Please take us back to my father," I begged. "He's in Cairo. The Ottomans will never get into the city. If you take me to my father's house, I can give you double the money you've paid. My father will thank you personally for your courage. You've saved my honor and dignity and my brother's life. You're the very best of men. Or you can take me to my aunt's house, even though it looks as if the soldiers have taken control of her quarter."

My words of praise seemed to have no effect on him whatsoever.

"Will you take me back to my father's house?" I pleaded. "Either that, or leave me at my aunt's house where I can take refuge?"

"No," he replied resolutely.

"I realize that the trip is dangerous. Perhaps I could send a message to my father, and he'd come to pick us up. Or take me back to my aunt's house. Do you hear me, my brother?"

"Enough talk!" he said impatiently. "I'm not your brother!"

I looked all around me in despair and then at my brother. He was crumpled up in a ball and shaking in fear. I calmed down and let my heartbeats slow down. The realities of this dreadful morning now came pouring out. Was this man a hero or demon? I began to have my doubts . . .

"You're an Egyptian like me," I begged him. "You know the Mamluks and their lies. You know about the cruelty of the Ottoman soldiers. Let me be! May God give you a good reward for rescuing a Muslim woman from these savages . . ."

He did not respond.

"How much did you give them?" I asked, clutching my brother to my chest.

"Enough to buy you and your brother," he replied casually.

I gasped on the spot. "My brother," I begged, "I admire your courage. My father can increase the amount five- or tenfold if you take me back to him. What are you going to do with me? I won't bring you any benefits. For that amount of money, you could buy a girl a thousand times prettier than me."

He did not respond.

At that point, I seriously thought about jumping off the cart. Maybe I had to do it.

He seemed to read my thoughts. "If you jump off," he said, "I'll leave you for the soldiers. Don't worry. You'll only be alive for another month at most. The soldiers will take turns with you, thirty or more every day, till you die like a wild beast. Then they'll do the same thing with your brother. He'll only last a day, I swear to you. He doesn't have your endurance."

I held my breath for a few moments. "I wasn't planning to jump," I said.

After a while, he stopped in front of a house and pulled me and my brother off the cart. He banged on the door, and it was opened by a woman in peasant dress.

"Who are these people, Husam ad-din?" she asked.

He pushed me inside the house. "She's a slave girl I've bought today, and he's a young slave we can use for profit in the future."

He grabbed my hand and shoved me into his room. "This is my room," he said. "You'll stay here all the time and do what 'Adlat tells you. Everyone here has to work. 'Adlat is the wife of my elder brother. She'll teach you everything."

I collapsed to the floor. "My brother," I said, "I'm not a slave girl. God curse any man who kidnaps a Muslim woman and turns her into a slave girl. That doesn't happen in Egypt. No one can enslave Egyptians."

"It happens every day," he said without the slightest reaction. "I didn't kidnap you. I risked my life to rescue you. You remember that, and I paid a lot of money for you. From today on, you'll obey my instructions and forget all about your previous life. Otherwise I'll use the whip to punish you."

He went out of the room and left me to my first defeat.

⌐

I'll tell you the truth, my Aunt. Husam ad-din never touched me. He was not concerned about me as a woman; in fact, he never even looked at me. He kept me in his room, and I discovered a corner where I could curl up at night with my brother, covering myself completely as though I were a corpse. He hardly even sensed my presence, which led me to imagine that this terrible episode would come to an end; my sufferings were no greater than those of Job or Jonah—peace be upon them both!

'Adlat was brutal and stupid. I hated her from the very start, at least a little bit. From the very first day, she would hit me on the shoulder. "Get on with it!" she would yell contemptuously.

I'm a spoiled girl who would only eat after the slave girls insisted, someone who had spent her life in the havens of wealthy homes. Now I was being beaten on the shoulder by this peasant woman and told to work. I would be scolded if I burned the food or did not clean the house properly! A few days later, I heard her tell Husam ad-din that I was not fit for work. I was spoiled and poorly brought up; I neither accepted nor acknowledged orders.

After the very first night, my initial shock lessened. I tried to understand what was happening all around me, who had rescued me, who had kidnapped me, and how I might escape. 'Adlat's husband's name was 'Abdallah. He seemed to be at least ten years older than Husam ad-din, and he was nicer and kinder than either of them. I do not think he was a peasant, but had a profession; he used to carve and draw things every day. I watched him from a distance and thought about what I would say to him; how I would ask him to take me back to my father. I noticed Husam ad-din talking to his brother; he used to sit with him often in the evening. I also saw Husam ad-din transcribing poetry; the two of them seemed like calligraphers rather than peasants. Their script was really beautiful. 'Abdallah's carving revealed a huge talent and the creativity of a real artist. After they had eaten supper together and gone out, I slunk into their room and looked at the things they had drawn. I was dazzled by the sheer creativity of it. My father always maintained that creative artists were kind-hearted and sensitive. My own rescue would thus have to be coming soon. I understood that the two of them used to work in the field in the morning, and it was hard. They needed water and soap to wash their hands, then they would eat together.

I spoke gently to 'Adlat on that first night. "I see that your daughter, Sitt ad-dar, is beautiful, as beautiful as you are."

She gave me a contemptuous look. "You're talking as though we're friends," she said. "You're a slave girl. You don't comment about anything. You don't talk to me. You just obey instructions . . ."

"You're my mother's age," I pleaded. "Feel sorry for me. I'm not a slave girl. My aunt's house is two or maybe three hours from here. Come on, let's go there together."

"Didn't Husam ad-din pay a lot of money for you?" she asked without thinking. "If so, then you're a slave girl."

"If you'd just take me back to my aunt," I told her eagerly, "I'd give you a lot of money."

She gave me a push. "Start work here," she said. "Clean the dishes and room before you go to sleep."

I did not know how to clean. I dearly wanted her to go away and leave me, but instead she stayed there, waiting and watching me. I tried to take a broom in order to clean, but she berated me and slapped me on the shoulder.

"You're hopeless," she said, "If you don't clean, there'll be no food."

I was furious, and my face reddened. "Don't hit me!" I told her.

She slapped my shoulder again. "I'll hit you whenever I want," she said.

Within a day, I had discovered all the members of 'Abdallah's family. They had a daughter aged fifteen who was convinced that she was a paragon of beauty. I am embarrassed to state this, Aunt, but, from the outset, I felt that she was spoiled and wayward; no one could control her, and she refused to listen to either her father or mother. She used to give me orders, when I am the daughter of honorable parents. One day she punched me and yelled at me, but I bore it all patiently in the hope that God might do something about it all. I heard that 'Adlat had seven sons, all of whom were working as tradesmen in Cairo. I gave praise to God because they were not here; otherwise, I would have to serve all of them as well. Truth to tell, she gave my brother and me plenty to eat, and we used to sleep huddled together in a corner of Husam ad-din's room.

However, after three days I could no longer stand the lazy girl's arrogant attitude or her mother's.

That day, Husam ad-din came into the room but did not look at me.

"'Adlat's complaining about you," he said. "She says you're hopeless and don't do enough work to cover what you eat and drink."

"She's a nasty woman who hits me," I replied bitterly. "Can you believe it? She hits me! I'm not a slave girl. I've told you several times: if you take me back to my father, I'll give you ten slave girls."

Now, maybe for the first time, he did look at me. "Ten?" he said, pretending to be amazed. "What does your father do?"

I hesitated for a moment. "He's very rich," I replied.

He gave me a lengthy stare, as though seeing me for the very first time.

"My husband and son need me too," I added immediately.

"Your son?" he asked, again pretending to be amazed.

The story immediately took shape in my mind. "Yes," I replied, "I'm a wife and mother. I was scared for my son, so I left him with my husband and family. He'll pay you."

Then he sat down on the bed and stared at me. "Even if your father is rich," he said, "he'll never be able to keep any of his money once the Ottomans enter Cairo. Actually, he'll be lucky to stay alive."

"They'll never enter Cairo," I replied immediately. "Poor Sultan Tuman Bey is a man amid cowards. If the Mamluks fail in Egypt the way they did in Syria, then it's going to be bad for all of us!"

The discussion was clearly interesting him. "You talk about politics as though you know a lot. Do you think the Mamluks are going to fail?"

"Brother," I replied at once, "thieves do not give protection, and protectors don't steal."

"Yes, you're right," he said.

I tried to be nice to him so that he would leave me alone. "I've seen your calligraphy," I told him. "It's very creative. You should be doing it on mosque walls."

"You're talking to me as though we're equals," he said suddenly, "as though
you're a friend or companion. I don't like that."

I said nothing.

He was still looking at me. "Does 'Adlat make you do too much?" he asked.

"Yes, she does," I replied at once. "I can't do all this work; I'm not strong enough
to carry grain and knead dough. She hits me on the shoulder, brother, as though
I'm a servant. She has a spoiled nasty daughter, brother . . ."

He lay back on the bed, as though he had just noticed me. "Come over here,"
he said all of a sudden.

I gasped in spite of myself. I looked at my brother and gave him a hug. I stayed
glued to the floor as though asking it for help.

He looked at my brother, as though he had not noticed him before.

"Tell the boy to leave," he said.

"I can't," I replied immediately. "He's not yet six, and he's always scared when
he's away from me."

He gave me an angry stare. "Get him out of the room!" he yelled.

I whispered in my brother's ear to leave the room.

"You've been kind to me so far," I told him, once the boy had left. "Please continue to treat me kindly."

"Take your clothes off," he said, without even looking at me. "I haven't seen
you yet. I want to look at your body."

"I'm not a prostitute, brother," I stuttered. "I've a husband and son."

"A husband and son," he repeated dryly. "That's what you've said. I need to
make sure."

I put my hand over my mouth, and my whole body started shaking
uncontrollably.

He stood up calmly, grabbed my arm, and pulled me toward him. I screamed
in spite of myself. He put his hand over my mouth and pushed me down on his
bed. I tried to resist, but it was useless. I fought him with my hands, arms, feet, legs,
teeth, and heart. I kicked him, but, within moments, he had me completely under
his control. My body was suffocating, almost dying under the weight of his body. I
realized that this was the end; defeat was inevitable. Even so, my body rebelled, gave
a big shudder, and sprang into action to resist this assault. I could not breathe, and
my face was turning blue, as though I had crushed my soul and sacrificed my heart.

Our eyes met. As I opened mine, I bit his hand hard. I still could not breathe.

"I'll leave your mouth alone," he said after a while, "but, if you scream, I'll
whip you in front of everyone."

He took his hand away, and I tried to breathe but could not. I had no breath. I gasped, panted, and tried to breathe normally. Breathing had become costly and hard to do.

He stared at me. "I'll leave you for today," he said angrily, "but just for today. But tomorrow, if you turn into a stiff corpse on this bed, you'll be mine. Do you understand?"

I nodded eagerly, unable to speak.

I kept gasping, only wanting to breathe. He left the room and locked the door. Meanwhile, my entire body would not stop quivering.

Salar's Testimony (1)

Abu al-Barakat, I will tell you about something that has happened.

Today I received news that made me happy. Salim Shah has asked for the heads of the three of us: Inal, Salar, and Qansuh al-ʿAdili. Three Mamluk amirs, and he wants our heads. For each head he will pay the equivalent weight in gold. If one of us is brought before him alive, he will double the amount. It is a long story, Abu al-Barakat; telling it will take hours of time. But these days, courage has its consequences, and free Mamluks are not like those mercenaries who fight for money. We three belonged to the cavalry, trained together in the Citadel, and were brought from the same Qipchack region. They kidnapped us from the same village; we all knew each other. They took us away; at the time, the one who cried the most was Inal. He missed his mother and brothers. We massaged his shoulders, then punched him in the stomach. He ran after us to get his revenge. Our friendship became our refuge and family. When we all missed our family and longed for a life with no return, we used to play together, run races, talk in our own language, and remember or try to forget.

We were trained for Egypt; it was constantly in our sights as we carried on living. We learned things from one legal scholar, another commander, and yet another teacher. The ultimate goal was those sands mingled with river silt and the vestiges of civilization past. Egypt was always my particular focus, Abu al-Barakat. I fought for it with my own self and body; ever since I was nine, it was our goal. You were born in Egypt, Abu al-Barakat, and became an Egyptian. We—Salar, Inal, and Al-ʿAdili—adopted some of that river silt and learned to love the country. Do you understand? You have no choice when it comes to your birthplace, but, when you risk your own life for the sake of a country, it definitely becomes your own. I was not born in Egypt, but it has grown up inside me. The fall of Syria is the death of part of me, it being Egypt's major artery and an arm of Muslim territory. But, if Egypt itself were to fall, then the keys to the Kaʿba in Mecca would be in the hands of Salim Shah. Mamluks would have either to commit suicide or don women's clothing. I have vowed that it will never fall as long as I am still alive. And yet, treachery is threatening an eventual solution. Incurable disease and plague can eliminate any human beings. When they come from the very soul, Abu al-Barakat, they can cause damage; indeed they can kill or almost.

After the Battle of Marj Dabiq and Sultan Al-Ghuri's defeat at the hands of Salim Shah in Syria, and following the discovery of Khayir Bey's treachery and the retreat of the left flank of the army he was commanding, there had to be a search for the traitor himself. Khayir had betrayed his sultan for his own ambitious purposes. Egypt, he wanted it and loved it, but he did not defend or appreciate it. Egypt is no servant woman, Abu al-Barakat, doing whatever her master's whims decree. No, Egypt will defy traitors and even loyalists. He wanted Egypt for himself and paid the price by selling his soul to the devil forevermore. Salim Shah promised to make him ruler if he was victorious, so he betrayed the country.

All that happened a while ago. I do not want to go on too long. I was the one whom Sultan Al-Ghuri originally asked to command the left flank, but, between night and day, he changed his mind. He made Khayir Bey commander. Why? Have you wondered perhaps, Abu al-Barakat? Has anyone ever told you why Sultan Al-Ghuri changed his mind? What I am now going to tell you must remain inside your heart; you must not tell it to anyone or write it down. My own sense of defeat is like no other. My revenge will be forthcoming, and it will take the form of killing the traitor, or rather all traitors.

Khayir Bey was aware that the sultan had asked me to command and defend the army's left flank at Marj Dabiq. He managed to convince the sultan that I was not the right choice. I was still ranked as drum-major amir while he was governor of Aleppo. I needed to stay close to the sultan to protect him. That is what the traitor said. I was indeed close to the sultan and protected him. At this point, you might well ask, if I was protecting him, how was it that he was killed in the battle? I will tell you, Abu al-Barakat, and this is my story, one that you can write down. He was killed by an Ottoman general when his location was revealed by some Mamluk mercenaries. Al-Ghuri carried on fighting till his dying breath. War had broken out, and the fighting had become intense. The Ottoman general's sword split the sultan's belly open, and soldiers gathered around, eager to steal the corpse. You are aware, of course, Abu al-Barakat, that, for Egyptians, corpses are holy. I am Egyptian; I am one of them. I know that corpses are something holy and realized what Salim would do with Al-Ghuri's corpse if one of those soldiers mutilated the corpse of the Mamluk sultan. It would bring shame on all of us for the rest of time. I went on the attack with sword and dagger, all in defense of Al-Ghuri's corpse. The general wanted to snatch the corpse away from me, and a soldier slunk behind me like a hungry hyena. I kept on fighting, but now there was only one solution . . . something that would preserve the reputation of the Mamluks and their sultan.

In mere seconds, I cut off Al-Ghuri's head with my sword, ran off with it, and left the rest of the corpse where it was for the Ottoman hyenas. There is no point in having a corpse with no head; if they did not find his head, no one would believe that he was dead.

I mounted a horse with the head next to my chest. I set off as fast as I could, until I reached a river's edge. I stopped, grabbed my sword, cut up the head so that nobody could recognize it, and tossed it into the river. Egyptians still believe that Al-Ghuri will return; he is not dead. I have kept that dream alive so that the pestilence of defeat will not affect the heart. Were it to do so, there would be no cure.

When I returned to Egypt, Abu al-Barakat, I felt crushed. It was not the defeat at Marj Dabiq that slew my heart; rather it was my personal defeat, my shame, and the end of a love story that had lasted for years, only to be ended by treachery.

I returned to my house as usual and looked for my wife to give her a warm and loving hug. She was a spectacular beauty; I had never seen her till our wedding night. She loved me, and I was well aware how much she adored me, as she hovered around me, lighting up my every day. For seven long years, none of our children survived. Every time we grieved over our loss, our love for each other only intensified. You know how it is when you find a wonderful fruit in a rotten patch of trees. That is the way she was. But do you know the plant from which her luscious fruit came into being? She was Khayir Bey's daughter!

Yes, Khawand Sa'adat, my wife, was the traitor's daughter. But then, I told myself, someone who has committed one sin will not necessarily commit another. In times of defeat, love has to serve as intermediary. That is what I told myself throughout the conflict. Treason is like a skillful architect: It can set up barriers and sturdy, lofty fortresses in less time and with less effort. For me, that same barrier grew bigger, thicker, and stronger, but it reached its pinnacle whenever I thought, understood, and confirmed.

It is hard to choose between your love and your own father. Both are part of you. What a hard time it was. I feel sorry for her now.

She greeted me as usual, but, this particular day, she hugged me harder than usual, with tears streaming from her eyes.

"Thank God, you're safe," she whispered. "You're all I was thinking about."

She did not notice how rigid my body was, or how my heart was encircled by marble slabs. Her love was coursing without restraint.

She sat down and rested her head on my chest. I pushed her away.

"As you know," I said, "I was supposed to be commander of the left flank. You know that; I told you before I left. But the sultan decided otherwise. I wonder. Who told your father that I was going to be the commander of the army's left flank? Who revealed the secret in order to change history?"

She froze in place. "I didn't want you to die," she said sadly.

"But you preferred the death of an entire army," I responded coldly.

"You're my husband; I have no one else. I begged my father not to let you command the army and be killed. I didn't reveal any secret. Sultan Al-Ghuri listened to my father and sent you away from the left flank. It was the sultan's decision, no fault of mine. There's no way to avoid surrender. Salim's army is invading the whole country, with more than a hundred and fifty thousand men. Fighting is hopeless."

"Did you ask your father to serve as commander himself? To get the sultan to dismiss his loyal supporter and choose the traitor instead?"

"My father's not a traitor," she responded angrily. "He wants to save Egypt the agonies of war. He knows and understands."

Our eyes met.

"I told you the details," I said quietly, "when you were in my arms. That was my mistake. I too must die as a traitor. I told you to cheer you up, so you'd know. But you revealed your husband's secret to your father. You did it."

"I kept you safe, and I don't regret it," she replied calmly. "It's war, and that's out of our control."

For a few moments, I looked down. "Our life together is at an end," I told her. "I'll take you back to your father today."

Her eyes opened wide in amazement. "You know I love you," she said, tears pouring down her face.

"Yes, I do."

"And I didn't betray you."

"Yes, you did. Everything's over."

"You're treating me unfairly because I wanted you to live. You want to take revenge on me because of the defeat, but I'm not the cause."

"It's your father who's the cause. He's a traitor and sold himself."

"No, he understood and foresaw what none of you did."

"That's the difference between us, Sa'adat."

She looked at me. "You're taking revenge on me," she said, holding my hand, "because you hate my father. Where's your sense of justice, Amir?"

"Soldiers will accompany you back to your father's house."

"Salar," she whispered sadly, "my compensation is that you're alive. One day, you'll come back to me. You'll understand and see things differently."

"Even if I became a slave in irons being dragged around the markets," I told her firmly, "I would never go back to you."

I knew Sa'adat and her pride. She did not prostrate herself and beg me; she did not sob in weakness or defeat. Even so, her eyes gleamed and glistened, sighing, asking, and hoping. I stood up coldly and instructed the soldiers to make ready to leave. Those seven years collapsed. The savor of a lengthy love mixed with the blood of betrayal. Fortresses had been built, and everything was over.

The Testimony of the Translator Mustafa Pasha Al-'Uthmani (1)

I want to tell you about something that has happened, but you need to understand, Abu al-Barakat, that Salim Shah is the greatest sultan on the face of the earth. You will never encounter anyone with his courage, sense of justice, and piety. He sympathizes with the weak and overpowers the ruthless. With religious scholars and judges he displays a modest streak; it is only with enemies that his decisive and cruel streak emerges. Do you want to record the truth? Then listen to what I have to say. He would never have come to Syria if the religious scholars there had not sought his help against Mamluk outrages. Listen to me, brother, and do not get angry. Mamluks are thieves by nature; their mercenaries kill for money and fight for spoils. I will admit that some of them are not like that; I have met some whose piety and modesty match those of the Ottomans. But, my brother, there are few of them in Islam. In wartime, you do not expect soldiers to separate men from shaykhs or children from the aged; it is all chaos and obliteration, like the end of the world. Every war has its victims, and every victory brings cruelty and violence. That is the way of the world, and anyone who says otherwise, brother, is a liar. However, I have had the honor of accompanying the Servant of the Two Noble Shrines, Lord of the Two Lands and Seas, crusher of two armies, the all-conquering monarch, Salim Shah. I can vouch for the fact that he is the most upright person I have ever seen. I can testify to have seen the letter that the shaykhs and judges sent to him. He read it for himself, but he always wanted someone to translate it for him even though he knows Arabic perfectly well. If that shows anything, then it is his subtlety, his thoroughness, and his fear of injustice. He did not come to Syria for personal gain, as some people have suggested, nor did he proceed as far as the Egyptian border because he was out to control all Muslim territories, as biased people have maintained. No, it was a cry for help from the shaykhs of Syria to a pious Muslim ruler who loves goodness and justice.

When it comes to his dealings with Tuman Bey, I have checked the correspondence myself. Several times, he asked Tuman to surrender, pay taxes, and acknowledge that he was sultan of Egypt. Tuman Bey refused, and so did the Mamluk amirs. They even killed the letter carrier. To be honest with you, I actually negotiated with the Mamluk amirs, and discovered a kind of vanity in them, although I had no idea how they had acquired it, and an overwhelming self-confidence. I did not like dealing with them and will only acknowledge their courage in war and their perfect knowledge of Arabic—nothing else.

I have to tell you, brother, that some of the things that Ottoman soldiers did were not part of our ethical system. Salim Shah, the all-conquering monarch, certainly did not know about it. They were infringements committed by soldiers in the desert, resulting from hunger, thirst, tiredness, and exhaustion, no more than that. In fact, I will go even further, and note that the sultan heard that one of the soldiers closest to him had assaulted a peasant woman in Sharqiyya province and raped her in full view of everyone. They had been forced to watch but not defend her; after all, Ottoman swords were poised over their necks. No sooner did the sultan learn about it than he ordered that soldier to be killed on the spot in front of everyone. Have you ever seen and lived under a kind of justice better than that? Does any invader or pious shaykh behave that way, brother? Do you want to record the truth? I am telling you now and witnessing to it.

The only time I have ever seen the monarch hesitate was on the edge of Cairo. The city of Cairo has an unrivaled aura to it. In our country, we say that its special feeling of awe comes from that magic statue of the Sphinx and the three pyramids. Salim Shah was dreaming of seeing them. He had also heard about a particular building in Cairo, a gigantic structure that he planned to visit if he managed to get into Cairo—an awe-inspiring mosque named the Sultan Hasan Mosque. We know that he was a sultan and was killed by Mamluk amirs. No other building in the entire Islamic world can rival it. Sultan Salim had heard about it, and vowed to visit the pyramids for a single day and the Sultan Hasan Mosque for several days. I do not know what it is that attracts him about large buildings, but he would always say that civilizations consisted of major buildings—no more, no less. Without architects there would be no history, place, or victory. He is a wise, just, and modest monarch, the very best that Muslim territories have engendered.

Hind's Testimony (2)

I will tell you, Aunt, about what has happened; and what an event it is! All humanity has been struck by it.

All that night, I kept thinking about a way of escaping or wheedling my way out of the situation. The next day would be the end of me, the climax of my defeat. My mind kept toying with me and soothing my heart's anxieties. One man is better than a thousand, it kept saying; being a slave girl was better than being a piece of rag in the hands of an entire army. Husam ad-din was young and not all that evil. Even so, the hatred I felt for him was as tall as a palm tree and as deep as a river. Even though he had rescued me, I still felt disgusted by what he wanted from me and what he had almost managed to do. As you know, Aunt, if someone were to ask you to rip off your own skin and replace it with another one, and then told you that this was your fate which was better than the alternative, what would you do? I was my father's only daughter. I was spoiled and lived happily in my father's house along with brothers and other honorable people. Now I was at the mercy of this peasant and ignorant people. I had made up my mind to try once again. Money was bound to entice him and satisfy his personal greed. I had to resort to trickery and cunning. Either that, or run away. I realized that running away would inevitably lead to destruction. The reason for my profound hatred lay in his deceit or my own self-deceit when I had thought for just a moment that he was as pure as a cavalier, whereas in fact he was greedy and wicked, merciless and untrustworthy.

This Husam ad-din was a jinn from the very depths of the sea, but of a lower category. I cursed him, his family, all Ottomans, and everyone in Balbis.

Next morning, I decided to take the risk and run away with my brother. I looked for him in the house, Aunt, but did not find him. The house had three stories. I thought he would be in the shed. I was alarmed, and asked 'Adlat. She told me not to worry; Husam ad-din had taken him out with him today. It was at this point, Aunt, that I realized for sure that my struggle was not like others; my army had no soldiers. He must have realized that I was planning to run away, and so had made sure that my brother would spend the whole day with him. Not only that, but the house door was locked. The key, it seemed, was kept by 'Abdallah. I kept pacing around my room, like a bird that has made a hole in a narrow room but does not know how to get out. My heart was pounding, and I was shaking, but it was sheer fury that was overwhelming me, fury at people's evil and depravity.

All day, I worked eagerly with 'Adlat. I asked her to intercede on my behalf with her husband's brother. She stared at me in amazement. "Ask him to treat me mercifully," I asked humbly.

She did not reply, nor did she ask him for anything. When he came home at night with his brother, I hurried over to 'Abdallah, grabbed his hand and kissed it.

"Brother," I said, "I'd like you to save me so that God may bless you in your own daughter."

Husam ad-din stood up, looking astonished. 'Abdallah looked at me in alarm, then at Husam ad-din.

"I seek refuge with you," I went on quickly, "and ask for your protection."

"Protection from whom, my daughter?" he asked.

I looked straight at Husam ad-din as though he were a wild beast about to pounce on me. "From your brother," I said.

He smiled and looked at Husam ad-din who had nothing to say.

"He wants me to anger my God," I continued immediately. "I refuse to do it. Don't let him do things to me that you wouldn't want to happen to your own daughter. Devotion to God is a salve for the heart."

He bent over and lifted me up. "You're a slave girl, my daughter," he said.

"Has he told you what happened?" I asked emphatically. "Has he told you how I became his slave girl?"

"By God," 'Abdallah said, "no, he hasn't."

I then quickly told him everything, without looking at Husam ad-din. Hope giving me both strength and life.

He listened to me in silence.

"If he purchased you from the soldiers," he said, "I don't know how I can help you."

"Do Ottoman soldiers have the right to enter Egypt?" I asked insistently.

"No, they don't," 'Abdallah replied emphatically.

"Then what gives them the right to buy and sell me?" I asked. "My brother, since when have Egyptian women been sold to soldiers?"

'Abdallah looked at Husam ad-din who was still saying nothing. For the first time, I actually thought that he might be ashamed of what he had done and was planning to do.

"Husam ad-din," he told his brother, "treat her properly. She's the daughter of an illustrious house. Time humbles all . . ."

"Thank you, brother," I said in triumph.

"I'm like your father, my daughter," he said kindly. "I'm not your brother's age."

He looked at Husam ad-din and stroked his shoulder. "Will you be nice to her?" he asked.

Husam ad-din gave me a look that I did not understand. "Yes," he said, "I'll be nice. I promise that I'll be nice to her."

He then disappeared, and I felt more relaxed. However, I did not go into his room, but stayed in the hall, hugging my brother and wrapping us both in a large blanket. My brother fell asleep after midnight, but I could not fall asleep. I was still feeling worried, not knowing whether or not he had been persuaded by his brother's words. If not, then what would he do? I thought about going out into the fields, but, every time I remembered what the soldiers had done to me, I felt scared. I started rocking back and forth, holding the blanket around me. Then I heard footsteps coming toward me. I closed my eyes, hoping that the footsteps would go away and the person involved would realize that I was asleep.

It was Husam ad-din. No sooner did he see me than he yelled to me: "Leave your brother here!"

"Your brother interceded for me," I begged. "I've a husband and son. Be nice to me. Let me go."

"Go to the room," he said as though he had not heard me.

I left my brother and was about to rush over to the door. He caught up with me, grabbed me with my hand clasping the door handle, and dragged me to the room.

"Don't you dare scream!" he said threateningly.

But I did scream. He put his hand over my mouth till we reached the room. He pushed me inside and locked the door. I tried pleading with him.

"Your energy's a male trait," I said. "I'm a wife and mother. Don't humiliate me, I beg you. You've protected me and rescued me. Carry on with your honest labor. You will have your reward. My brother, you're the best of men!"

He interrupted me. "Don't say 'brother' again," he said as he took off his shoes and clothes. "Say 'my Lord'."

"Yesterday you were generous to me," I stuttered, my own heart within earshot. "I'll never forget that generosity as long as I live. If I don't pay you what you paid, do whatever you like. That's your right, but only if I don't pay you."

"Yes, it's my right," he said as he looked at my body like a piece of merchandise. "You're my property, and I can do with you whatever I want, today, tomorrow, every single day. Take your clothes off and stop talking."

I sat on the floor. "At least, listen to me," I begged.

"I beg you," I said in a humble tone that I had never known before. "I'm going to die if you do this to me."

He sat down in front of me and grabbed my head. "I don't want to listen to you," he said. "Your words mean nothing to me. I don't want you to talk today unless I say so."

In seconds he had lifted me up and put me on the bed. He smothered my body, and I let out a scream. He covered my mouth and pinned my arm behind my back.

"If you scream," he said, "I'm going to tear you limb from limb in front of your little brother. Then I'll sell him to the Ottoman soldiers so they can castrate him if he's lucky and doesn't die at their hands. Actually I'm going to do that now if you resist."

I did resist, but did not scream, fearing for my brother what might happen to him or what he might be about to watch. I struck out with every limb in my body and all the strength that I had. I expected him to slap me, beat me with a whip, or leave me alone, but he did not.

What can I say, Aunt? I wailed as though I had lost my entire family. A weak scream emerged from my mouth loaded with all the bitterness of defeat.

"Do you know how much I detest you?" I asked him.

I groaned as I felt him inside me, and my entire body shook, but no tears found their path to my eyes. I groaned in pain over what I had lost and what had been violated. If it had been in my hands, I would have keened then and there and seen my very self dissipate in the climactic groans of sorrow in the air.

He left his marks on me, sealing my body with fire so that he could be sure that I was his servant. He had burned the very depths of my soul, but, in spite of him, my soul remained free. It was my body that had been defeated by an enemy and coward.

Once he had finished, I buried my head in my hands in shame. At that point, I had nothing: bodies needed to be crushed; throttling and subduing free spirits was a noble activity.

He looked at me in amazement. "Why all this torment?" he asked. "It's happened, and now it's over. As I knew and expected, you were lying. You don't have a husband or son. From today on, you're my slave girl."

I sank to the floor, but did not cry. I stuttered isolated phrases, while my entire body quivered in its rebellion against him.

"I shall curse you with every prayer I utter," I said. "What you've just done is a serious crime."

I also told myself something in a muted tone of voice. "You're more despicable than all the Ottomans together. You decide to overpower a free woman to turn her into a slave girl, against her will and by sheer force. You only rescued her for personal reasons. The hatred that I feel for you has no parallel. One day, I'm going to slaughter you with my own hands; I'll split your guts open while I'm still alive, and eat your liver as Hind, the Caliph Mu'awiya's mother, did. But, in your case, I'm going to do it while you're still alive. I won't wait till you're dead."

"What's that you're muttering?" he asked after a while. "Come over here. You're not going to sleep on the cold floor.

"If you obeyed my instructions," he declared, "you wouldn't have to work in the house. You'd have a different status than all the other slave girls. I'd buy you silk and attend to your needs for a while."

"Then look for a prostitute," I replied.

"Why look for a prostitute when I have a slave girl?"

"Even if you cut me up into equal pieces, I would still resist you every day and every minute, till my life came to an end."

At that moment, I swore never to beg again. Hatred would soothe the thunder inside me. Hatred afforded a security only known to the oppressed.

"We'll see," he said casually.

The morning after that ill-starred night, my brother Shams gave me a sympathetic look.

"What were you scared of last night, Hind?" he asked me.

My entire body was throbbing with hatred. "Yesterday I wasn't scared of anything," I replied.

"I thought I heard you screaming," he said softly.

He opened his hand, stared at it, and gestured with his finger. "Just one scream maybe," he said.

"I was dreaming," I told him, "and had a terrible nightmare."

"What kind of nightmare?" he probed. "When are you coming back to our house?"

"Soon," I replied sadly. "I don't remember the nightmare."

"You must have been remembering the soldiers and their red standards," he said enthusiastically. "They were trying to kidnap us. Hind, I hate and fear them."

I did not respond, but stayed where I was, as sheer hatred oozed from every part of me.

'Adlat started scolding me and making me work. One day I yelled at her: "Enough talk! I don't want to hear your voice."

I remember that I poured water all over her face. She wanted to kill me and finish things off. Sitt ad-dar looked at me in alarm. 'Adlat grabbed me by the hair, tugged it, yelled at me, and slapped me on the face. I put up a fight and yelled as loud as I could. 'Abdallah was at home. No sooner had he come into the kitchen than 'Adlat stopped tormenting me and froze in place. She was still clasping my hair, while I was bent over and unable to stand up straight. He looked at the spilled water, then at my hair.

"What's happened?" he asked. "Let go of her hair, 'Adlat."

She let go of my hair. "This she-devil spilled the water," she said tearfully, "and was about to hit me. Tell Husam ad-din to whip her."

"Leave her alone," he said. "She's like your daughter. Believe in God through her, woman."

"You're siding with a slave girl against me?" she said angrily. "I'm going to tell your brother."

He did not reply. It seemed as if he was the weakest element in the household and the person who was kindest and most sympathetic.

I did not cry, but went to the room with my brother, determined to wage war again.

When Husam ad-din came home, I confronted him.

"Don't touch me again," I said. "I hit 'Adlat today. I'll scream, leave the house, and ask for help. If the Ottoman soldiers kidnap me, I won't be bothered as long as they kill you."

"You won't be bothered," he responded in amazement and with a degree of sarcasm, "just so long as they kill me. If I tore you limb from limb now and flayed you alive, what would happen?"

"That would be the best thing you could do," I replied bitterly. "Go ahead and tear me limb from limb, but don't touch me."

"There's no fear in your heart, Hind," he said. "Is that because I killed it yesterday, and now there's no longer anything to be afraid of? Or rather because you always defy the people who own you?"

"God alone owns me," I replied defiantly.

He hugged me to him. "No," he responded in a foxy tone, "I'm the one who owns you. I owned you yesterday and I'll own you whenever I want. All you have to do is to hear and obey, daughter of noble parents."

He took hold of my brother and carried him out of the room. He grabbed my hand.

"Don't make me hurt you or your brother," he said. "I'm going to throw him out into the fields."

This situation lasted for several days, Aunt, and I would rather forget them. He would rape me; I would always resist, but he always won. He did not beat me. I think he did not do that because he did not need to; he could simply use sheer force and threats to make that impossible. I endured it for a week without screaming for fear of scaring my little brother. However, I was sure that I would not put up with this forever; self-sacrifice for my brother's sake did not demand killing the soul and digging a hole for its corpse. I made up my mind to run away.

Meanwhile, 'Adlat avoided me altogether. It seems that she did not complain to Husam ad-din. Sitt ad-dar gave me some trivial things to do, which I ignored sometimes and carried out at others. I did not eat a lot; I gave it to my brother and wanted to die.

I realized that, if I ran away, he would sell my brother to the Ottomans. This peasant was like sin, latching on to the lowliest. If only you realized how much I loathed him and want to kill him! No matter. I decided to run away; either that or commit suicide. I do not want to say much about my feelings and sense of humiliation sticking to my body. When he disappeared from the room day after day, I decided to go out at dawn and take my brother into the fields till we found someone nicer and more honorable. After all, Egypt as mother had to produce someone preferable to Husam ad-din who turned a free woman into a servant and a respectable woman into a cringing sex object. I vowed to myself that, one day, I would find him again and get my revenge. I would take out his liver and eat it while he was still alive, so he could see and understand.

I grabbed my brother's hand. The only things I was carrying were some bread and fruit that I had stolen from 'Adlat's kitchen before we left. Fate was coming to my aid; I found the door open and went out to freedom after the humiliation of prison. The fields seemed calm, and the sun came out confidently and knew its path without fear or hesitation. It is those moments of hesitation that lead to defeat.

How was it that I had not planned to escape before? Why had fear won out till what happened had happened? I breathed joyfully and started running toward Cairo, or, at least, that is what seemed right to me. The only people I saw were farmers. It was as if the Ottomans had vanished, and the entire country was safe and normal; no war going on around us, and no invaders.

"Where are you taking me, Hind?" Shams asked after a while.

I was panting hard from all the running. "Away from the evil-infested house," I replied.

My feet sank into the moist soil, and I mowed down a lot of fresh green trees, but I did not care. After a while, I heard shouts all around me, but did not know where they were coming from; but they were all around us. I went back and hid in some trees and clutched my brother in case I had to protect him, or him me. The shouts were coming from women or perhaps children; girls, for sure, and maybe mothers, a kind of screams I had never heard before. It took only a few seconds for me to realize that the Ottomans were selling off peasant women from girls aged two to mothers in their forties. I swear to you that I saw a young girl being sold for five dinars. With my own eyes I watched as Egyptian Muslim women were being sold off in their own country and in front of their own families. The sword poised over their family's necks was enough to squelch any breaths and neutralize any idea of male protection. How I hate men, Aunt, but I shall talk about that later.

If I had moved, they would have sold me too. Someone else would have bought me for a dinar or less. What a miserable life we women have today after the Mamluks failed to protect us! How I despise them! If I stayed where I was, would they find me or not? Some other man could then rape me and take control of my body, this time an Ottoman, a soldier who had come as an invader, and who would now kidnap my brother, and rape him or worse—who knows? How vile wars are: they bring nothing good, nothing constructive. I covered my brother's mouth and stayed motionless where I was; now all I wanted was to go back to Husam ad-din's house. I stayed there maybe for hours; I have no idea how long. Eventually the market was over, and everyone went their own way. The soldiers disappeared.

For a few seconds, I looked all around me, then told him to run as fast as possible back to the defeat that we knew we would face and the injustice that we could live with.

I was panting as I banged on the door, terrified. 'Adlat opened the door alarmed.

"Just wait to see what Husam ad-din is going to do to you," she said. "You tried to run away, didn't you? How despicable you are! After everything we've done for you. You've no gratitude or sympathy in your heart. If only they'd sold you today, and we'd be finished with you."

I did not respond. I went into the kitchen, grabbed a big knife, and hid it in my clothes. Then I went into my room and waited for the punishment or total humiliation. Now death would be the best solution and the proudest too!

When he came home at night, 'Adlat told him the whole story. He came in, whip in hand, and hit the floor with it. He looked at me as I sat there on the bed, calm, fearless, and unalarmed, while my brother sat shivering on the floor. He told my brother to leave.

He was still staring at me. "When a slave girl tries to run away," he said, "she has to be whipped. You leave me no choice."

I did not respond, but I swear to you, Aunt, that I preferred whipping to what he kept asking me to do.

"But you came back of your own accord," he said. "Why?"

I did not reply.

He looked at my hand clutching my heart and the knife. "You're a fighter," he went on. "You know when to surrender and when to attack. Here your war's easier, but you're still bound to lose it with Ottoman soldiers. What are you hiding, a knife?"

My equipoise was unshaken and strong. "If you come any closer, I'm going to kill you myself," I said.

"Why don't you try to kill me now?" he asked.

"If I did, someone else would take me prisoner and turn me into a slave girl. I was created a free woman."

He nodded as though he understood. "Why can't you accept your fate?" he asked. "All of us have to do that. These days, free people are killed or enslaved. Maybe sometime you'll get your freedom back."

That was the very first time that he had spoken to me as though I were a human being.

"Ottoman soldiers were selling peasant women today," I said firmly. "One for less than five dinars. Why don't you buy five of them and let me go? I've promised to repay you what you spent on me. I swear to you."

"You lied to me," he said, sitting beside me. "You told me you were a mother and wife. You played games, complained to my brother, and did a number of other things which led me not to trust you at all. Maybe you don't have a family."

"I can forgive you for what has happened," I pleaded. "If you took me back to my father, I could reward you. Then everything would be over."

"I'm going to whip you today because you tried to run away," he said softly. "I'm going to stop you leaving the room, take the knife away from you, and prevent you from getting close to any knife or sword. You'll be available to me whenever I wish and obey my every command."

"Just try!" I said without even intending to do so.

Before I could shift the knife and thrust it into my heart, he grabbed me and the knife.

"Are you challenging me," he said, "because you're holding that puny knife? What kind of nonsense is that?"

"I'll find some way to die," I replied. "I'll stop eating and drinking till I'm dead."

He pushed me away and grabbed the knife. He then smothered me with his body as he had done before. I was about to scream, but then he spoke to me.

"I want to make a deal with you," he said. "You'll like it. Listen to me."

My heart was throbbing. "Anything," I replied hysterically, "just don't touch me."

"Three days."

"You won't touch me," I insisted, not even hearing what he said.

He brought his mouth close to mine. "I won't touch you for three days," he said.

"No, for the rest of my life."

"You'll sleep here and let me kiss you if I want. But I won't make you my slave girl for three whole days."

"What kind of rubbish is that?"

"I'm going to whip you now, and you won't be able to run away again. You're going to eat. Even if you stop eating, I won't let you die. Today you'll be my slave girl, tomorrow, and every day. If I leave you for three days after pledging to do so, maybe I'll get tired of you and leave you alone. Who knows? It's an opportunity not to be missed."

"You're torturing me as though I'm one of them?"

"One of whom?"

"The Ottomans."

"But I'm an Egyptian like you."

"As I've told you before, I curse you with every prayer I make. God hears my prayers. You've wronged me, forced yourself on me, and turned me into a prostitute. I am a free, chaste woman."

"No, you're my slave girl," he insisted again. "I spent everything I own in order to purchase you. I bought both you and your brother. You keep challenging me in a way that not even my own brother's wife manages to do. She's like a mother to me. My patience with you is beginning to wear thin. Beating you is really easy."

"I'll do anything, absolutely anything. But promise me you won't touch me again."

"That's not going to happen."

"I'll clean the whole house on my own, I'll cook, and carry out the animal dung by hand."

"Three days. Who knows? Maybe the Ottomans will kill us. If you were a professional fighter, you'd make use of the truce period to mobilize the army."

"A week," I said, covering my head with my hands.

He stared at me in amazement. "Are you negotiating too?" he asked. "A week then."

"Don't touch me at all," I replied, somewhat relieved.

"I won't be spending any time with you, but I've the right to kiss you whenever I want."

"Why do you kiss someone who loathes you?"

"What have kisses to do with love, Hind? How naïve you are!"

"No kisses."

"No agreement without kisses."

"If you suppose, man, that you're going to turn me into a slave girl who's happy with her lot in life, then you don't know the difference between a free woman and a slave girl. Anyone who can see the sun and know its warmth can never live amid darkness. Anybody who can sniff the pure Nile air can never live amid the rot of prisons."

"Just one kiss," he said after a pause.

I gave him a hateful look as I pushed him away. "Will you leave me now, my Lord?" I said dryly. "Then I can breathe in peace."

⟶

I wanted that week to go on forever; either that, or for the Mamluks to win. Then the Ottomans would disappear, and I could get out of this ill-starred house. On the first day, I started planning and thinking about ways of escaping. I thought that Sitt ad-dar might help me. I asked her and promised her a lot of money, but she was always distracted, singing songs and, so it seemed to me, thinking about men. From the very first day, this week seemed different from the first one that I had spent in this house. I think that 'Adlat's hatred disappeared; she asked me to undertake some more difficult tasks such as carrying heavy water buckets. For the first time, she asked me to clean out the animal dung in the stables. The work disgusted me, but she had the whip in her hand. She threatened that, if I did not do what she told me, she would whip me, tell Husam ad-din, and ask him to punish me. I was worried that, if she told Husam ad-din that I was not working, he would break his pledge. So I patiently endured the toil. You will not believe this, Aunt, but Hind, the girl whom you raised and know, started cleaning out stables, sweeping, and carrying water on her back. After three days, I would go to sleep in the corner of the room as though I were dead. My knees ached, my hands were swollen and blistered, and blood oozed out between my fingers. Husam ad-din would come home at night and go to sleep without talking to me.

After three days, my Aunt, he came over to me while I was sound asleep. He grabbed my hand, and I shot up.

"How sorry I feel for you, Hind," he said softly.

My whole body recoiled, and I moved away, feeling utterly tense.

"Come a little closer," he said, still holding my hand.

I pulled my hand away. "I'd like you to keep your promise," I told him.

He pulled me toward him till I was touching his chest. "I'm not fond of a lot of argument," he said, looking into my eyes. "Otherwise, I might just go back on my promise."

"What do you want from me?" I asked with a mixture of defiance and fear.

"Don't you feel any gratitude because I rescued you from the Ottomans?"

"You saved me to turn me into a slave girl and rape me."

He ignored my words. "Who are you?" he asked.

"One of the people's children," I replied proudly.

"You mean, a Mamluk child?" he asked in amazement.

"I tried to tell you from the very start. If you'd listened to me, none of this would have happened."

"What was going to happen was going to happen, and this particular episode as well. Why should I be bothered about your lineage? If the Ottomans enter Cairo, all Mamluk daughters will become slaves. Who's your father? An amir?"

"My grandfather was one of Sultan Barquq's amirs."

"Sultan Barquq!" he said derisively. "He ruled over a hundred years ago. You're an Egyptian, just like me. After three or four generations, you can't even count the number of sons of the people. Do you have any Egyptian blood, or is it all Turkish?"

"It's just my grandfather who was an amir," I replied without hesitation. "He married an Egyptian woman, and so did his son."

"So, you're Egyptian then," he said with certainty.

"That's the way it is with Mamluks," I confirmed. "Egypt is all they have."

"Do you really believe that the Mamluks are Egyptians?" he asked in amazement.

This conversation was interesting me and making me forget that I was in his room and under his total control.

"My father says they're Egyptians," I said.

"Is your father always right?"

"My father knows everything. He reads and writes."

"What's his name?"

I hesitated, and then tried to change the subject. "Do you believe the Mamluks are Egyptians?" I asked him.

"That will become clear shortly if they fail to defend Egypt. They have no homeland and deserve to die."

"The Ottomans will never get into Cairo," I said enthusiastically. "They won't be able to do it."

"Why so certain? There's treachery in the air."

"Traitors never win, if you only knew it."

"To the contrary, traitors are the only winners, did you but realize it."

"What will you do if the Ottomans enter Egypt?"

"They're already in Egypt, Hind."

"Egypt means Cairo."

He remained silent.

"Are you going to work in agriculture all your life?" I asked him immediately. "Have you had any sword training?"

"I've never held one," he replied assertively. "I don't like fighting."

"But you steal what's not yours."

"No, I saved a jewel from being indiscriminately crushed by animals. With that in mind, don't I have any rights?"

"What you saved, my Lord, is not an object. It's a person who has feelings and can hurt."

"In wartime we're all objects: treasure, sword, and crops. Didn't your father teach you that?"

"My father doesn't like wars."

"How did you learn about wars? You fight, you defy, and you dare to argue with me."

"By God, I won't do it anymore," I pleaded immediately. "Forgive me. I've lost everything I own."

"You've lost, and that's over," he responded casually. "Whether you go back to your father or stay here, you've changed, understood, and come to a realization. Why not accept your fate, if only for a while? Do you think I'm going to be patient with you forever? When this week's over, if you so much as resist, argue, or dare to say something I don't like, then I'm going to use the whip without hesitation. I've been merciful and patient with you. I'm not usually so patient."

"But you have nice handwriting," I said, trying to convince him. "Your heart must be full of mercy."

"That's true," he said with a sarcastic grin. "My heart is full of mercy."

He took my hand and looked at the cracks in the skin. I felt alarmed and kept trying to pull it away.

"You'll be getting back to work," he said. "We all work here."

He grabbed my chin and lifted it.

"Hind," he told me, "you must lower your eyelids when our eyes meet. Don't look at me as though we're equals. We aren't."

"I'll try," I replied, lowering my head.

Salar's Testimony (2)

I will tell you about something important that has happened . . .

In times of danger, Mamluks remember the goal, probe profound truths, and are mindful of the risks involved. What shame would await them if their own dynasty were to disappear like the ones before theirs, and every trace of them vanished from the face of the earth? Dear colleague and friend, I shall not deny anything or lie to you. Injustice has spread and avarice has planted its roots among the Mamluks. Assaults are now permitted, and violence is required and obligatory. With so many pleasures on offer, the main goal has been lost. But, as you and I both know, this is Egypt, with its own special magic to intoxicate the mind and its particular treasures to tempt any believer. With its fascination and kindly soul, it is able to prompt passionate feelings, not a lot of shouting or moaning. Aggressors assume that she does not care or express regret. No matter. The amirs were well aware of the danger, that time was not the same time; it was over a century earlier that the Mongols and Crusaders had been defeated and left. But the Ottomans are cleverer and stronger, and their soldiers are tougher. Their arrows never hit hearts in throats, instead they are out to pervert and crush people's souls. They know how to seduce, to betray; when to advance and when to hold back.

Abu al-Barakat, danger drowns in water the same way that pitch chars faces. Sultan Al-Ghuri was killed, and the amirs woke up to find themselves facing a disaster which they had shunned and ignored just as Noah's folk had done with the flood. They had supposed it to be all illusions and crazy dreams. They all looked totally stunned, as the grip on the jewel that opened the gates of the sacred city grew tighter, that being the goal of Salim Shah. He was well aware of the extent of the risk involved and the value of what he was about to acquire. That applied even to this utter barbarian who had butchered all the male members of his own family, his brother and nephew, and who appreciated the significance of risk-taking. People say that he had deposed his own father and killed him. I know all about the magic of authority and the way that rulers tread its path alone, as though it always involved reckoning and a journey to the end. I realize too that Egypt is the goal and desired target. This man, Salim Shah, who fears no wild beast or weapon, is frightened by Egypt. He paused, took some time to think, and sent messengers, trying to get the Mamluks to surrender, but without success.

We three—myself Salar, Inal, and Al-'Adili—got together with the Mamluk amirs. We decided to appoint Tuman Bey as sultan, he being a just man untempted by greed. But he refused.

The three of us then headed for the house of a shaykh respected by everyone in Egypt. He had renounced everything, withdrawn, and abandoned this lower world, all in order to strive for the ultimate achievement. He was spending years of his life with no need of man or beast; he ate only a little, wore coarse clothes, and lived far removed from earth's treasures, and all in a quest for what would touch the soul, enrich the body, cure the thirst for greed and passion, and use its steadfast will to defy bodily desires. You know who it is; you must know already, Abu al-Barakat. We were heading for the house of the one who knows God, Abu as-Sa'ud al-Jarithi. When we met him, I was the one to initiate our explanations. I was seated in front of him, filled with awe, despair, and alarm, fully prepared to gamble with everything in the cause of victory.

"How is it possible," I asked in frustration, "for the Mamluks to be defeated and their entire dynasty to disappear? They were the glory and defense of Islam, defeating invasions and winning at a time when all other regimes were vanishing. When ignorance was widespread, they were eager for knowledge; they were building things while others destroyed and torched everything. They spent precious resources for the sake of Muslim lands. There's no dynasty like them, no knowledge such as theirs, and no mosques and buildings like theirs. Shaykh, Cairo does not have a single caravanserai, fountain, or school that wasn't built by them."

"Every age has its allotted book," he replied quietly without looking at me.

"Our time hasn't arrived yet."

"Dear amir . . ."

"Please call me Salar."

"My son, individual initiative always brings success. Just look all around you. Allow your insights to counteract your eyes so you can really see. Think carefully and confirm. What do you see?"

"Decline and intrigue in every sector," I replied after a pause. "Some people have not forgotten the eventual goal or lost their way."

"Injustice always defeats and erases."

"But, Shaykh, 'God knows the evil from the good.'"

He gave me a lengthy stare. "You've come here with a pure heart," he said, "looking for deliverance and justice. Make your request, my son."

"Tuman Bey is the best person to lead and govern Egypt now. He's honest and courageous."

"He is indeed."

"But he's refusing. He's scared of government intrigues and amirs' corruption."

"His insight is obviously very powerful."

"In times of great peril, bonanzas surface. We have to take risks. Surrender will mean death for us all. Do you understand me, Shaykh?"

"Yes, I do," he replied softly.

Salar said: "Salim Shah has proposed to us that we acknowledge him as sultan of Egypt and pay taxes to his country. If we did so, then we would become subjects of his empire and squeeze out the food of Egypt's poor for his purposes. How are we supposed to give a vote of confidence to someone who relies on betrayal? Perhaps you've heard about Khayir and others. He's promised them a lot and exploited their greed."

"Sometimes that's the way of the world," the Shaykh replied gently. "Cruelty overcomes courage; killing and slaughter eradicate entire civilizations."

"So, if justice disappears, there's no hope for us?"

"I don't know, my son. Does the existence of justice give you hope, or snatch it from your hands? God does what he wills. You have to defend your own home."

"Egypt's our only home. If we surrender, then Egypt gets absorbed into Salim's lands, and darkness will descend on us all. Without the sun's warmth, you die; there's no life without it."

"Consult your own heart, my son. You've come to see me with an obvious purpose. What do you want from me?"

"That the amirs should all swear on the Holy Qur'an in front of you to give authority to Tuman Bey and to cease all in-fighting and conflict."

The shaykh said nothing.

"They'll swear not to fight each other," Salar went on, "or act disloyally. If they agree to do that, then Tuman Bey will agree to govern Egypt."

"Salar, your heart has all the courage of a knight, the enthusiasm of a warrior, and the piety of a searcher for redemption. Your request is granted."

The amirs all swore on a copy of the Qur'an in front of the shaykh, and Sultan Tuman Bey agreed to govern Egypt. I was fully aware of the burden he was taking on and his own sincerity. I was part of his own personal weaponry.

After the sultan had sworn his oath, the three of us gathered and agreed on the battle plan and its aftermath: what was going to happen if we won or lost.

"Khayir Bey's head is what I'm after," I said with determination.

"Your wife's father?" Inal asked.

"You know she's not like that anymore," I replied.

"You want his head for personal reasons, Salar. Be careful; there are risks!"

"No, I'd like to kill all traitors," I made abundantly clear. "Khayir's head and the person commanding him."

The two of them looked at each other.

"You mean, Salim himself?" Qansuh al-'Adili asked fearfully.

"If he died, we'd limit the amount of blood spilled."

There was another oath that the three of us swore: to kill Salim.

Now, my soul felt relieved, and I was able to sleep after a whole month of non-stop agony.

Hind's Testimony (3)

Fateful events, Aunt, come as surprises and convulse existence. For the first three days after the agreement with Husam ad-din, he did not touch me. On the fourth day, I started to feel better, but my body was still exhausted by the hard labor and having to wake up at dawn every day. The brutal way that 'Adlat was treating me made her the person whom I hated the most in the household, apart from Husam ad-din, of course. On the fourth day, 'Adlat woke me up as usual, left my brother where he was, and left the room, while I was still rubbing my eyes. Husam would always leave immediately before dawn and not return till late.

That particular dawn, she told me to clean out the stables. I was about to leave, but then Husam ad-din stopped me by the door.

"Leave Hind alone today," he told her firmly. "I need her help."

'Adlat gave him an angry look. He grabbed my hand and led me into the courtyard. We sat down together in the sunshine. He sat next to me, Aunt, so I moved away a little. He did not try to come closer. He brought out some pieces of paper and his inkwell.

"I'd like to teach you how to do nice calligraphy," he told me. "I may need your help."

I gave him a dubious look. Aunt, I had no idea how convey to him my absolute hatred. As you know, there are some bodily scars that can heal over time, but there are also others in the heart that linger and oppression that stays in the soul forever. I did not know what to say, Aunt. Every time he was intimate with me against my will, he was killing my heart or almost. Then I started thinking that the next time would be better because my heart was already dead. But it would revive and die all over again, multiple times. Forgive me; maybe I'm exaggerating. You may be telling yourself that my fate is simply that of many women, and it's not the worst imaginable fate. But I used to be Hind, maybe different from all other girls; my self-esteem and pride were my most precious assets.

He looked at me as though he was well aware of what was going on in my mind.

He began writing slowly. "Look," he said.

I looked at his fingers which were drawing careful lines. For a few seconds, I tried to forget what he had done to me, so that he would not get angry. If he did, he might well annul our agreement. Who knows?

He handed me the inkwell. "Here, now you do it," he said.

I had never been bothered with handwriting. But, at this juncture, I was eager to do anything to get him to leave me alone. I wrote something badly, just a few words.

"What kind of writing is that supposed to be?" he asked critically.

He grabbed hold of my hand to pull it over the paper. I tried to pull it away, and he looked annoyed. I let him hold my hand. With a frown, I did my best to concentrate on what I was doing.

'You're hopeless, Hind!" he said after a while. "What do you do well? Just defy and talk?"

"I'm sorry," I responded quickly, lowering my eyelids. "I'll try."

"No, don't try," he replied, taking the paper from me. "Just talk while I'm working. Tell me about Cairo and your house. Do you have servants and slave girls?"

"Yes, we do," I replied eagerly, missing my father very much. "Have you ever visited Cairo, my Lord?"

"My Lord, you say!" he repeated happily. "That's much better. You've started to understand, Hind."

"Do you make your money from farming or calligraphy?" I asked.

"Both."

"If you moved to Cairo," I suggested, still eager, "you'd make a lot more money. You could work for my father and do calligraphy for his books in your beautiful script."

"Your father will accept me and work with me," he asked sarcastically, "when I own his daughter?"

"You'd free me, of course. He would pay you a lot."

"Of course!" he said with the same sarcasm. "Now tell me the truth. Why didn't you get married all this time? How old are you? Eighteen?"

"Nineteen," I replied shyly.

"How come you haven't been married?"

"I've always preferred knowledge and learning. My mother died, and the time wasn't right."

"You preferred knowledge. Why didn't you learn about love? That's knowledge too."

"My Lord," I replied fearfully, "you promised."

He laughed, maybe for the first time. "I didn't expect that the very first slave girl I've bought would turn out to have devoted herself to knowledge. What kind of luck is that?"

"That's why I've asked you to buy someone else," I told him, still eager.

"And I've told you that I don't have the money."

He looked all around him. "Come to our room," he said.

My feet weighed me down. I had sworn that I would not plead with him.

"I beseech you," I begged in a whisper in spite of myself, "you gave me a promise."

"I'm not going to do anything," he replied, pulling me behind him. "What's the matter? I'm just going to kiss you once, as we agreed. Then you can leave."

I shivered. He sat me down on his bed, and I closed my eyes. It was as though I was expecting to be beaten by the teacher because I had not understood or remembered.

"Come on then," I said, hugging myself, "do what you want."

"You're angry with me," he said. "Why?"

If only I had had a knife at that point to thrust into his heart and tell him why.

"You make me hate you so much that it's intolerable," I said bitterly. "People are kind to animals and don't force them. Maybe if you thought of me as your donkey, you wouldn't be so cruel."

He ran his fingers over my hand. "Do you feel that?" he asked.

"Yes, I do."

"Does it hurt you?"

"You've no idea how much hurt and loss I feel," I replied sadly.

"But sometimes I have the impression that you're not feeling anything," he said. "Anyone who can feel sad can be passionate as well. You have no heart. Do you have one, Hind?"

I pulled my hand away. "Yes, I have a heart," I replied. "It refuses to see me treated like some inanimate object, my Lord."

He looked into my eyes. "You never cry," he said. "You're not even good at begging either. You've suffered degradation and have lost everything, and yet you've never cried. Can you be in pain and not cry? I didn't realize that there were women who could suffer pain without crying. You've no heart."

I did not respond.

He ran his fingers over my face, then drew close to my mouth. "If you stopped resisting," he said, as though he had not understood what I had said, "what would happen? You're my property, whether you resist or not."

"If I stopped resisting," I responded angrily, "and surrendered like some slave girl, I would certainly die. Death's preferable to surrender."

He rubbed his chin over my cheek. I hugged my body and closed my eyes, as though he were flaying me as never before. He kissed my cheek gently and started kissing my neck all over. His breathing was burning my breasts. I covered them, with my hand over my heart.

"You promised me," I told him firmly.

He ran his hands over my hair. "Surrender would bring with it unimaginable pleasure," he whispered. "Why torture yourself? Let your body control the reins so it can seek and feel. Hind, you need someone to look after you and show you affection. At times like these, affection is in short supply and costly. You need to grab it when you're miserable about your loss of status and working intolerably hard. If you'd let me take care of you, all your sufferings would be at an end. Just remember: your sufferings haven't really started yet. Maybe you'd be a lot older if the Ottomans entered the country. You'd be looking for someone to look after you, and would find no one. You're clever enough. You have to know when to resist and when to give in."

My entire body was shaking as far from him as possible and recoiling in preparation for some new assault. "You've kissed me," I said quickly. "That's it."

"It's not over yet," he replied, kissing my eyes, ears, and cheeks.

I opened my mouth to object. He gave me a strange kiss, Aunt. At first, it was gentle and unhurried. But then it infiltrated my heart, bound it, and assumed control. I did not resist him till I had carried out my side of the promise. But, when I started feeling giddy, reality became all confused, my body lost its ability to resist, and my heart felt—I do not know—either hatred for him or anger at myself, I was scared and angry at myself and the evil lurking inside me. I pushed him away as hard as I could.

"You promised me," I said.

"I'm keeping that promise," he replied, giving me a hug.

I pushed him away and wiped his kiss off my mouth as hard as I could. "Are you going to leave me alone now?" I asked.

"Yes," he replied, standing up. "Why are you so alarmed? Is it me or you?"

I did not respond. I pursed my lips so I would not yell right in his face. He went out and left me, as angry and aggravated as I have ever felt. I groaned in sheer fury, wiped off his kiss as hard as I could, and cursed him. There are times when the devil takes hold; you know what I mean, Aunt? His words were like misgivings inside my heart: "in times like these, affection is in short supply and costly. You need to grab it."

That day, he did not come back to the room, but slept in the hall. For the very first time, I could relax and sleep peacefully in his bed along with my little brother. It was before dawn when 'Adlat woke me up as usual, and he disappeared from the house.

'Adlat started making things even harder for me. If I was slow or took a break in the middle of nonstop work, she would grab a stick to beat me. I got the impression that, when Husam ad-din left and she knew that he would be away for a night or two, she would treat me much more harshly. That day, she told me to clean out the animal stables in the house basement. I defied her, refused to do it, and told her that I would be telling Husam ad-din. But she insisted, and seemed nervous and sad. I did not know much about her own life. She handed me the brooms and water, and pushed me toward the piles of animal dung. If only I had remembered, Aunt, that I would have preferred to clean up animal dung every day rather than be touched by that man and turned into his concubine or slave girl. I had the impression that my wish had been granted, and I was now to clean up the animal dung every day. My entire being was revolted by the job, and I kept my nostrils closed while I was doing it. A week went by without problems. He had gone away before the weekend and before touching me. After several days, something distressing happened that I need to tell you about so that the rest of the story will be clear. In fact, I started the day cleaning out the buffalo and cow refuse.

I put my hand over my nose because the stench was suffocating me, almost enough to make me faint in sheer disgust. I used a large cloth to wipe off the residue, feeling utterly nauseous. Just then, I heard a weird noise in the next room.

They were groans, not screams; laughter, but not cries for help; a plea mixed with passion, but not fear; whispers in a shaky voice, a playful mind, and a drunken, boisterous heart. I knew that voice, Sitt ad-dar, 'Adlat's daughter. I headed quietly to the next room and stole a glance into the room. What I saw was a dream or nightmare, I don't know which. But I swear, Aunt, that that is what I saw. Forgive me, Lord God, for what I am going to say. I saw Sitt ad-dar splayed out on the straw, semi-naked or naked. Over her was a man whom I did not know. They seemed to be having sex, but, unlike me, she was not screaming, asking for help, and loathing every minute. For a few seconds she spotted me watching and ran to the door as fast as possible. A hand grabbed me and pulled me inside.

"What are you doing here now?" I heard Sitt ad-dar ask.

The man was still holding my hair. "We'll kill her now," he said forcefully, "and bury her. She's a slave girl, isn't she?"

She may have said his name at that point; I don't know. I did not get a good look at his face. He had vicious features, and his eyes radiated evil. I hated him before I even set eyes on him.

"Let go of my hair," I shouted. "I'm going to complain to Husam ad-din. God knows, that's for sure."

He gave Sitt ad-dar a frown. "Is she that man's slave girl?" he asked her.

"Don't touch her," she replied sadly. "We mustn't annoy my uncle."

He grabbed me by the neck, squeezed my throat, and throttled me as hard as he could. I could not breathe and saw the world vanish around me. I thought I was dead and had gone straight to hell. Raising his hand, he brought it down hard on my cheek, and I fell to the floor. He kicked me as hard as possible on the back and stomach several times. Then he grabbed me by the back and buried my head in the dung.

"I don't care who you are," he said. "I'll cut your tongue out and pull out your eyes too. You're going to eat shit in front of me right now so your mouth won't say anything."

He pushed me down so that I was totally immersed in dung, almost dying from the foul stench and the disgusting taste in my mouth.

"Leave her alone," she said. "If she dies, my uncle will kill me."

He clenched his fist and punched me hard in the back. "I want to kill her so we can relax," he said. "She wasted our love-time, my darling. She's a devil."

"She won't talk," she told him, holding his hand. "Let her go."

She grabbed him by the hand and looked over at me, buried in the animal droppings with no part of my face showing. "You won't say anything, Hind, right?"

I could not speak without swallowing more shit. I just nodded my head eagerly. The vicious man grabbed some more and shoved it inside my mouth.

"Swallow it now, or else I'll kill you," he said.

My mouth would not do it, so he hit me on the shoulder.

"Swallow it," he said again.

I did swallow it, Aunt. Can you believe it?

He pushed me outside the stables. I was barely outside before he grabbed me again.

"Now I'm going to take your eyes out and cut out your tongue," he said.

I shook my head again and ran off as fast as I could.

As soon as 'Adlat set eyes on me, she shouted angrily and told me to wash. I did that, as my blood mixed with filth, my nose bled, my head throbbed, my face was swollen and blue with bruises, and my back was burning as though I were in a fire-heap. I claimed that my feet had slipped and I had fallen over inside the stables. I headed for my room, called for my brother, and locked the door. I hoped that Husam ad-din would not come and see how I had been so humiliated and quite how responsible he was for the sorry state to which his own errors and sin had now brought me. The taste of dung inside my mouth did not leave me for days, and I was unable to eat or move. My brother Shams kept asking me when we were going home and why we were visiting these peasants and who were they. I could not come up with a response. Do you realize, Aunt, that humiliation can intensify to such an extent that your mind is completely unable to function; you get the feeling that you are part of a nightmare that renews itself every single day, and there is no escape? That is the way I felt, and I simply preferred to keep my eyes closed and not say anything. I was convinced that, if I did speak, the shit would come out of my mouth, lots of it. In fact, I had dreamed that the slippery shit would come cascading out of my mouth like water from a powerful waterfall, nonstop and without mercy. I had tried to scream during my dream, but had not managed to do it. Every time 'Adlat came in to see me, I pretended to be asleep. One day she shook me.

"You're not going to sleep forever," she told me. "You have to go back to work."

She seemed hesitant. "When Husam ad-din comes back," she said, "I'm going to complain. You're hopeless!"

She went out and left me alone with the nightmare: what was lost and gone and what remained. For most of the day, Shams kept playing all around me.

Thank God, for several days Husam ad-din did not come back. The visible signs of the beating had gone, but I still had my back pain. 'Adlat asked me again to clean out the stables.

"No," I replied.

I expected her to hit me and give me a whipping, but she did not. She left me, cursing and swearing as she did, and went about her own work. I kept bathing over and over again. The kicks and swelling were still clearly visible on my back, and the pain was unrelenting.

Salar's Testimony (3)

Al-Ashraf Abu an-Nasir Tuman Bey was sultan, with his splendor, greatness, piety, and pride. He was a Mamluk. He did not arrive as a hired, thuggish killer like the mercenaries. To the contrary, he had been trained as a Mamluk, just like Inal, Al-'Adili, and myself. He was my teacher, and I owe him my entire life. This time, I have sworn to name every traitor, coward, shirker, and hypocrite. This is an era for courage and risk-taking. Among Mamluks, there is no place for traitors. I requested a meeting with my teacher, the sultan, and took a list of traitors' names. He read through the list carefully.

"Amir Jad Badri al-Ghazali?" he read out. "How can you be sure?"

I explained to him how I had confirmed the information. He already knew that, for the past month, my task had been to spy on Mamluks, particular Khayir Bey's allies and supporters. Killing Khayir Bey had been my principal goal, and still was.

The sultan frowned. "I trust you," he said, "but I can't reveal that to my army or confront the amir with what you've said."

I opened my mouth to speak, but he stopped me. "Some Mamluks only fight for spoils," he said, "while others like to fight because they're aware of the need and purpose. Still others appreciate the purpose but still want the spoils. Most important, they want to stay alive. If I were to tell them that one of the most important Mamluk amirs was an ally of Salim Shah and another one had formed an alliance with him beforehand, I would be destroying their morale and creating even more traitors. Salar, this list is for me alone. Don't mention the names to anyone else."

I was not persuaded by what the sultan had said. I understood his strategy, but was not convinced. I would have preferred to butcher Amir al-Ghazali in full view of the Mamluks and make his corpse an example. In times like these, I preferred absolute power and ruthlessness. However, I was well aware of the scale of the crisis and size of the armed forces, so I said nothing more.

"We're going to proclaim a general mobilization," the sultan told me. "This isn't a Mamluk war, Salar; it's an Egyptian war. Egyptians have to defend their own country."

"The Mamluks are Egypt."

The sultan smiled, and, as long as I live, I shall never forget that sarcastic grin.

"That's what Mamluks believe," he replied, stroking my shoulder, "and that's their big mistake. Mamluks are a small segment of Egypt. The Egyptian population has to fight the Ottomans; they have to join the army group. When danger is at the gates of the city, Mamluks need to explain their position and get off their high horse, if only for a few days. Salim Shah has a hundred and fifty thousand soldiers. Egypt won't be like Syria. They must be annihilated before they enter Cairo, even if that means women going out to fight them."

That is what the sultan said, Abu al-Barakat. He then went out in person to dig a trench at Ridaniyya. I watched as he dug it by hand. The amirs all looked appalled as they watched the sultan digging a trench around Cairo and joined in. He wanted to meet Salim Shah's forces in Sharqiyya province which was derelict and starving, but the Mamluk amirs did not agree. No matter. That's something else that we can discuss later. Can you believe it, Abu al-Barakat? At this critical moment, many Egyptians joined the Mamluk armed forces, and the army size grew to ninety thousand, half of them Mamluks, the other half Egyptians. Moments when you can see such a spirit of harmony between the two sides are rare indeed. Mamluks were not arrogant, and Egyptians stopped their grumbling, complaints, and sarcasm. On very few historical occasions has Egypt turned into a single entity. Even Copts and Jews flocked to fight the invader, women, boys, the entire Egyptian population. In a moment, I'm going to tell you everything that I witnessed. It was a splendid event, full of moments of glory and pride.

I will tell you about three horsemen from the same regiment who became amirs. Inal was the most pious and earnest in his faith. He was married to Khundtatar, the daughter of a Mamluk amir. She had been his entire life, ever since they had been married ten years earlier, and no slave girl and no war could pull him away from her. She bore him three sons and consolidated her total control over him, so much so that we used to tease him during our meetings. I have never seen another man who could focus his vision on such a small area when the whole wide world was open to him. We could not understand why or how. A true warrior can control both heart and passion, but how can he control even his own vision and then tell it not to see, object, and dream? We never saw his wife; he kept her away from the world as a whole. People said that she was very beautiful; even slave girls admired her loveliness. Whenever he came to nightclubs and singing events with us, he would always sit there, uneasy and worried as he contemplated the possible consequences. We would tease him all night and count off for him the slave girls' assets and their different types and colors. We did our best to convince him that love was an adventure; warriors did not indulge in just one risk, or else they would become ascetics and worshippers. They should indulge in thousands of adventures. In both war and love, practice and risk were requirements. But he never listened or understood. We were different. He had an innocence and courage that surpassed those of any other amir I saw.

Qansuh al-'Adili was positively buried in wives and slave girls. He had three wives and any number of slave girls; he used to buy one every month or two, and then sell her. He could not understand Inal and work out how he could be so content and happy. But you know me, Abu al-Barakat. I prefer to postpone talking about myself for a while or maybe forever. I'll tell you about Inal. He is the brother whom my mother did not bear, my colleague on the long road in the mountain citadel. One day, Al-'Adili purchased a slave girl who was renowned for her magical beauty, her sweet voice, and her provocative dancing. He decided to give her to Inal, but he refused without even seeing her. Can you believe that, Abu al-Barakat? He said his wife would not allow him to own any slave girls and she would be incredibly angry. When he talked about the things his wife would want and permit, he sounded just like a eunuch or servant boy. That is the way that Khundtatar dominated and controlled him. Both Al-'Adili and I loathed her even without having seen her. No sooner had I set eyes on that slave girl than I told Al-'Adili that I wanted her and would buy her from him. Such beauty as that had to be purchased and its preservation was evidence of ethics and principles. My wife at the time, Sa'adat, Khayir Bey's daughter, did not object or say anything; she was aware of her limits and obligations. She never compared herself with slave girls; they were like pots and bottles. There could be no comparison between them and wives. Who would ever compare themselves with a pot? But Khundtatar always had her own opinions and different ideas. I want you to know that so you will understand what happened and was going to happen.

Hind's Testimony (4)

This is a bewildering event, Aunt.

When Husam ad-din came back, he came into the room looking worried and sad, all of which gave me the hope that he would not be touching me today. I sat on the floor and did not move. He took off his clothes, and I looked away.

"'Adlat's told me that you fell in the stables and hurt yourself. You can't do any hard work."

"Yes, that's what happened," I replied agitatedly.

He suddenly looked at me, then pulled my hand away from my face. He did not see any marks or wounds. He looked at my face.

"Where are the bruises?" he asked.

"After a few days, they disappeared," I replied.

"And what about your body?" he asked blithely.

"No bruises there," I replied quickly.

For a moment, our eyes met. He stood up and left the room, apparently getting ready to meet his relatives. 'Adlat asked me to put some fruit and baked goods in front of the guests and to keep my veil on the whole time.

I headed for the stairway with the food and listened to what some of the guests were saying. There were five men along with Husam ad-din and 'Abdallah. One of them kept cursing the Ottomans and their sultan, while the other was urging the Egyptians to attack the invaders. A shaykh insisted that any Muslim killing another Muslim was a crime, while the Mamluks were continually fighting unbelievers even though they were not Muslims themselves. How could that be when their invaders and opponents were also Muslims?

"If a Muslim were to be an invader," one of them responded eagerly, "then he'd have to be killed. The Ottomans have to be wiped off the face of the earth, to the very last drop of Mamluk and Egyptian blood.

"The Ottoman invasion will be a disaster for Egypt," he continued fervently. He himself intended to grab his sword, face them at Ridaniyya, and either die or kill every last one of their soldiers before they started investing Cairo.

Husam ad-din listened to what he was saying in silence. The man's eyes encountered mine; I recognized him, and he did me. This crude man was wearing a gallabiya, and his expression was filled with violence and maybe passion as well. His malign enthusiasm was filling the whole room. I lowered my head and almost threw the food on the floor. Husam ad-din signaled to me, and I went over to him. He seemed to have noticed the hateful glances that I had exchanged with the man.

"Why have you come here?" he whispered. "Did I tell you to come?"

"'Adlat told me to bring in the food," I whispered back.

I ran out as fast as I could, catching my breath. By now, I had made up my mind to tell him the truth. Husam ad-din was an evil man, but it was an evil I could live with or adapt to, whereas this other man positively oozed a much worse kind of evil from every pore. Would Husam ad-din protect me? Would the other man find out, and then pluck my eyes out and cut off my tongue? Why should I trust that rapist who had so mistreated me? Why should he protect me? I was really scared of that vicious man and ready to use rocks to protect myself against him. I was afraid that he would follow me now and have his suspicions as to whether I had told Husam ad-din everything. I was afraid that he would be coming after me now and would cut out my tongue and torture me. At that point, I was on my own: no father or brother to protect me, just a weak, submissive woman. I told my brother to return to the room and go to sleep.

I sat there, listening to their conversation, my hand poised nervously on my cheek, totally unbothered about 'Adlat's scolding and the orders she had given me.

I noticed Sitt ad-dar looking over at the window to see her lover, passion leaping out of her eyes. When she noticed me, she gave me a bashful look.

"We're going to be married, Hind," she told me. "He's going to ask my father either today or tomorrow."

I did not respond.

The gathering went on and on, for hours perhaps. At midnight, 'Adlat came in to go to sleep. She told her daughter to go to her room, and Sitt ad-dar went away grumbling. I kept looking down on the gathering from above. People started to leave. Just when the vicious man was about to depart, Husam ad-din asked him to wait. When everyone else had left, Husam ad-din looked at his brother 'Abdallah who excused himself and went into his own room.

The fact that the vicious man was still there scared me. I worried in case he was a friend of Husam ad-din. Even though I was sure that he actually hated him, I was not sure what was going on around me. The two men looked straight at each other.

"Do you hate the Ottomans?" Husam ad-din asked him.

"I'll do anything," the man insisted, "to make sure they don't enter Cairo."

"Anything?"

"You know, and I know."

"You know, and I know," Husam ad-din repeated.

Suddenly, Husam ad-din drew a sword from its scabbard and put it on the man's neck. "Who sent you?" he demanded.

"What are you doing?" the man asked in alarm. "Are you out of your mind?"

"Who sent you?"

"No one sent me. Why are you doing this?"

I watched as the man drew his sword from inside his clothes as quick as a flash and pointed it at Husam ad-din's stomach. A fierce struggle ensued; I don't recall exactly, but that's what I believe. I was shocked and scared. At that moment, I hoped that Husam ad-din would kill that dreadful man, but worried that Husam ad-din might be killed and the other man would torture me. I clenched my teeth as not to scream, my eyes following the sword thrusts. I had the idea that, if they both died, I would either be saved or destroyed—I did not know which. Here injustice was intertwined with an attachment to life. If Husam ad-din were to die, I had no idea what would happen to me. After a while, I could see that the dreadful man was dead. I swear to you, Aunt, Husam ad-din butchered him like an immature little lamb. He almost completely beheaded him, then dragged his body outside the house. I can still see the man's eyes staring up to the sky and his forked tongue still trying to talk, as though to mouth groans of pain; indeed those marks of pain would remain on his dead face forevermore.

My whole body was shaking, as though I was the one who had just been butchered—not because I was afraid of death; by now, I was used to it. Instead, because the whole thing had been done so quickly and expertly by someone who claimed he had never killed anyone.

I curled up in my room along with my brother. After a while, Husam ad-din came in, after washing and praying. He sat down on his bed.

"Ask your brother to leave," he said.

I did not argue, and asked my brother to leave the room. I stayed where I was.

"Come over here," he told me, as he stretched out on the bed.

I did not move, so he pulled me unwillingly toward him. I pushed him away, hoping all the while that he would kill me on the spot. I can swear to you, Abu al-Barakat, that death no longer scared me. I dearly hoped that it would relieve me of much suffering and humiliation that had made my life taste like the shit that had still not left my mouth.

I pushed him away as hard as I could. "I've told you," I said, "I won't be your slave girl."

He twisted my arm around my back. "And I've told you," he replied, "that you're my property. I paid everything I own to buy you."

I tried to escape his clutches, pushing him away and putting up the vigorous resistance of someone defending her honor and very essence. However, he put pressure on my arm till I cried out in pain.

"Stop resisting," he said. "I don't have any patience today."

The pain brought tears to my eyes, but I did not cry.

"I'll be resisting for the rest of my life," I stuttered.

"What kind of woman are you? You want me just as much as I want you. Do you think I don't know?"

"It's your own delusion and dead conscience that makes you imagine that. You attack me and hurt me. God will never forgive you for that."

He did what he did, Aunt, with me resisting all the way and my heart groaning silently in defeat but otherwise uninvolved. I moved away and hugged myself.

"Come over here, Hind!" I heard him tell me.

He started pulling me toward him, and I leaped up. I pulled my wrap around me and fell to the floor. "Leave me alone!" I told him.

But on this day, he did not do that. Instead, he carried me against my will and threw me on his bed. I tried to move away.

"You're going to sleep here," he insisted, "and you're going to tell me everything. Don't defy me, I warn you. As I've told you, I'm out of patience today. If you stay where you are, I won't have sex with you again, but, if you resist, then I will. So choose now."

I lowered my head and started rubbing my arms nervously. When I looked away, I could still picture the dead man's face.

Now Husam ad-din's hand was on the same spot in my back where that man had kicked me, rubbing and circling the exact spot where it hurt the most. I groaned in pain, then stood up and stared into the darkness all around me.

"Get away from me!" I said.

"You're a fighter," he replied gently. "If the Mamluks were all like you, then the Ottomans would never be able to get into Cairo. You never surrender or follow your heart's passions, fears, and desires. How beautiful you are! You're not a slave girl, Hind; you could never be one."

His words surprised me and calmed my nerves. "But you make me your slave girl or prostitute. I don't understand!"

"For a while," he replied, still stroking my back.

"What do you mean by that?" I asked. "Are you going to let me go?"

For a moment, he said nothing, but then he grabbed my shoulder and turned me toward him. "Do you know that man?" he asked. "What are those marks on your back? I noticed the way you looked at him and he at you."

"I saw what happened," I replied in alarm. "You said you'd never killed any-one, but I watched you slaughter him. You did it, and then washed yourself as though you'd been slaughtering a chicken."

"That was the first time. He had to be killed. What did he do to you? How do you know him? He arrived while I was away."

There is no release from degradation. Humiliation gnaws at the heart like worms in the guts of corpses. I clutched myself and said nothing. He hugged me, and I did not resist.

"If you hug me," he said affectionately, "it's no surrender. Let me hug you, and I won't do anything else. You need my arms, I understand that."

I put my head on his shoulder. His bodily warmth calmed my heart. "How do you know?" I asked.

"What did he do to you? He knew you were mine, but hated me. It's my fault. I should have realized that he would come. I left you and thought about other things. I failed to protect you. He must have beaten you and tried to humiliate you. I know."

I buried my head in his chest. "How do you know?" I whispered.

"Tell me."

My memory of that man's words frightened me. Everyone around me was scary; I could not trust any of them. Even the elder brother, 'Abdallah, was power-less when compared with Husam ad-din. I gathered every ounce of courage.

"I saw him with Sitt ad-dar in the stables," I said. "I think he'd deceived her. She's young, and . . . I hope you won't hurt her. Nothing happened; she was just talking to him."

He kissed my hair and ran his hand over my head. "What did you see?" he asked.

"Nothing," I replied. "They were just talking. When he spotted me . . ."

Now he ran his hand over my arm, hair, and back, his affection combined with determination. "What did he do to you?" he asked.

Every time I recalled the taste of that animal dung and the utter humiliation, I choked and almost moaned. He seemed to hear my choking breaths and remained silent, while his hand staunched the wounds.

He hugged me even tighter till I could feel the blood coursing in his veins. I felt scared, broken, shattered. His arms had soothed my fears. As I put my arms around his shoulders, I did not even know myself.

"Please," I begged him, "take me back to my father."

"What did he do?" he insisted yet again.

I felt angry at the world as a whole. "Yes," I replied, "he beat me. He kicked me in the back and stomach and slapped my face. He made me swallow shit."

He still said nothing as he ran his hand over my body and massaged the bruises on my back, making them feel less painful.

"Now he's dead," he said, kissing my forehead, "and it's over."

"If Sitt ad-dar were to find out," I said, as though I were sharing my innermost thoughts with my father, "she would carry out his threat against me. He said he'd pluck my eyes out and sever my tongue. Maybe she'll do it!"

"No, she won't," he made clear. "He's dead now, Hind, and no one will dare hurt you."

"I don't deserve it," I replied.

"None of us do."

"No, I mean the sheer humiliation. I was a spoiled lady. Why have you done this to me?"

"Go to sleep, Hind. Tomorrow will be better; that's for sure."

At that point I felt the effects of oppression blended with a peculiar kind of shame, as though time as a whole had breathed its last in my soul.

I closed my eyes. "If Sitt ad-dar finds out," I told him again, "she'll take her revenge on me."

"Nobody will be able to touch you," he insisted again. "I've told you that. For a while, I was distracted, but that won't happen again. I promise you."

"I don't trust you," I told him honestly. "These days, I don't trust anyone. I don't know what's happened and what's going to happen."

"Forget about that for today," he whispered as he kissed my ear.

I did not respond, but, after that, I did not know my own self. I slept well the whole night through in his arms. I'm telling you the truth, Aunt, and I need you to realize that defeat can blind your vision; dejection opens the doors to temptation. All night his hands kept easing my back pain, soothing and massaging the bruises. In fact, when he stopped doing it, fell into a deep sleep, and pulled his hand away, I found myself, still asleep, grabbing his hand again and putting it on my back. That way, he kept relieving or increasing my pain, I do not know which.

The thing that baffled me at the time, Aunt, was how frank I was with him. I was well aware that I would be too embarrassed to tell my father and mother about eating shit. Maybe that had done away with my sense of pride. Now there was nothing that I felt like keeping hidden inside my heart, because it had been shamed and humiliated. Odd things keep happening in these times, Aunt.

I woke up after dawn. I was afraid that my honor's sun-disk had been eclipsed or its moon looked wan. But I had never surrendered to him. I swear that, every time he had asserted his control over me, I had put up a fight. He might own me as a slave girl, but I kept resisting. I may have slept in his arms, but I never gave in.

His arms were wrapped around my shoulders, and my head was on his chest.
I remembered what he had said: he promised to take care of me and protect me . . .
he promised . . .

The truth descended from my head like the arrow fired by a professional killer.
I clutched his chest.

"Did you realize," I asked him, "that 'Adlat was making me work so hard? Did
you ask her to make me clean out the stables? Did you ask her, Husam, to soften
the dough?"

"You never call me 'my Lord' anymore," he replied, eyes closed. "When will
you learn to do that?"

"But you aren't my Lord."

I leaped up and slapped my face. "Good God!" I said. "Why? What do you gain
by humiliating and crushing me? She does everything you tell her. If you said that
she was working me too hard, she would obey you. But you asked her to make me
to do that, from the start, from the very first day. Why? Am I not a human being
just like you? Am I not an Egyptian like you? Why are you doing this? Actually, I
know. Good Lord, how can you be such a . . ."

I was planning to drown him in curses. I felt like telling him that he was despicable, evil, depraved, oppressive, and unjust.

"You've a lot to say," he replied. "I don't like it!"

"I get it. You wanted to wear me out so that I would submit; I'd be broken and
give in. You wanted to let me choose between cleaning out the stables or sleeping
in your arms. You've said that before. Why do you keep trying all these tricks on a
helpless woman like me? Why?"

He sat up and looked at me, but said nothing.

"I know," I went on sadly. "It's your pride that's been wounded by this unknown
girl. How can she possibly not be happy to be your slave girl? What woman would
refuse to melt into your arms? I had to be punished. If you had done it, I would
hate you, but, if 'Adlat did it, then it wouldn't matter. Why should you flay me if
someone else could do it instead? Why scold me for objecting and rebelling when
'Adlat could deal with it? What . . .

"What a devil!" I whispered in a voice that only I could hear.

I slapped my face again. "I actually thought that you pitied me," I repeated. "I
really did. Can you imagine?"

I was about to stand up, but he grabbed my hand. "Hind," he said, "you're cleverer than I imagined. But don't forget who you are and who I am."

I said something in a weak voice.

"What did you just say?"

"Nothing."

"What did you just say?" he asked again.

"We're all God's servants, my Lord. But, for the God of those servants, some of us are better than others. Do you have any instructions for me?"

"No, I don't," he replied angrily. "Try to stop thinking and reflecting so much. That's hurting you!"

That upset me. "I don't know why," I replied hesitantly. "You didn't know that I'd find that man inside the stables or that he'd hit me the way he did. Isn't that right? Or did you have a deal with him?"

Our eyes met, and he looked furious.

"I'm sorry," I said. "At this point, everything's a jumble."

I was already aware that he had not known. I had deliberately wronged him, maybe to give him a taste of humiliation, at least once.

He leaned over and grabbed my wrist, till I could feel his breath on my lips.

"Why are you so concerned about me?" he asked. "Why bother about my good and bad points? Am I not a man who's forcing you to have sex and to stay here? So why all this thinking about my intentions and goals? Explain it to me."

My heart was pounding, and I had no idea whether I was simply annoyed or actually hated him. "You've infringed on my boundaries, my Lord," I told him. "Forgive me . . ."

"No, I won't. You know that I'm your Lord, don't you? Are you going to push me away and keep resisting, or come willingly?"

"Even if I died today," I replied firmly, "I would never come to you willingly. If you butchered me and cut my body up into equal segments, I would not do it. If you made me eat shit as that other man did, that would be preferable as far as I'm concerned."

Our eyes met, and, for a moment, I thought he was going to hit me. Maybe he thought about it.

"These are obviously inklings of doubt," he said instead. "Your vigorous objections hide a good deal of acceptance. I won't allow you that either."

With that, he stood up and left.

I stayed on the bed, exhausted perhaps and despairing about what had happened. This was possible. A great deal had happened yesterday, and even more would be happening today. After a while, 'Adlat came in with a smile on her face. Can you believe that, Aunt? She gave me a smile and brought in a tray with food and a cup of milk. She put it down in front of me.

"I didn't realize you were sick," she said eagerly. "Don't get up today. I've brought you some food. I'll prepare breakfast for my darling Shams. What a beautiful child he is! He reminds me of my own children . . ."

I gaped in amazement.

"Here, drink this," she said, bringing the cup to my mouth. "No time for work today. Drink up and relax, my daughter. I'll take care of you myself."

I closed my eyes, then opened them again. Maybe the dream was over. But it was not a dream. I was sure that Husam ad-din had spoken to her; he had been giving her instructions all the time. All that day, I stayed in his bed; I looked at the place where he slept, and everything had turned into a jumble for me. What had happened yesterday and would be happening today . . . it was war. War involved deceit, planning, and weapons. He had tried cruelty on me, then the soft touch. How unutterably evil the man was!

'Adlat was determined that I would stay in bed the whole day. She would bring me food and water herself.

He came back in the evening. "Do you want to sleep in my arms again tonight?" he asked dryly.

"It won't happen," I declared.

He held my hand. "I'm not going to force you," he said gently. "You need someone to soothe the pains in your back and stomach."

I hesitated for a moment. "I'd prefer you not to do that," I replied.

He seated me on the bed. "Are you afraid of yourself?" he asked. "I gave you a promise. Don't be afraid of me. You don't trust your own self."

He sat down beside me. "What do you say, that we just talk, then you go to sleep in my arms? I know you're tired."

"Why did you kill that man?" I asked.

"Why do you need to know that?" he asked, lying back on the bed. "Isn't what he did to you enough?"

"No, that's not enough to kill a man."

"We'd had problems for some time."

I felt the same shiver as I did every time I remembered what that vicious man had done to me. "He seemed to hate you," I said, "hate you a lot. What had you done to him, I wonder. Flirted with his sister perhaps?"

He pulled me to his chest. "Put your head here," he told me with a smile.

He put my head on his chest and wrapped his arm around my back. He started massaging the bruises. I felt really tired, Aunt, and the bruises were hurting. I let him soothe my bodily aches and buried my head in his chest.

He kept massaging the bruises on my back and stomach. "Does it hurt you?" he asked.

I let out a groan. "Yes, it does," I admitted shamefully.

He muttered a stream of curses against that vicious man and kept easing my pains.

That day, Aunt, we talked. My feelings were a mixture of relief and caution. He did not try to kiss me or have sex. A devil kept toying with me for a few seconds and whispering why not just surrender. He might treat me like a princess and even perhaps get married to me after a while? I thrust that cursed devil right out of my mind and despised myself because I had allowed it to beat on the door of my own soul. That vicious man and the way he had beaten me had changed everything. He seemed to have broken my spirit or almost so. I did not sleep that night, nor did he.

Each of us pretended to be asleep; I do not know why he did it, but, in my case, I was doing my best to protect myself against its evil impact. I regretted having responded to his call and slept in his arms. How could I have thrown myself into such sinful behavior and then expect to find a means of escape? What I needed was affection and a curing hand. Husam ad-din had perfected both injustice and affection. When the two traits were blended in the heart of one man, one era, one house, and one country, the mind goes crazy. Resistance turns into seafoam, and affectionate touches are like magic charms, controlling the will and robbing the mind. Even so, I suppressed my heart's iniquity, the same way the genie is imprisoned inside an ancient lamp.

The night hours were bound to come to an end, slow and painful. After dawn, I could sense him slinking out of the room.

That same morning, Aunt, something odd happened. I smelled something burning; actually, I could hear the regular, quiet sound of fire in my ears. I did not hear anyone shouting. When I left the room, I saw 'Adlat frowning, and Sitt ad-dar sitting but not moving. She did not scold me, blame me, or even greet me.

"Where's Husam ad-din?" I asked in alarm.

'Adlat was putting a lot of things into a huge basket. "He's burning crops with the men," she replied.

I opened the house door and grabbed hold of my brother. I saw the men carrying grain into large granaries, then burning it. Husam ad-din, 'Abdallah, and a lot of peasants were working with them and Mamluks in their obvious uniforms were watching from a distance.

After a while, I gathered that the Ottomans were on their way into Cairo. Burning crops would leave their horses hungry. Peasants preferred losing their crops to leaving them for the invaders to use.

Several hours later, Husam ad-din came back and, along with his brother, loaded the camels with baskets full of foodstuffs, flour, and dates. I did not try to help them, but held on to my brother. Then I looked at Husam ad-din, who lifted me up and put me on the camel without saying a word. He then put my brother in front of me.

"Where are we going?" I asked.

"Cairo."

"Why?"

He did not reply.

———

It felt as though life refused to manifest itself, and the heart declined to calm down and relax. What can I say, Aunt? He wronged me and tortured me; hatred and something else that I cannot identify blossomed inside me. His steps preoccupied me, and his existence, whether near or far, filled the gaps in my heart. Fear prevailed inside me, duly jostled by anger and something else . . . a regret that I am ashamed to mention now. I do not understand it. After I had slept in his arms, he had missed me perhaps, then had gone away and left me to be humiliated by that vicious man, and after my doubts had grown regarding my heart's attitude toward him. After all that, my feelings were all muddled and intertwined.

When we reached Cairo, we entered a small house, and he gestured to me to go into the room. As I did so, I was thinking about a way of escaping to my father's house, now that it was feasible and that much easier. There were no Ottomans around us anymore. I asked myself why he had brought us here, knowing that I would run away. Did he want me to escape?

After a while, he came into the room, carrying some papers.

"Are you pregnant?" he asked suddenly.

His question shocked me. It served to remind me of my defeat and dejection.

"I don't think so," I replied somewhat shamefully.

Our eyes met. He sat down on the bed and told me to do the same. I sat in front of him.

"Keep these papers with you," he told me. "Don't read them now. They're your certificate of manumission, witnessing that any child of yours is mine."

"You're letting me go?" I asked him sadly, swallowing hard.

"Not yet," he replied. "Keep them with you till the time comes."

"When will that be?"

"When? When I'm dead, disappeared, defeated, victorious, or else forget all about you. When, you ask?"

"You're going to forget about me?"

"Why are those the only words you ever hear?"

I grabbed the papers. "Thank you!" I said.

"Have I been generous with you?" he asked dryly.

"No, you haven't," I replied. "You know that."

"I took what I deserved, what I'd earned. That's what soldiers do."

I looked into his eyes. "Are you a soldier?" I asked without thinking.

Maybe for the first time, he smiled. "Are you a slave girl?" he asked.

"No."

"We all live with names and selves that aren't ours. We pretend, make claims, and believe our own pretenses. We live out personalities that we don't recognize. Hind, I'd like to sleep for a while. After today, there won't be any time."

He seemed exhausted; it had been a long ride, and he had not slept for a day or more. I did not say anything. I watched as he lay down beside me, buried his head in the pillow, and fell fast asleep. Sleeping there at that moment, he looked handsome. I had hated him, you remember, but now I was looking at those closed eyes of his, the nose and lips, and found my hand heading for his beard, stroking it with soft touches. I pulled the covers off his shoulders a little and looked at him for the first time, or maybe the last; I don't know. I pulled the covers even further back, as far as his stomach, and could see his whole chest and back. I ran my hands over his shoulders. I have no idea, Aunt, what hit me; maybe a devil. But I rubbed a number of scars and wounds; some of them were fresh, less than a month old, while others maybe went back years. He had claimed he had never held a sword. He had lied.

He had claimed he had been honorable toward me. He had lied.

He had claimed he was Husam ad-din. He had lied.

The gaze of that vicious man had never left me, as he was dying, his curved tongue trying to say a single word to a mother—no more, no less.

I picked up the papers and read them. He had not lied to me. They were a certificate for my manumission. He had signed them, using his real name: Salar!!

At the time, I did not even think about his lies, his deceit, and his strange way of leaving.

I looked at his head, buried in the pillow and his back, something that I had never seen before in the course of my resistance and defeat.

I put my hand on his back and moved closer to him. I will tell you the truth, Aunt. I had no idea what I was doing when I gave his back a fleeting kiss. Then I plucked up my courage and gave his back a slow, lingering kiss and brushed my lips over some of the scars. The devil took control of me, it seems, and affection for him overwhelmed all thoughts of hatred. The sense of imminent separation alarmed and baffled me.

"Stay with me," I heard him whisper, without moving. "Why are you standing up?"

My heart was pounding, and I stayed where I was. I turned to look at him, and he sat up.

"There's not much time left," he said, holding my hand. "Today or tomorrow, I'll take you back to your father. Hind, I want you to come to me willingly. You want me, don't you?"

My heart leaped with both passion and despair at once. "I'll never come to you as a slave girl," I replied weakly.

He grabbed my hand and put it on his chest. Then he brought it close to his mouth. "Never for a single day!" he said.

I moved closer to him without even willing to do so. My breaths were searing his neck. "Not even for an hour or less," I said.

"Why?" he asked, kissing my forehead. "If you came willingly, you'd soothe all your wounds and calm your soul. We could erase everything that's happened, everything that's troubling you today."

Now I asked him the question that had been nagging at me and that I had not dare ask. "Do you have a wife?"

He did not respond, but ran his hand over my hair. "If I take you by force now, knowing that you long for me," he asked, "what will you do?"

"I'll resist you as I've always done. I'll never come to you willingly as a slave girl. I'm not a slave girl, and you're not Husam ad-din."

He pulled me toward his chest and wrapped his arm around my shoulder. "Stay in my arms for a while," he said.

"I don't trust you, and I don't trust Mamluks. You're a Mamluk amir, aren't you? Salar, that's your name."

He hugged me so tight, Aunt, that I could feel his ribs against my breasts. Our breaths mingled, and, to tell you the truth, I felt things I'd never felt before: bitterness, elation, longing, anxiety, and everything in between.

He pushed me slowly toward his bed and kissed me on the mouth and forehead. I closed my eyes in the hope that the world might come to a halt, and he might say something I wanted to hear. Maybe, maybe . . . In wartime, recording the risks of affection needs a lengthy book, Aunt; it is one that I could write myself and spend some time talking about despair and the occasional longing for his touches. He poured out his entire affection, something I had never encountered before. He was a rarity indeed, and I both needed and deserved him. When I felt his hand making its way to my breasts, I grabbed it and pushed it away.

At that moment, I recalled Sitt ad-dar lying in the arms of that vicious man. As I pushed him away, breathing hard, I was resisting my self's own devil; it felt as though my breaths could not work out how to distance themselves from his, nor could I understand why, for the first time, I was actually crying.

"I'm not Sitt ad-dar," I told him, "nor am I a prostitute or slave girl. I'm no less than your own wife, if you have one. These times are regularly humiliating honorable people."

As though struggling with himself, he said nothing. "Why are you crying now?" he asked as he stood up. "You've never cried before."

Do you know why I was crying, Aunt? Yes, you do. I was crying because I actually longed for him when my very soul lay between his ribs and in his heartbeats. He will never understand, Aunt. Do you know why I was crying? Because he had assaulted me and done me wrong, planning carefully, making his decisions, and abusing my body. Then he had crushed my spirit as well . . . Because I can never forgive him or expunge him from the recesses of my soul. These are treacherous times, years of stupidity in which you cannot tell enemy from friend.

"Hind," he said, holding my hand, "everything will be over soon. The Ottomans will never get into Cairo. They'll withdraw and be defeated. When that happens, everything will be different."

I swallowed hard and looked at my hand in his. "Different, how?"

"You know," he replied, looking down. "I tried to break you; I won't deny it. I found your pride peculiar. It shocked and challenged me. I tried all the persistence and violence that a soldier possesses, but you were not defeated. You still look me straight in the eye when we're talking, without even lowering your eyelids, as though we're equals. Even my wife doesn't do that."

If he had known how defeated I now felt and could have understood and sensed my own longing, he would not have said that.

"What kind of woman are you?" he asked. "I had a loyal and beautiful wife and lots of slave girls."

"You don't need me," I replied, wiping away my tears. "I'm not as beautiful as your wife, nor as seductive as your slave girls."

Our eyes met.

"Remarkable fates these are!" he responded. "I thought of you as my spoil, grain, gold, part of my property under my control. But magic took over your body, and the gold sprang up and rebelled against its owner. The crops were scattered, and the sword refused its master's orders. It was as though I had discovered a living soul amid the inanimate mire, and what a soul it is! Your resistance annoyed me; it provoked my sense of pride, and I was out for revenge. You'll never understand. You aren't a man or a soldier. Never mind, you're here, safe and sound."

With that, Aunt, he left the room. To tell you the truth, the devil kept toying with my heart, and I felt a certain regret. If I had let him wallow inside my body as he had with my soul, what would have happened?

Were I to surrender and accept a fate other than my own, a master other than my own, and a different role and personality, what would happen? Why can the heart be defeated this way?

I did not stop crying or longing for him . . . I wanted him to go away and leave me. For the first time, Aunt, I was afraid of my own self. Do not think badly of me, but it seemed he had managed to break me. He had certainly defeated me. I am just a helpless girl. I'll be frank, Aunt: all day I've been going through hell.

Sitt ad-dar came into the room, walking somewhat bashfully. "I want to thank you, Hind," she said, "for not revealing my secret. I'm sorry about what happened."

I did not respond.

"Do you know anything about the man who was with me?" she asked. "He disappeared suddenly. Did he try to threaten you or see you? I wonder, was he scared of my uncle? After he came to visit us, I haven't seen him again. I miss him. After what's happened, I'm afraid he'll discard me. Will you help me find him?"

"Maybe he was afraid of your uncle," I replied, "although he's not actually your uncle."

She gaped in amazement.

"I know everything," I told her.

"What do you know?"

"I know he's not your uncle, and that you're all lying. It's almost as though I'm watching a shadow-play in Bulaq!"

With that, she called her mother in, and they both sat in front of me.

"Who are you," I asked, "and who is Amir Salar?"

'Adlat was shocked. "No more talking," she said. "It's more than we can bear."

———⌐

He returned at midnight. I was curled up in a corner of the room, along with my brother. This time, his presence would be protecting me from my own self.

"Ask him to leave," he said blandly.

I whispered to my brother, and he left.

As he took off his clothes, I said nothing and did not move. He lay down on his bed. My entire body was shaking, Aunt, and my throat was on fire. It felt as if I had caught a fever. He did not ask me to come over to him or order me to have sex with him.

He turned his face away. "You can sleep here," he said. "I'm not going to force you."

"I can't," I replied.

"Are you scared?"

My eyes were fixed on his back, and I could imagine my hand around it. If only I could go to sleep in his arms, if only, if . . .

"Yes, my Lord," I repeated, "I'm scared."

"Of yourself or me?"

"Of myself," I stated, "not you."

"You'll regret it, and then you'll realize. When I leave in an hour, Hind, I may never see you again. If I die, at least you're safe. In Cairo, you're safe. If I die, 'Abdallah will take you back to your father."

Those words of his made my body shake. My soul gave way, and my mind went on the attack without mercy. I stayed there, silent and motionless. Today, he was torturing me—in a whole new way, it seemed.

"What's happened, my Lord?" I asked bitterly. "Why aren't you forcing me like all those slave girls?"

He turned toward me and sat up. "That's impossible," he said. "Now that's impossible."

I did not understand why or what had changed. In fact, I wanted him to embrace me, bury me inside himself, and then kill me and dismember or burn my corpse. After today, I would have no life. I praised God that he had left me alone and had not forced me, a limitless mercy. But wars involving amirs are full of surprises.

He stood up, extinguished the lamp, and sat on the floor in front of me. He reached over and grabbed my hand.

"Hind," he said affectionately, "come into my arms. You long for me, and I for you. There's just one hour, and then I'm leaving."

My breaths came out in short bursts. I pulled my hand away, unable to speak.

He looked at me, and I could see his eyes gleaming in the soft light. I was crying silently.

"You said you wouldn't force me," I pleaded.

"I didn't intend to," he replied gently.

He grabbed my hand again, opened my palm, and stared at it. "Sometimes," he said, "I see you with all the power of a soldier, then, at others, you seem as weak as an orphan in war, never crying."

He gave my hand a kiss that pierced my heart.

I wiped away my tears with a shaky hand, and then pulled it away again. I curled up again in my corner, clasping my heart. Perhaps my breathing would give in to my will, and the nasty taste in my throat would not affect and pollute my every breath. His kindness was much more dangerous than his cruelty. Wars involve deceit, and amirs have no sense of loyalty.

He went back to his own bed. I did not see him or know if he closed his eyes. Was he thinking about me? Did he still desire me? Why had he not forced me? Why not push me to his chest, and then demolish and fragment my mind?

I chewed my fingers in anguish. I seized my hand so it would not grab hold of him and run over his back and chest. I would not give him a long kiss like the one he had surprised me with before, the one that had penetrated my veins and the arteries of my heart. Love, Aunt, involves the kind of grief I had not known before, leaving behind a bitterness that surpasses that of plague, war, and invasion combined. There it is, before me, just a few steps away, and yet far enough that I cannot reach it and hug it to myself. He is the one who constructed the barrier, Aunt, not me.

Salar's Testimony (4)

Do you want to tell the story of the disaster of mankind, Abu al-Barakat? I shall tell you stories, fateful events, the era of cowards and traitors, but also of courage and horsemen. I informed the sultan that General Jad Badri al-Ghazali was as much of a traitor as Khayir. The people betrayed fell into a sea of lust and greed. Salim had promised him Syria, and Khayir Egypt. What amir could turn that down? I knew all this and wrote it all down for him. When there is treachery around, no ditches are of any use, and no pit can protect you against an enemy who strikes from behind. I investigated the situation for months and spent all my time tracking Ottoman movements and those of Bedouin, Mamluks, and Egyptians all around them. They gathered together everyone with a weakness or craving, like a reptile that sucks blood from the dead and the living. I spent an entire month, investigating and understanding. My identity was only discovered two or three days before the battle. Khayir sent someone to look for me, kill me, and spy on me. When he arrived and seduced Sitt ad-dar, I could tell from his expression who he actually was. I could recognize the symptoms of treachery and understood them full well. He spoke eagerly about his hatred for the Ottomans, but, when liars are talking, you can see their eyeballs quivering in an unusual way; only someone who recognizes treachery and its poisonous sting can detect it. In less than an instant, I recognized a traitor and had no hesitation about killing him. I realized who had sent him and why he had come. You will not believe this, Abu al-Barakat, but the man was a Mamluk soldier pretending to be an Egyptian; like me perhaps, but with despicable intentions. Egypt was not his purpose, but rather his temptation; he wanted to crush it beneath Ottoman feet. From his stance and movements I could tell that he was a liar: I needed nothing more than his quivering eyes, his stance, and his hand gestures. What he did to Hind . . . Unfortunately, I only found out about that after his death; otherwise, I would have split his guts open while he was still alive.

A day or two later, some spies brought news that the Ottomans would not be entering Cairo by way of Ridaniyya, but via the mountains. It was Al-Ghazali who had suggested that plan. Can you imagine, Abu al-Barakat, fighting your own body and blood along with the enemy? Can you even believe that such treachery could emerge from within your own heart and ribs? I shall never be able to forget or understand that.

Cairo closed its gates: Bab an-Nasr, Bab al-Bahr, Bab ash-Sha'riyya. Egyptians waited, anticipating and worrying about the enemy: would they get in or would a son not make it back. I told the sultan that Salim was now approaching from the mountains and would not pass by the trenches we had dug. The army prepared to launch an attack, and, with my own eyes, I saw Egyptian men who, I assumed, were not trained to fight, wielding swords and fighting like the best trained soldiers, the courage inside their hearts soothing those same hearts and giving hope. I swear to you, Abu al-Barakat, and I hope that you will record all this in your book. Write down the truth, even if it offends a few Mamluks. You are bound to annoy the Ottomans in any case, but writing the truth is itself a kind of battle and victory. Recording events is a means to certainty and a source of stability for the heart. Fate is forever playing with us and our destinies, but we stand with our feet firmly planted on antic soil whenever we record the truth with no fear of either weakness or strength and show no favor to brother or clan. History, Abu al-Barakat, serves as a block to oblivion, heating frigid buildings and guarding against the evil intentions of the greedy; that is, provided it is recorded by a reliable hand and catalogued at the hands of men of learning and knowledge. Record in your book that, with my own eyes, I saw Egyptian men fighting with courage and self-denial, eyes gleaming bright—competent, perfectly devout servants of God, and with all the enthusiasm of lovers and rebels.

This land will always defy its enemies. Anyone who imagines that he can dominate it is fooling himself. Its people cannot be coerced or suborned. Sometimes, they can be governed with ease, and their hearts are often unruly, with no ruler or sultan filling their eyes.

We fought hard, and some people died. The three of us plunged our way into the enemy lines in a dangerous foray. We had decided to fulfill our promise and kill Salim. If you are making war on the whale, then you have to strike it between the eyes. If it is a seahorse you are fighting, then you must find a way to its stomach so that you can squeeze the spirit from deep inside. Tuman Bey was aware of our plan. You will not believe the decision he made on the spot. He decided to run the risk with us. He, the sultan of Egypt, went with his horsemen and slunk into Salim's tent amid all his soldiers and army in order to kill him.

However, it was the fates that decided things for us. When we attacked Salim's tent, he was not there. The chief minister, As-Sadr al-A'zam, Sinan Pasha, the second most senior Ottoman official, was killed, but Salim escaped. After some brutal fighting between us and the guards, we managed to get away.

Salim uses cannons and rifles for protection. What general uses gunfire and treachery to fight wars, rather than showing an appreciation for chivalry and the honor of battle? No matter. Half our army was killed, and a third of theirs or less.

I saw men fall from gunfire, tumbling to the ground like stars from heaven. After some hours, there was the stench of rotting corpses. Our army withdrew and faded in the gloom into the inner depths of Cairo. Salim stood there on the outskirts of the city, with the road wide open in front of him and the Mamluks vanishing away. Now the bride was in his hands, for him to toy with as he wished. Even so, he hesitated and did not enter the city.

The Testimony of the Translator
Mustafa Pasha Al-'Uthmani (2)

Cairo surrendered to us in a day or less, Abu al-Barakat. The soldiers eagerly asked Salim to pierce through the darkness and head for central Cairo. They had heard about the pyramids and the wonderful, lofty stone buildings, mosques high enough to reach the very stars in the sky. Travelers and scholars had written about them and every kind of ascetic, worshipper, anyone with a craving or desire, made it their destination. But Salim, King of Kings, was not that eager. He kept trying, time after time, to use his good offices to bring the conflict with the Mamluk sultan to an end. But Tuman Bey did not accept the offer; he was stubborn and impetuous, did not appreciate either how much had been lost, and was not aware of his own personal status. No indeed, Abu al-Barakat, Sultan Salim, King of Kings, never liked war. To the very last moment, he favored a peaceful resolution and was never impetuous. His soldiers kept asking to enter the city; some of them were after Cairo's treasures, its food, honey, pastries, and women. Others were eager to return home after months spent in the desert amid piles of corpses. The King of Kings stayed put and did not enter Cairo. For three nights he remained in his camp. Whenever a general asked him, he replied that it was not yet the right time.

I do not know why he hesitated. Was he scared of the location, or did he have a sense that the conflict was not over? He was a general and warrior, well aware of when to hold back and when to advance. I did not dare to ask him, but learned later that he did not feel confident with Tuman Bey still alive and hiding in Cairo and Mamluks and Egyptians regarding him as an invader and aggressor. Traces of them were still to be found even though they had turned away for a while.

After three days, he was convinced that the road was open for him to seize the very heart of Islam and become caliph of all Muslim territories. He set out with the rest of his army, unimpeded by fortress or gate, and entered Cairo as victor. His janissaries had opened Bab an-Nasr for him. As he entered, he granted a pledge of safety to all Egyptians—may God glorify him and give him strength! That Friday, shaykhs in mosques prayed for him. He issued a decree to the effect that any Mamluks who submitted to him could save themselves, their property, and their family. To us, the city seemed devoid of Mamluks, sons of the people, Copts, Jews, and even Greek merchants.

Some Mamluks responded to his offer. Three hundred of them surrendered in defeat to the King of Kings, every rank from amir to soldier, and they remained in his hands. I swear to you that I saw a company commander, drum majors, and lots of soldiers being reprimanded by the king because of their sultan's stubbornness and hostility to the emperor. He then put them all in prison. It was his intention to release them as he had promised, but events were to turn out contrary to our expectations.

Hind's Testimony (5)

I will continue my story, Aunt, and I hope your heart will want to hear the truth. Telling it may soothe the troubled soul. When Husam ad-din, or Salar, left, I felt desperate. The world seemed gloomy and unclear. 'Adlat did not make any demands of me; she seemed nervous and scared. Three of her own children had been fighting in Ridaniyya; if her husband had not been ill, he would have gone too. For the very first time, 'Adlat and I were talking to each other. Her roving eyes and dreading heart made me feel sorry for her. She sympathized with me as well, due perhaps to the despair she noticed in my expression. She then told me everything frankly. I think that Salar had given her permission to do so before he left. She proceeded to tell me a tale much stranger than anything in shadow-plays or jinn stories.

Salar grew up in the Citadel, and, from a young age, was trained to fight and to study jurisprudence and Arabic calligraphy. At the time, 'Abdallah was the calligraphy instructor. Salar joined his class when he was ten; a friendship grew between the two of them, since they were both fond of script and writing. The relationship continued beyond the end of Salar's training, and he asked 'Abdallah to keep teaching him calligraphy. When possible, he would visit him every week. After a while, he became amir of the drum regiment, with forty soldiers under his command. The sultan gave him an estate in Balbis, and he asked 'Abdallah to oversee it, moving there from Cairo along with 'Adlat. All 'Abdallah's sons had their own professions, so they preferred to stay in Cairo. Salar was busy in Cairo, so he did not visit his estate; he did not know the peasants nor did they hold meetings with him. When the Ottomans entered Syria and were on their way to Egypt, it seems that the sultan asked him to undertake some investigative task, spying on the Ottomans in Sharqiyya province and Balbis so as to prevent them entering Cairo or to fight them in its outskirts. At that point, Salar decided to don peasant dress and claim to be 'Abdallah's brother who had come from Cairo to spend some time with him. No one doubted him. Even Sitt ad-dar swore not to say anything, in case the Ottomans killed her father and mother. 'Abdallah's loyalty was to Egypt. Salar, whom he had considered a son and companion for some time, perfected the role of Husam ad-din, so much so that even 'Abdallah regarded him as the peasant who loved Arabic calligraphy and worked in the fields.

I was stunned as I listened to all this, Aunt, but I was curious to find out more.

"He had slave girls as well, of course," I said to 'Adlat.

"Yes, he had lots of slave girls in his house in Cairo," she replied.

"He can't tell the difference between a slave girl and a free woman," I said regretfully. "He's used to being obeyed and having women fawn over him and begging him to spend the night with them. That's why he was determined to humiliate me; I said no when they all said yes; I kept saying no when they all set their sights on him and wanted him to acknowledge their existence. Amirs, my dear friend, know nothing about women."

'Adlat did not understand.

"Did he have a wife?" I asked, fearing what her response would be.

She seemed to hesitate. "Yes, he had a wife," she replied. "I think so."

"Did he leave her?" I inquired.

She looked as though she did not want to say anything, so she did not reply. I let the suspicion gnaw at my mind. That night, I could not sleep. I felt like yelling right in his face, clenching my fist, and giving him a big punch in his stomach and face. If he had so many slave girls, then why all the aggression and lust toward me? Why did he hate me so much for things I did not want? Did he need a slave girl in Balbis as well? Did he find some solace in spending a different sort of time observing my collapse and defeat?

I was thinking about him and his feelings toward me. Why had his treatment of me changed? At first, he had not even noticed my existence; I did not feel that he even viewed me as a woman. But then, something happened to make him want to force me to have sex with him. I tried to think what might have been going through his mind at that point. If he had wanted to have sex, he could have done that on the first or second day. And yet, he did not seem to even notice me. But then, in a night, it all changed. Maybe something happened to annoy him, and he decided to take his revenge on me; it might have been something I said, even though I was trying to avoid speaking to him. One day, I complained to him about 'Adlat, and then he took notice. That I can recall. That day we talked about the Mamluks. Do you remember what I said, Aunt? I do. I told him that thieves do not give protection, and protectors do not steal.

He told me that I was right. At that point, I did not realize that he himself was a Mamluk; in fact, the idea never occurred to me. Maybe my words hurt him, or made him despair and take his revenge. That same day, he told me to take off my clothes and treated me like a piece of baggage. Then the incident in the stables happened, and things changed, Aunt. Was it a sense of guilt toward me that made him show some affection and sympathy? After that, why did he say that he could not force me any longer? Fateful events were toying with both of us; sometimes he would be punishing me; at others, showing sympathy.

At all events, he is an evil man, no word to be trusted and no promise. I waited for him to come back so I could tell him that and then leave. Do not ask me, Aunt, why I did not leave the house easily at the time and return to my own father's house. I have no ready answer for that.

Two or three days later—I do not remember exactly—'Adlat started screaming and wailing. I found myself hugging her in sympathy; I did not expect, Aunt, to find a place for her in my heart. She lost three of her sons at Ridaniyya, and now was left with three others, Sitt ad-dar, and her husband. We told her that the boys had died as martyrs; they had shown more courage than all the mighty generals like Baybars and Qutuz. Even so, she kept on screaming, Aunt, till I could barely hear. You had to shout for her to hear what we were saying. She rolled in the dirt and lost consciousness for several hours. The keening women and other women from the quarter all gathered around her, weeping and praying to God for help. 'Abdallah sat there with the rest of his sons, listening to the Qur'an, tears pouring down and heart broken. At that point, Aunt, I decided that, if I saw Salar (or Husam ad-din) or that other man who had so overpowered my soul, I would hurl myself into his arms and do anything to keep me with him, if only for a day. I was not crying or shaking. Life was refusing to evacuate my veins, rebelling against my limbs, and demanding to go out into the forests. As you know, days that are steeped in death will always extract reckless instincts from the very depths.

I sat in my room and put my hands over my brother's ears so he would not hear the screams. I knew that Salim had entered Cairo and the city's mosques were praying for him. I could have left yesterday or today, but I did not; I could not.

I started to be scared of the Ottoman soldiers. Maybe they would invade people's houses and slaughter women and children. Who knows? I stayed in my room with my brother, not moving.

My brother looked anxiously around the room. "Where did Husam ad-din go?" he asked. "Is he dead too? Did our father die, Hind?"

"Don't say that!" I replied impatiently.

He looked doubtful. "Don't get angry with me, Hind," he said.

"Why should I be angry with you?"

"You hate Husam ad-din," he replied, "but I don't."

I was shocked. "Why don't you?" I asked.

He stood up and started pacing around the room, unsure how to respond. Shams was always more honest than me, Aunt, but he had no idea about what fate's disruptions can do to the human heart.

The door opened, and there he was.

When I looked at his face, I could see that he was exhausted and all his clothes were bloodstained. I felt like throwing myself into his arms and kissing him all over, but I did not. I had the impression that he had not left the battlefield yet.

"You're fine!" I said. "Thank God, you're safe!"

"No, I'm not," he replied in a tone I did not comprehend. "Today nobody's safe. Come on, I'm taking you back to your father."

I wanted to be sure myself before reassuring myself about him. "You've come back safely, haven't you?" I asked. "The war's over, isn't it?"

"No, it hasn't started yet," he replied. "None of us can possibly be safe as long as Salim's in Cairo."

"Don't hurl yourself to certain destruction," I said emphatically. "This is a trial, and we have to endure it patiently, Husam."

He gave me and my brother a hug. "No, we can't endure this patiently," he replied. "Come on."

Today he had no cart with him, instead a powerful horse. He seated me and my brother in front of him. For a few seconds, he stared at me.

"What happened is past and gone," he said. "You've no choice; forget it all."

"Will I see you again?" I asked sadly.

For a moment, our eyes met. Then he left without saying a word.

BOOK TWO

WHAT HAPPENED

How easily humanity can vanish! After the plague, I was
aware of mankind's paltry insignificance. Do you realize?
You have to realize that, if we do not record wars and
immortalize them in buildings, then they simply vanish
like dust in the air. No plague will ever kill buildings, and
no treachery can destroy them.

—The architect

The Testimony of the Translator
Mustafa Pasha Al-ʿUthmani (3)

Salim Shah, King of Kings, is governing with unprecedented wisdom, whether in Muslim lands or elsewhere. War does not distract him from contemplation, taste, and the pursuit of knowledge. He had a piercing gaze and clearly focused eye. What a great ruler! Once Cairo opened its gates and we set our eyes on its treasures, buildings, streets, and mosques, our soldiers were totally taken in and fascinated by it. That worried the King of Kings, who stopped any soldier from getting married to an Egyptian woman, whether daughter of a Mamluk or from the common people. The sheer attraction and magic of this country troubled him, as strangers adapted to it, and all notions of origin and purpose were forgotten within its recesses. That is what happened, Abu al-Barakat, or almost so. I will tell you about a visit that the King of Kings paid to the mosque of one of the sultans in Cairo, named Sultan Hasan. He had wanted to visit that particular mosque for some time. When the opportunity arose, that mosque was where he intended to go. That day, I went inside with him, and I watched as his gaze wandered over the various alcoves and surveyed the designs and decoration. I saw him right in front of me, carefully examining the marble work in the mosque floor. That went on for an hour or more till I was exhausted and needed to sit down, but did not dare say anything. Then I watched as he looked up, examined the lamps, and absorbed their light like a monk or Sufi. He climbed the minaret and leaned his arm on the wall.

"Who built this amazing structure?" he finally asked.

We all stared at each other; at the time, no one knew the architect's name.

"The architect's name," one of the soldiers said, "was Muhammad ibn Baylik al-Muhsini, a son of the people."

"A son of the people," the sultan repeated as though he was not listening.

He looked all around him. "From this minaret," he said, "you get the impression that you're ruling the entire world, that you're actually nothing. You're aware of how utterly puny you really are. This minaret is scary. Do Mamluks pray here?"

"Those criminals have no faith," I replied, knowing the answer. "They use mosques as battlefields, my Lord King."

"They don't deserve it," he responded at once. "They don't deserve buildings like these. But they do love to fight. Did you but know it, they need to be around."

"You've told us to kill them," one of the soldiers pointed out hesitantly.

"I'd like to," he said, "but I don't know if I can. Being at the very top of this minaret shows you something. Power is intoxicating, ambition is both blessing and revenge. We have to do away with them."

He started descending the staircase. "Mustafa," he told me just then, "if you saw beauty like this, what would you do?"

"I'd grab it for myself," I replied immediately.

"No, I don't want it for myself, but for my own country. I want a mosque just like it, with marble, lamps and lanterns to light up the world, brass designs, and Qur'anic verses to show the path. Take a few lamps from here—lamps, brass, and marble."

He thought for a while, then added: "And all the professional artisans."

I did not understand what he meant. "My Lord . . ."

"These Egyptians make things like this every single day," he said. "Now the fighting is over, we must think about building."

"What a great sultan you are. Do you want to build a mosque in your name in Egypt?"

"No, in my own country, one that's no smaller than this one, the mosque of Al-Mu'ayyad Shaykh, Barquq's mosque, and those of all the other Mamluks. We need men and gold. Take them from here."

"Men or gold?"

"Take both. Gold alone doesn't build structures, and men with no gold cannot create glory! Take them both, when the time's right."

Salar's Testimony (5)

I had done some research before and knew a lot about Shaykh Shihab ad-din, he being the shaykh for the mosque of Shaykhu al-'Umari an-Nasiri in central Cairo. We needed someone like him for the fight that had not started yet. War, Abu al-Barakat, is not simply a battle directed by generals. No, it is continuous conflict among peoples and countries, involving quarters and alleys. Did the Egyptian people learn how to love and live with the Mamluks, or was it that they hated the idea of invasion and realized what kings usually do when they enter a village? In those days, Egyptians possessed all the sagacity of scholars, so they resisted and fought just like the ancients. I saw it with my own eyes.

We were looking for a mosque that would be easy to reach and large enough to hold both soldiers and civilians. It would serve as the focus for resistance and war involving Cairo's districts and alleys. Abu al-Barakat, I proposed the Shaykhu Mosque to the sultan, not only for its position and importance, but for its shaykh. He was the mosque; his words could move the heart, and his steadfast attitude helped us more than any number of swords and guns. I proposed Shaykh Shihab ad-din after doing some research on him beforehand. I had listened to several of his sermons. He was my age, thirty or slightly older. What bound me to him were his powerful eyes, his weighty words, and his complete self-confidence. I knew that he came from a family of religious scholars; his great-grandfather was 'Abd al-Karim al-Manati, and another of his ancestors was the famous Shafi'i "Judge of Qus," 'Amr ibn Ahmad ibn 'Abd al-Karim al-Manati. So, he came from a noble and devout family, renowned for its sense of justice and its learning. He was still living off an endowment from a Mamluk amir named Amir Muhammad al-Muhsini.

I went to see him at night, a few hours before the dawn prayer. I was aware that he would always spend the night in solitary devotions inside the mosque. I was dressed in civilian clothes. When I went in, he did not realize I was there. He stayed where he was, reading the Qur'an and praying.

"Shaykh Shihab ad-din," I said after a while.

He turned to look at me. "My brother," he said, "you've come to pray for Egypt."

"No," I replied firmly, "I've come to fight for it."

"To covet it or love it?"

"I don't know. Both maybe."

"Lovers can't covet, and coveters can't love."

Our eyes met. "Shaykh," I said, "we don't come here under compulsion, but always as volunteers. That should be enough to grant success to those who persist with courage. The deserving should be granted success."

"Who might that be, Amir?"

"How did you know that I'm an amir?"

"Your eyes and your words. You talk of success and conflict, but you don't ask me about what's more important."

"I don't know what that is," I replied immediately. "However, for me, fighting is an obligation, something fated. I want to protect this country. I don't want to see any woman being seduced, humiliated, and overpowered by an Ottoman soldier. I don't want children to be enslaved and men killed. I am deeply concerned about this land and I'm worried about thieves and invaders."

Shihab ad-din smiled in silence. "The robbers all around us, Amir, are Mamluks and Egyptians as well, not just Ottomans."

"Leave the local robbers for me; I can handle them, but I can't guarantee what foreigners might do. Do you trust me, Shaykh?"

"How can I trust you, Amir, when I don't even know you?"

"Now you do."

Shihab ad-din stared at me hard for a while. "A year ago," he told me, "a woman came to see me, crying and asking me for help."

I listened patiently.

"Do you know about the killing of the donkey-man?" he continued.

I did not respond.

"He was a poor man who only owned a donkey and cart. A Mamluk soldier, who seemed to be drunk, asked him to take him across the bridge. The donkey-man obeyed his orders and did so. When he asked to be paid, the soldier refused to give him anything. When the donkey-man insisted, the soldier smashed his head in and threw him in the river in front of everyone. What did the Egyptians do then, Amir?"

I knew what had happened, but had no idea why Shihab ad-din was raising this now. I was furious and said nothing.

"The Egyptians surrounded the soldier," he went on, "and hit him, but they didn't kill him in the hope that justice would prevail. They took the soldier to the governor who immediately ordered the soldier to be punished. Everyone was happy, and justice seemed to have prevailed."

Shihab ad-din drew closer to me and stared into my eyes. "You know this, don't you?" he asked.

I did not reply.

"The Mamluk amirs got together and decided to challenge the governor and punish him for insulting the soldier's honor. The soldier escaped, and the governor was deposed. The amirs proceeded to crush all requests and everyone who nursed some hopes. The man's widow came to me, crying and asking for help. I gave her some money, but I had nothing else. The amazing thing, Amir, is the way that the Mamluks reacted, their intense anger at the way the Egyptians had dared to attack the soldier who had killed the donkey-man. They actually demanded regulations that would prevent Egyptians from confronting soldiers. Do you remember?"

"I know what happened," I replied. "The soldier committed a crime."

"I realize that you weren't one of the people who raised objections for the soldier's sake."

"No," I replied firmly, "I was not."

The shaykh smiled. "But then," he said, "you didn't offer support to the poor man either."

"Sometimes Mamluks go astray," I replied equally firmly. "But they're part of us and work for us. Tuman Bey strives for justice, and I support him."

"Do you strive for justice to save the Mamluks or for the country's sake?"

Just then, our eyes met. "You know the answer," I said.

"Why do you need a powerless shaykh like me," he said, "someone who can't even punish a Mamluk soldier?"

I sat up. "In wartime, risks have to be taken," I told him in all seriousness. "Is Salim an invader or caliph? Up till now, is everything that I've seen so far the staunching of wounds or rather killing and robbery? Who attacked whom? Who comes from Egypt and who stays? Do we even know the difference, Shaykh, between invader and sultan? Invaders win their victory and then leave with the spoils. Sultans, on the other hand, die amid its mud and are buried in its earth."

"So then, you really love Egypt and have no ambitions."

"Yes, that's right."

"What do you want from me?"

"This mosque. I want you and the mosque, obedient to the sultan, as a safe haven for fighters and others who wish to join them, a refuge for every refugee and injured person."

"Tuman Bey is a wise man," Shihab ad-din said. "All Egypt loves him. He arrived at a time when prudent thinking was a disease and loyalty was a crime. Justice demands the availability of punishment. The Egyptian people are with you, Amir, all of us. I'm not a man of war, and yet I pray for something more precious. Don't ask me to curse anyone or to prevaricate and lie."

I was delighted. "I'll promise you that," I replied.

He gave me a long, hard stare. "I've seen you before," he said. "Once or twice at Friday's prayers. You were listening closely and understanding. Search in your own depths, Amir; you can't really know yourself as yet. When the conflict is over, start a search so you can discover. Whoever searches, finds; whoever doesn't, fails. People who grieve over this lower world vanish inside it; those who transcend it reach for the eternal. We'll meet again soon. We'll talk about that on another occasion."

"I dearly hope so, Shaykh."

I stroked his hand. At that moment, my war had started.

The Testimony of the Translator
Mustafa Pasha Al-'Uthmani (4)

The King of Kings was peacefully inclined. He gave Egyptians a pledge of security. However, incredulity is a known human trait, and that, along with the Egyptians' refusal to acknowledge his good intentions, annoyed him and all of us. How was it that Egyptians preferred a foreign tyrant who arrived as a slave, then proceeded to humiliate them, instead of a free ruler from a Muslim country who had been giving them justice and security? Prompted by the Mamluks, they were utterly confused. The battle for Cairo began, Abu al-Barakat, and it was the fiercest fighting I've seen in my entire life. The Mamluks emerged from every conceivable foxhole, along with their wives, children, artisans, and peasants; to us, it seemed as though all Egyptians were with them. It was a veritable flood of people that spread all around our men, and drowned them. We knew nothing about Cairo's quarters and streets. Even our Mamluk soldiers were shocked by the attacks. A commander and his soldiers were killed on every single street, alley, and crossroads. Even the King of Kings was exposed to some attacks with swords and arrows; one day, he was hit by a stray arrow even in the Citadel fortress; but for the doctors, he might have died. What kind of devil has taken possession of the Egyptians these days? Did our soldiers slacken off, were they surprised? I do not know. However, they did lose their ability to fight back and their courage in the face of the terrifyingly sudden onslaughts. The Kings of Kings was more furious than I have ever seen him. He gave orders that any Mamluks who surrendered should be killed; the number that day was three hundred. He gave orders for them to be butchered in their prison and for their heads to be hung on a rope-chain extending from the Island of Roda all the way to Bab an-Nasr. That length required more than three hundred heads, and so he also gave orders for all Mamluks and sons of the people to be killed. Do not blame him, Abu al-Barakat. If you had been in his place, you would have done the same. Yes, he had given the Mamluks a pledge of security to surrender themselves, but, as you well know, they are traitors by nature, and the Circassians in particular are veritable personifications of evil.

I myself saw that rope with the heads stretching across the Cairo districts and watched as Ottoman soldiers hung the heads on the Cairo gates, caravanserais, and Egyptians' houses; so much so that there was no house in Cairo without a Mamluk head in front of it. If any Egyptian tried to take the head down so as not to frighten his children, he too would be killed and his head put up in place of the Mamluk. In war, Abu al-Barakat, terror is a weapon, but in Cairo the war did not come to an end and its impact did not lessen. Our soldiers were not any more powerful; indeed lots of them were killed. The King of Kings did his best by finding out who was in charge of these raids with Tuman Bey. Three days later, he had found out for certain.

It was three drum majors: Salar, Inal, and Qansuh al-'Adili. Salar was the most dangerous of the three. No sword could scare him, nor could his loyalty be purchased, not even with the promise of land or a governorship. Salim immediately gave orders for them to be killed and promised that whoever brought their heads to him would receive the equivalent weight in gold. Salim always keeps his promises, but spies told him that the Mamluk stronghold in Cairo at that point was a mosque named for a Mamluk amir, Shaykhu, who was a contemporary of Qala'un's sons. The mosque had been turned into a location to bring people together and welcome Egyptian and Mamluk rebels. It seemed that Shihab ad-din al-Manati, the shaykh of the mosque, was turning people against Salim. Can you believe, Abu al-Barakat, that an Egyptian shaykh would turn people against the Muslim caliph? Why? Because this caliph is a foreigner? The Mamluks are foreigners too, are they not? What is the difference between Salim and Mamluks? Egyptians say that Mamluks have no other country than Egypt; they build and grow things there. Salim's country, on the other hand, is far away, and he wants to make it the core and shield of Islam. What kind of idiot thinks like that? Salim came to save the Egyptians from Mamluk oppression and injustice; they did not understand or even try to do so. Salim gave orders for the shaykh to be killed immediately. Treachery is punishable by death, and shaykhs are by no means immune to error. In fact, he wanted to hang Shihab ad-din's head alongside the other three amirs and take them round the Cairo districts. Salim swore that he would do it. He is both powerful and capable; when he swears to do something, he carries it through. But the fighting did not come to an end, Abu al-Barakat. The arrow that hit the King of Kings struck him in the neck, and he was forced to disappear from view; actually it seemed that he had vanished and retired. Something totally unexpected happened, Abu al-Barakat, as though the days were spinning fast and indiscriminately like new waterwheels. The Ottoman forces were being beaten or almost so. What was baffling was that the Mamluks took off their distinctive uniforms and put on civilian clothes. It was impossible to tell them apart from ordinary Egyptians. When it was time for Friday prayers, the shaykhs in the Cairo mosques prayed for the sultan, but they did not pray for Salim. Instead, they prayed for Tuman Bey as sultan of Egypt!

Salim was furious when he heard that. "If any soldier slacks off about killing Mamluks," he said, "he's to be killed on the spot.

And the war continued.

Hind's Testimony (6)

You will remember, Aunt, how I felt when I returned home and how happy my father was about my brother and myself. I did not tell my father everything; I felt too ashamed to mention all the details about my humiliation and defeat. I just mentioned a few things. At that point, my father asked me for the name of the man who had first rescued me, but then grabbed and kidnapped me. I hesitated for a moment, but then I realized that the time for concealment was over and Salar was not be bothered any more about who knew the truth. I gave my father his name, and I told you, Aunt, what had happened. You read the certificate that he had given me; your heart cracked, and you frowned, realizing full well what had actually happened to me. My father never saw it, and I did not dare talk to him frankly about it. I simply said that the Mamluk amir had made me work as a servant in his house—no more, no less.

I stayed in my room for hours. You were my only friend; perhaps you understood more than most people. You had lost your husband immediately after getting married and had not had any children. I was your daughter. You had never been married to anyone else. I was your friend and companion. Do you remember, my Aunt? I stayed in my room for hours, unconcerned about the fighting in Cairo or what was happening outside. I was trying to understand my own self. I had come home now, but was still where I had been. For my father, the fighting in Cairo was his conflict. He welcomed wounded people into the house and asked us to help them. We did that every day. I would emerge listless from my room to give them some food, wearing a veil to cover my face. When we met Ziyad for the first time, he was one of the resistance fighters confronting the invaders who had been wounded during the fighting in our quarter. My father had picked him up, taken pity on him, talked to him, and learned a good deal about him. He was a merchant's son who worked with his father. These were hard times, and it was doubly hard for me because my heart was troubled, sad, angry, and vengeful.

"Hind," you said at the time, "I need to talk to you."

I looked at you, but said nothing.

"I realize that you've been through a real trial," you told me, "but I'm feeling a bit baffled. Are you upset about what happened, or for some other reason?"

"About what happened, Aunt," I replied immediately.

"You realize that Ziyad's asked your father to get married to you when the fighting's over. He only saw your eyes, but he's from a good family."

"He doesn't know anything about me," I replied without thinking.

You understood what I was meaning, Aunt.

"I told him everything," you said bashfully.

I gaped in amazement.

"I had to tell him," you went on. "That only made him more insistent. He realizes what happens in wartime. He knows your inner strength and excellent lineage. What happened to you was against your will and has left its scar on you. He knows and understands."

"But I don't want him," I said.

You looked at me. "Why?" you asked. "I can understand. After what happened, you hate men and having sex with them."

I clutched myself, as though begging my Lord to help me transcend this torment.

"He left me like a piece of broken glass," I said. "He rolled me up in a corner and left. How could he?"

You kept staring at me in despair, Aunt. Did you know? Have you delved deep inside me and uncovered my heart's secrets? I believe you have.

I buried my head in the pillow and closed my eyes. The image of him was constantly in front of me.

A few hours later, my father came into the room to see me. "The man who kidnapped you . . ." he said gloomily.

"What's happened to him?" I asked anxiously.

"Are you scared for him or of him?" he asked with a frown.

I sat up. "Forgive me, Father," I said seriously.

"I thought you were dead, and I grieved over you. Now I've found that you're alive again. You saved your brother and yourself. Your personal courage is unparalleled, Hind. Amir Salar. Now I know who he is."

"What are we going to do?" I asked.

"It's war, Hind. There's nothing I can do now. We have to wait first for it to be over. It might lead to our destruction. Do you know who his wife was?"

I swallowed hard and shuddered. "Who?"

"Khund Sa'adat, Khayir Bey's daughter."

I put my hand on my chest. "Did he leave her?" I asked.

"Perhaps, I don't know. But, even if he'd done that now, he'd take her back after the war. She's from the same stock as him. A traitor's daughter, to be sure, but at this point he's the most important man in Egypt. If, God forbid, we're defeated, then he's bound to go back to her. The same if we win. She'll have no one else."

As my father looked at me, my throat was on fire. I did not say anything.

"In wartime," my father went on after a pause, "good and evil are confused. All colors are dark, and the heart's light is extinguished. Be patient and steadfast. I don't like the times we're living in."

"Forgive me, father. I'll feel better, I promise you."

"You'll be married," he declared, "have children, and forget what's happened."

"Give me some time," I responded painfully, "so I can inure myself to defeat."

Salar's Testimony (6)

The core stabilized and calmed down, Abu al-Barakat. The traitors moved away, becoming like puny ants that have lost their way and will be crushed by soldiers' boots. Amid the mosque's alcoves, I breathed in the fresh air and shook hands with the shaykh and Egyptians. We all sat in a circle around Shaykh Shihab ad-din. The Egyptians said that they had endured much injustice from the Mamluks, but that we three amirs deserved to rule Egypt and Syria along with Tuman Bey. We were courageous fighters and strove for justice. That is what Egyptians said. It was not right for foreigners to make off with their treasures. These were very different moments for us. I will tell you about them, Abu al-Barakat, so you can record them. If we do not do that, we are bound to forget them. The Mamluks will remain as slaves of a different kind, quarreling with each other over trifles, while Egyptians will remain a clump of people who never really got to know the Mamluks and their fighting skills. In those moments, Mamluks and Egyptians came together and shared jokes and tales that poked fun at us. We laughed along with them, prayed, and made plans. I used to train them in fencing and spear-throwing. Those were days indeed; they went by like a dream, or maybe a glimpse of paradise that passes us by without stopping to confront recalcitrant sinners.

We saw all the heads hanging. I was a soldier and realized that such ruthlessness on the part of a king was not an expression of confidence, but rather of fear. Such displays of cruelty by a sultan or warrior were a sign of an imminent end. We took off our Mamluk uniforms and put on the clothes of ordinary Egyptians and peasants. That way, it was difficult to tell Egyptians and Mamluks apart.

Some Egyptians gave me a list of demands, and I promised in front of Shaykh Shihab ad-din to fulfil them all when I was sultan, provided that we emerged as winners and expelled Salim and his army.

On Friday, the sultan himself came to the mosque in disguise, met Shaykh Shihab ad-din, and thanked him. He listened to the shaykh's sermon, then shook hands with the local commanders and Egyptian notables. He told them who he was, and they all declared that they were ready to sacrifice their lives. He was honest, not a common trait among sultans. He would squeeze children's shoulders and listen to complaints from the elders. I read out the list to him, and he promised to lower taxes, reduce the heavy impact of the Mamluks, and make a clear distinction between them and Egyptians. He would alter unfair laws, like the ones that penalized any Egyptian who argued with a Mamluk soldier. After the sermon that day, the sultan declared that God had created us all equal. The Egyptian people were defending their own country; he was just a servant carrying out their orders. At that point, the Egyptians bowed down and cheered him, so much so that I was afraid the sound might reach as far as Salim in his citadel. Our sultan now adopted the Shaykhu Mosque as his own house and refuge, a citadel from which to launch attacks on the enemy invader.

You recall, Abu al-Barakat; I told you about three horsemen who were with Tuman Bey throughout the war. We all understood each other through a mere glance or gesture. Together we planned raids that were bound to eliminate the Ottoman army. If Salim chose to use treachery to fight, then Mamluks had to perfect that game too. We bribed Ottoman soldiers with grain and gold and finished them off in the city quarters and mosques. They used the Al-Mu'ayyad Mosque as a refuge and stole its lanterns, brass, and silver. They killed Egyptians, the weak, and children. Inal pretended to be an upper-Egyptian peasant and brought honey and bread to sell to the soldiers. They would let him in, and, once they were not looking, he used to open the main door. We would be right there, behind him. Some Ottoman soldiers surrendered, others decided to fight, but we beat them. Now it was our turn to collect heads and terrify the invaders and traitors. We then urged them to go chasing after women, and, when they did so, we pounced on them and arrested them in houses and stores. We heard some of them pleading and pledging allegiance to Tuman Bey. We had attacked at midnight, and, by sunrise the next day, the Ottomans could go round and pick up their soldiers' corpses, their hearts torn to pieces as sheer terror directed and toyed with their swords.

Tuman Bey insisted on taking part with us in raids and attacks. Al-'Adili and I rode on either side of the sultan, accompanied by a large group of camels, as we made for Salim's encampment. Our camels were loaded with grain. We were wearing Bedouin dress and had our faces covered. We stopped at the entrance to Salim's camp and asked the guards if they needed any grain. We had mixed chaff in with the grain, and it looked as though the soldiers were going to steal our camels and grain and kill us, as we were expecting. We set fire to the wheat and chaff, and beat the camels with our whips, and they rushed into the camp and burned it. We entered with our swords and horses, killed a lot of them, and took many prisoners. Their sultan either fled or hid somewhere, but I could smell fear all around us and heard pleas for help and cries from those who had escaped the slaughter, were scared, and had surrendered.

Victory secured, we returned to the Shaykhu Mosque.

"I have to check on our children," Inal said quietly.

"No," Al-'Adili mocked, "it's your wife you want to check on! It's wartime, man, so forget about your wife!"

Inal was furious. "It's my children I want to check on," he said, "that's all!"

"We're not leaving the mosque till we've finally won," I said. "Your children are perfectly safe."

By now, our success had calmed my spirit. "Or maybe you're longing for your wife," I joked, "as Inal put it. In wartime, men forget all about their women."

"You've no heart," he retorted angrily. "You know nothing about women."

"We know everything about women," I stated confidently. "If you'd joined with us in the past, then you'd have learned a good deal about them so that none of them could control you and make you forget that we're facing the Ottomans here."

He gave us both a furious look.

"We were joking," Al-'Adili and I both said. "The time is now, then the war will come to an end. At that point, go back to your wife and children."

I then looked at Al-'Adili. We started planning our next attack on the Ottomans, my gaze all the while fixed on the sultan.

The resistance and attacks on the Ottomans continued. Eventually they came to realize that Mamluks are not like other fighters; they are more courageous and fearsome. The Egyptians knew and understood that and could distinguish between the various dangers. The Ottomans were defeated, Abu al-Barakat; record that in your book. The quarters of Cairo defeated them, Abu al-Barakat, even though the Battle of Ridaniyya had not stopped them from entering Cairo.

The Testimony of the Translator
Mustafa Pasha Al-'Uthmani (5)

The sultan's health improved, but the soldiers were in bad shape, whether from illness or wounds. Some of them were coming back with wound-thrusts from women. Can you believe it, Abu al-Barakat, Egyptian women coming out with kitchen knives and stabbing soldiers? When hundreds of women unite to attack soldiers, there is no hope of escape. Their fighting is much more savage and painful. They are stabbing at manhood and honor. What Egyptians need, Abu al-Barakat, is a decent upbringing and solid administration. The Mamluks failed in their training and teaching; their schools taught jurisprudence and hadith, but not ethics. In our country, which woman would ever dare raise a weapon in a man's face? No matter. I will tell you the true version of what happened. I hope you will record it accurately and not follow your own whims. If you were an Egyptian, you would be writing the true story; if you were to consider yourself a son of the people, you would do the same, all so that Mamluks and Egyptians could learn a lesson.

When the fighting intensified and victory seemed to be favoring the Mamluks and Egyptians, some kind of strategy or resolution of the conflict was clearly needed. The fighting was wreaking havoc on the Mamluks, Egyptians, and Ottomans. We did what we did because we wanted to save the Egyptian people rather than destroy them. Sometimes a commander has to bring a conflict to a conclusion, even though it may lead to a lot of bloodshed. Join me in doing the math, Abu al-Barakat; you are familiar with accounting. If our ensuing actions led to the deaths of ten thousand Egyptians or more, of half of all Mamluks or less, that is still a trifling number when compared with the number who would have died by the end of a war that went on for years. Decisions have to be made. The number of dead Egyptians and Mamluks was indeed large, maybe five thousand or more. I do not recall. But the number of Ottomans killed was also large, perhaps half that number. In any case, once the sultan had recovered his health, he gave instructions that the war was to end in a single night. He ordered heavy guns and canons to be mounted on the roofs of Mamluk mosques; they were to be fired nonstop until Cairo surrendered. He said that he wanted to go in person to the Sultan Hasan Mosque and fire cannon himself from there. That is what we did. The war came to an end, and Cairo burned.

Hind's Testimony (7)

I will tell you, Aunt, about fatal misfortune. My longing for him was mingled with a certainty that he had died or been killed. Every time I spotted a head hanging from a rope, I looked at it closely, expecting to see him. Can you understand how much I suffered? I wanted to talk to him just once perhaps, about the love that had been born out of his unkindness and oppression toward me. I wanted to kiss him once. Forgive me, Aunt, I'm pouring my heart out to you because you are the person closest to me.

I left the house without telling my father and looked all around me: smoke from fires, and corpses piled up in the streets. The fire was not dying down, as though the smoke would last forever. They kept firing, Aunt, pulverizing my country. I saw a woman carrying her husband's corpse; she was crying and begging a soldier to carry it. She just wanted to take the corpse and bury it. Her husband was a Mamluk soldier. I heard her pleading with the soldier. She handed him her ring.

"I just want to bury him," she said. "Don't leave him in the street."

But the soldier insisted on beheading him first. Salim had issued that order for all Mamluk heads, whether alive or dead. The woman agreed and dragged her now headless husband's corpse away. I suppressed my utter shock and went back home, my heart in shreds and all hope collapsing at the thought of witnessing such a thing again.

The following day, Aunt, Cairo was still on fire. I went out again to look for corpse remains or children's limbs so I could collect them and return them to their owners. The fire's red glow was stronger than the sun in the sky and spreading unprecedented pollution. The sound of ʿAdlat's voice was deafening my ears, superseding every house and mosque. People died, but those who survived were worse off by far. My entire body was shaking and my eyes kept wandering, as I made my way around the house. I was not sure how I could help her or make her feel better. Every time a new corpse appeared, it broke my heart.

A few days later, the big news arrived. Another conspiracy and a double defeat. Sultan Tuman Bey had hidden himself with Hasan ibn Marʿi, a Bedouin shaykh, but the shaykh had betrayed his pledge and sold him to Salim. It seemed that treachery had its own particular seasons, times when it would spread, just like the plague. Egyptians could not believe that their sultan was now a prisoner of this foreign invader. Not only that, Aunt, but I received information about the Ottomans and their revenge. They burned the mosque of Shaykhu al-'Umari an-Nasiri, entered the mosque sanctuary, and butchered him mercilessly. They also burned a number of other mosques where Egyptians had hidden or resisted the invaders. I heard, Aunt, that they put women in prison. Can you believe it? They imprisoned Mamluk widows and their women folk specifically. Some of them were tortured, while others were forced to pay over everything they owned and to give the soldiers all their gold in order to stay alive. Those days were all darkest night, no stars falling, no lightning flashing, then disappearing.

The Testimony of the Translator
Mustafa Pasha Al-'Uthmani (6)

Victory always belongs to the one who is powerful and just. War involves deceit and weaponry. Do not blame the victor and sympathize with the loser simply because he has lost. The Mamluks are no angels. They do not fight on behalf of religion or country; they fight for money and gold. They have turned their imprisoned sultan into a saint and martyr. I do not know whether it is because of their love for saints and martyrs like the Copts, or whether it is just naiveté and ignorance. I saw and watched the sultan's meeting with Salim Shah. This is what happened. I will give you a completely honest version.

Tuman Bey stood in chains in front of the sultan. Salim, King of Kings and caliph of Islam, looked at him.

"I asked you to surrender once, twice," Salim told him. "Instead, you preferred to shed blood."

Their eyes met.

"I wanted to defend my country," Tuman Bey replied defiantly.

"It was stupid of you to declare war when you weren't prepared for it."

"Yes, it was. But you used fire power as a weapon, whereas we only resort to traditional chivalry."

"Mamluks don't have any traditional chivalry, man," Salim responded mockingly. "There's none of that in war in any case. War uses deceit, weapons, and force. We've learned that, and so have you. If you'd surrendered, I would have made you governor of Egypt."

"It's already mine, alive or dead. While I'm alive, I'm sultan, not governor. If I'm dead, then I'm a martyr, but I still die as sultan, not governor."

"We're no different: you arrived here as a foreigner, and I did as a ruler."

"I came here for a country; I have no other. You've come to take its treasure back to your own country. We're not the same."

"You're answering one word with another. If you'd shown some regret, I'd have forgiven you."

"And have people say that the Mamluk sultan was defeated and begged Salim for forgiveness? I'll never do that."

"They'll say that whether you do it or not. Egypt will fare better under my rule."

"It was the glory of Islam and heart of the world. Do you want it for that reason, King, or for your own country?"

"I want it for all the Muslim territories."

Now it was Tuman Bey's turn to smile. "I construct and build, then you arrive to destroy and oppress. Which of us deserves to rule? The Mamluk monuments will survive to show what has happened, what the Ottomans did not build, what they stole, and whom they killed. It will all be recorded by scholars. Buildings are what remain, General, and provide witness, no more."

"Buildings are what remain," Salim repeated. "Your brazen behavior leads me to think of some humiliating way to kill you so that you can be convinced that, in wartime, buildings are of no value."

"I was making it clear to you, General, that a victor is someone who peoples the earth. 'As for froth, it disappears without trace; what is useful to people remains on the earth.'* Thus said the Lord of Servants."

"You build monuments to immortalize your own rulers. Then you proceed to tyrannize people and do evil on the earth."

"If we agreed in our view of Egypt and government," Tuman Bey stated clearly, "then there would be no war and no enmity. But that's impossible. You have your war, and I have mine."

At that moment, I thought the caliph of Islam was going to kill him. I can swear that I saw some admiration in Salim's expression.

"The true warrior," he declared, "can smell courage from a distance and appreciate the intrepid warrior. I admire and esteem you; you deserve that. But, for your obstinacy and opposition, you also deserve to die."

He gestured to the guards, and they took him out without any further word.

The war came to an end, and defeat was the Mamluks' lot. Mamluk heads illuminated Cairo like so many lanterns.

Then Salim extended his generosity to every corner of the land. He pardoned Mamluks and Egyptians, and gave the Egyptian people a pledge of security. In times of victory, the true greatness of kings emerges. My own king gave money to the shaykhs and went to the Al-Azhar Mosque in person to pray, listen, and give the mosque his blessing.

At times, I had the impression that all Egyptians were alike—Mamluks, Jews, Copts, Byzantine and Muslim merchants—the same shape and appearance. Once

* Qur'an Sura 13:17 [Thunder]

the Mamluks had disappeared into the fields and peasant lands, it was impossible to distinguish them from the rest of the population. Without their flashy uniforms, there was no difference between them and Egyptians. For that reason, you cannot blame our army; they had no other choice. They hit back at anyone who attacked them, and made no distinction between Mamluks and the general population. That was not feasible: the Mamluks disguised themselves as Egyptians and sought refuge among them. Guns were our only resort.

I am not going to talk about the thefts, because it is all a pack of lies. Every army needs weapons. In wartime it is the defeated who have to pay for the losses. The Mamluks will claim that we stole gold and silver, marble and wood, even the doors of mosques. We took it all out of Egypt . . . but what we took were simply our rights after a ferocious conflict. We did not leave Egypt in ruins. No, we left it in Mamluk hands, just as it had been before. But this time, we have also left a devout overseer there, someone who knows how to curb Mamluk ambitions.

Hind's Testimony (8)

The day when our sultan was killed was a very sad day indeed, Aunt. I wept on the bosom of a Coptic woman who made the sign of the cross on her chest, tears pouring from her eyes. It was the major Coptic festival, Good Friday, when heroes die so the world can live; tears are shed throughout Egypt, and martyrs are celebrated. He was a sultan whose spirit engendered hope for purity of heart, defeat of evil, and unity of humanity as a whole; an end to betrayal, perfidy, greed, and killing. They had once sworn allegiance to their sultan, but such times never last. Instances of success pass by like momentary pleasures, never lasting except for those people who succeed in the end and abandon the world.

They hung him up on the Bab Zuwayla. For the first time, I noticed how handsome and proud he was, with his calm, penetrating eyes. He had asked us to read the Fatiha of the Qur'an for him three times, realizing and anticipating what his fate would be.

He told the man to do his job. I saw him hanged right in front of me. His soul left his body to hover all around us, and I can swear, Aunt, that the women present saw him soaring above the clouds with a smile on his face. That memory has stayed with us all in Egypt till today. Cries of woe arose, and the keening started, with the whole Egyptian population mourning his death. I was there, and my eyes kept searching for him, Salar. If he were still alive, he would come today. The war was over, and Salim had pardoned all Mamluks and Egyptians. For one final time, he demanded that swords be lowered and defeat be acknowledged.

I was searching for him among the Egyptian populace, but did not find him. I returned to the house, my heart burning with Ottoman gunfire.

"A sad day indeed, Hind," my father said as soon as he set eyes on me.

"A sad day indeed, Father," I replied ambiguously.

I went into my room and closed the door. Do you remember, Aunt? You came in just then and calmed me down.

"You have to forget him," you told me. "It was a trial, but now it's over. He was the first man in your life, so you're attached to him. That's the way we are, my daughter. We always get involved with the first man to hurt us and invade body and soul, even though they treat us harshly and cruelly. Don't repeat my mistake. I regret my loneliness and weakness. You need a companion, not a lover."

"I need to die," I responded bitterly.

You stroked my hand. "That's stupid," you said. "It's not the kind of thing that Abu al-Barakat's daughter should be saying."

I started feeling hopeful again. "Will you go with me tomorrow to Bab Zuwayla?" I asked her.

You replied, Aunt, that you could not stand seeing the sultan's corpse hanging there for three days.

"I'm going there every day."

"To look at the way our sultan's been humiliated?"

"To see the sultan."

Next day, Aunt, I went there, but did not see him, and the day after that as well. Everyone was in tears. As I circled his pendant corpse, I kept bumping into people, one in tears, another shrieking, still another moaning. And then, in the midst of the crowd . . . I saw him.

He was tall and stood proud. That day, he was wearing his full amir's uniform. He was staring at the corpse, his eyes gleaming and stony. I could not tell whether he was crying or his eyes were expressing bitterness, hatred, and fury. They were riveted, focusing solely on the dead sultan's eyes. I looked at his face, the longing that I was feeling springing from my own eyes. I wanted him to see me, to notice that I was there. He stayed there for an hour or more, not moving or looking around, as though he were a stone statue. Then he saw me.

Finally our eyes met. Mine called out to him, but his gleaming eyes did not even see me, like two glass eyes bypassing my face to a distant horizon that I could neither reach nor comprehend. He did not speak, smile, yell in my face, or even show any sign of recognition.

I did not dare say anything. I was afraid he would not reply. He would leave me and depart, destroying the vestiges of my life.

I cannot begin to describe, Aunt, my sorrow and fury as I stood there in front of him, while he treated me as a total stranger, as though he did not even know me, had never humiliated me and forced me to have sex with him. He had toyed with me, deceived me, and then toyed with me again. Today too, he was humiliating me and forcing me to leave. If only I had yelled in his face or hit him in front of everybody.

When I went home, my sense of defeat was spreading and expanding to the ocean limits. I blamed myself. Maybe if I had submitted to him and shared love-making as he had wanted, he would have at least greeted me. Perhaps if I had shared my personal feelings with him, maybe, maybe . . .

At that moment, the widow of the slain sultan came to my mind, now in a dark prison after losing both husband and lover and being tortured for the sake of some gold. If only existence could be adjusted by the flash of gold and the weight of dinars!

That day, my father came in to talk to me. I was sitting there, dry-eyed and speechless. I stared at the wall, but could not make out its shape or color.

"You're my favorite daughter," he told me gently. "These are sad times, as you know. I want to be sure about you before I die. Don't disappoint me."

I realized what he meant. "I'll never do that," I replied sadly.

"You'll be married to a man whom I've chosen for his morals and learning."

I was unable to respond and said nothing.

"If I ever met that amir," he went on, "I'd kill him with my own hands. He must have died with all the others. Is he dead, Hind?"

I realized why my father was asking that question. "No, he's not," I replied.

"How do you know?"

"I spotted him among the people bidding the sultan farewell."

He nodded. "We're completely erasing the past," he said, "its sorrows and its defeats. We're beginning again, for my sake . . ."

"Wait a little," I replied sadly. "I need some time."

He looked at me as though he realized what was going through my mind. "You've learned," he said. "By now, you've understood and learned."

"Please wait a little," I pleaded, "so I don't hurt people who only deserve the very best.

"Okay, Hind," he replied seriously.

You were scared for me, Aunt, I realize that. When I went out into the garden, I found Ziyad right in front of me. I was wearing a head-veil, but my face was uncovered. I felt upset and was about to go back inside, but he stopped me.

"If you'd allow me," he said politely, "I'd like to say just one word. Then I'll feel happy for the rest of my life."

I looked all around me. "Go ahead," I said.

"I'm a colleague of your father, and I've learned from him," he said. "I thank fate that I was wounded in the fighting. Your father took care of me and encouraged me when I was in despair. He's an important and wise man."

"Thank you," I replied without looking at him.

"Allow me, Khund Hind," he went on. "I know what happened and how much you've suffered. In wartime we have to stand together and be united."

I looked at him. He was a really good-looking man with a well-meaning demeanor.

"Why did you fight with the Mamluks?" I asked him.

"I was fighting for my country, not the Mamluks. I much preferred not to see men's heads rolling and women being stripped and raped in the streets. But it seems that it was all fated. Egyptian women are my sisters. Their honor and sanctity is mine too."

His gentleness and morals seemed the very opposite of Salar: no rape, no theft of my heart and body, no injustice and oppression.

"You're a fine person, my brother," I told him slowly. "I wish you well."

"And I hope that you'll consider your father's suggestion," he said. "I realize that times are hard, and the memories are painful."

I looked down. "My brother," I told him, "God's servants have suffered enough. I won't treat you unjustly, when you are the best of men."

He looked wounded. "What happened is no concern of mine," he said. "Your aunt has told me everything. That only makes me even more convinced that you're the best person in Egypt and the purest of women."

At the time, I had no idea how the soul could attack the mind that way or how the heart could combine with it in order to destroy me! I could not manage it.

"Forgive me, brother," I said softly, "but . . ."

"If your heart is in darkness," he interrupted, "then you need some time for it to be lit again. You need someone to help you see everything. I can understand your sorrow and aversion."

"You're right," I replied, "my heart is in a dark place. But, in the hands of mankind, the light is only one. Without light, the heart cannot give. Forgive me, brother. I want you to be always safe with the one you value and love. You deserve only the best."

With that, I left without saying anything more.

⁓

Aunt, this passion is intolerable. Life no longer has any taste in my mouth or any color. I had lost my mother and some brothers, and realized that such losses were part of the baggage of these times. The loss of the man who had wronged and enslaved me would make me happy, would it not? But he had managed to gain control of my heart, Aunt, and squelched any confusion and hatred.

Most of the day, my hand was propping up my chin; I only left the room for short periods.

How had his eyes managed to penetrate my very existence, as though I were nothing, a cloud that dissipates with the first gust of wind or disappears completely, leaving nothing behind except time passing? How could his cruelty have reached so far?

I was orbiting around him and still am.

Memories of those humiliating days would not leave me. Sometimes, I would hate him and vow revenge; at others, I would miss him; at still others, I would long for his arm to be around me at night. One day, I was surprised to receive a visit from Sitt ad-dar. She was alone, and her face looked pale. She said she wanted to find out how I was and to hear my news. I asked her how her mother was and apologized for not visiting her. As I recall, she stayed for an hour or less.

"I think my beloved is dead," she told me sadly before leaving. "He's left me like this."

"You need to be careful," I scolded her. "It's not so easy to downplay your own honor."

"What could I do now, Hind," she asked in tears, "if people found out?"

I suddenly understood what she meant. I was shocked, and put my hand over my mouth. She was obviously pregnant, in her fourth month at least.

"Can you help me?" she asked.

"Help you?" I replied. "How?"

"I don't know," she said, "but, within days, everyone will find out. The scandal will kill my father."

For a few seconds, I said nothing.

"You realize how many girls were raped by the soldiers, don't you?" she said. "Lots of them . . . In wartime, women are all legitimate."

"Are you going to claim that you were raped by Ottoman soldiers?" I asked angrily.

"If they'd found me, they were going to rape me for sure. They did it to others. I'm not lying."

"They did it to other women," I insisted. "Yes, true enough. But not to you."

She gave me a defiant look. "I came to ask you to help me," she said. "I thought you had good feelings about us. I gave you protection. Do you remember how kind my father was to you?"

"Why don't you ask Amir Salar to help you?" I said. "Isn't he a family friend?"

She shuddered. "He'd butcher me if he found out," she said. "Are you crazy?"

"I didn't realize he was that concerned about girls' honor," I said bitterly, "and worried about their reputation."

"Are you angry with him, Hind?"

"Why should I be?" I replied angrily. "There's nothing between us."

Silence followed. Sitt ad-dar stood up listlessly and left my room.

I whistled angrily at her stupidity and my own problems. They did not involve a child in the womb, but instead a demon that would not leave my heart alone or show mercy. At that point, I almost went out of my mind. How . . . how could he not have seen me when he was looking straight at me? How could I not have left a single trace inside his heart?

My father started insisting that I consider Ziyad's offer; he would not be waiting forever.

"I don't want to do him wrong, Father," I said, tears pouring down my face. "I'm not right for him."

He gave me a long stare. "Why?" he asked.

"My heart's in shreds," I replied honestly, "and my mind is all over the place. Now that I've plunged into this deep well, I can't get out."

"I don't understand what you're saying. I asked you to think about it."

"I swear to you that I'd be married to him if it were not doing him an injustice. I can't stand being that unfair to anyone."

My father left angrily. I do not know what was affecting me: a touch of the jinn perhaps or a demon.

That night, I did not sleep. I was tossing to left and right. As dawn was rising, I heard my brother's voice waking me up. "Hind, Hind," he whispered, "he's waiting for you outside."

I knew he liked to joke, but at that moment I did not need it. "Leave me alone!" I told him.

"Husam ad-din," he said. "He's waiting for you by the back door."

I clutched my heart and almost fell flat on my face. I put on my robe and ran to the back door as fast as I could.

I looked all around me, but saw no one.

"What kind of joke is this, Shams?" I yelled. "Don't you dare try this on again!"

He slunk up behind me, covered my mouth, put me on his horse, and made off, as though it were all a wonderful dream that would never come to an end. There he was, holding me to his chest and not moving. He stopped in the desert and lifted me down without a word.

Today he was Salar, not Husam ad-din. He was not wearing the amir's uniform, but his gaze was that of a warrior, and his sword was clearly visible in order to terrify any opponent.

He looked all around him. "How are you?" he asked.

I was filling my gaze with the sight of him and did not respond. I wanted him to stay there in front of me forever; I just wanted to look at him, to know he was well, and that he was with me and all around me.

He stared at me for a while. "Hind . . . ," he said.

I bit my lips. "I'm not well," I told him bitterly. "I'll never be well again."

He looked away. "These are times," he said, "when darkness is intensifying all around us. They too shall pass; they always do. No disaster can be as bad as defeat. . . ."

When he looked at me again, my eyes were calling him longingly.

"Keep a small segment of your heart to remember what is past," he told me, "then move on."

"Why have you come?" I asked him angrily. "I assumed you'd forgotten me. Times would continue—that's what you told me."

"Why are you so angry today?" he asked tenderly. "Give me your hand."

I looked around me for a moment, then stretched out my hand and clamped it on his.

"I've come to ask you a question that's puzzling me," he said.

"Ask away, Amir."

"Why didn't you go back to your father while I was away? You could have walked to his house in less than half a day, but you chose to stay in my house till I returned from the Battle of Ridaniyya. Why?"

"For the same reason," I replied deliberately, "that made you wait till you got back from Ridaniyya to take me to my father's house. Why did you return me to my father's house before the war, Amir? You were eager for victory. If you won, what were you going to do with me?"

"That's all past now," he said sadly. "Today, I've also come to explain some things to you. You may be confused about them. Do you realize what's happened to the wives of amirs and Mamluks? Even the sultan's widow is being tortured in a dark dungeon. Animals, all they want is her gold. We're in times when there's no difference between king and slave, good and evil. It's a time for spoils and theft. Any Mamluk amir's wife is now facing a dire fate. Impossible . . ."

"What's impossible? For you to be married to me?"

He held my hand even tighter. "To be married to you," he replied clearly.

I made an effort not to understand his words. "What triumph is there," I asked, "in defeating me? Have you come here today to revive a wretched passion or to kill off the vestiges of a wounded heart?"

He moved closer. "I came here to see you," he said softly.

"Why?"

"When times are risky, soldiers need to preserve a sense of tranquility. For me, your face gives me that feeling and assurance."

"You were looking for traitors, Amir," I whispered tearfully. "You were delving into people's hearts in order to confirm their intentions. Isn't that right?"

"I know," he said after a while.

"Do you know about the contents of my heart and what it has to endure? For your sake, I will suffer, I'll be patient. If you'd only promise to come back, to give me some hope . . ."

He brought my hand up to his mouth and kept it on his lips. "I wronged you once," he said, "but I can't do it again. Even my own egotism has its limits. If only you knew . . ."

I grabbed his hand. "Cruel injustice only ever happens once," I said, "but, after that, nothing is the way it was. It's gunfire, Amir, burning and destroying, leaving nothing to be saved or destroyed."

He pulled me toward him and hugged me. I leaned my head on his chest and placed my ear over his heart in the hope of finding what I was looking for.

"These are times of defeat and oblivion," I said. "Egypt is being hit by fire without a single scream being heard. I'm dying every single day, without a single scream. There's no point in blaming and censuring anyone."

I kissed the spot where his heart was. He hugged me tighter than ever before, till I thought that my ribs were going to crack and burn as well; I did not care. I put my arms round his back and whispered his name twice; once as Husam, then as Salar.

"You didn't respond, Amir," I said. "I'll ask you again. What happiness was there in making me suffer, and what kind of victory in my defeat? Did you come to pervade my every day, drown what remains of my heart, and then leave?"

"No, I came to explains things to you, in the hope that one day you'd understand. My marriage to you either today or yesterday would be exposing you to suffering at the hands of someone with no understanding or mercy. You're a fighter, Hind, and you always win. No fire can destroy you, no swords can scare you."

I kissed his chest. "If I were actually fighting swords and guns," I replied bitterly, "then I could stand it. But you've grabbed my very soul. I can't win."

He kissed my cheek and ear. "I long for you," he whispered.

"Who am I when compared with princesses and governors' daughters?" I asked. "My love, Amir, is a blend of doubt and despair. It inspires the soul all the time."

"There exists a soul as weak as Job's after he has been afflicted by adversity but with no assurance of redemption. Such a person is not a prophet. You were saying that the soul's defeat cannot be reversed. You've just said that."

"The war's over. Let's start again together."

"As far as I'm concerned," he replied bitterly, "it's not over. That would be the end for me. That's why I've come to see you."

I felt shattered, and a dark cloud descended on my heart. "I have a lot to tell you," I said.

He stroked his beard with my hair. "I know it all," he replied.

"For just once, let me decide."

"Don't ask about me or look into my situation," he declared firmly. "It's all over now. If times were more settled, I'd stay with you all the time, my entire life . . ."

He kissed my hand and let me go. "Get married," he said, "forget, and grab whatever happiness fate reluctantly lets you have. You have to grab it, Hind."

With that, he put me back on his horse and returned me to my home. He then vanished, just like life, heart, and soul.

Salar's Testimony (7)

We need to record what happened after that, Abu al-Barakat. Once the last Egyptian sultan had been killed, no other followed. There would be no other ruler with his proud mien. When he was killed and his corpse was hung up in front of his men for three days, we had either to take revenge or die. For a man, such shame is akin to castration. Death is the more merciful and honorable course. Salim Shah issued a general pardon to all Mamluks and Egyptians, but there was no mercy or sympathy involved; simply self-gratification and oppression. As a soldier himself, he knows the significance of loss and weakness. He had won the war by firepower, not through military strength. For us, war involves rituals and ceremonies, with its own morals and customs. People to whom we have given a pledge of security are not to be killed, and mosques and homes are not to be burned. The Egyptians realized that; they knew for sure who was for them and from their own number.

No, Abu al-Barakat, we refused to accept defeat. We three amirs never forgot our pledge. We would kill Salim Shah, and then the traitor. We planned an operation from which we knew that we would not emerge alive. Inal would make his way to Salim's encampment disguised as a reliable driver. Al-'Adili's and my role involved waiting till Salim transferred to the Nilometer with his entire camp. We would then swim across the river and get into his quarters from the Nilometer's base. While Inal was offering his soldiers water and wine, we would butcher some of them, then get inside and kill Salim Shah—or one of us would. There were three of us. We swore that any of us who fell into Ottoman hands would never abandon his companions, whatever the cost. The agreement was that anyone who did fall into Ottoman hands would never be tortured for years, have his limbs cut off or his guts cloven in two pieces. No, he would be killed on the spot. One of us would do the killing, as an act of mercy and loyalty to a friendship that had lasted for years and a lifelong rapport.

I realized that I was bound to die. I did not want Hind to be tied to me and to have Salar's name linked to her. The plan worked perfectly. While Inal distracted the guards, Al-'Adili and I swam across with our weapons. I went in first, had a fight with the guard, and killed him. I then moved on to the second and third guards; the target seemed really easy. Al-'Adili and I ran as fast as we could, and got to Salim. We heard his screams and saw his shocked expression. But one of the guards stabbed Inal in the arm and grabbed hold of him. The screams woke up a second and third guard.

"Get out of here," Al-'Adili yelled at me. "Quick, dive into the river."

He disappeared into the river. Before I did the same, I aimed one arrow at Inal's heart and another at Salim, but instead it hit a guard who was sacrificing himself for his commander. I dived into the river and heard gunfire as Salim ordered the guards to fire on us in the water. I was hit in the foot, but we continued swimming. For a while, we stayed underwater and then hid among the water-hyacinth.

I looked at Al-'Adili's face. He was panting as the river water dripped from his face and eyes.

"The arrow didn't hit Salim," I said.

"It didn't hit him," he repeated. "Did you kill Inal?"

"Yes," I replied.

He looked satisfied. "If we want to escape," he said, "then we need to hide from view and never get together till the crisis is over or we're gone."

For a moment, I thought about going back to Salim's tent. In my imagination, I could see myself pouncing on him and throttling him to death. Then, once he was dead, the guards would kill me. I would have throttled him, not killed him with a sword."

Al-'Adili raised his hand to start swimming away. "This completes the defeat," he said. "Do your best to stay alive, if you can . . ."

I watched as the gunfire hit the river waves, then quieted down, and gradually faded away. I could feel the bullets buzzing and the water boiling all around me. The darkness soaked up the sound of gunfire and rifle shots, erasing everything that was and had been.

Words were ringing in my ears; imagination shrouded my eyes and erased the path. I kept seeing my hands around Salim's neck and watched as soldiers threw Inal's corpse into the river. If only I could swim back now and get to Salim! Why run away when there was no escape from death and bodily demise was blessing, relief, and deliverance? I was aware that I might have lost my mind for a while. Killing Salim now was just as impossible to achieve as victory. Recovering those moments of achievement was impossible too; moments when Egyptians and Mamluks had come together, Mamluks had donned peasant clothing, Egyptians had clasped Mamluk swords. All injustice, anger, and pride had vanished. Just then, we had been victorious, if only for a while. After such a triumph, defeat's impact was that much harsher, as heavy as elephants and hippopotami.

Then Al-'Adili and I fled.

That day, I had been hit on the left foot and had killed my friend with my own hand. It may have calmed my troubled soul, but my sorrow only intensified.

Thereafter, every Friday was equally miserable: all hope dissipated, and the sense of defeat was total.

I fled to the mountains and headed for Abu as-Su'ud al-Jarihi, the holy man of God. I stayed there for a while, but at first he would not talk to me. He let me share his domicile without saying a word. A day later, I asked him if my presence was annoying him.

"Everywhere is God's place," he replied. "How can I be angry when this place isn't mine? We come to believe that places and things belong to us, but then we die. We either leave them all behind, or else some stupid foe grabs them, apparently thrilled to own something that won't last. The material of this lower world seems near, but is far distant; it can't be seized or controlled. Stay anywhere you wish, my son. Both you and I are borrowing from God."

I said the prayers behind the shaykh, then sat in front of him, my expression completely grief-stricken. To tell you the truth, I wept, maybe for the first time, with no feeling of shame or humiliation. Shaykh Al-Jarihi is not like other human beings: his soul is pure and has transcended the details of the ephemeral life that neither eats from hunger nor drinks from thirst.

He massaged my shoulder without saying anything. I had a great deal pent up inside me. The defeat was mine alone, or at least that is what seemed clear to me. The traitor had been the winner, and the greedy commander had emerged victorious. They had even burned buildings. If they had been able to cart off the pyramids' stones, they would have done it.

"If you could confirm that the world was just a silly game," he went on after a while, "you would not be weeping. If you realized that it was all vanity, then you could move beyond your grief to something loftier and more significant. Wars, my son, are a game in the hands of men. Winners and losers return to their places. After a while, the whole thing dissolves—no benefit to victory, no spoils compensate. Did you not realize that you were dead and so were they? Come to see me after a while, and we can talk again. You wanted to slay the traitor and invader, didn't you, but you did not succeed. The soldier inside you won out, not the calligrapher who contemplates God's words. Recollect and understand, then be reassured and move on to another shore. If you don't kill the traitor, you'll die; if you don't kill the invader, you'll die. When the times comes, neither victory, territory, nor money will matter. This land that you're defending is wonderful and enduring, but we're ephemeral."

"My defeat is gnawing at my heart, leaving no place unsullied, like an attack of leprosy on the limbs."

"You've done what you have with a sound heart," the shaykh said. "Start afresh. That other game is over; the players have all gone home. Stop, and start again.

Victory comes in the beginning. By transcending defeat with patient resolution, you shame the enemy attacker."

I stopped crying. "It's that starting point that baffles me," I said quietly. "I can't work with the Ottomans. I can't pray for their sultan and eat at their tables. I can't die like Inal, and leave chaos all around me. If only I could be something other than a soldier, could stop riding horses with sword fights boiling and seething in my very veins. I'm not a hireling for the Ottomans, nor am I an Egyptian, an artisan, or a scholar."

He smiled. "You haven't crossed the river yet," he said. "You're only thinking about yourself and how to fill the cavity in your heart. You have yet to move beyond this world. Traverse the river of the heart to contentment; you'll get there."

"I don't possess your ability to turn away from the world."

"Set yourself to work and don't belittle it. It's not your heart's task to dictate to you who you are. Don't make it the stronger part; it's weak. Before achieving godliness, there is depravity."

"How can I do that?"

He smiled again. "Don't ask me about things I don't comprehend. Don't remind me about the mind's flaws and limitations. You need time. Fighting with swords is swift and simple. With the heart, the struggle is a lengthy journey, a crossing, and a sacrifice."

<hr />

Al-Jarihi, that man of God, left me for several days without saying a word. He would contemplate, read, and eat only a little. Occasionally, he would go out into the desert wastes, and only come back after a day or two. I remembered days gone by; the world was in my arms, and my legs could extend all the way to the clouds. We were three, laughing together and playing a lot. At the time, none of us was thinking about death or evanescence. Hours were witness to our frivolity, self-confidence, and indifference to authority, and to the lure of weapons. The three of us would go out together to hunt, relishing the desolate surroundings and talking about what was to come. We would seize opportunities, pounce on animals, declare war on clouds, and win.

The entire world was subject to our will. Everything in it was goods and wheat that we would purchase, sell, and distribute to our friends. We would return from our hunts with spoils, go to music halls, listen to the singing, and enjoy the dances. We would select the women we wanted for a day or three, then exchange them and purchase some fresh, attractive slut who was calling out to passersby. There were times when we would purchase the world, without realizing that it does not like to be fettered. It would slip between our hands without our hearing or seeing.

It would take revenge, and bang us hard on the head. Self-confidence and ability would crumble.

A few days later, the shaykh came over and looked at my foot. "You're neglecting it," he said. "You need to treat it. It needs to be amputated."

I looked at him, but his words did not surprise me. "The wound fractured the bone in my foot," I said. "Gun wounds are hopeless. They destroy, then the wound gets infected."

"My son," he told me thoughtfully, "when that happens, you have to amputate. Otherwise you'll die. When a wound's infected, it poisons the whole body."

"I know," I replied firmly.

"If you know, then why haven't you done something about it? I wonder, are you supposing the amputation will kill your injured soul and help you forget the defeat? The amputation will involve your foot, not your mind or your heart. Do you realize that?"

"Yes, I do."

"It's your pride that can't accept defeat."

"It's not in my hands. I've tried."

"You've deceived yourself. It's making you think you're still capable. You haven't realized how feeble and weak you are. It's all fate, I've told you that. The only people who emerge defeated are those who've already lost their own soul."

With that, he grabbed a knife carefully, stuck it in the fire, then amputated my foot at the ankle. He cauterized the veins and closed up the wound. I did not scream, but it did feel as though a raffia rope was strangling me. I cleared my throat to get my breathing regular again, and sucked all the air out of my lungs, hoping that some fresh air would clear my chest. With vomit all over my chest, I cleared my throat again and took another deep breath as he plunged the knife into my flesh. I cannot recall how I managed to endure such pain; at the time, defeat had robbed me of my mind, like poisoned wine. I lay flat on my back, staring at the distant horizon. I was thinking about this shaykh, who had grabbed the knife so cautiously, as though he were planning to cut off the sultan's head in front of his own soldiers. He had clearly never done an amputation before, nor had he killed or slaughtered anyone. His hand was shaking, and he did not do a competent or professional job. He kept reciting Qur'anic verses and asking me to suffer in patience. My mind was far away, and I could remember my mother's steady gaze . . . my mother, I can't even remember her all that well.

He looked at me. "Did you want to die, my son?" he asked. "Did you let the wound fester with a personal goal in mind?"

I was still staring at the distant horizon. "You spend a lot of time contemplating, Shaykh," I said, "but you're not good at surgery. You're asking me that question after reassuring yourself that I'm safely relieved of my heart's secret longings which I haven't achieved."

He massaged my shoulder. "You put up with all the pain without a single scream," he said. "Be patient and take stock. It's only proud hearts that suffer the world's degradation and the braggart's success, but they never submit. Even when the conflict is over, they can still appreciate the significance of great triumph and the soul's desire to please God."

I smiled bitterly. "How many people have you killed?" I asked.

He was stunned. "Is killing someone that easy?" he replied. "If I were to kill anyone, it would be my own self and part of me. The truth has created us from a single self."

"It's all fated," I replied at once. "You've never killed anyone or done any surgery. If you'd studied surgery, Shaykh, you could have spared me all that pain. But you're no good at it."

"Forgive me, my son. I didn't mean to cause you that much pain."

"I'm not blaming you, Shaykh. Your discernment surpasses that of others. You know what I mean."

Our eyes met. "I hope I'm wrong in my understanding," he replied sadly.

He prepared some food for me. "When you've eaten, pray and ask God," he said. "Maybe memory will help you."

I looked at him. "Will you lead the prayer?" I asked.

He smiled. "Some prayers promote serenity, while others inject life into the heart. In such prayers, you need to pray on your own. It is the process of harmony between you and God that brings healing, mercy, and control. No imam can intercede, and no congregation will come to your aid. You need that control over the unruly heart and the shadows of His mercy cast over the vagrant soul."

I nodded in agreement. I took a look at the remains of my now severed foot and envisaged it as Mamluk heads hanging on Salim's gateways.

If only I had managed to kill Salim Shah before I killed Inal! If only I had thought about the thing we had come there to do and sacrificed the horseman! Maybe Salim would have survived and Inal been tortured—who knows? That day, I prayed and kept my head close to the ground, as the smell of soil injected some life into the dying mind.

I can recall the day: three children. One of them was crying nonstop, calling for his mother, and cursing the man who had sold him and forever changed his lot in life. That had been Inal. Another one stayed riveted to the spot as he was sold; that was me. Do you want the details, Abu al-Barakat, so you can record them in your book? I will tell you about a child who was not snatched from his mother's breast and did not run away from the slave traders. I will tell you about a child whose mother woke up in the morning, helped him put on his best clothes, and combed his hair.

"What do you see?" she asked him, looking all around her.

"Our house," he replied involuntarily.

"It's a den where not even mice want to live."

I did not understand. I noticed that the roof was threadbare, high, and distant. I had not seen or even met my father. He seemed to have disappeared before I was born. I saw brothers and sisters, lots of them. My mother clasped my hand.

"You're going to sleep on silk," she told me enthusiastically in a tone of voice I can never forget. "You're going to become an amir like the ones in Egypt. You're going to escape and be happy."

I did not understand her. I had no idea where Egypt was.

She kept holding my hand the whole way. Every time I tried to pull it away, she clasped it tighter. When we reached the market, she opened her left hand, which was large with powerful fingers and nails full of the clay that she worked with every day. A man placed a money purse in her hand. She took it and turned to me.

"Go with him," she told me. "Don't look for me or be angry with me. You don't know."

I did not cry at that point. That lofty ceiling came crashing down on my head, and the earth shook.

"Mother!" I said as she vanished from in front of me.

With that, she ran. I have often imagined her weeping, regretting, and missing me. I never told Inal or Qansuh al-'Adili that I had not been kidnapped by slave traders as they had. My mother had sold me. She had to have chosen me because I was stronger and worthier to become an amir; she was thinking about me, my life, and my future. She made a sacrifice for my sake and deprived herself of her heart's own darling. Her heart was still a void. Once in a while, I wondered if she had not really wanted me, and I had done something to really annoy her. But such doubts did not linger, and only forced themselves upon me on those occasions when defeat materialized and the dim glow of impotence shone forth.

After a while, one, two, three days, I was aware of him stroking my head.

"The fever's gone," he told me.

Sweat was pouring off me as I turned my head to look at him. "How long has it been?" I asked.

"Two days," he said. "You were speaking in Turkish. Do you know it well?"

"Yes, we all do."

"You were calling out to someone in particular. When people have a fever, my son, the truth always comes out. We remember those people who overwhelmed us with injustice, and other with passion. Both remain in the memory. If you could be sure that His love was enduring and all other loves were transient, then you would be able to achieve tranquility."

I did not respond. I could not remember whom I was calling.

Shaykh Al-Jarihi kept reciting Imam Al-Shafi'i's verses in a melodious tone. I repeated them, sometimes not understanding them at all, while, at others, doing my best to understand—but, at all events, with an unprecedented level of appreciation:

Let the days do as they will;
Should fate so decree, then be of good cheer.
Be not alarmed by the events of time,
For this world's happenings are not ever here.

The Testimony of the Translator
Mustafa Pasha Al-'Uthmani (7)

One of the traits of the King of Kings was his mercy; he was always magnanimous. As you know, Abu al-Barakat, some Mamluk amirs were angry after the defeated sultan was killed. They tried to kill the King of Kings; you must have heard about that major event. They came very close to achieving their goal; in fact, I have never seen the King of Kings as shocked as I saw him that day. God curse treachery and its practitioners! They are without religion or homeland, those Mamluks, no sense of loyalty and no mind, did you but realize it. A widespread ignorance of infectious diseases and their epidemics must have affected the Egyptian people, so they now need someone who will make them see and understand after they have spent a period of time neither understanding nor discriminating good from evil. As yet, we do not know who dared to commit this crime. One of the Mamluks died before he could talk, and Khayir Bey was unable to identify the culprit. He had brought a number of Mamluk amirs to stand in front of the King of Kings and proclaim their allegiance. The King of Kings pardoned them, a whole lot of them. One of them was an amir named Qansuh al-'Adili, whom Khayir Bey brought to stand before the King of Kings. As I recall, he had disappeared to Upper Egypt and was living with the Bedouin. Khayir Bey interceded with the King of Kings on his behalf. To tell you the truth, Abu al-Barakat, I do not have a great deal of respect for Khayir Bey. He reminds me of the desert snakes that I have seen during our travels in Egypt. His twisted methods were very different from my own, whether in war or peace. I preferred honesty and frankness when dealing with friend or foe. I have no idea what made Khayir Bey focus his attention on this particular amir, but I was led to understand that he was arranging a governorship or other post for him.

The King of Kings demanded that Qansuh al-'Adili come before him and ask for forgiveness for the things that he had done during the resistance and fighting in Cairo. Failing that, he intended to tear him apart and impale him, then kill his entire family in front of him before parading them around the streets of Cairo. I heard that Khayir Bey spoke to Qansuh al-'Adili for a whole day (or half a day), then told him to shave off his beard because that reminded Salim Shah of the Mamluks. He ordered Qansuh to swear allegiance to Salim Shah. I was present at the time and watched as Qansuh al-'Adili, whom I believed to be a powerful amir, entered with Khayir Bey. He greeted Salim Shah.

"I was wrong," Qansuh al-'Adili said. "I've come to beg for forgiveness and pardon."

Salim thought things over for a while. "Killing you would serve as a warning," he said, "but victory leaves a sweet taste in my mouth. I don't want to spoil it. If you swore allegiance and you and your soldiers worked with me, your life could still see its triumphs."

"I'll do it at once," Al-'Adili replied.

"Will you come to Istanbul with me?"

Silence ensued.

"No, my Lord," Khayir Bey said, "he should stay here and help us. His presence here represents a triumph for you of unprecedented proportions. I know him. By pardoning him, you're providing a model for all recalcitrant Mamluk amirs. Caliph of all Muslims, they will be saying that Al-'Adili the rebel asked the caliph for forgiveness, stayed in his presence, and kissed his hands in obeisance. From today on, there'll be no more opposition."

Salim thought for a moment. "You own an estate and soldiers, don't you?" he asked.

"They're at your disposal, my Lord."

"They'll stay at my disposal. Half the revenues will go to the janissaries for a ten-year period. Swear to that."

"I swear."

With that, Al-'Adili bent over and kissed the sultan's hand. I could see his resentful expression, facial scowl, and deep-seated hatred. Those amirs have no sense of loyalty. I walked with him and Khayir Bey to the palace gate.

"Today you've saved yourself," I heard Khayir Bey tell him.

"I know," Al-'Adili replied gratefully.

"There was an attempt to kill the Kings of King. Do you know anything about it?"

"I swear, I know nothing about it."

As Al-'Adili left the sultan's quarters, I could see the rancor in his expression. He may have saved his life, but there was little gratitude in his heart. You can write that in your book, Abu al-Barakat: however you treat slaves, they will never show any gratitude.

Salar's Testimony (8)

After a while, I went back to Cairo to look for Al-'Adili and get his news. I knew that Khayir Bey had arrested him, then released him the same day. He had promised him a governorship and other benefits. I also knew that Khayir Bey was looking for me, desiring to build bridges to a friendly encounter. I realized what his intentions had been and was aware of his goals now. I never despised someone as much as him. And yet, it was a visit that was inevitable, as inevitable as visiting the dirty tombs of people you do not even know.

He shook my hand warmly and asked how I was. "What happened to the Mamluk amir?" he asked, looking straight at me. "He's lost a foot? Was it during the fighting, or was he running away from something?"

"For commanders," I replied coldly, "losing a limb is a mark of honor. Always better than surrendering."

He smiled. "Well," he said, "you've surrendered and lost your foot. You've managed to do both, Salar. I've been looking for you for quite a while. I wanted to talk to you."

"I know. That's why I've come. But I've no idea what the governor of Egypt wants with me."

Silence prevailed.

"I did what I did," he said, "to save the Mamluks. I realized that, if we didn't surrender, they'd all be killed."

"The Mamluks didn't surrender."

He ignored my response.

"After I'd interceded on their behalf," he continued, "Salim Shah pardoned them. There can be no Egypt without Mamluks. I defended them for Egypt's sake."

"Without Egypt," I stated firmly, "there would be no Mamluks."

"They're going to rule for many centuries, and history will recall the true purpose of what I did. I made the right decision in a moment of crisis. You can govern with me. We can work together as we did in the past. I realize, Sa'adat is expecting you . . ."

"Governor of Egypt," I replied thoughtfully, "once the keys to the Ka'ba were in our treasury, you started getting orders from Istanbul. What honor can there be in that? You've shut the gates of glory and opened others for dependency and darkness. Dependency means darkness. Mamluks before the invasion are not the same as they are after it."

"Poetic words do not suit a warrior."

"To the contrary, the warrior knows the difference between those who will cooperate with you and those who will refuse."

"Those who work with me will guarantee that the government of Egypt will return to the Mamluks at some point. Those who refuse realize that they're inevitably beaten. You'll understand that one day and realize that it's true—after a year, five years, a hundred . . . You'll realize that Egypt is the Mamluks, and the Mamluks are Egypt."

"I know and realize full well that their influence will never wane," I replied emphatically. "Their properties will never be touched. They're good at Arabic and work well with Egyptians. They'll be effective rulers. But now, Mamluks are people who have had to deal with defeat and are used to treachery. I cannot work with them. Let me leave in peace. You can govern, and I'll have my own life."

"Your life won't be the same, Salar," he said. "You can either be an amir, with troops to defend the country, or a defeated soldier, with no troops or weapons."

I looked down. "Do you want an amir with troops to defend the sultan in Istanbul," I asked, "as though I'm protecting a brothel with my sword until the whole thing is over?"

"How dare you!"

"Someone who has no troops or anything to be scared of can dare, Bey. You have soldiers. If you so much as touch my wealth, I'll fight you to the very last day of my life and turn every Mamluk amir against you. They'll say that Khayir Bey is grabbing the amir's money and collecting it to send to the sultan in Istanbul."

"You deserve everything that's happened to you, and more. It's the victor who deserves to succeed."

"Victors are people deluded by time for a while, as it toys with their greed."

"So now, you've turned into a Sufi! Where's the Salar who used to grab everything he set his eyes on?"

"There's no longer any justification for recklessness and acquisition."

For a few seconds, he was silent. "Sa'adat wants to see you," he said.

I did not respond.

"If it wasn't for her," he said in a slimy tone, "I would kill you once, maybe twice. If not for her, I would split your head open and take the brains out for soldiers to cook."

"The living emerge from the dead," I said, "and the dead from the living."

"What do you mean?"

"Your daughter is a blessing from God."

"Do you still want her?"

"I have no experience with the dictates of the governor of Egypt's daughter. Marry her off to one of the Ottomans you're working with."

"No, I'm going to marry her to someone a thousand times better than you, someone with a complete body, not crippled."

Our eyes met. "When I marry her off, Salar," Khayir Bey went on, "it'll be to someone who will bring your defeat to completion and remind you of what was."

"Such a man doesn't exist," I responded.

I walked over to the door and saw her standing there, with a pained expression and frowning visage.

We greeted each other. "I wish you well," I told her affectionately.

"I cannot be well," she replied quietly, "when I am far away from you."

"Your father wants a whole man for you," I said firmly, "not a cripple like me."

"My father wants the best for me. You're the best for me, Salar. Don't let hatred change our hearts. What's happened has happened, and it's over."

"Forgive me my selfishness," I replied, meaning everything I was saying, "and my inability to forgive. It's a calamity and a sin, but there's nothing I can do about it. You'll be fine and safe inside palace walls. Forgive me, Princess."

With that, she left. I was looking for the three horsemen, but did not find them.

BOOK THREE

DAYS GONE BY

We were three horsemen crossing the bridge together. The beast emerged from the depths and breathed fire on the bridge. It collapsed, or almost.

Salar the Mamluk

Hind's Testimony (9)

After my meeting with him, Aunt, I went back like someone touched by magic. I felt sure he was going to do something risky; nothing would stop him. He might be killed before I had the chance to tell him what he had done to me and what had happened; the event that had come to fruition inside my heart and soul. How cruel that amir was, in victory and defeat, in war and peace, in love and hate. When my father asked me yet again to give Ziyad a chance and take my own initiative, I replied firmly that I could not do it. My father seemed to understand and did not force me. He is a scholar and shaykh, who writes history and knows the laws and pressures that impact the heart.

Salar asked to meet me, and he did.

He clutched my chest to bury it in his, and he did so.

He had come to tell me to forget him. He did that too.

He knew I could not do that.

On the day the sultan died, he both saw me and did not. It was as though somehow he had lost all feeling; I cannot be sure.

When I searched for his heartbeat, I found some reassurance.

He must not have forgotten me. I had the sensation of him being around me all the time. Can the heart be deceitful? If it were your heart, Aunt, why would it deceive you? Do you understand?

He had wronged me twice, and the second time was even more cruel, if only you realized. The first time, he subdued my body in spite of me; the second time he subdued my heart, again in spite of me.

Every time I recalled what had happened between us from the very beginning, I had the feeling that a huge falcon had snatched me up, clasping my head in its talons. It had taken me and flown over the whole of existence, with me screaming. Then it had dropped me and let me plunge into the river where I had drowned. But if only he had let me drown. He had plunged in, searched, and pulled me out before it was all over. He was still hovering over my existence; I had found no peace, and he had not let me die.

At first, for him I was simply a piece of property, like all the women in his life. I was a thing, no more. He neither thought about nor understood my suffering. But then, he changed. I realized that he had changed. He loosened his grip and opened his hand, revealing a generous side, someone who knew neither generosity nor mercy. What can I say, Aunt? He made me mourn what was lost and what remained.

My mind was left wavering between doubt and certainty. I did my best to gather up the remains of the story, just as I had watched Mamluk wives collecting the remains of their husbands' corpses. He was in disguise, and had rescued me. Why had he kidnapped me? He had lots of slave girls; maybe he had been looking for some distraction in Balbis while all his slave girls were back in Cairo. Who knows? I have no idea how men think. Perhaps treating me badly gave him some kind of entertainment and even relief for his anxious soul. Why did he force himself on me, when there were all those other women who were eager to attract his attention? Was he actually playing some kind of game part of the time, as though he were on a hunting trip with his friends? Would he come back loaded down with birds and animals, stuffing some and cooking others? Perhaps I will never really understand.

A few days later, I received some news that shocked me and made me believe my father about fate's creative instincts and the fragrance of miracles. Sitt ad-dar came to visit me again for no particular reason or justification. There was no friendship between us, and we had nothing to say to each other. Even so, I received her. Day after day, she kept coming to see me. It was later that I discovered that she had persuaded Ziyad to be married to her. Can you believe that, Aunt? A relative told me that he had been sitting with my father every day. On her first visit, she had greeted my father when Ziyad was there with him. In him she had discovered her target, and she came back again in the hope of seeing him. She saw him, spoke to him, and told him how she had suffered at the hands of the Ottoman soldiers. That is what my relative told me. Ziyad's heart softened. He was already troubled because I had refused to be married to him, and felt an obligation toward an Egyptian girl for a sin which was in no way her fault. He decided to be married to her, and my relative informed me that they had actually been married a few days earlier. I was outraged and furious at her deceit. I told my father what the story was with her and what I had to do. I told my father that she had deceived that poor man. My father listened to me.

"The marriage has happened, Hind," he told me. "I can't do anything now. He knows that the child she's carrying is not his, and he's agreed to that. I don't need to cause a scandal or talk about women's honor."

My father was right. I smiled sarcastically at the "wonders of fate." I felt really sorry for Ziyad, poor man with his simplicity and pure heart. I hoped that Sitt ad-dar would realize the enormity of her outrage and sin, and turn out to be a loyal wife. I was by no means convinced that she would be that, either today or the next day. I was afraid that my own rejection of Ziyad had been the reason for his rapid marriage. I begged God for forgiveness if I had done wrong, but I was still unable to contemplate getting married.

Salar's Testimony (9)

The things that happened after all that, Abu al-Barakat, were a continuation and maturation of the defeat. You realize, Shaykh, that we soldiers have no idea of the impact of killing when we are doing it, nor do we realize the weight of loss involved. We have learned that there is no loss in death; that is decreed by fate. Salim may have been a soldier who killed people in cold blood, and then strutted his way through the streets of Cairo in celebration of his triumph. When people started laughing at him in their grief, he squelched their laughter and decided to ban shadow-theater performances throughout Egypt. No fun, no argument. It was a time just for eclipse and burial. Excuse me, Abu al-Barakat: the conflict was one thing, and its consequences were another. The invader stole gold and silver and left with ships loaded with our treasures. He stole marble from mosques and even from the Citadel which he ordered to be broken off and loaded on his ships. He stole mosque lanterns, even brass-inlaid wooden doors. He stole all that; indeed he forced Alfi, my own craftsman, to go with him. 'Abdallah, my own teacher, was one of them too. None of them had any choice, 'Abdallah and his craftsmen sons. The Ottomans dragged him in and asked him to provide a guarantor. He brought his son, and the same thing happened. Then he brought in his other sons as well. Ottoman chains were wrapped around them, and they were on their way. I saw the dead expression on his wife's face in their house; he offered to let her come with them, but the sultan gave him no choice. If he refused to go, the sultan was going to kill him or kill his guarantor, namely his own son. That day, I was there in order to bid him farewell. I expected 'Adlat to travel with him; he was all she had. But she shook her head to left and right.

"I'm not leaving my country," she insisted.

"Umm 'Ali," he told her bitterly, "we've no choice."

"'Ali's dead."

"Come with me. The ship's waiting, and all the children are going. Don't stay here with no husband or children."

She did not hear what he had said. He yelled in her ear. When she did hear, she gestured with her hand.

"Go where you're told," she said, "and leave me here. I'm not going to work for people who have killed my children. I'd much prefer to die here."

'Adlat had a warrior's determination. I promised 'Abdallah that I would take care of her and not leave her. 'Abdallah and his sons left. I was still searching for my comrade, Qansuh al-'Adili, the only one now left from the time when a plan had been hatched by a clever draftsman.

Several months later, I heard the details of Qansuh al-'Adili's arrest and subsequent release. He had spoken to Khayir Bey, who had convinced him that there was no point in fighting the new sultan. He should ask for a pardon, which the sultan duly gave him after Qansuh had promised to work with him and acknowledge him as sultan. It seemed that he too had no other choice.

I had to check on Inal's wife and three children and make sure they were well. I already knew what had happened to his wife: prison, humiliation, torture, abuse. The children were living on the streets or in the Citadel prisons. For several days, I went to the prison where Khundtatar was imprisoned and demanded to see her. After I had paid some bribes, the soldiers allowed me inside. I went in to see her. It was actually the very first time I had set eyes on her; she came out with her face uncovered and a veil wrapped around her head. She looked exhausted, and her eyes were not focused.

"You're Amir Salar," she said, "Inal's friend."

"You're going to get out," I told her firmly. "Don't be alarmed. Today or tomorrow, I promise you. Where are your children? I didn't find them inside the palace."

She looked all around her. "Did you see him before he died?" she asked me.

Our eyes met. "Yes, I did," I replied. "He asked after you, and entrusted your care to me. He loved you, Khund, and valued you greatly."

Her tears fell. "How did he die?" she asked.

For a moment, I said nothing. "He was completely surrounded by soldiers," I said, "and fighting them off. He managed to kill a lot of them, but then one soldier stabbed him in the heart and another in the back. He fell to the ground and died instantly. He died as a hero, after courageously killing many soldiers. I was with him and saw it all."

"Where's his corpse?" she asked.

"I drowned it in the river so the soldiers would not mutilate it."

"Where was that?"

Her questions were beginning to get on my nerves.

"You'll be getting out," I said.

"Can you get me out?"

"I'll do it before tomorrow. Where are the children?"

"With a slave girl whom I trust. I'll give you her name. I've asked to talk to Salim."

For a moment, I thought she had lost her mind. "Which Salim?" I asked.

"Salim Shah."

"Whom did you ask?"

"The guards. Which sultan puts women in prison and tortures them for the sake of gold and silver?"

"That'll never happen," I told her. "What ruler will ever respond to a prisoner's request to meet him? Wait for just a day. I'll get you out tomorrow, I promise."

"One of his men is coming today to talk to me," she confirmed.

She seemed to be talking nonsense. I did not want to waste time talking, and agreed with the guards to smuggle her out before dawn. But the guard was shocked when he came to me and said that he had not found her in her cell.

I do not know, Abu al-Barakat, whether to laugh or cry. I heard what had happened from some guards and spies. Maybe you want to know so you can write it down in your book. Or perhaps you would rather meet her or him. Who knows?

I will tell you what happened.

It seems that Khundtatar's tears were combined with the money that she promised to some of the guards. She asked them to bring one of the king's and new sultan's men so that she could tell him about the unjust way that she had been treated. The information reached Mustafa Pasha, the translator who accompanied Salim everywhere. He decided to meet her so as to put an end to her nagging requests. He decided to punish her and order that she be whipped because she was roiling the atmosphere for the sultan and his men. Mustafa Pasha went to see her.

"Stop complaining," he told her dryly, a frown on his face. "You're no different from everyone else. All the wives of slain Mamluks are in prison. Why do you want to meet the sultan's men?"

Khundtatar did not respond. Mustafa Pasha looked up and noticed her face, her long, chestnut-colored hair, and the tears glistening in her wide eyes.

"What do you want?" he asked gently.

Her voice was all sorrow and weakness. "They've sent the very best of men to meet me," she said softly. "Is that to make me suffer even more in my total loneliness? They have deceived me and told me that Ottoman soldiers are cruel and uncouth, whereas I'm only used to dealing with determined fighters and attractive saviors."

"What's all that rubbish, woman?" he responded angrily. "How dare you speak like that!"

She bent over and kissed his hand. "My Lord, she said gently, "I just want to fill my eyes with your lovely face. I want to tell you about someone who has been humiliated after a life of glory and who now spends her days alone and unjustly treated in your prison."

Mustafa Pasha looked at her in shock. Like many sons of the people, she was speaking fluent Turkish.

"I've given money to the soldiers," she told him imperiously, "so that I could complain to you about my situation."

He looked all around him, then fixed his gaze on her. "You want to get out of prison?" he asked.

"That's what I was hoping for," she said, "but now I'm not so sure. If I get out, then I won't see your lovely face again. If you wanted gold, my Lord, I could tell you where it is. You deserve it, but I gave it to the soldiers."

The soldiers shared those words with each other and were hesitant as they gestured to each other: "If you wanted gold, my Lord, I could tell you where it is. You deserve it." They talked about how perplexed and tense Mustafa Pasha looked. Her beauty, it seems, was enough to make a man lose his mind. A few days later, I learned that Mustafa Pasha had been married to Khundtatar and brought her children into his own palace. Sultan Salim was not happy about the marriage. The idea that Ottoman soldiers should marry Mamluk widows did not appeal to him. However, the situation was unusual, and shaykhs contracted a number of marriages that way. I will not hide from you, Abu al-Barakat, that I was very annoyed and accused her of treason and vulgarity. Now however, I have a different take on things. Even though I will never forgive her for being married to an Ottoman, I cannot say for certain that it was treason. It seems that she was a woman with nothing but her beauty, with three children who would be lost without her. Even if I had managed to get her out, I would not have been able to guarantee her a life of honor and security all the time. She joined the victorious army so as to carry on, or so that her children could carry on. Was that because she loved Inal, or because she did not care about him? I do not know. I have never understood women; everything they do is unexpected. If she had been my wife, I would have risen from my grave to slaughter her, then died again and rested in peace. Every time I recalled how loyal to her Inal was and how he refused to purchase a single slave girl, I smile bitterly. What went on deep inside her is difficult to understand and evaluate.

Hind's Testimony (10)

I was asleep on my bed as usual. My mind kept wandering as I waited for news about him. Sometimes, Aunt, I was certain that he adored me even more than I did him, but there were other times when I thought that he did not care about me, but only thought about his defeat and himself. Then he came.

He arrived with no advance warning. He knocked on the door and asked for my father, Ibn Iyas. My heart leaped in both fear and delight. I clasped the wooden window frame with quivering fingers and recited some Qur'anic verses. I hoped that my heart was right about his reason for coming and that my father would be able to forgive . . . I took some deep breaths so as not to faint and tried to hear what they were saying.

"I've come to ask for your daughter's hand in marriage."

"Another man has made that request, and everything's settled."

For a moment, he said nothing. "Has she agreed?"

"Do I have to answer your questions, Amir?"

I was stunned and put my hand over my mouth as I did my best to control my anxiety.

"I deserve her more than he does," Salar stated.

"You have no rights regarding her or me," my father said decisively.

"Listen to me, Abu al-Barakat," Salar went on, "I want her. I've wanted her from the very beginning. I was afraid that, if she were linked to me, she would be maltreated. I was thinking about her and her safety."

"You were thinking about her and her safety!" my father replied in a fury I had never seen before. "By God, if I didn't know what happened, I would kill you now, here in my own house and in front of my children."

"Abu al-Barakat!"

"You did not deal honorably with her," my father went on. "You did not treat her fairly and were unable to differentiate between a free woman and a slave girl."

"Indeed, I realize that," Salar responded clearly. "It wasn't just that I was confused. Those were times of defeat that only made the confusion and desperation even worse."

"Are those days at an end?"

"No, Abu al-Barakat, they're just beginning. But now I know a lot more."

"What do you know?"

He looked down for a while. "I realize that those times of confusion and desperation will be much easier for me if Hind is with me. When she was, Shaykh, those were the best of times. You're a shrewd man and can tell the difference between truth and falsehood. I swear to you that I'll take care of her and treat her like a princess."

"What about your wife?"

"I haven't had a wife for some time."

"Why did you divorce her?"

"Doubt was all that kept us together. It was her father who separated us, the same way that wars separate soldiers and their land."

"You're leaving the governor of Egypt's daughter? You must be thinking of going back to her."

"You and I both know how he became governor of Egypt. Egypt doesn't have to kowtow to traitors."

"What crime did his daughter commit?"

"Predestined fate. Living together became impossible. It wasn't her fault. Her father built the ramparts."

"How many slave girls do you own?" he asked after a while.

"I no longer own any, nor do I plan to buy any."

"Why do you want my daughter? Is it your conscience that has brought you here or some other reason that I don't know?"

For a few seconds I stopped breathing. My whole body was shaking.

"Your daughter has a free heart and proud soul," he replied. "She will always be reminding me of my defeat and will give me hope that my own free spirit has not been vanquished. I need both memory and hope."

My father seemed to be affected by what I had said. "She'll never agree," he said.

"I'll ask her myself."

"Don't you trust me? The way you treated her is worse than anything the janissaries do."

"That's all in the past; such things often happen in wartime. In desperate times, insanity and desire regularly show themselves."

"Are you sorry?"

Salar did not reply. I started pounding my mouth with my hand. I wanted my father to say yes, but he did not.

My father asked the question again. "You're asking me a question that I don't want to answer," Salar replied. "If I do, I'll be lying, and I've sworn to tell the truth in front of you."

"So you're not sorry?"

He did not respond. I saw that my father was on the point of getting up and attacking him, but my elder brother grabbed him. "Calm down, Father," he said, "and listen to him."

"If I could have been married to her before," Salar said, "I would have done it. I didn't want to hurt her. Even now, I realize that life with me is a hardship and that the person whom you have chosen for her is better than me. He'll never have to live amid the folds of defeat and the burning fires of despair. But selfishness always dominates, and the life-instinct always triumphs over the desire for oblivion."

"It's as though you've saved her in order to torture her slowly."

Silence ensued. "I'll give it some thought," my father said, "and I'll ask her."

"Let's do that now," Salar said vigorously.

My father gave him a defiant stare. "I'll ask her and let you know her response," he said.

Salar retorted in the same tone. "Forgive me, Abu al-Barakat," he said. "I've lost a great deal in life, and I don't want to spend the rest of it waiting."

My father stood up and moved closer to him. "I'm not one of your soldiers to be ordered around, Amir," he said softly. "I told you I'll think about it and give you a reply in a few days."

I really wanted to talk to Salar and give him a hug. I was eager to quench the flames of my fear and longing. I lowered my head, realizing that my father would be speaking to me.

Salar left, and my father came into my room. "I've come to see you," he said despairingly, "but I already know the answer. Passions of the heart always win over the mind."

"Father," I pleaded, "you know people and can assess their hearts. Has he been truthful with you?"

He was silent for a moment. "He doesn't tell lies," he said, "but he's boastful and self-centered. Or, at least, he was before the defeat. Most of the time, defeat will crush conceit and promote self-denial. Aren't you worried, Hind, about his amputated foot?"

"No, I'm not," I replied sorrowfully.

"Living with a defeated soldier could be hell itself," he told me after a pause. "As far as he's concerned, the fighting isn't over. The words have never left his mouth, and life has not stabilized. He'll be hurting you as well as himself."

"It's not his fault," I replied. "He fought and did his best."

"I realize that. I want you to know and to be patient. You've chosen to live in the caged lion's den. Can you train him?"

"I'm going to try," I replied eagerly.

"His affection for you may well save you from his despair and greed. The only thing that will come to your aid will be the variety of feelings he has for you. Have you realized that? Whatever happens, you must make sure that he still feels that way."

"I understand what you mean, Father," I replied. "He fought for all of us."

"He lost his foot for all of us and for Egypt."

"Yes, and that's in his favor."

A few days later, my father asked him to come and hear my response for himself. Salar lost patience and asked him what my reply was. My father refused to tell him and asked him to come to the house. My father sat down and seated me next to him. When Salar came in, all words disappeared, leaving only eyes and hearts. For several minutes, we did not speak, but then, my father spoke to him.

"Amir," he said, "you've come to ask my daughter for her opinion. Do you remember?"

"Yes, of course," Salar replied impatiently. "Your father says that someone has come to ask for your hand in marriage."

He looked at my father who seemed to be reading a book and not looking at him. He looked furious; it seemed that he had run out of patience.

"When I asked you to continue our relationship," he went on angrily, "I imagined that you would wait. But it seems as though women can forget quickly and erase anything that spoils their life."

"I didn't expect to be blamed, Amir," I responded firmly.

"You can't discard everything that we had between us like a piece of rotten meat," he went on angrily, "and then get married."

For the first time, I realized that I possessed a certain degree of power in this situation. "What if I did? I could do that, you know. You saw me, and pretended not to know me. You abandoned me with no promise and no hope. I'll do whatever I want."

He looked all around him. "You can't," he declared, "not today, not tomorrow . . ."

I was feeling happier than I had for some time. "So what if I did that and chose some other man?" I replied defiantly. "You would abandon me without a single word, then ask me to forget it all and resume our relationship. . . . that's what you've asked, isn't it?"

"That'll never happen," he retorted angrily, "and you know it won't. You know why I went away and why I came back."

I looked at him "What would you plan to do, Amir?" I asked, my heart hovering around him.

"What I did before, Hind," he replied defiantly.

"Kidnap me?"

"Yes."

"Humiliate and torture me?

"Maybe that too."

I looked down at his foot and saw the scar from the amputation. Affection now overwhelmed both my joy and fury.

I looked at my father, then at him. "How would you have known whether or not I was married?" I asked "You deserted me without knowing anything about me."

"To the contrary," he replied, "I knew everything when I deserted you. I had news about you from the very first day."

"I understand," I said accusingly. "You abandon your baggage, then collect it again when the time's right."

"What's the point of blaming me?" he asked impatiently. "I don't like that. You're going to be married to me, and that's the end of it."

I went to open my mouth, but he gave me a cruel stare that silenced me.

"I couldn't do it, even if I tried," I said involuntarily. "I couldn't be married to anyone but you, not now, nor in a thousand years."

I gave my father a bashful look. "I agree, Father, if you do."

At the time, Aunt, you gave a sarcastic grin. You wanted to talk about girls' naiveté and things of that kind. My father gave his consent reluctantly, but he asked a lot of Salar. He asked him to make a copy of his book in a beautiful, clear script and to spend an hour or two every day recounting to him everything that had happened so he could put the finishing touches to the history.

The Testimony of the Translator Mustafa Pasha Al-'Uthmani (8)

Before the King of Kings left Cairo, he asked to climb up to the roof of the Sultan Hasan Mosque one last time, as though he realized that he would be never be visiting Cairo again; he did not have all that much time left in life. When he reached the roof, he looked all around him.

"In my hands are the keys to the Ka'ba and the keys to Islam," he said.

He then looked at the chief minister, at that time Yunus Pasha.

"Do you remember, Pasha?" he said disapprovingly. "You said that the conquest of Egypt was impossible, and we had never been involved in a war like this one. Which of us was right? I'm returning to my homeland with the keys to the Ka'ba and all the Holy Lands are in my hands."

"King of Kings," Yunus Pasha immediately replied without thinking, "I still think the conquest of Egypt's a disaster. You're going back to Istanbul with half your men. The other half have been lost; children have been orphaned and wives widowed. You've handed the governorship of Egypt to a traitor who betrayed his sultan. So what about the Ottoman sultan?"

For just a moment, I gaped in astonishment. I did not know whether Yunus Pasha had lost his mind, or this was some kind of game between the two of them. However, without any warning, I watched as the King of Kings, Sultan Salim, drew his sword and plunged it into the heart of the chief minister, Yunus Pasha.

"Idiots don't hang around with kings," Salim said. "Otherwise, their resolve is broken, and there are doubts about their triumphs. Take his corpse away. No, throw it off the mosque roof in front of me so soldiers and Egyptians will be scared."

Then he looked at me. I was shaking like a kitten.

"Mamluks used to fight each other inside these buildings," he said. "They didn't find them beautiful, awesome, or devotional. They don't deserve it all; I've told you that before. Even so, they're the best people to govern Egypt. They know it and still fight each other. Do you understand, Mustafa?"

"Yes, I do understand, Caliph of Islam," I replied without thinking.

"They know it and fight each other," he repeated. "We don't speak their language or know how to deal with them. To me, it seems that Egyptians have no sense of gratitude. They're stubborn by nature; it's difficult to satisfy them or earn their loyalty. They need someone who knows them by heart in order to secure full control. The Mamluk amirs know them well and speak their language. They're used to dealing with them. I've no desire to destroy Egypt; I want it to survive. It's the Mamluks who will virtually keep it that way. Their proclivity for fighting guarantees that Egypt will still need the caliph's resolve and justice. It provides Istanbul with a reserve of force and Egypt itself with a compliant attitude. Egypt must survive and remain compliant. Do you understand, Mustafa?"

"Your every word is a model of prudence, Caliph of Islam," I replied.

He looked all around him. "When I go back to Istanbul," he said, "I'm going to build a mosque like this one, only bigger. I can promise you that. Ottomans will never fight each other in it; in fact, they'll never fight each other!"

"They're the guardians of Islam," I responded without thinking. "Their wisdom is that of religious scholars."

I will tell you the truth, Abu al-Barakat: I really wanted to stay in Egypt, but did not dare say that to the King of Kings. I was afraid he would cut off my head. He was punishing any soldier who married a Mamluk widow; many soldiers did that. My heart was in Egypt with Khundtatar; she was very different from my wife in Istanbul. I can never forget how beautiful she is; her gentleness can melt your heart, and her affection was enough to make me lose my mind. She gave me an unprecedented kind of love, drowning mind and memory. One month after our marriage, she was pregnant with our son. I could not leave her. She wept in my arms and begged me to stay. All my life I had been a soldier; crying had no effect on me, and women never dominated me. But she was a Tatar, someone who could so distract a soldier in her land that he thirsted and hungered in her arms. I promised to protect her and the child all their lives, but she told me that she needed to have me with her. She really loved me, Abu al-Barakat. I had never learned anything about love of women. My wife performed all her duties perfectly, with a frown and with no words of love or longing. As I see it, she believed that love was for slave girls, not free women. Any display of passion would diminish her status. I did not want to go back to Istanbul or to my wife.

Hind's Testimony (11)

I can remember our wedding day, Aunt. It was a victory amid defeat. You know, that day I felt like a duckling that has been rescued when the rest of the family has drowned; it does not know whether to be happy to have survived or sad about the ones who have gone. However, the love in my heart was different from all other types of love and torture. I had loved him as a peasant, then as a Mamluk; I had given him love twice. His passion had drowned my heart, erasing the past and forgiving all sins. At first, my memory was both enemy and invader, searching fearfully in the body for a past full of injustice. I was afraid that my anxiety might show, and memory might overwhelm passion. He looked at me for a moment, then he put his hands around my face.

"Do you want me?" he asked, as though to counteract my memory.

I lowered my head, doing my best to hide the tension all around me. "Yes, I do," I replied.

He clasped my shaking hand. "You're shaking," he said. "Is that fear or passion?"

I clasped his hand, but said nothing.

He ran his hand over my face. "Calm down," he told me. "You know how crazy I can be, and you've had a taste of my cruelty. Maybe there was a time when you thought that cruelty could be an obstacle to betrayal, a way of resisting defeat. But there's no betrayal around you any more, Hind . . ."

He brought his mouth close to my face. I closed my eyes, not really understanding what he had just said. I let him kiss me, as love proceeded to crush all memories.

Our wedding night was one of reassurance for the soul and ridding the heart of both sorrow and doubt. I gave myself to him with both pleasure and passion. For the first time, I was his. That is what he told me.

"It's like the very first time," he told me gently as he hugged me to him.

"It's the same for me," I replied bashfully.

He hugged me harder. "If only the Mamluks had learned about resistance and victory from you," he said.

"But I didn't win. You did."

"No, you've won once, twice maybe," he responded. "You've no idea how much you've won. I'll never tell you."

I put my arms around his neck. "Will you tell me whether you prefer me compliant the way I am now, or whether you preferred it when I resisted?"

He smiled. "Your heart doesn't know the word compliant, Hind," he said. "I prefer you now, happy and agreeable."

Love, Aunt, is as sweet as refreshing water, erasing all evil and injustice. And yet, he was a different kind of soldier from all the others: dreamer and lover, not just concerning me, but his entire makeup and identity that was spread out before his own eyes. After several days, I knew all about plunging into the soul of a defeated soldier; I recognized his bitterness, and loved him even more. My feelings never wavered for a single day, and my affection never stopped. He realized that.

I have never cried a lot, Aunt; you know me. I want you to know that, whenever I set eyes on the stump of his severed foot, I burst into tears. He was splayed out on the bed, with me beside him. When I looked down at his foot, I could see the skinless, fleshless bone. I could only imagine the impact and pain when it was amputated. It was obvious that the person who did it was not qualified or a doctor. I ran my hand down his leg, tears still pouring.

"Does it shock you to see the stump?" he asked casually.

I decided to try a little humor. "Not as bad as seeing the neck of that gross man you killed," I said, still crying. "Do you remember?"

"Why are you crying?" he asked.

"Because of the agony you went through on your own. I would have liked to be there with you."

"You'll be with me for the rest of the suffering," he responded with a bitter smile. "Don't be afraid."

"You won't suffer any more," I said affectionately. "That's all over."

But he was still suffering. I was well aware of that.

He used to wake up at midnight, and either sit where he was or wander around the room. Then he would go out without saying a word and look up at the stars. I would stand behind him, sit beside him, and massage his shoulder every time. I would ask him to go back to sleep, but he did not answer, as though he neither heard nor saw me.

Sometimes he would get on his horse and canter through the darkness for hours. When he came back, he would fall asleep as though he had never left my side. After some time, I was able to see that, for those hours of darkness, he needed no one. He saw no one and needed to immerse himself in his own soul. I often detected agony from his amputated leg in his expression.

"Salar," I used to say next morning, "you need to sleep at night. You never do."

He looked at me, but said nothing.

I could feel his bitterness in my own throat and around my eyes. Once he was putting an iron foot on his amputated leg.

"Maybe, if I cut off the other foot as well," he yelled in utter frustration, "it would be easier to walk."

I rushed to help him without saying a word. He did not like a lot of talk. That day, he was nervous and impatient. He snatched the iron foot from my hand.

"You'll never understand," he told me. "Let me put it on. Leave the room, go on . . ."

I refused to leave as he had told me. I stayed where I was and let him put it on, watching the frustration boil enough to come bursting out of his veins. He kept muttering oaths under his breath and snorting in anger. At moments like this, I was really afraid of him. I will not lie to you, Aunt. But I still could not leave the room. I kept staring at his foot, as though, that day, I had somehow lost all understanding.

Once he had put the iron foot on, he stood up and was shocked to see me still there.

"What are you doing here?" he asked. "Didn't I tell you to leave?"

I stood up and headed for the door with a frown. He stopped me. "Never mind," he said, "you can stay."

I pretended to be making the bed. "I thought you might be needing something," I said. "That's why I stayed."

He gave me a long, hard stare, but I could not understand why he looked so distracted. At that moment, he did not seem to be with me. His mind rebelled and plunged him back into a past that I did not even know. I was scared, Aunt; I felt he had gone somewhere far distant, and I did not know whether he was alive or dead. I grabbed hold of his arm.

"Salar!" I said in a panic.

I was right. He did not respond, as though he had not heard me or even realized that I was there. I gave him a powerful shake.

"Salar!" I said again.

All of a sudden, he looked at me, as though only noticing me just then. "Yes, what are you afraid of?" he asked.

"Of what you were thinking," I replied, heaving a sigh of relief.

"I wasn't," he replied blandly.

I was still clasping his hand. "Sometimes," I said, "you wander far away, and I can't find you."

"I'm here with you. What happened to you?"

"No, you weren't with me."

He looked perplexed. "Maybe," he said, "once in a while . . ."

Those were scary moments, Aunt. I don't know whether it was my love for him that made me sense when he was pulling his mind away from the world, or the fact that I was so close to him, or some kind of suffering that was difficult to hide. But he came back to me; he always came back. I smiled and kissed his hand. He looked at me in amazement, then went out. Salar, Aunt, is a man who never gives up on your mind for a single instant; you are always preoccupied with it or dominated by it. He has his own special magic that can crush any angry feelings you may have toward him. I myself had taken the plunge into his blatant ruthlessness and forcibly extracted an affection that only showed itself to me.

I became pregnant with our first child. I told him hesitantly, realizing that he might never be happy. Such feelings never entered his heart, he told me.

He was writing a lot of words on a sheet of paper. I sat down in front of him.

"What beautiful handwriting you have!" I said.

He did not reply.

"What name do you prefer," I asked, "Husam ad-din or Salar? Whenever I see you writing, I prefer Husam ad-din. I like both of them together. I love you, without any name, place, or time."

He stared at me. "Thank you," he eventually said.

"You know, I think I'm pregnant," I said hesitantly.

He stopped writing, but did not look at me.

"You're familiar with that peculiar feeling," he said, "that you're involved in some ongoing, endless task. That's what I'm feeling. How miserable these times are! How unpleasant is this incomplete work!"

I still clasped his hand. "But we're together," I insisted. "Being with you is complete happiness and pleasure. You want to have a baby with me, don't you?"

"No, Hind," he said after a pause, "I don't want children. I don't want anyone to live in these times of defeat and corruption. But I realize that you want to have a baby; that's your right. No matter."

I swallowed hard and did my best to control my anger. "Maybe a baby can give us some compensation for the defeat, who knows? Maybe it'll bring us a victory."

"Victory will require centuries of time," he replied assertively. "In wars like this one, you have to wait for fate's verdict. It's difficult to rebuild what has been destroyed, and there's no way for us to find what has been lost."

"I'm convinced," I replied at the time, "that the government of Egypt will revert to the Mamluks once again."

He looked at me. "Perhaps," he said. "But the Mamluks now are not the same ones who fought with Tuman Bey. Defeat has crushed the pride of the elite and removed their aggressive instincts."

I could find no way of getting him to share my joy or to understand how happy I was to be having a child with him. I clasped his hand.

"You realize how happy I am with you, don't you?" I asked.

"I realize that you're putting up with me, yes," he replied with a bitter smile.

"But, when you take me in your arms at night," I insisted, "the world means nothing and tolerance has no place. My love for you will never flag. When I'm with you, my desire will never be vanquished."

He stroked my hand, but said nothing. I was not lying, Aunt; it was the truth. Salar never talks about his feelings; he has never told me, even once, that he loves me. Even so, I knew and felt him, inside me and next to my chest. He hugs me and strokes my hair. He has been my entire world, and I have been content with him and my child.

Salar's Testimony (10)

I have told you before, Abu al-Barakat, about what happened to the three horsemen. As you know, I saved one of them myself; my arrow hit him in the heart, so he now sleeps in peace. After the defeat, there was no life to be led; he did not shave his beard and don Ottoman dress. He became one of them after being a pillar of the country and guardian of our home. He died a martyr, and I have often envied him his death inside Salim's camp. Qansuh al-'Adili honored his friendship and his oath, but shaved his beard and let his mustache grow till he looked so like a janissary soldier that you could not tell them apart. We all changed. I was a peasant, calligrapher, and amir, although I no longer knew who I really was. I settled down with Hind in Balbis and started organizing the agricultural business myself after 'Abdallah had left. I asked 'Adlat to join us and built her a small house to live in. I really wanted just to be a peasant and calligrapher, but the amir gave me no choice. He was a prisoner of his own self, seething, smashing his restraints, realizing full well that the wars to come would be completely hopeless. What was I supposed to become? Community shaykh? Who was I protecting, who was I supposed to be fighting? Peasants? Was I going to fight Egyptians or pretend to be protecting them? Should I be using my whip on them to extract dinars and hand them over to Salim in his far-off country? What kind of work was that? In my own location, I was lord and king, master of everything. I was perfectly content with my estate in Balbis and the revenues it produces. I turned my back on politics and government. Qansuh al-'Adili was very happy when Khayir Bey interceded on his behalf with the invader sultan. The sultan chose to pardon him, whereas he could have slaughtered him and split his head open. But he did not do that. How merciful is Salim Shah, and wise too!! That is what Qansuh told me when we met a few years later, and he was a community shaykh, controlling Egypt or part of it. He had purchased slave girls and settled things for the future of his children. Maybe he managed to sleep in peace, whereas my own eyes had no taste of either peace or tranquility.

Qansuh visited me in person. "We misunderstood Salim Shah, Salar," he told me with conviction. "It was war, but now it's over. He hasn't touched the Mamluks or their property."

"To the contrary," I replied with a scoff, "he's hung their heads on a long piece of rope, stretching all the way from Cairo to Alexandria."

586

"There was a war," he went on. "We fought in it, and now it's over. He's left us alone. You have to make adjustments to the new situation."

"Do you know how the janissaries treated Khayir Bey?" he went on emotionally. "They put him in prison in the Citadel, humiliated him, and demanded money and their salaries. The only thing he could do was to ask the amirs for help and impose heavy taxes. He needs us, Salar. Our strength now is much greater than before. If we got together as we did in the past, as though time had not passed, it would be better for us and the country as a whole."

"What is it you want?" I asked directly.

"Khayir Bey will give you back your soldiers and appoint you as shaykh of whichever town you like. You'll be protecting Mamluks and their property, not Ottomans and their soldiers. Do you understand?"

"Forgive me, my friend. I'm totally confused. You want me to protect Khayir Bey?"

"He's a Mamluk first and last. We need him to live."

"Have you heard about injustice in the land?"

"There was injustice in the land before the Ottomans came. Whether it involves them or other people, there are always people who go astray. That's human nature."

"No, the people's suffering is much worse, and they've been inventing whole new ways of punishing people that are more cruel and painful. Just forget about me."

He stopped talking, and our eyes met. "No one hates the Ottomans as much as I do," he told me softly.

"You were just saying that Salim Shah is not that evil."

"I say what I say, my brother, and I fight my own way and on my own behalf. The day will come when Mamluks again have sole control over Egypt. Mamluks are the only ones who can do that. This sultan's like the phoenix: you hear about him, but you'll never see him. He'll stay in Istanbul, and we'll be in Egypt, all of it. He demanded that I pay his janissary soldiers, and I immediately agreed. Then he left, and I did not pay a single dinar. My money's not for the Ottomans. As we learn during our training in the Citadel, Salar, the warrior needs to be flexible, fleeing through the narrowest of apertures and getting his limbs to dodge and take pain. Khayir Bey is not that bad, and his daughter was your wife. You used to say that she was a good wife."

"That's all past. It's over."

"That's why I've come."

"To convince me that Khayir Bey's not that bad?"

"No, for his daughter's sake."

I looked at him without understanding.

"I want to marry her," he told me, "and you're my friend and brother. I have to ask your permission. I realize that your relationship with her has been at an end for some time, and you now have another wife. But I don't want to sever the solid ground and friendship that still exists between us both."

I smiled bitterly as I recalled Khayir Bey's words. "Being married to her, 'Adili, will never create a rift between us. Don't worry. It's your long mustache that'll do that."

"If I behaved like you," he responded with a smile, "constructing a fortress around myself, and cutting myself off from the world, how could I serve Egypt and its people? How could I help the Mamluks? They're my primary concern."

"But you're collecting taxes for the Ottoman sultan," I replied thoughtfully. "He's your boss. Forgive me, my friend. Salim's the one who humiliated and killed your teacher."

"You're talking as though all Mamluks consist of me, you, and Inal. You know full well that many Mamluks killed their teacher or his children. Don't let the defeat distort your memory. The people who killed, terrorized, and betrayed were all Mamluks as well."

"They were all Mamluks as well," I repeated.

"No matter," he said. "I would like to visit you once in a while."

As I shook his hand, I was aware that the paths between the two of us were separated by rivers and seas. Memory no longer existed.

We were three horsemen. Inal was the only one who had escaped. He had died a martyr and had not had to live with shame.

I spent the rest of my life searching for the vestiges of the conflict, for people, places, and weapons. What had been stolen and destroyed. My first search was for Shaykh Shihab ad-din's family. After he had been killed, I went to visit his wife and sons. I learned that punishment did not end with his killing; all his property had been confiscated, even the endowment that he had inherited from across the ages; Amir Muhammad al-Muhsini's endowment had been taken away by Khayir Bey, and now the family had no source of revenue. I decided to serve as sponsor for his wife and children, my hope being that the spirit of resistance would continue in this house and family. I did not know what the future held. At this point, Egypt seemed to be humbled and adaptive, but the country never ceased to amaze in its ability to recover from illness and rouse itself from indolence. I had been responsible for Shihab ad-din's death and the loss of his endowment. From now on, I was going to be responsible for his wife and children who would be getting a monthly payment larger than what the endowment had provided. Every month, I kept track of his son's studies at Al-Azhar; I could see in him a shaykh and fighter just like his ancestors. That was a small victory, one to light up the dark recesses of injustice and make the colors less deceptive. They had burned the mosque of Shaykhu al-'Umari, but it was still standing; it is difficult to triumph over stones, Abu al-Barakat, and Egypt is full of them. I still walk past the mosque and observe the signs of burning and the defiant presence of the stones.

"When the fighting's over," Shaykh Shihab ad-din used to tell me, "go seeking, and you will find. He who seeks, finds; he who shirks, does harm; he who grieves for this world, disappears in it; he who transcends this world, achieves eternity. We'll meet again soon . . . and talk about this another time."

But we did not meet again and talk. I have been seeking, but have not yet found. I have tried to use my own judgment, but, so far, I have not acquired any knowledge. Those simple phrases emerged from his mouth so easily, but now, they are utterly impossible to achieve, rebuilding what has been destroyed and injecting life into those who have died. There was no other meeting or explanation. I used to watch his son as he recited the Qur'an. I could see the crushed expression in his powerful eyes, his sense of defeat, and his steadfast attitude. That gave me some hope.

I kept running out of breath as I chased after an era gone by, an ancient victory, a kind of powerful force of which I was no longer a contemporary. I went to visit the tomb and mosque of Amir Muhammad al-Muhsini in order to chide myself for what had been lost and the treasures that we could no longer preserve amid such despondency. I was curious to find out about this Mamluk amir and his family and how and why he had managed to bequeath an endowment to Shihab ad-din's grandfather. Why were so many tales of courage and justice, of generosity and mercy, attached to his life story? I went to his mosque and asked about his life story. I vowed to remember it all by heart. If we do not reach the desired goal, then we need the warmth of the past for life to continue; if we do not manage to remain, then we need tales of heroes so as not to disappear. Amir Muhammad al-Muhsini was like me perhaps. He came from his country far away; he had no choice in the matter and no idea about what was to come. His heart settled in Egypt, and it became his source of sustenance and passion. He was a warrior and victor. I was a warrior with no chance of victory. He had come at a time of power; I had come at a time of weakness. He was part of me and like me. I pictured him in my imagination; whenever I looked at his face, I saw myself. As I imagined him, I would put my sword in place of his and my corpse instead of his. I would never have the opportunity to build the way he did. I would be wandering around the desert, like some infuriating vagrant, self-denying and closing my mind to everything around me, just so I could have some kind of life. There could be no accommodation with what was current and ongoing. I was living with injustice all around me, watching

it spread. It was as if the Mamluks had realized that life was short and desert out-
laws were not all that different from them. Each of them had his allotted time span
and end, Abu al-Barakat, whether today or tomorrow. It is not a characteristic of
soldiers to live on the victor's garbage, but I have come to believe that some Mamluks have preferred to do that.

We were separated by two centuries or more. I was him, or I wanted to be.

I ran my hand over his tomb and that of his Egyptian wife, Zaynab ibn Abi
Bakr al-Maqsha'i. She must have been a fighter, just like Hind. Any woman who
can tame a soldier has to be a fighter herself. If she were still alive, Hind would
have found a sister and friend. But, thank God, she had left before the end and the
completion of the building. If I had a son, I wonder if he would be able to build a
mosque like the mosque of Sultan Hasan. Would he become an architect like Amir
Muhammad's own son? But why build anything now, and for whom? The heart of
the sultan in Istanbul resides over there. He knows nothing about the stones and
buildings of Egypt.

The Testimony of the Translator
Mustafa Pasha Al-'Uthmani (9)

Salim Shah was the greatest king of all time, Abu al-Barakat. He possessed the ruler's prudence and the general's intrepid instincts. His death came as a shock to all of us. As yet, we do not know how he died or what the strange disease was that afflicted him three years after the conquest of Egypt. What really saddened me was his unfulfilled dream. Life did not give him enough time to build his mosque, so the Sultan Hasan Mosque in Cairo is still a unique example, unrivaled by any mosque in Muslim territories. He collected both men and property, but the passage of days let him down and pounced on him in a single night. There were any number of rumors. Some said that he was poisoned; others that he contracted the incurable plague; still others in Egypt suggested that the curse of Bab Zuwayla had fallen on him. Egyptians have been expert magicians ever since olden times, and they have a special curse that they use with anyone who kills their ruler; it devastates the body and sends it to oblivion. Here in Istanbul, people say that the sultan was struck by some evil magic that killed him. When Tuman Bey ordered Egyptians before his death to recite the Fatiha of the Qur'an three times for him, he was actually telling them to recite an ancient spell known to the Egyptian Copts, one that devastates the body and takes revenge on the soul. Everyone walking past the Bab Zuwayla recites this spell. But do not believe, Abu al-Barakat, that everyone passing by the gate recites the Fatiha three times to curse the sultan's soul. Most of them, Abu al-Barakat, do not know how to recite the Fatiha. The caliph has died, Abu al-Barakat, without achieving his dream. He has died under the curses of the assassinated Egyptian sultan, as is the case with a number of others in ancient times. Such magic curses in Egypt are well known to us. However, they have managed to liberate me from the trammels of my own personal sorrows. My son was born, but I could not see him. Khundtatar has been sending me love-letters every month; she has told me that she is keeping to her pledge and agreement and sometimes accuses me of forgetting all about her and going back to my wife. I have crushed her loving heart, she says. Those words of hers have torn me apart; I have never forgotten her. For three whole years, Abu al-Barakat, I have never dared ask to return to Egypt. But, when Salim died, I asked his son, Sulayman, to send me to Egypt. I found that Khundtatar had indeed kept her pledge and was still as beautiful as ever. I am being totally frank with you, Abu al-Barakat, because, like you, I am in search of the truth.

Hind's Testimony (12)

He has not changed over time. For him, everything came to a halt on the day he saw the sultan hanging at Bab Zuwayla. I made a point of handing our son, Muhammad, over to him in the hope that he could establish some kind of bond. After a while, he did that. One day, I saw and heard him talking to Muhammad while he was still asleep.

"Don't be sad," he told his son, "and don't believe what they're going to write. Your grandfather knows the truth. Read his book. When you're older, I'll explain it all to you, everything: who was the traitor, who fought, who was defeated, and who died. Then you'll understand and know."

He insisted on calling his son Muhammad. When I asked him why, he told me that there was a Bahri Mamluk amir named Amir Muhammad al-Muhsini. He said that he wanted his son to remind him of that amir's life story and lineage. In times of weakness and despair of any relief, such memories were useful. I did not object.

He then started telling our son, Muhammad, again and again about the three horsemen, the same story each time. Every time it was told, Muhammad listened eagerly. He used to listen as Salar told him: "We were three horsemen crossing the bridge together. The beast emerged from the depths and breathed fire on the bridge. It collapsed, or almost. One horseman said: 'My armor will protect me from the fire.' Another said: 'My sword is my assured defense against the wild beast.' The third horseman claimed that the beast was not that evil. If we were willing to listen, then perhaps it would let us carry on peacefully. The first horseman drowned, the second was defeated, and the third's whereabouts were destroyed by fire. No one knew anything about him."

Muhammad used to ask what had happened to the sword and armor. He was eager to find out which of the three was his father. Salar ignored his questions and kept on narrating the story. Once he had finished, he felt anxious at first, but then somewhat relieved.

For him, the most difficult time of day was noontime. He would wander around the house like a caged lion running in a narrow space, hovering around his own self in sheer frustration. Every day, at that specific time, I learned to stay out of his way. I would go to my own room or Muhammad's and leave him alone till he calmed down. Once he opened his sword-case which he kept in the basement and started practicing fencing and spear throwing. Then he put the swords back in the case.

"Burn it, Hind," he said emphatically. "It's no use."

I closed the case. "Let's just keep them in the case," I said.

"When I order you to do something," he yelled at me, "do it with no argument."

I lowered my head and said nothing. He started wandering all around the room while I stayed put.

"What do you want?" he asked.

"Nothing," I replied softly.

"There's something you want to say," he told me. "What is it you want? Why don't you want me to get rid of my swords? What can I do with them as a cripple? Which amir ever fights without a foot? Who am I supposed to fight? For what?"

"Those are memories that we hold on to, with their share of bitterness and suffering."

"I don't like these arguments," he said angrily. "You argue a lot and disagree with me. That's got to stop."

Suppressing my anger, I remained silent. I had a lot that I wanted to tell him. I felt like yelling in his face and leaving the room in a fury. But I could not do it. It was not that I was afraid, Aunt, but rather that he had managed to grasp the edges of my heart with a stone hand that no one could smash. The slightest sign of sorrow in his expression would make me worried.

"I didn't hear you promise to stop disagreeing with me," he said angrily.

"I'll stop disagreeing with you," I replied.

With that, he left the room and went out into the fields. He only came back in the evening. I prepared dinner for him and sat in front of him, frowning. He did not eat anything.

"Salar," I asked, invoking a love that managed to counteract my anger, "are you still angry?"

He looked at me with a shocked expression. "Why should I be angry with you? I'm not angry."

I massaged his shoulder and kissed his hand. "So eat then," I said, "for my sake."

He stayed silent. He went into the room, but did not go to sleep or say anything. I hugged him, and he did not resist. I did not say a single word till next morning, my heart being crushed by my worries about him. He was better next morning and went out to check on his estate. Then he came back and started transcribing my father's book for multiple copies. I could see a certain serenity making its way into his expression, and that made me relax and feel more normal. I started to get used to his moods and mental states and came to realize that, after his journeys into the past and its sorrows, he would always come back to me. I was stunned by his precise memory and broad understanding of details of battles and the number of soldiers and weapons. He was preserving history like mosque walls; he would know who had prayed, who had been killed, who had been overcome by his own greed, who had sold himself, who had purchased his soul, who had gone astray, who had returned, who had disappeared, and whose name was forever preserved by the walls.

Do you still remember, Aunt, 'Adlat and her daughter, Sitt ad-dar, who was now married to that fine man, Ziyad? She gave birth to a son, but, less than a year after the marriage, Aunt, she ran away, abandoning her husband and the boy who is not actually his and her mother who had lost a great deal. None of us had any idea where she was, but I heard some rumors that I will not repeat here because they involve women's motives and are extremely malicious. She did not show herself again, which means that she had enough money. All of which makes the rumors more persuasive, but I will not go into such motives. It was terrible for Ziyad. He had no idea what to do with the child, but, because he has such a generous heart, he decided to raise the boy himself. He used to visit 'Adlat every month, sometimes every week, and devoted his life to the child and to learning. You are going to smile, Aunt, when I tell you what happened. Salar found out that Ziyad had wanted to be married to me; do not ask me how he found out. He would only let me see 'Adlat when he was there too; he was afraid that I might set eyes on Ziyad by chance. Actually, he argued with me about it on one occasion.

"I'm going with you when you visit your father," he said. "Ziyad keeps coming there without an appointment."

I tried to dissuade him. "Salar, I said, "my father will protect . . ."

He interrupted me. "When I give you an order," he insisted, "I don't want any argument."

On the day he found out about Sitt ad-dar's flight, he was a bundle of nerves and anger. He cursed and swore at all women and their fickle behavior. I stayed where I was, not saying a word. On that particular day, my happiness was combined with a certain apprehension: after so many years, I had learned to be afraid of his wrath and knew when he was going to blow up. While I was somewhat happy that he was jealous, I was also worried about his loss of confidence.

"It's not all women, you realize," I told him after a short pause.

He looked me straight in the eye. "What are you implying by that sentence?" he asked. "I've told you: no visits without me. That's it."

"As you wish," I replied.

For just a moment, our eyes met. Then he surprised me by putting both hands around my face and giving me a powerful kiss on the lips. With that, he left, still cursing and swearing at all women. He was still furious.

I came to realize that his moments of calm would come when he was riding his horse. He could forget about his amputated foot, and be as dominant and wild as he wished without any restraints; the vicious streak inside him could have free rein. There were times when he would be calm, carefully transcribing words from the Qur'an or poetry and wandering around another world, one without violence and defiance, consisting entirely of careful, slow work, of rules, symbols, numbers, and letters that never left the memory. Sometimes, I would sit beside him, knit my eyebrows, stare admiringly at his hand, and enjoy those few moments of calm without saying a word. I would even breathe as lightly as possible so as not to disturb him. Often he would pretend not to acknowledge that I was there or not notice at all, while, at other times, he would look at me for a moment, then go back to his script.

One day, he smiled at me as he was writing. "I can write down your stories for you as well," he said.

I looked at him, stunned. "What stories?" I asked.

"Your testimony, Hind," he replied, "the stories you tell your aunt. Will you tell me what you tell her?"

I did not ask him how or what he knew. "Women's chatter is not that important, Salar," I replied.

He kept his eyes on the letters. "Women's chatter represents the truth of the oppressed and the cries of the humiliated," he said. "You above all realize that."

I swallowed hard and put my hand on his shoulder. "What is it that I know?"

"The agonies and insanity of war."

"I promise you," I replied firmly, "that I'll only tell you the truth and . . ."

He interrupted me. "I've no doubt about that," he said. "Your frankness has often surprised me. You reflect on things like your father and believe that writing history is a cure for the soul."

"Why do you talk to my father," I asked out of curiosity, "and then write?"

"Your father, Hind, listens to a large number of stories. He's patient and possesses an ear that can distinguish truth from lies and sift reality from sheer fancy."

"If you're tired of it, I can tell him."

"No, Hind, stories are my reason for being alive. There is a particular kind of victory to be had in writing things down and making a text. Only a true scholar can appreciate that. Your father knows."

He put his arms around my shoulders and handed me a pen. "These sheets of paper are very expensive," he said. "You must learn how to write well. Come on, I'm going to teach you calligraphy. Then you can record your own stories."

With that, he took my hand and rubbed it over the piece of paper. I was no good at writing, but I could feel his breathing all around me, his powerful hand grasping my fingers, and his kisses on my neck.

"These pages are very expensive, Salar," I told him in a weak voice overwhelmed by passion.

"I know," he replied as he kept kissing me.

I dropped the pen and gave him a big hug. "I'll tell you everything," I promised.

"Your stories don't worry me," he replied, as he kept kissing me. "I want to teach you some things," he went on, "so that you can stop sitting there for hours in front of me while I'm transcribing."

"I won't stop," I replied defiantly.

"You're stubborn and defiant by nature," he said. "Even so, I'm going to teach you some lessons."

At the time, he kept laughing, and I laughed too, just like a child amid the palm trees, a time of freedom and anticipation. It is hard, Aunt, to write about those times. In my imagination, Egypt was like the moon's sphere, its light shining on mankind while events of time failed to reach its elevation or brilliance. I have no idea what to say about Salar: events came all clustered together, giving my life a faint glow while covering me in an affection that shielded me from all evil.

⌒

The death of Khayir Bey both delighted and scared the Egyptian people. From women I learned that he had been cursed, just as Salim Shah had been before him. He had died in agony, having been afflicted for a year or so. He had had no idea how to lessen his suffering. People say, Aunt, that he spent a lot of money giving alms to the poor, his condition being that they pray to God for him, either for a cure or else for death. But it seems that he had no luck in purchasing mercy; the world of the unseen remained in God's hands alone. He put on banquets and, when the disease intensified, threatened to kill them all if they did not pray for him. They all did so in loud voices, but it seems that all the threats and menaces were ineffective in curing the disease or saving him from hellfire. Shaykhs in pulpits, sword at their backs, prayed for him, and the city chief also prayed for him as he impaled someone who had stolen oranges in the market. Janissaries prayed for him too, as they proceeded to collect taxes by force from certain merchants. However, none of these prayers made a difference. When Khayir Bey died, he was the richest man I had ever known in Egypt. They found six hundred thousand dinars in his possession. He never got to enjoy it himself or leave it for his children. The Ottomans took it all. His loyalty to Sultan Salim, as a traitor, made no difference, nor did all the taxes that he had collected from Egypt for his master in Istanbul.

People say, Aunt, that both he and Sultan Salim Shah were cursed when Sultan Tuman Bey was betrayed and Sultan Al-Ghuri before him. They say that ancient Egyptians had perfected the arts of magic. Anyone who betrayed their legitimate rulers would be struck down by an incurable curse. I believe that, Aunt, even though I realize that magic is forbidden. But how else are you to explain this sudden onset of death and pain so soon after the death of Tuman Bey? My soul is now at peace, and I still walk past the Bab Zuwayla and recite the Fatiha for the last Mamluk sultan.

Then I recall very well the day when I was visited by two women, both of them beautiful and both of noble heritage. The difference between them was obvious enough, and the visit of the second worried me a lot, while that of the first did not.

Khundtatar came without making an appointment and asked to talk to me; me specifically, and not Salar. I had heard about her from Salar and knew her story. I knew as well how angry Salar was with her and how he had refused to see her after she was married to Mustafa Pasha. Even so, I welcomed her warmly and offered her some food. I was stunned by how beautiful and slender she was; I actually felt a bit jealous and praised God that she was married. The dream kept floating through my imagination that Salar might have been thinking about marrying her so as to offer her protection, but I had dismissed such devilish notions. Since we had been married, Salar had never thought about betraying me or about any other woman.

The atmosphere was tense. I had no idea what she wanted or what I was supposed to say. She greeted me with a smile, but stayed silent. I waited for her to say something.

"Salar knew how to choose his wife," she said after a while.

I thanked her, somewhat embarrassed. I felt like telling her that I was not as beautiful as she was, nor did I possess her poise and wealth.

"Salar doesn't want to see me," she said directly. "I realize that."

"No, no," I replied, "he's just busy and . . ."

She interrupted me. "No matter," she said. "I've come because my husband has asked me to do so."

I swallowed hard. "Your husband, Mustafa Pasha?" I asked hesitantly.

"I don't have any other husband, Hind."

"Of course. Forgive me. What does your husband need?"

"He wants to talk to your father," she replied softly. "He knows that your father's writing the history of Egypt and wants to tell him the true version of what's happened. The scholar has to listen to all the different points of view and not separate one version from another purely on the basis of his own heart's inclinations. That's what my husband has said."

"My father will be delighted to welcome Mustafa Pasha and hear his testimony," I assured her. "In fact, he's been looking for people to give him different perspectives. He's searching for the truth, Khund, not for some personal inclinations."

"Don't call me Khund. Use my real name, just Tatar."

"Tatar," I repeated," my father will be glad to meet your husband."

"Will you tell your husband?" she asked.

There was silence.

"If I told him lies," I said, "he would get angry. That scares me."

She gave me an affectionate smile. "Yes," she said. "Inal used to say that he would get angry very quickly and change his slave girls every month, as though he was buying new clothes. True love has changed him, I believe."

"It is circumstances that have changed us all," I replied bashfully.

She gave me a fixed stare. "You realize, Hind, don't you, that this is a war which gave men the impression that they fought in it, whereas it's only women who have paid the price. Who fought, who lost, who resisted, who was destroyed, it is us women, not men."

At the time, I could not explain how it was that I felt so drawn to her, as though she were not the creepy devilish female that my husband had spoken about.

"You're right," I replied softly.

"You're different from Sa'adat," she said. "She was my friend."

"Different how?" I asked.

"More ruthless and fierce," she replied. "Forgive me! I'm being frank with you. The warrior needs to be married to someone who can parry his thrusts and not submit so that he can treat her like a piece of old clothing he can put on for the sake of some lovely memory or to fulfil some obligation."

I was shocked and surprised. "I'm fierce?" I asked.

"You're fierce and ruthless inside, Hind," she said. "I can see it clearly. Gentleness and affection are like kohl you put on your eyelids. We have to put it on every day, or else your face looks pale."

"I realize that you suffered in prison," I said sympathetically. "Inal's death must have been hard on you."

She gave me a smile that I will never forget as long as I live. Was it love, surrender, or defiance? "God has given me the compensation of a wonderful husband," she said. "He fills my entire life, Hind.

"My entire life," she repeated.

As she left, I promised her that my father would listen to the testimony of Mustafa Pasha the translator and record it all. I felt sad and disheartened; I did not know whether it was her own internal sadness that had spread all around me, or rather it was all a consequence of my own imagination and vision of love. I could never be sure. But the second visit that evening was far more serious and filled my heart with genuine sorrow. It was Sa'adat who came to visit me after her father's death and her divorce from Al-'Adili. Misfortune had struck Khayir Bey's family and their wealth had been sequestered.

What really pained me, Aunt, was the yearning in her expression. I wanted her to be like her father, hateful and greedy, but I did not know if she was like that. I had loathed her for some time, and worried about his affection for her and a life before me. I did not know whether it was simply my own selfishness or rather love that dominated me and made me not want him to see any woman other than me. But, in those times, nightmares were always turning into reality. She came to his house, and I was the one who opened the door. As she greeted me, her eyes looked downtrodden and defeated. She asked to meet him. What a nerve is that, Aunt? What kind of affliction?

I offered her some sweetmeats and juices, struggling all the while to keep my own inclinations in check. For just a few seconds, I hated him and hated myself as well. I blamed him for not giving me any choice before.

She gave me a sad look. "How's Salar?" she asked after a pause.

I could not work out how to hate her; it was impossible. "He's okay," I replied distractedly.

She smiled affectionately. "Is he still as stubborn and domineering as usual," she asked, "or has he changed?"

When I looked at her, I could see the years between them. She had known him and been a part of a past that I could not reach. I was jealous of her and her past. I was sure that there were things I didn't even know about.

She lowered her head. "Forgive me, Khund Hind," she said. "I've come without an appointment, and I'm sure that my visit is troubling you."

"Khund Sa'adat," I replied, "I'll welcome you at any time."

The yearning look was still in her eyes. "It's difficult not to fall in love with Salar," she said. "You know he's just like a leopard or panther, like savage beasts. His skin gleams with eye-catching colors. Just for a moment, you can forget that he is capable of killing you in a few seconds. He'll deceive you, drown you, and leave your heart suspended in mid-air."

Those words of hers started annoying and unsettling me. She knew them by heart. Nothing is worse for a wife than the existence on earth of another woman who knows and understands her husband.

I did not respond.

"Please forgive me," she said after a pause. She looked all around her, then continued, "You're a woman. You know . . ."

"What do I know?" I asked dryly.

She stared off into the distance. "He would often consort with slave girls for a day or two," she said, "but I wasn't jealous. What's the point of being jealous? A slave girl can never give him what a free woman can. I just wanted him to be happy. If he liked a slave girl's voice or dancing, I'd let him be for a while, completely sure that he would come back. He always did. Does he still do it now?"

I did not like this conversation. "No, he doesn't," I replied nervously.

Our eyes met. "You don't let him," she asked, "or he doesn't want to?"

I did not respond.

"Will you let him talk to me?" she asked after a pause.

"Of course," I replied in a blend of sympathy and worry.

"If we were to meet at some other time," she said calmly, "and there wasn't an amir standing between us with one sword on my heart and another on yours, we could become friends."

I stood up. "I'll call Salar," I said.

I told him what Sa'adat, Khayir Bey's daughter, wanted. For a few moments, he said nothing, but then he went to see her. I kept track of his eyes and hers through my window and listened in on the conversation. I shall never forget it as long as I live.

Her head was lowered, and she looked tired and troubled. She sat in front of him.

"I always accepted my fate patiently," she said, "but you were unkind to me, Salar. You killed me."

He kept staring at her, but said nothing for a while.

"How are you living?" he asked.

"I'm not," she replied softly, while I was trying to listen in. "You know I'm not."

I watched as he looked down at the designs on the floor rugs. "It's all predestined fate," he said.

She hesitated. "You rejected me," she said, "the rich daughter of the traitor, a woman who dominated the entire land and owned everything. So, now that I don't have my daily bread, what are you going to do?"

He looked at her for a moment. "As long as you're alive," he said, "I'll never see you with your head lowered, nor do I want to see you in need of anything."

I clutched my heart, and my breathing came in spurts. I swear, Aunt, that I could see affection in his eyes. Just then, I felt an indescribable hatred for him; at that very moment, I dearly wanted to be able to scream in his face.

"Do you know what you did to me?" Sa'adat asked him bitterly. "Do you know what I felt and how I suffered being married to one man while my heart and soul belonged to another? You showed no mercy or understanding. You know about love for the impossible, the sense that what's happening is somehow divorced from the human soul. The soul hovers in some kind of space outside the body. Qansuh al-'Adili was married to me because of my father. As soon as my father died, he divorced me; he was only thinking about his own interests and profits. When my father died, Qansuh told me he realized that you were the only one I loved. He told me that he hated me, and hated and despised my father."

She was silent for a while. "He beat me," she went on tearfully. "He told me that I deserved to die because I wasn't faithful to him and only thought about you. But I was faithful to him, Salar, at least with my body. But my heart was not faithful; it tortured me, and apparently him as well. I've never begged you before; my own pride has stopped me. You realize that."

He frowned. "I do realize," he said, "and you're not going to beg now. I'll not see humiliation in your expression ever again. You deserve to be treated properly."

"You're the only one in my life who can do that," she replied sadly, "even though I'm just a part of your life and not all of it."

As he looked at her, I clasped my hand while my heart kept pounding in my chest.

"I'll rent you a house," he told her softly, "and you'll receive what you need every month. That's my obligation, and not any kind of exceptional gesture. You were and still are a princess and the best of women. If you need anything, come to see me."

Their eyes met, and she smiled sadly. "You know what I really need," she said, "but I realize that you can never give it to me. Never mind! Is it the anger you feel toward me that has erased all feelings inside you or is it your own pride and the Mamluk defeat?"

"You're an ornament among women!"

"I don't forgive you."

"I don't forgive myself for a lot of things that I've done."

"I don't need your money, Salar."

"Yes, you do," he insisted. "Forget your conceit and pride. It's your right, the time we spent together."

"Sympathy and affection are no substitute."

"It's your right, Sa'adat. Once or twice you saved me. Do you think I don't know?"

I put my hand over my mouth and sobbed.

She looked at him, then stood up. "What do you plan to do?" she asked.

"Today you'll be moving to a new house," he said. "We need to find someone who deserves you."

"You want me to be married off," she asked dryly, "the same way my father did it? Maybe you're forgetting about your own cruelty and lies."

"Maybe I am forgetting my unkindness," he replied affectionately, "not to mention the bitterness of betrayal and the fortresses constructed between us."

"Do whatever you like with me," she said sorrowfully. "Marry me off, and give me money and a house. I know that you were monarch of the heart's profundities and would never give up on your kingdom and throne."

Their eyes met, but I could not see his expression. I was struck by the evil feeling that she still owned part of his heart. I almost lost my mind and purpose.

"My one solace," she told him softly, "is that you're alive. I've told you that before, and I'm going to say it today and every day."

The echo of her words kept ringing in my ears. "Once or twice you saved me," that is what he had said. She wanted him alive, even far away. That is what she had said.

I avoided him all day and slept in our son Muhammad's room. Actually, I did not sleep that night, and he did not come looking for me. I realized that he needed to be alone for a while; the affection inside him was deep-rooted and enduring. Ah for the agonies and cruel games of time!

That day, I hugged my son, doubt doing away with certainty and success never complete—indeed, never complete.

My son shook me, as I sat there riveted in place. Those words would not leave me alone, whether asleep or awake.

"Mother," he said, "you're just sitting there. It's as though you've been bewitched. Are you feeling well?"

"I seem to have caught something," I replied bitterly. "Don't worry, I'll be fine."

Next day, I did not go back to our room or say a single word to him. When he came by at night, I was hugging my son and pretending to be asleep.

"You're coming back to our room now," he insisted.

"I'd prefer to sleep here," I replied softly, my eyes closed.

"You're going to come," he insisted. "I need to talk to you."

I grabbed my neck, fearing his words and expecting some act of betrayal. "I'm staying here," I stated firmly.

He grabbed my hand. "Come on, Hind," he said.

I went to his room and sat on the bed, without saying a word.

"Why are you avoiding me?" he asked.

"Do you love her?" I asked without intending to do so.

He did not respond.

"Do you want to go back to her?" I asked bitterly.

"She loves you," I went on before he had a chance to respond. "She still loves you. She's not that evil. I was expecting her to be a wild animal, but she came here, defeated and still in love. I know the truth. I saw it for myself."

"If you knew the truth," he said defiantly, "then you'd know the answer to your questions. You're always searching for words that respond to the will but don't mean very much."

"Do you want to go back to her?" I asked again in a choking voice.

"No, I don't," he replied firmly.

I hesitated for a moment, still feeling the bitter taste in my throat, jealousy overwhelming all my love.

He grabbed my arm and pulled me toward him. "Come here," he said.

I made for his arms and rested my head on his chest.

He wrapped his arms around my shoulders. "Don't leave our room again," he said.

There was a lot that I wanted to say. All night I kept thinking about what had happened in the past. Had he made me his slave girl, I wonder, so he could forget her? Had he forced himself on me because he was really in love with another woman? Was I the bottle in his hand, something to plunge into the ground so he would be cured by the sound of it breaking? Did his defeat lead him to despair, so he got rid of it all inside my body? Did he ever feel any regret, or did he regard me as his spoils and property? Why had he changed? Did he finally feel sorry for the unprecedented level of agony he had caused me? Once that other uncouth man had appeared, what had happened to him and me? It was as if that individual had arrived to bring our fates together forever. These were all questions that kept gnawing at my mind, and they in turn ignited a feeling of jealousy, creating a fury that squelched all love. I was in love with him. At this very moment, I wanted to melt into his arms and have him help me struggle with my doubts. But it seemed to me that he was not going to do that.

His arms were still wrapped around my shoulders. "I can feel your anger in the way you're breathing and your body's pulling away," he said. "What's the matter?"

To tell you the truth, Aunt, I did not dare tell him what I was actually feeling. There were times when I was afraid of him. At this particular moment, I was afraid of his words more than anything else.

I tried to push him away gently, but he only hugged me harder. "Stop your thinking," he told me," and stop pushing your mind so far away."

"I've lots of questions," I said, "but I don't know the answers. In the past there was some insanity and a whole lot of sorrow."

"Listen, Hind," he replied thoughtfully. "I can ask you to erase the past and I myself can try to drown your memory. But genuine victory demands that we retain memories of evil and injustice, of good and compassion. Victory means accepting the past without wallowing in its defeat. This world of ours involves a short attempt at achievement, no more. If we chop off half of it, what's left for us? Do you understand?"

I looked down for a moment. "I'm not sure you're convinced by what I said."

"For me, knowing the road and not heading in that direction is preferable to endless wandering through the wilderness."

As I wrapped my arms around his neck, I felt scared by his complete control over me and my own annihilation in his midst.

"Why did you marry me?" I asked after a pause. "Was it to forget her?"

"I don't like these questions," he replied. "You know that."

I had hoped that he would say it was because he loved me and could not bear to live far away from me; that I was his only love, that his love for me had crushed every past, that . . . that . . . I knew he would never say that. He never had before.

I searched for something to say to quench the burning fire in my heart. "Aren't you going to marry her?" I asked.

"No, I'm not."

I was still in his arms and needed nothing else. "But you're not happy," I said. "Were you happier when you were with her, I wonder?"

"Forget about her, Hind," he insisted. "Don't talk about her again."

I remained silent. I moved away and looked at him. "Have you forgotten about her?" I asked.

He gave me a hard stare, and I expected him to lose his temper.

"Forgive me," I said quickly. "Jealousy's an incurable disease."

"I've told you I won't answer your questions," he replied impatiently. "Find your answers inside your own heart. Once you toss jealousy aside, the truth will be patently obvious. No more talk today."

I moved closer to him again, his anger roiling my heart. "Forgive me," I said. "I'll do it, I'll toss my jealousy aside. But you're not happy. I'd like to make you happy, but realize that I can't do it."

He leaned his chin on my head. "You make life bearable," he said gloomily, "but all happiness disappeared on the day when I saw the last of the Mamluk sultans strangled with a paltry, thin rope and hung up for days in front of the Egyptian people. You know that as well."

"The sultan died as a martyr hero," I replied, holding his hand. "Conflicts are like life itself: the strivers are not always the victors. Will I ever get to see you with a happy expression?"

"Don't ask me for something I can't do. It's just a few days we get to spend with those whom we love, then we leave them and it's over."

I rested my head on his shoulder and said his name. It was the first time he had ever used the word "love." He did not mean me specifically, but, that day, I still felt that particular word erasing my heart's doubts and my soul's wanderings.

That day, he made love to me, as though he were showing his love and loyalty to me and honoring my own vicious streak in wars. I called out to him and told him how much I loved him. I slept in his arms, wanting times to settle down and the rest of humanity to disappear. Khundtatar's words were always with me, and her smiles were etched on my heart; I had no idea why. He got up at midnight as usual, and stayed there sitting on the bed, as though he were semiconscious and half-alive. He went out, rode his horse, and came back at dawn. I was waiting for him. When he came in, he took off his outer clothes and sat on our bed.

"Do you think it was the guns that defeated us," he asked, "some hidden iniquity in the amirs' actions, or betrayal?"

"Salar," I replied gently, "the war finished five years ago."

"But Salim Shah has died," he went on as though he had not heard what I said. "He'll never come to Egypt again. People say he wanted to build a mosque like the Sultan Hasan Mosque, but he couldn't do it. Do you know that?"

"Salar," I said, running my hand over his face, "the war's over, Salim's dead, and the Mamluks are still governing Egypt."

"'The Mamluks are still governing Egypt,'" he repeated. "What kind of deception is that? The defeat hasn't even started yet, and the enemy to come is even fouler and more rapacious. That may be from Crusader lands. Who knows?"

My eyes were half-closed. By now, I was used to this conversation every night, as though he were trying to bring the conflict to a close on his own terms, every night and every dawn, but not succeeding.

"Come on," I told him lovingly, "get some sleep."

"Sleep can't put out the fire in my heart or give it any peace."

"We need you," I told him sadly. "I'm worried about you."

As I closed my eyes that night, he turned toward me and placed my head on the pillow. "You go to sleep," he whispered. "You have to put up with me, I realize that."

He kissed my forehead. I smiled, reassured of his love, and slept peacefully.

Salar's Testimony (11)

I could not teach my son how to fight; in any case, I did not want to do so. I felt sorry for him every time I looked into his eyes and saw my own. He had arrived during the dark times linked to the defeat. I hoped that I would not need to talk to him and explain the causes and underlying aspects of the defeat. I hoped to talk to him about the glories and triumphs of the Mamluks. But fate denied me that.

Holding his tiny hand, I took him outside on my own for the first time. I took him to the Sultan Hasan Mosque. We climbed the minaret, and his eyes opened in amazement as he looked out over Cairo. He was maybe four at the time, so he did not know a lot and had not seen much either.

I told him about the fighting and what had happened. He frowned as he listened to me; I am not sure whether or not he understood. He asked me if the three horsemen had taken part in the fighting. I told him that they had.

"When did they cross the bridge?" he inquired.

I thought for a moment. "When the fighting was over," I replied.

I told him about Shaykh Shihab ad-din and how he had been killed. His eyes teared up.

"Don't worry about him," I reassured him, stroking his hand. "He's in a better place now, and his children are entrusted to my care. They're studying jurisprudence, and they'll be just like their father or even better. After a few years maybe, they'll resist and win. As long as that family's in Egypt, there's nothing to fear. His great-grandfather was a contemporary of some of the great sultans, like An-Nasir Muhammad ibn Qala'un. His name was Shaykh 'Abd al-Karim al-Manati."

I heard a voice behind me. It was Mustafa Pasha. I frowned and did my best to suppress an incurable hatred I had been nursing for some time.

"Is that your son?" Mustafa Pasha asked.

"Yes, it is," I replied coldly.

"I heard you telling him about Shaykh Shihab ad-din who defied the Ottomans."

"Is there defeat in mere words, Pasha?" I asked. "Why fear words?"

"As though the Mamluks weren't afraid of words!" he said sarcastically. "You were talking about his great-grandfather, Shaykh 'Abd al-Karim. I'm interested in that family; I've done some research and found out various things. Do you also know, Amir, how he died and what his end was like?"

Our eyes met. "The truth must be told."

"Well then," he went on defiantly, "tell your son that the Ottomans killed Shaykh Shihab ad-din, and the Mamluks put his great-grandfather, the illustrious Shaykh 'Abd al-Karim, in the Citadel prison. He died there amid the darkness and filth. Speak the truth, and all will be well."

My eyes bored into his as though it were a sword fight between eyeballs.

"Who stole the lanterns from the mosque?" I asked.

"War involves victory and spoils," he replied at once. "You're a fighter. You know that."

"Isn't it a crime to steal the light and leave darkness to ravage the mosque's alcoves?"

"If you wish, you can change them and bring in copies," he said. "Make some lanterns just like them and put them up in their place."

"It seems, Pasha, as if you're asking me to make a new foot like the one that I've lost and replace it."

Mustafa Pasha stared at me long and hard. "I get the impression I've seen you before, or, at least, your eyes. You had your face covered, but your bearing and appearance . . ."

"The spirits of fighters are forever coming together," I replied bitterly.

"Could it be that you tried to kill the King of Kings?"

"Why should I kill him," I asked, "when death is his fate in any case?"

"Talk about him with respect," he said. "He was the caliph of all Muslims and Servant of the Two Sacred Shrines."

I turned away and said nothing.

"I've a son the same age as yours," Mustafa Pasha said after a pause.

I gave him a phony smile.

"Did you come here to tell him about the mosque?" he asked.

"No, about the Mamluks."

Mustafa Pasha sat down confidently in the mosque courtyard. "I'd like to listen to you," he said.

"You won't like what I have to say, Pasha," I told him.

"I've already heard about your daring," he said. "Go ahead, and don't bother about me."

"Do you know who built this mosque, my son?" I started. "Muhammad ibn Baylik al-Muhsini. He was a son of the people. His father, Amir Muhammad, was one of the bravest and most powerful horsemen. Like your own mother, he was married to an Egyptian woman, and she bore him five children. The youngest was Muhammad, the architect who built this mosque. No other building like it was ever constructed. I named you Muhammad so you could become like the father or son."

"How did Amir Muhammad die?" Mustafa Pasha asked.

"I believe he was killed."

"By the Mamluks?"

As our eyes met, I understood his intent. "A Mamluk amir killed him," I replied defiantly, "because he was both courageous and fair. In the cause of justice, he had no fear of blame. It was an era of illustrious cavaliers; Egypt was the glory of Islam, and travelers and scholars came there from all directions."

At the time, Abu al-Barakat, I did not notice that a number of people had gathered around us and were listening to the information. It was a large circle, with me in the middle and Mustafa Pasha in front of me. All the vacant space was filled with people, so much so that, if you had approached from far away, we would have seemed featureless and unrecognizable to you. The gentle light eliminated all differences, and the circle fused together and gradually faded. I could no longer see Mustafa Pasha, nor he me. Colors all blended together; there was no red for Ottomans, yellow for Mamluks, no white, black, blue, or green. I stopped talking so that people might break up and move away and Mustafa Pasha would again appear in front of me, defiant and triumphant. But the crowd only grew larger; colors were completely erased. The shaykh of the mosque intoned the call to sunset prayer. The rows straightened, and I stopped talking. Cairo seemed far away, sad and proud, with stone buildings yet to be completed. There was a hidden sense of victory lurking in the depths that I would never get to see or witness. Today, the atmosphere was absorbing all colors and all faces.

ON THE MARGINS OF HISTORY

Ibn Iyas (Abu al-Barakat) wrote his history, *The Loveliest of Flowers Concerning the Events of the Ages*, based on the testimony of Mustafa Pasha, Amir Salar, Hind, and others.

The Mamluks continued to govern Egypt until the massacre in the Citadel at the hands of Muhammad 'Ali in the nineteenth century. However, the golden era of both the Bahri and Burji Mamluks had long since passed, coming to an end when the Ottomans entered Cairo. The Ottomans never had complete control of Egypt. In fact, the Mamluks kept trying to regain independence for Egypt until the French invasion (1798). Once in a while, some of them were successful.

Right up to today, Egyptians still call the day of Tuman Bey's death "gloomy Friday," and some people still recite the Fatiha three times as they pass by Bab Zuwayla.

The buildings still bear witness to what was and what happened. The mosque of Shaykhu al-'Umari still stands stolidly there in the Khalifa quarter of Cairo. The mosque of Sultan Hasan continues to store history and recount it every day.

In the final section of the story, Josephine, Dr. Salah's granddaughter, discovered her goal. Tales of defeat stimulate life, not death; they touch the heart, and remind it of the final stage. Loneliness was firmly settled inside her. All persons, human beings as a whole, were part of her experience. And yet, it was still meager, with no horsemen or invasions, a modest experience of a journey with loneliness and defeat. She knows Amir Muhammad and Zaynab, 'Amr and Dayfa, Salar and Hind; they are all still friends who engage with loneliness and inspire a feeling of confidence that her story is not unique and her destiny is not unusual. She realized that love stories help bring about a spirit of harmony, if only for a while; they can convince people that death is not the end, and life is not the goal. A certain amount of sympathy and affection can be found within the vicissitudes of time. Josephine did not find the serenity of love during her journey and came to realize that she never would find it. Amid the upheavals of time, occasions when spirits coalesce are rare indeed; they deserve contemplation and a written record. The heart's defeat is something that we get used and adapt to, just like bloodshed during wars. Sorrow has a dark hue that can obscure the sun, but it can be pierced by moments of total harmony between lovers. It illuminates the heart with lanterns that cannot be stolen.

A sense of security resides in history. After it is read, no catastrophe can shock and no triumph can encourage boasting. It is what happened and is over. She has now told what happened, or she has tried.

GOD BE PRAISED, THE WORK IS FINISHED.

Afterword

By any evaluative yardstick that one might wish to apply, Reem Bassiouney's novel *Awlad al-Nas,* which I have here translated here as *Sons of the People,* is a significant addition to the tradition of the modern Arabic novel, and of the historical novel in particular. It is steeped in history, and specifically the history of Egypt and its capital city, Cairo. As such, it joins a number of other novels in Arabic, composed over the course of the last century or so, that have invoked history and historical records in order not only to provide fictional insights into the past in and of itself, but also to present to the contemporary reader of fictional narratives examples of human behavior and political decision-making that will often serve as relevant commentaries on the historical present in all its complexity. Such is certainly the case with *Sons of the People.*

Sons of the People is then a quintessential historical novel, and, as such, a successor to a long-standing tradition of that particular genre within the modern Arabic novelistic tradition. Many novelists who have penned novels that they themselves or others have linked to the subgenre of historical fiction have heartily endorsed that opinion. In the particular case of the Arabic novel tradition, a listing of such works would be extremely lengthy, but mention should be made of the great pioneer of the genre, the Lebanese writer Jurji Zaydan (1861–1914), and, in the context of more focused and contemporary examples devoted to Egypt and its capital city, Jamal al-Ghitani (1945–2015) and BenSalim Himmich (b. 1948) from Morocco.

This novel is explicitly historical in its setting in both time and place. As already noted, the focus of place is Cairo, although, in the different segments of this three-part narrative, local activities take place elsewhere in Egypt—the city of Qus in part two, for example, and an agricultural region outside the city in the earlier sections of part three. The first part of the novel also establishes a yet more specific spatial focus within the city of Cairo, in that it is much concerned with the construction of one of the city's greatest monuments, then, as now: the mosque complex of Sultan Hasan, still rising in all its magnificence from the lands immediately beneath the Cairo Citadel constructed by Ṣalah ad-din (Saladin) in the 12th century CE.

The overarching historical context within which the events of this novel need to be placed is a consequence of the lengthy and complex transition from the

Ayyubid dynasty founded in Egypt by Ṣalah ad-din in 1171 CE to the gradual assumption of power by the Mamluks—trained soldiers imported as boy slaves to Egypt from the regions of Turkey and the Caucasus and initially employed by the Ayyubid rulers in their conflicts with both the invading Crusaders (the so-called Seventh Crusade under King Louis IX of France) and the Mongols. Many of the consequences of that transition process, one replete with conflict, intrigue, and family rivalries, are reflected on the pages of this novel.

The time context, or rather contexts, are clearly established by the citation of specific dates at the beginning of each subsection of the novel. Each of the three parts is concerned with a particular historical period, and the narrative is placed, with considerable scholarly expertise and textual authenticity, into the political, social, and cultural milieus of the time. As if to underline the linkages that connect this narrative to the historical record, the story includes what we might term "cameo appearances" by two of the most famous practitioners of historical writing in Arabic: Ibn Khaldun (1332–1406) and Ibn Iyas (1448–1502). In the second part of the novel, Ibn Khaldun, as chief judge of the Maliki school of law in Cairo, is anxious to share with his judicial colleague 'Amr, the "Judge of Qus," his impressions of the complexities involved in serving in the senior judicial post in Cairo in such complicated times (that itself being one of the principal themes of BenSalim Himmich's historical novel devoted to the later years of Ibn Khaldun's career spent in Cairo, Al-'Allama [2001; The Polymath, 2009]). In the third part, two narrators—one Mamluk, the other Ottoman—provide "Abu al-Barakat," to wit, Ibn Iyas, with entirely different narratives detailing and justifying the fraught circumstances surrounding the Ottoman invasion of Egypt, led by Sultan Salim Shah (generally known as Selim I), and the subsequent capture of Cairo in 1517.

In the prefatory section, a narrator explains that the papers that she is now going to present to the reader are the result of research conducted by the daughter of a man who worked with Hasan 'Abd al-Wahhab, the Egyptian archeologist who, in 1944, discovered an inscription inside the Sultan Hasan Mosque, indicating the name of its architect: Muhammad ibn Baylik al-Muhsini. That identification provides the initial linkage to a particular family, one that is to represent the blended category of "sons of the people" through contacts and relationships between Mamluks and Egyptians, and that, through three different generations, is to be the focus of the narrative that is to follow.

The first section, entitled "The Mamluks," is dated to the year 1309. The government of Egypt is still far from stable, as the children of Sultan Qala'un (1279–90) vie for power. One of his sons, Sultan Nasir ad-din Muhammad, has returned to power for a third reign, having been twice replaced by Mamluks of his own father. But alongside these political complications is the far more deadly scourge of the plague, which manages to wipe out entire families and large segments of the Egyptian populace as a whole. The second period is set half a century later, in 1353, during which time a number of Nasir ad-din Muhammad's sons have ruled Egypt for short periods before being deposed or killed. This section introduces the reader to the figure of Barquq, who was to become sultan in 1383 and was himself deposed and sent into exile in Syria before being restored to power in 1390. The third and final part of the novel, "Event of Nights," is set significantly later, in the period 1517–22, and, as already noted, adopts a multi-narrative format in order to present to the reader (via the historian Ibn Iyas) a record of the circumstances surrounding the Ottoman invasion of Egypt and eventual capture of Cairo, an event that put to an end the Mamluk era in Egyptian history.

While these are the novel's three historical frameworks on the broadest scale, it is within the daily life of Cairo, and in both the public and private spheres, that the primary fabric of the narrative is located. The "sons of the people," referred to in the novel's title, are the result of the mingling within this social framework of Mamluks and Egyptians, and, in particular, intermarriage between Mamluks and Egyptian women, thus producing such "sons of the people." When, in the first part of the novel, Ahmad, the son of an Egyptian merchant, Abu Bakr, clashes with some Mamluk soldiers, he is arrested and brought before the Mamluk amir, Muhammad al-Muhsini. Ahmad's sister, Zaynab, rushes over to plead on her brother's behalf and catches the amir's eye. The stage is set, as it were, for what is to follow.

Abu Bakr asks his close friend, Shaykh 'Abd al-Karim al-Manati, a much respected figure in the Cairo quarter where he lives, to intercede on his son's behalf. The shaykh is pious and judicious in his opinions, traits that bring him into dialogue, and occasionally disagreement, with the Mamluk authorities in Cairo who prefer direct applications of the law rather than more nuanced interpretations of religious doctrines and legal precedents. In the second part of the novel, those same traits are amplified in the career of his precocious grandson, 'Amr ibn Ahmad ibn 'Abd al-Karim, the "Judge of Qus," who is portrayed from an early age as being totally devoted to knowledge and the further acquisition of religious learning. His career is to be marked by his application of effective justice through the vigorous application of the Islamic principle of "*ijtihad*," the invocation of independent judgment in the formulation of legal opinions as opposed to a sole reliance on precedents. Needless to say, the novelty of this decision-making process earns him much popularity in Qus and also much resentment and opposition from traditional authorities. His friendship with Sultan Barquq, cemented during their joint exile and imprisonment in Syria, leads initially to his appointment as chief judge of the Shafi'i legal school in Cairo. However, when the Mamluk amirs surrounding Barquq engineer 'Amr's dismissal, he starts teaching in the Sultan Hasan Mosque in Cairo (its construction being, as already noted, a prominent feature of the first part of the novel) and attracts an ever increasing number of students. Many generations later, the Mamluk amir, Salar, who has been working as a spy disguised as a peasant named Husam ad-din, joins two of his colleague amirs in selecting the Shaykhu Mosque in Cairo as the headquarters for the armed resistance to the invading Ottoman army. There they are welcomed by the mosque's shaykh, Shihab ad-din al-Manati; that last name linking this popular religious figure and preacher to his 14th century ancestors depicted in the previous parts of the novel.

Each of these significant participants in the religious and social life of Egypt and its inhabitants over centuries and generations also plays a central role within the private sphere of family life. For this reader of *Sons of the People*, it is in this particular domestic context that the richness and originality of the novel emerge to their fullest extent, in that we are introduced to three remarkable female characters, each of whom is to play a major role in the life and demeanor of the male figures who, as just described, perform a variety of religious, social, and political functions outside the home environment. In the first part, Zaynab, the daughter of the merchant Abu Bakr, is, as noted above, married to Muhammad al-Muhsini, a Mamluk amir. Their son, also named Muhammad, shows an early and abiding interest in architecture and is to become the obsessed designer and builder of the Sultan Hasan Mosque. In the second, Dayfa, the beautiful and wayward woman from the Egyptian south, is eventually married, after much trial and tribulation, to 'Amr, the judge of Qus. And, in the third part, Hind narrates her own account of her kidnap by the Mamluk amir, Salar, and her fraught relationship with him.

All three women are forced to endure terrible hardships as part of their developing relationships with these men. Zaynab, initially recalcitrant, is imprisoned by Al-Muhsini while the fate of her brother is being decided. Dayfa is cruelly whipped by her father and abandoned by her feckless husband before 'Amr, as judge of Qus, decrees her divorce and is married to her himself. Hind, born a free Egyptian woman, is purchased by Salar (at least, as he sees it) and treated as a slave girl before he eventually decides to "manumit" her and return her to her father's house. While the stories and experiences of both Zaynab and Dayfa are recounted by an external narrator, Hind, who is eventually revealed to be Ibn Iyas's own daughter, is allowed to tell her personal story (to her ever attentive aunt) in her own words and in multiple segments. Within the set of complex external and internal situations and networks that we have just outlined, the gradual process whereby the relationships between these women and their male consorts are shown to develop may be different in each case. However, all three women are of one mind in their determination to confront and defy the negative consequences of their fates, to endure and overcome the violence to which they are subjected by their relatives, husbands, or owners, and to use their own inborn instincts and persuasive talents to curb the worst character traits that the men show towards them and others. There is a real sense in which this novel is best seen as a series of narratives about three remarkable Egyptian women whose lives, misfortunes, and loves are portrayed in such a way as to offer an accurate reflection of the tumultuous period in Egyptian history in which they lived.

The text of *Sons of the People* clearly sets out to identify itself as a document of record, from the explanatory letter with which it opens to the utterly different (purportedly "truthful") accounts of the Ottoman invasion of Egypt dictated to the Egyptian historian, Ibn Iyas, in part three. Within this work of fiction, history and the historical record are presented as variable narratives, thus providing the reader with a vivid illustration of the contentions put forward by, among others, the historian and literary critic Hayden White (in both *Metahistory* [1973] and *Tropics of Discourse* [1978]), namely that history operates along a narrative spectrum that proceeds, via biography and autobiography, towards fiction. In his iconoclastic series of statements, *Reality Hunger: A Manifesto* [2010], David Shields provides a further relevant comment on the specific generic interstice within which history, fiction, and narrative creativity are fused:

> The line between fact and fiction is fuzzier than most people find it convenient to admit. . . . The distinction is easy to voice but hard to sustain in logic. For imagination and memory are Siamese twins, and you cannot cut them so cleanly apart. There's a good case for arguing that any narrative account is a form of fiction. (65)

Sons of the People thus provides its readers with an example of the novel as fictional genre, indeed the historical novel, fulfilling its generic purpose as Lionel Trilling's "agent of the moral imagination," and doing so in a thoroughly creative way that serves both to please and to instruct.

In conclusion, I would like to express my thanks to Reem Bassiouney, the author of the novel, for her constant interest in this translation project and for her willingness to offer information and advice on points of detail. I would also like to thank my colleague and friend, Michael Beard, one of the editors of the Syracuse University Press translation series, for initially drawing my attention to the novel. Since then, he has been a constant source of encouragement and advice and has contributed in important ways to both the translation and format. The staff at Syracuse University Press have been of great assistance in the preparation and publication of this English translation of a wonderful new contribution to the tradition of the Arabic historical novel. I thank them all.

Roger Allen, February 2020

List of Principal Characters

Barquq (d. 1399): Bahri Mamluk sultan, who ruled Egypt twice (1382–89 and 1390–99), interrupted by a revolt led by Yalbugha and Mintash during which he was kept prisoner at Kerak Castle in Syria

Dayfa: daughter of Al-Ridawi and eventually the judge's wife

Amir Fakhr ad-din: the governor of Qus

Jamaq: son of Amir Fakhr ad-din

Shaykh Al-Mahmudi: a Mamluk solider who studies with ʿAmr at the Sultan Hasan Mosque, later Mamluk Sultan Al-Muʾayyad Abu Nasr Shaykh al-Mahmudi

Al-Maqrizi (1364–1442): Egyptian historian of the Mamluk era

Maryam from Abyssinia and Zubayda from Yemen: two friends of Dayfa

Mintash: governor of Malatya, and, along with Yalbugha, a conspirator against Sultan Barquq

Al-Muʾayyad Shaykh (d. 1421): Mamluk sultan, with a renowned Cairo mosque to his name

Umm Hasan: a salt-seller, mother of a boy killed by Jamaq, and the judge's loyal servant

Shaykh al-Qumati: traditionalist opponent of ʿAmr, "Judge of Qus"

Al-Ridawi: a merchant and Dayfa's father

Amir Saladun: governor of Cairo

Imam al-Shafiʿi (767–820): Muslim theologian and founder of one of the four schools of Islamic law which bears his name.

Taqi ad-din Ahmad ibn ʿAli al-Maqrizi (1364–1442): prominent Egyptian historian during the Mamluk period

Yalbugha al-Yahyawi: a major Bahri Mamluk amir who consolidated power around himself during the sultanate of the young Al-Hasan

THE FINAL STORY

ʿAbdallah: Salar's elder brother

Abu al-Barakat Ibn Iyas (1448–1522): prominent Egyptian historian during the Mamluk and later Ottoman periods, and father of Hind

Abu as-Suʿud al-Jarihi: a Sufi to whose mountain retreat Salar flees after the failed attempt to assassinate Salim Shah

ʿAdlat: ʿAbdallah's wife

al-Ghuri (1441?–1516): Mamluk sultan at the time of the Ottoman invasion of Egypt in 1516

Hind: daughter of the historian, Ibn Iyas, captured by Salar whom she eventually marries—one of the three narrators of "The Final Story"

Inal: along with Salar and Qansuh al-ʿAdili, three Mamluk amirs opposing the current regime

Jad Bardi al-Ghazali (d. 1521): a Mamluk amir who defected to the Ottoman cause during the Ottoman invasion of Egypt in 1516; in 1519 he was appointed Ottoman governor of Damascus

Khayir Bey (d. 1522): Mamluk Bey who treacherously assisted Salim Shah in the conquest of Egypt

Khawand Sa'adat: daughter of Khayir Bey and wife of Salar

Mustafa Pasha al-'Uthmani: official translator for the Ottoman sultan and one of the three narrators of "The Final Story"

Qansuh al-'Adili: along with Salar and Inal, three Mamluk amirs opposing the current regime

Salar: a Mamluk (using the name Husam ad-din) who captures Hind. Along with Inal and Qansuh al-'Adili, he is one of three Mamluk amirs opposing the incoming regime imposed by the Ottoman sultan; one of the three narrators of "The Final Story"

Salim Shah: the Ottoman Sultan, Selim (1470–1520)—known as "Selim the Grim," who conquered Egypt between 1516 and 1517

Shaykh Shihab ad-din: descendant of both 'Abd al-Karim al-Manati and 'Amr, "Judge of Qus," and the shaykh in charge of the mosque of Shaykhu al-'Umari an-Nasiri in central Cairo during the Mamluk opposition to the Ottoman invasion

Sitt ad-dar: 'Adlat's daughter

Tuman Bey (1476–1517): the last of the Mamluk sultans who was imprisoned and put to death following the capture of Cairo

Ziyad: prospective fiancé for Hind

REEM BASSIOUNEY is the author of nine novels and a scholar of Arabic linguistics. She was the first woman to be awarded the prestigious Naguib Mahfouz Award from Egypt's Supreme Council for Culture for the best Egyptian novel of 2020 for her bestselling novel *Sons of the People*. Bassiouney's novel *The Pistachio Seller* was awarded the King Fahd Center for Middle East and Islamic Studies Translation of Arabic Literature Award in 2010. She also won the 2009 Sawiris Foundation Literary Prize for her novel *Professor Hanaa*. Five of her nine novels have been translated into English, Spanish, and Greek, including *Sons of the People*; *The Mamluk Trilogy* (forthcoming) and *Fountain of the Drowning* (forthcoming), both translated by Roger Allen; *Mortal Designs* translated by Melanie Magidow; *Professor Hanaa*, translated by Laila Helmi; and *The Pistachio Seller*, translated by Osman Nusairi.

Bassiouney is a professor of sociolinguistics at the American University of Cairo. She has published eight academic books and is currently the editor of the Routledge Series of Language and Identity.

ROGER ALLEN retired from his position as the Sascha Jane Patterson Harvie Professor of Social Thought and Comparative Ethics in the School of Arts and Sciences at the University of Pennsylvania, where he also served Professor of Arabic and Comparative Literature in the Department of Near Eastern Languages and Civilizations for forty-three years. Among his published studies on Arabic literature are *The Arabic Novel: An Historical and Critical Introduction* and *The Arabic Literary Heritage*.

He has translated many fictional works by modern Arab writers. He is the celebrated translator of the Egyptian Nobel Laureate Naguib Mahfouz, including translations of a collection of short stories *God's World* and the novels *Autumn Quail, Mirrors, Karnak Café, Khan al-Khalili,* and *One Hour Left*. Other Arab authors he has translated include Jabra Ibrahim Jabra, Yusuf Idris, 'Abd al-rahman Munif, Mayy Telmissany, BenSalim Himmich, Ahmad al-Tawfiq, and Hanan al-Shaykh.

For a full list of titles in this series,
visit https://press.syr.edu/supressbook-series
/middle-east-literature-in-translation/.

Author's Acknowledgments

Thank you to Michael Beard for all his support. Thanks to Adnan Haydar.

Special thanks to Arwa Al Hinai for reading the translation and sending suggestions.

Thanks to Syracuse University Press for taking on this project. It is always a delight to work with you. Thank you, Deborah M. Manion and Lisa Kuerbis.

Very special thanks to Roger Allen for an inspiring journey and translation. I am honored to work with you.